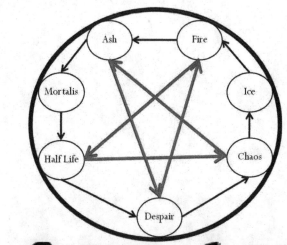

Succubus

Book 1 – Seven Hells

By Juan Crazy

Order this book online at www.trafford.com
or email orders@trafford.com

Most Trafford titles are also available at major online book retailers.

Printed in the United States of America.

ISBN: 978-1-4269-6733-7 (sc)
ISBN: 978-1-4269-6734-4(e)

Trafford rev. 06/09/2011

 www.trafford.com

North America & international
toll-free: 1 888 232 4444 (USA & Canada)
phone: 250 383 6864 ♦ fax: 812 355 4082

'We always knew there were gates,
we just never knew how to open them."

—Etch T

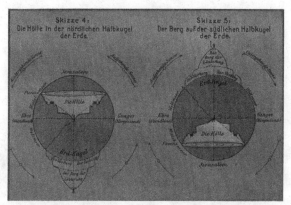

Dante Alighieri, Albert Ritter (Hrsg)

Dedication

To my parents, Erwin and Louise: do you regret creating passionate children?

To my wife Shelagh, driven to re-education, to fulfill a lifelong passion.

To my children, I hope you find your passions and balance them with their respective costs.

To my friends and fellow global road warriors: you already know our costs are higher.

To Stephen D., your passing pushed me to finally start writing.

Contents

Introduction

Passion is what defines us as individuals. The greater frequency and the depth to which it motivates, establishes what we are and what we will become.

However, there are costs to be paid and the more grandiose the goal typically the greater the cost. The problem is, these costs are never quantified up front, or levied upon delivery of goal. The fees are paid, day after day and typically over several years. Then, after achieving our goal we realize that the costs sometimes were much higher than we had ever expected.

This story is a journey of passion as seen from the eyes of three main characters, each motivated by different things: ambition and duty, love and revenge.

A bloody start

The two young princesses sat cross-legged on the massive canopied bed and although their attire indicated that they were prepared for the nights slumber, the noises they were making seemed to suggest that sleep was not to be any time soon. The long flowing, heavy velvet canopies barely muffled their shrieks of glee, giggles and laughter.

Beyond the canopied bed within the large chamber, two of their three handmaidens were busy taking the princesses' ball gowns and placing them on their custom dress dummies.

Tira, lady in waiting for the visiting Princess Elle, had just finished tying up the girl's beautiful, delicate dress and was about to lift it and take it to her lady's room when she was halted by mistress' voice calling from behind the closed canopies. "Tira, could you bring us the small balls from my room? I have bet Mindy a silver Nail that you and I could beat her and Diri in a game of Pila."

Tira turned and looked over at the bed. "It's got to be two AM my lady?"

Mindy laughed in response to the Tira's objection. "Your lady has claimed that you Montterran's are superior then us Terrans when it comes to the game. Your princess is now honour bound to prove out this claim. Besides," Mindy Princess of the Terran lands continued with a laugh, "my mother has set no curfew so we shall not sleep until we drop from exhaustion. Or until we see the light of day!"

"Yes my ladies." Tira responded. Curtsying, she then quickly turned and exited the room, carrying with her the mannequin with the flowing party dress upon it.

Elle, a cheerful girl of fifteen, turned back to look at her friend Mindy, the princess of Terran. Her best friend was tall, well tanned, and aglow with joy at turning sixteen. They had both just spent the most exiting night of their lives, dancing and celebrating Mindy's coming of age, and though they should have been exhausted, they weren't. In fact, Elle hadn't felt more awake in all her life.

Elle, smiling, looked enviably at Mindy. Her friend was very pretty, with shoulder length, curly brown hair that Elle simply adored and not so secretly coveted. "Your hair is just so nice. I wish I had curly hair," she pouted unexpectedly.

Mindy smiled at her friend's aggrieved expression. "It's such a pain. You at least can curl yours when you want to. I have to spend painful hours sitting while Mira tries to comb mine out and straighten it enough to put it into a bun or braids."

"Besides" Mindy continued slyly, "did you see Terris almost break his neck when he turned to look at your long, sleek locks? He is quite the man isn't he, so tall, and with long, dark hair."

Mindy paused and her dark eyebrows raised as her eyes widened. "And did you see the charger he road in on? That horse must be worth a kingdom by itself, never mind that his saddle was studded with rubies to match the red in his doublet!"

Elle blushed. "Did he really? I didn't even notice, and I wouldn't have thought you would have either. I didn't think you and Larot ever once broke eye contact. That boy is absolutely smitten with you…." Elle giggled and then gently jabbed her friend in the arm. "What's that? Oh wait, am I hearing wedding bells?"

"LIAR", shouted Mindy giving her a playful shove. "You did too notice Terris. He was the first man you danced with, and at these sorts of events, that is clearly showing favourites! Maybe it's you who will soon be married. AnnonTer might be one of the colder places to live, but coming from frigid MountRyhn you likely would find the place a warm one to raise a family. He's the Duke's oldest son you know, and Duke Rudolph Ygor is going on 70, so Terris stands to inherit soon. He's one of the finest catches in all the Kingdome!"

Elle shook her head. "Terris didn't stop talking about him the entire time we danced. He kept trying to impress me with all his talk about his cloths and money. He might look like a catch, but I disagree. He didn't succeed in whatever he was trying to do. There is also something devious about him as well, like he's always thinking about something else, about how to get things he wants…. I don't really trust his looks. You know what I mean? Like a wolf."

"A wolf can be fun for a romp, Elle," kidded Mindy.

"Larot on the other hand" interjected Elle very enthusiastically "Now there is a piece of flesh. Mindy, if you don't land him soon another of the court will – he is a prize! There wasn't one lady there tonight that didn't hope he would walk their way."

Mindy sighed happily. "He is dreamy isn't he?"

Mindy paused then, a sad look crossing her features. "I don't have much to say though, about who I will court or marry. In the end Father will make up his mind. For all I know he might even try to marry me off to a Mohen, or a Masti nomad King's son, just to improve trade." Mindy looked down and her frown deepened.

Elle reached over and gave her friend a little hug. "I think well of your father. He was a very proud man tonight – he couldn't stop smiling and you never left his gaze. He loves you dearly and will allow you to follow your heart when the time comes. YOU are his most prized possession."

"And did you see," Elle continued enthusiastically, "your mom had a tear in her eye when you danced with Larot! She gave your dad a hug right then and there in front of the whole court. I guess I can believe you missed it, considering you were lost in Larot's arms."

Mindy looked up and brushed a little tear from her eye. "Really?" she asked sheepishly.

When Elle smiled, Mindy beamed and began to perk up. "I noticed you danced three times with Darn, Elle." she said, her tone playful. "You know, the shorter lad, with fair hair. The one with the plain doublet, with some type of green plant sewn along

3

the hem?" she teased, knowing full well from the glint in her friend's eyes that Elle knew exactly whom she meant.

Here Mindy paused, and then continued in a much more serious tone. "Three times is playing with fire Elle. Showing that much favouritism? Tomorrow the entire court will be talking about you two!"

"Hmm, Darn. I could have melted in his arms." Elle said, ignoring the warning and falling back slightly, pretending to swoon. "He was soooo gallant and charming. He's such a wonderful man."

Mindy took Elle's two hands in hers. "Not that I would stand in the way of 'true' romance Elle, but, ahem…you know Darn's father Carton is only a Barron. The Tunis family are 'named men' governing the Cliff Mines. They run the place for my father, but they don't own the lands - he isn't royal Elle."

Mindy paused, testing her ground, wondering how much she could really say to her friend without upsetting her. "I'm not sure your father would approve. You are, after all, a princess. You can't forget that Elle. I know my father might let me follow my heart, to a certain point, but he would never let me forget that I am of royal blood."

Mindy continued her speech, trying to move Elle in a different direction. "Terris on the other hand will be a Duke when his father dies. A marriage to him would make our countries even closer."

Elle looked away in stony silence and Mindy, seeing how the statement had hurt her friend, tried to cheer her up again. "Hey, if things really are that serious all you need do is talk to my mother. She loves you like a second daughter and you ARE related. I am sure my mom could convince father to make Darn a Count. Perhaps as a marriage gift to your father?"

Elle beamed in response. "Did you see his belt and stockings? They had lilies on them or something. One thing for sure, I would have to teach him a thing or two about fashion." Both Elle and Mindy broke out into girlish laughter.

Mindy gave Elle a little shove. "That is 'high' fashion in the south I want you to know." she joked. "It's all the rage on the coast to wear doublets sewn with seaweed!" Elle exploded in laughter and tears streamed down both of the girls cheeks as they fell over with mirth.

When they had settled, Elle affected a disinterested air, trying to hide her obvious curiosity, and appeared to examine the patchwork of Mindy's duvet. "He must be what now, eighteen?"

Mindy grinned and indulged her friend with what details she had. "Almost, he turns eighteen in the spring. Let's see, what else can I tell you…? He is one of the best that I have seen at our jousts. He always ranks high with a crossbow and he's amazing on his horse. The men of the south fight with lances and he can throw them very far. It must be from their experiences trying to spear fish in the ocean. Ahhh perhaps an ocean voyage for the honeymoon…"

Elle blushed and quickly decided to switch the topic back to Mindy. "With you turning sixteen, that makes you courting age. I am sure there will be a very long line tomorrow at your father's throne, and I would bet a talon that Larot will be there at the front. You will be married a good year or more before me, I would wager."

Mindy turned and laughed lightly. "I hope so. I'm getting bored here. I want a change. I want to go out riding with boys on my own, to travel. My father is soooo very protective. I can't go anywhere without a chaperone. I really don't care 'how' long the line is – I just hope my father lets Larot court me."

"If I know your father, he will make sure of the lad by making it a long courtship. You aren't out of the castle yet my friend!" Elle giggled.

Mindy nudged a little closer to Elle. "My father won't let me out of his view unless he is absolutely certain I will be safe. The more he frets about his Kingdome the shorter my leash."

Mindy sighed. "Father Mellon sent his regrets for not coming to the party. It appears there are all manner of strange happenings

5

in the North. Father would tell me little except that there were an unusually large number of strange beasts reported in the Northern Mountains. It has father terribly anxious."

"There is always something that makes Kings nervous." Said Elle glibly. "If my father isn't worried about one thing it's another."

"Yes, but this is different." Mindy continued. "Father Mellon is a close friend. He promised me he would come down for the party. It was breaking that promise that rose Father's greatest concern. The Lord Drakon would not have broken his promise to attend and celebrate with us unless there was something seriously wrong in the North."

Mindy continued with dropping spirits. "Nothing is certain for our kingdom. The Masti and Tock are forever raiding our northern settlements; the Mohen are so large and strong and always at our door. My father might love me dearly, but he would think first of his kingdom. I do very much fear that he might end up betrothing me to a Mohen Duke's son simply to create a sense of security for our people."

"Oh, well then you had better start pouting now, and tell your father that you are in love with Larot. If you tell him soon you and your mother can convince him that he should get one of your cousins to marry some Mohen lord or something." Mindy shrugged. "That wouldn't be enough I'm afraid. It wouldn't ensure a binding tie between our nations."

Holding back a tear, Mindy smiled bravely. "Now you on the other hand, lets see. We would absolutely need the Lord Drakon to travel west to wed you in the halls of Mount Ryhn. I will have to start working on him the next time I see him to ensure he doesn't get 'distracted' when the time comes."

Elle looked a little glum. "In truth, I'm not sure what my father has in mind for me either. Last time he ordered a council meeting the Duke of Oathos brought his sons. The younger one was nice, but..." Elle's voice trailed off.

"But they aren't Darn." Mindy continued and both girls smiled with understanding.

A little head appeared from behind the canopy, accompanied by two small arms holding a small tray with feet. Mindy turned. "Oh great Diri. Thank you so much, we're starving!"

Diri, the oldest of the three handmaidens, chastised the two girls. "I watched you both. Neither of you ate a bite all night long. All you did was dance and talk. You will both get sick if you don't get some food in you – AND some rest."

Mindy took the tray and set it down between herself and Elle. It was stacked with both hard and soft cheeses, crackers and small, blackish fruits. Mindy picked up one of the latter and took a nibble. "Mmmm. Have you ever tried a blackberry? I don't think they were in season the last time you visited. They just ripened this last week, and ohhh they are soooo good."

Elle took one from the tray and looked at it. "No, but I had some of the jam you sent me and it's my favourite." She popped the entire berry into her mouth, rolled her eyes and moaned with glee.

Mindy finished hers off and started to cut off a piece of dark orange cheese. "This Ferro cheese is good too. I could eat a brick of it in one sitting – but then I wouldn't be able to fit into my dresses. The Holy Knights of the Temple Guard make it. Back before he became the High Drakon, Father Mellon use to bring us kilos of it every time he visited us, which back then was virtually every other month."

Mindy took a nibble of the cheese and rolled her eyes in enjoyment. "It's made from the milk of a small Masti animal called a Blood Ferret. The creature's milk is said to be the sweetest of any. Unfortunately, not too many of our local farmers raise the small creatures for they have an evil disposition and wickedly sharp pointed teeth."

Elle's laughter filled the room. "I would give a golden talon to see one of those Grand Knights trying to milk such an animal."

"They all look so 'staunch' and proper." Elle continued. "Except for that one that wore the poncho... what was his name again? I've never seen them so much as crack a smile. All of them always doom and gloom... but his outfit! For a Knight?"

Mindy laughed. "Can you believe it? I used to tease all the Temple Guards so. The uniform fabric is so rough."

Mindy moved a little closer to share her gossip. "You know, Mira's parents lived in the area, and she says that the soldiers of the Holy Guard don't wear long under garments. Can you imagine how that would chafe?"

Elle cringed and shook herself. Both girls fell once more into a fit of giggles.

Mindy sobered up a little. "It is sad that your dad couldn't come. My father and mother really were disappointed when he said he couldn't. I hope he's ok."

Elle shrugged her shoulders. "He took a very nasty fall. He tried to jump a fence and his horse didn't make it. When he fell, the horse fell on top of him, pinning him to the ground. At first they thought he might have broken his neck."

"Ends up he is very bruised, his leg is badly hurt, and he also broke a few ribs. He tries to act as if he's this 'invincible King'. He says that it wouldn't be proper to come with a cane and all. However, I am thinking he's hurt a little more then he lets on. When he was brought back, we were all very scared."

Mindy nodded. "My father acts the same way – as if nothing can hurt him. But that's not just kings you know, it's all men. Still, I wish he were here to see you dance in that gown he gave you. It's gorgeous, I love the green, and it goes so well with your eyes."

Elle smiled and then winked at Mindy. "Well I preferred that he wasn't here and let your mother lay the rules for the night. Are you kidding, if he had been here I would have been up to bed by 11. And if Darn or any other boy had so much as approached me to ask for a dance my father would have likely had his sword out in two shakes of his broken leg and gutted the poor boy!"

Mindy screeched with laughter and Elle accompanied her. Both fell over holding their sides as laughter and tears broke the early morning stillness. They had been up all night, and it was coming close to daybreak. Both were obviously getting a little giddy.

They froze however, as the sound of a sharp and distant scream. At the second scream, they sat bolt upright in their bed. Elle put her arms around Mindy seeking reassurance.

In the chamber beyond the curtained bed, the two maids ran over to the window to peer out.

"What is it?" Mindy asked to the maids, still hiding behind the heavy canopies. Mira turned to the princess and shrugged. "It's hard to tell. The moons have set already, yet the sun does not rise. There is no light to see what's going on in the streets below the keep."

Diri was stretching all she could out the open window. "I see something in the court... White streaks and something large is walking up to the keep's doors."

Mindy stood. "Where are the court guards, and those of the keep? Can you see them respond?"

Diri shook her head as Mira tried to push in next to her.

"I see no guards, only a fog of sorts, or ...."

Diri grabbed Mira's arm with her right hand and pointed out excitedly with her left. "And there – Mira – do you see it...? There, by the keep gate. It's tall, and the other – like a small mountain cat."

Mira gasped and put her hands to her mouth. "What is it?"

The curtains of the bed pulled back and Mindy ran to the window. "What is it, where are the guards? Mira – go out into the corridor and see if we have guards on the floor."

Mira turned and anxiously headed for the door of the royal bedchamber, shaking her head. "Your mother wouldn't allow guards on this floor. I'll go down to the great hall and see if the captain of the watch knows what's going on."

"Have him send up a guard to stand by our door, just to be sure!" Mindy yelled as Mira closed the door firmly behind herself.

Elle wrapped her arms around herself in fright. "Mindy, I don't like this. I'm scared. I've never heard such a scream. Something horrible is happening."

Moments of stillness passed, and then came another high-pitched scream. This time however, it came unmistakably from within the keep itself. Mindy ran back to Elle, and held her in her arms.

Diri, still by the window, kept looking out, straining her neck and arms to see around the curve of the walls. "I can't see anything now. It's like the thing at the gate isn't really there. One minute it was standing there, another not…. And the fog! I haven't even seen it's like when down by the sea, and we are far from the ocean! Perhaps it is not fog, but smoke or… or ghosts. Whatever it is, it is moving through all the streets that I can see."

"Ghosts? Diri, you're scaring Elle, speak no nonsense." Mindy stroked Elle's hair. "It is just a fog, nothing else. And what you saw earlier is likely nothing more than a small animal that has spooked those within the castle."

"Perhaps a few dozen stink-rats have gotten into the kitchen again. You'll see Elle. Nothing to be afraid of." Mindy said reassuringly.

Mindy continued stroking Elle's hair and held her tight as she whimpered, far from comforted.

The door to their chamber burst open, and Elle's maid Tira came running back into the room, crying hysterically. "I was down by your room my lady. I can see the court from there clear as day - and parts of the city. My ladies, there are shifts, shifts that fly. All that they touch disappears like vapour. Armed men race to them, and they disappear. All the keep's guards are gone…."

Tira turned and slammed the door shut and put her back to it. "The key, where is the key?" she called out hysterically.

Mindy ran to her dresser and took out the key from her top drawer. Elle jumped back onto the bed, pulled the canopies closed and then peered out through the slit between the great folds of purple velvet.

Mindy twisted and threw the key to Tira, but the throw and catch were not clean and the key skidded on the hard stone floor, bouncing off the bottom of the door.

Diri raced from the window to help bar the door. She reached for it and grabbed the lever to hold it closed while Tira scrambled for the key.

Mindy took three hesitant steps towards them; hands clenched together in fear, watching Tira try to pick up the key.

Diri yelled. "Hurry, I hear something. There, hurry, hurry, someone is on the latch! Fast Tira, fast, I can't hold it!" Diri knelt and put her shoulder under the lever, her two fists clenched white with strain. Perspiration dripped from her face.

Tira screamed. "I have it – hold it a moment more!" She reached up, placed the key in the lock and started it turning. There were a few clicks as the lock fought valiantly and then a massive bang as the door exploded inward.

The flash of force split the door down its center. Half of the broken beams carried Diri off with them to the right, where she landed in a crumpled heap; the left fragments took most of Tira with them in the other direction. Blood from both women sprayed outward, showering Mindy, who had been knocked backwards and to the floor.

Mindy crouched, and then pulled herself to her knees, visibly dazed by the explosion. Elle, still mostly hidden by the canopies, peeked into the room. Her eyes widened in disbelief at the carnage before her.

Mindy's face and arms were covered in blood, and her white nightdress was stained a deep red, almost black, with the same. She looked up through her dripping hair towards the gaping hole that now marked the entrance to the chamber.

A small creature, no more than two feet tall, appeared in the opening. It bounded into the room in a half-crouch, using its arms to hasten its movements. It was red as the blood that ran down Mindy's face, with a thin, whipping tail and a small, horned head.

The creature uttered a high-pitched snarl and picked up a piece of what had once been Tira, sniffing it. A small pink tongue protruded from between delicately pointed teeth and licked the bloodied flesh.

Mindy cringed at the sight of the creature's small needle-like teeth behind its dark red lips. It took one step forward and then turned around, seemingly cowed, and moved hastily to the side. It glanced sideways then, directly into Mindy's eyes, and laughed a high-pitched, sickly laugh.

Mindy turned back towards the entrance, once more allowing her eyes to linger for only the briefest of moments on the bed where her friend remained hidden. Then she turned her face back to the door, and all her half-formed thoughts of escape vanished. There, framed by the splintered wood of the severed doorframe, stood the most beautiful woman she had ever seen. As their eyes met, Mindy froze, her fear and tension inexplicably gone.

The lady that entered the chambers was almost as tall as a man, clad in translucent fabric that swayed gently, as if in a constant breeze, though the early morning air was deathly still. It hung loosely from her shoulders, and plunged to her naked navel. The lady's skin was pale beyond comparison, not ashen, but almost a glowing white, which radiated beneath the light fabric of her outfit, leaving nothing to the imagination.

All sense of doubt, all fears, all concerns melted away from Mindy – sloughed off like a snake sheds its skin. Surly nothing could hurt her or her friend, she thought, now that this beautiful angel was in their presence.

The mysterious white lady gazed down at Mindy, and in the lady's strange eyes Mindy saw her entire world. They were completely black - deep pools that you could drown in - and in the pools there were swirling shadows and shapes. They drew nearer and bigger as the lady approached. Beneath the eyes, blood red lips parted in a smile.

As she watched the lady make her way into the room Mindy was filled with warmth and happiness she couldn't remember ever experiencing. It was as if she was two years old again, and had fallen and scraped her knee. She looked at the mysterious woman now as she had looked at her mother then, with longing. She yearned for the lady's embrace, to be held and looked upon lovingly.

The white lady stopped in the middle of the room and spread out her arms. The gossamer fabric of her sleeves hung down and drifted lightly, brushing the floor.

Mindy stood slowly, hesitated and then raced into the white lady's embrace.

The caress was tender and sweet. Mindy looked up lovingly into the dark, black, all encompassing eyes and cried. Such joy she felt, such warmth, such belonging and love. Endless, eternal… Her body felt so close and she pressed even closer to the lady's perfect form. She felt so secure, so unabashed, so at ease and protected.

The eyes that held her stare never wavered, but the eyelids widened slightly as the lady's smile became a grin.

Elle, dumbfounded by Mindy's response, was startled and looked across the room as the little red creature, forgotten until this moment, began to chatter excitedly.

The white lady's blood red lips parted further, showing brilliantly flawless teeth, white as a fresh winter's snow. Mindy's mind raced with fleeting thoughts she could not seem to grasp. Elle, kneeling upon the bed, still hidden, was horrified by the seemingly mindless display of her friend, but remained where she was, fearful and helpless.

"Those lips, that mouth." Mindy said softly, as if in a dream. "What happiness I would have if they would issue to me a command."

Elle continued to watch in growing bewilderment and shock. There stood Mindy, covered in the blood of her handmaidens, embracing this most beautiful, scantily clad lady. While it should have been in some way comforting to see Mindy so at ease, it was so alien as to be disturbing, so bizarre that Elle cringed and shook with renewed terror.

Elle gawked as the white lady's embrace tightened and Mindy's grasp appeared to loosen. Ever so slightly at first, Mindy's back arched and her head fell, exposing her creamy white throat. Her eyes rolled back, hiding her pupils, the whites just showing from beneath her long dark lashes as they slowly fell closed. Elle could see Mindy's face, read her expression clearly. It was at first calm and serene, but in the next moment she grimaced in torment. Still Mindy uttered not a sound, and she made no move to free herself. As Mindy's tanned face and arms began to fall limp and turn red the little creature to the right of Elle suddenly fell silent.

Slowly, Mindy's lips parted as if she fought for breath, and then she let out an unearthly scream that shattered the keep's eerie silence like a knife.

The Terran Princess' skin darkened even further, and then, as Elle looked on, unable to turn her eyes away, every pore on Mindy's body seemed to bleed. It was as if her skin had turned to parchment and could no longer contain the life within her. It seeped from her head; her face, her body and legs, bathing her in blood and darkening the colour of her already stained dress.

Elle screamed then, the sound ripped from her throat by the sight of her friend's broken, lifeless body, and the little creature snapped its head towards her, where she remained cloaked by the thick velvet bed curtains. It ran and jumped at the canopies, tearing them open and leaving Elle exposed for several precious moments before she regained the sense to flee. Elle turned and bounded off the side of the bed then, and made a desperate attempt to reach the door.

The white lady didn't even raise her gaze as Elle passed around her, but rather, continued to look lovingly down at the blood-soaked girl in her arms. Bending, she made as if to kiss Mindy's cheek.

As Elle crossed the center of the floor the white lady's lips met Mindy's forehead. Mindy's bleeding skin, unable to contain the now bulging flesh beneath it, exploded, bathing the room and all of its occupants in still more blood and gore.

Elle screamed in horror, but even as she raised her arms to wipe off the blood now covering her face, she did not pause in her desperate race to escape. She jumped over a few fallen shards of the door and slipped on the blood where it had begun to congeal, but was able to regain her footing. Elle grabbed the doorframe with her left hand, hoping to make a sharp turn down the corridor in her quest for the stairs leading down and out of the keep.

Elle could hear the small red creature at her heels as she threw herself through the broken doorway and into the hall. She lunged out of the room and turned left into the corridor, another scream, of both fear and grief, welling up in her throat.

The next moment the scream was cut short, and all that issued from Elle's lips was a small gasp as she flew face first into a wafting white cloud. The cloud had hands that gripped like iron, and a body, and a face that seemed entirely filled by grinning white lips and empty white eyes. Before she could catch her breath and prepare to scream again, like a warm breath in winter, both Elle, and the wisp of smoke, disappeared into the night.

15

Diamond Mountain

To the east the ice on the mountains reflected back the sun's last light with blinding brilliance. Hues of blue and yellow flared out from where the snow met the hard ice.

To the west sheer cliffs rose dauntingly, frozen and capped with snow and ice. At the top of these a sharp spike of ice as old as time rose majestically, like a silver spear, almost as if it was trying to pierce the sky itself. The mountain's point was so sharp and so high no shadow from any other mountain on the range touched it. It shone like a brilliant diamond - fully encased in everlasting winter. It was for this it had been named Diamond Mountain.

From the peak of the mountain, cold air rushed down its sides like so much water. Flowing easily over the smooth ice it gained both a bone chilling coldness and tremendous momentum. Where the ice ran out, the flow of cold mountain wind hit the broken rock surface head on, making the air swirl like river rapids.

At the base of the ice floe the churning air currents hit small pockets of snow, tossing them into the air. These in turn blew over the mountain's face like white hairs flying about an old man's head.

As far as the eye could see snow-capped mountain peaks glistened where they touched the darkening, cloudless sky.

At this particular moment the sun was dropping in the western horizon, taking with it what little vestiges of warmth and light were left on the barren landscape. The valley below Diamond Mountain was already cloaked in shadows. On the eastern horizon nestled villages surrounded by giant trees that poked up through the darkness, almost like they were hands reaching out to grasp and cling to the last of the sun's warming rays.

As the sun eased itself down over the mountains the shadows visibly lengthened, stretching hungrily forward as though they sought to devour the giant trees and swallow the valleys whole.

The man walking alone, carefully picking his way along the warn mountain path, was in his mid-life; his face was hard and worn and his eyes showed signs of an age beyond his physical years. His stature was proud, yet he didn't stand tall. It was visible to anyone who cared to spare him more than a passing glance that his past had worn his soul thin, that the battles he had fought had drained him of his spirit. The lean years as a soldier had made him hard in body and in soul.

The cold airflow lapped up over Etch's feet, wrapped tightly in tough leather; and under his fitted buckskin pants. It was time to start back down to the cabin he thought. This day was well over and the night air was only going to get colder. Still he paused, looking out over the horizon with an air of expectation. This was his favourite time of day on the mountain, the time just as the sunset and the moons rose.

It was times like this that Etch felt he could afford to stop for a moment and reflect on his life and his family, when he could bear to look to the past, as well as the future.

Climbing mountains had been getting harder for Etch as of late. He reached behind him and touched his back, feeling his muscles twinge in protest. He had softened much in the last few years; marriage, stability and three square meals a day did that to a man. But the hardness he felt inside, made from experiences such as he could not share with anyone, not even his beloved wife, never truly disappeared. Rather, it lurked, hidden beneath new layers built by the passing of time.

Etch smiled as he thought of his loving wife, Rachael. Rachael, who had said, upon seeing him after he returned from the wars, that when she looked into his eyes, it felt as if he was seeing her from behind smoked glass. Yet here, on this mountain, looking out over the plains, the view was pristine, and he saw life with clarity he seldom felt anymore.

Etch's smile broadened as his mind continued its wandering. For a time, shortly after the children had been born, Rachael had looked at him again as she had years before. Even he had felt in those times that the world had regained some lost quality again, become that much more real. The 'smoke', as she had put it, that had long haunted his eyes had seemed to be dissipating, dissolving.

And then the children came bringing with them even greater clarity to his sense of being. They had given him and Rachel a sense of immortality, one he all to badly needed following the brutality of the front lines, along with a sense of destiny and definition.

"But they are no longer young children now." He said softly, fearing to raise his voice above a whisper, lest he break the tranquility of the moment and the feeling of peace that washed over him. The children were growing fast, and as they aged the clarity and purpose, the *passion* they had brought to his life were fading, and his view was blurring once again.

Etch loved to climb this mountain and to look out over the plains as he did now. It was the only way he knew to center himself, to maintain the tenuous link between the man he had been, and the man he had become. Etch had always needed goals, objectives to drive himself towards. He knew himself that he was a man that required a passion in order to live.

"Passion, without passion in life…" Etch said softly, his words virtually inaudible as the winds picked up and carried them away into the unhearing wilderness.

"Well now this mountain and what it guards is my passion." Etch said, raising his voice to match the new force of the wind as he turned his gaze to the point where the mountain met the star-filled sky. He squinted as his eyes touched the brilliant peak.

'How many times have I been up this mountain on this search?' Etch asked himself. 'This search, these ventures up this mountain, have been my one true passion now for many years.'

At this the tired, pensive man turned again, and this time cast his gaze down the mountain's long, cracked face, down far below to where he knew his home, wife, and children were. Down to shelter, safety and warmth. He feelings were torn, though home and hearth called – so too did the mountain keep its hold on him as it had for so many years.

He had uprooted his family and built their new home up here against its cold breast. He had done all of that and more so that he could be within the reaches of Diamond Mountain and its haunting summons.

"I guess this would be considered an obsession." Etch said to himself. The mountain, his ever-unmoving friend and enemy, did not reply.

Etch felt as if he had already lived a long life. Looking back, he knew that at forty-two years of age he had already seen more of the world than most any other man in the area. He had been ranked first scout in a large company, had fought in many battles and had earned the respect of many a knight and even a king. Few men could boast of that.

But here in the mountains there were few to boast to. He and his family now lived in relative solitude and socialized infrequently with those in the hills, even more infrequently with those in the valley now so far below.

On some of the colder winter nights he would sit with his family in front of a roaring fire and remember the days gone by. He would tell them of the lands he had seen, the people he had known. He wondered out loud with them and encouraged his family to speculate with him if the men and women he had met on his travels still lived, and how they fared. But outside, in the cold light of the rising moons, it seemed more than ever like an old man's activity to him, and he rebelled against the thought.

He was still young. Perhaps his heart and soul were growing old, but his body was still young. There should be more left to his life than just memories of the past.

Something was missing in Etch's life. Something in his mind wavered just out of reach, something that nagged him and left him feeling 'incomplete'.

Would he find that which he sought on this mountain – would he then feel 'fulfilled'? Unlikely, it would improve their life with wealth, but that would not be the answer to the riddle he faced now. The answer lay in something else, something more elusive.

Etch inhaled a great breath of the frigid air. The cold burned his throat and pierced its way down and into his lungs. As he exhaled his breath appeared as a fog. The moist air from within twisted a moment as the air currents caught it and then dissipated quickly to be carried away by the drafts.

Try as he might Etch couldn't figure out the elusive task could possibly make him complete. He knew not what he needed to do to finally put to rest his soul, what it was that would let hi, say that he had done all in life that he had ever aspired to do…

For years he had believed that finding the buried Drekian horde would do it. But now, after so many years searching and finding nothing, Etch was beginning to doubt that the call of the mountain was any more substantive than that of a siren, designed to lure those that answered further and further into oblivion. Yet here he stood, atop that same mountain, at the end of another searching trip, about to return to his family empty handed because he didn't know what else was left for him to do.

Etch looked up and beyond the horizon. Halos was visible now, its frowning, broken face illuminated the sky with a faint pink glow. Halos was always visible early this time of year, even when its face was broken as it was now.

Etch looked further down on the horizon, but knew full well the other mountain tops would block his view of where Detros was likely hiding, just below the horizon.

Detros' grinning face would be up all too soon. It was a period the superstitious village folk called 'seasons of sorrow'. Detros' broken face looked down from the heavens every few years but when his face was turned to look down on them – there were always hard times. Etch thought back recalling that in his lifetime; Detros had been present during each year that there had been a plague, or famine. Detros had looked down when first the Drekians had come too! Etch frowned looking up – Detros' smiling face had never in his lifetime brought with it a time of peace.

Detros followed Halos ever so, each face changing as they spun around the world they watched. Even though the sun was hidden for the night, when Detros' great face rose then the evening's sky would lighten once again. And when Detros fully faced them grinning as he would tonight from above, he was brightest. Etch, however, didn't want to wait to see Detros rise. The light already cast by Halos now was sufficient to descend and his left knee was already cramping with the cold, it was time to head down.

Etch took a careful step, watching how he placed his foot so as not to disturb the loose shale. The trip down the mountain would be slow he knew, as each step had to be taken tentatively. On every other footfall the grey rocks crunched and parts of the shale rock would roll down ahead of Etch, making eyrie, crackling sounds that echoed across the mountain.

Etch narrowed his eyes, trying to find larger pieces of shale to step on. Stepping slowly from one to the next he descended. A glimmer of blue light sprayed against the grey shale of the hill as Detros peeked from behind the mountains and sought to illuminate each of his next footfalls.

Etch took a larger step downward, bending his left leg so that his right could make it to a larger rock a full meter down the hill. His pointed toe reached the edge of the shale stone steadily enough, but the stone moved forward when he shifted his weight to it.

'It is too late! It was too steep! But he knew he was far to pull back.' He grimaced as the rocks began to slide.

"Damn the seven hells!" Etch swore softly.

He had to hope that the weight of his body would push down the top of the shale edge. Etch knew he was committed and had to complete that step or fall back against the hill.

21

Etch pressed down on his right heel – praying for it to hold… and it did! With painstaking slowness he shifted the rest of his weight and his left leg forward, making to entrench himself on the spot. The stones beneath his right foot took that opportunity to revolt.

The half of the stone on which he stood broke apart. For what seemed an eternity Etch watched as the front piece of the stone he stood on pointed up to the sky, then, with a finality that shocked Etch back into awareness the stone pulled free and started sliding down the mountain.

"Ahhhhh!" Etch screamed as his right foot shot up, and then his left. He fell backward, smacking his now uncovered baldhead against the mountain's hard, rock surface.

When the rest of his body collapsed against the mountain he knew he was in serious trouble. The rocks under him began to crumble and slide. Etch's weight turned the stones beneath him into a blanket that moved, gaining momentum as it slid over snow and ice.

The mountain growled as if angry at being woken. Etch's heart sank. 'So this is what it must have been like.' He thought to himself. 'I will be lost like all those others before me. This mountain will swallow me whole as it swallowed the entire Drekian army. I will leave no marker. My family will have no knowledge as to where I will lie.'

Unexpectedly, the mountain's growl stopped as quickly as it had started and Etch's downward movement halted.

"How lucky." Etch said softly, hoping that his slide was indeed stopped; yet fearful that even his laboured breathing might be sufficient to start the terrible fall again.

He lay quietly a moment, regaining his composure, and then craned his neck up and back, looking to gauge where he had fallen. He blinked as he noted the disturbed rocks above him. He was at least one hundred meters from where he had miss-stepped.

As he regained his breath and composure, he ever so slowly moved his head to either side to look at the surrounding stones on which he lay. With courage, he picked up his head and put the slightest of pressure on his shoulder blades. He paused a moment, ensuring that the rocks were holding and then he raised his head again and looked down to his feet. Both heels were dug in. His legs had created a small indentation in the soft stone.

"No broken bones," He said to himself a little louder, relief colouring his voice. Etch took a breath and flexed a few of his muscles. He was sore, very sore. Beneath his leather pants and coat he knew that he was deeply bruised.

"It should be enough to hold. "Etch said with a quiet voice. "Let's hope that my next stupid move doesn't send me the rest of the way down," he added under his breath, and with that he started to rise painfully.

It took Etch a good thirty minutes to stand and prepare to take his next step. It was going to be an even more arduous descent now than he had originally thought to make.

Etch's mind went blank, forcing his total concentration onto his steps as he made his way down the mountain. Half way down to the rock shelter he used as a way station he paused and took a couple of shaky breaths. He looked up at the now pale stars, overshadowed by the new source of light; Detros had risen. Its evil, grinning face was beaming down on him, smiling at his folly. The face was not welcome, but its light was, for it gave Etch the illumination to proceed.

Etch chuckled out loud. "I might not get the opportunity until tomorrow, but I bet I sleep soundly when I finally do!" He turned then, focusing back on the task at hand, and took another step towards safety and warmth.

Dimi

Years before the fall of the great city of Terran Add, in the southern Fendly Forests a small dryad nymph slept. It had been a very restful and much needed sleep for Dimi. But now the sun was rising and as it rose it shone down on her peaceful form, warming her, pulling loose from her mind the last tendrils of a sweat and peaceful dream. The sun's soft warm rays caressed her face coaxing her eyes to open.

The moss beneath her was warm and fragrant and she felt totally secure. The clearing she slept in, lying as deep as it did within the Fendly Forests, was entirely safe.

Dimi wrinkled her nose as it was tickled by a wisp of vapour that wafted up from the moist moss around her. "I guess it's time to rise," she whispered to herself. Then she groaned, "perhaps only a moment or two more?"

With knees drawn up and arms wrapped around her legs Dimi tightened her eyes and then blinked and then rubbed the sleep from the corner of her eyes. Fully recharged from her long sleep, she felt the pang of hunger, and her tummy grumbled, suggesting that she should rise and tend to her basic needs.

The dryad's green eyes glittered like emeralds as they caught the errant beams of light. Dimi squinted feeling a momentary pain as the bright light hit her eyes. She sighed as the sun shone down warming her, but its light was not all that welcome and she moved slightly to one side so that the beam of light no longer touched her sensitive eyes.

Dimi turned slowly in place, taking in the sounds of the morning. Birds nearby chirped as they built nests and foraged for insects or nuts. Small rodents chattered and squealed, snapping twigs and burrowing in the soft soil under the massive trees that surround the clearing. Where she stood however, within the clearing itself, there was silence, a silence hardly disturbed by her soft, short breath.

Sitting erect, Dimi stretched her arms up to the sky and moaned a sigh of relief. "Oh what a wonderful sleep." she said to no one in particular as she looked around.

Her voice was like a musical instrument. It was gentle and high pitched yet soothing. A few animals turn to look in to the clearing at Dimi, but none were disturbed, and they return to their activities quickly.

As Dimi started to rise, wings unfolded from her back and expanded outward. As they moved from her back their tops appeared to unfold and extend even further, coming to the point where from their tips to her back they are each almost as long as she is tall.

The wings at first appeared as if painted white, but as they expanded they let the light of the day pass through them and shimmered translucently. Dimi looked up at her wingtips and smiled as they gently stretched upwards, pulling her to her toes.

Glancing down, Dimi paused to brush off her green felt pants and brown leather vest and check her belt. Her wings, having stretched themselves to their full length, folded gently back and down again, until they rest tight to her back, almost invisible against her vest, which ends at the top of her waist.

Touching her chin first to chest then round to each shoulder, Dimi continued her stretches. Her short hair caught the sunlight as she moved, and shimmered in a range of colours, from moss green, to gold and then finally to snow white. Her eyes closed and then opened again quickly as she blinked twice in the bright sunlight.

"Humph, I'm hungry." she said with a childish pout.

"What do I feel like today?" she asked the trees aloud, almost as if she were expecting a reply.

Her musical voice sang out to the trees and a few birds paused in their chirping to hear it. "Something sweet I think, perhaps honey on Marlow leaf. Or Butter Bread toadstools smothered with blueberries."

25

Taking a few strides, Dimi started towards the clearing's edge. Being no larger then a human girl of eight or nine, her strides were short, yet amazingly light. Her small feet, clad in worn, supple leather, made no sounds as she stepped lightly over twigs and brush.

Faced with the brambles where the clearing turned to woods, Dimi closed her eyes and scrunched up her face. Then, raising her hands to her waist, she whispered something and the branches in front of her pulled apart to let her pass.

"Thank you." Dimi said respectfully. "I do so much love this place, and you all make me feel so safe." Her voice sounded like wind chimes and flute combined.

As she passed through the barricades made of thorn, twig and root, the branches swayed back into place. As they returned, Dimi heard the woods respond to her thanks with a warm, smiling sigh.

'Honey would be up in the northern low grounds beneath the small falls, where flowers are most easily found.' Dimi thought, licking her lips. 'But Butter Bread toadstools would be found among the darker caves and crags in the wetter places by the coast.' Dimi knew the place where all such foods abounded, for these were her woods, and its secret places were not secret from her.

Butter Bread toadstools." she mused. "Should I venture to my secret haven by the sea?"

"I really am hungry. Butter bread toadstools would be much more filling and fitting for a day such as today." Dimi said as she looked down at a small cylindrical container at her waist. She pulled at its lid and it popped as the two pieces separated. It was filled with a variety of small quills, some so slight that they were only as wide as a hair, others the sizes of long thorns. She put the top of the container back on and then looked inside a small pouch that was hanging on the other side of her hip.

Frowning, she sighed, "I guess it should be a trip to the sea caverns, for there I can find some Damas root. I'm getting a little short."

Thus decided, Dimi swept gracefully under the forest's branches without difficulty and like a deer, passed through the dense underbrush without hesitation.

There was not even the slightest pause when she approached the small river as she travelled south. Faced with the obstacle, her wings simply unfolded and she continued to run, seemingly on top of the river itself. From a distance one would have thought that she was made of air for her transparent wings were invisible to the naked eye.

Dimi's trip south was amazingly fast and quiet. The chipmunks didn't even stop their chattering and notice her passing when she jumped over them. The forests were thick, and the travel brought her to increasingly hilly terrain. She bounded up and over hill and through valley with unceasing energy – never altering her main direction or changing her pace.

It had been many years since Dimi had come down from the North to live in the Fendly Forests. It hadn't just been the idea of living closer to the sea, for she could have gone north to the Sea of Tears much faster. It was the warmth of the south, the smell of the southern forests, and the hot, moist breeze off the Sea of Capitherous that had drawn her here. And it was that same smell, the same moist breeze that drew her to the coast once again today.

Dimi thought back upon her earlier life in the North with a nostalgia tempered by both years and miles. She had come a great distance since sadness and fear had made her depart the lands where she had been born.

Dimi shook off the dregs of her last thoughts before they could become too melancholy – she was truly happy now, happier then she had been in centuries, and it showed. Dimi seemed almost to glow as she streaked through the dense forest.

"Ahhh, there." she said as she sniffed the air, not breaking her stride. She could just smell the sea, although she was still many hours away from it.

Dimi could have run with her eyes shut through these forests, sensing every branch, every twig, before she reached it. Still, she preferred to keep her eyes wide open as she ran, absorbing every moment of her joyous trip.

Through thorn and underbrush she passed – never scratching her skin or tearing her clothes. She traveled through the forests like the wind in the leaves - invisible and swift…. Dimi was content beyond belief, free, unfettered, and alive.

Dimi's journey to her special place by the sea slowed as she entered the denser parts of the forest. Here the forest was younger, much younger than those she had known in her youth. Her emerald eyes dazzled as she looked up to the leafy canopy, breathing in deeply the scent of the woods sweet perfume.

"You young trees smell gooood." Dimi said as she opened up her arms and tilted back her head to bathe in an errant beam of sun that breached the cover of the trees around her.

Dimi sighed and opened her eyes, bending to walk under two very low branches that stood before her. "Now you my little friends, what do you think you are doing here?" She said in a surprised voice as her head came up to notice that before her flowed a sea of one-meter high plants covered with brilliant orange leaves.

"Humph, Bushburn. I won't risk your burn." Dimi mused trying to assess the best way round the meter high plants.

"You are to tall for me to walk through, but too low yet to crawl under. But while I am here…" Dimi said to the bright orange blossoms before her. Dimi knelt down and reached to the base of the closest plant's stalk and then started to dig around it. Carefully, a moment later she was pulling out long strands of the plant's roots and putting them in the small pouch that hung from her side.

"Not bad." She said patting the little bag with her now dirty fingers.

Dimi look back at the plants and then giggled. "Too early for the fruit, but not too early for the burn." She turned herself around then and walked back under the trees.

"I won't let you burn my tender skin." Dimi said with a wisp of humour back at the plants as she turned to circumvent the large stretch of bushes.

"And where Bushburn grows, so too does dragon's teeth!" Dimi said as she walked around the small growth of orange plants. She moved up to her tiptoes as she spotted a black thorny busy sitting amongst the outer area of the sea of orange. A moment later she was pulling long black thorns from the tree and placing them in her little bag.

Dimi paused a moment looking at the orange bushes and the contrasting black, black thorny. But her growling stomach spoiled the perfect stillness of the moment. Standing back up Dimi rubbed her small belly. "A rare find." She said to herself and smiled once more. 'What a wonderful trip.' she thought. "But I had better continue!"

Dimi's mouth began to water as she started back to her spirited run southward to the sea.

On over root, past trees she bounded. When space permitted, her little wings would extend and a leap would bring her forward in massive bounds over larger stretches of rough terrain. And as she ran she hummed.

Her progress was amazing and unfaltering. Only when she finally reached the start of the peninsula did she slow.

The valley before Dimi had turned from light green to that of dark green and brown. Stretched out before her were ever-taller trees, covered from tip to root in mossy strands. And to the right and left the peninsula's seaward walls rose ever higher. She knew that in but a kilometres the walls of the peninsula would be over two hundred meters high and that they would draw together ever so slowly like a funnel.

Dimi hated this part of the trip. With the moss strung trees, and heavy undergrowth 'anything' could be hiding. Predators of all sorts would sit within the branches or lie quietly beneath the roots. Other pack animals would wait until something entered the valley and then would trap them there.

The old woman peninsula was a scary place, filled with dark and foreboding shadows and real danger. Never once had she passed this way that there hadn't been a carnivore present, lurking.

"But what good is a secret place, without a guard?" Dimi said to herself as she steeled herself to go forward. "I will just have to be careful." She paused, closed her eyes and sniffed the warm moist air and listened. Behind her the forest was live with the sound of chattering rodents and cawing birds, but before here there was a stillness, and great silence. Then smiling opened her eyes and started forward at a slow walk.

Dimi pressed her shoulders back ensuring her wings were tightly pressed against the back of her leather vest for she knew that they would be of more a hindrance within this terrain then of benefit. She would have to run and jump like a hare, not attempt to take flight. Above in the trees, she knew were tree massive snakes a plenty, waiting patiently for bird to alit on a branch or to fly by. 'No, she would not be taking flight no matter what the situation.' She assured herself.

Nervously Dimi continued on, slower, with more caution and attentive to the sounds around her. Occasionally she looked back and noted just how much more the valley had tightened around her.

As she progressed, the long winding trail that flowed through the valley became darker. Steep ridges and sheer rock cliffs overshadowed the valley floor. After a few hundred meters the winding path she had been following disappeared having been swallowed up by dark brown and green moss.

As Dimi moved into the ever-darkening shades of the narrowing valley she noted the change in vegetation. The valley walls, floor and trees were all covered in moss, making the trek along this stretch of the valley floor dark and foreboding. No birds flew up within the trees, and she ever felt as if she was being watched from above. 'Why am I doing this again?' She asked herself silently.

Many a tree clung to the valley's walls, bent out horizontally. On all these trees hung long, wide, heavy strands of moss. The moss and leaves were like many levels of curtains ahead of Dimi as she moved forward. Travel was slow as she duck under and cut through others with her small dagger.

"Quieter than a moth," thought Dimi as she slowly stepped over twig and root, landing lightly on some small rocks by the base of a tree.

Her green leather and felt outfit matched the colour of the moss that hung down around her. As she pressed through another living curtain of moss her sandy brown hair picked up a few of the strands making her appear as if she was a creature of moss herself. 'Butter bread toadstools.' Dimi thought. 'Not too much farther then there will be a large warm open area, dry and bathed with light and warmth.'

Dimi took a few more confident steps forward and parted another thick strand of moss. As she took half a step forward a few errant strands of sandy brown hair stood up on the back of her neck, and she froze. 'Something is up ahead.' she thought to herself. Then she looked around, wondering if her paranoia was overwhelming her, or if perhaps that what she was feeling was from being watched by those silent slithering creatures within the trees. Her eyes narrowed, and she held a breath as she watched what she had though was a massive trunk three meters before her move. It had hung partially suspended from the massive moss covered tree. Slowly it coiled and then slithered up further into the moss and branches far above.

Dimi smiled and took half a step forward, but then froze again as she spotted slight movement from up ahead. Holding her breath she crouched down slowly and opened a bag hanging from her belt. From it she pulled a small leather case that had been folded in half. Within the unfolded leather was a neat arrangement of black darts tipped with various colours of waxy substances.

Dimi crouched and looked down then with lightening swiftness un-strapped a small reed from the side of her calf and brought it up to her waist. Extracting a small green animal quill from her leather flap she slid it into the end of the reed. Two others darts she held between her fingers as she folded the leather together and returned it to her pouch.

"No wind, no wind." thought Dimi. "My scent must not move."

The smallest of currents brushed her arms and face and Dimi relaxed marginally as she caught the scent of salt. It was coming from the sea. Dimi smiled knowing that her scent had not likely been detected by whatever was in front of her for the wind was still blowing towards her and not towards the sea as it often did in the night.

Dimi breathed lightly and regularly almost in tune with the sea breeze. 'There!' Thought Dimi as her slightly pointed ears caught the ever so slightest sound. 'A step it took; it walks heavy though it walks on moss. It must be large not to fear that snake!'

Dimi strained her eyes. There were too many shadows ahead to see clearly. Whatever it was, it was well hid beneath the many layers of canopied moss.

Dimi became somewhat frustrated, as she crouched motionless half way through a long strand of moss. She had come upon many strange beasts on her trips these ways, and each brought its own challenge. Dominion of the peninsula apparently was continually fought by different predators – 'what predator considered the old maid's peninsula's there's this year?"

'There are too many trees and too much moss!' she cursed to herself as she crouched there listening and sniffing the wind. The large trees reached up to the sky all covered in moss blocking out the sun and casting weird shadows down upon their limbs. The dark moss that clung to everything swallowed up what little light did reach the valley floor.

Dimi glanced nervously behind her, wondering if she should turn and skip this trip south. But a gust of wind blew against her turned face. She shook her head, knowing that now if she turned, she would be the hunted and not the hunter.

"Tooth or nail? Tooth or nail?" whispered Dimi to herself in the softest voice only the caterpillar climbing up the moss beside her could hear. "What type of beast are you?"

"Hmmm, butter bread toadstools." Dimi said trying to regain her confidence. "I should fear nothing within this forest." She smiled as confidence once again ran through her veins. "Lets dance this dance then." She whispered again but this time not quite as softly.

Dimi moved from a crouch to a crawl and crept forward at a deathly slow pace. Not a sound could be heard as she moved; even her breathing was synchronized with the sighs of the breezes within the trees.

After moving forward another few meters she once again moved to a crouch and picked up a small moss covered stone. Gingerly she held it in her left hand smiling as within her right she once again held her blowgun and darts.

In one quick movement Dimi's arm rose and snapped and the stone took flight up and through the moss. The stone was small and it made only the slightest noise as it hit moss-covered branches on the way up, and then a moment later there was a small thud ten meters ahead of her as it hit the floor of the valley.

There was a moment pause, like after a flash of lighting before the thunder. But then the forest awoke as something massive slammed forward through the moss and trees towards where the stone had fallen.

Dimi stood up catching a glimpse as a massive reptilian creature, easily two metres from the tip of its long reptilian mouth to the end of its black and yellow swishing tail raced forward in amazing speed under the upper canopies of moss towards where the stone had fallen.

It stopped momentarily at where the stone had hit and then its elongated head surged again forward to a small bush where it obviously thought its prey was hiding.

The creature's massive maw opened and snapped at the shrub sending twigs and moss flying in all directions.

Dimi could smell the creature from where she stood and the odour turned her stomach. She knew at once that within its mouth was the foul decaying flesh of its previous victims. "A lick from your tongue will rot one's flesh, and in a wound your spit is fatal." Dimi said to herself, her voice less than a breath in the wind. She stood up and brought her blowgun to her lips – waiting, watching for the perfect moment.

Frustrated that it had been deceived the large black lizard snapped at the remnants of the bush and slashed its head back and forth ripping what remained of the plan from the earth and sending it flying. It then turned quickly to face back towards Dimi; its yellow vertically slit eyes dilated as it searched for that which had deceived it.

Dimi blew hard into the reed - aiming for the creature's eye - but at the last minute the animal blinked and the dart bounced off of its tough hardened leather eyelids. Then, its mouth opened ever so slightly revealing hideously yellow needle thin teeth. Black strands of rotten flesh fell from between the teeth down and over its red gums. The beast smiled evilly as it spotted Dimi.

"No, no, no." said Dimi out loud knowing that the time for stealth was over. She frantically looked around her, trying to get her bearings, and trying to judge how fast the creature would be able to reach her.

Dimi stood up and slipped another dart into her gun. She paused a moment, wondering if instead she should reach for her small dagger but then shook her head knowing that if she was within reach of it, one bite would be her ending. Even if nicked, the poison within its mouth would overwhelm her small body in seconds.

The creature's front feet suddenly pumped pulling its massive body forward but so too did Dimi move, but at thrice the speed. However, instead of running away, Dimi ran headlong straight for the beast.

The creature's large body bent back and forth as its three-meter long body was propelled amazingly fast-forward by its four stubby legs. Just as they were almost to each other Dimi leapt.

"BITE ME!" Dimi yelled as she soared up and over the head of the beast. As she landed on its writhing back she turned to watch its head wrap round, its maw snapping open and shut as it pursued her.

"PFFFT" Went the blowgun as Dimi in blinding speed raised it to her lips. The dart flew invisibly fast from it towards the creature and down and into its throat.

"Done!" Dimi yelled as she jumped backward avoiding as the mouth snapped less than a hand span from her face. Dimi danced backward and then leapt as she coughed. "FOUL BREATH!" She called back to the creature in a mocking voice as she raced amazingly fast down its tail.

The lizard coughed and turned its massive body to pursue Dimi. Its massive head shook back and forth frustrated as its eyes blinked, searching for its prey.

Dimi danced forward and under a large curtain of moss and then rounded the tree that it had hung from hoping that the creature had not been able to sense her movement. She held her breath as she rounded the large trunk and looked into the small open area where the beast stood.

Her dash within the moss had been successful, the creature charged where it had seen her enter. Dimi watched as it ran forward. When it reached the curtain of moss its maw opened and snapped, open and close it banged ripping moss in each turn.

Dimi ran back to where she had previously stood and turned, loading in another dart into her blowgun. "HEY STUPID!" She yelled at it.

The creature growled like a bear in heat as it turned lightning fast around to face the small creature that had alluded it. Its eyes were like giants saucers and its mouth was wide open, waiting to grasp its prey.

"SLOWPOKE!" shouted Dimi and she lowered herself into a crouch reading once again to spring.

The creature charged forward, its head, with open mouth moved left and right as it ran forward in its charge, the forest echoed its chomping as its mouth opened and slapped shut over and over again.

Dimi jumped once again, but this time the creature expected her and it stretched its upper body up onto its front toes, hoping to catch the creature before it could reach its back.

But Dimi, smiled, expecting the feint. Her wings opened up in a flash and flapped once sending her a meter higher then flooded again before she hit the branch above. As she descended Dimi's blowgun pointing down expelled another dart – down deep into the beast's throat.

"Pffffft" the dart flew. And then her wings extended and blinked open and closed, giving her just enough lift to land her at the tail of the beast. The beast screamed and roared in frustration and slashed its tail at her.

Dimi, danced over the waiving laughing loudly back at the creature, taunting it. "Is that all you got?" She asked it. "Not much of a dance!"

The jaws on the foul beast snapped shut and then opened as the beast coughed as it tried to turn once again to catch its prey. But then its stubby legs faltered and the creature's pupils narrowed.

The massive lizard froze a moment and then its massive long snout opened and it coughed. The cough came from deep within the beast and its tail swished as it coughed. The maw snapped shut; only to open again as another cough shook it from tail to the tip of its nose.

Confidently, Dimi strode forward out from the moss. "Foul mouth, now has foul throat!"

Dimi's voice sounded comically childish. "Tried to bite me did you? Now your throat's a little tight? Are your eyes a little blurry? Is your sense of smell all gone?"

The beast's mouth opened again widely as it coughed, it was no longer concerned with its prey, but was now totally focused on breathing.

The beast's next cough wasn't loud and ended with a gasp as its throat-swollen shut. With realization of its imminent demise it began to thrash, desperately trying to inhale.

Open and closed snapped its mouth, once, twice, three times as it thrashed back and forth. Its long tail sending moss covered rocks sailing around the little clearing.

"Nasty, nasty foul mouth!" Dimi said almost sadly to it. "You would have eaten me so it serves your right!"

And then suddenly the creature's back arched and its mouth opened again, stretching the sides of its jaw to the point of cracking. The lizard's eyes were wider then plates, frozen in a state of fear as it sensed its own imminent demise. Then, slowly the eyes glazed, its body sagged and its tail went limp. Its massive mouth snapped shut one last time and it lay still, finally dead.

"So sad, you died. Foul, snapping mouth. "Dimi said as she started tentatively back towards the creature.

Dimi stepped lightly over the end of the beast's tail and cautiously worked her way up to its head, watching it intently for any signs that life still beat within its chest. Her head tilted to the side as she crouched down by the lizard's elongated snout. Absentmindedly Dimi dropped her hand down to her pouch and extracted the leather quill packet.

Slowly Dimi pulled out a Dragon Thorn and pinching it at one end, slid the pointed end along the creature's mouth. Green slime slipped up the dart, carefully Dimi turned the dart and once it was covered almost all the way to her fingers she placed it on the ground. One by one she did it to the others then she sat back on the ground and rested her head on her hands. With elbows propped up by her bent legs Dimi sat back and admired her work and waited for the darts to dry.

Of times not long past

Despite the fact that Detros now smiled down on him and the valley below, Etch's mountain shelter was virtually invisible to him from above. Even after all these years on the mountain he often had to actually pass by and approach from below the entrance in order to find it.

The slopes of Diamond Mountain were steep and each step on the loose rocks was treacherous. Small rockslides were frequent all year round, yet lessened in the late fall as ice descended down the sides of the mountain and grabbed hold of the loose shale. Then when the face of the mountain did move it roared as entire ridges fell away.

Etch took his time in his descent, carefully picking each foothold, watching as he lifted his back foot. Crevices and cliffs abounded below. He had been lucky before, another misstep here would likely result in the ground turning liquid and sending him over one of the cliffs. He often wondered what the experience would be like, flying down hundreds of meters, watching the earth race up to kiss you good bye.

Etch wound his way down carefully. Very slowly he moved down the steep incline towards the entrance to his cabin, finally visible in the pale moon glow. The icy air currents were colder, and occasionally now slipped up the back of his legs and up and under his jacket sending shivers down his spine.

A cold rush of wind was in full flow down the mountain. "It will be good to get out of this cold tonight!" Etch said softly as he took another step. His back ached and his head throbbed from where he had banged it when he fell.

The cabin was nothing more than a stable bubble beneath the seemingly solid rocks above. It had likely existed for hundreds of years, formed when a few larger boulders were forced tightly together during one of the countless rockslides that characterized the region. The slide had passed over the larger boulders leaving a convenient gap directly behind them.

He had found it five years ago and quickly made it his mountain camp. It had saved his life a number of times already as a shelter from the sliding rock and biting wind that the mountain threw at him.

Small flakes of snow and ice dust clung to his beard's three days of growth. The stubble of hair on his head and face itched. 'When I get into the cabin I'll start a fire and shave.' he promised himself. Etch enjoyed the feeling of being clean-shaven, and the prospect made him smile.

Etch reached up and touched the back of his head where a bump was starting to form. When be brought his gloved hand back down, he noted that the tips of his fingers were darkened with blood. Grimacing, he reached into his pocket and pulled out a small leather hat.

Etch stepped down another half meter, digging his foot into the shale. Small stones tinkled down a few meters from where his right foot now rested. Gingerly, he pulled up his left foot and stepped the rest of the way down.

"Just cause it's cold – don't go rushing off and kill yourself." he said softly to himself.

He was within twenty meters of the rock ledge that marked the start of the last leg of his journey, and his last chance stop and rest safely. The shelter beckoned just ahead, but he knew it would take him another thirty minutes or more to make that space. The rocks in this specific area of the mountain were not especially loose, yet he always took the most care here. He wanted to ensure this area had the least disturbance. 'When you make a shelter – never leave paths straight up to it. You never know what company might drop by.' he reminded himself as always.

As Etch came within a few more paces of the shelter's entrance he caught a faint whiff of smoke, and saw several tendrils issuing from the cracks along the upper left side of the rocks that formed the better part of the shelter's cover.

Quietly as he could, he edged to the crack on the left and then, just as he was about to step in, he banged on the wall at the entrance and growled as loud as he could. "Graaaar, I am a savagely hungry mighty mountain beast and I smell fresh meat!"

There was the slightest of moments of silence and then a voice came from within. "Very funny, Dad. Not this time."

Etch smiled and then took two more careful steps around the opening.

"Chad, what in the world are you doing up here?" Etch asked as he pushed himself through the narrow crack and into the rock cavern.

Chad was sitting on a stone he used as a chair, poking at a small fire with a piece of wood. He looked up and smiled at his father, and then dropped the stick on the hungry flames. Etch paused for a moment to watch the branch hit the fire. It crackled and caught almost immediately. 'The fires up here burn too fast,' he thought as he looked at the flames, 'and yield too little heat. But my, it does look so lovely warm.'

"How many times have I told you that I specifically didn't want you scaling up to the cavern? Especially without me!" Etch half yelled at his son as he emerged from his reverie and took another step in to the fire's gentle warmth.

"Had to Dad. Mom sent me up to find you. Two men came by yesterday looking for you. It must be something important." These days Chad spoke with ever increasing brevity, as if issuing that extra word in a sentence was just not worth the effort.

Etch looked at his son. 'My has he grown.' Etch thought to himself as he walked over to where Chad sat and ruffled the boy's hair. 'Twelve seasons already, and the lad is as tall as his mother, and with feet bigger than my own.' Etch's smile lessened for a second and then returned. 'It won't be long now and I'll be looking up to my own child.'

Chad was tall and stringy. In the summer, without his shirt, he looked as if he had no meat on him at all. His ribs stuck out and when he bent over and moved his arms, his shoulder blades looked like they would break clean through his skin. He was growing so fast; his body hadn't time to fill out.

Chad's blond, almost white, hair was close-cropped, a simple bowl cut that his mother, Rachael, performed every few weeks. She razored his neck and back of his head with Etch's filleting knife, keeping him clean. Etch expected that the bi-weekly tradition would soon end, as Chad was getting to consider himself to be too much of a man for such things. He was all arms and legs and sinewy muscle. He was always anxious these days to show off just how much strength he now had.

Chad looked over at his dad and smiled. Etch smiled back, then took a few steps towards his son and bent over to give him a big hug.

Etch's hug was welcomed and returned warmly with a big ear-to-ear smile. But Chad's smile turned to a frown as he looked at the bloodstain on the top of Etch's hat. "You're bleeding Dad, sit down – let me take a look."

"What kind of men Chad?" Etch inquired as he plopped himself down on the cold rock floor in front of the stone his son was sitting on.

Hoping to get a fast glance at his son, Etch bent his neck to the side. "What were they wearing, were they village folk, traders, someone mom knew?"

"Stay still Dad." Chad replied, turning his fathers head to point forward once again.

"Soldiers, king's guard." Chad said nonchalantly. "They wore the king's personal insignia on their chests. The king's marking of a shield with a unicorn on it. One had a sword and shield, and the other a spear. Looked like they were regular soldiers, maybe even castle guards."

Etch could feel Chad pushing and prodding on the cut to see how deep it was, and trying to remove a few pieces of stone that had partially filled it. "Man, you did one number on your head." He said as he pulled out yet another small stone. "It's cut wide open in the back. Your hat is soaked with blood. What did you do, bang it on the ground looking for stuff?"

"Very funny. No. I fell. Damn ground moves like quicksilver." Etch struggled as Chad held his head but managed to turn around and look into his son's eyes. "Little more movement and I would have been here a heck of a lot faster, but likely in a few more pieces."

"I wonder what they're doing out here this time of year?" Etch mused out loud, his thoughts returning to his unexpected visitors. "The king hasn't sent his own men this far out for years, and never in the dead of winter like this. With Margrave Mard Devmond so close by he could have just sent a bird to him and had him send someone over."

"Why would he send his own men? I wonder what they wanted? Did you hear anything about what they said to your mother Chad? Did they bang on any others doors in the village below or just ours up here?"

"Don't know." Chad replied. "You got a needle here and some string? I think I should stitch this up."

Etch turned incredulously around to look at his son. "You came halfway up this mountain and you didn't bring along your kit? What type of son did I raise? What did you do, just jump out the door, grabbing your shoes on the way? I didn't raise an idiot did I?"

"Go blow on a snake! Mom said, go up and fetch your Dad. So here I am. I don't need to bring a needle and thread up here, because only an old fool would need one. Any other person wouldn't be so daft as go up on this fool search, never mind to bang his head on the way back down."

Etch scowled, and Chad flinched. His son wasn't quite sure if he had crossed the line and was now somewhat apprehensive. He wasn't going to push farther, but he wasn't going to apologize either. Etch turned back around and reaching into a small pocket on the inside of his jacket pulled out a small leather pouch, which he handed to Chad over his shoulder.

Chad took the pouch and removed a long heavy needle and some coarse thread. "This is a thick needle for the head, so it will hurt some. I hope I don't tear your flesh."

Etch sat still. "Just take your time. I trust you won't - not if you want to sleep on your back tonight."

Etch sat quietly for a moment while his son worked. The needle stung as his son slowly repaired the cut.

"It ain't a fools quest you know." Etch said in a brooding tone. "We know the Drekians marched up this mountain in retreat from Gallant's men. They got most of the way up there and then the mountain just gave out. Swallowed up the entire lot of them."

Etch went on in a dreamy sort of tone. "Every time I'm up here I can 'feel' something. Like something darting just out of sight, something standing in the grey shadows of a cave not quite visible. I can feel it - there is something on this mountain, something of value, something of power."

Chad sighed and paused slightly to look down at his dad. He knew this was an obsession with his father, one unlikely to end soon, but he couldn't help commenting on it. "The king's men spent years looking for it before I was even born. You've been searching all those years, and all the years that I've been alive… and for what? What's gone is gone. This mountain is not going to give them up."

Etch turned back towards his son. "You don't understand. That army of 2000 men, all on foot, had looted and plundered a dozen castles. They did it because they could, and they *took the riches with them.*"

Etch turned back around so that his son could continue his sewing. "They did things we couldn't explain - they must have had magic. We always appeared days behind them in everything they did and everyplace they went. Only on a few occasions did some of our advanced troops ever catch up with them – and then it always cost us those groups. They traveled amazingly fast, though no one knows how they could keep the pace that we on horse could not sustain."

"Then one day Roehn guessed right as to where they would hit next and we sent all our men out to confront them face on – all on blind faith, for nothing else was working. Two thousand men on horse rode to battle this mysterious army. Any man or horse that travelled too slowly was left behind. We rode hard and fast and men and horses dropped like flies."

"And all for naught." Etch continued sadly. "They must have seen us coming or known somehow that we were there. We never got to face them for a final battle. But when they got here – the mountain did what our best forces were not able to; it swallowed them up whole. It did with one blow what our entire army could not."

Etch looked at his son and pointed with his index finger. "Never underestimate the power of a mountain."

Chad laughed. "Yeah yeah yeah, blah blah blah. I've heard this story a hundred times. Stay still now or I'll stick you and prove there aren't any brains in this skull."

Chad peered down, pinched his dad's skin and started poking the needle through again. "It's a good thing you're bald up top, makes this easier."

Etch winced. "Ouch, just don't make it worse then it already is, and don't pull the thread too tight."

"Quite whining, I thought you were some great warrior or something?" Chad replied.

"No, never was the strong stupid type you seem bound and determined to grow up to be. I was a scout boy that means fast, smart…. I was a well-known expert tracker. They said I had eyes like a hawk, and brains to out-think any enemy. I was not a pike or sword man." Etch replied with pride.

Chad met his father's verbal parry and poised for a thrust of his own. "You mean to say, you ran from the battles, not to them."

"Funny, Chad. We were sent to them precisely to hit fast and retreat, to draw the enemy out so we could weaken them and truly know their numbers, and when fighting the Drekians that wasn't easy! I was the only one from our group of scouts to live long enough to see the end of the Dreks."

"Yeah, and one of the last to join the group if I recall correctly. Drafted weren't you?" Chad said putting great sarcasm into his tone once again.

"Nothing wrong with that. Old enough to know that soldiers die, and young enough to join with grinning face when called by my king." Etch responded, his voice still proud. "Never lied about that to no one. And once you're in the thick of a battle it doesn't mean much anyway."

Chad looked down at his dad as he finished sewing. He wiped off the needle and replaced it in the leather pouch now sitting beside him. "The king tore half the mountain down looking for them, and never found hide nor hair. What makes you so sure you will? If they're buried the way you say they are, they must be 10 meters down or more. You could stand right on them and never know it."

Then quickly, to redirect the conversation in a vain hope for victory in the conversation Chad added. "That's it – got a knife?"

"A knife? "You don't have a KNIFE either?" Etch bellowed incredulously as he wrenched around to face his son.

Chad chucked and pulled his knife from his belt, holding it up before his glowering father. "Gotcha. Now hold still or I'll cut you."

"Idiot boy." Etch grumbled and held still while his son cut the thread close to his head.

Chad replaced the remaining string in the pouch and handed it back to his father. "So, lets go. It's too damn cold up here to spend the night."

"I don't think so." Etch replied as he shook his head. "We have jerky and hard loaf and a few apples for dinner. We have a nice warm blanket we can share. We'll head down in the morning. Going tonight would be a fast way to make your sister an only child and your mother a widow. The cold drafts from the peak have made the slopes slick with ice. How do you think I banged my head, fool child?"

Chad looked disappointed as Etch turned around on the floor to face him. "Ah, Dad, I was hoping to put my new string on my bow tonight. I got it from town. It's made special, and the man said it will shoot twice as far."

"Well then, likely you were robbed. Nothing will outshoot the gut string I set for you. If you need more distance then it's time for a new bow – one that will make your arms hurt from pulling."

Chad smiled back at his dad. "That would work for me too. When can I get one, or better yet, can I have yours? Don't you need a new one?"

"I think not," said Etch in reply. He stood up, brushed off the back of his pants and went to the back of the cave behind the small fire. There he pulled back a large rock and felt back into the crevice it revealed. With a long hard pull, he drew out a bag, tied tight with a heavy string. He gave it a big pitch and sent it flying to his son. "Grab this and make yourself useful. Cut us up some tack and bread and then let's get some sleep. I think we're in for a long day tomorrow."

Montterran and the King

The liege Lord of Montterran, Roehn the Third, looked out of his study's window, set high atop the castle's keep and strained his eyes into focus. He hated staying within the castle and yearned for even a glimpse of the fields of Montterran. In the distance beyond the portcullis, he knew the men; women and children of his realm were hard at work reaping the results of a bountiful summer. How he desired to be out riding among them enjoying this fall day and revelling with his people during the harvest.

Roehn leaned heavily on his walking stick and looked down at his legs. His right foot, thickly bandaged with white cloth, peaked out from beneath his long blue tunic. His page had split a pair of hose so that he could at least cover his other leg but it was blue as well, making the bandaged foot stand out that much more.

He wanted to pace he was so frustrated and it only served to irk him further that pacing was out of the question. He couldn't bear to stand still and yet here he stood – his folly visible for all to see. The price of an afternoon's sport had been steep; it had cost him much more than just bruised ribs, a hurt back and a broken foot.

The King turned with difficulty and looked at his aide. "Why is it taking so damn long? If I don't get some good information soon – all may be lost!"

Lord Mitos, the viscount of Passion Mont and aide to the King, knew the severity of the situation in front of his liege. More importantly however, as the King's trusted advisor and confidant he knew the personal trauma his dear friend was facing.

Lord Bartholomue Mitos returned the King's visibly distraught gaze as calmly as he could. He had to try to determine not what to say, but in what tone to say it. After all, most of the information that would be forthcoming the King already knew.

The viscount cleared his throat and then responded in an even tone, his voice leavened with a hint of understanding. "There isn't much we can add to what you already know my Liege. We have already sent for the merchant who has just come back from TerranAdd. As you heard, reports have arrived stating that upon return he informed the captain at the Eastern gate that the great city and castle of TerranAdd stands empty, that it is devoid of all men, women and children. Even the cats and dogs, he claims, appear to have vacated the Terran capital city."

"He says that the castle gates stand wide open, yet there is no sign of siege, battle, blood or arrow visible in or around the city." Here Lord Mitos paused, allowing his words to sink in.

"Captain Thesra has informed me." Lord Mitos continued. "That rumours are coming in that another rider has returned from the city with similar claims; that of the thousands that lived in and around that vast city there was not to be found neither man, woman, nor child. But until we can talk to someone that has actually been there that is all we have – rumours."

Mitos knew that beneath his official concerns, there was even something deeper disturbing his liege. Princess Elle, the king's only child and his most precious possession, had been visiting that same city and was now in the host of thousands counted missing.

King Roehn had himself planned on journeying to TerranAdd with his daughter that same day, and would have had he not hurt himself while hunting. Mitos knew that what truly nagged the King now was the unspoken thought that, had he been there, he would at least know what had befallen his daughter, and perhaps could have protected her.

Mitos rose from his chair beside the King's desk and approached Roehn, imbuing his voice with as much hope as he could muster. "All the trades people, everyone in the city, know that we will pay for good information. We know as much as anyone within these castle walls. One hundred of our best and fastest armed soldiers have already been dispatched to investigate. Still my Liege, you must realize that it will take days for word to get back to us as to the true fate of TerranAdd…and your daughter.

Mitos took another step towards his liege, and spoke again, this time as a friend. "The thread merchant was exhausted and scared to death when he got here, he drove his rig as fast as he could to return to Mount Ryhn with his news. Perhaps your daughter and her guards had left before whatever emptied the streets, and in his haste and fear the merchant didn't notice her, or rode past her caravan in the night. Our own men may stumble upon them at any time, safe and away from TerranAdd."

King Roehn breathed a sigh, turned back to the window and then glanced over his shoulder at Mitos. "If I wanted a fool's advice, I would have hired someone from the local tavern to be my aide. Speak not to me of an impossible hope."

"Talk to me of things real, Lord Mitos. If something attacked and brought TerranAdd to it's knees – brought the mighty King Tar and his great court and castle down, then what befell him and his befell my daughter Elle as well."

The King bent over and touched his bandaged leg absentmindedly as it pained him. "Elle dotes on Tar's daughter Mindy and loves her as a sister and the Terran King and his Queen Terresa love Elle as a daughter, she would not have departed early from their celebration."

King Roehn paused, the weight of his fears visible in the lines creasing his brow. "There is also but one main road between there and here; I doubt the merchant could have missed my daughter's guarded caravan."

Mitos had to nod in agreement with the King's observations. He knew the chance of Elle having left early was slight, but he felt compelled to offer the King what little hope there was.

"My liege, there would have been thousands of additional people within the city walls this week for the festivities. Her father would have had visiting lords from PlanTer, Santer, and AnnonTer and even possibly from lands further to the east, and those lords would have had their guards as well. They would have all been there, just as Elle was there. Everyone was bid come by the Tar to celebrate his daughter's sixteenth birthday. There would have been tens of thousands of people within those gates. Surely some of those knights and lords would have made an escape and taken your daughter with them for safety and honour's sake."

Roehn turned to face Mitos and rubbed a hand across his brow wearily, as if seeking to erase the lines, which appeared as a testament to his tension. "And then where did they go? How could it be that no other word then got out? I find this all very incredulous. With five thousand men at arms I wouldn't be able to pull TerranAdd down in less than a month. And what army of that size could get within distance without notice? And why, if they were attacked, did no runner come to us to ask for aid?"

Mitos looked solemnly over to his King. "I know my liege." Mitos knew as well, that Roehn was punishing himself for not accompanying his daughter on the trip. Roehn was a proud man and after the fall he hadn't wanted anyone in TerranAdd to see him with his cane in hand, unable to sit through a feast. He was worried that they would think him weak, so he had sent his daughter alone. Now he was regretting it bitterly.

Roehn took a halting step forward with his bad leg and cane and staggered to his desk. He sat down hard and pulled in his chair, wincing as he did so. "What befell that city has befallen my daughter, and even as we still search I grieve, but still bigger problems face us. Do not think that all I contemplate is my own loss. If an army of such size as to take TerranAdd has manifested itself here, then it were meet to take action ourselves to prepare our own defence."

Mitos moved nearer and sat back down in one of the large, armless chairs facing the desk. "And if others know that TerranAdd stands empty then indeed we must think of our own people and their safety. As we discussed, all men at arms both within our walls and without are on alert. Captain Thesra has been summoned and should arrive shortly."

Mitos opened up a roll of parchment lying on the desk and looked over the numbers written elegantly on it. He turned it slightly to show the King his reckonings. "We have been more than prosperous of late, and you have been frugal in your spending, our coffers are full and we have adequate funds to finance both an expanded call to arms and also to purchase whatever we need to fortify our city."

Roehn looked at the parchment, laughed without humour, then frowned and sighed. "With a threat such as this one may prove to be, we will find our coffers slim pickings in a short time. I fear that we are not looking at a small group of raiders. My first thought is of the Drekians, come again across the sea and down from the north. Quickly in and out with no survivors is their trademark."

Mitos shook his head. "But they have never hit a city of this size. Also, the merchant indicated that there were no carrion birds circling the city, no bodies in the streets, nor nearby. There were also no signs of arrows or spears, stuck in either ground or body, nor damage to the turrets or walls. If an army hit the castle of TerranAdd, then there should have been lots of bodies, or burning pyres that could be seen for miles. This is very strange, and seems to suggest something new."

Roehn nodded. "It has been decades since the Drekian siege, and if it were they, then surely Lord Bothos on our Northern borders would have noted their passing. We expanded the Orthos castles and watches to ensure that they would never again surprise us. Surely if it had been them, or the Tocks, we would have heard by now.

The King, sounding increasingly weary, continued. "Mitos, you must think me a fool to worry about them still after all these years, but I've always thought we haven't heard the last of them. Yes, this does feel different, but they pillaged countless of our castles and destroyed both Terran and Montterran strongholds and settlements. Entire villages were simply gutted and abandoned."

Mitos nodded. "All of us within these lands remember those days and still fear the return of the Drekians. Yet, never did they have the audacity to attack the capital city itself; TerranAdd was always too well fortified. Also, when they did attack, although they moved like the wind and seemed to know our every thought, they were still flesh and blood. They always left bodies."

Roehn stretched his neck, looking up at the ceiling in wordless entreaty, and then sighed heavily. "No matter who, we will not be slow to wake this time. I want our battlements fully armed day and night with archers. I want our horsemen ready to ride on the second and our foot soldiers battle ready and stationed within the barracks around the city walls."

Roehn raised his voice and directed his next order across the room. "Page! Call in Thesra. And someone find me that merchant already; I want to see the man myself!"

A boy, no older than eight and practically invisible in his neat grey uniform, jumped up from the small stool at the back of the room where he had been seated until now and ran for the door. He threw it open and in his haste ran full force into a man, fully clad in chain mail, who had been standing just outside the door.

Captain Thesra strode forward, tall and proud. His head was uncovered and his long black hair brushed the collar of his blue surcoat, which opened to reveal Roehn's crest, a silver shield and unicorn, emblazoned on his chest. His chain hauberk rustled as he moved forward, and swayed slightly. Scale greaves shone brightly overtop his shiny polished riding Sabaton He turned as he entered the room - "Theta, you ok boy?

The page nodded and looked up reverently as Thesra strode past him towards the King. "Yes, my Lord."

Theta picked himself up off the ground and brushed the dust from his simple linen tunic, then turned and bowed low to the King. "My liege, is there anything else I can get for you? Perhaps some wine?"

Roehn smiled at his nephew, relieved that he hadn't been hurt in the collision. He winked at the lad and shook his head. "No, clear heads are needed tonight, rather bring us some talc and cheese. We won't be interrupting our planning for dinner."

"Yes my Lord." Theta responded with another low bow, backing out of the room and closing the door behind him.

Thesra strode over to the King's desk, bringing with him a long, rolled piece of parchment. Roehn motioned him to sit in the last chair beside Mitos. "Thesra," Roehn started. "Where do we stand with men at arms?"

Thesra leaned back in his chair and nodded. "As you know 'The Fist' was sent immediately to TerranAdd to investigate. They travel without wagon or accompaniment, so as to make better time. If you want to march on TerranAdd in force, then I can field five hundred more knights, a thousand men at arms, and 300 archers that could march from Mount Ryhn within two days notice. It will take me those two days to assemble enough supplies and wagons. That would leave us with a home guard of 100 knights, 500 men at arms and one hundred archers to defend the walls."

Mitos looked over at Thesra, "What of the lords of our court? What can they offer us in terms of men at arms?"

Thesra shook his head. "As yet I know not the sum of what the lords can bring to aid us. Once the news of TerranAdd spreads they will likely come forward freely to offer men and aid. Men from the countryside and city are not of short supply, the winters have been gentle and the crops good for many a year. We should be able to recruit quickly, but it will take a few months to fully arm and train them. Most are, after all, busy with the harvest."

Thesra looked over at Mitos as he continued. "I suggest that we ensure the defence of our borders. Let the lords of our court start recruiting, but do not draw their men into the city just yet. Let them rather start building boundary defences. Mount Ryhn's back is to the mountains, unlike TerranAdd. Our focus must be on keeping our forward defences up and strong – and building them ever stronger. I can start sending them word immediately – but I know their first question will be of cost – they have been at peace a long time and not had to pay much in taxes as of late."

Mitos thumped his fist on the desktop emphatically. "No loyal lord would worry of cost at a time like this. We will simply tell them to do it, and we will determine the payments later. But we must also tell them to keep good records of all their expenses and that I myself will audit their records before a single coin is paid."

Mitos turned back to Roehn. "My liege, you should call them all to court for immediate council."

Roehn nodded. "Done. Make a note and send out birds in the morning Mitos."

Thesra nodded, and then added. "It isn't just men we will need, but armour, swords, horses... We can ask the Lord of Sieren to send out his trade fleet and start purchasing. Their trade routes are good. They should be able to obtain whatever quantities of other stuffs we will likely need for now."

Thesra slowed somewhat in his speech here, not quite comfortable in this realm of finance and accounting which he was now forced to consider. "To grow to any sure size it will take time to recruit, dress, train and armour. We will not have the time to set our own blacksmiths to work. My liege, our lands have been too long at peace; we will have to buy most of what we need.... It will be an expensive expansion if we wish to move quickly."

Lord Mitos jumped up then, casting an angry look in Thesra's direction before returning his focus to the King. "Do not think about the cost at this time. Our coffers have more than enough to start this. My liege, you must move now, you must move men at arms of sufficient strength to TerranAdd to defend it from any other who would add their pillaging to the chaos."

"I beg you my liege," Mitos continued emotionally. "We have talked of this already - if we know of the fall of TerranAdd then so will the Mohen, the Tock and the Masti. The Mohen are only slightly farther from those gates then we are, and the Masti have longed to regain the lands they lost during the blood wars."

"Further," Lord Mitos continue slowly. "If TerranAdd is left undefended and you can secure it – men of Montterran will farm the surrounding lands and count themselves doubly blessed. We will not want for income next year, for the Terran soil is rich and rewarding. The Cliff Mines alone will pay back your costs in but a few months. You must act now, and act with sufficient force. Take the risk of exposing yourself here for a short while."

Thesra grudgingly agreed. "What Mitos says is true. Although costly, we must move. Our back is to the wall, but if another comes to claim TerranAdd our cost will be greater still. We are very dependent on our trade with the Terrans. If the Mohen, or worse, the Masti, take TerranAdd – we would be backed into a corner. We should start now with thought of expanding and defending not just Montterran but also TerranAdd and the counties surrounding. Whatever has come, it has crushed an army of significant size already. The more I think on it, the less I think this the work of the Drekians. I do still fear though, that if word gets to them of our weakness here, they too will come to continue the slaughter.

Roehn stood and nodded decisively. "By our friendship with TerranAdd we are already ourselves declared in war, although with no face to name our enemy. We need to recall all solders and men to defend our walls, and within weeks, not months, I want a full two thousand foot solders and a thousand archers stationed to guard this city, ready to move at our command – more if we can. Start now setting up for armouries. We must think battlements and defences with a single goal – to leave no area uncovered."

Roehn walked around the desk and perched on the edge looking down at Thesra. "Start a full conscription. Our neighbour's capital is open and her people all gone – likely dead. Others will follow, but not us. We need to defend ourselves, and also to raise an army to confront this foe. .

"Mitos, send birds to all the other lords of the realms. I want each lord to start building up their own strength of arms to defend our regional cities and towns… and we will use them to help expand our battlements around Terran."

Thesra stoop abruptly. "A quick, mobile army and defences for a major siege. I understand my liege and will get on with the task right away."

Mitos stood as well and turned to Thesra. "We must keep our eyes and ears as open as possible. We know not what we face. The army that took TerranAdd may have been quick at their job, but it still would have had to be massive to carry away and dispose of the bodies. We must take no chances this time, but neither can we be slow to act."

Roehn pulled himself to his feet and grabbed the cane resting against his desk. "Thesra, I want battlements established around our lands. Extend them first to the southern border we share with the Terran. Build towers that can defend smaller groups – buildings that we can establish runners or signals from. We need to ensure that we can see this enemy before it is upon us. The lack of such towers is what almost lost us to the Drekians. How lax we have been not to have built them since!"

Thesra's eyes narrowed as he stepped towards the King. He unrolled the parchment he carried, which proved to be a map of Montterran and its surroundings. "We should position the bastions in places with the greatest vantage points, but also in places where warnings can be sent by both bird and man."

Thesra pointed at the middle of the large map. "I would suggest we build beyond the river that separates our lands from Terran, up in the hills, just before TerranAdd. A wall of battlements could oversee the plains on both sides. In this way if Terran lands are besieged we can fall back to the high ground of the hills. If that line fails, then we can fall back to the river. By the time they cross the river we will be ready for them within our castle gates. Our own city walls should also be shorn up. We will need men to work on them."

"The King of Terran and I have always been good friends." Roehn said quietly. "His daughter Mindy was Elle's closest friend. Never would I have thought to lay claim to his lands. But if TerranAdd has fallen the Tocks will move in, and most certainly – if it wasn't already the Mohen to blame for this travesty – they too will be on the move. The Mohen have long begrudged King Tar their eastern lands. PlanTer stands as a thorn in their side. It is the strongest of Terran defences, guarded by the most men at arms of any region for that fact."

Thesra shook his head. "No, had Mohen attacked PlanTer first, King Tar would have known of it and made ready. He would also have called for our aid."

"Perhaps in some way the Mohen bypassed PlanTer via TenTor?" Lord Mitos speculated. "Mohen soldiers could have used boats to reach the southern shores. But then, there are the castles of SanTer and TenTor... Hmm this is a great puzzle."

Mitos shook his head to clear it. "Also, if the prize was the city itself, then there would be new soldiers there, it wouldn't be standing empty. And if they had landed at TenTor their first move would have been to SanTer and the Cliff Mines, not to TerranAdd."

"The only given truth we have," Mitos, continued. "Is that TerranAdd stands empty, and King Tar is no longer there to guide what people remain. It was fortunate that many of the Terran lords did not attend themselves, but instead sent their sons and daughters else there would be no order left within the land at all. However, what little power and order remains within the lands will not be sufficient to hold back the Masti. Those carrion will be out in force to pick at the bones of that once great land – attempting to regain what they lost in the blood wars."

Thesra piped in. "The Tocks are also a concern. The towers of NinonTer and AnnonTer are strong and well armed, but the Tocks have ever been a race to challenge poor odds. If they have heard of the fall of TerranAdd then I am sure they are traveling south as we speak." Thesra. "But of greater fear would be the Mohen. IF the emperor turns his eyes west... We can only hope that his ambitions have waned as he grew old."

"First we must prepare I think for the Tock. We should get word to the battlements at Oathos to be on the lookout." Thesra added quickly and then slowed to a more controlled tone. "My liege, I have already called back to service all known scouts and officers just recently retired. A few scouts have already been sent north and south to search for signs of the aggressor – several will be sent to the Sea of Tears and others to our southern coast."

Roehn stood and hobbled back over to the fireplace. "To search for a faceless enemy that has vanquished an entire city. We face an enemy who would take a capital city only to leave it open and untouched. It makes so little sense that all of its people are gone. No one can move that many slaves that quickly and leave no trail behind."

All heads turned as the door opened and Theta re-entered carrying a heavily laden platter. The page quickly set the platter down, poured 3 short glasses and handed them to the men. A large block of white cheese along with a small loaf of bread and a knife he left sitting on the platter as he strode over to the fireplace and started to work at assembling wood in the hearth.

"Yes, a fire to warm us and keep our thoughts clear. " Roehn said and then winced. He turned slowly and walked back to his desk, taking his seat once more.

Thesra moved forward and cut off a piece of cheese. He stuffed it in his mouth and washed it down by draining the glass of talc. The dark liquid was cold and bitter. 'That was a large gulp of talc to consume this late in the day.' Thesra thought to himself. 'I won't be sleeping at all tonight.'

Upon swallowing the talc Thesra raised his head and spoke loudly "The search, my liege, will be by the brightest and best this country has to offer. If there is any sign of the enemy or our princess, our men will find it."

Roehn turned red in the face, lifted his arm and pointed at Thesra. "I have just said this to Lord Mitos not ten minutes ago, and I do NOT want to have to repeat myself to every fool in this world – so mark my words and spread them around. Our country, and the lives of ALL our citizens are at stake here. Your men go to search for our country's enemies and not just for the whereabouts of my daughter. If in their travels they happen upon her – then indeed I shall rejoice, but at this point my belief is that she is lost."

"My will, the will of the King, and all our resources, will be focused on one objective and one objective alone, and that is the protection and safety of the people left alive. Do I make myself clear to both of you?"

Thesra and Mitos both nodded solemnly. They knew their lord's heart was breaking – but would not offend him by showing it.

King Roehn looked at Thesra. "I want every man able to hold an axe or bend a bow to be prepared to be mobilized if need be. I leave it to you to ready them and to ensure we have the arms to support and defend this realm. I don't want a rabble of farmers I want a well-trained army. And find me a count fast as to what my lords should be able to field so that I am prepared when they arrive."

Captain Thesra spoke with uncommon clarity and confidence now. "I agree. I would rather have one soldier over four farmers. Leave it to me my liege. We will start the conscription and ensure that every person in this city knows what to do should we be attacked. Every man able to hold a club will be organized. I will start to properly arm another five thousand men within the next three months and you should have another group of that same number ready by the summer."

"Good. Do it. Start now." King Roehn said shortly. "Make my people feel safe tonight and tomorrow. Have a visible presence at the walls. Keep fires burning around the city for everyone to see! A people that don't feel secure cannot sleep nor work. Our people must continue with their harvesting, their tanning and canning and their preparations for the winter."

Lord Mitos nodded. "I will start coordinating the creation of a large caravan, obtaining as many wagons as we can – and I will also start looking for workers. We will be moving more than soldiers into TerranAdd – we will need cooks, blacksmiths, bakers…"

Roehn nodded as he envisioned the pieces coming together. "Go then Thesra, start preparing our defence and armies.... I will announce tomorrow that you have been appointed General of the Combined Montero Forces and you can start organizing my lord's men. We have been so long at peace; it will be a challenge. However, the time is come to bring the Montterran forces together again as one. The call to arms must be sounded."

General Thesra stood and inclined his head to Roehn. "My liege."

Thesra turned smartly, strode to the door and started to exit but stopped when Roehn called. "Each day, at this hour, we will meet to discuss our strategy. Bring with yourself any new captains you think need come." Thesra turned and nodded once more, then opened the door and exited the room.

Roehn sighed and sat down. "Mitos, my fear is that these one hundred riders of the Fist will arrive at TerranAdd and that they will be able to tell us little more then what we already know. We need to start working on a sounder intelligence strategy. Any ideas? Who within court can we bring to our council that can help us there?"

Mitos was quick to respond. "I will send birds and runners out with word to all the lords of the realm that there will be both a senior and general Council of Lords."

Roehn shook his head, stood and staggered over to the hearth where the fire was starting to crackle under Theta's watchful care. As the boy noted Roehn's approach he stepped aside and moved to take a seat by the end of the mantle but paused when Roehn nodded in the direction of the door. "Theta, please leave us." the King commanded. "I have things of confidence to talk with Mitos about."

Theta nodded sharply and jogged out the door, closing it softly behind him.

Mitos followed the boy with his eyes, ensuring that he and the King were in no danger of being overheard before speaking. "We need men of 'intelligence' at these times you said, I imagine your majesty means spies and informers?"

"I will need your help Mitos, if we are to persevere. We must have information." Roehn said.

"Build yourself a trusted staff my Lord Mitos." King Roehn continued softly. "You must be our General of Intelligence and Security. Find me a replacement to work as chancellor; someone that can keep an eye on our finances, for that will soon become a full time job, and I will need you and yours elsewhere."

King Roehn reached down and massaged his hurt leg. "If there is a threat from within or dissention among the lords, I want to know about it. I want to know about what my people fear and how their trade is faring. Are they venturing into the hills and mountains or are they too scared? I need to know it all." "Hmm, tall order to ask for intelligence from those within court." Mitos replied with a touch of humour in his tone. "Let me make a rather radical suggestion my liege. Have you ever heard of a man called Dimo Misinton? He is quite well known throughout the less savoury taverns in town as the master of our cities Thief's Guild."

"Thief's Guild? No such thing in our town." Roehn said sardonically.

Mitos continued. "Misinton is the man currently in charge of the Guild. No one is exactly sure of how old he is, but he has definitely seen a few more winters than most. He has a daughter, one Dimona. I hear tell she is now the heart of his intelligence operation. She is renowned not just for her work with knives, but also for the fact that she seems to know about every noble, and where every coin or jewel resides within the walls of our city. Dimona also appears to have quite a few interests outside the walls."

Roehn nodded his head. "So you have some candidates for your team. I will leave you to it. Just keep me at arm's length. It would not be meet for the King to know too much about dealings such as these. And remember, my people's safety comes first."

"Aye, my liege." Mitos said, rising. "Let me be off then too. There is much I have to do. I will take your leave sire, and start my planning. Is there another that I might call on for you, or something else that I should look to do?"

"No, go." Roehn said and pulled himself up again to stand.

Mitos took a few steps towards the door and then stopped. "My liege, no matter your focus, you know the people also bear the same hurt you do at the absence of our princess. Our prayers will be made nightly for her safe return."

Mar Roehn, for a moment just a man, the father of an only child now lost, looked up at Mitos, a single tear visible but held stubbornly back. "My daughter is lost Mitos, gone with the thousand other souls of TerranAdd. I am alone now. My beloved Mary I lost at her birth, and now she too is gone."

Roehn sighed deeply and looked down. When he looked back up the man was gone and the King had returned. "But we will only truly be alone when we lie within the damp earth – and that day shall not come for us or for our people if we do what must be done. We must be prepared, we must work hard and above all – we must be smarter then our enemies. Never stop thinking of what we should be doing. No idea is to be overlooked…."

"Aye my liege." After a moment of silence, so heavy Mitos could barely bring himself to return the King's impassioned stare he turned to leave. As he opened the door Theta slipped back in.

"Shall I prepare your quarters sire?" Theta asked from behind Roehn 's chair.

Roehn looked back over his shoulder at his page. "No. Go now and take your own bed. I will stay up a while yet and think."

Theta nodded and then walked quietly over to the door. As he opened and exited he turned. His voice was soft. "Then I will go to the chapel before bed and say a prayer for Elle. She was so kind to my brother and me, I often thought of her as our sister. I will miss her."

As his page closed the door Roehn lowered his head to his hands and began to weep.

Of ButterBread Toadstools

Dimi smiled as she passed under the last of the moss curtains and entered the massive area under the towering cliffs that marked the end of the Old Woman Peninsula. "My private and most secret place." She said lifting a hand to shield her eyes as she walked forward into the warmth of the sun.

The peninsula ended spectacularly. A white sandy valley floor stretched before Dimi, nearly a hundred meters round. The Sun shone down from directly above, reflecting off of the curved two hundred meter high cliffs that terminated the valley.

Dimi caught her breath as the heat of the sun reflected off of the cliffs hit her. It was stiffening hot, and the sand beneath her leathered shoes almost burned the soles of her feet. Dimi smiled as she stepped forward towards the cliffs, looking up at their pockmarked faces.

Caves of all sizes dotted the sheer cliffs, but Dimi knew them all very well. Confidently she walked forward keeping her eye on them getting her bearings and searching out the one she was looking for. She licked her lips as she envisioned the look of the large golden toadstools bathed in the moisture created by the meeting of hot air and moist salty winds from the sea.

As she approached the base of the cliff Dimi strained her neck and looked all the way up. Way atop seagulls screeched and soared in the warm rising air currents.

Dimi had only once climbed to the top. She loved to watch the birds, but had soon found out that a few of the caves within the wall went all the way through. By traversing fifty or more meters in the darkness she could get to a ledge and be able to sit comfortably and watch them while being protected from their droppings.

"I will picnic there." She said to herself looking up to another large cave entrance a good fifty meters up from the ground she now stood upon.

Dimi climbed skilfully. She climbed with confidence and sureness, moving slowly up the side of the cliff, her tiny fingers finding almost invisible finger holds, her thin leathered feet pressing hard against the stone she lifted off of the ground and rose up the cliff's face.

The cave that held her prized food was not up too high, and Dimi made it there confidently in but a few minutes. She turned momentarily as she entered it pausing to breath in its moist cool air.

Dimi took a few steps into the cave and then sat down and closed her eyes. The cool cave air felt very refreshing after the hot dusty climb. She paused with eyes closed, hoping to adjust them to the darkness before her.

In her mind she recalled her previous trips into the cave. 'Thirty metres then the crumbling stones and where I must crawl through the small opening. Then back and to the left where it opens up, where the moisture drips down from above onto the bed of toadstools!

In the past she had brought torches to this place to explore. Her night sight was spectacular, but back deep within the caves; there was no light what so ever. But now, after venturing to these cliffs so many times, torches were no longer needed and they were definitely not desired! Their smell seemed to defile the sanctity of her special place the darkness within the caves now almost felt 'pure' and the sweat scent of the toadstools had an almost hypnotic effect on her. It was the closest thing Dimi could have to a religious experience. There was no other thing in life that had ever made her feel better, or more at one with the world or nature then finding the toadstools and eating them while watching seagulls soar over the cliffs and the sea.

Dimi's memory was excellent and her sense of hearing was beyond superb. She opened her eyes and stood, knowing that for many more paces she would not need to crouch. She walked forward slowly yet confidently rounding stalagmite and stalactite sometimes sensing them before she could even feel them with her outstretched hands. The cave rounded slightly and narrowed, cutting out all remaining light and within ten more strides the last green glimmer from within her eyes dissipated and even when she brought her hand in front of her face, she could not see them. She paused and then continued her slow, confident walk listening intently for the echoes of her footfalls against the cave walls.

It had been only her third trip into the caves when she had ventured forth unaided – this was part of the excitement – "The 'treasure' hunt begins!" Dimi said to herself in a whisper. Her words echoing and reflecting back to her.

After a few more strides Dimi moved to a crouch and then began to crawl as the cave's floor rose up to meet its ceiling. Even though she crawled, her pace quickened as she realised that beyond the narrowing would be a larger opening. Just ahead was her intended destination – a large open towering cavern, filled with moisture. A pool of water would be at one end, fresh and clean filled from a bubbling spring, and against the other wall, continually bathed from dripping water from high above would lie her treasured feast!

Just as she was pulling herself through the last of the narrowing, onto the floor of the opening Dimi froze as she inhaled. The sweet scent she had expected was not there. Instead, in its place, was the scent of decay and death.

Dimi halted, frozen in her crouch. She hadn't even sensed it, nor smelled it – yet something was there ahead of her, waiting for her in the absolute darkness. She froze and held her breath and listened intently. Then, ever so slowly she breathed out and in – trying to discern the first scent she had smelled.

'Was I spooked by the foul mouth, or do I smell his scent on me?' She thought to herself for now, the scent of toadstools was all she could smell. Pausing a moment more, listing her hand reached forward in the darkness searching out the next spot her knee should go.

Nothing she had ever seen nor ever heard of could have moved as fast or as silently as what then raced over and scratched her hand. Dimi brought back her scratched hand and clutched it to her breast. Her heart quickened its beat as adrenaline surged through her – 'What creature could move so fast and sure in this darkness that it might scratch me and run back to cover? She froze and breathed in deep hoping for a scent of it. She brought up her hand; it smelled of dust and burnt coal. "Bats?" She whispered as she listened intently for the sound of possible leather wings.

"Mouse, bat, or rat." Dimi whispered to herself after a moment of silence had passed. "Mouse, bat or rat." Dimi turned her head from left to right hoping to catch a sound. She breathed in deep but still heard and smelled nothing. 'Perhaps my nose is just spoiled from having been so close to foul mouth.' Dimi thought as she bent down trying to see if the scent she had caught a moment before had come from her pouch.

Dimi took another crawling step forward and something scurried up behind her and bit the back of her heel through her leather strapping. "Ouch, damn RAT." Dimi shrieked, her high-pitched voice shrill and echoing in the cave. She kicked out with her leg lightening fast and flailed with her now drawn dagger in the area the critter had been – but felt nothing on the tip of her blade but the hard rock covered ground.

Her heart raced, this time, she had heard it move. It had walked, crawled with sharp clawed feet, but if it was a rat – it was then a very large one and one almost a third her own size. Dimi swallowed and concentrated trying to slow her beating heart.

She turned back to face the cave's entrance but stopped and did not move fearing that if she turned to crawl back she would give the creature an opportunity to attack her from behind. Instead, she turned and her softest, friendliest, most musical voice echoed gently through the cave. "Are you guarding your littler – little one? I won't hurt them, I promise!"

Dimi's emerald eyes were open as far as they would go; yet she could see nothing. "I should have brought a torch." Dimi whispered to herself.

"You don't know just how stupid you were." A high-pitched, scratchy voice whispered in front of her sending shivers down

Dimi's spine and raising up all the fine hairs on the back of her arms and down her neck.

The voice was higher as her own, but rather than musical it was rough and torn. Dimi's fear seated itself deep within her stomach as she recognized at once that this creature was more than a simple carnivore – more than a simple hunter… This one was intelligent and enjoyed the hunt and the kill…'There was evil in its tone!' she thought.

Dimi had no idea what was in front of her, but the scent she had first smelled came back wafting to her nose – it was old, decaying. Her eyes widened as memories of many, many years past came flooding back to her. 'Noooo, please no." She said out loud to the creature. "You are not alone are you little one?"

The only answer before her was a snickering that appeared to move silently before her, almost in mockery to her blindness.

Dimi strained here eyes before her, hoping in vain to catch some shadowy shape. "Let me be and I will let you live little one – I will leave." Dimi said in an un-quivering voice.

"I don't think so," responded the voice. Dimi spun for the voice had moved, and had come from a mouth no more than a meter from her. Blindly she lashed out with her dagger, but it swished unobstructed through the air and was met only with another mocking light laugh.

Dimi went up onto her toes and stepped as far back against the exit that she could. With her left hand she felt for the top of the roof wondering how fast she might turn and crawl through the opening – and wondering if the creature would pursue her.

"Think again sweat little one." Came the voice again, but this time to her right.

Dimi's lightening reflexes shot her arm and blade out, its tip connecting something but the blade tip hit and slid off of the creature as if it had hit glass.

Dimi knew of most every creature, both mundane and magical that walked, slithered or flew in these parts but she had no sense of what this creature was... 'But the smell!' The 'smell' she did recognize – and fear now grew as she heard something move from deeper back within the open cavern. "Call off you hound. There was nothing ever between us. We were as you were, trapped by the master, made to do his bidding. Why would you torment me?"

"Bites you I will." came the dry rough voice again and Dimi swiped her blade in front of her again, again the tip connected but was effortlessly deflected by the creature's smooth hard skin.

Dimi went down on all fours and started to push her feet back into the caves opening, hoping to back away and out. But rough, long clawed hands grabbed her shoulders and pulled her and drove her face down into the rocks of the cave's floor.

Dimi spat out stones as she scrambled forward trashing with her blade back and forth grappling with her arms, hoping to catch the creature that had assaulted her. Four five steps inward she lunged and then she spun and turned as the creature slapped her rear and laughed. "Arrrrr!" Dimi growled and her voice echoed around the room.

"Not to leave yet." The voice called back to her. "More sport, plus my master needs to study you."

"Your 'master'? So it has come to this then?" Dimi called back to the back of the cave – "you aspire again to be what he was? Did you not suffer enough under his twisting thumb? Haven't you learned yet the cost of such dabbling? That such power corrupts?"

"She has made many wondrous things she has." The creature cooed back to Dimi as it danced around her just out of reach. "But the old master thought your kind were his masterpiece. Transmogrification of an entire village, the establishment of an entire new species with just a single incantation!"

Dimi slashed out mindlessly at the voice and then paused a moment as she heard once again movement from the spot beside where she knew the pool of water was.

"Wings." The creature purred. "Wonderful, translucent wings. By dissecting you, she will learn his last great ways – she will be able to go beyond where he did." The creature laughed. "And for this insight." The creature giggled. "I am promised the pieces of you after she is done!"

Dimi took three fast steps to the left making for a spot where she remembered the ground as being flat and pebbled with small stones. The stones were soft and would 'crunch' when her assailant moved forward, even if he weighed little.

Dimi turned slowly around searching with her senses for her assailant; no longer confident that it was still at the spot it had been when it spoke. She crouched and her right hand moved slowly back and forth in front of her, silently slicing the air with her thin dagger – 'surely it would have eyes of sorts,' she thought.

There was no light within the cave to sparkle off the blade, yet its tip glowed ever slightly green with poison. 'I am leaving now, get your last laugh in you evil creature." She said hoping to taunt the creature to attack.

"Oh, so you would prick me… poison me?" Came the voice from the darkness around her, echoing off the cave walls.

"Yes. One prick and you will be dead, dead, dead," replied Dimi in as commanding a voice she could. "Dead, dead, dead" her echo retorted almost mockingly. Dimi breathed deeply, balancing herself.

"Dead, dead, dead." Said the rough voice, closer again than Dimi had thought possible. "I bet your fresh blood is very tasty. Is it tasty dear?" Dimi froze in concentration. Her blade delicately balanced in her hand pulled back waiting to strike as the voice drew closer. "When you cut your thumb does it taste …? Tasty?"

On the creature's last syllable Dimi struck out with her blade – up and forward to the tormenting mouth. But her slice cut only air as the creature jumped back. Almost without thinking Dimi spun and slashed out. Again nothing, but this time she felt air brush back the slender invisible hairs on her hand. This time she had almost had it. She heard a quick intake of breath as it dodged and spun. "I almost got you that time!" She yelled out at the creature. "What is your name? SO I can carve it on your tombstone. That is before I default it – you evil beast."

"What a mouth?" Came the reply now from back of the cave. "Too late the courage and too little spent." The creature replied. "Mistress is ready for you now... the spell is set. Your time is up."

Dimi's heart skipped a beat as she inhaled quickly. She turned to dive to where she believed would be the cave's exit.

A crackling blue electrical bolt slammed Dimi down and into the ground. The charge hammered her lungs and froze her heart in mid beat and then jolted its way down her arms, legs and up her neck to her head. With teeth clenched tight together she groaned in pain. For a moment there was light and in her pain Dimi turned her head slightly. There not two meters from her stood a small red creature, a lesser demon, a familiar. "You are nothing but a new pet for the new master." She groaned out in spite.

As the light dissipated from her limbs, the last she saw with its light was the creature, bowing low with an over glorified bow. Its pointed tail swept up from the ground to point above its head. As it bent forward it tucked its arm gracefully under its belly in a mocking bow. "Keek".

Dimi, gasped in pain as the bolt released her. Desperately she pushed herself up to her hands and knees and then grasping her dropped blade she rose and turned to face the back of the cave. With a last great ask of defiance Dimi crouched down and readied herself – her poisoned blade held at her side.

Keek ran beside her and scratched at her leg, but she ignored the pain – she was after larger game. "I will stick you for that Sarta Pensor!" Dimi said defiantly.

Seconds passed until the rest of Dimi's senses returned. Her body ached and her muscles burned as she moved. She held her breath, trying to judge where her last lunge would go.

A biting cold blast of air hit Dimi in the face burning her eyes and face. She staggered back as step and then bending forward lunged with all her might. "Karatora!" Came a woman's voice from before her and Dimi froze mid step with one foot suspended above the ground mid stride. Every fibre in her body froze in place, every tendon stretched, every muscle pulled, yet no movement could be bought from them. Even her eyes were locked in place staring into the empty darkness before her."

Tears of fear and self-pity began to stream down the side of her face. With all her might she tried to move her hands to wipe them away as if in shame, but they would not obey.

"Zezat tol deh". Came the voice from the back of the cave, and Dimi winced as biting cold crept into every hair, every pour, it flowed like water down into her stomach, it seeped like air into her nose and down to freeze her lungs. The pain was excruciating as she was frozen in pace – yet the pain did not bring sweat unconsciousness. Dimi prayed within her mind that her eyes could close, that the darkness around her would take with it her mind. She prayed that she would pass out so that the pain would end.

But the pain did not – and as the cold continued to burrow into every part of her body her pain increased… and beside her Keek's mocking voice whispered now into her ear. "Cold, so very cold – aren't you?"

"Far too late little one." Keek said as it stroked her frozen cheek.

A slow glow began to form around Dimi's feet. Although she could not look down, she could now make out the form of Keek as it poked and prodded her frozen body. It turned and looked back into the darkness. "Fresh is soooo much better." It pleaded. Keek hands went and stroked Dimi's outstretched hand, still holding the dagger. The little red creature licked her fingers and then looked back longingly to the darkness. "A finger first? Surely Keek has earned a finger?"

Darkness came forth from the back of the tunnel. Dimi tried to scream in agony and in fear, but her jaws, and all the muscles and bones within her body were frozen solid... "Let me die then." She finally hissed out from beneath clenched teeth with all what remained of the air within her throat and lungs. The pain in her chest was like a great tearing as her lungs vainly tried to stretch and pull more air back within them.

Without air, without breath – yet Dimi's eyes did not dim. Her mind although cold, was not numb but continued to writhe in agony.

"Can I have a taste? A small bite and nibble?" came the question from Dimi's feet as Keek encircled her leg like a puppy dog might to its master. It pulled itself up and wound its way around her legs, sniffing and climbing up her midsection until its arms encircled her neck.

The creature brought its face up close to hers. "A nibble from her ear, a precious green eye?" It licked its lips, its dark red tongue dancing millimetres away from her eye.

A small spark of electricity lit up the cave and slammed into Keek sending it hurtling off of Dimi. "Not yet." Came a faint feminine voice.

In the corner of her field of vision Dimi caught her second glimpse of Keek. It was unclothed and hairless and red all over, it had the figure of a very small man, but it had small pointed horns and a whipping tail that was longer than it was tall. It pulled itself back to its feet using its small-clawed hands. As the electricity that hit it dissipated Keek looked over at Dimi and smiled, its sharp pointy face and evil tipped ears echoing the points of its horns.

Then as the last of the light upon it failed, Keek's gaze went back to the creature now approaching Dimi. "I deserve it. I told you how to capture it!"

Dimi could now sense the presence of the other as it moved forward towards her. It was covered in black flowing tattered rags that hung over its head and flowed down over its hands and face. As it moved forward Keek snickered. "Silent little frozen one, she had not fed for many a day and you would be a most tender morsel."

"Older perhaps than she prefers." Keek added as it drew near to Dimi once again. "But no. This form is not hers for feeding; it is the other face she draws. She must concentrate and not be swept away with blood lust."

"Right master?" Keek implored as the shrouded creature stopped before Dimi and Keek.

"You must not eat it." Keek stated as a matter of fact. "You must study it only. If you turn you will not be able to concentrate."

Long wrinkled fingers poked out of the end of one sleeve, illuminated by the ever-growing green and blue light now bathing the lower half of Dimi.

The hand reached up and pulled back the shredded hood uncovering what Dimi first thought was a mummified head but later realizing that the female face she was able to see was not bandaged with cloth, but rather that the skin was so loosely tied to the ladies skull that it flapped almost as if unattached. Gaping holes around the black, empty eyes showed flashes of white as the creature's skull showed through.

The lips peeled back to reveal blackened, rotting teeth. "Dimi. It has been so long." A crooning voice said. "Did you miss me?" The old, deathly figure laughed lightly and the sound was like autumn air passing through dried, dead leaves.

The hand returned down and stroked Dimi's face, down the bony hands passed from face to neck as the witch walked round her prey. The fingers lingered on Dimi's back. Gently she stroked the wings, from tip to end; back and forth her fingers fell.

"Can you smell it Keek?" The old crone's voice rang out as she paused mid stroke.

"Yes, I smell the fear mistress – but you must not. You asked that I be strong, that I remind you... remember?"

The witch's robes brushed Dimi as it reached over her. She could feel its tattered robe flapping and rubbing against her. The creature leaned in close to Dimi, almost embracing her.

Dimi cringed as it drew near. Underneath the stringy mildew of the robes she felt a skeletal frame being press against her.

The creature of death and decay shifted and turned while still towering over Dimi. Its frame seemed to grow as it pressed against her. It became soft, and its garments, once tattered rags, now felt like silk and smelled of spring grass and pine.

"NO MASTER. You must control yourself." Keek yelled out in panic.

The witch halted and the softness dissipated, and once again she smelled of tattered rotting flesh. "She would taste soooo good. There is so much life force here, it is too hard to resist."

"If it dies, you cannot finish your study." Keek demanded. "Take it, take what you came for now and let us depart. IF you need more we can return later!"

The crone groaned and hesitated. "You are right my friend. After all." The witch laughed, her voice dry and devoid of any humanity or compassion. "Where will she go? We can keep her here in this endless death for all eternity?"

Keek laughed. "Yes, yes. Come back for parts as we so like."

Dimi's head swam as she was enveloped in pinpricking electricity that flowed like tiny fingers all over her body. 'Unable to move; unable to turn. No ability to touch; no thought to flee. Why the torture?' Dimi thought. 'Why can I not scream? Why can I not die?'

The little creature was close. A small tongue licked and encircled her ear. "My lady can bring pain AND pleasure. Yes she can. But she won't bring you pleasures, right master?" The creature inquired in almost a warning tone. "Master needs something else, remember master?" it asked.

The creature, back to its originally stinking self stretched long bony fingers and stroked Dimi's cheek. Jagged, chewed nails brushed her cheek, sending rivulets of moisture down her cheek to her chin. The thin fleshy tissue behind the short nails felt so cold even to Dimi's cold face that it burned her. Dimi wanted to scream but had no breath. She strained to draw breath, but could not. Still she was deprived the release of unconsciousness. It seemed she no longer needed to breathe. It was only the unnatural feeling that compelled her continually to try – causing her massive pains in her chest.

Keek's small voice came from where he had fallen. "Frozen, frozen, frozen. No way to scream, always awake but not moving, always in pain but not crying… forever screaming a silent scream."

"Please master, a toe?" Keek pleaded. "Keek finds it. Keek deserves a toe!" it begged as it circled.

She could feel the loathsome creature pulling on her frozen foot trying to lift and pull the shoe off. Then it started to chew on the front of the shoe in an attempt to bite through to her foot.

Keek screeched as it was hit and sent thudding against the wall of the cave once again.

Then the long bony fingers of the witch returned to stroke Dimi's face and neck – again they travelled down her back and rested on her wings. Dimi felt pressure on her back and neck. Pain shot up her spine and down to her tailbone as the fingers started pushing and pulling on her frozen wings.

Dimi would have fallen to her knees with the pain but her legs were locked, frozen in place.

Sound built up in Dimi's ears, the sound of her brain screaming and the sound of her nerves splitting as the hands pushed harder on her wing joints.

"SNAP"

'Oh gentle darkness take me!' Dimi's mind screamed silently as the pain in her back bore into her very mind rending all sense of rational from her thoughts. The pain and cold took her mind and swirled it downward into the deepest depths of her mind – down into the dark recesses she pushed her soul to escape the pain of her body. Time stood still for Dimi as she stood frozen, in the darkness of the cave, and in the darkness of the deepest recesses of her soul.

A city and princess gone missing

It took Etch and Chad a full day to get down the mountain. All the way down Etch seemed distracted and their conversation was disjointed. Chad could sense there was something bigger at play.

"Why do you think the king's men were here?" Chad asked. "Will you be going off to war or something?"

"I don't know, Chad. I haven't heard anything lately to make me think there is anything going on, but then again, we live in the backwoods of this empire. We might be behind in the news. We have had peace since before you were born, but there are always mountain raiders and clans that cause occasional problems." Etch replied somewhat distractedly.

"Think the Drekians are back?" Chad pressed as he took a step closer to his dad.

"That's putting the cart before the horse I think Chad. It's far more likely there have been some local raids and they are looking for information on a clan or something. Still, I went up past the Toris Pass when I was under the command of Thesra and King Roehn during the Drekian Wars as lead scout of the Fist. I was the one that tracked the Dreks to the Sea of Tears and proved that they had come from the western continent. Perhaps they are looking for more information about what I found back then…. Who knows for sure?"

"We're almost there — lets go for it." Chad said and started to jump and run ahead. Although each step was precarious and started a small slide, Chad's amazing agility kept him upright. Etch watched as his son continued to accelerate down the slope.

"Fool boy, you could get yourself killed doing that!" Etch yelled after his son. But the boy's spirit was contagious and soon Etch started running down the slope himself. In a matter of minutes Etch was just to the side of Chad, but Chad, seeing now that his father wasn't too upset with him, increased his pace and started moving full out.

Etch let his son pull ahead. Chad had no fear of being hurt, but Etch knew better. They might only be a short distance from the end of the shale, but in that short distance they could both be seriously injured. For Chad a broken bone would mean a few months of discomfort, for Etch it would mean a harsh winter for the entire family. If maimed, it would mean poverty and hunger. 'Better to slow down.' He thought.

Chad hit the end of the shale in full stride, with little slides following every footstep. He didn't stop running, but changed his jumping into a more consistent gait over the larger boulders that marked the end of the shale.

By the time Etch stepped onto the boulders, Chad had already reached their home. The two-story log cabin was exposed from above on the mountainside but was sheltered from below by the tree line. Giant hemlocks spread out and down to the valley from there on. Etch had built the cabin several seasons ago in order to have a continuous view of this part of the mountain from his front window. He had spent many a night seated before it mapping out where he would dig or search next.

Smoke billowed from all three of the chimneys; Rachael was cooking and the upstairs fireplace had already been lit, warming the rooms for their evening's rest.

Chad didn't get a chance to reach for the door knob before Lys pulled the door open so hard it hit the wall and ran out screaming to jump into Etch's outstretched arms. Beaming ear-to-ear Lys buried her face in Etch's neck and groaned as she gave him the hardest hug she could muster.

"Dad, I missed you." Lys said as she kissed his cheek.

"And I missed you too!" Etch responded as he set her back down to earth. Etch smiled as he looked down at his nine-year-old daughter. 'My,' he thought. 'She is growing quickly too!'

Etch gave her a kiss on her forehead and she turned, taking his hand and leading him back into the cabin. "So Lys," Etch asked cheerfully, "what have you and your mom made us for supper?"

"Yeast dumplings and roast pork!" Lys replied with an excited smile.

"Wow, what's the occasion?" Etch asked loudly as he entered.

Etch's wife of fifteen years, Rachael, stood with her back to the door, her attention focused on the cast-iron stove. A large pot steamed furiously, occasionally sputtering out water onto the stovetop. Smaller pots simmered nearby as the stove sizzled in reply. The room was filled with the rich smells of meat and yeast.

Rachael looked up from her task. "We thought you might be a little hungry and Lys wanted to make something special. She has really helped me a lot today so we had time to work on a bigger meal than we originally planned." Rachael turned to pull the large pot of boiling water off of the stove and set it aside to cool.

Rachael pointed backhandedly at her son who was now sitting by the fireplace with his feet hanging over the chair's large arms. "Chad on the other hand, bolted from here after your friends came and left us without so much as a stick of wood!"

Chad didn't even look back before responding. "There's tons out there around back, I don't know why you need another pile inside the house." Chad rose from his comfortable seat to pick up a poker and began adjusting the logs in the fire. He turned to grab another piece of wood to add to the growing blaze and realized that there was none. He scowled and started heading for the door. "I know, I know, I know. I'll get some now."

"Put on your shoes if you are going out. I don't need you with a cold." Rachael yelled after him as Chad stepped barefoot out of the house.

"Stubborn boy!" Rachael growled as Etch stifled a laugh. "Your son…" Rachael let the familiar refrain trail off.

Etch removed his jacket and hung it on a peg by the door. The cottage was very cozy. The thick wood walls made it well insulated and inviting. Under the entrance it opened up to the full second floor, separated by a three quarter wall. Stairs in the back right of the cabin went up to two small, separate rooms just large enough for a bed and dresser each. Every stick of furniture Etch and Rachael had made from scratch. They were very proud of their home.

"I am going to miss being home." Etch said quietly to himself. He knew what was coming. The elaborate dinner was proof of his suspicions. Rachael knew what the men had come for and was making him a dinner to ease him into the mindset. There was no use talking about it right now, it would only upset Chad and Lys. It was best to wait until later.

"Mountain looks about the same as always I assume?" Rachael said teasingly.

"Yeah, pretty much." Responded Etch. "Nothing new again this year. I'm not sure if I'll even make the trip next year. We could use the extra time for hunting; it would mean another set of skins to trade."

"We don't really need any more meat than what we have, and we have plenty of money. It's good that you take a rest once a year, you work hard and you deserve it. Plus, when you're out of my hair I can get more done. Right Lys?" said Rachael.

"We worked on your birthday present when you were out!" Lys said. "But I won't tell you what it is, it's a secret."

Chad came back in then, covered in sawdust and holding a large bundle of split wood.

"Wipe your feet or you'll be scrubbing the house!" Rachael yelled at Chad. "Why do you refuse to wear shoes anyway? Your feet growing so rapidly they feel restricted? Don't you feel cold walking outside without shoes?"

Chad stomped his feet and walked over to the hearth. Etch gently shook his head and walked over to the kitchen table. Lys was busy setting the table and pouring apple cider for everyone.

"Cider too!" Etch exclaimed. "Wow, you girls are going all out!"

Lys beamed. "I told you he would like it!" she said to her mom.

Dinner was a quiet affair with each member of the family deep in their own thoughts. Afterwards Etch sat down in the big hide covered armchair and Chad and Lys played cards in front of the fire. Rachael brought over some apple pie for dessert.

Etch wolfed down the pie and then looked up to Rachael, who had just seated herself in the rocker beside him. "So, who were they?"

"Two of Sir Beston Thesra's men. A couple of soldiers on horseback who looked more like boys then men. They came to ask a 'favour'." Rachael replied as she looked up from her pie.

Rachael's voice was low and she spoke slowly, knowing the direction the conversation was going to lead. "Appears as if there is something happening in Terran. They didn't give much information, just hinted at rumours of bad things. What they did say was that Princess Elle was to have been in Terran until recently and she is missing now."

"Missing?" Lys said, turning from her cards and looking over to her mother.

Etch leaned forward in his chair and motioned to Lys that she should keep her mind on the game in front of her and not on her parents' conversation, although he knew that in these small confines both children were actively listening to what was going on. "Missing!" Etch echoed, "Roehn must be going crazy. What happened?"

"The soldiers were very vague, I don't think they knew that much Etch. Thesra must have sent them right out when he heard that she was missing. Either that or perhaps no one knows."

Rachael paused and looked down then back up at her husband. "What they both did know was that Thesra wants you to come to TerranAdd and then go out and search for Elle. Not as part of the Fist this time, but alone… as a sole scout reporting directly to him and the king."

Etch didn't reply. Instead, he looked up to the ceiling and sighed.

Rachael continued, still slowly and deliberately. "Thesra is now captain of the King's army, he should know more when you get there. Sir Thesra Beston they said wants his best tracker looking for the king's daughter as soon as possible. They were quite anxious for you to head towards MountRyhn and I think if you had been here, one of them would have escorted you."

Etch sighed again. The weight of the news felt heavy on his shoulders. He glanced over at Rachael and then at Lys and Chad. Both of the kids were looking at him expectantly. He smiled reassuringly in reply to their unspoken questions.

"But you weren't," Rachael continued, "and they talked and then decided to go try finding Toe. I told them where they could find him in the hills. I was just up there the other day dropping off a few things for Memdy." Rachael looked at Etch with her 'I know' face and then smiled.

"How is she doing these days?" Etch asked a little apprehensively.

Rachael shook her head. "Not well, the dear. She hasn't been herself since last spring. Always has some cold. Toe isn't all that well these days either. But I left her some vegetable stew and some jarred peaches. They have enough food for the winter; Toe is a good hunter. I'm just worried for them. If they ask Toe to help them Memdy will be left all alone."

"I know Toe; he loves Memdy. He will decline the offer. Did the soldiers say they would be back this way after visiting them?" Etch asked, looking back over at the fire.

"For soldiers, they both seemed a little too nervous about traveling into the hills. They said they 'might' check back in on their return. They did leave a pouch of gold to help pay to get you supplied and to purchase a horse. I looked in the pouch; there's a lot there – more than a tracker's fee for a year. Obviously there is more to this story than what they are saying. It puzzled me that they said nothing of having Toe work with you. Do you think perhaps they are going to have him do something else?"

Etch stood up and walked towards the fire to warm his hands. "Hmm, who knows why they want Toe. If they were young soldiers then they were smart to go up into the hills together; there are lots of things there that could take down someone inexperienced. As for the fee, we are talking about the princess after all."

Rachael stood and stepped behind her husband. "Etch, I don't like this. You left the service a long time ago. We need you here yes, but most of all we need you alive and not in harms way out who knows where. It's hard when you leave and we have to sit here not knowing where you are or if you're alive or dead!"

Etch turned to face his wife and whispered. "If the king calls me, I cannot say no. This is the king's daughter we're talking about. Of course I'm going. You know that too, that's why you made the fancy dinner."

"I know," sighed Rachael resignedly. "Your travel pack is already assembled. Lys oiled your bow and it's hanging unstrung, along with your sword. You can leave in the morning. I asked around and you can buy a horse from Mar in the village with the gold they left. Take the rest with you – we have enough here to keep us for quite some time."

Emotions played on Rachel's face. Etch looked deep into her eyes as she spoke to him. "The kids and I will be fine. I'm just afraid, etch. There's something that they didn't say, something about this that makes me feel uneasy. This is big Etch…"

The suddenness of having to leave his family and home came rushing in on Etch. His neck muscles knotted and the cut on his head began to throb. He tried to re-center himself, for his sake and that of his family.

"I trust your feelings Rachael, you have always sensed the coming storms and predicted their size. I will be careful and I'll send word when I can…. But you know it will be hard. On the road I won't need much. I'll take a look at the money and leave what I can spare – I can't really say how long this is going to take."

Chad appeared at Etch's side – "Can I go too? I can sit behind you, I'm as good with the bow as you are and I have twice your eyes and legs!"

"Ah, let me think for a second." Etch started sarcastically and then added very quickly before Chad could say another word, "No Chad. Your place now is to do all that I was doing here. You will be busy enough. Your mom will keep you hopping and you need to keep everyone fed and clothed…. this is no small task I am leaving to you."

"Thought so." Chad replied disappointed and sat back down with Lys. "My deal?" Lys handed Chad the cards then looked over at her father giving him a reassuring smile and nod. She stood suddenly then and walked over to him, gave him a big hug and returned silently to the fireplace where she resumed playing cards again with Chad.

"I will be off at first light." Etch said, his mind made up. "With any luck, I will be back before the winter comes."

Rachel knew better, and her tone reflected the fact. "If it was simple Roehn would have already found her. Don't go risking your neck by trying to return before the snows start falling. If it starts to snow before you can get to the pass then stay the winter, we'll be fine until spring."

Etch looked up at his wife. If it had been something simple, he knew he wouldn't have been sent for. This wasn't going to be settled fast. Etch knew that he was likely going for at least six months. He knew it, she knew it and from the look on Chad and Lys' faces, they knew it too. "Ok Chad," he said with forced enthusiasm, "deal your mom and I in on the next hand. Let's move to the dinner table and make this a real game."

The Road to TerranAdd

Hundreds of hoofs pounded the dry earth and dirt and then flung it towards the sky. Only the first eight of the one hundred Montterran soldiers were fully visible; a cloud of dust obscured the rest. Hanging in the sky it trailed the company like a long, ashen snake.

The pale brown dust from the parched road was chokingly thick. All of the soldiers had been forced to tie small strips of cloth over their faces under their helms and chain veils in an attempt to help their breathing. After the first day of riding their clothes and mail were white and caked. Even the horses were protected, their riders having tied loose cloths to their armoured chamfrons to protect their noses and mouths from the thick dust. Through the biting heat the Fist of Montterran thundered east past the thousands of hectares of farmlands that marked the eastern reaches of the Montterran lands.

Each knight balanced a two and a half metre lance on his stirrup and every one of those lances' flat, polished spearheads acted like a mirror. Reflecting the light they flashed and sparkled. Thousands of harvesters in the eastern fields turned to watch as the Fist rode by. Living as they did a full day's ride from the castle, few common folk had yet heard the rumours of ill tidings in the East.

This was Montterran's first guard called the Fist of Montterran, and they were magnificent as they made their way along the road at a fast trot. At the front of the company road a tall man who held high the company's standard, its split tail flapping in the wind. As the flag passed peasants paused in their labour. Men and women alike pointed at the company with pride and children ran to their parents shouting with enthusiasm.

Miathis derCamp, commander of the Fist, rode beside Tunder, his first, the man he had also chosen to bear their standard. He glanced back to survey the company but was disappointed. Beyond the first two rows of riders all the others were blurs in the dusty air.

The ride had been relatively good, for the ground was solid, but the dust was making all of the company irritable. Miathis turned back to the road trying to visualize where on the map they were now. Tiran Falls was to be the company's first formal stop; it was not all that far away and resided safely on the Montterran side of the Tiern River. From there they would cross over into Terran lands. It would be a hard ride up and down the Terran Hills, but after that TerranAdd would be before them.'

Miathis' mood was solemn. They had given him little information as to what he could expect when they arrived. The uncertainty of their ride to TerranAdd had already sapped the spirit from every man within his company. What would they face, Mohen? Dreks?

Each man within the Fist feared something different, drawing as he did on the stories told to him in his youth. Miathis had even heard some of his men speculate that the wizards of old had returned, 'even though none have been seen for several generations.' he thought.

"Fear" Miathis said aloud. His voice was dwarfed by the thunder of steel shod hoofs slamming the earth. He had to ensure his company thought and fought like a single man, and most importantly, a man without fear. It was for this reason that, although he commanded this group, he was about to rein in his horse and ride a spell at the end of the company, even though the dust would choke both him and his mount. He needed to ensure that all of his men thought of themselves as part of a bigger whole.

Miathis knew that although the Fists' training had been rigorous, and their reputation for victory unbroken, this new company of men had never been driven very hard. There had never been any need, for Montterran lands had, for the most part, been at peace for years. 'How I wish that even one or two old-timers or northern riders had been assigned to the company. They could have brought reality to bear when the new soldiers started to voice concerns about the pace of their travels'. Miathis knew his plan would mean driving them much harder then they had ever been driven before.

'Perhaps', he thought. 'shared adversaries will bind the group better than anything else could.'

Miathis pulled his reins to the side and slowed his mount, signalling Tunder to continue leading the group forward as he fell behind. It was something he loved to do. Moving up and down the ranks gave him a good chance to inspect the condition of both men and horses and to note how well they worked together. It also made him feel more a part of his company.

Miathis knew that as the youngest ever commander of the Fist he needed to earn the respect and loyalty of his troops. They had trained and drilled together certainly, but now they were venturing forth to fight, and possibly die, together…. Miathis knew in his heart the difference between the two.

The commander of the Fist had not allowed his men to sleep the night before, nor to rest their mounts. The road was dry and Halos and Detros had given enough light to ride by, so he had made them ride. He needed to see where the weak links were, and how well his company would respond to his command. It was crucial that he know their true worth before they faced situations where that knowledge would be critical.

As a result of this the Fist had maintained a fast trot all through the night and had stopped only briefly to inhale food, check their mounts and to give their horses feed and water.

'There will be time enough for breaks once we are on Terran soil,' thought Miathis. 'Once we cross the border there will be homesteads and farms for the scouts to investigate while the main group of men sleep.' He planned to rotate his men nightly. Some would stand guard, some would scout out the surrounding areas, and others would rest. He needed them to get into a frame of mind suited to war now. He also wanted to obtain maximum information about what might have transpired in TerranAdd before actually arriving. If a large company of soldiers had advanced there was bound to be evidence of it outside the capital city. If he didn't find any evidence on the main roads he would surely find it in the surrounding fields.

'One cannot simply erase the movement of a few thousand men, especially if they had siege engines with them.'

Miathis had grown up listening to his father tell stories about the days of the Drekian Raids. He had always thought his dad's company a group of old, daft men stumbling about in the dark. 'The stories that speak of a Drekian return are just that, stories, and I'm going to prove it.' He grinned under his face cloth and chain veil. 'And if by some chance this was the work of that illusive band of raiders, I am going to be named as the man that figured it out.'

Miathis nudged his massive black mount, the largest of all the horses within the troop. He had spent half a year's wages on this horse, a beautiful mare standing just over 17 hands high. His father had said that it was vanity to spend that much on a horse, but he knew that this beast was destined for greatness. Miathis wasn't a large man himself, and he looked even smaller on Koal, but together with his magnificent horse Miathis was still half a head taller than any other rider in his company.

In a moment Miathis was riding to the left of the last contingent of the Fist. A few pack horses were being led behind them and they were definitely struggling with the pace. Miathis wondered how fast and hard he could push these beasts of burden.

"I sometimes prefer rain, this dust is terrible!" Miathis yelled above the thunder to a soldier at the rear. The soldier's head turned slightly as he listened to his commander. Miathis could barely see the man's eyes even though he rode close to him so thick was the dust.

"The first night we will rest well," Miathis yelled. "Tieren Falls will have water to wash your outsides with and you can have a pint of ale to wash your innards with." Miathis couldn't see the faces of the men riding beside him, blocked as they were by their helms, but he knew they were smiling beneath their chain mail and makeshift duct filters.

Miathis tried to remember the names of the two men riding at the very back. He was fairly sure it was Mort and Dar, judging by their size and the way they held themselves. It was a little hard to discern just how large they were; he glanced down at their horses and confirmed his first guess.

The two had tethered leads to the back of their saddles that attached to the bridles of two other horses, each bearing two fifty kilogram sacks of grain. Man and beast would eat light on this trip. The horses could graze when they stopped, but Miathis didn't want rests to last long and he wanted the horses in top form so he had brought along one hundred and fifty kilos of grain to supplement what they found for themselves. The men were provided only with hard tack. They would hunt when they could and stop at the river to replenish their packs and establish a supply replacement.

Miathis didn't quite know what to expect in terms of supplies once they reached TerranAdd. 'Will we find food and grain, and can it be trusted if we do?' In his discussions with Thesra they had worried about food poisoning and other such maladies

"Mort, Dar keep an eye on the pack animals." Miathis yelled. Both turned to look at the leads that dangled behind them.

'With one hand on reins and the other holding a lance there's no chance to catch the cord if it works itself untied.' Miathis thought to himself.

Both men checked their lines and nodded back to Miathis.

Miathis looked again at the packhorses. The bouncing of the sacks likely felt unusual for the horses and they bore them differently than they would a man. Still, both horses were rather large, each almost 16 hands and weighing four hundred and fifty kilos or more, so they bore their sacks no worse than they might an armoured rider. "They looked ok!" he yelled motioning with his hand towards the two horses. Mort and Dar both nodded in reply.

As soon as he had entered the regulars, Miathis' intelligence and his skills with bow, lance, and horse had marked him as an exceptionally talented youth. So skilled was he that even early in his youth his father Drion had known that he would do well at soldiering.

Still, despite that, Miathis was not a pretentious person. He was quick to say that much of his advancement as a soldier was because he was a lucky person. It was all a matter, he said, of being the right person in the right place at the right time. His philosophy had long been that luck governed one's fate, not effort nor the gods.

Miathis' grandfather had hailed from a vale between the Casten and the NorWestern mountains. He had fought in the very first Drekian Wars and had been awarded a small area of farmland by the Count Palatine in gratitude for his service. His father had been a freeman, a 'sell sword' and then later a soldier. His reputation and skill had earned him some local renown and he was accepted into the Fist late in life. It was those connections his father had made within Mont Ryhn and the company that had led to Miathis being accepted to the Fist.

Then it had been a sheer stroke of luck that Miathis had come into command. One autumn day three of his superiors had fallen violently ill after sharing a meal. He had been asked to lead a group of men to investigate a disturbance in a nearby village. Being somewhat cocky and inexperienced his small group rode right up to the village without first scouting it out. What the group stumbled on was a well-armed mountain clan raid. The clan had come down in force on the little village with 30 men, heavily armed. Miathis' crew numbered only a third of that.

Although undoubtedly a force of men required great skill to best a company three times its size, Miathis always described the situation by saying they had been "extremely fortunate". The larger group of clansmen had been ill prepared and had virtually walked into their lances and swords.

In reality though, it was not luck, but rather Miathis' unpretentious, positive attitude that marked him and made him the man he was. Miathis was known for his directness of speech and understanding of men, it was his approach to life that set him apart. It was also, in part, why Thesra had named him to lead the company despite his youth. Miathis was a born leader.

Koal coughed. Miathis leaned forward in his stirrups and noted that the cloth covering his horse's nose and mouth had detached itself. "This dust is not good is it?" He said to Koal. The horse's ears turned back upon hearing her master's voice, and she bowed her head slightly in response. In reply, Miathis sneezed. The finer particles of dust were penetrating his loosely tied cloth. Miathis spurred his horse on to move them both back up to the front of the line.

"Enough time spent at the rear. If I can't see what's ahead, I can't really lead the men" Miathis said out loud. The noise of the horses and armour drowned out his words. 'Between the noise and the dust, it's a lonely ride within the ranks." Miathis thought to himself.

The Fist made a good forty kilometres an hour on the flat ground and the company all knew that they were expected to keep up the pace for most of the day. They looked forward to making the Tiren River, where they would slow down considerably in order to take more precautions as they moved into Terran lands.

Miathis pulled up beside Tunder, his best friend, who was still carrying their colors. Tunder was a massive man and held the long shaft of the Fist's standard straight up, its butt balanced only lightly on his stirrup. The lance measured four metres long and was a brutal strain for most to hold. No other man in the crew could hold the flag for anything longer than a few hours, the flapping of the streamers tiring their arms.

Tunder his arms thick as tree trunks, never appeared strained. He had grown up the son of a blacksmith and had hammered and performed hard chores lifting stone and wood since he was able to walk. Every night he continued to build his muscles with exercises until long after most within the company were fast asleep.

"The chain of your flail is hanging too low and rubbing your mount!" Miathis yelled over to Tunder. Tunder looked down and back as far as he could but his massive build wasn't very flexible. He passed his reins from left hand to right along with the standard. He then reached back with his left hand where the flail was strapped. He could reach the handle well enough but not much else.

Miathis pulled his horse up close to Tunder's and leaned out of his saddle. With his right hand he reached down behind Tunder and grabbed the heavy link chain where it was dangling down. With a quick flip of his hand he looped it over its handle, securing it. "Good enough for now. At least your mount won't be sore by the time we stop for rest!" Miathis yelled.

Miathis looked back over at Tunder's flail. It was an ugly and ungraceful weapon. The shaft was over a metre long, made from gnarled and knotted wood. At the end of the slightly twisted shaft hung a heavy length of chain that ended with spiked, very heavy iron ball. He always enjoyed watching Tunder practice with it on horseback. It gave him amazing reach on the attack. It was not, however, a delicate weapon and one wrong flick of the wrist could send the ball screaming into the wielder's back.

Tunder looked over, his dark eyes wide open and excited. "So we're actually stopping for a rest tonight?"

Miathis smiled and nodded. "The horses aren't used to this either, and I don't want any of them going lame. This dust must be even harder on them."

Tunder nodded then looked forward again.

'This is what Tunder lives for.' Miathis thought to himself. 'Riding down a road at the head of a column of soldiers holding their standard up high, all the surrounding villagers, and their daughters, looking up at his massive stature as he rides past.'

By nightfall it seemed from a distance as if the riders and horses had just come out of the mountains covered with snow. Every inch of every man and beast was caked with dirt. When the men dismounted most pulled off their helmets, took a mouthful of water from the skins strapped to their horses and spat. Many started coughing when they took off their helmets and the cloths bound to protect them, but all went swiftly around their mounts, grabbed their reins and continued forward at a walking pace.

One of the soldiers, Tirad, pulled his horse around the others and started walking beside Miathis. "I can hardly wait until we make the Tiren. I plan to ride across and not take the bridge. Perhaps then I'll be clean again!"

"We have a long ride before we will see her gates and if you break from our ranks and ride to the river, even as a jest, I will make sure you won't be clean for a month," Tunder's voice bellowed from the other side of Miathis. "Consider yourself very lucky that Miathis is having us stop along the way at all. I expected us to ride harder and longer and then straight in to battle."

The mentioning of battle had done what he had expected it to do – it had brought the soldier's chatter to a cold end as the all their thoughts turned inward. Tunder watched as the younger ones reached down and touched their sword or adjusted their mail. He had serious concerns about this young group of men, too few had seen real battle and for most of them this was an exciting trip to break up the otherwise monotonous daily drills. They had been at peace too long, been too soft on these men; life had been just too good.

Miathis looked back too see how his royal charge Bettham Bethos was doing. The son of Duke Bethos of Oathos hadn't been quite as 'bad' as he had feared when originally ordered to take on. Miathis winced remembering the conversation he had when he was given the charge - Lord Bethos had quite the political clout he had been reminded and there would be hell to pay if the lad was killed in some silly drill. Smiling inwardly he glanced over at the young lad that road beside Bettham. There rode the Duke's son opposite Tirad Mismar. Coming from a family with no real money or lands the lad had dogged determination, and had made it in to the company with hard work and demonstration of uncanny innate skill.

Tirad also was Bettham's contrast in that the lad, although modest still exuded self confidence and he had quickly made friends with everyone within the company, including, and especially, Tunder.

Miathis took off his own helmet and shook his head. Sand and dust flew from his head revealing short-cropped brown hair. He sneezed and squinted as the dust fell into his eyes and onto his nose. He and Tunder had driven the men many days on long hard trips to condition them, and several on hot days where the road had been dusty. He wasn't sure now if it was because this day they ventured forth in earnest or if the road really was dustier than any other they had ridden. Either way, he had made up his mind – they would stop at least once along they way. He really didn't want them walking in blind to Terran Add. 'Someone, within the area must know something.' He said to himself.

"We are making good time," he yelled back at Tunder with intentional loudness so a few of the closer men could hear him. "We'll stop for a bit longer break when we hit the Tirin Falls to wash ourselves up. It will be a short stop to rest the horses, pick up a few minor supplies and a very early start before dawn."

Those men that heard Miathis let out a small cheer.

"Hold your tongs lads that just means harder riding to make up the time lost, and the dirt is better then rain. If it were raining we would be spending the nights oiling our gear!" Tunder yelled back at them.

Tirad called back a rhetorical question, "Can we not clean up before we ride in to town so we can impress the ladies?"

Miathis yelled back at the rambunctious lad. "I wouldn't piss on Tunder's boots Tirad, he's just as likely to stick them up your butt for comments like that.

Tirad looked over at Tunder, his expression momentarily one of fear, and then he smiled and nodded his head at Bettham. "Girls like a rough and ready soldier – either way works for me!"

Bettham remained silent and shook his head in disbelief at Tirad's boldness.

The night was uneventful, as was the next day and the following night. The men and horses alike got in to a sustainable rhythm and stride. The nights were still relatively warm and the road was good albeit dusty. They make excellent time.

Occasionally a lead man was sent ahead to ask a question to those along the fields but few if any had heard anything about the great city to the west. The harvests had been excellent this year and the countryside abounded with food all the farmers were most concerned about pulling in their bountiful harvests.

It was dark and late when they finally made it to the large four-meter walled gates of Tiren Falls. Upon seeing the riders the gatekeeper swung wide the large double doors that had already been closed for the night.

Tiren Falls was an old town; long ago it had been a border fort. Now it was a resting place for weary travelers, and housing for local merchants who built tall dwellings on the eastern side so that their rooms could overlook the river. The city was very nicely maintained; fancifully painted signs adorned the streets proclaiming the trades of those within the buildings and in the center of the town stood a large stone watering hole and fountain that was powered by a small windmill.

"Tunder", Miathis called.

Tunder reined his horse closer to Miathis, "Aye?"

"Go over to the stables with a man or two and ensure our mounts are well taken care of. And send a few others out to replenish our supplies, I don't want any men eating any food or drinking any water when we get within a days ride of Terran Add. When all is squared away, get a barrel or two of ale for the men but keep them together and try to keep them from getting into the taverns we will be leaving early tomorrow.

Miathis pulled out a small purse, looked at it, shook it, and then tossed it to Tunder. "Have Bettham and Tirad work the merchants for our supplies but whatever you do, don't let Tirad out of your sight for long, I don't want a scene with any merchant as a result of Tirad having a romp with another married woman."

Tunder smiled as he caught the purse. He knew that for all his faults Betthem was a clever lad, and especially good at haggling with merchants. After every purchase made for the company they always ended up finding enough spare coin to buy something extra for the company's officers. Plus, giving Tirad a task would keep them busy and out of trouble.

Tunder turned to two other soldiers and then pointed at Tirad and waved them forward.

Tirad smiled as he approached Tunder, already having an idea what was going to be asked of him and eager for the task. He had grown up fairly poor compared to most the other people in the company. His father had sold most of their sheep to pay to ensure that his son would not be a simple foot soldier, nor be taken to work in the castle. His parents might not have been well off, but he had always worked hard and was considered a smart lad. After only a summer at Mont Ryhn he had learned how to read and write. It was his intelligence and not necessarily his brawn that had enabled him to join the Fist. Tirad had been one of the first additions to the company after Miathis was named commander.

Tunder smiled as Tirad approached and tossed him the bag of coins.

The gatekeeper must have either known they were coming, or had seen them from afar, for he opened the doors before they had a chance to call out a greeting and waved them through smilingly.

After receiving his instructions from Tunder, Tirad pulled up next to Miathis and launched a jibe. Pointing over at Tunder he leaned in and said, none too quietly, "The wind is to the east, they must have smelled Tunder coming! I'm surprised that having caught his scent they haven't barred the doors!"

"I wouldn't be so cocky Tirad." Miathis retorted. "Tunder is second in command and he is about to decides who is standing guard all night. I wouldn't want him overhearing something nasty if I were you."

Miathis winked at the lad, then urged his horse forward through the village gates and into the city streets.

The villagers opened their shutters and peered down at the company when it came to a stop by the fountain and market area. When the men were all within the large open area Miathis ordered the company to dismount but stayed seated himself. "Tunder has already named a few of you who will help with the purchasing of supplies and then carrying them back to the horses."

Miathis moved his mount so that it pointed in the direction of the general stables, which lay in the north-eastern part of the village. "The rest of you, take your horses over to the stables. Wash them, brush them down and get them food. When your horse is well cared for, I want you to check your gear. Check, clean and oil your swords and armour. Then and only then, you can hit the pubs for *one* pint or *two only*. And remember, we are the Fist and you are expected to comport yourselves as such.."

Miathis paused to let his orders sink in. "You will be bedding in the stables with our mounts. I expect all sergeants to be the last of their men to the pubs - I want everything in order for us to leave in the morning. I also want every man as clean as he can get by morning, and *not* hung over."

A small grumble came from a few of the men scattered about the troop. But then the four sergeants started barking orders to their men, and the complaints were forgotten. The sergeants pushed for fast action, eager to get to a pub themselves.

Miathis looked around him. The fountain was surrounded by a stone wall half a metre high. In the center stood a carving of a young boy holding up a fish from which water spouted. The white mortar and wood buildings surrounding the large open courtyard were all well maintained and very clean.

There was no doubt in Miathis' mind as to where he was headed. It was over to the Porker Barrel for some smoked ribs and a tall pitcher of ale and perhaps a kiss or two from the barmaid, and the keeper of his heart, Bess.

The Porker Barrel was a good step further into town and off on a side street. It wasn't a highly trafficked place for it was more expensive than most, the food was good but the service was what drew Miathis to this place.

Miathis stepped through the front door and was greeted joyously by Bess, who had spotted him as he passed the pub's large front window. Running to him she threw her arms around his neck and exclaimed, "I thought you might be out and about now that there's trouble brewing. My luck has improved."

Bess' feet lifted off the floor as Miathis straightened himself and pulled her up into his arms.

"Ah, she's supposed to be waiting tables Miathis, if you don't mind," came a shout from behind the bar, which was nestled in the back right corner of the restaurant.

"My good friend Jent Porter, looks like life and business has been good to you!" Miathis said loudly as he came up for air, not releasing his hold on Bess just yet.

"Do you have a place I can clean up Bess?" Miathis inquired as he looked down into her deep brown eyes. Bess' hair was sandy brown and hung all the way down her back. A small cloth pulled it back from her forehead. His eyes lingered over her, tracing her figure as she pressed tight against him. "Now Miathis," Bess said chidingly as she watched his gaze wander.

Bess gave him a sarcastically prudish look and pushed away from him and down onto her own feet. "Of course we have a place. The king's mark and your coin is always good here – Right father?" Without waiting for a reply she pointed with her thumb to the stairs. "Up and second door on the right. Go and get cleaned up, take off that chain mail and by the time you come down a feast will be waiting."

Miathis smiled and after giving her a peck on the cheek walked over to the stairs and went up to the room. It was small, but neatly maintained, and would suite his needs for the night. He went over to the bed and started taking off his greaves and mail and then pulled off his heavy leathers and piled them on the chair by the bed. He turned to the dresser and noted the washbasin there along with a pitcher filled with cold water. He started towards it but was interrupted by a knock on the door.

"Don't dally." Bess said as she opened the door, not waiting for his permission to enter. "Your ribs and beer are already on the table. Here," she said as she entered the room and crossed to the dresser. "I brought you a pitcher of hot water, you're a mess." Bess turned and smiled at him, noting that even though his leathers had covered him, dust still clung to him all over. His face was ashen, as were his arms.

Miathis smiled and took the pitcher of warm water from Bess' outstretched hands. He then turned slyly and tried to grab her waist, but she dodged him quickly and pushed him away with a laugh. "Don't start, or my dad will be up here in a minute and make you marry me tonight. He doesn't trust us much as it is, and he did see me come up."

Miathis smiled and set the pitcher on the dresser as Bess turned and left. He watched her petite, well-rounded backside as she exited. "One day, I will have to marry that girl." He said to himself smiling. He turned then and picked up the pitcher of water again, splashing some on his face in an attempt to regain his concentration. He was not, after all, there on a personal trip.

***

The dinner was indeed a feast to Miathis who had grown up with meagre fare, having lived his early years eating bland NorWestern cooking, mostly steamed fish and rice.

He noticed Jent walking to another table, a pitcher in each hand, and shouted out his thanks. "Jent, compliments to the chef, he's outdone himself tonight! Please, sit down and spend a minute with me."

Jent smiled and without asking refilled Miathis' stein and then sat down in the seat opposite him. Miathis reached over to the pitcher in turn and filled the glass in front of Jent. "Wet your whistle, you've been working a long day as always."

Jent sighed and nodded. Every time Miathis looked at the man, he looked less the father and more the friend. Miathis' perspective on age had changed as he saw more of the world and interacted with more people. He felt much older as of late and no longer liked to think of a man of forty-five as 'old'.

"Aye, business has been grand." Jent said as he picked up the drink. "Though I'm thinking I should be raising the prices again if the likes of you can afford to frequent my establishment."

"Long summer with lots of rain and a great hot fall. Times have been good." Miathis said and took a swig from his ale. The beer's foam splashed his face as he took a deep pull. He smiled with satisfaction and wiped his face off with his sleeve. "Excellent beer. You can always tell a good harvest by the taste of the beer. Barley was fresh and strong this year."

"But all good things have a tendency to end, eh Miathis? I assume you are off to TerranAdd with your men to find out what has happened?" Jent asked with a questioning eye. It was a look that appeared to have some knowing to it.

"Yes, as fast as we can." Miathis said softly in reply and glanced around to ensure no one was actively listening in on their conversation. There were a few other patrons in the place this evening, but they were mostly merchants and couples that had come in from the rural areas to sell their wares in the city. None of them gave Mathias pause.

Miathis looked back at his friend with a questioning look. "But what do you know about it? Surely there have been a few people from those parts in through here recently that have shared some information?"

"Not a soul, not even the regulars. And what's more – same is for all the merchants." Jent said in an tense voice. "Sure we've still got the local regulars," he said as he looked around the room, "but at this time of year, I usually have a lot more from the east. I've had not one of my regulars from TerranAdd these last two weeks."

"Something very queer is up." Jent added sourly in a lower tone. "I have good friends a few days ride from here, the Makays, that I'm starting to get worried about. I would have gone myself to check on them but I have a business to run. I've been urging a few local merchants to send out their apprentices or to hire a lad to go and check out the different farms and villages east of here. A couple of lads went out, not far mind you, just a ways…"

Jent paused then leaned forward. "*Everyone*, not just one or two, but *all* of the farmers near TerranAdd… gone. The animals are in the pens, the horse in the stables, but all the folk are gone. Whatever befell the city, it didn't stop there."

Miathis leaned back in his chair. He picked up a large rib and took a bite. After washing it down with some more beer he smiled. "Excellent seasoning Jent." Pausing he leaned forward. "What did they see at the farms themselves?"

"It just wasn't natural." Jent replied as he squinted at Miathis. "Meals on the tables, pipes on the dressers, sometimes boots by the door. No blood, no burning, no bodies, nothing. No man leaves his farm at harvest time, it isn't natural."

"Surely there must have been some trace of where they went. Hundreds of farmers and thousands more from within TerranAdd don't just disappear." Miathis said as he pulled a pipe from his belt and started stuffing it. "There must be some hermit or recluse left up there that noticed something."

Jent smiled wanly. "Right now those that have heard aren't asking too many questions. Instead they're taking night trips to the east. I expect as others start thinking more will be leaving to pick up a new horse or to find some sheep."

"They better not be doing much of that, the king will be sending out a lot more than us shortly, of that I'm sure." Miathis took the candle from the table and lit his pipe. "We are at peace with the Terrans, they'll be back or their other lords will claim title and then what – a war with our allies because we are perceived as raiding their lands?"

"The locals of TerranAdd will not be coming back, I feel sure of it." Jent said simply. "Bob Makay comes into town every month to buy fresh herbs for his Dad and drops in for a pint before leaving. Normally you can set your calendar on it, but he didn't show up two days ago."

Jent shook his head and sat back; he looked right and left then back at Miathis. "Old Man Makay, Bob's dad, never leaves his house. He was an ox of a man in his time and always had several mean dogs to keep him company. Bob says he has a cross bow and sits up by a window on the second floor. Most of his neighbours don't come to see them because they're afraid the old man will shoot them on the doorstep. It would take a good crew to come and roust someone like him without sign of struggle. You ought to go check them out, talk to Bob and his dad and see what they have to say about this."

Jent reached forward to grab his stein and took another long pull of his draught. He tilted the stein back too far and some of the beer ran down the side of his clean-shaven face. He looked old, old and worried. He had been hearing a lot and didn't like it.

"The question isn't just where all the people went." Miathis said as he leaned in to the table and whispered. "It's why they went or what took them. If you come to raid the place, you come in, kill a few to get them in order, rob them and go. But it's too much work and mess killing them all unless you've got a mighty bad grudge, and then, unless you plan to come back and live there, why do anything with the bodies?"

"Aye, it's very weird. You be careful when you go. If Bob or his dad are around, you mark their words. They're smart in the sense of things even if the old man sounds a little nuts. He knows things, he does. There's something unnatural about there, some magic at play, I'd bet my life on it."

"Magic? There hasn't been a real wizard around since before my granddad was born. And even from the stories of old, there weren't any that could do something like this to an entire city. Nor were they ever inclined to."

Jent leaned closer too, his voice barely a whisper. "Always there has been magic, it grows and wanes in unknown cycles. In my granddaddies time it was said to have been up a bit, but not the way it was for his granddad's time before him. Perhaps it isn't going away like we all thought; perhaps it circles back. Listen, you go find the Makay's place and talk to the old man. If he isn't in the house, try the hills out back."

Jent took a pull from his pewter mug and wiped his wet lips off with his sleeve. "He built a burrow in a hill back behind the house, tucked away on the edge of the forest. If there is anyone alive in those parts, it will be Bob or his dad. They were the men that remembered and told the legends. Go there and see, if not for you, for me. The Makays are well remembered around these parts by some of us. If something has happened to Bob then the old man will need to be helped. If Bob isn't there you tell the old man to come visit us for a time won't you? You will make it up there right?"

"My task is to not just to make TerranAdd, but to check out places between the Tiren and there, so yes, I will check in on the Makays. I can't afford much time in side trips, but it would be good to have a local man that can tell us something. If we find the old man alone I will tell him your words. But I don't have time to coddle him – nor can I spare a mount. If he doesn't go willingly I will have to leave him. You understand that right Jent?"

"Aye, I hear you. And thank you." Jent said as he placed his hands on top of Miathis'.

Miathis leaned back, his voice louder and clearer as their conversation ended. "Enough talk for tonight, I have an early morning and there's a long week ahead."

Miathis drained his cup, as did Jent, and both stood and shook hands. Miathis then reached down and pulled open his pouch and handed Jent a few coins. Jent looked as if he might refuse but Miathis nodded emphatically. "I will find your friend and his dad, and if I can't, I will find out what befell them."

Jent nodded and accepted the coin and the words then picked up the pitchers and headed back to the kitchen.

Miathis stretched and headed up the stairs to prepare for bed and what would be his first good sleep in three days. A lit lamp was waiting for him when he entered the room and his bedding had been pulled back. Fresh, cold water was in a pitcher on the dresser.

He yawned and pulled off his leather trousers and then crawled between the sheets and stared at the ceiling before turning onto his side to extinguish the kerosene lantern. "Magic, that's just about all that I need to face now." Miathis said to himself. The faint light of the city's lanterns came through the open window and bathed the room in a soft, warm glow.

***

In the dark of the night Miathis awoke with a start to two cold feet slipping into his bed. Bess curled up in Miathis' arms and sighed. Her petite body nestled against him as her face nuzzled in to his chest. He reached around her with one arm and drew her closer to him, feeling goose bumps on her arms. She shuddered slightly as his warmth pulled the chill from her limbs.

In the darkness Bess looked up at Miathis. Hope, desires, and fears were in here eyes. "Be safe Miathis, be safe ok?" Whispered Bess.

Miathis responded with a kiss and hugged her closer, reassuring her the only way he knew how.

The king's thief

Dressed in plain clothes Bartholomue Mitos, Viscount of PassionMont, entered the Cloven Hoof tavern, not that the sign above the entrance marked it as such. The sign swinging above the door bore the image of a hammer and anvil and proclaimed the establishment as being the same. Mitos however, knew that every type of villainous man or woman would know this place as the front office of the underbelly of Mont Ryhn. Beyond its doors and front tavern existed another, one that was not easily accessed, especially by one such as he.

"Good evening sir" called a wench by the first table and the crowd in the tavern grew quiet as all eyes turned to face the door.

"A pint when you have a chance, eh?" Responded Mitos as he headed over to the only open table in the room. Every nook and cranny here was taken, people even stood apart in the corners. Only here in the middle of the room, directly under the glare of the kerosene lamp, was a table available.

Mitos was ill at ease. He was sure that any number of individuals within the room would kill him if they even suspected who he was. He had taken great pains in working out his disguise; dirtying himself, removing all jewellery and even practicing his speech and walk. At first, in fact, he had thought to hire someone else to go in his stead, but the task at hand was too important.

Mitos believed that the safety and prosperity of Montterran people rested very much on his shoulders. In his opinion, while the king and his formal council of lords occasionally dirtied their hands, they never had the stomach to go the distance. Often times, he thought, things that had to be done for the Kingdome were best done by those more inclined to the task, else they might never be done at all.

'Into the belly of the beast.' Mitos thought to himself as he strove to remain inconspicuous. 'Keep your eyes down and don't look around, these people come here to meet but not to be seen. If you look curious, they'll know you for an outsider.' he thought as he sat down at the table.

A elderly bar wench appeared before Mitos with a tall pewter stein filled with what looked like flat beer. It appeared as if something was floating in the top… something white and not quite dead. "Here you go mate, enjoy!" laughed the wench and turned to leave. The front four of her upper teeth were missing, and the only two Mitos could see before she started to turn were black. Her hair was dark and greasy, Mitos had no idea what colour it might have been under all the dirt.

Mitos' right hand shot out, grabbing her wrist and holding it tight. "One second please." He whispered in his most villainous voice as he twisted her around, letting the words lilt slightly to bring in a Sieren accent. "You obviously know I'm not from around here, but don't insult me with this slop." Mitos pushed the stein away from him and stared at the wench.

He continued then, much softer and adding to his speech a southern Terran drawl "You and likely every one else in this room knows I'm not from here, that isn't the point. What is the point is that I want to talk to Movin. I know he's here, he always is."

The wench, turned round by Mitos' rough pull on her wrist, froze at his words and blinked at the mention of Movin. At first fear streaked across her face. She had taken him for a citizen lost and unaware that he had walked into a lion's den but now she wasn't quite sure. The mentioning of Movin the Sieren speech and the glint of his eyes made her fear she had misjudged the man.

Regaining her composure and confidence she smiled an ugly toothless smile. Mitos almost cringed. The wench obviously chewed Bardos root, for her mouth and lips were grey. "Oh you do, do yah? Well if you see him you go get him yourself." replied the wench as she tried to pull away.

Mitos held fast to the woman's wrist and wrenched it hard. "Get him here…" Mitos reached into his belt with his free left hand

and pulled forth two Terran silver nails. Forcing the wench's hand upward he placed them in her palm. Smiling slyly he closed her fingers around them. "Please?"

The wench looked up and around, then put the coins down between her breasts where Mitos heard them click against her existing stash. He shuddered internally, wishing he had not watched the wench's placement of the coins. She was not a handsome woman and the sight was somewhat disturbing.

"I'll see what I can find." the wench replied pulling her wrist away as Mitos released his grasp.

Mitos looked down and then glanced around through the corners of his eyes, trying to assess how many people had been listening in. It couldn't be helped, and he was sure that everyone in the room now believed that Movin the Thief was having an out of town visitor.

Mitos sat back and pulled an old pipe from under his shirt. He pulled out some rather nasty smelling Mohen leather leaf, stuffed it in the pipe and lit it. Everything, down to this last detail, had been planned out in his mind to create the illusion that he wasn't who he seemed. Still the image was almost ruined as he gagged on the smoke filling his mouth.

A moment later Mitos noticed the wench addressing a man half obscured by shadows sitting in the far corner of the bar. The man looked over to him, nodded ever so slightly, and then motioned with a gaze that he should exit. The slippery looking man then tipped the wench and stepped quietly out of the tavern.

Mitos waited a few minutes then followed the man out the door. As he exited the pub he pulled out his dagger. "I'm not stupid." he said softly as he entered the dark street.

"What can I do for you Bart?" Came a voice from behind him. Mitos spun. This man was very quiet. Mitos tried to conceal his frustration at being recognized and hailed by an abbreviation of his first name. He had hoped for greater secrecy. Obviously, although a lowlife, this man had an eye for those within court.

"I need to get a message to Dimo or his daughter Dimona." Mitos said quietly as he took a step closer and placed his blade back into its sheath under his shirt. "I have a gold piece if you give them the message that I would like to meet with them."

Mitos couldn't make out much of Movin beyond the fact that he was dressed very plainly, neither well, nor poorly. His features were plain as well and his hair was actually clean, although not well combed. Overall, Movin was a very unassuming individual.

"Be at the White Stag for dinner in two days, the back room." said Movin. "They knew someone from the court would be asking for them and who might be doing the asking as well. They might show up, they might not, it's none of my concern."

The grace of Movin's movements as he stepped in to grab the coin amazed Mitos. He immediately recognized his peril in coming down to make the exchange. Had Movin wanted to kill him he would have been dead.

"You scared of me, gov'na?" Movin questioned with a voice like a viper. "That's good. But I ain't nothing as scary as the two you're asking after. I'm to tell you this too. No matter who you are, how well you think you can hide, if you double cross them, you and yours will all die most horribly."

"Got that Bartholomue?" Movin added with a wink.

Mitos nodded. A moment later Movin turned and disappeared into the shadows. Mitos looked up, feeling suddenly exposed and alone. He quickly started to walk back to the better lit streets and to the carriage and guard he had left several blocks away.

***

Two days later Mitos was sitting in the back room of the White Stag sipping on a rather tasty and unpolluted beer. When he arrived he had been ushered into the back room by the barman where a table was waiting, already set with roast chicken and bread. After waiting half an hour he had started to nibble on what had been set out. Fearful that he might have a long time to wait he decided to make the best of things.

Mitos was desperately hoping that Dimo would make an appearance. The price his informants had told him was the cost of asking for a meeting was jingling in a pouch by his belt. Just to be sure another of like size was wedged underneath his belt as well. He hoped that that the old man's price would pay for Dimona's attendance as well, but he sincerely doubted it. The second pouch, and yet another concealed beneath his black vest, were there as additional recompense should it be required for what he wanted to ask of them.

Mitos had found out the day after his meeting with Movin that the White Stag, located as it was on the wharf, had two special properties. The first was that it was in a fairly well trafficked area, so comings and goings weren't that noticeable. The other was that the White Stag had a trap door in the floor by the wall that opened to a ladder that led down below the wharf to the water. The pub had supposedly served as a meeting place for the Thieves' Guild and 'outsiders' such as some of the shadier merchants for many a year.

The White Stag it seemed, was considered neutral ground, and was protected by both the underhand merchants of the area and the guild. It was safer in that building than in church, Mitos had been told. Any crime committed near it was punishable by the guild leader and that was something feared by any with sense enough to know.

Mitos was eyeing the trap door when the door to the private room opened. Noise spilled in from the busy tavern beyond. A very tall serving wench, much prettier then the last wench he had dealt with, came in and brought two tankards of mulled wine. Mitos smiled, sure that the two glasses indicated that Dimo was indeed coming and would be there shortly.

As the wench shut the door to the room the trap door opened and a man climbed out. He was small in stature and very old. His face was lean and his skin hung loose and wan where it showed above his drab brown robes, which were clean but well worn and patched. What little hair remained on his head was white, and his eyebrows were thick and full.

Mitos kept a stoic expression as he stood to greet the man. He knew Dimo MisinTon, head of the Thieves' Guild of Montterran, was one of the most powerful men in the city even though he was extremely diminutive.

'Powerful and dangerous.' Mitos reminded himself. He had been informed that last year this small man had personally gutted three visiting thugs who mistook him for a grandfather and an easy mark. Their intestines had supposedly hit the ground before they even knew that he had the jump on them.

"Good evening my friend." Mitos said as Dimo straightened himself up and shut the trap door.

"Good evening to you sir." Dimo replied cordially. "Things are well I see. Isn't that a new vest? And my those purses you are wearing are just lovely."

Mitos chuckled looking down at himself, wondering how the thief could have spotted them so quickly. To his eye they were well concealed. "Is there nothing your eyes don't catch?" he asked smiling and proffering his hand in greeting.

"I heard those purses chink when you reached for that beer five minutes ago while I was still below the wharf." Dimo said ignoring Mitos' hand and settling himself in the chair opposite.

Mitos nodded then pulled one of the purses from his belt and slid it over beside Dimo. Dimo didn't touch it, but rather grabbed a fork from the table and pushed it back towards Mitos. "My time here is free, as long as you tell the King that his pain at Princess Elle's loss is felt even by us. She was a ray of sunshine in this town. You may tell him for me that any news of her will be passed to you for no charge. "

Mitos' eyes lifted. "That is a very generous gesture Dimo, and your heartfelt statement will, I am sure, be appreciated by the King, though he assures us his focus is on the Kingdome and not his daughter."

Dimo stabbed a piece of chicken on the platter and looked up at Mitos, meeting his eyes. "First, don't say my name aloud here, even these walls have ears. Secondly, between the two of us – it isn't a generous move at all. There is nothing more dangerous than a man in power looking for his only child… and that danger more than doubles if that man is a king and that child is a young girl. I want it to be clear that we are here to help him. I know full well that if he thinks we have any knowledge he will burn down his own city to get it…. I know I would."

Mitos reached out and pulled some bread off of a loaf on the table and dipped it into the mulled wine. "Roehn isn't quite like that, he values his people above all else. He is, however, a man of deep honour and your genuine comments and gesture will be appreciated. Never forget he is the King and must always act as such. He will not be held to any future account for information you might pass on later."

"No notice will be expected. I just want him to know that should we come to know of Elle the knowledge will be passed to him in good faith."

Dimo paused, then looked up at Mitos. "Why did you want to see my daughter Mitos? She is as precious to me as Elle is to Roehn . Do you know how dangerous your request was? I had a few thoughts of not coming, or perhaps visiting you personally later and thanking you with my knife for passing around my daughter's name to the likes of Movin."

"My apologies." Mitos said in earnest. "I didn't have another method of asking and the request was honest. What little rumours there are of her is that she is a very gifted woman."

Dimo raised his voice slightly. "I told you already, any information we gather you will get. She will find what can be found and we will pass that information on to you."

Mitos raised his hand up to his belt. "I would actually like to ask something more of you." Mitos paused, trying not just to pick his words properly but also his tone. "What I would like to do is make an arrangement to hire you and your men."

Dimo's eyes rose slightly at the unorthodox request. "To what end?"

"You have obviously heard of the fall of TerranAdd. We want it searched. It will undoubtedly hold some treasures that the raiders did not happen upon. I would expect that you will be sending people there to 'collect' those items not already being watched over. My, or rather, our, offer is this. The King and his officials will turn a somewhat blind eye should you perform some *controlled* looting and in return we ask for a favour."

Dimo laughed out loud and held his small belly. "Our city is now almost devoid of thieves, every one of them is heading to TerranAdd." Dimo shook his head. "No, if you want some of those coins, you should have left a day ago! What type of gift is this, to give us something we can do already? How would the court restrict our ability? What would you offer for us to control that which we take or to work with you in this regard?"

"First, soldiers are on their way to TerranAdd as we speak. They have instructions to hang any thief they find within the city and to lock down its treasures. What we offer to you is legitimate access. We're not talking of robbing a store, but of the opening of thousands of stores, of the castle's entire wealth."

"Concealing such wealth, and such goods as will be found will be.." here Mitos paused for effect, "difficult for even the best fence."

"What we offer is that we will turn a blind eye should you work with us and also to some extent limit your take. If not, Mont Rhyn will become much more difficult for you to work in. Further, for their aid your men will be listed as privateers, and as such we will turn a blind eye should you need to protect your new found wealth from other thieves."

Dimo looked up apprehensively at Mitos, trying to assess the threats and benefits of the offer.

Mitos leaned back in the chair. "We would not be stopping what you are doing now, just restricting it slightly. And for us to allow all this we ask but one thing. We want information. We want any and all information about whatever your men find out or even suspect has happened at TerranAdd."

"The key phrase here is 'risk free and legitimate'. You will have access to goods under the domain of the Montterran forces. The gold you find and loot you take, of which we will want an inventory, will be totally unsoiled. Just think of all that gold, legitimate and clean."

"It legitimizes your organization and activities... to a point." Mitos added. "Who knows, with a dowry such as that in a few years Dimona could be married to a count and you could have a grandson of nobility."

Dimo sat back in his chair, looked down at his plate and pulled on his ear. "Not sure if Dimona will agree, and mind you, she just might box my ears for even thinking about this but... if we can keep two coins for every eight we find you have a deal. It will be worth it if I don't have to worry about hiding the stuff from your guards."

"At three to ten then, my good friend?" Mitos responded.

Dimo looked up again and frowned, then smiled and nodded. "I think you have a deal. Three coins in ten of all we find we will keep, the rest will be passed to you. Any coin or object inventoried to you will be considered our property by law."

"Dimona will assess the worth of our findings and inventory what we take and I will pass it on to you along with your, shall we say, commission."

"Done... but remember the information we seek about those that were at TerranAdd." Mitos added.

"Of course." Dimo acknowledged.

"Excellent! So when will you speak with Dimona? How soon can you know her response?" Mitos asked as he rose. "I had hoped you would have brought her, but obviously I overstepped my request and for that I apologize once more."

Dimo smiled at Mitos. "She couldn't be here – she was already on her way to TerranAdd three days ago."

Mitos nodded, then smiled broadly at Dimo's words.

Dimo went to the door and said something to the serving girl. In a few minutes she was back with a small quill, ink and some parchment. Dimo sat down and wrote a note. It was a short note of only a few lines and he in less than a minute he was passing it over to Mitos , unsigned, unsealed and unfolded.

Mitos looked quizzically at the note, then turned it upside down and squinted at the parchment.

Dimo chuckled, "I doubt if you will be able to read that, it is in a rather obscure language that very few people alive now know. The way it is written and the words used will authenticate it to Dimona. You will need to send it with one rather polite and trusting man to the Black Water pub in TerranAdd. It's a small place east of the main citadel. He should be dressed as a soldier, and have him tie something white to his belt. With luck he won't get his throat cut before being able to hand the note to Dimona, but there's no guarantee. Either way, if the note arrives in TerranAdd it will make it to Dimona so I wouldn't send someone you can't afford to lose."

Dimi stood and nodded to Mitos as he walked over to the trap door. "I wouldn't delay in getting that note to your man. My Dimona has a very keen eye and she reads people well. She will be likely a good source of information about what might have happened at TerranAdd. She also works fast. If you wait too long she might be finished picking TerranAdd clean before your men even get there. That daughter of mine can ride like the wind." he added proudly and then descended the ladder and vanished into the night.

MountRyhn

The mountain pass was shrouded with extremely thick fog. The once warm valleys were loosing their battle with the cold winds flowing down from the mountain peaks.

Etch had descended to Verin in the early morning. It was an easy walk over the rolling foothills to the small village. As he entered the town he looked back at Diamond Mountain, its peak invisible through the clouds that clung to it and covered it all the way to below where his wife and children were, still asleep in their beds. He sighed as he turned and began winding his way towards the blacksmith's, where he hoped to find a mount.

Unfortunately, the only horse the blacksmith would part with was a very old one. Its back was sagging, its feet appeared tender and what teeth remained were rotted. Its only redeeming quality was that the blacksmith wasn't overly aggressive in his asking price and Etch managed to purchase it for a few silver claws. He opted not to purchase any of the saddles offered for he wasn't sure the horse could bear the weight. Instead he bought a simple blanket, bridal and bit.

At the eastern outskirts of the village Etch carefully climbed on the animal's back and cringed as the creature shuddered under its new burden. As it started forward at a rolling, steady walk Etch became a little more confident that it would live until he got to Mount Ryhn.

Etch didn't pause along the route, eating his dinner while still moving forward. They kept a steady pace until the horse slowed somewhat entering the hills leading to the Verin pass. Etch looked up to the pass and tried to assess the risk. He knew he had to get through quickly if he was to beat winter's chill. The soldiers had told Rachael that their trip through the pass went well, but Etch knew from previous years that you took your chances from one day to the next. Once the heavy snows fell the pass would be closed and those within the Verin vales would be isolated from the rest of the world until spring.

"Giddy up…" Etch said to his mount, giving it a gentle nudge with the heal of his foot. "During these fall days, it can snow at any time up there. And given your bad legs, I don't think you would enjoy walking through knee deep snow." The mount's pace didn't waver and it continued to trudge along at its same slow rate.

So far Etch had seen no one else on the road east. Often at this time of the year the pass roads were busy as villagers and easterners shuffled quickly back and forth making their last trades of the year. Today however, the road was empty and the tracks suggested that only two other horses had gone east in the last few days.

The narrow road wound its way up through foothills and eventually took Etch to within the pass itself.

The pass itself didn't feature much of a road, but rather a worn trail up and between the shoulders of two mountains that hunched together protecting the vale from the east. Snow often drifted down from their peaks, creating drifts four or five metres deep. Some old tales told of people that had crossed the pass in the winter, using snowshoes, but there were far more stories told of men and women and entire caravans swallowed whole by the mountains, only to be found when the snows receded.

Etch knew that there were two spots in the pass that were especially dangerous. The first was a section that was spotted with large boulders. The boulders were so smooth that climbing them was extremely difficult and they were so close together that to pass them you had to carefully wind around and through them. When snow did come, the winding road between them was blocked. Often early in the winter season the snow that rested on top of these massive blocks would fell down on unsuspecting travelers and trap them between the frozen sentries.

The second area was near the end of the pass. One long crack, fifty meters deep, four hundred meters long and only five meters wide passed through the last of the mountains and led to the foothills of the eastern Ryhnian lands. Rocks fell freely down from the cliffs on either side here, as did snow. During the winter the pass was not navigable, for the snow created pockets of air meters below the surface that would swallow anyone who passed overhead

As Etch entered the upper reaches of the pass he turned to look back to the west one last time. As soon as he rounded the first of the smooth boulders he would lose sight of Diamond Mountain.

Etch frowned in disappointment. The view to the west wasn't much to fuel any future memory. The clouds still hung on the massive mountain, virtually obscuring it. Etch turned his horse once more and nudged it forward, winding his way around and through the massive stones.

"Most are still home in bed at this hour, or looking out of their window while at breakfast - gazing at the fog coming down from the mountains." Etch said to his mount as he pulled up his collar to ward off the cold drafts that slipped through the stones.

A few droplets of water from Etch's collar spilled down his back sending a shiver up his spine and making the blond hairs on the back of his neck stand up.

Etch reached forward to touch the horse's mane and tiny drops fell from it, running down its neck. The horse didn't respond but just continued to tread along at its moderate pace.. As he stroked the horses' neck he mused, "I will have to think of a good name for you my friend for we will be each other's sole company for some time to come I expect."

Etch smiled looking up. They were making good time despite his horse's shortcomings, good enough that they might reach the long narrow passage locals called the Crack, the last part of the pass, by nightfall. If they could get through there while it was still light enough to see he could ride on beyond it through the night. Once through the Gateway there was no way to go off course for there was only one navigable route. He would make the hills by the morning, and Mount Ryhn by early afternoon.

It had been a couple of years since Etch had last traveled to Mount Ryhn. The most recent trip had been to pick up some herbs for

Rachael to go in a healing poultice she made. She had used up all of her original supply after one of the villagers lost a leg in a landslide.

Etch's nose cringed at the memory of his return trip. The herbs had really smelled badly. As per Rachael's instructions he had made sure that they were fresh, and had wrapped them in three layers of leathers, yet even bound as they were the acrid smell had reached his nose, leaving him coughing and sneezing the entire way home. 'It took me a month to get that scent out of my clothes!' Etch remembered with a grimace.

As darkness enveloped the mountains he reached the Gateway. Tense, he braced himself to continue. Traveling the passage was unnerving at the best of times; many horses became skittish in the close confines, surrounded by the high walls. Etch had hoped that in the darkness his mount would fare well and that he might be able to sleep a spell while the horse continued its trek but it was not to be. Occasionally stones fell from the cliffs above and hit the trail either before or behind them, the sound making the horse stop dead. It needed constant reassurance to continue along, which meant Etch would get no rest at all.

***

As the morning sun rose Etch could just smell a hint of grape on the air. Sometime just before dawn he had entered the Ryhnian foothills, known especially for their vineyards. The early morning sun glistened off of the thousands of rows of staked vines that grew to either side of him. Men, women and children were already out checking on the crops. Several farmers were pushing massive wheel barrows full of grapes down the hills to the large buildings where the grapes were pressed.

In the distance down the slopes Etch watched as massive horses pulled large wooden barrels towards Mount Ryhn.

The castle of Mount Ryhn itself was visible now in the lowlands to the east. Its magnificent towers stretched to the sky topped with cones and massive flags whose crest could be seen even at the great distance. Roads from the highland pastures and vineyards wound down and joined a single main thoroughfare that led to the city. All around Mount Ryhn were massive farms, their fields checker-marked by smaller roads. Small cottages appeared as dots on the roads that crossed through the golden valleys.

Etch smiled in appreciation. The vineyards to his right and left were heavily laden with fruit and the fields below waved in the distance; massive stalks of corn, great golden seas of wheat, and fields dark green with vegetables.

Etch's first stop as he entered the great walls of the city was at the Wicked Witch. The Witch was a sort of general store and pub combined and Etch intended to grab a few odds and ends he might need on his trip, items he knew would be harder to come by in any other merchant's quarters.

He knew that the Witch was an excellent place to find rare herbs and roots, as well as the latest information. The man that ran the small shop always worked on the razor's edge of the law, trading in materials and goods that were either somewhat 'suspect' or were down right illegal (which were only to be purchased by those of acquaintance).

Etch knocked on the door, entered and immediately sat down at a table. A man around sixty-five years of age walked through the hanging curtains that separated a back room. "Hello, Etch. Been a very long time – nigh on two years now isn't it? You were in for some Tuffle root for your misses last time through if I recall. How did that work out?"

"Worked fine, you sold me good fresh stock she said. She made tea from it and also a poultice that helped the lad she was tending at the time. I ended up using the tea she made on her that winter, she caught a nasty cold and bad fever. Three times a day I gave it to her and in ten days she was up on her feet. I am much obliged for your help my friend." Etch said as he stood to greet the man. "You are looking good Datos. Time is treating you well."

"Please sit Etch. Yes, thank you, I am faring well. The summers have been warm and the winters not too cold; business has been steady.

Overall, I am a contented man. So, your family is well then? Your wife, I am sorry for I've forgotten her name, and your children?"

"Thank you yes, all are well." Etch responded, but didn't elaborate.

Etch never spoke much of his family, and never mentioned their names. His work was his work; his business was business, and his family entirely separate. Etch cherished his family's detachment from what he did.

Etch had often needed to work on the edge of the law and occasionally had dealings with individuals like the man before him. He liked Datos, but when working on the borders of the law, the less that people knew about you and yours, the safer you were. It was a mark of his trust in Datos that the man even knew Etch's real name and that he had a wife and children at all.

"So, what can I do for you Etch?" Datos asked cheerily.

"I need some Tygor leaf and Pylor. Basically, if you could set me up with a large travelers healing kit, a good one, it would be much appreciated." Etch replied. "It's been a while, what will a good setup cost me?"

"A full three gold for a good setup," Datos replied, "if you want fresh material. By saying a 'good kit' I get the feeling you want roots and herbs for a variety of ailments and protections and probably anti-venoms for the more common poisonous snakes. How far will you be going? If you're going to the marshes then I would recommend taking along remedies for the Water Moccasins for I hear that Moss Landing is overrun with them this year."

"Not sure where all I will be headed, so make it well stocked and label the contents." Etch smiled, and reaching under his gray cloak pulled forth his purse and set it on the table in front of him. From it he pulled four gold coins and one silver and pushed them over to Datos.

"I have learned that a well-stocked bag from you can save more than my own life. I wouldn't think of traveling without one of your kits now – they're more important than food. You told me that once, and I have learned to live by that lesson."

Datos smiled and stood up. "Give me a few minutes. I don't get many requests for a full travelers bag so it will take me a moment or two to get it together. I'll just label the bottles and bags with what it is, how to use it and what to use it for."

"Oh, one thing." Etch added with a smile and a wink. "If there is something besides Tuffle root that can do the same, give me it instead. Otherwise I'll pay the extra silver and you can put it in a bottle with a solid stopper. That stuff stinks!"

Datos chuckled. "I thought of that after you left the last time. You bought it the day after I pulled it from my garden in the hills; it hadn't even had a chance to dry out a touch. . I bet you smelled like a skunk for a day or two after returning home."

"A *month* I smelled of the stuff. It took all my courage to make the tea and smell it again when I needed it."

Datos chuckled and then nodded and turned to the back room. Etch sat back and waited while looking out of the shop windows at the people on the street. He never grew tired of watching the human traffic in the city. "So many people." Etch said to himself.

Etch could hear bottles and jars being opened through the doorway behind him. Without turning he called back to his friend. "Listen, Datos." Etch said loudly. "What's happening these days in court and in the guard? Any new players? What should I be wary of?"

"Not much has changed in the last few years Etch. Roehn has kept a stable court and the same players are there as were there two years ago. Dukes and counts are behaving themselves, although I hear the Duke of Sindor continues to walk the edge of legality with some of his trading … much of my more 'special' ingredients come via his ports. But he has on the whole been keeping in the background."

"But the happenings of TerranAdd, now there's a lot of talk about that. And here you come, asking for a traveling kit, a big one at that. I've seen several people I don't normally see these last two weeks. There is lots of speculation about, but not much fact. What do you know of it Etch?"

Etch leaned forward a little. "Not much, and very likely far less then you. That's one of the reasons I'm here Datos, to hear what you know of the goings on at TerranAdd. What do you know of the happenings? And what is being said of the King Roehn and his family?"

"By family, you are of course talking of his one and only daughter and by the question I can guess you already know something of her disappearance. Yes, she is missing. She had gone to TerranAdd to visit Mindy Bestinor, King Tar's daughter, on her birthday."

Datos, still hidden behind the curtained arch, talked while opening and closing bottles and jars. "If you believe the gossip then TerranAdd is totally vacant, all the people for kilometers around missing… just plain gone."

Datos' head peeped out through the curtains. He looked seriously at Etch as if trying to discern if he was telling him new news or reciting what Etch already knew. Etch kept his card playing face on, trying to not let Datos read his thoughts.

"No blood, no bodies, no nothing." Datos added, and then turned back to his work.

"Lots of talk within the city walls, but frankly that's the all of it. No one *really* knows anything – all the rest is just speculation."

Datos came back out through the curtains again, this time holding a large pouch, and sat back down at Etch's table, leaning close. "Mark my words though, dark work must be afoot to make an entire city's folk disappear. That is the one thing all those in my inner circle are saying… and feeling."

Datos looked up over Etch's shoulder to the window and then back down to Etch. "Those that I know who deal in charms and they say they felt something, but are keeping their mouths shut. They're all very scared and none too sure of themselves these days.

Many of the true ones, the ones with real gifts, are hidden away in reclusion, locked up in their homes."

Etch had traveled far and had always considered himself a man with an open mind. Still, he raised his eyebrows at the mention of 'gifts'. He never had fallen in for luck charms or the concept of magic in general. He was a little disappointed with Datos for even mentioning it. "Even 'true' workings do but little. Why the interest Datos? What is the relationship of charms with TerranAdd? Why would they speculate dark workings and what do they mean by that?"

Datos leaned back in his chair and looked soulfully at Etch. "Most of the charms you see in the city are just thrown together by charlatans for the villagers and passersby who don't know any better but as of late there have been a few vendors that really do seem to possess the skill. One woman in particular is now a steady customer of mine and I have seen her do things with herbs and the like that I would never have believed had I not been witness to it."

"According to my friend, the ability to do magic, like create charms and the like comes and goes in unusual cycles that span generations of time. In her grandfather's time she says, the creation of charms to ward of beasts or vipers was quite common and you could actually see the impact of the charms on the beasts. Then suddenly those same charms of old seemed to loose their power and became nothing more than bobbles and trinkets best used for fooling tourists."

"Lately it seems there has been a recurrence of these powers. I have seen her with my own eyes take a lock of dog hair and create a charm that makes any dog you see run from you. Not walk away nor try to bite, but if you approach it, it runs from you... and it isn't by smell."

Datos smiled. "Some of her charms work too well. Thankfully she charges a fair price for her work. For ten gold you can get a good charm to ward off moccasins..."

Datos leaned back in his chair. "Trouble is, no guarantees from her. She admits without hesitation that she has no idea how long the charms will last. She says the powers could last months before they peak, last even longer, or end tomorrow. She doesn't know."

"What is the connection then, between these powers and TerranAdd?" Etch asked quietly, still not seeing the point.

Datos leaned forward and responded, his voice almost a whisper. "She can't explain for certain but she says she feels sure that there must be a connection, she just isn't strong enough in her art to know what."

"Only one thing will she say can be known as truth. If what befell TerranAdd was done by magic, then it was the biggest magic act done in centuries."

"Where would I find this woman so I could talk with her?" Etch asked.

Datos looked up at Etch frowning. His face and entire body seemed to wrinkle all as one. He looked much older than he had when Etch first walked in. This subject was troubling Datos. The tension in his voice was very noticeable; he was scared and wasn't enjoying the conversation. Something was shaking him up.

Datos frown deepened. He was still not sure if he should divulge the information to Etch.

Etch smiled, reached in under his cloak and pulled out four more gold coins and placed them on the table.

Datos' eyes brightened. "I think I can trust you Etch. But I have to warn you, if you seek her out." Dato paused for a long moment and then bit his lip. "Most that go see her are never seen again. She tolerates me because I trade for some of the herbs she can't grown in her own garden. I can tell you how to get there, but I can't guarantee the reception you will get when you arrive."

Etch pushed the coins forward across the table but left his hand by them waiting for more information as to the location of this old lady.

Datos smiled and nodded. "She lives by the Smite River falls, ten kilometers south of the main Tiren bridge on the east side of Tiren Falls. The area is very hilly and heavy with trees so it's slow traveling. Her house is surrounded by small gardens. You can't miss it if you stick to the road below the falls."

"She enjoys her privacy, as attested to by the large cats that guard her. She always knows when she is being approached. If you see the cats, run." Datos grinned. "Not that it will make much of difference."

Datos leaned forward and started picking up the gold coins. He looked up at Etch and whispered very softly. "Her name is Stymar."

Etch paused a moment then reached up and scratched his two days' stubble of beard. "Is there something I should bring her? Will she deal in information for gold and if not what would such a woman desire?"

"Good thinking." Datos said. "I can pack you a small bag for her, the type of rare herbs she usually looks for."

With Etch's nod, Datos stood and motioned to the back room with a wave of his arm. "This stuff isn't cheap."

Etch nodded, "Nothing here ever is Datos." In the next few minutes he spent another three gold for a second small bag of herbs. Etch looked in his purse and frowned at having spent much more already then he had planned.

"Thank you friend." said Etch as he stood to leave. "I have business elsewhere, but I will be back after dinner to pick up my purchases."

Datos smiled at Etch. "I'll throw some Tygor leaf into your travel bag as well, it could be a long journey."

Etch smiled and shook the man's hand. "On cold nights there's nothing like a small leaf to make the evening pass eh?"

Etch exited the small shop and untied his old horse. The city streets were bustling with people. Merchants' windows were overflowing with produce and at every street corner sat a farmer with a wheelbarrow of vegetables. Sweet smoke filled the air as butchers busily cured beef and pork and citizens ran about in and out of the shops with arms stacked high with food and material.

"Business in the city is good I see." Etch said to his horse as he started heading in the direction of the barracks.

Etch tied up his mount and entered the large barracks located on the northern wall of the city. He was quickly directed to the eastern rooms where he was told he could find his old friend Thesra.

He felt a little awkward walking down the long halls. All the other men in the building wore the markings of the Kingdome and it had been a long time since he had worn the garb of a soldier. Many men watched him pass but none questioned him along the way. 'They've grown lax in good times.' Etch thought to himself as turned a corner and headed towards where he had been told he would find the general's quarters.

As Etch turned down the next hall he almost collided with a soldier standing guard. "This hall is off limits to civilians." the soldier said as he blocked Etch's way.

The soldier was about thirty and was armed with both sword and dagger. Etch smiled. "Not quite a civilian." He said to the man. "My name is Etch, Etch Tarrow, one time scout in the Fist. Sir Beston Thesra is expecting me." he added when the soldier failed to look suitably impressed.

The soldier looked him up and down and then nodded. "Follow me then." he said as he turned and started down the corridor.

When they reached the officer's quarters, the soldier instructed Etch to follow, knocked on one of the larger door and then preceded in.

As they entered a waiting room Etch noticed a few empty chairs as well as a table and chair where another soldier sat reviewing some parchments.

The soldier that had brought him in turned to him. "You may sit here." he said and then walked over to the other soldier and leaned forward. "This man is Etch Tarrow. He claims that Sir Thesra is expecting him."

The sergeant at the desk stood up, looked quickly at Etch, who had remained standing where he was, and nodded. He turned to the other soldier, nodded again and then looked back over at Etch. "Yes, the man is expected." He knocked smartly on a door to an inner room and then entered it quickly, closing the door behind him.

Etch stood waiting for only a moment or two before the sergeant returned and motioned that the soldier should escorted Etch into the inner office. As Etch entered his old friend Thesra, garbed in the uniform of an officer, stood up from his desk and walked over to greet him. "Etch, it's been a long time. How are you doing?"

Etch shook the man's hand as Thesra put his arm around his shoulder and walked him to a large chair by the desk. "Come in, come in. We have a lot to discuss and not much time. Please sit."

Etch took a quick look around. The office was very large and well appointed. To one side sat a strategy table with miniatures representing the kingdoms around Montterran. The desk behind which Thesra now sat was massive and piled high with parchment.

There were over a dozen chairs aligned in front of the desk, obviously intended for briefings. Many memories of serving under Thesra came flooding back to Etch as he took in his surroundings.

"You know why you are here, I'm sure" said his friend and one time captain. "But let me start from the beginning anyways for I am not sure where our knowledge might overlap."

Etch sat down and looked over to the general who threw a few parchments off to one side to make room in the center of the desk. "TerranAdd stands empty and undefended. We have no idea who or what hit the city, although rumors and suspicions abound. All citizens in the city and in the areas just surrounding the walls are gone. All the men, women, and children, even the very old and very young, vanished in a single night."

Thesra slammed his fist on the desk "They are gone and we have NO idea how or why! You can't believe how frustrating this is Etch – to prepare to fight a battle with an unknown foe!"

Thesra calmed himself quickly and then eased back in his chair. "There is no trace of them, nor trace of where they went."

"What we have done so far," Thesra continued, "is send the Fist. One hundred men left with all haste a few days ago."

"Their objective is to scour the city and surrounding areas to try and find out what befell our neighbours."

Etch shook his head in bewilderment. "Movement of that number of people must leave a trace. Movement of any army that could capture TerranAdd without their being able to send word must have left some sign."

"Who, how and why – all these questions are unanswered." Thesra said and then looked down at the strategy board and parchments. "Our first thought was the Drekians, but this doesn't have the feel of them... unless their skills have greatly improved in the last few years or they're being aided by some unknown force."

The knight stood and walked around the desk, sitting down on the edge in front of Etch.

Etch leaned forward. "How can I help?"

Thesra nodded approvingly. "I knew I could count on you. We have hired and brought back to service quite a few of the old company these last few days. What has transpired will destabilize the entire region and I expect that the Masti will not sit still for long."

Thesra looked across at Etch assessing him, determining how much of the old scout was still in front of him now. He smiled in relief at Etch as he saw within his eyes the same spark he had once known. "However, what I would have of you is something in a bit more of a personal mission."

He paused a moment and then continued with a lower voice. "Princess Elle was in TerranAdd when all this transpired. I need a single minded, well-trained tracker to search out and return our princess to our kingdom, and her father."

Etch nodded, understanding the entire picture. This was not a fully sanctioned order from the king, else Thesra would have noted that somewhere in his request. This was a special mission the general had come up with himself, one the king was unaware of. "What aid will I have, and how much time can I take in order to accomplish this task?"

Thesra stood again and walked back around his desk. He opened up his drawer and pulled out a large purse, tossing it to Etch who deftly caught it with his left hand. "There is a fair amount of gold in that purse and three rare stones of good quality."

"I trust you Etch, or I wouldn't pick you for this quest. If you need more within reason – you can sign a note for it with my name and I will ensure repayment. You know more than most men the sufferings of war. We likely wouldn't stand for open war as it relates to the cost of the Princess – but up to that I would risk just about anything. No man should stand in your way. I do not endorse any wrong play and will not promise any general amnesty but…."

Etch stood, lifted his chin and interrupted Thesra. "Enough. I know enough of what you are saying. I have funding and purpose enough to drive me. I take my charge. I will find King Roehn 's daughter. I will not falter, nor cease until my quest has been fulfilled."

"Well said, well said." Thesra remarked. It looked like a weight had been lifted from his shoulders.

"Take this note that has my mark and orders on it. It marks you as my man and, should you need it, it will give you the same authority and command as a lieutenant in our army."

"Unfortunately, beyond the words I have said, this purse and that letter there is nothing more that I can offer. We have no better information or guidance to give you… no starting place to search save TerranAdd, no hope greater then that of a man who speaks for a king who cannot."

"I understand." Etch said. "Then I will leave. I have a thought as to where to start. It isn't much, but I will find more. I will send word from time to time when I can, or if I find specific word about her whereabouts. One thing I would ask. The mount I ride is a tired, miserable animal. I would like your permission to have a trained horse and pack animal for the trip. I could purchase one within the city, but I would like it trained for battle."

Thesra nodded. "That I can get you, I should have thought of as much. One moment." The general walked out the door and Etch could hear him speaking to the soldier sitting in the waiting room. Etch followed slowly behind.

The general turned and motioned to the soldier who had brought Etch in. "The guard will take you to the stables, you can have your choice from any of those available. The arms keeper will also be so instructed, should you need any mail or a shield."

Etch shook his head and looked down. "As far as sword and shield, I have what I need. I will travel as light as possible. Armour or more weapons would mark me as a soldier and might stop others from talking to me. I take enough risk riding a soldier's mount. I sacrifice that only to gain the speed it will give me."

Etch extended his hand and Thesra took it and gave it a solid shake. "You have work to do, as do I. I have what I need and will get the rest." Etch said and smiled at his friend.

Thesra smiled. "I only wish there was more time so we could reminisce about the old days."

Etch chuckled. "There will be time enough for that when I return with my charge. You can buy me a pint or two then."

Thesra laughed and patted Etch on the back. "Indeed, more than two if you return with your charge."

With a final nod from both, Etch strode forward. The guard, having noted the friendship to his commander stood tall and at attention before Etch, then turned sharply to lead him to the stables.

TerranAdd

At first glance you would never have thought that Dimona was related to Dimo MisinTon, King of the thieves. Unlike Dimo, who was a man short of stature and grizzled looking, Dimona was statuesque, almost elfin. She was also extremely beautiful and had an eternally youthful appearance. With her long blonde hair and shapely body she captivated most men but her most memorable attribute was her steel blue eyes. With a glance even the best-trained thief, those that prided themselves on their self-control and steady hands, would stutter and trip over their words.

Still, everyone in Dimona's command knew that she had inherited some of her father's other traits. First, she was extremely intelligent, but even more obvious were her keen sense of perception, her street smarts and her amazing dexterity and agility. Dimona, much like her father, was also a merciless, cold-blooded killer.

Despite her aptitude, perseverance and training, Dimona had found it difficult to follow in her father's footsteps. As a young apprentice thief she had done amazingly well but as she grew into her beauty her ability to remain unseen and to be quickly forgotten disappeared. There were few fair-haired girls around Mont Ryhn, and none that looked quite like her. Once spotted she could never blend back into a crowd.

Dimo had realized early the potential of his daughter and also how her good looks might be to her detriment so he had trained her for leadership and for the solicitation of information and trade of intelligence, places where her beauty would be an asset. After all he reasoned, a beautiful woman can get more information from a knight than any man could in her place, no matter how he might threaten.

At the same time, Dimona's striking appearance was a risk even in the intelligence business. Rather than attempt to hide her beauty however, Dimona did the opposite, flouting it for all to see. If you can't hide – "Be inconspicuously conspicuous" was her current motto.

Dimona was, like her father, also a master of disguise. In gossip throughout the countryside Mont Ryhn was attributed to have within its walls dozens of the most beautiful women in the world. Only a few within the guild knew that most of those descriptions could be attributed to a single lady.

It was widely agreed that Dimo had trained his daughter well. As she truly flowered though, finding her duties became harder and harder. It was a challenge finding assignments that would keep her away from the darker sides of the trade, things like blackmail and assassination. Fortunately for Dimo his daughter had an exceptional mind and quickly developed a unique skill that gave her a competitive edge. Dimona could read people; she could understand how people thought just by looking at them.

"If you are good at knowing how people think then you can predict what they are going to do even before they know themselves." Dimo had said to his daughter at age ten and obviously the comment had stuck. Dimona had applied her sharp mind to the task and honed that skill above all others.

At age thirteen Dimona bested a trained assassin sent by a neighbouring guild to kill Dimo. When Dimo asked her of the fight she stated matter of factly that by simply looking at the man she had known how he would fight and by extension, how to defeat him.

Dimona's pursuit of the understanding of human motives quickly became her passion. Dimo encouraged her by sending her to study with the Temple Guard when she turned fourteen. For four years she studied anatomy, languages, and religion. Then he sent her far and wide to expose her to different customs and traditions. With her keen insight and observation she truly came to understand the human spirit and body. Those skills, when paired with her early training in theft and knife fighting, made her what she was today – a woman not to be trifled with.

At present Dimona sat tall in her saddle atop her mottled, brown and white horse. Her profession made it impossible for her to ride Lady often, for the horse's markings, much like her owner's, set her too far out in a crowd. However, whenever Dimona traveled far from Mont Ryhn she always made an exception.

Dimona had put forth little effort today to conceal herself. She wore a stark white blouse and a long blazing red cape fell back down from her shoulders to cover her horse's flanks.

Those sitting on their mounts in front of Dimona contrasted her dramatically. Six non-descript men sat atop standard fare horses and every one of them looked extremely ordinary. No man, women or child would spare a second look for these men or their mounts, and indeed none did. Neither man nor horse was tall nor short, fat nor thin, they neither dressed well, nor poorly. The men had neither scars nor mottled skin, yet they were not comely by nature.

Any individual, seeing one of these men riding through the countryside, would have thought nothing of him. They would perhaps label him a merchant or a farmer, someone of no consequence, and definitely not an individual to be concerned over.

It was only Dimona's trained eye that noted each man's coiled stance hidden beneath his brown or grey cloak. She could see the ripples in the cloth where their trousers concealed blades. In their eyes she caught a glimpse of thinly veiled malice and a shard of darkness. These six before Dimona were the guild's most adept thieves and assassins. She had selected them personally, each and every one, for this assignment.

Dimona addressed her company of thieves in a formal manner to set the ground rules and to ensure that her authority over them was well defined. She knew that ruling these men would require especially strict control, for men of their talents believed themselves above most authorities and respected only those whose raw power exceeded their own.

She straightened herself authoritatively and began her address in a loud, commanding tone "Good afternoon gentlemen. For those of you that have joined us as of late, and even for those of you that have ridden all the way here with me, let us again go through our main objectives for this venture."

As each word issued from her mouth Dimona watched the eyes and features of her men, constantly evaluating. With each subsequent glance she varied the pitch and tone of her voice as she targeted each man individually to ensure she had his attention.

"First and foremost, you were each 'requested' for this activity because for some reason or another you have either pleased the guild, or pissed us off." Dimona smiled and a few of the men, sensing her ease, chuckled at her words.

"Whatever the case you are mine for the duration of this assignment. Deviation from the tasks assigned or 'side trips' for personal gains will be frowned upon." Dimona said, pausing to look each man in the eye and drive her point home. Nothing else needed to be said following that. Every man there knew that to cross Dimona would mean a swift death, or worse.

"First, all other thieves within the guild have been told that TerranAdd is ours for the next week and they aren't to be within a stone's throw of the city. If you happen across someone too stupid to abide by that arrangement you have my permission to slit their throat. Just do it quietly and ensure you dispose of the mess. This town is supposedly devoid of bodies, so should a soldier find one they could easily come to the conclusion that it came from us."

"Secondly, each of you will be assigned a specific area to search and loot and at least one additional special objective. There is great wealth within these walls." Dimona raised her hand and motioned to the city gates and castle walls behind her. "However, my father has listed specific items that we must return with. Some of these you might find of little worth, that isn't the point. If it is assigned to you to find you will do so."

"Third, unless you are dead you are to meet me at the entrance to the Black Water pub by midnight so that I can inventory what you have found."

"I should not have to state the obvious, but in the interest of clarity, I'll spell it out for you. Keep your horse's tracks to a minimum, go to our area and store your horse in a vacant building where it won't be found should there be any others nosing around. Also, hording what you find for personal gain will be dealt with most severely. Each of you will get the percentage of the total spoils that was outlined when you were taken on for this assignment."

"Those of you that know me well know that I don't have patience for people who step out of line on assignments that I am running. If you find something of specific note we might be convinced to alter your compensation, however, if you try to conceal it from me your life on this earth will end most miserably."

After a short pause, Dimona grinned wickedly. The faces of the men remained stony and impassive, but she could see from the tension in their gaze that she had made her point. "Remember our secondary purpose here is to find out what happened to these people. Find out what you can as you search. Are there signs in your area that suggest a meal was being eaten? Was it breakfast or dinner? What clothing and weapons lie in the cloakrooms? Observe everything, but leave no signs of your search."

Dimona looked around at all the men, one by one. Only one man was looking away for her. She followed his gaze to the flapping flags atop the rampart of the castle. "Bek, do you understand?" she asked sharply. Bek was grinning when he turned his head back to her and looked into her eyes.

"Yes, I understand exactly." Responded Bek as he leered at her. All the others remained silent.

Dimona looked at Bek, who was, if anything, a little on the scruffy side. He hadn't shaved that morning, perhaps thinking that he didn't really need to look that inconspicuous in a city that was supposedly abandoned. Dimona liked the confidence and cockiness that it implied. Bek was one of her most self-assured assassins.

Dimona noted that Bek had come to the venture extremely well armed. He wore a long robe of heavy weave that hung down to just above his knees. Although the fall air was chilly the robe was warmer than necessary, better suited to the heart of winter or the mountains. Dimona knew that the man wore it not for warmth, but rather so that he could conceal the dirk and three daggers that he wore beneath it. In addition, Dimona noted by the way it hung that the robe was also lined with many small pockets.

Bek's returning stare broke under her gaze and he looked away from Dimona and shifted in his saddle. Dimona didn't break her gaze or change her expression but she noted to herself that her point had been made. In that one look Bek knew that he had no chance of concealing anything from her.

"Well then, let us start our task." She said as she turned her mount to the gates of TerranAdd. "We will meet tonight as promised."

Dimona turned her head slightly and addressed the man now directly behind her. " Bek, draw closer before you go. I have changed my mind for your task. We need to talk."

As they were dismissed the other five thieves kicked their mounts and started trotting into the city. Each turned within a horse length of the other, disappearing down the side streets.

"Bek Hassfoot," Dimona started with a sultry voice. "I would take you for a man who knows his way around the brothels."

Dimona listened carefully and heard the man shift uncomfortably in his saddle. Had any other said as much to him she knew he wouldn't have so much as blinked an eye. Bek had had a crush on her for many years and Dimona knew her question was cutting a little closer to fact than he was comfortable with her knowing. Dimona on the other hand, was specifically trying not to disillusion the man, she had no interest whatsoever in a personal relationship with him.

"No need to be coy with me," Dimona added in a level voice. "I know you frequent them often. So your task is to search the two larger brothels of the city."

"You should find a fair bit of coin if you locate the madam's quarters. But of utmost importance is that you search the rooms and buildings themselves. Most of these places have hidden entrances, exits, rooms and the like for special guests. If there is anyone left alive in this city the only hope would be that they are hiding in those."

Bek nodded. "You plan to supervise me Dimona?" His tone turned to one that exuded lust in stark contrast to Dimona's coldness. "I'm sure we could find a room to ourselves."

"My, you do have high expectations don't you Bek? Unfortunately, for you, I will be too busy to dally the day away with you. I will be searching the TerranAdd Thieves' Guild."

"I tell you now that I will be in the city's guild because I know that would be one place you yourself would head straight for. Don't. I will be there and if I find you around that location I will gut you like a fish." Dimona turned in her saddle as they passed under the walls of the city. She looked Bek straight in the eyes and held his gaze. "Understood?"

Bek frowned. "I once lived in this city, I have friends here. I would like very much to know what became of them. Not to mention the guild master here, Thomas, kept some of the best tools of the trade I have ever seen. I need a few replacements to do my work… for our guild of course."

Dimona turned to look forward again as her horse moved up the main street of the city with a slow and graceful gait. "Of course, for the guild. I know you were once of this guild, perhaps then… Yes, ok, as long as you are with me. Together we can look at the guild. Dimo warned me that this Thomas fellow was not a trustful man and will have left traps to guard his spoils. Lead the way Bek, we will go there first."

Bek spurred his horse to take the lead. They twisted and turned randomly through the narrow alleys. Dimona knew that this wasn't the direction of the guild's quarters, but rather that Bek's intent was to ensure their horses' tracks wouldn't show them traveling through the main gates and straight into the city proper, something an average group of thieves would naturally do in their hurry to take what they could.

'He's a good thief.' thought Dimona. He wasn't entirely trustworthy, no thief ever really was, but he had been around for some time and knew a great deal. Dimona had known when she chose Bek that he had originally come, or at least most recently come from, TerranAdd. It was one of the main reasons she had handpicked him, plus there was the incident two years back that made him to here just slightly more expendable then the others.

"Unless you want to spend a lot of time trying to hide, I suggest we take a small detour and head there now. Any trained eye still alive would note our coming regardless." Bek pointed down and behind him at the tracks their horses were leaving. To both of their eyes the tracks stood out as new. Dimona noted that there were no other tracks in the streets newer than a week or two old. "We could ride on the side of the paths, close to the walls, but it will still be seen." Dimona mused.

"See how the streets have dust and sand settled on them already? There has been no rain these last two weeks." Bek said. "So daily traffic should have disturbed it. There hasn't been much activity here for a week, perhaps more."

Dimona nodded in silent agreement and then looked up at the dwellings. "Most of the shutters are closed. Whatever happened, it took place at nightfall or in the early morn. Only a few are open, perhaps some had time to look out and see what was going on."

Bek looked back at Dimona, still focused on the task at hand. "Our people's passing through the city will not go unnoticed. It will be hard to conceal our tracks here. It's like a rich man spreading flower out on his floor, unless you plan to spend the time re-flouring our passage will be noted."

Dimona nodded. "We don't have that much time. I am sure men are already riding from Mont Ryhn and I wouldn't doubt traders coming here have already returned to tell tales to the Tock, Masti and Mohen. If the Tock have heard about this they will be quick to send men and women to strip this town down."

Bek looked up greedily at the tall merchant dwellings. Signs announcing various trades hung sporadically along the street. "This city is worth a lot."

Dimona sighed. "The surrounding lands too are worth much. The farms we passed were empty. Each farmer's son in Montterran could be set for life should they ride here and lay claim. Those crops need only be harvested and the youths would be set and Montterran women riding out to wed them."

"Unless of course the lands are poisoned, plagued or ... cursed?" Bek said quietly, looking up at the empty plaster and wood buildings they rode past.

"This place is quieter than the grave. Not even the sound of hounds. Smell the air – it's too fresh. There's no scent of hearth fire, of smith fire, nor of baker or tanner. No trace of the smell of home cooking. It's too clean here."

"I was thinking the same." Responded Dimona as they rounded another corner.

"Hold on for a second, here, there's a tavern of some sort... the Rusty Knot." Dimona said loudly as she dismounted. She tossed her horse's reins up to Bek, "Stay here, I'll be back in a second."

Dimona cautiously opened the door. A few tables had been set, but no food was laid on the plates. Flies were buzzing around one table in the corner and she noted that a piece of sausage, the only food she could see, had maggots all over it. Wrinkling her nose she walked over to the bar and peered behind. Nothing much back there, a towel lay on the floor right next to a few coins. They were copper so she didn't bother to round the counter to pick them up.

Quietly and cautiously she walked over to the left and entered the kitchen. The stoves were all cold and empty. She opened one and peered in, the fires inside had long since burned out. Pots and pans appeared to have been just warming up, their contents only half cooked. They held mostly breakfast foods; sausages, eggs…. She opened the big oven and looked in, a set of burnt loaves of bread were sitting on the baking rack. Having seen enough, Dimona exited the kitchen and the tavern and took her reins back from Bek.

"Very early morning, about four or five at the latest." She said to Bek as she rounded her horse and mounted it. "They were just preparing for merchants and travelers that might want to depart early. Only one table had food, so only one person was up to break fast. The meal is half eaten and the chair is away from the table but not turned over. If the person was rousted, or aware, it hit them so fast that they didn't even get a chance to stand."

Bek shook his head incredulously. His voice echoed his surprise. "We're a good five hundred metres from the gate and yet they had no forewarning? All the doors are closed? This is unbelievable. Raiders don't close doors as they exit and even if they did, there are no signs of any type of struggle."

Beck kicked his horse forward. Over his shoulder he voiced his growing concern. "I have to tell you Dimona, not much can get under my skin but this scares me. A city full of people doesn't just empty. This is the result of some great curse."

Dimona said nothing but smiled slightly as she noticed Bek's becoming ever increasingly ill at ease.

Bek rose in his stirrups every so often or hung low from his saddle to peer in to a window as they made their slow progress through the back streets. Bek shook his head. "There aren't even dogs about. What would keep strays from this place? I wonder if there are horses in the stables. If they were left without food and water they will be in bad condition." Bek said, pulling his horse up short.

"Keep going, I thought of that. We have a man going there already. Horses are worth a lot. If they were left with enough feed and if they had troughs for water they might still be alive. What is found alive will be moved elsewhere. Anything dying will be left. We can't afford to be blatant about our presence. Killing them would leave an obvious mark."

Bek was used to this cold side of Dimona. Still, he hated the thought of the animals dying. In many cases he had more compassion for animals than he had for mankind. He really hadn't wanted to go to the stables for fear of what he would have seen, and knew in his heart he would have had a hard time walking away from a horse dying of thirst. Shaking himself he turned his fears around with a brief flash of hope. "Horses can live a week with only a little food and it's likely that most would have had access to water in their stalls. They will be hungry and weak, but they probably only lost the very young or old." Bek's spirits picked up at that and he quickened his pace.

"Slow down again, I noted a shop with it's door open." Dimona chided as her horse sped up to match Bek's increased pace. "There, up that side. I want to go in and check it out."

"It's a tailor's shop, see the needle sign? Nothing much of value there." Bek said with little interest. "Another two streets up and to the left is the entrance to the guild, I'll meet you there."

"No Bek. Stay here. We will go into the guild together. " said Dimona as she dismounted once again and tossed her reins to Bek without another word.

"We're wasting our time." Bek complained as he held the horse but Dimona didn't turn back.

Dimona entered the tailor shop easily through the open door. There was a stretch of cloth on the big cutting table with half a pattern cut, but no sign of the scissors. Three spools of thread were on the floor, obviously knocked off the stitching table. She walked in further and noted that the side door was open as well.

Dimona looked around, trying to recreate what had transpired in her mind. 'Someone ran from the shop.' There were three dramatically deep footsteps in the soft dirt path outside the side door. Three strides and then... nothing. No back steps, no other footsteps, nothing. A man had run out of the store, presumably holding the scissors. He must have seen something come in or looked out of the shop and noticed something amiss. 'He tried to run and then... then what?'

Dimona reached up and pulled her long hair back behind her head, as was her custom when she was nervous or tense. She reached in her belt and pulled out a small twist of leather that she used to restrain her hair. Shaking her head, she exited the shop.

"Very odd" said Dimona out loud. Her usually strong voice sounded hollow and thin in the stillness of the city. She turned around to glance back at the tailor's shop and out of the corner of her eye saw a bird on the roof of the neighbouring building suddenly take to wing, disturbed. Startled Dimona followed the pigeon with her eyes for as long as she could before turning again and heading back to Bek and the horses.

When she approached Bek, Dimona didn't relate the bird's sudden flight. Bek was already scared; there was no benefit in mentioning what was probably nothing.

"Well, this far in the people obviously heard something. Whatever they saw coming must have scared them for one in that place attempted flight." Dimona related evenly.

"And yet no bodies and no blood." Bek said shaking his head vigorously. "I've never seen anything like this."

"Nor I, but can I tell you, I have never seen such opportunity either. There were full rolls of silk on the shelves. Each roll worth its weight in silver and just sitting there for the taking. Think what wealth we have here... a full city and we can just walk in and take what we want!" Dimona beamed and looked at Bek who was almost visibly drooling at the prospect of the unmentionable wealth.

Bek's face fell then and his voice was without its usual bravado and confidence. "Unless whatever attacked comes back for its own spoils. You thought of that yet? Whatever attacked them, it's still out there and if it comes back it will get us faster than it got them. We should take what we want and leave. Something dark is about, something bad, something, something,...evil."

Bek pulled his horse around the corner and stopped in front of a rather unassuming home.

"This is the back way into the guild. Only supposed to use it on occasion because it's a personal residence that has a door into the back of the pub the next street over but somehow I don't think they'll mind."

"Just a second." Dimona said as she dismounted and hurried over to where Bek had pulled up. "Let me go in first, I want to check how things were left. Will the door be locked?" Dimona tethered her reins to Bek's mount and he dismounted as well. She knew the horses were well trained and wouldn't leave the spot unless something disturbed them, and they weren't likely to be stolen in this city!

"No, never locked. Every old thief knew this place and none with any sense of self preservation would wander into the guild without a purpose. But once we get within the front room the doors that separate the rooms within will all likely be locked and have traps set on them. Let me go first, I'll go slowly and not disturb anything, but I know their work, I can spot the traps."

Bek dismounted and pushed the door. It was not only unlocked but had been partially opened. "Either partially opened or partially closed." Bek commented as he walked through into the main anteroom.

"I would say the latter." said Dimona. "Look how the door's weight pulls it almost closed." Dimona pushed the door slightly and it swung in and then back out. She then pushed it again slightly, looked down at the floor and entered the room.

Here it was evident that the thieves at least had put up some type of fight, or had known they were about to be attacked. All three of the large tables in the room were thrown over, as were the dozen or so chairs that had at one time been around them.

As Dimona followed Bek in she noted that the door couldn't be opened all the way. A knife blade and two crossbow bolts stuck in the back of the door preventing it from opening flush to the wall.

Dimona looked up at the lintel and then at the right side of the door jam. Three more crossbow bolts had obviously been fired towards the door, the bolts now jammed deep into the frame. Four other bolts were stuck in the wall that faced the street.

Pointing up she motioned to the bolts. "Something came in, and the thieves tipped over the tables to hide behind, then used crossbows with the hope of a staving them off."

Bek looked down at his feet. "The thieves here were skilled, bolts shot, knife thrown, yet look at the floor. No signs of blood anywhere… neither attacker nor defender. A bolt at this distance would go straight through chain or plate mail." Bek motioned again to Dimona who followed his incredulous gaze. "Look at the floor!"

Dimona acknowledged his comment and agreed with his observation. "If the men were hiding behind that table and set of chairs," Dimona continued thinking aloud, "unless their opponents jumped over the table, grabbed them and jumped back with them in their arms …no, nothing could explain this."

Bek walked over behind one of the tables. "There are three crossbows still here with bolts unfired."

Dimona motioned to Bek and pointed at the door on the far wall. "Keep on. Whatever is done is done. Open the next door, but be careful for traps. If they knew something was coming, they would have trapped or barred the other passages." Dimona said as she drew a small dagger from her belt.

Seeing Dimona's action Bek drew his own dagger and approached the second door. He peered at the small key hole in an attempt to verify visually if it was still closed and locked.

"They must have left that other door slightly open as an invitation; this one is closed and locked." Bek whispered.

Bek spent another minute looking at the door and latch then pointed down and motioned for Dimona to take a look. "Look there by my knees, two holes. If you bang hard on this door it will shoot out poison darts."

Bek sheathed his knife and then from under his heavy cloak he pulled out a small leather case and extracted a thin metal wire. He manipulated it into the lock with a small twist of the wrist, listening closely until he heard a click. He motioned with his hand to Dimona to keep quiet and to stand back.

When Bek looked back to ensure Dimona was not going to be in line with the potential trap Dimona signalled with her hands that she was prepared and that from then on they should use hand signals just to be safe. Bek responded in kind with a few subtle gestures, returned his pick to his cloak and pulling out his knife turned the knob of the door.

There was a slight pop and two darts sailed out of the holes. Bek nodded and his fingers started their complex twists and turns. The signing was something her father had established in their guild. It gave them quite the advantage when stalking pray or when inside a house. Silence was a thief's best friend but on larger projects you still needed to be able to work as a team. Only the better thieves, those that often worked in groups, ever even tried to learn sign for it wasn't overly simple. It worked well for those that started as pickpockets for it required very flexible digits, not the types of hands that had spent years with hammer or hoe in them.

Dimona watched Bek's hands sign out his comments 'set to go even if unlocked' she read in his signs. 'Interesting,' she thought.

Dimona signed back with her left hand, 'There will be other traps beyond. Poisonous or vapour?'

Bek nodded his head and signalled back to her. 'Not likely vapour, probably more poison darts.'

Bek cautioned her with his left hand as his right pushed open the door in front of them.

"Zing", a very small blue crossbow bolt streaked from behind the door and connected with the wall behind them.

Even though they had been prepared for it, the shot was still unnerving and when Bek turned around he noted that Dimona was crouched on all fours awaiting the next attack. He had a look of surprise on his face having just now realized how fast and silent his friend was. Dimona smiled in return to his surprised gaze. Then she nodded her head upwards egging him on. After another moment of hesitation she finally whispered. Get on with it." whispered Dimona. "The city is dead. The house is too quiet. Why would anyone still be hiding after this long?"

Bek struggled for a reply to his courage having been challenge. "If I step on a trap or set something off I want to hear it first."

Dimona's smile softened ever so slightly. "We don't have all day ant this is a big city and you and I both know that if you hear a trap it is already too late!"

Bek looked around the corner of the doorjamb and then at the ground and the ceiling just inside the door. Seeing nothing he gingerly stepped in. As he set his right foot down he froze, and pulled it back up. He paused a moment, then set it down again just to the right of his original placement. Dimona noted his foot's position and started after him, following in his steps.

The next room had a table pushed up on its end. A small crossbow had been nailed to it and small cords, levers and strings had been tied, linking it back to the door itself.

Dimona pointed to it. "Hurriedly set up. This wouldn't have been the type of trap left set-up all the time. It has to have been erected quickly as an aid to offset a new threat."

At the side of the room more tables and chairs were pushed to the walls. Bek pointed to them. "Men would have been in here with swords drawn to wait. It would have been close quarter fighting for any more than 2 or three defenders. There are two swords on the floor, so there were at least two men at one point. Nothing alive could have made it through the door and over to the men. Nothing could have shot through the door fast enough after the lock had been set."

"The trap had not been sprung." Dimona said, suddenly realizing the significance. She motioned to the next door on the opposite side of the room. "If that door is locked then we will have proof that whatever took them away spirited them straight through the walls."

Bek looked nervously back at Dimona. "Magic then." Dimona nodded slowly.

Dimona lightly snapped her finger and Bek turned to look at her hand as she began signing again. "How many doors, how many rooms, where are we headed?"

Bek's hand flexed and turned with small movements. "Next door leads to a hallway. Right branch goes to the pub. The left is guild master Thomas' office.'

Bek went to the next-door and looked at it. Again he set aside his blade for use of his pick. There was a definite click and Bek turned and signalled with his hand at Dimona. "This door locks only from this side, no trap." Dimona nodded. They had one answer to the puzzle, although the answer raised more questions then it resolved.' If the door was still locked, then unless there was another secret passage the residents could have only exited by extraordinary means.'

It was a slow walk to the end of the left hall. Bek diligently pointed out to Dimona a few places not to step and where on the walls specific traps had been laid.

As he approached the guild master's door Bek looked at the floor, then dropped to his knees and crawled forward slowly inspecting each inch. As he arrived at the door he went up on one knee and inspected the door and keyhole of Thomas' office.

Bek scratched his stubble. 'His beard is showing white.' thought Dimona. 'So that puts him around forty. He's likely been rubbing something on his hair and kept himself clean shaven to make himself look younger.'

Dimona could, as a result of her training, tell someone's age simply by how they bent over. However, she also knew that all thieves by trade had to be masters of deception and that they also had to stay nimble and flexible. A thief who acted forty could often be as many as twenty years older, assuming of course, that they lived that long. Dimona looked at Bek and smiled, she guessed somewhere around forty four, at the surface to others he would have been able to pass himself off as younger, but Dimona read the years in his eyes – he had the look of a man that had lived his entire life dancing on the edge of a thieves blade.

Bek stood up suddenly, startling Dimona who immediately dropped to the floor.

Without even turning around Bek grabbed the knob turned it hard and swung the door open. There was no click, no bang, no crossbow bolt, nothing.

Bek continued to astonish Dimona as he walked straight into the office without even looking around. "Come on in. Thomas was here, but he must have gotten out ahead of whatever got the rest." Bek said aloud in an even and confident tone. "He went fast, the traps weren't set as he left."

Bek walked up to the desk and prodded the chair with his dagger. "But don't sit on or touch the chair. First thing someone does if they break into an office is feel out the power and sit in the chair. It likely has a poison sprayed on it that will eat through your skin."

Bek used his dagger to pull the chair away from the desk. "Look, a note!" he said surprised.

Dimona approached slowly, taking in the room, which was furnished like a small, cozy library. She rounded the large desk to look at what Bek was pointing at.

Bek turned it slightly with the tip of his blade so Dimona could see it and then stepped back a little. "Wasn't that nice of him? But I don't know what it says. Nothing but scratches and lines on it."

As Dimona looked at it Bek started examining the room. "It does look a little like your father's work. I've seen similar before, when I delivered a message to him from Thomas a few years back."

Dimona read the note silently to herself. 'Dimo, I am sure that by whatever means, you are likely reading this now, or perhaps your lovely daughter. Either way, my regards and apologies for the brevity of this note. We within the guild heard nothing as they attacked. Only moments ago a few startled screams and some scuffles came from the gates. I sent men out to investigate, but none returned. A few others have spotted strange white forms in the streets that appear to be able to move through walls and floors without worry. When they touch a man, both disappear. They work the city as if well in control, and look not for treasures but smell out man, woman and child. I am doubtful if we can hold them off, for no weapon appears to damage them and I fear that hiding will not avail us. I will, however, give escape a try. This old thief has a few surprises yet. With luck, should I succeed, I will send you word... Sincerely, Thomas.'

Dimona looked over at Bek who was now looking at her. "They heard something moving fast up the streets. It's just like we surmised, whatever it is can move through walls and when it touches a man they both disappear. Thomas said he was going to try to get out of the city, how would he do that?"

Bek motioned to the floor. "Tunnels I'm sure, leading from one basement to another around here, and eventually out to the eastern wall. We're only about five hundred metres away. The last house sits against it and two iron doors guard it. Besides Thomas, perhaps one other might have a key. It would take thirty minutes through all the tunnels and doors to get out from here. Think he made it?"

"I hope so." Said Dimona softly. "If anyone got out, it would be him." Dimona looked at the walls that were covered in shelves holding books, small boxes and jars. She winked at Bek who smiled in return. "So, Bek. Where would he keep the good stuff?"

149

Bek walked over to a bookcase against the left wall. He pushed it further to the left and it slid easily on the smooth hardwood floor. On the wall behind the bookcase was a small metal plate with a keyhole in it that had obviously been mortared into the wall itself. "This little safe is only about 12 inches deep but it will hold the valuables."

Bek turned and motioned back to the desk where Dimona stood. " Be careful, but check the top right drawer. If he left in haste you might find a rather nice dagger he enjoyed toying with when he had special company."

Dimona turned to the desk and its right double drawer and looked at the lock. Carefully she manipulated her dagger and popped out a few levers that were cleverly worked on the underside of the bottom drawer. Pulling it open she then proceeded to engage a few more cleverly concealed switches under the top drawer before pulling it open.

She smiled as the top drawer opened smoothly, exposing a variety of jars and purses. Resting atop of a stack of parchments at the back was the dagger Bek had spoken of. The scabbard was black with small black stones set around its neck. The handle too was black as night and was capped with a large black stone.

"What type of metal is this, that it is so black, and what are the stones?" Dimona asked as she picked it up and held it for Bek to see.

"I don't know." Bek said without turning, still working with his small pick on the wall safe. "I only saw him use it once."

"Thomas was a little, shall we say, over excited when we brought him a thief that had been stupid enough to talk to the local authorities about a pending activity. Thomas made an example of him. He took out the dagger from there and while we held the man he pulled it out and cut him on the face." Bek turned and used his hand to demonstrate that the cut had been small. "Just a nick mind you, like shaving almost. The man thrashed so hard we had to let go of his arms. He kicked and gurgled on the floor for ten minutes before finally going quiet. In the end his face was a sickly greyish and the whites of his eyes had turned."

Bek chuckled. "I would suggest you not cut yourself with that blade."

Dimona picked up the scabbard and tried to pull the dagger out, wondering if the blade itself was black or if the poison was discernable. As she picked it up she felt unevenness on the back of the scabbard and flipped it over. Some symbols had been etched into the tough leather. A design of leaves entwined around a skull.

"Whoever made this was an artist." Dimona said as she tried again to pull the blade out. No matter how she pulled, it didn't move.

"Do you know the trick to unsheathe it?" Dimona asked, but just as she did she noted that some of the stones around the neck of the scabbard could be pressed in. 'Careful' she thought, 'it might bite back.'

"No idea, Thomas pulled it out fast enough. Damn this is a tricky one." Bek swore. "Three tumblers at least, wow!"

Dimona turned over the dagger and closely examined the different stones. Almost all, she realized now, could be depressed. Obviously pressing one or more would unlock the dagger. Dimona doubted it would be sequences of buttons, for the scabbard was too small to hold a complex locking mechanism. She put the scabbard in her left hand and felt two of the buttons under her left index finger. She pressed them both at the same time and pulled… nothing. She stretched her finger so it covered a third button on the edge and squeezed. The dagger slid from it's sheath, its blade as black as the rest of it.

"Very weird colour, and it has markings all down the blade. Doesn't look slick either; if its dried poison the scabbard must have something in it. Look at this, it's matte black, but it looks like metal, not wood or ivory." Dimona swished it through the air and faked a stab, she put her left hand out and balanced the blade on it using just the inside of the handle. She then deftly flipped it in the air and reached out to catch it by the handle but pulled her hand straight back at the last moment, letting it fall to stick into the desk.

"Careful! Are you mad?" yelled Bek. "Didn't I say a nick would kill you?"

"Weird, it balanced perfectly, but when I spun it, it turned slow." Dimona said as she pulled the dagger out of the desk and inspected the tip. She smiled when she noted that it hadn't even smudged the finish of the blade.

"The handle is filled with some heavy liquid and it has a small bubble in it, that's the problem. I wonder if that's just air that got in over time or if the liquid is the poison?"

Dimona looked down, her eye almost level with the desk where the dagger had gone in. "The wood that is cut isn't wet and doesn't appear to have anything on it. I would like to have a mouse with me right about now. I could stick its nose in it to see if the poison was secreted when the blade hit."

"Must have been. How else would it have worked?" Bek returned sardonically.

There was a resounding clink from the strongbox. "Ta da!" Bek laughed. "Open."

"My you are a talented man Bek, "Dimona said sarcastically. "Pat yourself on your back later – in the meantime pull out its contents and lets take a look?" Dimona asked as she returned the blade to its scabbard. She turned to face Bek and while walking over placed the sheathed blade on a strap that hung on her back under her cape.

Bek grunted but didn't look back at her. "Our friend Thomas was in a big rush he left many of his ledgers and notes. And he must have thought it was very important to take the time to write your dad a note rather than to pocket these." Bek pulled out two large blue stones and a massive ruby. They were easily ten carats each and sparkled in the thin light from the window behind the desk.

"This is odd. I know these are getting more popular, but why throw junk in here?" Beck put his hand back in the safe and pulled out three small leather strings, each with a small stone on them. The stones were all polished white and smooth and drilled so the string could pass through them. "Perhaps his kids wanted him to keep their stuff in here?" Bek joked.

"Put the larger stones in your coat and remember I counted them and pass me the necklaces. You know Thomas didn't have any kids." Dimona said briskly.

Bek held them up while still kneeling in front of the box and Dimona picked them from his hands. "Very unassuming," she said. "To store them there must mean they have some value. One square, one sphere, one pyramid. How cute... and not quite smooth. Or rather, they are, but something is either inked on them with a very fine quill or was baked into them. Writing of some sort, something I haven't seen before."

"A script even *you* don't know. Now I've heard of everything!" Bek laughed as he pulled out a stack of paper and a small pouch. "Markers, wow, some rather prominent people too. Too bad they're worthless now." Bek threw them on the floor and peeked in the small bag. Not seeing anything he poured the contents out into the palm of his hand. A dozen small black pearls spilled onto his hand. He poured them back into the pouch and handed them up to Dimona who was now looking over his shoulder.

"Too hard to sell, even if I wanted to, and not worth my time. But on a lady such as yourself the string would be dazzling." he said smiling.

"Why thank you Bek." Dimona said in a feigned lady like way. "You are 'such' a gentleman." Bek seeing the sarcasm in her tone chuckled a little in reply.

"Well, that's about it. Not quite as much as I expected."

Dimona nodded, "He had other less obvious places likely to hide bulkier valuables – we will search for them later. I was really looking for stuff he wanted us to find hoping he would give us some leads."

"We still have no idea who it was or why they did it though. But after reading the note, if Thomas didn't know – I doubt we will find many clues elsewhere in the city. You can make your way to the brothels when you're done here; check out their strongboxes, especially the madam's quarters. At least you will find money and likely a few jewels there. I'm going to head to the inner citadel to meet up with Henk and see what we can find in the court and lords' chambers." Dimona turned to leave.

"You sent Henk because he's too poor a lock breaker to open a king's strongbox didn't you? Funny, you don't seem to trust us much do you?" Bek said as he stood and brushed off his jacket, dusty from leaning against the wall.

"I trust all of you about as far as I can throw my nice black dagger." Dimona said smiling.

"Always remember, it doesn't fly far, but when it hits it leaves a terrible mark."

Old Man Makay

Koal neighed and stomped her back feet when Miathis reined her in. The massive horse was tense, but she was truly in stride today. "Hold!" Yelled Miathis. The Fist, as one pulled back on their reigns and ground to a scuffling halt.

It had been a long days ride past Tiren Falls, and into the Terran hills for the men and horse alike. Their ride had improved for the elevated Terran lands had received much more rain than what had fallen around Mont Ryhn. Miathis turned to look back at his men and their mounts and noted how much better mood his company was in, now that it wasn't as caked with dust.

'Not only where they in a better mood, but they were getting into stride.' Thought Miathis. 'Both man and horse was showing better discipline. However, the entire company of men also knew they were getting closer and there appeared to be a certain tension in the ranks.'

"We have a good company." Miathis said to Tunder who turned his mount to stand beside Miathis. Tunder's lance was still held amazingly high, the banner of the fist flapped in the late fall breeze. Miathis smiled as he watched their standard flap. The clenched hand on a shield of grey brought great pride to his heart. The Fist was the best company of men Montterra could field – and today, for this great adventure he led them.

Tunder nodded proudly as Miathis turned his mount and started riding down the length of the men to inspect them. Each soldier had their now shiny shield strapped on to their left forearm. Their helmets gleamed, as did the mail that covered their faces and necks. The dust cloths tied to their horses had been removed and the horse's coats glistened.

Bettham, a slight built soldier dismounted quickly and stepped forward to Tunder in order that he might take the company standard and allow Tunder to dismount. Bettham looked up hesitantly at his large sergeant, second of the fist.

Bettham father's lands were at the northerly part of Montterran where the Tiern River separated their country from the Terrans, and the Tocks. Bethos, Bettham's father did rather well as a Lord for he controlled the mines that supplied all the country's requirements for steel, copper and bronze. The mines weren't as profitable as the fabled Terran Cliff mines that spat forth silver and gold, but they were still very profitable.

Those within the company all knew Bettham's lineage, and as such few gave the lad much time and most of the soldiers gave Bettham the cold shoulder and given any chance they could they saddled the lad with the worst chores.

Bettham worked hard at every task assigned; however, in most instances the harder he tried at an activity the worse his results. Bettham strode forward nervously for this evening he was especially leery. Tunder suspected him of having been the source of a boyish prank played upon the sergeant the night before – something he had NOT been responsible for. He feared that any small discretion on his part this evening would mean extra duty.

Bettham was very tired having ridden all day and he wanted nothing more than to grab a bite and go to sleep. Extra duty this night was something he wanted to avoid at all cost.

Tunder looked down at Bettham and then passed down the standard to him. He bent low down from his saddle to ensure Bettham could grab the middle of the lance with both hands.

Bettham reached up and grabbed the massive standard as it flapped in the evening breeze. In his gauntleted hands the shaft was much wider than a lance making it hard for him to hold. He knew that letting the standard fall would bring down Tunder's wrath.

"Grab it fast Bettham!" Tunder growled. "If you drop it, I will make you brush down a dozen horses before bed."

Tunder was hard on Bettham, in his mind it was for the lad's own good. He knew that Bettham's father was a large burly man that ruled the north with a strong fist. Bettham had been assigned to the Fist to 'toughen him up' and to 'make a man of him'. Tunder intended to do just that. It was his personal mission to drive Bettham the hardest, and with luck build a much stronger man out of the slight built youth before him.

"Bettham, grab hold well!" Tunder bellowed seeing the lad's hands shake. "Are your hands too small to hold the standard of the fist?"

Just then a stronger breeze hit the long flapping standard pulling it backward. Bettham had not the chance to lower the stub of the pole to the ground. The standard flapped and pulled the tip backward over his head dragging him backward and to the ground.

Tunder shook his head. "Somehow I think this will be a long night for you Bettham."

Miathis returned on his horse from inspecting the troops. He looked over to Tunder who was dismounting, grumbling and shaking his head. "I don't think Tunder is amused, Bettham." Miathis said noting the standard on the ground and Bettham struggling to get back to his feet. "I would be picking that up fast if I were you!"

The rest of the company started laughing. Bettham was more gangly then strong. He appeared very awkward as he attempted to rise to his feet in all his mail. "Sorry Sir. I slipped."

Tunder picked up the end of the standard and brushed off the flag. He then lifted the long pole up again and held it out for Bettham. "Balance boy, balance." Tunder said looking at the young man. "All a soldier is - is balance."

As Bettham stepped forward to receive the standard Tunder placed his right gauntleted forefinger on Bettham's shoulder and pushed slightly. Bettham staggered backwards and only barely stopped from falling again to the ground.

Tunder shook his head in disapproval. "Stand always with your feet slightly staggered with one in front of the other. Bend always slightly in the knees if must be – but always think balance. "

Tirad Mismar walked forward to the head of the company and grabbed the reigns of Bettham's mount. Tirad had been the last man to enter the Fist. He had come from a fairly poor family but upon entry he quickly showed all that he was very capable with a lance and sword, and that he was exceptionally quick of thought. It took Tirad no time what so ever to fit in and gain the respect of every seargent of the company – they all thought that one day he would prove to be a very capable knight. However, although capable of chumming with more senior members of the Fist, Tirad had kept apart from them and had elected to befriend the friendless Bettham. Within less than two weeks they had become inseparable friends.

Miathis looked down from atop his mount as Tirad walked forward. He wondered if it had been Tirad that had pulled the prank on Tunder the night before. The lad looked slightly upset and Miathis wondered if he felt guilty that his latest act of trickery had put his friend in some peril of additional duty.

"Tunder's breath knocks you over again Bettham?" Tirad asked jokingly to Bettham in a not so quiet voice. A few of the other soldiers nearby chuckled as they heard Tirad's jab however others busied themselves not desiring Tunder's retribution.

Bettham's eyes widened with fear as he glanced at Tirad and then back to Tunder. 'His friend had gone a little too far with that one.' He thought. But he relaxed a little noting that Tunder had turned a deaf ear to the comment and was now issuing orders to the company to dismount and to establish camp for the night.

Bettham shook his head and took the standard and headed over to where the rest of the company would be setting up their camp. Although disappointed that he now had to brush down horses before dinner, he did not complain. He was more upset with himself that he had failed at this simple task than he was upset with its consequences.

Tirad followed behind Bettham leading both horses behind him. "You try to hard Bettham. You know that is your problem don't you? You are too tense around Tunder. Whenever he isn't around – you do fine. But when ever he is around, you bumble around like a ten year old boy."

"I know, I know." Replied Bettham soulfully. "He just makes me so nervous."

"He isn't anything special." Tirad added. "Just another man. A big man mind you, but a man none the less."

Tirad liked Bettham most because of how he acted. He had been raised in a poor family and their only exposure to those of court was when a baron or lesser count would visit their families shop. Most were audacious and rude to his parents and walked with a air of superiority sometimes not even recognizing his existence. Upon joining the Fist Tirad had seen that Bettham was different. He treated everyone as a better, not even an equal. Bettham worked very hard at trying to improve himself and 'never ever' used his title or talked about the money his family obviously had.

Tirad lead both horses and followed his friend. "I will give you a hand with the horses." He said. Then in a softer voice he added. "Bit of my fault, it was I who put the mud into Tunder's boots yesterday morning. I had no idea you had been instructed to polish them that night."

Bettham shrugged as he walked ahead of Tirad and then spiked the standard at the edge of the campsite and returned back to Tirad. "I don't think that matters much. Tunder simply had it in for me today – I could feel it."

"I'm telling you – you just need to relax around Tunder and Miathis." Tirad pulled up close behind Bettham as they walked to the area where the horses were to spend the night. "Hey I have an idea. I overheard Miathis mention to another sergeant that he and Tunder were going to ride out and check out some farm close to here. If we get done fast we might be able to go with them!" Tirad added excitedly.

Bettham looked back at his friend bewildered and shocked. "I am bagged and sore." Bettham responded. "What you want to go riding more today, just for fun?"

"Listen, 'that' is what you need Bettham, to see Tunder and Miathis apart from the company. You have to relax around them, and let them see what you are capable of. Besides, a little action could be fun." Tirad added glibly.

"One thing at a time." Replied Bettham as they made it to where most of the company had gathered by a small grove surrounded by a few trees a couple of hundred meters from the road. "First we have to help brush down all the sergeant's horses." He turned to Tirad. "Still game to help?"

Tirad nodded and Bettham smiled. "Thanks Tirad. Can you take the horses and hobble them, I will get Tunder and Miathis' mounts – I'll be back in a minute."

Tirad took the two mounts round back behind the company where a few other newer men were tethering the horses which shone with sweat.

"Hey Tirad, your but sore yet?" Mort Rindos asked. Tirad turned and looked over at Mort and his friend Dar Jentri both were standing behind the tethers untying the large sacks of feed that had been tied to the packhorses.

"No, not yet. May is holding out well too." Tirad said as he motioned to his mottled brown mare behind him. "Now that she isn't coking on dust." He added remembering the end of the previous night's ride.

Dar looked over at Tirad and nodded. "You should try it all the way at the back of the company. No matter how much beer I drank in Tiren Falls, I could still taste that dust.

"Least you got time to have a pint Dar!" Scoffed Tirad. Miathis and Tunder had me running errands well into the night, I never made it to the pub!"

Taramst Bestown, the senior soldier assigned to supervise the company's mounts looked up from behind a horse he was tending to. "You in trouble again Tirad? Tunder sent you here to help?"

"Bettham's been assigned to help take care of the sergeants horses again." Tirad said looking over to the old soldier. "I came to help, I heard that the captain might be going out to check out a farm near here and thought if I lent a hand you might let Bettham go a little early."

Taramst looked over sceptical at the young soldier. "We'll see." He said with a noncommittal tone. "Depends on how much you two get done."

Tirad reached up and started taking off his horses saddle and bridle. "Same drill as last night?"

"Yes." The old soldier said while turning and walking away. "Once you do your own horses you need to do all the sergeant's horses too."

Tirad went to the tethering line and tied up his and Bettham's mounts and continued to take off their saddles and bridles. A moment later, Bettham was back leading in Miathis' and Tunder's horses.

"Just as you said Tirad." Bettham said as he tied Koal to the tether. "They said they are going out and want them to be the first to be watered and fed. Did you talk to Taramst?"

Tirad turned and nodded to his friend. "If we get ours and the sergeant's horses done in time, then I think he will let us go."

Bettham nodded, he wasn't all that eager to work fast for in some way he hoped that they wouldn't be ready in time. But after he noted that Tirad was working as hard and as fast as he could. Bettham leaned in to the chore at hand.

Taramst came back up the line an hour later to check their progress. "Another day's extra duty Bettham?"

Bettham nodded in reply. "Yes, you will have to put up with me once again."

"And then you plan to going riding?" Taramst asked jokingly. "Bit of a sucker for punishment if you ask me. This trip is just started, you two should pace yourself for who knows what tomorrow will bring."

Bettham grumbled. "That's what I thought. I am bagged but Tirad thinks that we should join them tonight!"

Taramst pulled a pick from the back of his belt and tossed it to Bettham. Bettham reached up to grab it but he fumbled the catch and the pick fell to the ground. "Check all their shoes."

"I got it." Tirad said as he reached down and picked up the pick and winked at Bettham."I'll work on their feet, and you finish brushing them down, that way we will be done in no time." He then turned to Taramst. "What do you think? Can we go when they come?"

Taramst didn't look up but instead proceeded to look over Bettham's horse. "Fine, fine." He grumbled. He then looked up at Bettham and motioned with his pick at Tirad. "But when you get back, it will be you brushing down yours and their mounts and not me."

Bettham looked over at Tirad who nodded. "Ok." Tirad said enthusiastically as Bettham forced a smile. "Works for us."

Tirad picked up the leg of his horse and started working the mud from its shoes while Tamarast looked down over his shoulder watching him work.

"Want to see if you can come too Taramst?" Tirad asked sarcastically, hoping that his question might stop the old man from looking over his shoulder.

"Ah, let me think a moment," replied Taramst as he stood up and looked at Tirad. "Ah, NO! Not I. I plan to grab a bite and sleep. This is just the start of the trip…. You have to pace yourself."

Bettham nodded respectfully as the old man looked over at him. "Hey, it wasn't my idea." He added sarcastically while pointing down to his friend.

Taramst shook his head. "The folly of youth. Wish I could bottle up your energy Tirad. I would sip from it every day." He said as he walked away still shaking his head..

"We need to hurry for they won't be long." Bettham said as he stopped to take off the rest of his mail. "And I heard Miathis tell Tunder that they are going to ride light tonight."

Bettham motioned to Tirad's mail coat. "You can take that off. No armour on the horses and they won't be wearing any themselves, just leathers and swords. They won't be going far, and he wants to ride quietly."

Tirad nodded and took off his helmet and then his mail coat and placed it by the tree by his saddle. "We can come back and pick up our armour when we return with the horses." He said motioning to Bettham to place his in the same spot.

Bettham moaned slightly as he lifted his armour up off the ground and stacked it by the tree. "I could do with an hour sleep and here you have us going out for a ride in the countryside." He laughed a little. "Why do I listen to you?"

"Oh hush up and keep brushing down the mounts." Tirad said with a laugh as he came over and slapped Bettham on the back and then rounded the next mount and lifted its back leg. "Soft ground, shoes are all fine." He said letting the foot down and then raising the other.

"Don't skimp on the job." Bettham warned. "Taramst would be make our lives a living hell if one of the sergeant's horses lost a shoe tomorrow."

"You know what Bettham? You think too much." Tirad said without looking up.

Bettham and Tirad worked hard right up to when Miathis and Tunder came to claim their horses. The two friends were drenched in sweat and smelled like horse themselves. Bettham looked up tiredly as the officers approached but Tirad stepped up and smiled.

163

Miathas looked down at the long double line of horses. "Looking good." He started as Bettham stepped forward grabbing Koal's reigns and passed them to his captain.

"I had some help." Bettham volunteered nodding to Tirad.

Miathis smiled as he took the reigns. "Tunder and I are off for a short ride to check out a nearby farm. We will be back in a couple of hours."

Tirad stepped forward leading Tunder's horse. Its coat gleamed from its recent brushing. "I was wondering if the two of us could come along tonight?" He asked as he handed Tunder the horse's reigns.

Tunder looked over at Miathis. Both men had obviously washed up; Tunder's red beard and hair were still wet and dripped down his leathers. Miathis had his sword strapped to side but Tunder was only wearing his dirk having left his flail back at his tent.

Miathis shrugged as he returned Tunder's questioning gaze. "Up to you." He said.

Tunder looked down at his horse and patted its head and then its neck. "Good job on the brushing." Tunder asked. " Who did mine? You Tirad?"

"Ah, no actually Bettham did yours sir." Tirad replied nodding over to his friend.

Tunder's head snapped around to look at Bettham.

"She is a fine, sturdy horse." Bettham said braving a smile at his sergeant.

Tunder took the lead from Tirad and walked round his horse. "Yes, she bears my weight well." Then he turned and looked at the two sweaty youths and noted that their mounts were already saddled, waiting behind them. "You two sure you are up to it? We will have another long hard ride tomorrow."

"Yes sir." Tirad replied eagerly as he turned and went for the reigns of his and Bettham's horses.

Tunder looked suspiciously at Bettham. "You sure?" He asked looking at the lad who was dripping sweat. Bettham smiled and nodded enthusiastically. "Sounds like fun." He lied.

Miathis chuckled as he went up on Koal. "Well, it seems like you both had this request well prepared. I am assuming Taramst has agreed?" He said looking round for the old man. He noticed the old soldier round the back of the tethering line. He motioned down at the two lads standing before them. "You ok that these lads come with us?"

"Yes sir." Taramst replied. "The horses are almost all taken care of – I can do the rest. The lads said they would take care of your mounts and their own when you return."

Miathis turned to look at Tunder who nodded shortly. He then looked down at Tirad and Bettham and smiled. "Yes, fine. We are only going a kilometre or so from here. Northwest into the hills to a sheep farm – scout out the area to see if we can learn anything before we reach TerranAdd. You are welcome to join us."

"What's the name of the owner?" Bettham asked boldly.

"MacKay. Jent said the man's name is MacKay. Older man with a son named Bob." Miathis replied taken back a bit by the bold question.

"That the man Jent told you about?" Tunder asked Miathis who turned and nodded.

"Who's Jent?" Tirad asked as he started to climb atop his horse.

"Jent is the owner of a pub in Tiern Falls." Tunder replied with a bit of an evil grin on his face. He then turned his thumb and pointed it at Miathis. "Jent is also the father of a rather pritty girl named Bess." Tunder chuckled loudly as he pulled up his horse next to Miathis. "Now there is a young thing I would like to saddle, wouldn't you Miathis?" He asked while trying to keep a straight face.

Miathis had always wanted the evening rides to be less formal as a break from the day's activities. But he was still startled a little by Tunder's comments especially in front of the Tirad and Bettham.

"Bess, I have seen her – at the Porker Barrel!" Bettham said niavely as he mounted his own horse. "The one whose bodice looks like it is about to burst every time she bends over!"

Tunder's tenor laugh boomed as he heard his joke gain momentum with Bettham's niave addition. He couldn't stifle his laugh, he bellowed full heartedly. Bettham looked back at Tunder who after a moment stopped laughing and wiped a tear from his eye.

"Oh bless me that was funny."

Miathis looked over at Tunder and gave him a condescending look and then he laughed himself. "Careful, or you and your men will all be doing extra duty tomorrow."

Tirad looked up surprised by Miathis words – a moment later realization came to both of their faces. Tirad laughed a little and tried to make light of Bettham's last comments. "I guess words out now captain. If you are stepping forward to defend her honour then she has you hooked!"

Bettham, finally realizing now that the lady he had just described was indeed Miathis' girl blushed. He stuttered, trying to back track his own words. "Not that I notice or, ah... I am sure she is quite the prize."

Tunder seeing Bettham's discomfort bellowed out another tumultuous laugh as he moved his horse forward. "Ei, she is quite the catch... and she snared Miathis' good!" He laughed and continued to wipe tears from his eyes. He looked up at Miathis who appeared to be getting a little bored by the conversation. He chuckled not wanting to end the teasing. "And best not talk too much about her in front of him, or tonight's ride will cause him great discomfort."

Miathis, thinking that the conversation had now gone on long enough spurred his horse forward and through the trees heading northwest. "LET'S GO THEN." He called back to them as he nudged Koal into a gallop.

With a spur Tunder was after him yelling "YOU CAN'T GET AWAY FROM IT MAN, SHE HAS YOU BY THE SHORT AND CURLIES NOW!"Tiran laughed as he spurred his mount trying to catch up to Tunder. "GOOD ONE TUNDER!" Tirad yelled forward to the sergeant.

"Lets go girl." Bettham said as he fumbled with the reign and nudged his horse forward to catch the others. The mare jumped forward and a moment later was surging forward with amazing speed.

Taramst smiled as he watched the four ride away. 'Amazing horse.' He thought to himself taking note of the animal Bettham was riding. 'Not as tall as Koal but every bit as good, or possibly even better.' He thought.

Taramast laughed as he watched the four depart, his keen eye for horses lingered on Bettham as he watched the lad lean in and let his speckled grey mare run. It had leapt forward quickly and its movement was very smooth, almost graceful. "Chasten no doubt." He said to himself as he watched the lad and horse surge through the trees after the others.

Miathis enjoyed the cool fall air on his now red face. Koal danced round and through the last set of trees and then before them were the rolling Terran Hills. He pressed his knees in and let loose the reigns and Koal shot forward and up the hill. At the top Miathis slowed Koal down to let the others catch up, but as they drew near he turned and continued forward. "Catch me if you can." He said almost to himself with a glib tone – feeling most confident that none other could match Koal's stride.

A moment later Miathis was surprised by the sound of horse and rider closing in behind him. He turned and looked back as Bettham and his mount raced up to ride less than a horse length back. He smiled and pressed Koal for greater speed but a moment later he heard the sound as Bettham and his mount matched their pace.

The four rode up and down the hills for over forty minutes with Miathis in the lead, followed closely by Bettham. Both slowed every other hill to let Tunder and Tirad to catch up and then they would race down and up the following hill or two.

Miathis laughed as he and Bettham bounded over each flowing hill for Koal was always able to keep just ahead of the lad. As they broached the next hill Bettham and his mount bounded forward in a great burst of speed so that they reached its top just ahead of them.

"Well done!" Miathis yelled over to Bettham as he reigned in next to the lad. The two turned and waited for their friends who were still more than fifty meters behind.. "Fine horse you have there." He remarked looking down at Bettham's horse. "A bit small, but she runs very very well."

Bettham nodded as he caught his breath. However, he turned his mount slightly and looked to the west. He didn't feel comfortable with others focusing on his rather expensive horse. "If we move straight west now we can cut a few minutes from our ride."

Tunder drew up next to them followed quickly by Tirad. "Why did we stop?" Tunder asked as he looked over to Miathis. "The path is over next hill to the North isn't it?"

Miathis shrugged as Tiran pulled up beside the other three. "Bettham appears to know the area and suggests a shortcut." Miathis turned and looked over at Bettham. "Bettham, do you know the Makay family farms?"

"My dad once mentioned him and pointed his farm out on a map." Bettham felt awkward again now as Miathis, Tunder and Tirad all now looked at him. He especially felt uneasy when the situation arose where he had to mention his family – and especially his father the duke.

"I understand that the old man had a reputation as a local hero." Bettham added. "The Tocks kept coming down to these hills to steel sheep, and one time they made the mistake of raiding the Makay's farm. They killed most of their hands and also Mrs. Makay. When he returned and found his wife dead the old man went crazy, and with his two sons tracked down and killed over three dozen Tocks. His one son died and his other, Bob, got an arrow in the knee. But the old man got his revenge on the lot - he tracked them all down and killed them. He turned a little savage himself; some of the Tocks they found were rather mutilated."

Bettham continued as the others listened to him while they caught their breath. "The Tocks never sent another raiding party south. Most of the other farmers in the area had died in previous raids so the Terran King Tar awarded Bob Makay full rights to the lands north of here as a reward for his bravery and valour."

Bettham very conscious that everyone was attentively listening to him added sheepishly, "we talk a lot about it in Orthos because of us being so close to the Tocks I guess."

Miathis nodded impressed with the lad's detailed historic review he then added what he had been told. "Jent said that his remaining son Bob stays around the farm taking care of the old man now. We should be a bit careful, for the old man supposedly has a crossbow he likes to keep by his side."

When the four and their mounts had caught their breath Tunder said with a smile motioning the lad forward. "Lead the way then Bettham."

As almost in reply to Tunder's words Koal snickered and shook its' head. "Ya, I know you like leading girl, but not now." Miathis patted Koal firmly on her neck and then motioned Bettham to lead them on. Bettham nudged his mount and it took off at a full gallop.

"NOT SO FAST MAN!" Yelled Tunder as he turned and swore to himself. "Damn boy is going to wear out our mounts."

"WHAT, GALLOP GIVING YOUR BUTT A RUB? Joked Tiran as he spurred his horse and it shot out after Bettham's.

"LISTEN BOY." Tunder yelled as he nudged his mount into a gallop. "YOU REMEMBER THAT I AM SECOND IN COMMAND OF THE FIST!"

Miathis laughed as he rode. "THAT LAD CAN PULL ALL YOUR STRINGS TUNDER!" He yelled as he came within earshot of the large man. Tunder growled in reply making Miathis laugh even louder.

Bettham slowed when they were less than a kilometre from where he thought the Makay homestead would be. He looked up at the sky and note that the sun had set, Halos was already in the sky and Detro was broaching the horizon. As the others came up from behind him he turned and got off his mount. "It isn't far from here."

Miathis looked ahead then back up to the dark sky and then nodded. "Lets go slow from here, try not to make too much noise. How much further?"

"Only a few hundred meters in and we should see the start of the Makay farms, the house itself should only be in another few hundred meters in past the farm's fences. They pasture their sheep on these hills." Bettham hesitated. "I believe so anyway. I only ever really just saw it marked out on a map a while ago. I have never been here before myself."

Miathis looked over at Bettham impressed that the lad remembers such details having only had the place pointed out on a map long ago. He looked over at Tunder who was obviously also thinking the same thing.

It took but a few minutes to reach the farms. As the men rode slowly down the dark path and entered the farm they pointed to each other different things that seemed out of place. There were large sheep pens all open and devoid of sheep, massive long sheering stalls, with metal sheers still sitting on stools...

"The workers had already been up early ready to start a long fall day of sheering when they were interrupted by something." Bettham whispered as he led them forward.

The four soldiers rode right up to the main dwelling and as they approached the house's front portch Tunder pulled on the reigns of his horse and rode around the building while the others dismounted. The three waited holding their leads until Tunder returned from his short trip round the house.

"Looks quiet and empty." Whispered Tunder as he pulled back up to the group and dismounted.

Miathis put his hand on the hilt of his sword as he walked up the three steps to the front porch and then to the door. Bettham followed Miathis but elected to pull out his sword from its scabbard. The finely worked slender blade glistened as if wet as it reflected the light of the moon.

Hearing the sword being pulled from its scabbard Tunder turned and looked over at Bettham. "Bit small of a blade." Tunder whispered. "Is that for cutting an apple?"

Bettham balked at Tunder's jab but Tirad quickly whispered a retort in defence of his friend. "Big doesn't always mean better!"

Tunder smiled, his teeth shining brightly from between his thick beard. "Just looked a little … don't know … boyish I guess."

Bettham shrugged. He knew that the blade was a little small, but he had found it harder to handle the larger blades. His brother Bartholm who was as big as Tunder wielded a bastard sword but he just didn't appear to have the skills nor size to use even a long sword – much to his father's chagrin.

Miathis tried the door, but it was bolted shut. Tiran pushed gently past Miathis and pulled out a dagger that had been strapped opposite to his long sword.

The dagger was small with an extremely thin blade. Tirad delicately slid the blade up the length of the doorjamb until it stopped just under the handle. He then angled the blade up and pushed hard and the latch was forced open. The door swung inward and the dried, rusted hinges groaned loudly.

"Very slowly" Miathis whispered. "Remember, the old man is known to have a crossbow."

"Interesting" Bettham said looking back to the farm and pens. "Sheep farm but no sheep... and no dogs."

Miathis looked back concerned, then nodded and looked at Tunder who was also now looking at Bettham impressed with his observation.

Tunder pulled out his dirk and turned around to face the treed area surrounding the house. "I noted a small shack out back that could house some dogs but it was empty."

"Some dogs don't bark much, like to sneak up on you." Bettham added. "But I think we would have seen or heard them by now."

"Yes, no dogs outside and we are not being that quiet." Miathis said in a regular voice. "If anyone is here, they likely already have heard us. Lets go in."

Tiran with a great shove pushed open the door the rest of the way and walked inside followed closely by Miathis then Bettham and finally Tunder.

It was very dark and they didn't enter very far. All the windows were covered with drapes or something and the only light came from behind them.

Tirad pulled a small strike stone and cloth out from a small bag from inside his leather shirt. In two strikes the small cloth was alight and he hastened over to light a small candle he noted sitting on a table by the door. Grabbing it he then found a lantern by a larger table and lit it with the candle. The inside of the house brightened.

"Doesn't look disturbed." Miathis said as he walked in further to the house. "Tunder, you stay by the door and keep an eye out. Tirad, come with me upstairs."

Miathis took the candle and started up the creaking stairs while Bettham looked through the pantry. Tunder walked to the right side of the room and pulled open the heavy drapes and looked out at the farm.

Miathis walked up to the landing trying to make as little noise as he could on the old wooden staircase. But as each stair groaned like an old woman he soon gave up and started walking up without as much care. Tirad followed – his small dagger still out.

The upstairs bedrooms were empty. When they entered the master bedroom Miathis noticed a large carpet covered in dog hair, beside the carpet was a chair that was positioned to look out the window that overlooked the path leading to the farm. A few extra bolts leaned against the wall by the window.

"These blankets are big." Tirad noted. "His dogs are rather large." Tirad said as he moved the chair to look out the window, which was uncovered. "It is getting dark out there – we should be heading back. There is nothing here, he is gone."

"We need to check one more thing." Miathis said as he walked back to the stairs and started going down.

"What?" Asked Tirad as he trailed behind.

Miathis descended back to the main floor and headed to the door. "Bettham, bring the lantern. I would expect that Makay's might have some type of cold cellar out back."

Tunder turned from the window he was staring out of. "I noted a path from the house that went back, I thought it might have gone to their outhouse."

It was still brighter outside then inside but the trees were creating black pits of darkness. The lantern burned brightly and Miathis winced as he looked around. "Bit dangerous with the lantern." He said. "Anyone watching now will see us for sure. Careful, we will make an easy target."

"Just up there, see the breaking and worked ground." Tunder said as he walked up behind Miathis. "Path is covered with pine needles and wood chopping so not to track mud when going from the house."

Miathis walked up the path about fifty meters then put up his hand. The others stopped. He then motioned to Bettham to extinguish the lantern submerging them all into total darkness. Miathis sniffed the air and smiled and followed the scent of a small fire to a small mound of earth that was piled high with roots. A few trees had been toppled over it to cover the mound.

While the others stopped in front of the berm Bettham walked around the right of it and then with his hands he motioned the others to come to him.

When Miathis drew near, Bettham pointed at a smallt hollow tree stump that poked up from the ground. A faint wisp of smoke was flowing up through it.

Miathis cleared his throat. Then with a normal voice he announced himself. "Anyone home? We are from Mont Rhyn. Jent asked me to drop by and see if his friend Bob Makay was ok."

The silence that followed was deafening. In the distance a twig broke and a owl hooted.

"We can see a mound with smoke coming out." Said Tunder as he stepped up and peered down the makeshift smokestack. "Hello down there!" His voice boomed and echoed in the smokestack.

A small shuffle came from behind them on the path, and then there was the sound of two very low growls.

Miathis put up his left hand while he the four men turned slowly to face back down the path. As Tirad and Bettham turned, both had their blades out.

"No sudden moves or one of you will have a new bolt to add to his ribs." Came a voice from the darkness before them. "Mind you my sons are watching too. Any of you move and we will drop you where you stand."

Bettham standing closest to the old man and his dogs re-sheathed his short sword. "We are friends. We mean you no harm."

"I will be the judge of that." The old man said as he stepped forward into the moonlight.

Two massive war dogs stood on either side of the old man – almost like bookends. Their eyes reflected back what light there was.

Bettham didn't know where the dogs started and ended they were so big and so black. But he knew that he didn't want to have to fight them in this dark. He held up his arms in a gesture of friendship and hoped the man's eyesight was as good as the dogs.

Miathis slowly worked his way around the other three. "My name is Miathis derCamp. I am the commander of the Montteran Company the Fist and friend to Jent Porter the owner of the Porker Barrel. Jent asked if would look in on you – as I passed by these parts."

The old man didn't budge, and neither did the dogs.

Miathis smiled and held out openly his hands. "To look in on you and your one son Bob who comes to the Porker every couple of weeks. Is he here – can I talk with him as well. Jent said I was to ask as to how his knee is."

Miathis slowly stepped towards the old man. But he stopped short when one of the dogs closed his mouth and growled deeply. "Jent also said if anyone could have survived out here it would have been you and that you would know what might have happened in TerranAdd."

The old man turned his head slightly and looked the four men over. Then he lowered the crossbow a bit and talked to his dogs. "Easy boys, back to the house."

The old man then turned and started walking back to the house. "Lets go back to the house and put on some light so I can see you better before I say anything more."

Along the way, Tirad took the lantern and relit it. The old man and the dogs led the four back to his home. He stopped as he put his hand on the door and pushed it open. "Just walked right in and made yourself at home did you?" He then glanced back at Tirad.

Tirad raised his hand and then shrugged as the old man pushed opened the door the rest of the way and walked in followed directly by his dogs.

"How did you lock it from outside?" Tirad asked as he followed the group in. "I didn't see a keyhole and there is only one window on the main floor and it doesn't open?"

"Never you mind; I have my ways young man." Replied the old man as he walked further in. As Tirad put the lantern down on the main table the two dogs sat down by the cold hearth at the back of the room, but both kept their eyes on the men as they came in.

"Trap door somewhere. Right?" Tirad asked as he walked towards the old man, but halted at two meters as one of the dog's eyes met his. "One that leads out from the house to back behind the woods?"

The old man just grunted, and continued to pull lanterns and cups down from the cupboard over the cutting board. "Don't be wise, and mind your own business."

Miathis approached the old man with hand extended. "Miathis derCamp is my name, I am the leader of The Fist from Mont Ryhn. He motioned with his hand at his companions. With me is Tirad Mismar, and Betthan Bathos, and the big man over there is Sergeant Tunder Warmar, second of the fist."

The old man looked up recognizing Bettham's surname. He then glanced at the others and then walked over to the fireplace. Bending down within three strokes of his flint he had the kindling burning. He didn't say anything as he piled a few small pieces of wood on top of the starting flames.

"What happened here?" Miathis asked eagerly looking over at the man. "Where did all your help go?"

"They are all gone." The old man started still looking into the flames of the fire. "Their screams are gone, it is quiet now. Quiet like it was when I first returned." He shook his head.

The old man then looked back at his dogs. "We went back into the berm when we saw them coming. Knew there was nothing that could stop them."

The old man proceeded to take a kettle that was sitting beside the hearth and hang it on a metal shaft that swung out from the fire.

Tunder sat in the chair by the window and Bettham, and Tiram sat down at the kitchen table. Miathis pulled out a chair and sat down as well as he watched the old man who stood up and walked over to a cupboard on the left wall and grabbed a few cups and a small container and proceeded to pile them on the table. He then sat down opposite to Miathis.

"What went on here? What did you see?" Miathis asked slowly.

The old man's eyes looked tired as he started across at Miathis. He reached up and scratched his face, which was covered in patches of white hair. For a fleeting moment his eyes stared back at Miathis with the spark of intelligence. "White shifts." He said simply. "I don't know what went on in TerranAdd but I assume it was there as it was here." He continued.

The old man stood back up to pull a pipe off of the fireplace mantle. He reached to a small jar by it and pulled out a few strands Tygor leaf and started to pack it into the pipe's bowel. Miathis looked over to Tunder who looked up and rolled his eyes as the old man lit the pipe with a small ember he pulled from the fire.

Miathis smiled as the man sat back down at the table. 'This man,' he thought, 'must have once been large and sturdy, but those days were long past. The winters had bent him and shortened his stance. Bits of bark and grass were intertwined in his clothing and hair. He was just generally filthy.'

"Would you like some?" The old man asked holding out his pipe to Miathis. Miathis shook his head. "No thank you." He responded kindly. "Can you tell us more? What do you mean by White Shifts?"

But the Tygor leaf was having its effect on the man, his eyes began to glaze and he looked back at Miathis smiling oddly. "Dogs and I eat fine. They brought me a few rabbits and squirrels yesterday, I could cook some up for you all if you like?"

"No we can't stay long." Miathis replied politely. "I just wanted to ensure you and your son were ok… and to see if we could find out anything about what happened in these parts. What has gone on here Mr Makay?" Pleaded Miathis with an elevated voice.

Both dogs raised their heads and looked at Miathis. Miathis sat back a little and then recomposed started again. "We have heard TerrenAdd is empty. Do you know what happened? We are in a bit of a rush here and plan on moving with all haste to that place and the more we know before we get there the better." The old man leaned forward and at once his eyes lost all sense of focus. They moved rapidly back and forth as he looked at Miathis he smiled. "Tree, and earth did scream that night. She opened the doors and letting the demons loose upon the land."

The old man put the end of his pipe to his nose. "Mark my words soldier boys. Mark my words - magic is going to rule this world again."

The old man relit his pipe and pulled slowly on it. The embers glowed and he blew out a perfect circle of smoke that drifted across the entire room. Miathis watched it move, a small realization came to his eyes and he looked back at the old man. "Where is your son Bob?"

The old man looked distressed at the question. He took a big sigh. "Silly boy tried to slow them down to give me more time." He shook his head slowly and then looked down at the table. "Now they are all gone."

"Magic." Tunder blurted out no longer capable of restraining his feelings. "I've heard enough. Magic tales are for crazy old men and children – no such thing."

The old man, noting Tunder's expression and gaze at Miathis became somewhat agitated. "I know, I saw! They came, white as mist, white as smoke. She opened the door and they came!"

The old man halted, his expression going to one of pain and sorrow. "The world screamed, the children oh the children oh the children." The old man started to cry and he put his hands to his face.

The kettle started to hiss and Tirad went to pull it from the fire using his sleeve as protection from the heat of the handle. He came back to the table and poured the cups half full each of the hot water for it was the entire kettle had in it. He then looked into the small tin of tea on the table but looking within it noticed that it was empty. He turned it over and shook it so the others could see. Tirad made a comical face to the others. Tunder smiled, but Miathis responded with a shake of his head.

"You need to take it easy old man, everything is all right." Miathis said with a quieting tone. "Listen. In the morning you go down to the Porker Barrel." He continued in his even voice. "Jent will make you up a good meal and a bed."

The old man looked up quickly and wiped the tears on his cheeks away with his dirty sleeve leaving a brown smudge upon them. "I won't leave this place again." He stated briskly, then looked back at the dogs and then at Miathis, Tunder, Tirad and lastly Bettham. His gaze almost looked like he suspected that they were going to run at him, tie him up and force him to ride with them.

Miathis added with his soft voice. "We are not going to force you to go." Miathis insisted. "I only meant to extend the offer that Jent ask that I relay to you."

The old man looked up briefly, and took another drag on his pipe. Miathis watched as the last spark of understanding that had once been in the old man's eyes was now totally gone.

"It is a long ride back." He added. "But I am sure you will be ok now, whatever as here is no longer around and your dogs will keep you well." Miathis nodded towards the dogs. "If you want to go, know that Jent's door will be open to you."

Tunder stood, "We should go. It's quite dark, we have to get back to camp and grab some sleep." He looked over to Miathis who nodded approvingly.

Tunder led the way back to the door. Tirad and Bettham followed directly, but Miathis stood slowly still looking at the old man.

"He will be ok here the night, and in the morning he can go back to town." Tunder said as he motioned to the door. "We need to get the men up and ready to take the ride through these hills tomorrow and onto the flats to TerrnAdd." Tunder added in a louder tone. Miathis getting the verbal nudge broke his gaze with the old man and started to the door.

"Nothing can stop them. If they see you – you will go too!" The old man said startling them as he followed Miathis out onto his porch. The two dogs walked silently behind the man. Tirad and Bettham, who had already climbed atop their horses turned to look at the old man one last time.

Old Man Mackay looked at each of them, almost frantically. He then turned and looked at Miathis. "Use to be stones that could protect little stones. You look for them, bound to be some in the city!"

Miathis, reached out and put his hand on the old man's shoulders, "It's ok. We will be ok. Listen, just promise me this – you go visit Jent ok?" The old man nodded and Miathis returned the nod and then patted the man on the back. As he climb atop Koal he looked back and raised his hand in parting to the old man, but received nothing but a blank stare back. "Ok, lets get back." He said turning to his men. "It is getting late. Detros is high and it will still guide our path for a few more hours.

"Detros, pah, Detros. The trouble maker." The old man called out into the night. "When Detros smiles chaos rules!"

Bettham turned in his saddle to look back at the old man who raised his hand and pointed at him. "You tell your old man the next time you see him to watch out. The moon no longer controls them. You warn him. Tell him that their fangs bring more then just death and to look to his back." The old man's insistent stare caught and grabbed Bettham. "You tell him that for me ok?"

"Ah, ya, ok." Said Bettham rather puzzled raising his hand in recognition before he turned back round.

Quietly they all rode back down the dark path. After the farm was no longer in sight behind them Tirad pulled up next to Bettham. "What was that all about, does he know your dad?"

Bettham shrugged. "Likely recognized my last name. Just a crazy old man I think."

Tirad shook his head. "Weird, he appeared crazy as a hatter one moment, and all .. I don't know – just weird the next."

"Too much Tygor leaf will do that to a man." Tunder said from behind them having heard their comments. "Start to see things in their smoke filled dreams, and later don't even need to smoke to see things. Magic – 'paaa' I say. Just a crazy old man."

Tirad rode for a moment trying to absorb what he had heard and seen. He then looked over to Bettham and then back to Tunder and Miathis. "He lost everything he loved, you can't blame him. He is old and alone now. But even… I don't know …"

Miathis nodded back to the lad and then looked over at his sceptical sergeant. "I know what you mean Tirad. Somewhere deep down you sort of felt the man had really seen something."

It was a long quiet ride back to the camp as visions of what the old man said haunted their thoughts. They all knew that what they were facing was not of this world – and ignorance fed the flames of their fears. Every shadow appeared alive, and behind every bush appeared a dark shape…with fangs.

Fables and Facts

It took Etch only three days to get to the east bank of the Tiren River. From there, however, his progress slowed considerably. Hundreds of years of spring floods had washed out the banks of the river leaving its shores studded with nothing but rocks and boulders making travel with the horse and mule miserable. Many times he was forced to re-enter the forest in order to make his way around rougher impassable sections.

"Keep on girls," Etch said as he urged the animals down the riverbank. "Two days along the river's edge – we should be close! Smite River must branch off soon and then we'll see the falls!"

The tall, black warhorse's ears turned forward to listen to Etch, but it didn't appear convinced and yanked back its head in protest.

"Oh come on!" Etch said shortly. "I don't like walking on this stuff either!" He turned and let the reins sit on his shoulder as he started pulling the animals forward in earnest.

Suddenly Etch stopped and turned his right ear south, trying to block out the constant sounds of the river beside him. A smile broadened his cheeks. "I hear faster water girls. I told you we were close!"

Half a kilometre further south the three weary travelers were finally greeted by the fork in the river they had been seeking. Etch looked up to the sky, trying to guess how much time he had before the sun set. Looking back to the ground he shook his head, knowing that it would be impossible to walk in the dark. He scratched the back of his neck and then pulled up the collar of his leather coat and frowned.

"Let's do it," he finally said after a moment's hesitation. "Datos said it was almost right after the fork. If we keep going we can get there before dark, and we can rest there." He pulled sharply on the reins with his final word and both animals begrudgingly followed.

The old scout was impressed with the Smite River Falls long before he saw them, for the roar of the falling water could be heard kilometres way, long before it came into view. At the falls the small river, typically only ten meters wide, fanned out to double its width before cascading down. Tall trees that towered on either side crowned its banks but over the falls nothing could be seen but sky.

Etch led the horse and mule off to the side and tied them behind a large fallen tree, sheltering them from the moist evening breeze that blew across the river. Carefully he walked forward, hoping to catch a glimpse down the falls before the last of the light left the sky.

Looking down, Etch watched as water flowed under the stones of the eastern bank. Near the edge of the cliff the floods had filled the gaps between the boulders with smaller stones, making the ground here almost flat – yet no more than thirty centimetres below the carpet of stone the river flowed. Large boulders poked out from the deep pockets of water. Some of the pools appeared deceptively calm, but Etch knew that below the surface the river swirled and pulled.

The falls themselves were strikingly beautiful and yet terrifying at the same time. The drop was far more than he had ever thought could have existed, and even the sides were sheer. Etch took a deep breath as he looked over the edge. "I hate heights!" he shuddered to himself as he stepped precariously close to the falls' edge. Far below the water bubbled and churned as the river fell down into its waiting arms.

"'Least I'm on the best side," Etch said, ever optimistic, as he continued to look down from where he stood on the eastern bank of the falls. Large rocks jutted out all the way down; although it would be a hard climb he believed he could do it. "Where there's a will, there's a way," Etch said to himself with confidence as he left the breathtaking view behind him and returned to tend to his animals.

"Well girls," the middle aged, bald scout said in a tired voice as he entered the shelter of the fallen tree, "we're finally here and the good news is you're both to have a day or two of rest!"

Etch patted the rump of his horse firmly as he led both animals further back from the river to the tree line and began to set up camp, pitching his tent and gathering wood which he quickly lit to ward off the coming chill of night. A sparse line of brown grass and weeds sprouted up behind the roots of the fallen tree. The grass was already winter brown, the result of numerous cold, wet frosts by the river, but it still looked like it would suffice as fodder for his mounts. Beyond the line of grass stood the forest – thick, deep and foreboding. 'Travel through it would be impossible with the animals,' Etch confirmed as he turned back to them again.

In the growing twilight Etch began to relax, and spoke companionably with the animals. "I haven't given you guys names yet," Etch said aloud, looking at his two new traveling companions. The mule stood solidly upon the stones, looking quite well considering the distance they had covered. In fact, as Etch looked at it, it shook its head as if it was almost eager to continue. "If this short stop is all it takes to get your wind back then you're quite the animal. Full of piss and vinegar and far more pepper than even I have!" Etch joked and a smile crossed his face.

"Peppy," Etch said as looked at the Mule. "Mule, I will call you Peppy!" Etch walked around the horse and patted the well-tempered mule.

Feeling left out, the dark horse nudged Etch's back. Etch laughed and patted her affectionately on the head and neck in turn. "And you girl?" he asked as he took another step back to look at his new horse.

The tall warhorse had not fared well these last few days. Etch had pushed too hard, rested too little, and hadn't spent nearly enough time brushing her down. Her coat was matted, small burrs and twigs were twined in her mane and tail and she stood a tad shakily on four very tired legs. "You've been through a lot already haven't you girl?"

"This isn't what you were bred for, is it? It's hard traveling, even for a mule!" Etch leaned over and began picking the errant burrs and twigs from her coat. Suddenly he laughed a little and then looked into the horse's eyes. "I know …. Mule!"

Etch burst out in laughter. "Mule, that's perfect! Horse, from now on I'll call you Mule!"

"You've fared better than any other horse I could have bought," he said, looking down at her legs. "Any other horse would have been lame by now. You've got the stubborn persistence of a mule, and you're going to need it, for our travels have just begun!"

Etch reached into his pocket and pulled out an apple he had been saving for his walk. He held it out and smiled when the horse chomped down. "Besides," said Etch, still smiling, "when we get back home Chad and Lys will laugh at your name and every time I call you, Rachael will cringe, making the kids laugh even louder!" The apple was gone in three bites.

As he stood picturing the scene Etch was bumped from behind by Peppy, who had seen the treat and obviously wanted some as well. Etch went back to the saddle bags and then returned with two more apples which he held out to the animals, who greedily consumed them in less than a minute.

"Datos said there were cats down below the falls – big cats. You girls will let me know if you smell anything strange, right?" The mule stood mute and motionless but his horse shook her body and swished her long dark tail in response. "As for me," Etch continued as he stretched and headed back to the campfire, "I'm going to bed. I'm bagged."

The evening turned into night as Etch sat watching the fire he had made atop the carpet of stone. Cinders dropped down through the cracks, hissing as they hit the water that flowed underneath. Although a mist appeared above the river the sky was clear. Stars sparkled as he lay back next to the fire. Pulling up his heavy woollen blanket he rested his hands behind his head and recalled nights with his family, wondering how they were and what they were doing.

'In the mountains the snow will already be deep and the pass to the lowlands is likely blocked.' Etch paused a moment reflecting on his errant thoughts. "No way back until spring," he said with a sigh as sleep came to his weary body.

The morning was cold and Etch awoke soaked from the mist of the river. The fire had gone out and what little wood he had left was too wet to light. Grumbling he got out from under his blanket, hoping that the pale morning sun might be warmer. Stretching as he rose he reached for an apple and some hard dark bread that was sitting just inside one of his saddlebags.

Breakfast was taken sitting on the edge of the falls – looking down. "Long way," Etch said to himself as he sat quietly, eating his meagre fare and watching the water race down over the top of the cliff.

After an hour of sitting, eating and staring bloodily at the falls, Etch fetched the rucksack he had brought with him from the city and turned to face his challenge.

The descent started well, for little water ran over the eastern edge. Soon, however, Etch determined that his originally planned path was not going to work and he was forced to move in closer to the flowing water. Handholds and footholds were slick and although the water pressed hard upon him, urging him on, at times he had to move painstakingly slowly.

"I would trade all my food for a long heavy rope!" Etch cursed to himself after he had been climbing for an hour. "Who would have thought it would have been as high as this." He paused to catch his breath on a small ledge and took advantage of the chance to look down. Far below he could see a large pool. Parts looked deep, but other parts had tree stumps popping out of them.

"I guess I could always jump," Etch joked to himself. He picked up a small stone by his foot and tossed it out about two meters in front of him, watching it as it fell and counting aloud. "One, two, three... eight, nine..." He winced as the small stone bounced off of a boulder at the base of the falls. "So much for that idea," said

Etch, looking over the ledge down the face of the falls. "Yeah right, like I would ever have the nerve to jump," he added sarcastically.

By midday he had finally descended to the bottom where he sat for a long time shivering and trying to regain his strength. His rucksack pulled and rubbed against his back where he had tightened the wet straps to ensure that when the water ran down atop of him the added weight would not dislodge him from the cliff. Eventually he rose again and started down the riverbank. The warming sun was a welcome sight as it appeared over the treetops.

"My back is going to be sore tonight." Etch said quietly. Then, as he caught a faint whiff of smoke he called out loudly, "Stymar?"

His boots sloshed as he stepped from stone to stone down the river's bank. "I hope this trip is worth my efforts!" Etch said as he jumped to yet another larger stone. His legs were numb and strained and his clothes and rucksack were heavy, soaked as they were, and he missed his landing. The river's cold lament was broken by Etch's startled scream as he fell sideways into the rushing water.

He sputtered and gasped for air in shock as his head popped back up. The swift current pushed him forward and into the middle of the river. Flailing his arms he was only barely able to push off of a smaller stone as he floated past it, finally attaining the eastern shore once more.

Puffing hard from the exertion and cold Etch dragged himself out of the water. Exhausted beyond belief he shrugged off his rucksack and lay on his back on the shore panting. "Lovely," he said out loud as he caught his breath.

"Why don't you come in and dry off?" called a voice from somewhere nearby.

Etch's wet, baldhead tilted backward as he tiredly tried to figure out where the voice had come from. Seeing nothing he grit his teeth and turned to his side to get a better view.

A small woman was standing atop a large stone another ten meters down the river's bank. Pushing slowly to his feet Etch raised a hand in greeting but the lady simply pulled her brown shawl over her shoulders and headed down a small path that led back into the woods.

"Stymar, I presume?" Etch said to himself as he picked up his rucksack and started forward. He sniffled as he walked and shivered as water sluiced down the back of his legs to fill his leather boots.

The small path wound briefly through the woods before entering a large clearing. The ground there was entirely worked, and some of the gardens still had plants in full bloom. As he stepped onto the first stepping-stone in the garden's path he hesitated and looked up, feeling a dramatic warming of the air. The clearing was sheltered, but the temperature seemed extreme. His limbs and face immediately began to warm, and his teeth stopped their forceful chattering. "Nice," he said to himself as he smiled and stepped onto the next stone.

A network of steps wound its way around the gardens and up to the small cottage whose door was open. Twice on his way Etch stopped; once, to inspect an unusual plant and again to admire a ripe tomato. Looking at the sky Etch tried to discern how it might be possible to grow tomatoes this late in the year. He shook his head a moment later and continued down the winding path.

"I have been expecting you, young man." Stymar said as Etch reached the cottage door. "Welcome to my home," she said, looking him up and down. "You're very wet, and very cold." Re-entering the cottage she returned a few moments later with a large blanket, which she threw to him. "Take off your wet things and lay them on the stones." She turned then and went back inside. "I will put on some tea for us."

Etch lay down his bag and then stripped down to his shorts and eagerly pulled the warm, dry blanket over him. With his free hand he arranged his clothes on the stones that made up the small porch in front of the cottage before turning to follow his host. Stymar had moved to the cast iron stove that dominated the cottage's main room and now held a steaming kettle in one hand and two mugs in the other. She smiled at him and motioned with her head that he should enter. "Much warmer I bet," the lady said as Etch wiped his wet feet and came in.

"The stones," Etch started, looking back, "the whole clearing." He hesitated a moment and then looked back at her. "It's all a lot warmer than along the river bank."

Stymar nodded. "Yes. It is nice, isn't it? My old bones don't take much to the cold anymore."

Etch gave her a startled look. "You're a great deal younger than I was led to believe," he said complimentarily.

Stymar laughed and her eyes sparkled as she motioned with her hand that he should sit in the wooden chair next to her rocker. A small table sat between the two and she placed the mugs on it and filled them with water. She then returned the kettle to the stove and came back with a small tin.

"Sit and drink some tea. It will warm you," she said as she opened the tin and pulled out some leaves which she put into the cups.

"Thank you, I will." Etch said as another shiver ran down his spine. "That water is cold."

Stymar laughed. "When you go back I will show you a much easier and drier path up."

Etch looked relieved. "I was planning to look further east for another way down, but the forest looks rather thick and I was a little afraid I might loose sight of the river. I figured the safest and fastest way was the direct approach."

"That was wise," Stymar said as she sat down in her rocker. "For you would not otherwise have found the way by yourself."

Etch held out his hand in formal greeting then, suddenly conscious that he had not yet told her who he was. "My name is Etch, Etch Tarrow, from the Diamond Mountain ranges."

Stymar nodded and took his hand. "You know my name already," she started, "or else you wouldn't have made it this far." She held on to his hand and then placed her other atop of it. "Very few brave the falls. Most try to work their way around the drop, and if they are successful in walking round then they end up much farther down river. If they attempt to return back north to the base of the falls and I am not expecting them... well, I have my cats to protect me."

Etch nodded, sensing a greater age in the woman's voice and tone then he noted in her features and the manner in which she sat. "Datos, a shop keeper in Mont Ryhn, gave me your name and told me where to find you. He also warned me about your cats. He said that of all the people he knew you alone would be able to direct me to what I seek... to answer the questions I have."

"Datos." Stymar said frowning slightly. "It was silly of me to ask for those herbs and seeds, but at the time I had need." Her frown faded then and she smiled again at Etch. "What did he tell you of me? What does he say in the city about Stymar? Does he talk freely of me now?"

Etch shook his head. "I don't think so. He doesn't say much. I think he knows me better than most, or...," he paused as he tried to put into words a definition of his relationship with the man. "We've known each other for some years. My wife is known for being a bit of a healer in the area I'm from, and I've done some business with him in the past. I guess he trusts me – if that is the word for it."

Stymar nodded. "So he isn't just telling every man and woman my whereabouts?"

Etch shook his head reassuringly. "No, not at all."

The lady relaxed into her chair and began to rock rhythmically, back and forth, suddenly looking much older than she had only moments before. She smiled at Etch and motioned to the tea. "Drink up."

Etch picked up the stone mug and sipped the warm tea. "Interesting," he said as he drank. The warmth spilled down his throat and spread to his entire body. "Mmm," he said as he warmed. "Very nice. I needed that, thank you."

Stymar nodded and smiled.

Etch felt a little uncomfortable, and continued rather hesitantly. "When Datos gave me your name he suggested that you might help me, given my quest."

"Harad said you are well supplied, as if for a long journey." Stymar looked over at the old scout and the sides of her mouth turned up slyly. "You know leaving your animals alone in these parts is a risky venture."

"Harad?" Etch asked. "I didn't see anyone, and usually I can sense when I'm being watched by someone."

"Harad is one of my cats." Stymar said. "He is the largest of the group and he really does enjoy horseflesh every once in a while."

Etch frown concernedly until Stymar laughed a little. "Don't worry. He won't hurt Peppy or Mule." Stymar shook her head and laughed. "You seriously named your horse Mule? My, you are a little twisted aren't you?"

Etch laughed weakly, his mind racing, trying to figure out the strange woman before him. He set the empty mug back on the table.

"Harad is one of your cats," Etch said in a confused tone, "and you can talk to him?"

Stymar nodded. "In a manner of speaking." She looked at his mug. "More?"

Etch shook his head. "Not just now, thank you. Perhaps in a moment or two."

Stymar nodded. "Relax. Harad will guard them tonight. You are cold and wet, spend the afternoon, sleep here in warmth tonight and return in the morning."

"That's very kind of you," Etch answered politely, "but I don't want to impose."

"No imposition whatsoever," Stymar replied reassuringly. "I don't get many visitors, besides, I can see in your eyes you have lots of questions and your mission is close to your heart. You have

191

already come a long way and will go much, much father before, or rather 'if', you are to return home."

Etch swallowed hard and ran his tongue over his lips nervously. "Not sure I like the sound of that 'if'," he said haltingly.

"Is the place what you expected? " Stymar inquired, pausing in her rocking and changing the subject as she caught his wandering gaze. "You were anticipating dangling chickens feet or the like I would imagine."

"Well, I must admit," Etch started slowly, not sure how to proceed. "Datos talked a bit of magic, which I never really much believed in, until, that is, I felt the warmth of your glen. And, and then you mention that you've been talking to a cat?"

She smiled, making him feel more at ease. "Harad was once an ordinary mountain cat. He and his sisters are much more than that now. I have been working on transforming them for over ten years."

"Transforming them?" inquired Etch, but his tone was soft and Stymar didn't pause in her story.

"I change them each subtly, one small thing at a time so as not to taint their true nature, and I talk to both before I do anything to them. Too much a change, too fast, can drive a beast or man mad you know… even if they ask for it."

"Datos Mrot told me that magic existed, but I didn't believe him. There have been some interesting things happening lately though, things not easily explained." Etch paused, looking first at the old lady, then around the inside of the small cottage. "Except perhaps by magic."

"Like how an entire city of people might disappear?" Stymar asked as she resumed her slow rocking.

Etch nodded and watched her. "He said that there has always been magic, but that it comes and goes in cycles. That all sorts of wizards actually did exist long ago, and are not just fanciful tales told to entertain children before bed."

Stymar nodded encouragingly and Etch continued. "Datos alluded but did not speak very openly of you or your skills. I would, however, be a fool not to think that the transformation of beast by magic is an awesome ability. Frankly, I'm a little surprised as to how lightly you speak of it to me."

Stymar nodded and looked at him with distant eyes. "It really is a small world we live in Etch Tarrow."

Seeing Etch's confusion at her words she laughed lightly. "Believe me, it really is, and so many of our actions affect much bigger things. One pebble cast down from atop a waterfall can kill a fish swimming below. That very fish might have been some other man's only food for his family. Each small action of even the smallest of us can affect great things. Yes," she added, almost to herself, "I think I will tell you what I can and answer most any question you pose."

Etch, now totally lost, and looked back at the old woman, wondering if he was to be answered entirely in riddles. In truth, he didn't quite know what question to ask next. "So, magic is real then?" he finally began, still somehow not fully convinced. Doubt filled his thoughts and he wondered if he still had it all wrong; if the lady before him was just touched and if at any moment he might see a small house cat bound into the room and onto her lap. But then he thought again of the warmth as he stepped into the glen and the vine-ripened tomatoes.

Stymar's hands rested comfortably on the arms of her rocker as she closed her eyes and began to speak. "It has existed without end since before history was first recorded, but yes, in some years magic is stronger. Those that can feel it and use it are stronger then too, but after a while it fades. The cycles can last days, months or even years and it can be generations between each cycle."

"In ages past," Stymar said with her eyes still closed, "wizards existed who could do great things. My work with my cat pales in comparison to what they could do, what they could create and transform."

193

"My grand mom told me of great beasts that hunted the forests," Etch began, remembering his childhood in the city. "Banshees that would feed off of the fear and pain of dying men, women or children, fanged beasts that roamed the mountains." He shook his head. "Childhood stories. I've been through those same mountains, travelled far to the north and although I've seen many strange animals, I've never seen such creatures as she described."

Stymar smiled knowingly, her eyes glowing with great wisdom. "Some, although not all, fables are at least founded on fact."

"Few from the west believe much of the tales anymore," Etch continued, "or even of the existence of magic. Tales like that are only told to children as bedtime stories."

"That is what happens when the magic wanes. People forget. Children are born and grow old never knowing and then they have children and the stories are twisted." said Stymar sadly.

Etch recalled some of the other tales he had heard, these ones not as long ago. "The only tale I was ever told about magic that I thought held any credence was a story told to me by an old Terran soldier that had fought in the blood wars. He told tales about the Masti blood priests."

Stymar nodded slightly and then opened her eyes to look at Etch, her face pale. "The Terran tales are true. Masti blood priests can work magic and their power is not affected by the cycles. They claim their power comes directly from their god but I believe as the Temple guards say, that the source of their magic comes from elsewhere. Their magic is unnatural and it is a shadow magic that is based on illusion. Unlike wizards, the Masti blood priests cannot create anything with substance."

Stymar cringed. "Whatever the magic is, and wherever it comes from, a blood priest only ascends to a level where he can command it through horrific acts. That is why the practice was outlawed in the East."

The old lady paused a moment to catch her breath and colour slowly returned to her cheeks. "True wielders of magic pull their power from the air and earth itself. When the cycles are high every rock on the ground and every breath of wind holds tremendous potential. With that power gifted wizards can do great things, but it takes years to learn how to control and wield it. Often times the cycles wane before they can learn how to bottle up the magic they need to keep themselves alive during times when the power is no longer abundant."

"When the powers of magic go, so too do most mages, for they can no longer sustain their life through their magical abilities. True, there are those who in times of high magic make runes that can be used to sustain them during an ebb in the flow but the length of these cycles can be very long, few are able to survive the longer droughts."

Etch looked at the woman before him, once again trying to ascertain her age in light of these new ideas. Her face was thin but not wrinkled, yet her hands looked well worn. Her hair was dark and only slightly touched with grey, yet her eyes... her eyes were deep. Etch shook his head, giving up, and focused again on the information he was learning.

"So magic comes and goes in long cycles measured in generations?"

Stymar smiled. "Yes. The cycles of magic come and go, and they have been on the rise of late."

Etch shrugged his shoulders, slightly cowed by his lack of knowledge on the subject. "Wizards and strange talking beasts, I can hardly wait to tell my kids," he said with a flash of humour. "What enables someone to use it? How do you do it?"

Stymar smiled. "A very few are born with the ability within them. However, without some spark or incident to ignite the skill they never even realize what they possess. Many of those who do realize their gifts go without training; few of them learn to do anything with it."

195

Stymar stood up and walked back to the kettle. She turned briefly and looked at Etch with an excitement in her eyes that left him vaguely unsettled. "More tea, Etch Tarrow?"

Etch nodded and the old lady turned back to the kettle. "There have been marked changes in the flow of magic these last five years or so. As I said, the tides are up, but even so, not even the greatest mage of all times, from all the stories I have ever heard, could do what has been done to TerranAdd."

"You're saying Magic didn't whisk them away?" Etch asked, once again confused.

"It definitely played a part, but no, I doubt any one spell wielded by even the greatest of mages could make an entire city disappear." Stymar said without looking up from the tea she was preparing.

"What then?" Etch asked. "What happened to them all?"

Stymar picked up the kettle and started back towards the table and chairs. Etch noticed that she used no cloth to protect her hand from the hot metal. "Hmmm," Stymar started and then paused looking down at her newly poured tea. "Let me start by telling you a little story, it might shed some light on what might have occurred."

Stymar poured Etch's mug full of water. She put more leaves within his mug and the scent of mint and herbs wafted through the air and tickled his nose. "This smells wonderful," he said, thanking her.

Stymar sat back down and started to rock slowly. The room grew quiet as they looked at each other. "Before I tell you my story though, tell me first why you would risk your life for these people. They lived far from your home. What is this princess to you?"

Etch was startled by the question and by how much information Stymar already knew about his quest. Sipping the tea with hesitation he smiled uneasily. Etch thought of his family back at home on the Diamond Mountains and chuckled a little uncomfortably. "Climbing down the falls, soaked and cold, I asked myself that very question. Perhaps I'm just a crazy old scout looking for one last hurrah. Perhaps I was foolish to leave my son, daughter and wife back in the mountains to fend for themselves during the hard winter."

Etch paused a moment, trying to figure out for himself why he was there, so far from the home and family he loved. "I guess I felt a sense of duty to the officer that I rode under for many years and to our king. I was there, I know what had to be done when the Tock hit Oathos, and then later when the Drekians came. I can imagine what it was like when the Masti rode south and killed all those in TieRei."

Etch paused as he looked up, reflecting back on his life as a soldier. "I fought in a few battles, I've seen some things I would rather not see again."

Stymar's eyes narrowed introspectively, then after a paused she asked a soft woreded question that came out almost in a whisper. "And in those battles, facing death as those around you died, what god did you pray to for salvation?"

Etch looked up hesitantly, searching the witches' eyes but only seeing a depth of darkness that hadn't been there before. "Every soldier prays at one time or another when faced with death, I was no different."

"Yes, but to who did you pray to Etch?"

Etch laughed, but Etch's laugh dwindled off as he looked at Stymar's eyes. "To anyone that would listen." He finally replied with some seriousness.

After a long and uncomfortable pause the old lady shook her head. "There are gods that don't need blood oaths to bind Etch." But no more than a heartbeat later, the darkness had disappeared from her eyes and the old lady's smile returned. "And after you find the girl then what?"

Trying to dodge her gaze he picked up the tea and took another long sip. Finally he nodded. "I am no fool, something is at play here, something bigger then any one of us." Etch paused as he thought of his family at home. "Some things you just can't run away from for after a while they will be at your doorstep."

"You have an honest face Etch," Stymar said in reply, "and unlike most, you have yet to mention once the prospect of a reward." She smiled and took her own mug, which Etch realized was still steaming. "You have travelled far from your family and home, and you will be going much much farther still…"

Etch laughed lightly and set his own mug back down. "Don't know if I like the sound of that, but since the snows have likely already fallen, the earliest I could go back now is the spring, so I have some time."

"Well then," Stymar said in a more serious voice, "let me tell you my story, for as I said it might shed some light on what has happened."

Etch settled in, tired, relaxed and warm. He eased back into the chair feeling comfortable and safe.

"In the time well before your father's grandfather there lived a wizard. He went by many nams back then, for he was a cruel man that had many enemies. named Patrick Kaynor. In those years, the cycle was full and the world was ripe with magic." Stymar sat forward eagerly as she began. "You could even smell it in the air."

"Patrick wasn't a nice man to start with, but the power he developed as a mage made him a horrible person. Even in his early years he had been noted as having performed especially heinous acts against those that were bold enough to be near him. Kaynor's talents appeared to have no end, his inner strength of will, his intellect and his passion fuelled his magical capabilities and he became that age's greatest wizard. Kaynor knew this, and relished in his power using it to his own greedy end and with absolute power came absolute personal corruption.

"Few lived long to ever grow close to Lord Kaynor, and Kaynor suffered few people for long. However, after many years Kaynor's need for someone to share his experiences with grew. One year when passing through a local village he spied a young girl. With his strong magical capabilities he knew immediately that the gift would be strong with this girl."

"Is this story about you then?" Etch asked with a smile.

Stymar laughed but shook her head sadly. "No, this girls name was Sarta, Sarta Pensor."

"She was a common peasant, born to a farmer and his wife. With many younger siblings she was forced to bathe, feed, and tend her sisters and brothers and cook the meals for the family as her parents scratched out a meagre existence for them on a small patch of land. She despised the lot the world had given her and as the months passed she grew bitter and desperate.

Kaynor stumbled upon her when she was thirteen. He entered the village along the main road where Sarta stood attempting to sell her family's potatoes. She didn't think twice when he asked if she would like to go with him. She dropped her basket and jumped on the back of his saddle. She didn't even stop to leave word for her father and siblings."

Etch nodded understandingly, having seen many a peasant farmer in his day. "Imagine yourself young, destitute, knowing that your life from birth to death would be one of hard labour," Etch said simply. "I've seen such girls in many different places and although it might seem selfish, I can't totally blame her."

"I agree," said Stymar, resuming her tale. "Imagine this poor young girl seeing a tall man riding down the road upon a great horse, dressed in fine silks with jewels and rings. She jumped at his invitation to leave her difficult life, but more than that. She had never seen anyone dressed so finely and although he was much older than her she was immediately smitten by his looks and overwhelmed by his wealth."

"The wizard took her into his towers, deep within the woods east of the Toris Pass. Kaynor instructed her in the use of her gift. She loved her instructions in magic and worked hard at her studies. In truth I think she always saw the old man more as a spouse then as an employer. To her, his power was intoxicating. Simply put, as the years passed the young lady fell in love with the man. Or so the story goes, I myself have other beliefs as to why she followed him so faithfully at the start. I always say, there are two stories but the only one remembered is typically the one told by the rich and powerful."

"Kaynor never really trusted her and as such, Kaynor treated her well but never returned her love."

Etch added knowingly. "He saw her as a pupil and nothing more. Not uncommon for a lord."

Stymar nodded. "And as years passed on he knew he wanted more so one day he departed from their tower and later that year returned with a very refined and beautiful lady, the daughter of a nearby lord." He then did one very silly thing for a person of his intelligence. "He came back and introduced Sarta to his wife as their maid and his apprentice."

Etch shook his head. "She would have been crushed."

"But he was blind to it," Stymar said softly. "Sarta was in shock. She had hoped that one day he would ask *her* to marry him."

"And what was worse," Stymar added, "the new mistress of the house was a true lady, and not accustomed to doing any cleaning or cooking."

"Sarta lived for her studies of magic and had only performed her chores as a matter of necessity, and also in the spirit of being the matriarch of the home she now lived in. Well, you can imagine, for the first while Kaynor wasn't very interested in tutoring Sarta, nor was his wife all that fond of him spending time with her. Sarta was given chore after chore by his new wife."

"Inside, she must have seethed," said Etch knowingly, "having to tend his wife."

"The breaking point came when Kaynor and his wife announced to Sarta that they were expecting to have a child in the spring!"

200

Etch chuckled. "She must have loved that."

"Remember where she had come from Etch, it was much more then anger that brewed in her stomach it was unadulterated hate. She loathed Kaynor's wife, and feared the lady would do nothing but produce babies now for year after year as her own mother had, and that she would be forced to live again as she had as a child. More than anything she feared that she would once again be nothing more than a nursemaid and have no time left to study the magic she loved."

"Over several months, Sarta poisoned Kaynor's wife. It was a slow poison, and by the time Kaynor suspected anything it was too late. The damage had been done and Kaynor knew that his new wife would not live through the winter.

"Sarta underestimated Kaynor's affection for his new bride, confronted she held out and admitted nothing taking his barrage of questions stoically. However, she noted in his eyes that his suspicions once sparked would not rest and fearing her life Sarta fled. Stealing what she could from the wizard she whisked away in the night."

"I would wager he was more than upset," Etch said. "Surely, Sarta wasn't stupid enough to think she could elude a master wizard for long."

"Ah, so here is where the story meets our current path. You see, over the time of study Sarta had been taught of the realms that reside beside our own. Over the years she had seen Kaynor open doors to those realms using focus stones of power. Remember, Sarta had some skill with magic by that time, and her ego made her think she could elude her master using those passage ways to other lands."

Stymar's hand came up halting what she knew would be Etch's next question. "Yes, other lands... other realms. Those childhood stories are also true, there are indeed other realms beyond our own.

"The seven hells do exist?" Etch retorted in a whispered question.

Stymar dipped her right index finger into her tea and then started to trace lightly on the wooden table. "The seven planes exist, and yes some could be seen as hells, but not all are. After all, our own world is one of the seven.

"Let me start by where we are, denoted by what is commonly referred to by wizards as Mortalis. For one item of note that has been verified is that only on the plane one is born, can one die."

"As her finger passed over the varnished surface it left a sparkling trail, a very faint, but visible, green line. She began by drawing a small circle and then, along the circle she drew spheres and from several of these, lines that jumped from one sphere to the other."

So here we are in the realm of Mortalis, named by us on this plane.

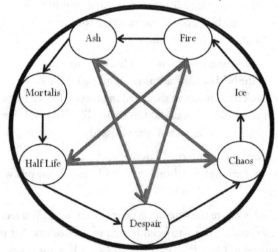

"There are direct paths from one plane to another, a circular relationship – allowing potential passage from one realm to the next, but these simple gates cannot be used to return back. If you are using these doors, you would need to traverse all the realms to return to your own."

"Then there are the higher gates, they allow faster passage – bypassing two gates and only five such planes are connected with these gates. The energy and complexity required to open these gates is massively higher."

Etch shook his head in amazement. "The Temple Guard preach of the seven hells. I had had thought it nothing more than a way to entice us to live well. So where do we fit in?"

"We are here, in Mortalis. Which, is the only gate to the greater circle and the Maker who looks and governs over all and from within we can see all and not be effected by the passage of time. With luck, we depart this plan and based on our journey end up there."

"However, if we are not worthy, we then pass to Half Life… and possibly beyond."

"Correct, and as we pass through to the greater hells of Half Life, Despair, and Chaos time does not remain constant. Patrick's theorized that as much as a century or more passed within Chaos when only a day had passed here. Yet the plane of Ash appears much closer to that of Half Life. "

As Stymar traced out the diagram and marked down Chaos Etch grunted. "The Masti worship the god of Chaos. Is that where this comes from?"

The old witch nodded knowingly. "Yes, twice removed from our own, the denizens of Chaos have held great power. Chaos by its very nature implies no order, instability and within that realm. In a year of our time a millennium may have passed there and in that time Demons would have risen and fallen from power – continuing the overall struggle and fight reinforcing chaos. For any people to worship One such being, implies it has survived a very long time in that realm. As to what end or what purpose it plans to influence us or what are its goals, that is unknown."

"Masti and the blood priests worship Andarduil, mistress of Chaos… for quite some time. That would put this Demon at being very very old in her realm."

"Yes, the Masti worship Andarduel and have learned to call to her using those types of sacrificial blood rituals. They have done so for hundreds of years, and as time passes, and the magic returns her gifts and influence have increased. Even from that great distance she can now bestow to her faithful great powers.

"So," Etch started, returning to an earlier thought, "if there are specific doors in and out, then if you exit our plane, your only way to return is to open another door."

"Exactly," said Stymar, pleased with his quick perception. "Mortalice is our plane, then round the we move to Half Life, then Despair and so on."

"So, Sarta opens a door to the second plane and in a flash she's gone!" Etch said. "Somehow, I don't expect that's the end of the story?"

"To open even the simplest of doors to these planes takes great power and if you do not sufficient power to move through others, you can be there for a very very long time. Over years Kaynor inbued crystals with power, so that he could on demand cast greater magics without consequence. But it would take years and years even for him to store enough power so that he could pass through seven doors so that he could return here."

"Sarta stole three crystals and one of these stones to open a door and depart our realm hoping to elude Kaynor."

Etch chuckled. "Uh oh, I get the feeling Sarta was in no small peril."

Stymar laughed. "Such a foolish girl. She had always suspected Kaynor's past was cruel, but was never convinced. He always seemed such a noble and wise old man to her. She was rather naive in the assumption that he would give up looking for her, or that he wouldn't be able to find her."

"So, where did Sarta go?" Etched asked looking back at the diagram on the table. "Half Life I guess? But then how did she get home with only three stones to open three normal doors?"

Stymar chuckled, "Ah, there is the rub. There was no chance she had the skill nor power to open greater door, but we also know that when Sarta returned, she was greatly changed and dripped of blood magic."

Etch looked back up at Stymar… "All this talk of Andarduel and the Masti is making me nervous."

Stymar nodded. "Sarta was in the realm of chaos a very, very long time." Stymar continued. "So long, that upon her return she had hoped that Kaynor would have forgotten her or perhaps even died of old age. But what Sarta didn't not realize was that time flows differently in each realm, what seemed a long time for her, was only a short time for Kaynor – a master wizard who could sense the opening and closing of doors out of and in to Mortalis. Sarta returned after many years, only to find Kaynor sitting patiently at the spot where she appeared.

Etch shrugged. "So you suspect someone in chaos assisted Sarta, letting her take a greater door to Ash, and from there she appeared back here to Mortalis, but to the waiting arms of Patrick? I can imagine her surprise, to see Kaynor standing there waiting for her."

"Kaynor was an arrogant and vengeful man and his hatred was ripe to the point of bursting. Sarta was tortured for months on end until it is said she was totally insane. But I myself wonder if she was already mad upon returning or if Kaynor drove her to madness after all she had spent a long time in Chaos likely under the whip of Demons that may make Kaynor look like a brother of the order."

"Yet she survived?" Etch asked.

Stymar smiled and then stood and refilled the kettle and put it back on the stove. "Yes, she survived the trip to Chaos and back, and survived his torture but at great cost, her very soul was shredded beyond belief."

The old lady looked out into the garden. "Kaynor cursed Sarta, as she was vain and pursued strength and personal gain, he left her twisted, old and in constant pain, a ugly shrivelled, wretched hag. He left her then, expecting her to wither and die."

"But," Etch began. "The story doesn't end there. She knew blood magic."

"Indeed, and with that knowledge, with help from likely the Masti and through the powers from the realm of Chaos Sarta has figured a way to return to a state of youth. Through a bloody ritual she transforms to a succubus to then pull the life force from others making her for a short time young and without pain."

"A succubus," Etch said, turning to look back to Stymar, who was again sitting at the table with another cup of tea waiting for him. "But her powers are limited?"

``She needs to perform blood rituals to obtain the power to transform. Then as a succubus she has even greater power. Once transformed she has the ability to bend any man or woman's will to her own, to make them do anything she so desires. Weak minded people would flay themselves alive if she asked them to. With escalating cruelty, I fear that she rises in interest to one in particular, and with that attention her powers will continue to grow. Whose attention do you think she holds now, whose favour?"

Etch visibly shuddered.

"As long as Sarta feeds, she lives and with each sacrifice she grows more powerful and earns greater favour and greater attention." Stymar concluded.

"A match made in hell." Etch agreed. "But to what end for Andarduil?"

"The god already had a taste for human sacrifice thanks to the Blood Priests, but never quite in the scale Sarta has gone to. It likely is now the start of a serious addiction. Plus, the bodies themselves appear now to be consumed or perhaps wisked away to Chaos itself? What would be an addicts next step?"

"Cut out the middle man and go for the source." Etch said in a whisper.

Both Etch and Stymar sat a moment in thought, sipping their tea.

"And what became of Kaynor? Is he still alive can he reverse this curse or put an end to her? If we break the link we end all this." Etch asked, hoping for a short, simple answer.

"He disappeared a few years after he let Sarta go. One can guess that as Sarta's powers grew she sought her own revenge upon him. Do not look for salvation from Kaynor, none will be found there."

Etch and the old woman sat quietly again for a long time until she finally rose and lit a candle. "It is getting late. You should rest," Stymar said as she brought Etch another blanket.

Etch started, looking deep into the lady's eyes, "So, an entire city consumed or whisked away to another plane all by the hands of one twisted old lady?"

Stymar nodded. "So it seems."

Etch's mind raced. "If the wizard is dead, where do I begin? I can't rightly go up against Sarta myself, will you come with me?

Stymar turned to look up at him. "I am bound to this valley now, I cannot leave it. But help can be found for those that need it."

"There is a creature, small but smart as a whip. Talented, and sufficiently motivated to help you. She hasn't visited me in a long time but I would know if she had passed on, and I have not sensed that."

With those words she walked over to one of her small dressers and opened the bottom drawer. Stymar returned to the table and placed a little yellow stone down in the centre, along with a small pouch that had a string attached to it. She will be able to help you find the succubus."

Etch looked down at the stone. It was a sickly yellow pebble with what appeared to be very small writing on it. "And this will help me find her?"

Stymar grinned, her kind face showed happiness worn down by many long years. "Yes, my sceptical friend. This minor focus stone will guide you to where she is. From there, I cannot fully see the path you will travel, but trust in Dimi, for all her failings she will not steer you wrong. "

Etch reached to pick it up, but Stymar grabbed his hand. She took the stone from the table and placed it in the little pouch and then placed the pouch into Etch's captive hand. "Now rest Etch Tarrow," she said as she motioned him to the makeshift bed. "You have a long road ahead of you and tomorrow you must begin."

The race for TerranAdd

Miathis tried in vain to keep a stoic, soldierly expression as he exited his tent. He was in a good mood and it showed in his smile as he looked around at the camp. Bending back his head he let the sun's rays dance across his face, warming it with their gentle touch. The night had been cold, very cold, but fortunately it had been dry.

The seasoned soldier knew very well that they had been fortunate. He had known when they departed that there was a good chance of rain and sleet at this time of year. He took a deep breath in through his nose and let it out through his mouth as he looked to the sky, trying to discern through scent and sight if there were any chance of snow that day.

As he exhaled his breath fogged in the still morning air, cloudy against the clear blue sky. Far in the horizon he could see the face of Halos. "Winter is almost here." he said to himself, trying again to erase the smile from his face. Miathis was excited, 'too excited in fact', he thought to himself. He needed to maintain at least a modicum of control; keep on an even keel. His men were already wound up as they raced to the Terran capital and it was his job to ensure they kept focused and vigilant, and didn't do anything foolish that might cause them to miss a hint en route that might help explain what happened. Simply put, he needed to keep the men in control of their emotions and if he couldn't control his own, then they surely wouldn't either.

Miathis looked around at the camp and the company of men who were tearing down their tents, putting on their armour and repacking their saddlebags. Sergeants were yelling instructions, trying to get the men to shake off the sleepy peacefulness that seemed to permeate the camp. He smiled as he saw Tirad and Bettham walk forward from the line of horses, bringing Koal and the other sergeant's mounts into the camp.

"Bettham says we should be in TerranAdd by mid-afternoon!" Tirad said with an ear-to-ear grin as he stepped forward and handed Miathis his reins.

"Perhaps, if we continue at the pace we did yesterday," Miathis said, patting Koal's forehead. The tall, dark horse's head came close to him and rubbed against his chest; her breath was moist and warm. "How are you doing my good friend?" he asked as he stroked the horse's mane. Turning to look at Bettham he smiled; the lad looked exhausted. "How are you holding out?"

"Well sir." Bettham said, trying to look more energetic. He glanced nervously around the camp.

"Tunder should be back from the latrine in a moment." Miathis said knowingly. "He, like all the others, appears to be in a good mood today," he added, almost as an afterthought.

Tirad strode past Miathis and started to take down the captain's tent. "The insides are still moist from condensation." Miathis warned as he watched the lad begin to untie the cords and pull the stakes from the hard ground.

Tirad's laugh rang out from around the back of the tent as he continued to fold it down. "Guess it won't matter much. After all, we'll be sleeping in beds tonight!"

"Let's not get too far ahead of ourselves." Miathis reprimanded. He looked over to Bettham and his face became stern. "I need everyone to keep an eye out as we ride. If you see anything unexpected, I need to know. We can't just ride into the city at full gallop. We're still not sure what went on there or who might be in the surrounding hills."

Bettham nodded as Miathis continued. "Everything has to be investigated, whether or not that means slowing or even stopping. Understood?"

"Yes sir," both lads replied.

"Good. Spread the word then." Miathis said curtly as he walked around Koal. Putting his left foot into the stirrup he pulled himself up. From his improved vantage point he spotted Tunder immediately. The tall sergeant was shouting orders at a group of men who were rolling up their tents. His voice could be heard clear across the camp. "Get going lads, we don't have all day!"

Miathis laughed and looked down at Bettham. The young soldier had heard Tunder's orders and was already turning to the direction. "Better be on your way over." he said as the young man turned to look up at him again. "He sounds excited."

Bettham didn't say anything, just started reluctantly forward with Tunder's sturdy mare.

The captain took one last look down at Tirad, who was still busy rolling up his small tent, and then nudged his massive steed forward. Koal responded eagerly, her shoes kicking up chunks of soil as she lunged forward. Miathis chuckled when he heard Tirad stifle a curse as he bent to brush off the dirt that had been unexpectedly tossed onto the tent's canvas.

In less than half an hour the entire company was mounted and ready to ride. The sergeants frowned as several of the men chatted excitedly with one another and speculated about how long it would take them to get to TerranAdd.

"Like a bunch of children." Tunder said as he pulled his horse up next to his captain's. "Are we there yet, are we there yet?" he continued, trying his best to mimic a child.

The captain laughed, though Tunder's deep tenor had sounded nothing like the sergeant had intended. His spirits soared as he looked at his company. The air sparkled with the reflected light that bounced off the small round shields his men all .

"Let's go then." Miathis said. "The capital awaits."

Tunder turned as Bettham strode forward. He was the last to mount, having had to fetch the company's standard, which was always left spiked in the ground until such time as they were ready to ride.

Bettham lifted the tall shaft of the standard up and Tunder reached down with one hand and grabbed it. He placed the butt of the lance down on the toe of his left foot as he turned his horse back to face the company. Then, lifting it high, he shouted to address the assembled men. "FIST!"

Pausing a moment again, he slowly moved the shaft around, letting the company's colours unfurl and flap in the breeze. His red-brown bushy eyebrows could still be seen poking out from under his open-faced helmet and as he turned the mail that hung from it jingled against his surcoat. "Forward!" he bellowed.

Koal needed no other encouragement; without so much as a nudge she started to walk. Feeling that Miathis didn't object the large mare then surged forward excitedly.

The mail covering Miathis' face felt cold as it splashed against his skin. It felt good and what was more, it let him smile freely without concern that others would think him giddy, which he admitted to himself he was in danger of being!

Miathis slowed as he reached the dirt of the road and pausing listened for the sounds that told him his company was following. Hearing that they were close behind he nudged Koal forward as he reached down for his own shield, which had been strapped to the mare's left side. With a graceful, practiced movement he pushed his left arm through the holder and then took the reins back into his left hand as his sword bounced reassuringly on his right side.

The morning slipped away in the drone of horses' hooves as all of the company rode forward, daydreaming of what they might find when they reached the capital. It was late afternoon when Miathis turned to survey the company as usual and noted that many of the men were now looking nervously around at the forests and hills on either side of the road. Miathis turned off the road and slowed, signalling to Tunder to continue forward. As the company passed he watched them closely, looking to ensure that man and beast were all in order.

As the last two soldiers rode past pulling the packhorses Miathis spurred Koal forward to ride beside them. "Beautiful day!" he yelled. His voice bellowed in his own ears as the mail reflected the sound back at him. Over the thunder of the beating hooves

Miathis looked questioningly at Mort and Dar, trying to ascertain if they had heard him.

Mort turned and nodded his head in reply. "Very nice," he yelled back at his captain.

Miathis looked at the leads the men had tied to the string of heavily laden pack horses that followed them, noting that one of the knots had not been well tied and was likely to soon come apart. "One of your leads!" Miathis yelled over to Dar, who always rode to the left of his good friend Mort. "The knot!" he said, pointing back to the lead that stretched out behind Dar's mount to the first of the pack horses.

Mort and Dar both tried to turn to look at their leads. Although neither carried lances, in their armour with their shields on it was difficult for them to twist in their saddles.

"Do you need us to stop?" yelled Miathis.

The soldier just ahead of Dar heard Miathis' question and looked back. He pulled his horse out to ride off the road as he assessed the situation and the quickly responded . "I got it!"

Dar nodded as the old soldier slowed slightly to fall back beside the trailing packhorse. "Thanks Taramast! If I try to pull on it, it might come loose."

Taramast took his lance into his left hand and let it slip down so that its shaft fell back atop his mount's flank. He bent forward then and moved himself closer to the trailing leads. With gauntleted hand he grabbed the horses' tethers and then sat back. With his own reins unattended atop his lap he looked down and retied the knot with his still-gauntleted hands. Content that it had been refastened he then let the tether fall again to hang between the horses.

Both Dar and Mort held their lances up high in a salute to their friend. Taramast returned the salute then started back to his position within the company.

"Well done!" Miathis yelled over at the old soldier. "I could use a hundred like you." he said in a lower voice, not intending any other to hear.

With inspection completed Miathis raised his hand again in acknowledgement to Taramast as he moved once again to the front of the company.

Realizing suddenly where they were, Miathis nudged Koal to hasten her speed, hoping to reach the front of the company before they crested this last high hill that marked the start of the Terran flats. "Let's go girl." he said as he leaned forward in his stirrups. "Over this next one we might even see the city."

He was within two horse lengths of the front of the company when Bettham yelled out a report, "nothing unusual. We should be able to see the flats from atop the next hill!"

Tunder turned in his saddle and even from beneath his mail Bettham knew that his sergeant was frowning at him for speaking without being instructed. "How are we doing?" Tunder yelled over as Miathis pulled up next to him.

"We've seen nothing." Tunder yelled over at Miathis, turning back to glance at Bettham and Tirad.

Miathis raised his hand in acknowledgement to the sergeant as he spurred Koal forward. Moving well ahead of the company he charged up the last hill. As he crested it he slowed down, searching for a sight of the capital in the distance. The day was clear and cloudless. The sun shone down and the flats stretched out down before him and on into the horizon, a brown and green checkerboard marked with fields of corn and wheat.

Miathis shook his head in awe at the sight. It was late in the fall and winter was not far off. He had half expected that it would snow during their trip here. "The fields should almost all have been harvested and turned by now," he said to himself, shaking his head.

Miathis raised his hand and behind him he heard Tunder's holler commanding the company to halt. He looked back and motioned Tunder forward to his side. The rest of the men grumbled as they were still mostly on the backside of the hill and could see little of the horizon. Miathis, however, wanted to look for a moment before his men rode over the crest and down onto the flats.

Tunder shifted in his saddle and let the shaft of the standard slip slightly so that it wasn't as high. The sergeant paused and Miathis looked over at his friend. "The fields...they should all have been taken in by now. It feels..." Miathis paused, "weird."

Tunder looked down and to the east. "I can see the city's outline from here. But look, there's no smoke, and the fields should be filled with people harvesting. The roads..."

Miathis looked down at the road they were on; it showed no track of horse and cart.

Tunder stood up in his saddle and looked now to the northeast. Miathis pulled his horse around and looked in the direction that his sergeant was gazing. "What do you see?" he demanded in a concerned voice.

"Thought I caught a glint," Tunder said hesitantly. He turned and looked at Miathis, unsure. "Perhaps not."

Miathis strained his eyes but couldn't see anything. He turned and waved forward the two lads sitting at the front of the company, "Bettham! Tirad!"

The two young soldiers approached and Miathis motioned them to the north and east. "What do your eyes see lads?" he asked as the two gazed to the north.

Tirad bent forward and then, in an amazingly fluid movement, with lance still held in his right hand, bent forward and pushed himself to stand atop his saddle. With his left hand he reached up and pulled off his helmet.

A moment later he gasped. "Someone's riding down from the northern roads, a troop. A large company of men, larger then our own judging from the trail of dust they leave behind them." he said, straining to see more. "It is hard to discern who they are at this distance, from the lack of reflection off of armour…" He paused as he looked back at Miathis. "Their number looks to match our own … at least."

Miathis looked over at Tunder. "Not armoured, so not Mohen." he stated plainly. "So Masti or Tock."

"My bet is Masti." Tunder said as he strained to see himself.

"How close to the capital would you estimate they are Tirad?" Miathis asked.

Tirad looked at the northern horizon and then to the east and the silhouette of TerranAdd. "A kilometre closer than we are perhaps more." Tirad said, looking over at his captain.

"But we will be riding downhill," Bettham interjected from behind them all, "and the north road is not as wide or as well packed as the east-west roads, and the winds there are stronger." His voice was excited as he raced towards his unspoken conclusion.

Miathis looked back at his company; the men sat confidently atop their mounts. The horses breathed easy and light. He nodded and turned to Tunder. "They will likely see us when we ride down the slopes, but the longer we sit the less chance there is that we will beat them to the city's gates."

Tunder nodded knowingly. "We ride then?" he asked.

Miathis nodded as he watched Tirad jump back down into his saddle. "We ride." he agreed.

As the men all turned one last time to look to the north a flash sparkled out from the distant force as an errant beam from the hot sun reflected off of a shield or perhaps just some small piece of metal that hung on a saddle.

"And fast." Miathis said as he nudged Koal forward and down the hill.

"Forward!" Tunder yelled back to the company as he followed Miathis.

Tirad and Bettham waited a moment and then nudged their mounts to join up again to lead the company as it approached.

"There! Due north!" Tirad shouted over to his friend, "Did you see it?" he asked, looking over at Bettham.

"Yes." Bettham replied. "But I don't think it's the Masti," he yelled back. "Masti blood warriors dress in dark colours and they never wear anything that might reflect the light. Even the grips and scabbards of their daggers and swords are black. Besides, if they had any priests with them, as they doubtless would, we'd never have seen them at all."

"You should have spoken up!" Tirad yelled back at his friend as the sound of the company's horses upon the hard road grew, along with their speed.

A cold shiver went down Bettham's spine as he noticed another small flash in the fields to the north of the capital. Looking down at himself and his own bright mail, and then back to his friend, he cringed. "They will see us for sure."

At the bottom of the hill, while still higher than the tall stalks of corn that stretched out and spanned the entire horizon, Miathis looked to the north one last time. A clear line of mounted men were now visible in the distance

"Their pace has increased, they must have spotted us!" Tunder yelled as he tilted the company standard back to point once again to the sky. The standard of the Fist snapped as the breeze hit it.

"Two hundred or more…" Miathis said, looking over at his sergeant.

"TOCK!" Yelled Tirad as he rode up behind his captain and sergeant. "Bettham says they are Tock!"

The company rode on down the long road that stretched straight to the east and the city, which now stood clearly discernible in the distance. For almost a kilometre or more they would ride, unable to see their adversary. On each side of the road stalks of corn stretched up, taller than even the largest of the company's war horses.

"Damn good harvest." Tunder yelled over to Miathis. "Never gets this high in the West!" He looked back at Tirad then, acknowledging his comments but at the same time dismissing him to return to the company. Before looking forward he tilted his head slightly to Bettham. "That lad's a smart one," he said under his breath to Miathis.

Miathis looked back a second and then, turning suddenly to face the distant gates once more, yelled back as realization hit him. "Making the city gates will do nothing for us."

Tunder nodded in agreement as he followed his commander's logic. "They may be locked! Besides, we haven't the men to guard the walls of a city that big."

"Better to meet them on an open field." said Miathis decidedly. The company continued to ride blindly forward as the sergeants passed the word to all the men. They stretched anxiously atop their mounts, desperately trying to see through and over the long stalks of corn. As they passed the small farming roads that wound through the fields every head turned in hopes of catching a glimpse of their foe.

Dust flew up from their hooves, leaving a long trail behind them that advertised clearly to their adversaries where they were. They, however, could see nothing over the long swathes of corn.

As they approached the end of the corn fields Miathis pushed Koal even harder. Standing in his stirrups he strained to find their rivals as they broke the cover of the corn. Frantically he scanned the north.

There, driving across the open grasses that encircled the city itself, rode a large company of warriors. "Tock for sure," Miathis said to himself, noting that the large company of leather-clad barbarians were riding without much order.

Miathis turned in his saddle, slowing slightly so that Tunder could draw near. The long split flag of the Fist continued to snap proudly far above him as he bounced forward. "No chance to make the gates." Miathis yelled. "They're far faster then we are."

"Two hundred or more!" Miathis added with a slight note of concern in his voice as he glanced back at his one hundred men.

The Tock, seeing the Fist exit the tall stretch of corn, wheeled to intercept them. As they turned they spread out and despite the distance Miathis swore he heard their battle cry.

Miathis shook himself inwardly, brushing aside the cloud of anxiety that gripped him. Looking forward down the road to the city he noted that the crops ended another five hundred meters away where they met the grass. Turning, he addressed his men, already at a gallop. "Faster!" He yelled, coaxing his company forward at break neck speed. "The time to pace is over."

"They have archers!" Tunder yelled from behind him. "We need to get in close!"

Behind the captain and sergeant Bettham turned to his left and looked into the eyes of his friend who looked back apprehensively.

As the two passed the end of broken ground Bettham yelled to Tirad. "They shoot well from their mounts! Force them to switch to axe."

The two good friends galloped forward, waiting for the call from Tunder that would turn them to meet the long line of barbarians that surged towards them.

Tunder spurred his horse and raised his lance high, then let the long spiked tip of the standard dip gracefully to the north. "Wheel!" he yelled and the company turned as one. The gallop they had maintained down the hill turned to an all-out run as the soldiers drew slightly apart.

Bettham moved his mount to be diagonally behind Tirad; his breathing was fast and furious. "Calm down, damn it." he swore to himself. "Save your strength you stupid fool."

The Tock before them raced at a full charge to engage. The barbarians rode with reins beneath their legs and guided their mounts with their knees. Arrows feathered brightly with red were notched and bows bent back. The barbarian line was broken and confused as it surged forward. Barbaric cries broke through the thunder in their ears as each painted warrior cried out for blood and urged his spotted horse faster so that they two could claim the first.

"Lances!" Tunder's voice commanded as the sergeant and captain moved their mounts to the center of the company.

"They outnumber us by more than two to one!" the tall sergeant yelled to Miathis as he leaned forward, letting his lance point down towards the barbarians.

"Keep them tight!" Miathis yelled as arrows started flying towards them.

With adrenaline pumping through his veins Miathis sat up in his saddle, pulled out his long sword and raised it high above his head, yelling out at the top of his lungs. "Feel the Fist!"

Behind him the entire company echoed their captain's call and the plains were split with the roar of voices. "Fall to the Fist!"

The first company of Montterran regulars surged forward and as they had rehearsed it a thousand times their lances tilted as one. The gleaming, polished metaltips of the lances dropped down from the blue sky. Down they tilted until they ran flat upon the air as if the blades themselves sought the flesh of the approaching enemy.

Arrows flew at the company like wasps on a summer's day. Even as their friends fell to the piercing stings, not one man among them wavered. They rode unfalteringly forward toward their enemy.

The tip of the Fist's standard led the way, held tightly under Tunder's arm. "The Fist!" Tunder yelled as he leaned forward in his saddle, letting the standard point towards the largest of the adversaries in his foe's ranks.

"Barbarian pig - I will set you on this great spit!" Tunder roared as he angled the standard towards the large warrior leading the barbarian charge. Tunder glanced down the length of the standard to its pointy metal tip. Beyond was his target, the massive warrior who held a large, bright battle-axe high above his head.

***

On the eastern side of the line of men and horses Bettham stared forward, focusing his eyes on the approaching force. At fifty meters his stomach flipped and fell as the long line of barbarians with painted faces came into clarity over his friend's shoulder. Many held bows but other, larger men, and women too, held cruel axes and massive war hammers. At twenty meters, when he heard the first of his company connect with the enemy, he squinted his eyes, leaned forward and prayed.

***

Tunder's smile turned to a frown at the last instant as the barbarian's horse turned, moving its master sharply to the right and enabling the Tock to avoid the long lance. Twisting, the sergeant tried to bring it around but the warrior was already inside the length of its and shaft was swinging his immense axe in a long horizontal arc.

The battle axe howled as the Tock swung it back. Tunder watched in horror and pulled hard on the reins of his horse, but it was too late. There was a sickening crack as the warrior's axe cleaved the top of his horse's head off and sliced through his reins. Blood and brains splashed back onto the sergeant's face and mail as beast and man fell to the earth.

Miathis blinked as he rode through the first line of barbarians slashing at the bodies that passed him. "Three hundred!" he yelled, turning to look for Tunder. At last he caught a glimpse of his friend, covered in blood, falling to the hard cold ground. "Damn you all!" Miathis screamed as he slashed and hacked his way through the barbarian horde, hoping to cut his way to open ground.

***

The reality of war and death gripped Bettham's very soul and shook it as an arrow slammed into the top of his helmet. He blinked, wondering if in a moment or two darkness would take him, unsure if he had just been dealt a mortal blow or if the arrow had merely grazed him.

But time to think was in short supply and he gasped as Tirad's lance passed by him on his right imbedded in a Tock. The yellow painted barbarian screamed in pain as he grabbed the shaft with both hands. Bettham let the horror drift from his view as he turned to face the front, desperately trying to regain sight of his friend.

***

Dar and Mort followed the company of men as fast as they could, however soon the charging Fist was well ahead of them and their packhorses. Dar looked over at Mort and pointed to the gates of the city "They're open!" he yelled. "Make for the gates!"

Mort kicked his horse as hard as he could, coaxing the last of its energy out from its legs. "Go girl, go!" he yelled. The horse's ears turned back and although already panting from exhaustion it pulled forward, yanking its tether and the following horses along with it.

***

Dodging an arrow, Bettham looked up and spotted a barbarian with a heavy cudgel riding to attack Tirad, who was busy exchanging blows with a Tock that swung a long handled axe. Grasping his lance he lifted it in the air and threw it with all his might at the approaching Tock.

The lance flew straight but the female barbarian saw it at the last moment and twisted in her saddle. The lance passed her by.

"ORRA!" Bettham let out a belated cheer as the lance struck another Tock behind his original target. Then his eyes widened sickly as the original target turned her mount and with cudgel waiving high in the air came screaming towards him.

The frightened lad reached down and pulled out his sword just in time to hold it up in an attempt to block the flying cudgel. The hard, knotted wooden cudgel was wrapped in iron and it slammed into his thin blade, cracking it in half. On it went, smashing into his chest, knocking the wind from him and sending him crashing backward to the ground.

***

Miathis looked back again, desperately hoping to see Tunder. He glanced around wildly, desperate to see his friend's helmeted head poking up above the other soldiers and barbarians who were now fighting on foot. His sergeant, however, had disappeared. Gritting his teeth Miathis turned his sadness to rage. With muscles bulging he slashed and hacked at each barbarian that dared to come within reach of his sword. Below him, Koal stomped and kicked as she ran sending countless of those upon the ground to their deaths.

***

Tirad was having a hard time of it; he had dropped three barbarians with little effort, but the one before him now was very skilled. Although he hefted a heavy hammer, the large Tock was fast. The young soldier's shield was twisted and bent from several glancing blows and his left arm felt as if it was nothing more than a dead stick. His right arm burned as spent adrenaline started to reclaim his energy. He huffed and puffed and slashed, pushing back the barbarian, but then cringed as yet another drew near. "Lovely," Tirad said as his heart sank, "an archer." Turning around he scanned for Bettham but his friend was nowhere in sight. "Just lovely," he said under his breath as he barely dodged another swing of the heavy hammer.

223

At that moment the barbarian archer circling Tirad from behind pulled back the string of his bow. He never saw Taramast's sword as it descended, cleaving his leather helmet and head in two.

Tirad turned quickly to his right after dodging the last blow from the hammer-wielding Tock, hoping that the view through his visor would be enough to show him where the archer was. He spun around and then flashed a quick smile, for where the archer had been, only moments before, Taramast now sat, high atop his horse. "Keep your eyes on your man!" Taramast yelled at Tirad, who turned just in time to see that the barbarian was once again swinging his massive hammer.

Tirad grunted and turned his shield in to face the oncoming hammer just in time. As he leaned forward the hammer hit, sending sparks dancing up into his eyes. He shuddered as the impact surged through his arm and then through his entire body.

"ARRRAAA!" he yelled. With what he thought was the last of his energy he thrust his sword forward and into the neck of his foe. The barbarian leaned back, hoping to avoid a killing blow, but Tirad followed him forward, sending the blade in deeper. Gasping and sputtering blood the barbarian fell backward, dying even before he hit the ground.

***

Tunder blinked surprised that he was alive. The giant of a man had been knocked senseless by the collision of horse, man and hard earth. He had fallen with his horse and had obviously hit the ground hard. The torn, lifeless form of his mount pressed down heavily on his left leg, pinning him helplessly to the ground. Tunder winced in pain as he pulled hard with hopes of liberating his bruised leg, but it remained immobile, entangled in his stirrups.

Looking around the sergeant noted that many men and barbarians were now on the ground, having lost their mounts as well. He searched the area frantically, hoping to see someone, anyone, from the Fist that might help him, but there appeared to be no one around with enough time to cut him free.

"What luck," Tunder said sardonically as his eyes met those of the barbarian who had decapitated his horse.

The ugly, painted barbarian walked slowly and deliberately towards him. Tunder marvelled at just how big the man was – 'a head higher then me still!' he thought to himself, then he smiled… 'But not as good looking!'

The barbarian was painted from head to foot in red. Even his brown leathers had been stained and his face was aflame with colour. As he walked forward a long, interlinked bone chain bounced upon his muscular chest. Tunder winced as he recognized the significance of the necklace. In the Tock tradition each link was made using a finger of a foe defeated in personal combat.

"No more links for that!" Tunder said as he frantically tried to free himself. "God's teeth!." he swore as he tried desperately to free himself. His leg twisted and his muscles burned but his foot remained trapped below his horse.

Tunder looked up as the big warrior pulled a formidable double-edged battle axe from off his shoulder. "Big axe for a big guy." Tunder swore as he pushed with all his might, his right foot against his horse in hopes of moving it with the added leverage. Even as it moved a hair, so too, did he feel his left leg get tugged along with it. "SHIT!" he swore again, looking up again frantically, hoping to see someone around that might intervene, knowing that his end was drawing closer.

Tunder kicked savagely at the dead horse and twisted until he thought his leg would break, but without avail. He stopped finally and turned to look again at the man approaching. Tunder had never really known fear until that moment. It welled up from his gut and moved into his chest before he choked it down with a laugh. "You wouldn't by chance use that wonderfully large axe to cut the straps pinning me to my horse, now would you?" Tunder called out to the barbarian.

The colossal Tock paused for a moment, looking confused. Tunder pointed to the saddle and then to the man's axe. The barbarian tilted back his head and laughed loudly. Looking back down at Tunder he brought forth his axe and smiled menacingly at the sergeant.

"I didn't think so." Tunder said under his breath.

Tunder pushed hard with his foot once more, a last desperate attempt, and heard a small metallic clink. Reaching down under the front of his horse he felt a link of chain and began to pull on it. 'My flail' thought Tunder as he pulled with all his might. The weapon came free easily enough, but after pushing again he realised it was not the cause of his predicament. Without a second thought Tunder lay on his back and started the flail spinning above him. The ball and chain swished over the horse and man. Using one arm he pushed himself up, moving the spinning spiked ball further up and into the air. Twice round it went before Tunder risked another look at the barbarian. "I might be down, but I ain't dead yet." he called out to him. Then he called the brute forward. "Come and get me you dumb bastard."

The barbarian shrugged, as if this last great act of defiance was nothing but a small impedance. Taking two more strides towards Tunder the Tock brought his axe around in a extended horizontal slice. At the last moment the blade twisted to its side and caught the spiked ball as it passed around. The axe head howled as it caught the ball and then chain. The warrior's arms bulged as he tore the flail's handle out of Tunder's grasp. With a loud bang the flail was gone, spinning in a giant heap into the air and far to their right.

Tunder gasped as the flail's heavy wooden handle was pulled from his strong grip. "I liked that flail!" he said, cursing the man in front of him with false bravado.

As the barbarian turned back from watching the ball and chain fly, he smiled again. Tunder's stomach fell. "Shit." he said to himself.

As his opponent took yet another step closer, Tunder could smell the barbarian. He was rank with days-old sweat and smelled of musty leather and smoke. Sniffing loudly Tunder looked up and smiled. "You stink." he said.

The Tock warlord said something in his guttural language. Tunder didn't speak Tock, but he understood the gesture as the barbarian wet his bare thumb and touched it to one side of the axe's edge.

Tunder growled and heaved, trying with all his might to reach forward and grab the Tock by the legs, but the man stepped back and avoided his reach. He looked down and laughed at Tunder then and once again touched his thumb to the edge of his axe.

The large warrior's face tensed as he moved the massive axe behind him, as if preparing for an executioner's chop. 'He means to cleave me in two.' Tunder thought with dread, 'Make a show of it.' Tunder grit his teeth, not looking around, and prayed that none of his friends would witness his humiliation.

"Just do it you BASTARD!" Tunder screamed at the warrior as the Tock began his great swing.

As the axe went back the warrior's face contorted and he shouted a choked and cracking battle cry. His chest swelled as his immense muscles, almost breaking through his leathers, pulled the axe around in a massive sweep.

***

Bettham cringed as a warm trickle flowed down from his hair onto his face and into his eyes. A moment later, blinded, he reached up and pulled off his helmet, threw off his gauntlet and wiped his eyes with the back of his arm. His sight returned faster than his breath as he gasped for the air that had been pummelled from him.

Looking up helplessly he spotted the female barbarian. Seeing victory before her she was turning her horse so that she could ride him down.

There was nothing left in Bettham, he was spent. His lungs ached as he pulled for air, his chest and stomach felt like they had been crushed. Still, with what little strength he had left he turned on his side and began to climb to his knees. Blood poured down his forehead and into his eyes.

Exhausted, hurt beyond belief, Bettham made it to his knees and looking up, watched the woman ride slowly towards him swinging her cudgel in a great circle. He raised his arms slowly as her cudgel swept forward, connecting with his chest and arms and sending him flying backwards once again.

Stars swirled and the earth spun as Bettham lay dazed, hovering between consciousness and oblivion. He heard, rather than saw, the woman turn her horse, he heard her war scream as she prodded it to run over him, to crush him and send him to his death. He closed his eyes and waited for the raining hooves as he listened to the sounds of the battle that continued to rage around him.

But the moments came and went, and still Bettham lived. He opened his right eye tentatively, expecting to see a horse's hoof descending to meet his face, but instead he saw nothing but blue sky. Turning he looked over and shook his head in disbelief at his friend standing in front of him. Tirad's long sword was angled up and into the barbarian woman, piercing her flesh just below the ribs.

As Bettham watched in disbelief, Tirad grabbed his sword's hilt with two hands and pulled down, yanking the blade out from the warrior. She looked up once in disbelief and then back down at Tirad before falling to the ground.

Tirad turned and walked to Bettham, holding his hand out to his friend and coaxing him to stand. "This is no time for a nap my friend!" Tirad said as he helped Bettham to his knees. Bettham wheezed and nodded as he tried to rise.

Tirad bent to offer him support and suddenly screamed. "TARAMAST!"

Two warriors were bludgeoning Taramast and another two stood beyond them peppering him with their arrows. Releasing Bettham, Tirad called out a question as he started towards the fight. "You OK?"

Bettham raised his hand weakly and Tirad sped off with sword swinging.

Bettham dropped back down to his knees then and doubled over, still trying to breath. Finally, after a few moments, he stood again and staggered forward, dazed, but alive. His eyes cleared slowly and his hands went down to where his sword should have been. Not feeling the hilt he looked down. "Gone, broken," he said as he started desperately searching for something to defend himself with.

Confusion and concern crossed the lad's face as his eyes spotted a long wooden shaft with a chain and spiked ball. Grabbing it he looked around for his sergeant.

***

Miathis looked about himself confused. Tock and Fist were bound in mortal battles all around him. The ground was soaked with blood and screams of terror and death now echoed louder than battle cries. He turned his horse and looked to the gates of the city. In the distance he could see Mort and Dar's horses standing before the gates. The Tocks that had ridden to intercept the two were on their way back. Miathis screamed, turned Koal around and charged.

Arrows shrieked at Miathis as he rode forward hunched low in his saddle. The two archers broke, one to his right and one to his left, hoping to keep their distance from him and his sword, but Koal was fast and surefooted and she turned in, giving Miathis the distance he needed to slash at the first archer. He went down with a howl, falling from his horse. As Koal turned around the second archer twisted in his saddle and shot at Miathis but Koal was already moving again and the arrow sped harmlessly past him.

"GET HIM GIRL!" Miathis yelled and Koal took off like the wind. Ground churned under her hooves as Miathis screamed again.

In three beats of Miathis' racing heart Koal was upon the second archer and his mount. Miathis turned her to the left, letting her chest hit the flank of the other horse and sending it stumbling forward. Then he rose up from behind them and standing in his stirrups, slashed open the back of the archer, sending man and horse to the ground.

***

Tunder looked up and gritted his teeth. The Tock leader's leathers were positively bursting at the seams. The muscles in the warrior's arms and chest bulged with unnatural size as he started the fierce swing of the mighty double-bladed axe.

The barbarian's face looked up to the heavens and through stained lips he yelled "TRUC O LO!" as he swung his axe behind him in one large arc.

Tunder held his breath and listened to the axe sing as it cut the air behind the massive Tock. He raised his head to receive the blow. 'I will look death in the face.' he thought. The axe began its rise to the top of the arch and as it rose the Tock went to his toes, straining to keep the tremendous instrument of death within his grasp. The double blade, already stained red with Montterran blood, glistened; runes cut in its side gleamed wickedly as wind whistled through them.

'I won't feel a thing.' Tunder thought as he listened to the blade hiss through the air. Suddenly, at the apex of the swing, the Tock warrior issued a strangled scream. At first Tunder thought it was a killing cry, a cry of victory, but then the Tock's hands did not descend; instead he halted as if frozen in time and released the axe. The heavy weapon, driven by its momentum, continued up into the air and went sailing over Tunder to land with a crash somewhere behind him.

Tunder watched in startled amazement as the massive Tock fell forward, collapsing to the ground before him. A round spiked ball protruded from the back of the warrior's head.

The sergeant's eyes traced back the ball to the chain and down the handle to the slight lad standing behind the fallen Tock. Bettham stood panting before him and between pants he smiled at Tunder.

"Lose something?" Bettham asked shakily as he yanked the handle, tearing the ball from the back of the barbarian's head.

The ball fell to the ground with a thud and Bettham turned the handle, offering it to Tunder.

Tunder smiled, then growled and yelled, "Behind you!"

Bettham's laughter stopped suddenly when Tunder screamed. Without even looking the lad spun, bringing the spiked ball around. Up and around him it flew, smacking another barbarian in the face as he approached at a run from behind.

The barbarian fell and Bettham turned back, a little shaky but still smiling. Without saying another word he walked around Tunder and his horse and sliced the leather ties that were holding the sergeant to the saddle.

As Tunder rose Bettham once again offered him the handle of the flail.

Tunder shook his head and laughed loudly. "You keep it." he said as he turned and picked up the massive Tock battle axe. "You seem to have the knack of it and I think I can make do with this." he said smiling as he felt the weight of the axe in his hand.

***

In the distance Miathis was swinging his sword wildly. 'The battle is turning!' he thought to himself with relief, noting that there were now more Montterrans then Tock still standing.

One of the few Tock warriors still on horse turned as he spotted Miathis and gave his spurs to his horse, hoping to escape him. Miathis let the man and horse go as he noticed another Tock on foot bearing down on Tirad.

Koal's neck lowered and the metal plate on her forehead slammed the barbarian's back, driving him under her hooves which then pummelled the man into a bloody mess.

***

The battle waned as what remained of the Fist continued to pound mercilessly at the Tock warriors. The Tock asked for no quarter and were given none. Soon, only the Fist stood or sat, their challengers lying dead on the ground all around them.

Miathis, still mounted, did a quick survey of the surroundings. There were only a dozen men still on horse, and a few of those were now slumping over with arrows protruding from their armour. There was less than that number again of his men yet standing on the battlefield. Bodies were strewn around; horses were standing loose where their masters had fallen. Here and there came groans from soldiers and warriors alike, badly wounded or dying.

He shook his head and sweat flew from his brow and dripped down into his eyes. Reaching up he pulled off his helmet and set it before him on his horse as he watched a large burly man holding a massive double axe walk towards him. "I thought you dead my friend." He said as Tunder drew near.

Tunder laughed as he looked up at Miathis. "So did I," he replied, shaking his head. Then, more seriously and with a touch of surprise, he nodded to the field around them. "We defeated them, at three times our number!"

Miathis nodded, "But it cost us dearly." he added solemnly.

Tunder surveyed the battlefield and then looked back at the city. "I didn't expect quite this type of reception."

Miathis turned his mount around to survey the city gates, which still stood open. In the distance, closer to the gates their packhorses still stood, but Dar and Mort were lying on the ground by their feet. From the distance they looked like pincushions, with dozens of arrows protruding from each.

Noticing Miathis' gaze, Tunder looked over at them. "They put up a good fight." he noted, pointing to a Tock warrior beside them. A lone soldier rode back from where the two soldiers lay, he rode slightly bent over his mount.

Miathis responded sadly. "We should have come with more men; a couple dozen archers would have made a world of difference.

Miathis looked over at Tunder. "We will risk going straight in to the city. Get the men in. Just past the main gates are the barracks, it has a well supplied surgery there."

Miathis noticed that the man on horseback was about to fall off his mount. "Taramast," Miathis yelled as he recognized that his sergeant had several arrow shafts protruding from his back and side. Rolling off his mount the captain made it to the soldier's horse in time to catch the man as he slumped and fell. Arrow shafts snapped against Miathis' arms as he caught the man, softening his fall to the ground.

"I'm ok, nothing more than a scratch" the old man said as blood trickled down the side of his mouth.

***

The sun had almost set before what was left of the Fist was finally inside the city's gates. They halted at the gatehouse which contained a small barracks and set the wounded down on cots. A few men tended the sick as the others went back out and led the horses into the city.

Miathis came over to Bettham, who was cutting out the arrows from Taramast's back. "The mail slowed many of the arrows down; most of them aren't that deep." the boy said softly. Then he looked up at Miathis. "But I fear one has pierced his lung."

Miathis nodded as he looked down at the soldier, who had fallen unconscious. Tunder came over then and Miathis looked up at his weary sergeant. "I know we are all tired, but once the men are in, those that are not tending the wounded must start to gather the bodies of our fallen. There should be enough wood around for a pyre."

Tunder said nothing in reply, only nodded and turned, signalling a few others in the room to follow him.

Bettham rose then from his place beside Taramast. "I have done all I can for him." he said quietly. Turning he looked over at Miathis. "If I might be so bold sir," he started.

233

Miathis looked up at the lad, surprised. "What Bettham?"

"Tomorrow we will need to clean the field as much as possible, burn what we can and bring what remains into the city." he said hesitantly.

"Why?" Miathis asked, bewildered. "We have no need of Tock bow or cudgel." "I think it would be wise." Bettham continued softly, but with growing confidence. "We should leave as little a trace of the battle as possible outside the city, just in case others ride by."

Miathis thought for a moment and nodded. "Tunder might not like the idea. I'm certain he thinks we should let the Tock rot out there." He shook his head and then rubbed his eyes. "I guess… makes sense." He concluded, but his voice signalled that his thoughts were on his fallen friends and not the bodies of his enemies

Standing, Miathis turned to face the other beds in the room. Six men with grievous wounds lay upon them, not one looked as if they would last the night.

Miathis wanted to linger to lend what aid he could to his men. But duty always calls the leader away, tears them from what they would like to do to attend to what is demanded of them. "What a price." he said sadly as he walked to the door. Opening it he hesitated as he looked out at the city, vacant and eerily silent. For the entire long ride here he had been anxious to enter the city and find out what had happened to its inhabitants, but oddly now he stood motionless as if almost afraid to walk out and enter it.

Inhaling deeply Miathis stepped forward out of the barracks onto the street and headed for the city's heart. After only a few minutes of walking he paused, suddenly ill at ease and unsure of the cause. Realization came quickly from all around him. For beyond his own footfalls Miathis could hear no other sounds.

The city all around the Montterran captain was beyond silent. Within the homes around him neither one man nor woman could be heard and the night was bereft of infant cries.

Proceeding in a slow and deliberate walk Miathis listened intently, hoping to hear something, hoping even in the darkness to see something that might shed light on what had transpired within the city. Still, behind each and every door he passed he heard nothing more than silence. In every alley he passed not one dog barked, nor cat meowed. The city was silent and still.

Miathis' pace increased as the hairs on the back of his neck rose. The city around him was vacant and deathly still, but even more than that there was something about it that made him uncomfortable. Although the streets were wide and empty he felt almost claustrophobic as he walked. To Miathis the dead city, its walls and buildings, seemed to exude ghastly, sickly feeling that made him shudder.

Although reluctant to stop, he did as he reached a major intersection. Pausing, he turned around slowly, looking up at the buildings around him and trying to ascertain the source of his ill feeling. A large pub on the corner that should have been filled with noisy and drunken patrons at this time of night stood empty and silent. And in the rooms above the pub and shops that framed the intersection no candlelight could be seen.

"What has happened here?" Miathis said finally in total awe of what he couldn't see. His voice carried and bounced off the walls, shattering the silence around him.

"What great evil hand ripped out this city's soul?" He said in a hushed voice as if now afraid to further disturb the silence.

"Whatever has touched this place," Miathis continued softly, "has left its mark."

Shaking the feeling of dread off of his shoulders the tired captain turned and headed further into the dead city.

The best laid plans of mice and men

King Mar Roehn the Third paced his study haltingly, a long, slender walking stick in hand, wincing with each step. As he approached the window he paused a moment; leaning heavily on the cane in his left hand he reached with his right to loosen the collar of his midnight black surcoat.

His hand slowed as the silver-threaded unicorn that was stitched on the breast of his jacket captured his gaze. The majestic beast stood up on its hind legs kicking defiantly at an unseen enemy.

"Elle…" he sighed softly to himself as his fingers slowly traced the sparkling outline. He smiled remembering how mesmerized Elle had been by the image when she sat upon his knee as a child. She would sit for hours tracing its outline and fantasizing aloud about why the unicorn's eyes were so wild with anger, and who or what it was trying to rebuff.

A loud crash disrupted the stillness of the morning. Somewhere down below his study someone had evidently dropped a large vase full of water. Roehn chuckled when he heard one of the chambermaids cursing the day as she prepared to clean the mess she had made.

The king stood a moment longer and listed to the activities in the rooms around his own. Closing his eyes he heard the bustle of servants as they ran from one room to another preparing the many bedchambers and studies. By the end of the day dozens of Dukes, Counts and Barons would arrive for the council meetings he had called and they and their entourages would need to be housed and provided for. The entire castle was buzzing with preparations.

Roehn sighed as his hand dropped away from the crest. He pulled back his shoulders and made to take a step closer to the window. As his left foot came forward he winced and leaned heavily on his walking stick. With a stagger he reached the windowsill and leaned on it heavily, taking the weight off of his hurt leg.

Supporting himself on the ledge, Roehn passed his cane to his right hand and considered it for a moment. He hated it and loved it at the same time, for although it was a well-crafted work of art, given to him by his brother-in-law, the Duke of Capris, he loathed being dependent on it.

Roehn shifted his weight again and held the cane's long, carved shaft in two hands. Smiling, he pulled firmly on its silver handle.

As he stood contemplating the delicate blade that issued forth from the carved wooden shaft Roehn heard his page and nephew, Theta Kathanor, approach him from behind. "It looks so very sharp." the lad said as he walked forward, hoping to get a closer look at the blade. "May I touch it?"

Roehn looked down at the lad and held the slender blade still as Theta reached up. "Only touch the flat of it, if you don't want to hurt yourself." he said.

"Your father is a smart man." Roehn continued as the lad looked up at him smiling. "He knew that I wouldn't like walking around with a cane, so instead he sent me a sword disguised as a cane."

The king looked down at his nephew. "I bet you have missed him dearly these last months. I know I have."

Roehn continued speaking as he examined the blade and the walking stick that had been deftly carved to resemble the horn of a unicorn. "You must be very excited to see your father again." He said rhetorically, looking at the young lad who so closely resembled his late sister.

Theta, having caught the king's distant gaze, knew that in his face the king was seeing his sister. He only wished that he could see the resemblance as well. He had never known his mother; she had died giving birth to him and his twin brother.

Theta shook his head. "Many of the council are within our walls. However, neither my father nor Duke Baras Bethos have arrived yet."

Roehn nodded and looked away from the lad, not wanting him to see the sadness in his eyes. Looking out the window he reached up with his right hand and undid the latch, however, with the cane in his left hand he had difficulty raising the glass. Theta stepped forward and assisted, pushing up the window. A cold breeze rushed in to meet the king's face and wafted up his grey-streaked brown hair. Theta stood back from the window as the cold air reached him.

"I'm sure all will come out as you plan my liege." Theta said reassuringly.

"I am sure it will." Roehn replied but then added with a sarcastic tone. "Assuming of course that Duke Bethos of Oathos and Duke Sirthinor of Sieren get along better than they did the last time both of them were here."

Theta laughed. "They really don't like each other.. but father never told me why, can you explain it?" Theta asked hesitantly, already knowing part of the story but wishing to hear more of the details.

Roehn laughed. "A long story likely best told to you by your father and not me." The king paused and glanced at the lad, who appeared somewhat disappointed.

"Oh, all right." The king relented, mussing the boy's hair. "At the last council Bethos heard Sindor Sirthinor suggest to the Margrave Devmond that the Duke of Oathos' eldest son Bartholm was the result of Bethos' having mated with a mountain troll. Sindor exacerbated the situation further by stating that the proof to his belief could be found by looking not only at Bethos, but also his wife and his younger son Bettham… all three together are not as large as Bartholm is."

"Bettham had just won the tournament and beat Duke Sirthinor's best knight hadn't he?" Theta put it, proud to show what parts of the story he did know.

Roehn laughed again and then added in a lighter tone. "Indeed – it was all sour grapes. However, the comments truly enraged

Bethos and had your father not held Duke Baras back, bloodshed and not wine would have ended the meeting and tournament."

Then, looking over at his nephew, Roehn continued in a more sober tone. "Bartholm was specifically not invited to this week's meetings, even though Duke Baras' eldest son is now of age and entitled to join us." The king paused a moment to reinforce his point. "Speak not of this to anyone. I tell you these things now only since you are kin and I have taken it upon myself to educate you in the politics so that one day you can rule a part of your father's lands yourself., Understood?"

The young lad nodded quickly, "Yes, my lord, very clear." Then a second later he added politely. "Thank you."

The boy paused a moment and then wanting to return something in exchange for being trusted so much by the king he added in a cautious tone. "Father doesn't much like or trust Duke Sindor."

King Roehn's eyebrows rose slightly, suggesting that the lad had divulged an insight that his brother-in-law might think personal, but then he smiled again as Theta's expression changed, realising his own foolishness for offering up his own family's secrets.

"Its ok lad, I knew that already. Just never forget the politics at play and that your loyalties must be clear; one day you might rule yourself." said the king simply. "Your father also knows that Sindor Sirthinor, the Duke of Sieren, is a key player in this current game."

Roehn went on in response to his nephew's obvious interest, explaining to the lad in detail. "The Duke of Sieren controls the largest fleet of ships we have and without him we will have a hard time ahead of us. Never forget, at one time the Sirthinors ruled the entire south. Their fealty was bought by your grandfather but only after much blood had been spilled. The last thing we need is for Duke Sirthinor to take this as an opportunity to retract his allegiance and start a civil war. Even beyond that – we will need his vote when we meet with the General Council of Lords. I need unanimous support for what I propose and there is much dissention among the council. Duke Sirthinor's agreement will be necessary in order to guide others onto the path we have chosen. If the Duke doesn't help me the general council will stay divided – which could mean the ruin of us all."

Roehn turned and walked past his page toward the large desk in the middle of the room. Theta followed quietly behind him, his mind racing with the politics at hand, until he realised his uncle was finished speaking and that his education was over for the day.

There was a knock at the door and Theta, relieved by the distraction, ran to it and opened it wide. "Good morning sir." Theta said as he bowed quickly to the man at the door, who stood between the two posted guards. Then, turning, Theta looked back to his king, who was now seating himself at the desk. "My lord, the Viscount of PassionMont is here."

Roehn looked up smiling and waved his friend in. "Come in Lord Mitos!" King Roehn called out.

Bartholomew Mitos, the Viscount of PassionMont, was Roehn's closest advisor and friend. He smiled warmly as he entered. Behind him followed his page Thero, Theta's twin brother, who punched Theta in the arm as he passed.

Mitos chuckled and shook his head as he watched Theta wince and then attempt to swipe Thero back. Thero however, dodged the punch and scurried quickly to the opposite side of the Viscount.

"You boys, never have I seen brothers so alike, yet so much at odds with each other." Lord Mitos said as he passed Theta and walked up to King Roehn. He gave a curt, semi formal bow to his liege, who was smiling at the two brothers and shaking his head at their antics.

"My liege," began Mitos in a formal tone. "Word has come that Duke Bethos is but a few kilometres away and should arrive in an hour or less. I have already sent out a runner who will lead them to their lodgings and ensure that their horses and men are quickly squared away."

"Good, good," responded Roehn who then motioned his friend to take a seat, "any word as to the Duke of Capris?"

"Not yet." Mitos replied, shaking his head as he sat down. "However, we still have some time. If we allow him a couple of hours to prepare, we can schedule meetings first with Baras. He is really the cinch pin to these discussions; we can always forego discussions with the Duke of Capris if necessary and trust that when he attends the senior council his words will be well placed to support our cause. It is Duke Baras that I have the most concern with. Should he attempt to fence verbally with Sindor it will be hard to bring Duke Sirthinor to our cause."

The king nodded in approval but then looked up as Thero, having walked around Lord Mitos' chair, prodded Theta in an attempt to provoke him into another response. Without turning Mitos rolled his eyes and shook his head. "Thero if you are so bored, go run and find Marinor. He should be around the kitchens. Instruct him that we will desire dinner for three brought to the council chambers in three hours." Turning to the king he winked. "Duke Baras is always much calmer after a good meal."

"Yes my liege." Thero answered as he bowed and turned to leave. As he turned, Theta put out his foot, forcing his brother to dance aside.

Shaking his head he turned to watch the boys. "Tell Marinor we'll have no wine; only beer is to be served. We will want Lord Baras' head clear for thought."

"Aye my lord," Thero replied as he exited.

Roehn, wanting to be alone with his confidant, looked over at Theta. "And you can go as well. Go find Sir Thesra and ask that he join us."

Theta nodded and hastened out of the room after his brother. It was apparent that he intended to catch Thero and continue their joust. Mitos smiled as he looked over at Roehn. "The twins are so very much alike…"

241

"I am sure both of them are quite anxious to see their father again." the King said as smiled at his friend. "It has been more than six months now."

There was a knock at the door then and Lord Mitos rose and turned to face it. "Yes?" he called out to the soldiers standing guard.

The door opened and Sir Thesra, general of the Montterran forces, stepped forward and into the room. Mitos nodded to the general and motioned him to enter.

"That was fast." Roehn said absentmindedly in greeting. "I only sent for you seconds ago."

"Theta just ran into me." Sir Thesra replied. "Literally." he added with a smile. "The lads were chasing each other down the hall and when they rounded the corner they both fell into me."

King Roehn chuckled as he visualized the lads crashing into the large, well-armoured knight that now stood before him. " I hope you cuffed them both on the back of the head and sent them off again." he said with a grin.

Mitos shook his head and resumed his seat. King Roehn motioned his general forward and pointed to a chair next to Mitos but Sir Thesra shook his head. "I would prefer to stand, if that's alright" the general said as he drew up in front of the desk.

King Roehn realizing again that his general was in full armour, nodded with understanding.

"I hope both lads still live?" Mitos asked dryly, looking over at the massive, steel-clad general. Large points issued from the generals knees and elbows and he was only now removing his helmet and his sharp, scale gauntlets, placing them all on the seat of the chair beside him.

Sir Thesra, having no great sense of humour, shot the Viscount a puzzled look, then, realising the man was joking, smiled in reply. "They do indeed live, though I had half a mind to send them to my sergeant for added duties."

"You should have!" King Roehn added encouragingly. "We should accelerate both lads' training…" He looked over at Mitos who nodded with understanding. "They obviously have too much time on their hands."

Turning abruptly the King switched gears and addressed Thesra again. "So what news do you bring then?"

"I was coming to inform you that the Duke of Capris was just sighted, not far from our gates."

"Well, some good news finally." said Lord Mitos as he turned to the king. "We will have this afternoon and evening to speak with both Karathor and Baras before Duke Sirthinor and Count Palatine arrive tomorrow."

King Roehn nodded in agreement. "And then tomorrow will be spent in convincing those two of the soundness of our plan. The general council can be held as scheduled the day after tomorrow." The king paused a moment. "Looks like you were right. It was a tight planning of dates, but with luck we will carry it off."

Lord Mitos smiled, and then turned back to the general. "Rumour has it," Mitos started, "that our friend Count Palatine has amassed quite an army as of late. Have you found out anything more as to the state of his defences?"

The general looked at Lord Mitos, then back at the king, and nodded. "The Margrave of Devmond is already here waiting for the General Council of Lords and has confirmed my suspicions. He is quite distraught that the Count, Lord Landor Rutt, who is his neighbour, has been hiring scores of archers."

"Count Palatine has been having some issues with coastal pirates." The king acknowledged, trying to think through why the Count, whose lands resided in the North-Western ranges, might be hiring large quantities of archers. "In our last meeting he mentioned that his merchant fleet was being raided, perhaps he is hiring them and putting them on his trade vessels."

"Perhaps," agreed the general. "However, according to the Margrave of Devmond the Count now has more archers than can fit on all his boats. The Margrave is a very nervous man these days and none too happy."

"Interesting," said Mitos absentmindedly as he licked his lips and continued thinking out loud. "Two of the five senior council members have been amassing soldiers for some time now… well in advance of the events in the east."

"The same two Lords," the king interjected in a slightly warning tone, "whom we need on our side in order to stand as one when we address the General Council."

Lord Mitos nodded understandingly at the king's undertone, but he did not give up his train of thought. He looked over to the general. "Have you heard anything more about the goings on in the South? What is our good friend Duke Sirthinor up to – how many ships and men does he really control now?"

"I have heard little – but hope to learn more when he arrives." the general replied. "Right now it seems either he has not been hiring as much as people are saying…"

"Or he's hiding his activities from us." Mitos said, finishing the thought the general had left unspoken.

The king, wanting to take the conversation into a more positive tone nodded enthusiastically. "Good for both of them General!" he said, looking over at Sir Thesra and then casting a pointed look of warning at Mitos. "We are going to need all of their forces and more for what we have planned."

"My hold over these few Lords is tenuous at best, they have grown strong these last few years and I did not put them back in place soon enough. As such our chore these next few days," King Roehn continued, "will be to convince both of these ill disposed lords that our direction is clear, that the course ahead of us cannot waiver and that all of these resources should be placed under your leadership, General. And we must with strength of conviction ensure that they all agree unanimously with the course of action when we present it to the General Council."

Sir Thesra nodded in agreement and then he looked over at Lord Mitos, who was also nodding his assent. "Before we finish, I should really tell you, the Margrave of Devmond would like to see you, your majesty," Sir Thesra said with a frown that showed more irritation than anything else.

"Why does he want to meet with the king before the council?" Lord Mitos asked in a perplexed tone, "to complain about the Count?"

The general shook his head. "I'm sure he will bring it up, but, that's not really why." The general hesitated a moment, cleared his throat and then continued. "It appears he is concerned that we have pursued men within his realm directly rather then to come to him first."

Mitos shook his head in bewilderment. "He will come to learn that for some things I will not wait, nor need I ask permission to pursue things within my own realm." Then curiosity came over him and he looked up at the general. "Whom did you send for?" Then laughing, he shook his head again. "Wait, don't tell me… I can guess. Why would the Margrave care about an old retired scout?"

"Insulted that I would rather have that man than come and seek out any of his own." Sir Thesra said, shrugging as he did so.

"I don't have time for petty squabbling." King Roehn said with finality. Turning, he nodded to Mitos. "Talk with him, placate the man. He just wants to be seen as being more important than he is."

Mitos nodded in reply to his king. "Done." he said, seeing that the King was uncomfortable with the conversation.

Roehn rubbed his temples wearily. "I'm already getting a headache from the politics of open court and we have yet to start the senior council. This is going to be a brutal two days."

Roehn looked up then and pointed at the Viscount. "Talk to ALL of the Lords and Barons before the general council – I want no bickering to deter our conversation from the important issues at hand. We have serious decisions to make. Ensure that they know in advance that we will be looking for each one of them to show how they can contribute in this situation and that favour will be given only to those that dig deep. There is no free ride to TerranAdd."

Mitos nodded. "I have already instructed some and will instruct the others as they arrive. All above the rank of Margrave will be housed within the castle, but all their entourages and all the Barons will be housed in the city. I have a list of where each will be and I will talk to them all before the general session."

"Thesra," Roehn said next. "Your task is to gain what insight you can from all the Lord's men as to the state of their armies."

Sir Thesra stood tall and brought his shoulders back as he nodded shortly, accepting his King's command in a more formal manner than was absolutely necessary within the close confines of the King's study. "Yes my liege. If I may, now that I have my orders I will take my leave. I want to be at the city gates to prepare for the arrival of the Duke of Oathos and Capris." Roehn nodded and Sir Thesra turned and exited the room, closing the door behind him.

Mitos turned and watched Sir Thesra exit, then looked back over to his King. "You need to be careful over the next few days. With all the Lords present it might be best to ask Sir Thesra to increase your personal guard – and we should look at other measures to ensure your safety and the safety of the other Lords. It wouldn't do us any benefit having duels break out in the city."

"Indeed." Roehn said, standing. "It is a shame that in days such as those before us we must guard our backs as well as we do our faces. Come now though, let us make our way to the senior council room to await the Dukes of Oathos and Capris."

Mitos nodded and together they turned and exited the room. The council chambers weren't far away, but the King had to stop a number of times to rest his leg. Mitos' concern for his King rose as he watched the strain on Roehn's face as they walked the short distance. Behind them, two guards followed at a distance.

The senior council chamber had been established in a small space at the back of the main citadel. The room itself had only one rectangular table in it. Roehn and Mitos entered without talking and the king proceeded directly to the head of the table, far from the door, as Mitos turned and closed it behind them, ensuring the guards were in position just outside.

An hour later the king and Lord Mitos were deep in conversation when there came a knock on the door. Both were surprised when Duke Hastor Karathor of Capris entered, having beaten the Duke of Oathos to the castle and to the meeting.

The Duke of Capris was still wearing his armour and riding gear and he appeared slightly out of breath. He looked almost as much a horse as a man when he entered, his face stern and clean-shaven and with a long mane of golden brown hair falling down his back. A few of his locks were braided and the ends were tied with coloured horsehairs, as was the tradition of the plains people of Piathis. The king rose to greet his old friend with a smile and a hug.

"We didn't expect you so soon." King Roehn said, looking the man up and down. "And I would have expected you would have met with your sons before coming to the council." he added. Looking back over at Mitos, who was standing just behind him, he paused a second in thought. "We should send for them!"

The Duke of Capris shook his head and the King saw small drops of perspiration on his brow.

Lord Mitos laughed as he stepped forward to extend a hand of greeting. "Sir Thesra should have known that a horseman of the south would not take long to make it to our gates."

"Especially when I heard that the Lord of Oathos might actually beat me here." Duke Hastor Karathor said with a laugh, finally gaining his breath. Then, turning back to his brother-in-law, he chuckled. "Sir Thesra made sure the rider sent to us let it drop that Duke Bethos was an hour closer to you than we were."

Duke Hastor took the King's arm and glancing only briefly down at his injured leg he then looked back up and smiled. Suddenly his eyes took on a pained look and his tone turned serious. "As I said in my letters, I will say again. If there is anything we can do to help find Elle…. anything…anything at all."

King Roehn nodded stiffly, trying to stifle his emotions. He motioned Duke Hastor to a chair. "Please sit down my friend – we have a great deal to discuss. There is much at stake here."

King Roehn sat down himself and then lifted the cane he had received from the man in acknowledgement. "Marvellous work." he said absently. "Quite thoughtful."

"It's nothing." Duke Hastor replied without changing his concerned expression. "You are looking better than when last I saw you."

"The King is much better." Lord Mitos interjected with an inflection that Duke Hastor picked up immediately.

"Of course." he replied knowingly.

Not more than five minutes later as the three men sat engaged in companionable small talk there came another loud knock on the door. When the King called for the door to be opened a short, stocky man sputtering from exertion entered. He looked wickedly at the Lord of Capris and then walked in quickly, making it to the King before Roehn could rise. "My liege," Duke Bethos of Oathos said as he entered. He immediately went to one knee and took the hand held out to him, kissing the ring.

"There is no reason for formality among friends." King Roehn said as he urged the Duke of Oathos to rise. "Come sit."

Duke Bethos walked around the table past the king over to Lord Mitos who stood and greeted him and then went back around to greet the Duke of Capris. "So Karathor, you just couldn't stand to be beat out by a Northerner, eh?" he said in a tone that was half joking and half serious.

Karathor stood and shook Lord Bethos' hand and greeted him with a smile and a laugh. "Never will it be said that any southern rider is anything less than twice as fast as our northern brothers."

Duke Bethos obviously now at ease, laughed and thumped the Duke of Capris on his shoulder with a short jab. "Well done, cousin." he added with a smile.

Both Dukes turned as the doors were opened once again and lunch was brought in. Three servants entered with tall plates of meats, bread and cheeses and behind the three stewards another followed with pitchers of beer and pewter steins.

"Ahh good!" Duke Bethos bellowed as he watched the men put the steins and beer on the table. "Nothing better to wash away the dust from the road." he said, reaching for the large pitcher.

"We have a long afternoon of talks ahead of us." chided the King in reminder as he watched his friend pour himself a large mug of ale.

The afternoon turned to evening as the senior Montterran lords discussed with their king the politics of the land. It wasn't until the wee hours of the next morning that they afforded themselves the luxury to retire so that they might be well rested when meeting with the other two members of the senior council.

The next afternoon, within the same chamber, all senior Lords were finally assembled and awaiting their king's arrival in order to discuss recent events and determine how together they might present their findings, decisions and requests to the General Council of Lords.

When King Roehn entered the room all the Lords stood and bowed and waited for him to greet them in turn. Lord Mitos watched closely the expression of the Duke of Sieren as the King passed by his chair and shook his hand. Sindor was just slightly taller than the Duke of Oathos but still an inch or two shorter than the king. Roehn purposefully stood tall and used his cane sparingly as he walked.

"How are you faring my liege?" Sirthinor asked with a tone that suited more of a conversation between peers then between a Duke and his lord.

"I am well, and you my good duke?" King Roehn replied without an inkling of emotion in his voice. He would not give the Duke the satisfaction of knowing that he had perceived the delicate slight just delivered.

"Very well," Sindor replied with a smile as he reached up and brushed back the dark black hair that had fallen down over his left eye.

Landor Rutt, Count Palatine of the NorWestern lands stepped forward. After bowing and kissing King Roehn's ring he stood back up and smiled. "It is good to see you my liege."

King Roehn gave the man a solid handshake. "You had the longest journey of us all, with the western passes now closed with snow, we are glad to see you."

Landor Rutt nodded. "It was my honour to come. We travelled by ship to the south-western coast, then rode east over the Serran mountains, whose tops are not yet covered in snow. And then east and north we went where we met up with Duke Sirthinor's caravan."

Lord Mitos smiled, knowing that King Roehn had already been aware of the Count's route and that he was only encouraging its repetition in order to make it clear to everyone that he was aware that Count Palatine and Duke Sirthinor had travelled together and that they were close allies and friends.

There was a pregnant pause as the message was delivered. Then the Duke of Capris broke the silence with a laugh. "Well I for one will never know why any man would travel by sail when he could instead have the company of a horse."

Sirthinor smiled slyly as he looked over and nodded to the Duke of Capris. "Not all of us prefer horse flesh above all others." he said dryly. "A few of us would prefer to spend a day under a sail riding a woman over a day in the saddle riding a horse."

Count Palatine laughed loudly at the joke, but although he bellowed, he could not entice the others in the room to follow suit. The Duke of Capris remained silent. The King smiled and nodded politely to Duke Sirthinor in recognition of the joke, but then moved around the table and purposefully took his seat.

"Thank you all for coming." King Roehn said quickly after taking his seat and motioning the others to join him. "We have much to talk about, so let us waste no more time. There have been quite a few changes in the east and we must discuss what strategy we plan to bring forth to the General Council to address them."

Sirthinor was the last to sit and chose the seat farthest from the King. To the left of the table's end sat Lord Oathos and to his right the Duke of Capris. Lord Mitos purposefully had chosen a seat that put him between Count Palatine and the Duke of Sieren.

Roehn looked around the table. "I'm certain that most of you have heard the rumours… and yesterday Lord Bethos informed me that others outside of our lands have already learned that TerranAdd has fallen and that Tar the Terran King is no longer unifying their lands. He believes that the Tock and the Masti will not wait long until they move to stake further claims on the lands of the east."

Roehn looked around the table, surveying his guests and judging their demeanour. After looking squarely at each man, he continued. "I have convened the senior council to ensure we have all agreed on a high level strategy prior to the General Council tomorrow. We need to ensure that our people feel a sense of unity in these trying times. We must emerge from this meeting today as one."

"We in the north are behind whatever plan you lay forth." Duke Bethos said, standing up to stress his point. The war hammer emblazoned on his tunic in classic northern style shone in the light as he leaned forward for emphasis.

When Bethos rose, the Duke of Sieren rolled his eyes skywards and sighed with exaggerated force.

Bethos cleared his throat. "The Northern men know the dangers posed by our foes and have rebuffed the Tock from our lands for decades. We will back any recommendation you make that will deliver a clear and decisive show of force to assure our people that we have the confidence to act."

"A show of force? " Landor Rutt asked curiously. "Do we fear the Tock and Masti now? Do we have now any clue as to what has really happened at TerranAdd – and who our foe is? Perhaps we should be shoring up the west and not the east – perhaps the Drekians have decided to bypass our lands and head further east? First let us know what foe is at our door, then let us talk of action." With his last words he looked at Duke Sirthinor who nodded in agreement but sat quietly.

Duke Karathor looked up at Duke Bethos, who, no longer quite so confident, sat back down. "Unless," he put in, "you have more information about the west Landor, there are few within this room who could be persuaded that the Drekians have returned. What most of us fear, but have not yet voiced, is that the Masti have risen again… or even worse, that the massive hand of the Mohen emperor is now stretching to the west. I would wager most within this room are worried about them and not the Dreks."

Roehn look over to his wife's brother and nodded slightly. Karathor, the Duke of Capris, was dressed in his normal, conservative grey tunic which bore a brown crest with a black stallion on a shield of silver. "Sir Thesra has confirmed that there have been strange occurrences and attacks in the Terran north… I have already talked with Bethos about sending some of his troops east to help those in Minon Ter. But my concern lies further east; the Masti WILL be looking to the south, and the Mohen to the west."

"Why would the Emperor now look west?" Duke Sirthinor asked bluntly. "When the old man hasn't been seen to have an ambitious bone left in his old brittle body. And don't say perhaps his son, for I hear Paxton prefers the pipe of dreams over the prospects of extending his father's domain of control."

"Besides," Count Palatine continued, convincingly carrying Duke Sirthinor's verbal charge, "the Temple Guard protects the north and the only one real door the Mohen have to the west is shut – bolted closed by PlanTer, which, as you know, houses the largest garrison of men the Terrans have and stands second to none in defences. And even the walls of SanTer that guard the great mines pale in comparison."

Duke Bethos realising that they were losing ground, looked over to Lord Mitos and then to the King.

Lord Mitos, seeing that Count Palatine and Duke Sirthinor were obviously working together in an attempt to move the senior council away from the action they knew the King was headed for, jumped into the verbal fray. "PlanTer is not so heavy a door, and the Temple Guard is much less than it once was. Tar Bestinor, the Terran King, is gone, as is the glue that holds those lords together, and his brother Methor was banished by his father to the south – not one of Tar's lords would follow under his banner. Should the Mohen or Masti march they will find little to no Terran resistance."

There was silence in the room as everyone paused, wondering who would speak next in an effort to stave off the impasse they were headed towards. The silence was broken by a knock at the door.

King Roehn looked up. "Enter." he commanded. As the door swung open Sir Thesra entered. The King motioned the general into the room. "I have asked General Thesra to give us a briefing of what our intelligence has learned. As you know, we sent the Fist to TerranAdd, however, we have not yet shared with anyone what they found when they arrived, or who they met along the way." The king paused as his general turned to face the Senior Council. Sir Thesra nodded to the king, then, standing with helmet held under his left arm, he started. "Simply put," he began, "the Terran lands have been greatly weakened. Our men rode to the capital and saw not one sign that there had been an attack – but not one soldier or civilian could be found alive nor dead within the city's walls."

"So the capital is secure now, the Fist are stationed there?" Landor Rutt inquired almost glibly. "Well then, that is good news - we have their capital and there is no foe to worry about… We should celebrate!" The count laughed but then choked his mirth when the King looked sternly at him….

"Please continue general," the king urged.

Thesra looked over at the Count and shook his head slowly. "The Fist was met by a company of over three hundred Tock who were riding down, likely to pillage the capital. Although my men bested a company thrice their size, they lost many."

"Alone they cannot hold the capital." Lord Bethos added as a matter of fact.

"They were never intended to hold the capital." Sir Thesra stated plainly as a reply. "They were sent as soon as we had word of the strange occurrences." The general turned and nodded to his King. "In part their mission was to return the princess, but they were also to investigate. Never did I think one hundred men could hold a city that size, even from a smaller company of Tock, let alone Masti or Mohen."

Lord Mitos watched Duke Sirthinor's expression keenly, noting that never once did the Duke look surprised by the news which they had kept secret until now. Count Palatine, however, was visibly shaken by the news and was looking questioningly back at the Duke of Sirthinor as if expecting him to reply.

Silence hung in the room until King Roehn spoke again. "Thank you General. Is that all?"

The general nodded and then snapping his heels together, turned and exited the room.

Bethos looked straight at the Duke of Sirthinor "We in Oathos are not quite as timid as you men are in the south. In a week or less my son and I will march to the east to help rebuff the Tock which are attacking MinonTer. For weeks already we have heard all manner of strange happenings and we will not leave people unprotected. Mark my words – this is but the start, and if the Tock pick up and ride south we will have our hands full."

Sindor Sirthinor 'tisked' and shook his head in bewilderment. He was a slightly built man, wiry, with the darker complexion common to those of the southern regions. He had shoulder length black hair and sharp looking features; his prominent nose was slightly bent and suggested the hard lines of a bird of prey.

The Duke of Sieren responded quietly, almost to himself. "The Tock are no more than vultures that smell blood. For all your bellowing of 'beware of the Tock' – I do not fear that they are a serious threat. They are merely riding south to pillage a city they have heard lies undefended. They are a scattered group of clans – no more. As for the Masti – the bloody Duke of TenTor's final act of genocide ended the Blood Wars. Too few of them remain to do much, and the Blood priests have all been hunted down by the Temple Guard."

"I still say there is nothing to fear in this, only opportunity to be exploited." Duke Sirthinor said slowly, looking around the room at the assembled men.

Bethos didn't look over at the Duke of Sieren, but rather, straight at Roehn. "The clans have been growing – they are strong and if the TeiRei, Count of MinonTer needs help, as we believe, then that means that the Duke of AnnonTer has his hands full with the Masti… for Rudolf's sister is TieRei's wife. He would not hesitate to help her if he could."

"All suppositions," Duke Sirthinor said viciously.

Bethos turned then, to acknowledge Duke Sirthinor. "My son and I will lead over two hundred and fifty knights, a thousand archers and a thousand infantry to the east – and still protect our own northern borders. What are you doing to protect our lands?"

Lord Mitos cleared his throat, stealing Duke Bethos' attention along with the others' in the room. He then looked over to the Duke of Sieren and Count Palatine. "What more proof do you need that we should direct the General Council of Lords to mobilize? Not one man among us disputes that TerranAdd has fallen – by what cause or to what foe we do not know. But additionally, although we hesitate to name it aloud, we also realize the great opportunity that this could represent to Montterran interests."

"There are rich lands to the east." Landor Rutt put in, almost too eagerly. "Their trade with the Farrows and Mohen…"

King Roehn had not wanted the conversation to turn mercenary in nature and he shook his head now, bringing Rutt's line of speculation to an end. "We were allies of the Terran people. We must first hold out our hand in friendship – not to usurp their lands when they are weak. We don't know for certain if Tar is gone. We must act as friends and extend our hand in aid."

"The same hope a father has for his daughter." Duke Sindor said in a low voice and all eyes turned to him. Duke Bethos and the Duke of Capris began to rise but King Roehn lifted his hands. "Keep your seats my lords." He commanded.

King Roehn smiled back at the Duke of Sirthinor and nodded. "A small hope, yes, but even should King Tar never return, I do not believe that his remaining lords will take it lightly if we start staking claim on their lands. With an unseen enemy; with the Tock, Masti and Mohen around us – we need to work together to shore up our defences."

"That's a significant risk for little gain." Landor Rutt said, looking back to the King. "Are you asking the Duke of Sieren and myself and all the other lords of the general council to risk our men, to open our purses to fund this venture… for NO gain? Then I say we should stay put and defend our own lands. Tar was a friend of yours – and you hope vainly that he will return with your lost daughter. I say there is little hope of that."

"Watch how you speak," the Duke of Capris said in a warning tone. "Never forget your fealty to your king."

Landor Rutt, shaken by the Duke's statement and tone, began to back peddle. "This is the Senior Council of Lords," he began with a slightly quivering and very defensive tone. "King Roehn has always asked us to speak our minds, to give him council as best we can."

"I tire of this." Bethos roared as his hand slammed suddenly on the table. "You both know that the Tock and the Masti are circling the lands, and you also know damn well that if PlanTer falls, the Mohen will walk right in and gobble up the Terran lands. You have all had it much too good. You know that the Mohen keep a short leash on local lords and taxes would be much higher if you had to bend your knee to the Mohen Emperor; what is it that you hope to gain out of inaction?" Then in a threatening tone he added. "And think my friends, what do you stand to lose?"

There was another long pause as everyone, including Count Palatine, turned and looked to Duke Sirthinor, awaiting his reply.

"I believe what Count Palatine is saying is that the General Council must be given some hope of potential future gain." With a silky voice the Duke of Sieren continued. "Should Tar not return, at minimum we must lay the grounds that after their investment of men and goods – restitution for the costs might be made from Terran coffers."

All eyes turned to the King. A moment later he nodded, but did not volunteer any additional comments.

"Then," Duke Sirthinor continued, "I believe we are in agreement in principle. It is the most honourable act to help one's neighbours. We will instruct the General Council that our efforts are to help them fend off the vultures." Then, turning to King Roehn he opened his hands, palms up, in a questioning gesture. "What would you have us do my King?"

King Roehn paused a moment. He, like the majority of others in the room, was in shock, totally surprised by Duke Sirthinor's reversal. The conclusion the Duke had come to was exactly what the King had desired. He had expected that he would have to make explicit and costly concessions in either lands or taxes before receiving Sindor's support. Part of him had even worried that his concessions would not suffice, and that he would need to threaten the Duke outright in order to receive his support.

Duke Sindor Sirthinor smiled calmly as the room stayed deathly quiet. Duke Bethos sat back down, totally speechless, as all eyes turned to the King.

King Roehn licked his lips and then replied in an even, unemotional tone. "With General Thesra's aid, Lord Mitos has defined a strategy that we believe will help the Terrans defend their soil, and yet not put our own lands at risk."

Duke Sindor turned smoothly to Mitos. "So then my dear Viscount, let us hear how we might help our friends in their time of need."

"Perhaps we could invite the general back?" Lord Mitos asked the King.

Roehn nodded and Mitos rose and went to open the door. The general, surprised at being called in so quickly, was slow in entering. When he did enter, he looked questioningly around at the Lords. Then from under his arm he took out a large map, which he hesitantly unrolled on the table.

The general pointed to the northern Montterran lands. "Lord Bethos has already committed what men he has to protect the north. He will head east to help in the defences of MinonTer against the onslaught of the Tock and shut their door to the south."

Turning to the Duke of Oathos he nodded and then continued, pointing to their capital. "I will lead what knights and men at arms we can assemble to defend TerranAdd." Then as he looked up to Landor Rutt he pointed to the north-western coastal area. "With reinforcements being supplied by Count Palatine and what other men at arms we can obtain from the other Lords within the general council." Looking up at the count he pointed to the map again. "Your men will need to follow the same route you took to get here, and then they will travel east along our supply route to TerranAdd, arriving there a few weeks later to defend."

The Count nodded curtly, but his lips were tightly sealed.

"We will need from you Lord Rutt," Mitos added as he looked directly at the Count, "as many archers as you can muster to defend the Terran capital's walls. They must move quickly to reinforce the general."

General Thesra looked over to Lord Mitos and the King, both of whom nodded, encouraging him to continue. Looking directly back up at the Duke of Sieren he continued to outline the plan. "PlanTer protects the only real passage through the eastern mountains and the roads from Mohen lands to TerranAdd. The Mohen's only alternative route is to attempt to slip around the south by ship. They would likely land at TenTor or SanTer. Our thought was to send men by boat from our southern shores to land at those ports. In this way the Mohen cannot circumvent PlanTer and should PlanTer be attacked we can quickly move some of these men north to assist in its defence."

Mitos looked around the table, but his eyes stopped when they circled back to the Duke of Sieren. "We hope to dissuade the emperor or his son from thinking this too easy an opportunity to miss simply by having our men in the Terran lands...as friends."

"And what of the Masti," Duke Sirthinor asked with a soft, but almost challenging tone.

Sir Thesra pointed to the northern Terran lands. "Once Lord's Rutt's forces arrive in TerranAdd I will move some men north to aid the defence of AnnonTer – thus completing the Terran defences."

Duke Sirthinor shrugged. "So then, what would you have of me and mine?"

Mitos rose from his chair and walked around the table to stand beside General Thesra. "We would like some of your ships to carry the Duke of Capris' men to SanTer; from there you will take your men and continue east to fortify TenTor. Both of you would then be in good position to send some of your forces north should we need them to protect PlanTer."

The Duke of Sieren looked over at the map without rising. Then with a smile he made a suggestion. "I would think it best if I stayed in SanTer and sent the good Duke of Capris on to TenTor. With his horsemen he would be in better position to ride quickly to the aid of those in PlanTer."

"After all," Duke Sirthinor added while looking back up at King Roehn, "if anyone has any chance of pulling together the Terran lords it will be Tar's brother, the great Methor Bestinor." The Duke smiled as he looked over at the Duke of Capris and then King Roehn, but there was no missing the icy chill in his voice. "And the future Terran King would likely receive your cousin better than he would receive me."

King Roehn's eyes never left Duke Sirthinor's gaze, yet in his peripheral vision he could see Lord Mitos shaking his head ever so slightly, warning his King not to take the offer.

King Roehn, however, had no ready excuse to offer Duke Sirthinor for his lack of trust, and so much depended on the Duke's assistance – without his ships they could do very little.

Without pausing further, King Roehn nodded. "Agreed – that seems best."

Turning, he looked over at the general and Lord Mitos. "Duke Sirthinor will entreat the Governor at SanTer and then head north when called. His ships, however, will move Karathor on to TenTor so that the southern horsemen can head north with all haste should they be called."

King Roehn looked at his cousin, the Duke of Capris. "You must entreat Methor Bestinor as my envoy – proclaim him the new Terran King. Perhaps our show of support will bring his own people forward to rally around his flag."

Karathor cast a suspicious look over at Sirthinor; he was obviously not convinced. Next he sent a questioning look over to Lord Bethos, who shrugged, not knowing what to say; the logic seemed plain. While fully five of the seven men in the room didn't want the Duke of Sieren anywhere near the fabled cliff mines, not one could argue against the logic put forward by the Duke.

All eyes turned to the Duke of Capris; he was well aware that now his agreement would seal the deal.

"It is highly possible," Sirthinor continued pushing his suggestion, hoping to crush what little hesitation still remained in the Duke of Capris' eyes, "that my ships will not even be able to dock at SanTer, for I hear that the governor there is not a trusting soul. I might end up having to keep all my men upon the boats – sailing around the southern shores protecting them from potential Mohen attacks from sea. The real question for you Karathor, is whether you would rather have your men and horses on a boat for this campaign or on solid ground – able to ride as you so love to do?"

The Duke of Capris conceded the point and nodded in final agreement. "Horses are better on land than water and I have heard the same of Carton Tunis' deep mistrust of outsiders." The tension around the table dissipated visibly.

"Done then." King Roehn added at last as he looked around the table to see if there were any other objections. "Our path is set." he said as he got to feet. Exhausted, the King grabbed his cane and then headed to the door.

Without turning King Roehn left the room and accompanied by his guards he made his way back to his private chambers. Entering the vestibule he instructed the guards and his page that he was not to be disturbed for the remainder of the evening.

King Roehn undressed and lay upon his bed, trying purposefully to push the events of the day, and the strain and stress he was currently feeling, away. Knots pained his neck and back and his head throbbed, but beyond that, the words spoken in that room had hurt him more than any there likely knew.

Over the last few weeks he had said so many times to others that they must keep their focus on the country, on the people, and not on the disappearance of his daughter. But not until this day, this last hour, had any other person spoken aloud what he feared most.

The King once again became merely the man and father. "So tired," he said softly to himself as he closed his eyes. He breathed deeply and willed his mind back to happy memories of his daughter sitting upon his lap. As he drifted off to sleep he smiled, remembering her voice and her soft touch upon his chest as she traced the unicorn.

A frozen scream

Etch looked down disappointedly at the cold, wet campfire, deliberating whether he should attempt to relight it or give up, break camp and share an apple or two with his horse and mule while riding. He rolled his head trying to relieve the stress-induced pain in his shoulders; spending the night sleeping on the hard rocks of the mountain road had not done his back or neck much benefit and the morning had come with fog and moisture that had saturated everything he wore, making him feel even more stiff then usual.

He looked down at the soggy remains of the fire and the stack of damp wood beside it and grumbled. "Damn mist," he said as he kicked the soggy sticks and coal.

"I'll be glad to get back into the forest," he continued, looking over at his two mounts, both in need of drying.

With the prospect of a warm breakfast unlikely Etch brushed down the animals and then packed the mule and re-saddled the horse. Taking a last look at his campsite to ensure he hadn't left anything behind he turned north, ready to set out and find the missing link and hopefully the answers to all the questions spinning around in his head.

Mule appeared eager for the trip. Choking up on the lead Etch reached forward and patted the horse's head "We're going back the way we came for a bit, then turning east." His tone was gentle and reassuring and the horse's ears turned forward; she nickered softly and butted his shoulder as if she understood his statement.

Looking back, Etch checked Peppy, who followed along behind, his lead tied to the saddle. "Just a ways further my mule and then through the forests south and east." Peppy, however, walked with head bent down, not seeming to care where she was being led.

Walking on the stony riverbank wasn't as painful as it had been; both Etch and the animals had rested and their footing appeared surer and less strained.

It wasn't until midday that Etch pulled out the string and stone Stymar had given to him. Closing his eyes he placed the stone in his uncovered hand and held it forward pointing due north. The stone warmed reassuringly as he started moving his arm to point south- east. Smiling he returned the stone to within his coat and patted his horse's neck – "Well Mule, looks like we have a direction. No idea how far, but at least we know which way."

Taking the animal's lead Etch crossed the bank and started pulling the animals into the forest. "We are going far, so until we are stopped for certain we will travel the way the crow flies," he said cheerily as he pushed aside a long spruce branch to enable the animals to exit the river's banks.

After an hour of hard pulling, with branches slapping and tearing at the animals, Etch stopped and after brushing them both down and ensuring they were secure he pulled out two blankets, which he draped over their sides. Then after checking them again, he continued forward, making slow progress through the dense forest.

Although Etch knew little of the dense, southern Fendly forests he travelled confidently, only occasionally checking his stone compass for bearings. He loved to walk in deep dark forests, for he found the stillness within them peaceful. The solitude made it seem as if the world was standing still, waiting patiently until such time as he would exit and enter once again the open world and civilization.

The day slipped away in twig and branch crunching strides. Although Etch found little difficulty in navigating through the branches, his horse and mule did not appear to enjoy walking in dim light over large roots and branches. As the afternoon's light dissipated their objections to his steady pulls increased. "I know it's tough walking, but we need to do better tomorrow," he said in a chiding voice before pulled off their protective blankets in preparation to stop for the day.

With mule and horse unloaded Etch pushed together a large pile of pine needles and made himself a soft bed under the long heavy bows of an evergreen.

"Much better than last night," he thought as he piled up more pine under the low hanging branches and against the sap-sticky trunk.

After stretching and checking the animal's leads he crawled under the branches to his new, soft bed and breathed in deeply the relaxing pine scent. Deep sleep came to him quickly and soon the sounds of the woods were accompanied by his loud snoring.

The next day proceeded as the first one had, as did several days that followed. The slow, monotonous walk under branch and over root would have worn down most men's minds to the point of exhaustion – but not Etch. For Etch each valley, each tree covered hill, held unique sights and each night brought to him a soft bed filled with the fragrances of the forest.

On the fifth day Etch woke to find the forest had changed overnight, from dark to light as an evening's heavy snow drifted down and through the tree overhang to rest in open patches on the ground around him. Feeling that change was in the air, he pulled out the stone and checked his bearings, somehow, he felt inexplicably closer. "Closer," he said in a reassuring tone to himself trying not to now figure out why he had such feelings.

The touch of winter was light in the south and as the sun rose to its apex most of the snow melted. It's appearance, however, had made the animals within the forest nervous. Just after mid day, when Etch was about to go once again into his pack for some hard tack and bread, he almost tripped over a pair of rabbits who were panicked by his steps. Knowing that had it not snowed the previous night the rabbits would have let him walk right by their burrow, the consummate hunter exploited their panic-stricken dash and with quick moves and deft hands caught one in each hand. Smiling, and feeling a sense of accomplishment and confidence Etch settled down early to make a hearty stew that he feasted on well into the night. As he bedded down that evening he somehow knew that by the end of the next day's travel they would be exiting the forest and that a change in scenery awaited him.

Etch was accurate in his assumption, and on the next day the forest thinned considerably. The open sky was a welcome sight, as was the scent of the sea, which inspired both him and his beasts of burden. Together they tripled the distance they travelled that day and by evening they were standing on the southern shores overlooking the Old Woman's Reef. To their immediate east were the cliffs that marked the Old Man's peninsula. "Good news girls," he called over to Mule and Peppy as he walked to the pebbled shore and reached down to touch the salty water. "Unless what we seek is in the sea or across it, it won't be too far now!" Returning to the horse and mule he started leading them quickly up the shoreline.

The southern shores rose up, slowing them only slightly but giving them an ever increasingly grand view of the Sea of Capitherous. When they finally reached level ground they could make out the full breadth of the peninsula as it extended down and into the sea.

Half way down the peninsula's western ridge Etch realised he had made a mistake. They had been following a man made path that had been worn into the cliff's edge by travellers who had needed to get around the coastal shores. The peninsula itself, however, was shaped like a hollowed out log or boat. If what they sought were within the peninsula itself, then they would need to depart the nice path and climb down the inner walls in order to reach the interior.

Etch pulled out his compass stone and cringed when it confirmed his suspicions. "We are going to need to either backtrack or descend," he said as he pulled Mule off the trail and moved away from the seaward cliffs to the drop off that would lead them down to the heart of the peninsula.

Before starting down the sharp incline Etch took one last, longing look at the peninsula's southern end. Seagulls flew above the cliffs, occasionally landing to nest upon its walls. Their calls were compelling, as if they were trying to dissuade him from his new course. Further out he could see the calm turquoise waters stretched out, smooth as glass until they reached the distant reefs.

Etch let the sunshine warm his face one last time before he got off Mule and started heading east. "Down we go," he said to the animals, hoping to keep them calm as he noted that the incline was steeper than he had hoped.

"Back to the darkness, eh Mule?" He asked as he turned after only a few steps to look back at his horse. Mule now stood with her hind legs almost a meter higher then her forelegs. Her coat was already matted with strands of moss that they had met part way down the incline. "Sorry, but it can't be helped!" he called back to Peppy who had as of yet not started his descent.

"With any luck it will flatten out soon," Etch said without much conviction as he turned and looked down the moss-covered slope that was shrouded with trees.

The descent was nerve-racking, for each step had to be tested out. The ground beneath them was soggy and soft. Etch pulled on the lead and the horse and mule followed behind him after he tested each step and sought out the best places to turn in order to wind their way slowly down the slope. It was tough going, especially for the trailing mule, who acted as an anchor for the threesome.

An hour later when they had still not reached the bottom of the slope Etch stopped and wiped the sweat from his face and head. The two animals behind him were panting with exertion and stood precariously, almost resting their rears against the ground.

Taking a breath Etch turned and took another step forward and pulled on the lead. He didn't even have a moment to turn before his arm was being yanked down. His horse lost her footing and began to half run half fall down the incline.

One moment he was looking forward, the next Etch was tumbling head over foot, banging off of trees and branches with his hand still clutching the reins. After his third impact with the ground he let go, but by then the cords had been pulled tight and they now held his wrist firmly. As a large tree knocked the remaining consciousness from his skull his last fear was that he would be making the trip all the way down to the bottom in tow behind his horse and under his mule.

Much later Etch's woke up, dazed and aching, with a dislocated arm pointing straight up to the moss filled canopies of the peninsula's valley. Still tethered to his twisted arm were Mule's reins. The leather lead was pulled excruciatingly tight and his fingers were blue from lack of circulation. Beyond the lead stood Mule, looking woefully down at him. She too looked weary, bruised and dazed. With eyes still blurry, Etch turned to his side, then with a lurching roll he launched himself forward. The lead snapped as Mule retreated instinctively, and her hard pull did the trick; with a resounding snap Etch's shoulder was relocated.

Pain erupted up his neck, down his back and into his brain, pushing him back towards the darkness and oblivion of unconsciousness. Holding on to his senses Etch turned his hand and pulled on the tether, freeing himself from the lead. His blue hand burned as blood returned and began to throb painfully. Content with his move he fell backward onto the soft mossy ground and let the darkness consume him.

Etch was woken by Mule who after a few minutes started licked his face and neck. "Bugger off." He groaned at the horse. "Let me die." He said as he opened his eyes to look around as to where they now were.

Mule butted Etch's head with her own as if testing if he was really awake. He reached up and patted her rumpled main, which hung down low over her eyes. "Sure drag me along with you." He said sarcastically to her. He grabbed firmly a hold of her main and instinctively the horse's head rose, pulling him to his knees and then feet. He reached up and patted the animal with his unhurt left hand. "I forgive you." He said to the animal in a mocking tone.

Etch barely was able to stand. He looked around while leaning heavily on the horse. Behind them both stood Mule – also still alive. Crossing the fingers in his good hand he slowly knelt down and inspected their legs.

"Thank my lucky stars." He said after checking out the last of eight equine legs. "No breaks." He immediately pulled off the saddles of the animals and checked their ribs... Contented that that would live and were even possibly in better shape then he was he sat down and removed the small pouch of herbs from under his jacket; he put a pinch of Tygor leaf between his lips and gums. Comfort came quickly to him, but beyond being able to unpack and drink some water he did little before slumping down into a drug induced haze and falling asleep.

The morning never appeared to fully arrive, 'or perhaps' thought Etch, 'my eyes are still fuzzy from the leaf'. Still very sore, and not desiring to rise he decided to wait a while to see if the day would turn brighter. He lay there on the soft ground for two more hours before he resigned himself that day really was upon them and that it was not going to get brighter where he now lay. Groaning he rose and while rubbing his eyes he peeked out through his fingers to look around at the dark mossy patch of earth that the threesome had ended up on.

He could see no farther than ten meters, for a multitude of long strands of dark moss descended from the extremely thick, branch and moss covered canopy above them.

Standing unsteadily he checked over the horse and mule once again, shaking his head as he did so. Both were badly bruised, their coats had long deep scratches down them, and their legs and feet looked tender, but as he had first observed neither were in too serious a condition.

Shrugging he rolled his shoulders. Although sore, he too was in 'repairable' condition.

"You girls OK?" He asked as he patted them down and checked their scratches. Down Mule's left foot there was a nasty deep gash he had not seen the previous day. Although it was already filled with congealed blood he cleaned it as best he could, packed with mud and moss and then tied up with a strip of cloth he pulled from his bag.

Contented that he could do no better for himself or his animals he focused on his quest and pulled out the guide stone. "Warmer."

269

He said as he smiled noting the direction it now pointed was due south. "It can't be too far." He said reassuringly to himself and the animals.

The valley floor was warm and little air moved within it. A small trickle of water could be heard in the near distance so Etch took hold of the mains of both animals and led them forward. Together they found a small pool that sat under a slow, but steady trickle of water that flowed down from the side of the cliff. Tasting it Etch verified that it was fresh and then allowed the animals to drink deeply. He splashed water on his face and neck before returning to drag their bags over to their new spot.

With his internal clock once again functioning Etch realized the day was almost spent. Still sore he resigned to spend another day in rest. However, promptly as the first light of day reached down through the moss he rose. After checking to ensure the animals were ok took out the stone and with nothing more than a dagger and a small leather skin filled with the sweat water he had just found he set off.

The path twisted and turned through the massive moss covered trees. Etch walked slowly sometimes using his dagger to cut his way through tighter stretches of moss. After a few hours he entered a small clearing, the trees above were less dense and sunlight sparkled down. He stepped forward and raised his face to the sky letting the warm rays warm his tired and bruised body. After a few moments of pause he opened his eyes. Skeletal remains of a very long reptilian creature lay almost concealed by moss in the clearing, its white bones poked up and through the moss, having long since been picked clean by insects.

"A year at least," Etch said looking over at the skeletal remains, "perhaps two." He said looking around now much more concerned about his own safety and wondering if he should have brought along his bow.

Hesitating a moment longer he looking at the reptilian bones. Deciding not to turn back to retrieve his bow he stood up and started forward, however, his dagger now was held tighter within his right hand.

His walk down the long peninsula continued to be uneventful, and almost pleasant. The ground was soft and easy to walk upon and whenever he grew tired he could find a soft place to sit down and rest. He stopped frequently to nurse his shoulder and bruises however never lingered long for the air was stiffening still and dank. By mid-day he had reached the peninsula's end and found himself walking out from a curtain of moss into an opening that ended in tall cliffs, pockmarked with caves.

The heat of the open area hit Etch like a sledgehammer. His nose hairs tickled in reaction to the sudden and drastic shift in temperature made him sneeze. The sneeze was followed by a dry cough for the air he now breathed in was burnt, almost voided of moisture and contrasted dramatically that which he had just left. He stood uneasily looking up at the tall cliffs at first thinking to sit down so that he could admire them without straining his neck, however, no longer was there soft springy moss beneath his feet instead dusty, hard packed sand exuded heat up and through the soles of his leather boots.

"Wow." Etch swore silently as he looked out at the opening covered in sun bleached sand. His eyes followed the cliff at the end of the valley up; up they rose to meet the sky. "Wow," he said again, as he removed his compass stone from his pocket.

"So, where are you?" Etch he said as he held it out. The walls of the cliff echoed his question eerily back to him as he stepped out from the shade of the trees and into the hot clearing.

With fingers tightly clutching the stone, he closed his eyes and started moving his hand out in front of him. Back and forth and up and down his arm went. At first, because of all the heat around him, he wondered if he was going to feel anything... But that thought only lasted a second as the stone quite suddenly, and very dramatically heated up.

Leaving his hand still extended Etch opened his eyes and found himself looking up to a small cave situated almost in the middle of the cliff face – it was almost fifty meters up off of the ground.

271

"How I in the hell will I get up there?" He asked himself as he lowered his hand.

Taking a few steps closer he looked up and yelled. "HELLO!" The cliff and valley echoed back his call. He waited a moment and then called out again, even louder. "HELLO, HELLO... ANYONE HOME IN THE CLIFF?"

His words echoed back again eerily, but beyond the echo there was no reply. "Great." He mumbled, realizing that his luck wasn't quite holding out as well as he had hoped.

Etch walked back and forth under the cliff looking up and down trying to map out how he was going to ascend. He shrugged his shoulders and rubbed his hands, hoping that they had the strength and now feeling much happier that he had rested well before continuing his journey. However, he realized he couldn't spend too long below the cliff for the air was hot there, and as he wiped sweat from his brow he realized that his water was almost spent.

After picking his route Etch walked back to the tree line and picked up a dried out branch that had fallen some time past. He then pulled out a thin leather string and after ripping off his sleeves, tied them both to the stick. Etch pushed the stick into his belt and headed back to start his climb.

He worked slowly and methodically up the sheer face trying never to put too much strain on his slowly healing shoulder. The cliff afforded him only small thin footholds and his fingertips were soon cut and bleeding.

"This had BETTER be worth it." He swore as he climbed with unfaltering determination.

It took him a long time to scale up up to the cave. Taking a deep breath, Etch finally pulled himself up on the ledge and sat for a moment looking down. He let both legs dangle as he regained his strength. After drinking the last of his water he tossed the leather drinking skin down to the floor of the valley. He counted as the skin fell, confirming to himself that had he fallen, he would not have survived.

Licking his lips as he rose again he pictured the small pool of water in the dark, mossy valley where he had left his horse and mule. "They better not drink it all before I get back." He said to himself as he turned to face the darkness of the cave.

Just as he had suspected after ten or more steps the cave closed in on him and grew dark. Kneeling, Etch placed the cloth tied small branch that he had dragged up to the cave on a small flat stone and pulled out from under his vest his flint. In three fast strikes the cloth was burning. Looking up, Etch knew he didn't have much time so he started forward into the darkness.

"Hello, anyone there?" He called tentatively out as he moved as quickly as he could forward and deeper into the cave. His voice echoed back revealing to him that the cave was long and deep.

As the cave narrowed and dropped in height he grunted as he crouched and then crawled forward.

"Hello, anyone there?" He said again and again as the passage continued to narrow. Etch frowned, as the torch flickered. Not having anything else to use he ripped of his other sleeve and quickly bound it around the sparking branch. The embers of the dieing flame caught hold of the slightly damp cloth and started to burn slowly. He was however, confident for the cave appeared to run in a single direction and he felt should his light die he would be able to retrace his steps.

After another two steps Etch paused and held the sputtering torch behind him having noted a faint glow ahead of him. The passage ahead however, was narrower still. As the torch again sputtered and started to die he resigned himself to the darkness and decided he would proceed a bit further to investigate the glowing object ahead. 'If he found nothing' he thought, 'he would need to go back down and make many more torches prior to coming back up.' He cringed at the thought of descending and then re-climbing with more branches in tow.

Just as Etch was convinced he could crawl no further the cave opened up. Moving to a small crouch he crawled forward to inspect the strangely glowing object that had drawn him deeper into the dark cave.

His first thought was that the small glowing object before him was nothing more than a moss covered stalactite. But as he drew nearer he noticed that the object was made all of shadowy white, semi-translucent ice and that the illumination he could see, came from deep within it.

Going with a hunch Etch pulled out the stone once again. "Weird." Was all he said as he confirmed that the stone definitely was indicating that the strange piece of ice before him now was what he had come all this way for!

Deciding to make the best of it he crouched down trying to figure out how he might get what was before him out of the cave so he could have a better light in which to inspect it with.

Keeling before it he reached out and touched it. Immediately his fingers felt deathly cold, he yanked back his fingers and rubbed them. "Ok, now that is downright freaky." He said as touched his still frozen fingers to his lips so that he could breathe warm air upon them.

"Unnatural…" He said rhetorically as he contemplated the source of the coldness.

The ice encased stalactite, shimmered in spots, but in other areas it was opaque – however he quickly realised that above all – all of it was very, very cold.

"Too cold," he said to himself as he noted that his breath would even fog when he was near it, although the air in the cave was cool it was still much warmer than the object in fact, it was almost as if the object was cooling down all the air within the cave!

Leaning closer he tried to look within the spots that appeared icy clear. Bending right up he peered in but then quickly pulled back startled by what he had seen. Beneath the ice had appeared before him a frozen, open eye. Etch looked at the now discernable ice clad creature and sat down on the cold, hard cave floor trying to determine his next steps. The base of it was wide and frozen to the floor.

Bending forward his hand brushed the ground; dust and pebbles parted …"Freaky." Etch said again as he felt with his fingertips something below the dust. In the gloomy darkness, lit only by a small faint glow that emanated from the statue his hand moved brushing back and touching the cut stone and earth that encircled the frozen statue.

Etch then sat back and tried to retrace with his mind, what his fingers had felt. After a few frustrating moments Etch realized that what was cut was either nothing at all, or symbols that represented a language he had never seen before. After a few minutes of thinking he decided that his options were limited. Pulling out his dagger he started scratching and chipping at the symbols – deliberately obliterating them.

As he completing the destruction of the symbols the ice statue shook visibly and seemed to glow brighter. Pausing he reached out to touch it but drew back his hand when the glow increased to a bright light. Wincing he shut his eyes as the ice statue flashed and then shattered sending shards of ice at him. Etch had instinctively closed his eyes, but the light had been spectacular and as he opened them up he saw nothing but spots.

He sat motionless for a minute doing nothing but blinking. Finally he concluded that he had either been blinded, or what little light had come from the ice before him, was no more. Tentatively he reached forward to where he remembered it sat.

Moving along the ground he brushed aside ice and dirt until he felt where he had used his dagger to chip away at the symbols. Then slower still his hands groped forward. Instead of ice, rock and coldness, however, his hands touched something wet and soggy. Flesh, still freezing cold… but flesh and … hair!

Elated and still scared that he had might have done something very wrong Etch picked up the still frozen creature that had once been encased in ice. Turning in the darkness he started crawling back from whence he came. Twice he had to crawl backwards dragging the cold and wet creature over the rocks and dirt behind him. But after much struggle he was at the cave entrance, and with the light of the afternoon sun was able to get his first real look at it.

The creature resembled a girl, frailer than his daughter but have approximately the same height. She was dressed in drenched and freezing cold wet leathers, and her short cropped blond almost white, matted, wet hair hung down just covering her eyes and ears. Etch reached up and pushed back her hair to get a better look at her face and noted that the tip of her ears were pointed.

The creature was still, deathly still and Etch felt suddenly sad wondering that if in his haste he had killed that which he had toiled to find. He drew the creature in to his chest and holding her tightly closed his eyes, hoping to feel her stir.

Not feeling anything he pulled her back and looked at her face, bending down to see if he could sense breath coming from her nose. Just as he bent forward to see if she was breathing her emerald sparkling eyes opened and she began to sputter.

Startled Etch's head snapped back as the creature took broken, sharp breaths of air. Then as it's breathing turned to gasps it started shivering, and then shaking

"We need to get you to a warmer spot." He said finally after a moment holding the small creature. "You are wet and too cold." "If we get down the cliff I can make a fire." He said looking down at it.

Etch peered down over the edge of the cave to the valley floor far below them concerned as to how to proceed. "Think you can hang on to my back?" He asked, wondering if the creature even understood his language.

The creature's blond, wet hair hung down almost covering her eyes. She nodded and then as quickly as a cat twisted and turned in his arms. With startling speed she was around him in the blink of an eye. With her arms draped over his shoulder and legs wound round his waist she whispered one single short word…. "Go".

The climb down was harrowing. Although the creature weighed virtually nothing compared to Etch, the bundle on his back still made it difficult to balance and move from foothold to handhold and his shoulders and hands were still very sore. Twice he lost his foothold and thought that they would both fall to their deaths. However, fortune continued to smile down to him and as the last of the light of the day disappeared they were on the floor of the clearing below the cliffs.

With the creature still on his back Etch moved quickly heading back to his camp, realizing that all his supplies, herbs and blankets were back where he had left the mule and horse.

The creature remained quiet as he jogged through the moss-covered vines. Almost total darkness made the tip difficult and slow and it was late into the night when finally the two returned to the camp and during all this time the girl moved little. Quickly he set her down and then pulled a blanket out from his bag and draped it around her as he turned to find wood dry enough to burn. A few minutes later they both sat beside a roaring fire.

Etch pulled some hard bread from his bag and handed her some and the two ate ravenously. "My name is Etch." He finally said as the creature looked up from her food to him. Her emerald eyes sparkled reflecting like a cat the light of the fire.

"Dimi," the creature replied back with a soft voice. Pausing a second she then added in an almost inaudible tone. "Thank you."

Etch nodded but didn't volunteer anything more. Knowing that when the creature was ready, if it wanted to, it would tell him why she had been sitting frozen like a stick of ice in a cave.

Dimi looked down at her fingers and hands, they were white and shaking. Etch looked over and offered her a drink from the cup he had just refilled with water from the pond.

"Want more water? Its warm." Dimi shook her head and Etch noted a small tear had formed in her eyes and she started to shiver. She drew up her knees to her chest and lowered her head and started to sob.

"That must have been unbelievably torturous." Etch said with as much empathy as he could muster. Then deciding that perhaps it was best now to ask, he did. "How long?"

Dimi's didn't look up, instead she shook her head lightly back and forth and her shoulders rose and sank indicating that she had no idea.

Etch looked around but with the light of the fire, he could see nothing more than a meter around them... the small circle of light that they sat within was warm and gave him a sense of serenity. The valley was deathly quiet and only disturbed by their movements and by the crackling of the fire.

"You ok? Etch asked with a soft tone. "Want some more to eat?"

Dimi looked and nodded at Etch who then handed her what was left of his last piece of bread.

Every few moments she shivered and drew her knees closer to her as she nibbled on the hard, crusty bread.

"You said your name was Dimi?" Etch prompted.

Dimi nodded, but remained silent.

Etch walked over to his bag and pulled out piece of dried meat from his bag and held it forth but Dimi shook her head. However, when he pulled out two carrots she lunged forward, grabbed them and started chomping fiercely on them.

"Hey, slow down. You will give yourself a tummy ache!" He said as if he were talking to a child.

Dimi gave him a flash of her eyes and they were filled with anger. "Not a child; likely much older than you!"

Etch cleared his throat. "Sorry." He began. "A friend of yours Stymar sent me to find you. The lady is old and wise I wouldn't be surprised if she somehow knew you were in trouble." Etch started looking at Dimi as she chomped on the carrots.

Dimi looked up hesitantly to Etch who took a bold step and said the lady's name, hoping for recognition and a response from the creature before him, "Stymar?"

Dimi nodded slightly but remained silent.

Etch looked at Dimi wondering just how old this creature was. At first glance he had thought her a child, but given her comment and now that he had seen deep within her emerald eyes, he suspected she was much, much older than he had first assumed.

Dimi shivered again and her teeth started to chatter. She pulled herself closer to the fire.

"What happened to you?" Etch asked.

Dimi looked up with suspicion in her look and didn't respond.

Etch smiled to reassure her then continued his tale. "She gave me something to help find you. She said she couldn't leave her home. You see this little stone." Etch pulled out the stone and held it lightly in his hand and then pointed it at Dimi.

Dimi looked up shaken and turned and backed away slightly. Etch realizing his mistake lowered the stone and put it back in his shirt. He then raised both hands in a gesture of peace. "It won't hurt you." He said reassuringly. "It just gets warm when it points at you."

Dimi looked a moment at Etch and then relaxed and moved again closer to the fire. "I am just a little shy of magic right now, that's all."

"And what a surprise I get, finding you - deep within the cave, frozen…" Etch continued with a half laugh, "especially since it wasn't that cold back there."

"There were symbols cut around you that I destroyed with my knife. Magic symbols I assume?"

Dimi nodded slowly but kept her gaze on the ground. She then moved closer still to the fire and let the blanket drop off from her shoulders so that she could use the flames to dry off.

Etch noted Dimi's back. The leather had a slit in it. At first he thought it had been cut for around the slit there was blood. However, as he looked closer he noticed that the two parallel cuts in her leather vest were exactly the same size and they had been stitched open.

"Are you hurt? Want me to take a look at it?" He asked as he pointed to the spots of blood on the back of her vest.

Dimi, looking back over her shoulder at Etch lowered her shoulder to take a glimpse of her own back. "I'll be fine," She replied solemnly, "I heal fast."

Etch shrugged in reply. "Just trying to help," he said casually.

They sat for moments in silence watching the crackling fire. Etch threw on some greener, mossier pieces to slow it down hoping to build up coals for the night, but the greener wood smoked burning their eyes and lungs. Coughing, Etch pushed the greener wood out of the fire and then tossed in a few larger drier pieces.

As if he could read her mind Etch smiled and calmly asked her. "Any idea how long you were in there?"

Dimi looked around her. Surveying the trees and moss trying to remember what they looked like when she had entered the cave. Trying to judge how long she had been frozen. Her voice, although still slightly rough was still the lightest and most musical voice Etch had ever heard, "years."

"Something was carved in the stones around you." Etch added. "The cave was dark so I couldn't see what it was, I tried to figure it out by touch but never seen the like before. Those were magical symbols kept to trap you there frozen, weren't they?"

Dimi nodded. "Magical runes, she froze me with a curse and then place the runes around me to keep me frozen."

"Why?" Etch asked slowly and with care.

"Mad, ugly, evil woman, she wanted me alive and conscious while she hurt me. Then likely as not, she thought it was more torturous to leave me frozen for all time then to simply kill me."

Etch looked away and then scratched his chin and then rubbed his baldhead. "Stymar told me a tale about a female mage that was turned mad and disfigured by an old wizard."

Dimi looked up, "I knew Sarta, long time ago she wasn't as mad. She had periods of calmness and lived almost at peace with her infliction. Kaynor was the one that 'changed me' so we had a common bond – she never so much as said a bad word to me in the past."

"Stymar says that her continual consumption of blood further corrupts her soul, that and it draws her closer to the favour of the god of Chaos."

Dimi's eyes flickered for a moment with that same fire. Etch catching the response pushed. "Evil has now fully consumed her if she worships Andarduel ."

"Stymar sent you to me?" Dimi asked as she held her feet closer to the flames. She winced and shrugged as she twisted.

Etch noted as she moved that her back had indeed been wounded and although it wasn't bleeding now, it had bled at one time. "Are you sure I couldn't help you by looking at your back?"

Dimi eased slightly then nodded. Etch pulled some cloth from his bag and walked behind her. He opened up the flap at the back and turned her so that the light from the flames could illuminate the situation.

"Bad cut," Etch said. He doused the cloth with a little water and gently wiped it. "But it looks like the skin is binding already.... When Stymar sent me south... I don't know. I guess I feel now that perhaps she also knew you might be in trouble, but couldn't leave herself to free you."

Dimi shrugged. "Like I said, I heal fast. But my wings won't return, they are lost and that loss won't quickly heal."

Etch paused a moment and then returned to his bag not quite knowing how to respond.

Etch prompted. "Where do you come from?"

Dimi visibly relaxed and then licked her teeth. Reaching down to the ground she picked up a small twig and started rubbing her teeth with it. In-between strokes she spoke. "Originally a small village in the far north east in the shadow of Kaynor's castle and power. One day he came to town and said he wanted a pixie for his garden, something he had seen 'elsewhere'. He spied me out and cast a spell upon me and then made me his servant. I tended his gardens. I ran when he left to pursue Sarta."

"Fables made real." Etch said looking at the diminutive little lady. "He gave you wings, how amazing." Etch added in an envious tone. "What's it like to fly?"

Dimi smiled a sad smile. A small tear formed in her eye and she brushed it away. "The transformation was brutally painful, and my change wasn't instantaneous. I wouldn't wish it upon anyone." Then looking back she shook her head. "They were more for show then function. I could get off the ground a bit, but I couldn't stay aloft very long."

"But I did grow accustomed to them, and I paid for them with pain so with pain I will return the favour."

"Why would she come after you, after all these years?" Etch asked in a confused tone.

Dimi smiled. "I don't know, my wings were magical transformation, perhaps she wanted to learn more by studying them."

"You also heal very fast." Etch said, "and you appear still very young yet you have said you have lived many years."

Dimi nodded. "Perhaps she hopes to unlock that secret to lessen her own curse. She sure was a foul creature, decayed and decrepit.

The years of blood drinking consumption has rotted her from the inside out."

Pausing a moment Dimi remembered the small creature. "There was something with her. Something I have never seen in all my years. An imp, a creature small even compared to myself with small horns, whipping tail and very hard dark skin. She called it Keek."

"Something from another plane perhaps," Etch added in a knowing way to impress his new acquaintance.

"Stymar told you of the doors, did she?" Dimi added in reply smiling. "Yes, from what I overheard in the gardens below the master's towers I would assume you are correct."

"We think it was Sarta," Etch added. "with the aid perhaps from those other realms. That whisked away all the people from an entire large city."

Dimi shivered. "The pain I endured, awake and frozen for so many years was immense. You cannot imagine the bite of burning cold that I have endured for so long I will not rest until she is paid back in kind."

They sat for many minutes in silence before Etch spoke again. "Our path appears linked, our quest similar. Given all that I have heard I fear Sarta is behind other troubles that have touched this land. Perhaps we can aid each other in what we both seek?"

Dimi smiled and nodded. "Sarta is beyond saving, beyond hope. Her corruption is complete, she is evil. But if she worships Andarduel and has the aid of the Masti she will not be easy to find nor kill." Slowly she looked back deep into Etch's eyes. "Are you there to the end whatever it might be?"

Etch nodded slowly and then reached forward and threw another few logs on the fire building it us and making the small clearing brighter.

She then smiled wickedly as her eyes narrowed and her lips drew tight. Very slowly she spoke, concentrating on each word Etch could feel the passion within her thoughts. "I will have to think of some nasty nasty poison to make her departure slow and torturous. And when she finally is dead, I will rip off her arms and beet Keek to death with them."

With eyes wide shut

With eyes pressed tightly together Miathis desperately tried to convince himself that he was not actually in a barrack in Terran Add, but rather in a boarding room at the Porker Barrel. He sought solace in his waking dream and forced his mind deeper and away from total consciousness. Perhaps if he really, truly believed he was there he would indeed find himself waking up to hear the familiar sounds of patrons calling for their morning eggs. He smiled as his mind's eye pictured Bess running back and forth in the pub below with stacks of sausages and bacon.

Miathis found himself mentally reaching out to her; as if he might catch the dream and make it a reality. However, a deep-throated snore broke the silence and pulled Miathis rudely back to a wakeful state.

Finally opened his eyes he lay there a moment longer looking up at the rough-hewn wood that comprised the barrack's ceiling. The Terran wood was full of knocks making the ceiling above look as if hundreds of faces looked down at him....

"Another day rises." He whispered to the faces above him. Although his words were as quiet as a breath the snoring in the bed across the room stopped abruptly.

Tunder's snore rolled into a throat clearing croak signalling his waking, a moment later the bed on which he rested creaked as he stretched and then sat. "I checked with the sentries an hour ago, everything is quiet and two of the scouts reported back saying it is dead quiet out in the surrounding fields."

"Too quiet." Miathis said as he rolled over and pushed himself up and out of bed. "I didn't sleep as well as I thought I would. I was dead tired, but the stillness of this city made me ill at ease last night. At first I couldn't figure it out, I kept waking but hearing nothing, now I realize that it was the lack of bustle and city noise that kept waking me."

285

Juan Crazy

"The city should be buzzing already, the smell from the bakers should be wafting in the air, the trades should be setting up their tents in the market areas. "It makes me uneasy." He said as he went to look open the window.

The cold air hitting him felt good and he embraced it and drew it deep into his lungs. His body was stiff and every muscle in it revolted and burned from strain. He looked down at his hands, which were badly bruised, as were his arms. His armour had shielded him from the bite of the blade, axe and hammer but the impacts had almost liquefied his muscles below. He felt massively hung over, yet he knew the effects were from lack of sleep and due to strain not due to the one pint he had had before retiring.

"It's going to be a long day." Tunder groaned as he rose and joined Miathis at the window. "I will go down and get the men moving."

"I'm starved." Tunder said turning to his friend. "Bacon, eggs, bread dipped field in bacon fat, smothered in melted cheese…. nothing like a good fight to increase one's appetite."

Miathis laughed "You are perpetually hungry." He paused a second and then added. "We need to keep an eye on the men, no fancy fare stolen from city stores until we check out a few things. Can't be sure what might be tainted."

When they entered the room one of the injured down the room noticed them. "ATTENTION!" He called. Several men, obviously injured started to rise from their cots.

"At ease men," Miathis responded quickly. "You all fought well yesterday and deserve a bit of a rest this morning. Tunder has already set the watch, and those able to help will be assembled not for another hour – you all have time to rest a while longer."

Miathis gritted his teeth and put on his best soldiering face started his walk down between the cots, looking at the many men who lay upon their beds. Several wore heavily, blood soaked bandaged. Although some were seriously injured, not a single man groaned out with pain or discomfort. A few of those that had lesser injuries sat next to and tended those more seriously wounded.

"How you doing soldier," Miathis asked as he paused by a cot. The soldier nodded back at his captain lifting his heavily bandaged arm. "I sent the Tock that gave me this to one of the seven hells sporting a smile that reached from ear to ear." Looking down to his arm he smiled. Bettham splinted it, and said it was a clean break and will mend well."

Hearing the name Miathis took a quick glance around searching for the lad. Before he could turn and ask his question to the lad Tunder stepped close to him. "He is in the side room with Taramast."

Miathis looked back with a visible question displayed within his eyes. Tunder looked back and slowly shook his head. Then with happier tone he nodded back to the soldier. "Bettham stepped in his place as surgeon last night. The lad has quite a knack with needle, thread and split."

Miathis inhaled deeply thinking about his sergeant. Then turning, he started to the side room reserved for surgery.

Pushing the door open Miathis entered slowly. Sawdust had been strewn across the floor yet so significant had been the blood lost within the room that the floor was still slippery.

Miathis first noticed the sergeants pale grey face upon entering the room and how still the man was lying upon the surgeon's table. The sergeant's gear had been cut away and his mid section had been heavily wrapped. The white bandages upon his mid section contrasted the dark red bandages that were wrapped around his head, shoulder and arms.

"How is our sergeant doing?" Miathis said softly as he went to stand at the edge of the table.

The lad inhaled deeply showing his weariness. "He has been going in and out of consciousness, lack of blood has made him week." Then using the sleeve of his blood splattered shirt he wiped the sweat from his brow. "I was able to seal most of his wounds, but

287

the wound to his stomach is the most grievous… I fed him some onion soup early this morning."

Miathis bent down and inhaled, smelling the definite odour of onion.

"It's been pierced." Bettham confirmed as Miathis looked up to look at him.

Taramast caught their attention as his dark, raspy voice spoke with a light note. "I've always hated onions. Makes my stomach sour and makes me rip some wicked farts. Its them you smelled not my gut. I'll be up and around in a few week. You won't get rid of me that easy, my pension is due at the end of the year."

Tunder stood by the edge of his bed, "So, you have just been dogging it then eh?" Turning he looked to Bettham. "You have to watch this one, he likely has been jumping off the cot mid bandage to steal swigs from the surgery rum."

Then moving to the side of the bed near the head of the table he looked down at his friend. "I will expect you up by the end of the week and if I catch you stealing any rum I might even have you dig a few latrines yourself!"

The soldier braved a smile back as he opened a swollen eye to look up at the towering man. Heavy bandages crisscrossed his blood stained head, a few which had just moments ago been white where now turning pink. The sergeant coughed but after clearing his throat, in a week voice responded. "We are in a city lieutenant; there is no need for digging latrines."

Tunder laughed heartily, yet he strained to fight back moisture that was building in his eyes. "I saw what you did." He added looking down at the man.

Bettham adjusting the bandage on the sergeant's arm looked up at the tall man.

"You rode your horse right at those archers, pulled their fire from the two lads." Tunder said pointing his thumb up at Bettham.

"Cut them down, but not before becoming a pin cushion in the process."

"I heard wearing feathers was all the rage in the big cities." Taramast added in a soft voice.

"Silly git, after all these years to get stuck by a Tock," Tunder added.

"There were six." Taramast responded with as much humour as he could muster. "But wasn't fast enough… Dar and Mort were lost before I could reach them."

"You did damn fine soldiering sergeant." Miathis added from the end of the table. "You saved many a lad yesterday."

Taramast motioned with his open eye over to Betthem. "They fought well, even this sorry excuse for a soldier. And I doubt I nor several others had made it without the lad's attention." Then with a laugh he started to cough; small droplets of blood sprayed the linen on his bed his body shook slightly after he finished coughing.

Miathis nodded in agreement then looked back up at Bettham. He didn't even bother looking around; he knew from the lack of faces that all the other healers had not survived the battle.

Tunder turned and seeing a large bottle of rum on the instrument table took it and popping the cork put the neck of the bottle to Taramast's lips.

"His stomach," Bettham blurted out, but Tunder's glance silenced him.

Taramast took a small pull from the bottle and then looking up at Tunder smiled. But the spirits had not fully wetted the man's throat when he started to cough again. This time, however, his coughing was extremely violent shaking his body. Blood, thinned by the brandy sprayed from the hurt man's nose and lips covering his chest with red specks and streaks.

Taramast looked up at Tunder. "Too few lads left to hold this city."

"Reinforcements will be coming shortly." Tunder added knowing that their orders were explicit and that Miathis would not leave the city even if he were the last man left within the city. "You let me worry about the men… right now you just worry about getting back to duty." He added.

Taramast laughter was cut short by more coughing. However, this time the coughing didn't end with gasps, but rather the man's face turned red and blood gushed up from his throat. His eyes went wide as he recognized his own mortality drawing near. Tunder dropped the bottle and reached out and grabbed the man's hand with both of his large mitts. Their eyes met and a moment later it was over.

They stood there looking down at their friend for few minutes before Miathis broke the silence. Looking at Bettham he nodded to him. "You've done a good job here tonight, You should get some rest."

"He saved Tirad and myself with that move … Bettham added looking back down at his sergeant."

Miathis smiled and then looked back at the old sergeant. "He has saved many a good man with his courage yesterday."

"He was the best." Tunder added proudly.

From behind the open door a few other soldiers stood and looked in, obviously recognizing the passing of a good friend. One of them, with a soft even tone began their traditional chant. "A man of the Fist is a man of stone." He started

Tunder turned and looked out at the group of men now gathering at the doorway. Their voices rang out with a deep, even and sombre tone. The man that had started the chant then continued; the others echoed in chorus. "We ride in the Fist."

"In the darkest dark before dawn on sentry he stands.

"We ride in the Fist."
"In the early morning he hones his sword.

"We ride in the Fist."
"In rain and snow… he will never slow."
"We ride in the Fist."
"Far from home with battle done yet on he'll go."
"We ride in the Fist."
"Until his enemies are gone and duties done."
"We ride in the Fist."
"As part of the fist, we are never alone."
"We ride in the Fist."
"With friend and comrade we fight, and sleep."
"We ride in the Fist."

The room grew still and Miathis forced a smile as he looked down at his old friend. "Rest now my friend, for your duty is done.

Tunder was the first to turn to leave the room. "I need to check on duty." Was all he said as he let go his friends hand gently, turned and left the room.

Miathis felt more tired now then he had right after the battle. His heart was heavy with the loss of his friends and the duty of leadership pressed hard down upon his shoulders.

Moving slowly, duty driven he exited the barracks he started his walk to the Terran pub where he was set to secretly meet with a contact from the thieves guild. It took him almost an hour to wind through the various back roads ensuring that none of his men followed him. Reaching the pub he stood for a moment to gather his thoughts and then walked up to the pub's door and entered.

"Hello." He said as he stepped in to the dimly lit room. He noticed that the windows heavily draped windows were only partially drawn back, a single long thin shard of light streaked from it into the room. In the corner of the room a figure stood and stepped forward into the sole shard of light. Miathis was startled to see the beautiful lady smile back at him and motion him to her table. "There is no one left in the city that cares about your comings and goings Miathis, please, come in and sit have some breakfast with me I made much more then I can consume myself."

Miathis walked over and extended his hand. "Thank you Dimona." Although enticed by the lady's tight clinging white blouse he resisted the impulse to give Dimona a 'quick once over' and instead looked directly into her steel blue eyes.

Dimona immediately noted Miathis' dark demeanour and smiled back warmly at him but didn't reach up to shake his had in greeting. "You look tired, Miathis." She said simply to Miathis with a tone to put him at ease.

Miathis sat down and grabbed a piece of bread from a plate and pulled it apart and started chewing deliberately on it.

"I have some bad news." She said as she looked down at her plate and started to cut a link of sausage. "We have confirmed that PlanTer has fallen, and the Mohen army appears to be on their way here."

Miathis had been about to bite down again on the piece of bread but instead looked up with a very tired expression. "Lovely." He said and then took another bite.

"How many?" Miathis said while he shook his head in bewilderment.

Dimona shrugged. "Even when your reinforcements arrive you will be outnumbered by five to one."

Miathis the ever optimist looked up at Dimona and smiled. "We will have to hold them until the Count Paltine's men arrive."

Dimona shook her head. "Do not count on replacements coming from the western shores. Word has it the Count has not sent a man to his King's aid."

Miathis, shocked shook his head as if to clear his thoughts. "What?"

"Landor Rutt is playing his own game, he did not send even one man east to follow your general, but instead has positioned his them on his eastern border. And the Duke of Sirthinor has split his men, half joining him to the Cliff Mines, and the other half he has stationed to protect his own lands. Both it appears have betrayed your king."

The captain's face turned white, he sat speechless with his mouth open. A cold shiver ran up his spine and the hairs on the back of his head rose. Then after a moment he regained his composure and letting his fork drop his hand turned to a fist, which he slammed down on the table making the plates upon it bounce. "Damn them both to the seven hells!" swore Miathis.

"With your eyes turned east you have neglected your back." Dimona added with a fatal tone

"What of those from the south?" Miathis asked. "Where now is the Duke of Capris, and has he convinced the new Terran king to assist us?"

Dimona shrugged. "We have little confirmed word from the south. All we know now is that the Mohen are only a few days ride from here and at their current pace they will be here before your general…"

"I would say run, but I do not believe you would take my advice. So instead, you will likely stay and die." Dimona's tone was more then a little sardonic.

Miathis put his hands to his face and rubbed the sleep from his eyes. "Good men died so that we could be here to explore this city and work with you to discover its secrets. And my orders were explicit – my men and I will stay here until our forces arrive or until such time that Sir Beston Thesera sends other orders."

"We have already done a fair bit of searching, I am not sure what else you will gleam from this city then what my men have already found out." Dimona replied unenthusiastically. "As you yourself have noted, the vast majority of the city stands empty of every living thing – man, woman and child. Dimona paused. "You should visit the inner keep. There are a few bodies of maids and I believe the Terran princes Mindy Bestinor – all were rather… well – lets just say their death were most unusual. There are no survivors nor true signs of any captives being taken."

"But the lack of bodies makes confirming her demise difficult." Miathis added hopefully.

Seeing the question in Miathis' eyes Dimona rushed in to add. "We found no trace of the Montterran princess Elle. There is no way to explain what went on in this city, you must search yourself and make your own assumptions."

Then after a long moment of silence Dimona's voice dropped to an almost apologetic tone. "My men and I will depart this city tonight, I have no desire to be here when the Mohen arrive."

Miathis looked up to the ceiling in despair. "How might I with so few men slow an entire Mohen army?" Then after a moment the captain looked back at Dimona. "Who leads the Mohen army?"

"They are being led by General Kikiltoe Mariard." Dimona replied. "Who is both smart and impatient? He knows Terran Add is the key to this country and as such did not dally after taking Plan Tar."

Miathis chuckled. "Lovely…. Couldn't have been the Emperor's incompetent fat son, instead we get the maniacal bastard genius son, the man who led the Mohen to victory against the Farrows… coming at us."

Miathis took another bite of bread and then after chewing and swallowing made up his mind. "Our orders are clear, we are to stay until the Sir Beston Thesra and his men arrive, and to hold this city until that time."

Miathis then looked deploringly over at the thief. "Is there no way that you and your men might be able to assist?" He asked.

Dimona's eyebrows rose, but softened slightly when she noticed the sense of desperation in Miathis' eyes. "My men are not soldiers, not one of them would be trusted to man a gate, even were I to order it." Then after a moment's thought and in a friendlier tone she added. "But we might be able to assist in slowing down General Mariard so that you might have more time for replacements to arrive."

Miathis paused, but then nodded slowly, "How?"

"We give them cause to hesitate." Dimona started as a smile started to form on the corners of her mouth.

Miathis looked back inquisitively, but remained silent.

Dimona took another bite of sausage as if to build the suspense. After chewing and swallowing she smiled at Miathis and he noted a side of her that he had not realised had been hidden beneath her beautiful demeanour. "It is likely the Mohen know as much about TerranAdd as we did before we arrived. Lets exploit the situation and create uncertainty as to what transpired here. We need to give them cause NOT to draw any nearer."

"Like what?" Miathis asked as he leaned back in his chair.

Dimona replied slowly, starting her words off with a sly grin. "Their scouts already draw near, but what if a few of them returned with stories of sickness and disease within the city?"

Dimona leaned forward and spoke in a soft yet confident voice. "We take a few of the dead bodies, Tock and Montterran, and fix them up to look like they died of the plague and place them at some distance from the castle in all directions for the Mohen scouts to find. Let me talk to a few of my men, we might be able to sell that image to some of the closer sentries."

"General Kikiltoe is said to be rather smart and not easily mislead by war tactics." Miathis added in an unconvinced tone.

Dimona's smile widened. "The General and I haven't crossed paths before."

``Complicated, but it might work, ``Miathis said as he watched Dimona stand and turn to leave. Dimona turned and headed for the door, her walk accented her hips and her feminine figure. ``Her walk definitely wasn't one of an assassin, ` Miathis mused as he watched her depart. Then as the door swung closed behind her he heard her reply. ``Only death is simple Miathis, keep your mind on that and you might survive."

Burning boils and deceptions

Etch was very impressed by Dimi's knowledge of root and herb. But what unnerved him was how quickly she obtained them. While riding Dimi would without notice or any slight indication that she had seen something on the forest floor below slide off her mount. Her small blade would appear as if by magic in her hand and flash once, twice and the next moment she was turning to jump back on Peppy. Typically, in the time it took him to pull himself from the fog of travel she had already harvested the plant.

"What have you fetched this time?" Etch asked as he watched Dimi vault back onto the mule with the bulbs of two wild plants in her hand. He glanced down at her waist but the lick of a blade was already invisible in its sheath. Etch knew that size mattered little when it came to an assassin's blade... even the smallest sharp blade could slit the throat of the largest warrior. He straightened his back and moved slightly in his stirrups. Its wasn't as if he felt in danger, it was just a subtle reminder to himself that he should never let himself be lulled into a sense of ease just because she was small and at first glance appeared harmless. There was this other level to Dimi he knew that lay just below her apparently tranquil surface; he had seen the flames of anger in her eyes more than once this trip.

"Radi tubers", Dimi responded as she looked down and plopped them in to the small bags that were slung over Peppy.

Etch groaned. "That stuff tasted really bad." Dimi didn't respond but rather focused on brushing off the bulbs of excess dirt.

Etch looked sadly at the saddlebags behind Dimi. Two days ago he had noticed that Dimi had at some time emptied their bags of any meat; when he asked her about it she had promptly assured him that he was better for it, as the meat was a corrupting influence to his body.

Etch's stomach growled in advance protest. Leaning down he patted the horse's neck and whispered softly in the ear that had turned back to him. 'Eating just herbs and roots is just not natural'.

Dimi looked back at Etch and smiled and laughed. "Like a horse would agree with you." Etch, wasn't all that startled to realize she had heard him. Looking up he noticed a small flash of fire in Dimi's eyes as she glanced back at him. It was a small indication that she knew that he was in a small way testing her. In as sincere a voice as he could muster he admitted, "Ya, ok I do 'feel' a 'Little' better for it." The small amount of sarcasm did not go unnoticed, and Dimi looked back round at him. "But that still doesn't mean I don't miss having a nice piece of salted meat to chew on every now and again."

"You were eating yourself to an early old age". Dimi responded with a conclusive tone. Etch shook his head and began to chuckle, a second later Dimi's laughter joined in.

Both riders mirth dwindled as they passed a last strand of forest and the wide planes opened up. Both caught their breaths as they passed the last strand of trees. It wasn't the unbelievable heat from the sun that now bore down on them that made them gasp, the rolling, golden fields ahead of them were breathtaking.

Miles and miles and miles of rolling hills covered in golden fields of hay spotted with splotches of tall green stalks that Etch assumed were plantings of corn. "Terran Flats." Etch said in a soft tone not to spoil the moment. "What a sight." Turning to Dimi he smiled as he pulled off his hat and wiped the sweat from his brow.

Dimi didn't look so impressed, in fact she looked a little uneasy and squirming in her seat she reached out and nervously patted the neck of Peppy and then very unexpectedly she reach back up and behind her with her left hand, feeling the empty spot on her back where once her wings were.

"It will be easy and faster riding even if a bit hotter." Etch said as he looked back at the hills hoping Dimi hadn't notice him observing her uneasiness.

"I prefer the comfort of trees." Dimi added.

Smiling he nodded forward and then he nudged his horse to take the lead. "What about Sarta? Where will she feel more comfortable and where would she go after leaving Terran Add?"

Dimi mused a moment and then replied with some small confidence. "Perhaps back to the master's old towers, I don't know. Perhaps..." Dimi's voice trailed off and then restarted with a little more confidence. "She is up to something, there is more to this then likely we know... I just feel it."

After a moments hesitation Dimi replied from behind him. "I could sense it even back then, there was something down within her. She was a raving lunatic, a savage but charming seductress when in human form and a carnivorous animal when not. The succubus in her had taken her over body and soul... She shouldn't have been able to plan or scheme beyond where her next meal was coming from."

Etch paused a moment in thought. "In league with another, or perhaps a tool of another. Perhaps we still can only see a small part of the puzzle. That other creature you mentioned that was with her is likely the key."

Dimi's lips turned to a vicious grin and her eyes sparked and dazzled with menace. "Keeker." She said softly. Pulling herself out of the self inflicted daze she added a bit louder, "A servant, likely nothing more."

"But not of this realm, and why would it serve her here." Etch added as their horses entered the tall grass. It swished around them as they road gently swaying and brushing their legs. The scent of the tall thirsty stalks was overpowering and pollen wafted over their tips. Etch immediately felt his nose begin to revolt and start to run. "Forget what I said about nice riding, this stuff makes me want to sneeze."

Dimi replied simply. "She pulled my wings off in an attempt to study how I was made, to look at the thread of magic within me... she was seeking a path to immortality."

"But that was a long time ago, she froze you and left you and never returned." Etch paused a moment. "She has moved now down another path. Perhaps that leads to the same ends, perhaps to another. Question is, is she being influenced or directed down a path. Where did Keeker really come from and why is he now loyal to Sarta and is his loyalty in earnest?"

They road on silently for almost an hour; it was Dimi that broke their deep thoughts.

"Something was different about her, she was more rank then even I remembered her presence to be. I thought at the time that she had just ripened, that the decay in her soul had just eaten more that once was her away. However, you could be right."

"I can't stop feeling that Sarta's mind was much clearer than it had ever been when I knew her. The old Sarta was an insane creature that fed and suffered only short bursts of sanity"

"How then," Etch said continuing her line of thought. "Did she come to such clarity once again to open the doors to let that creature through? How could she maintain such clarity and purpose to have a hand in what we both now fear she has?"

Dimi looked back somewhat upset with Etch. "I hate it when you finish my sentences for me." A moment later with Etch not saying anything more she continued. "There is obvious seepage between these worlds... Perhaps there are stronger ties." Dimi began.

Etch, deep in thought looked across the sea of tall grass and then to the sky. Detros' broken face frowned down from the otherwise blue sky. "There are a number of tribes that worship demons and demigods that apparently have no history upon this world. The Masti for example, are a tribe north of Terran Add dabble in blood magic. To practice the art has been outlawed for several years as is worshiping their god."

Dimi paused and then shrugged. "Give me a few minutes with Keeker and I will be able to tell you."

Etch looked over at Dimi with a smile. "Or perhaps she just like you said, rotted from the inside out. Imagine seeing yourself wither into a hag, and the only way you can look and feel better is when you feed upon the blood and flesh of people you used to live with. Ever insatiable and always at war with yourself, it would make a hard life if you ask me."

"Don't you even DARE to add a tone of pity to your tone!" Dimi spat back at him. "She would rather eat you then talk to you."

"Besides," She continued noticing that Etch was not about to contradict her statement. "I know Sarta. Sarta likely loves the powers she now has over others no matter the price. When she feeds, she can dominate any man or woman, and twist their will to her own. She can in that state enslaves them and they will smile as she sucks the marrow from their broken bones. It was her own greed for power that brought her to this fate and I am sure part of her is relishing in it."

"I am not arguing." Etch added in a agreeing tone. "I can believe Sarta sought you out to obtain the secrets of your magical capability…. I am just trying to get in her mind and figure out how she might be able to accomplish what we believe she did at TerranAdd that would take such great skill."

Dimi, looked over at Etch and paused a second seeing the question in his eyes. "Or the power of a demigod," He added finally.

Etch turned and looked back north, he chuckled and then rather loudly licked his lips. "So she eats fresh, bloody meat now eh?" He then looked back at Dimi a smiled as he licked his lips again while looking at her. "Mmmmm, fresh meat! Just saying it makes my mouth water."

Dimi frowned and then nudged Peppy forward. "You are incorrigible."

"Hey!" Etch called to her. "Don't blame me, I have been eating nothing but roots and twigs since we have met!"

Dimi didn't smile at Etch's joke but instead stopped Peppy again and looked at Etch. "When we meet her, and meet her we will…

remember just that her soul is black as pitch, darker then dark. You can't hesitate a second hoping that in some way we will find within her some redeeming value, that somehow she might be saved from her self. You need to move quick and decisive, even if that means the princess is lost... Sarta cannot be saved and will do more damage if she remains alive."

Etch's smile faded and he nodded as they both looked forward and continued their trek north over the Terran Flats. As they continued, Dimi would occasionally look behind them, and as the view of the forest faded Dimi became even more withdrawn. Her face was ashen white on the morning of the third day when they spotted the capital's high southern walls could be seen.

"What do you see?" Etch said as he turned himself to look north in the direction of the city, but it was still kilometres away.

"Not much activity for a big city. From this distance I can usually smell it all... but the smells on the wind are stale." Dimi leaned forward and squinted. "Black flags fly atop the center gates."

"You sure?" Etch said as he suddenly halted his horse. "Flying a Black flag warns travelers to stay clear. It means that the city is unclean, that it is suffering a plague." Etch said in a bewildered tone. "You sure?"

Dimi nodded. "The air carries an old odour of burnt flesh, but that scent is mixed with burnt leather... and not the scent of rotting flesh or sickness and there are no sounds of pain or distress upon the wind... it is deathly quiet."

"Leather and flesh," Etch paused. "Usually they are together when you build a pyre after a battle."

"I need to check it out." Etch said. "But perhaps it is still best if I meet you on the other side?"

Dimi chuckled and then clicked her tong and Peppy moved on again. "Don't worry about me getting sick, worry about yourself. Besides, I want to get out from these open spaces for a while."

301

Etch paused and then realized what he had just said. "Oh, right."

Dimi added quickly. "Someone is leaving the gates in a horse drawn cart."

"Unbelievable." Etch said in a surprised voice as he squinted and stood up in the stirrups looking north to the city. I can barely make out the walls! Your eye sight is fantastic!"

Dimi pulled her green felt hat down as far as she could over her hair and ears and an hour later the two unusual looking travellers were yelling up to what they at first thought was an empty tower.

"The city is closed, Keep safe, and keep far away from these walls." A voice called down from high above.

Etch smiled recognizing a distinct Roehn accent. Pulling the piece of parchment from his jacket he looked up and then held it up high. "I am a Montterran officer. I would speak with your captain soldier of the Fist."

There was an extended pause as from above Etch and Dimi clearly heard a young man cursing and calling down to his friend at the gate. "Tirad, you there, he says he is a Montterran officer."

"BETTHAM," yelled someone from behind the gate. "The man holds up a small piece of paper that you could possible read from way up there and you believe him? Tunder will have your ass in a sling and we will be brushing down the horses for a week!"

The soldier atop the wall motioned for the city's gates to be opened and then called down to the sole soldier below. "Too late now, better let them in now and take them to Miathis."

The gates were opened and a young soldier stepped forward to greet them. The lad only glanced at Etch's letter, but stood fast before them as he stared at Dimi. "Who is this with you?"

After a long moment of being stared at Etch replied, "of that I will speak with your captain, she is my charge and by our Lord's mark we shall pass. Now quickly man I am in a bit of a rush; your captain and I must have a word."

The solider made a quick move and stole a fast glance at Dimi. "Well at least your not Mohen… not with them ears and hair anyway." He said as he turned and pointed the direction in which they would head. "This way."

"Let's go." Etch implored as he nudged his horse forward. "Where is your captain? I can get there quicker then with you on foot."

"Meeting," Tirad said sheepishly then turning strode forward motioning the two to follow. "And you can't go off on your own, he would skin me alive if I let that happen. " Tirad reached up and grabbed the horse's reigns and led them forward. "Normally, I wouldn't take you to him right now where he is at, but somehow I don't think this is a normal time or that you are normal visitors." Turning he looked up at Dimi and smiled and gave her a wink.

When the three entered the Black water Pub Miathis almost jumped out of his boots. Dimona, however, simply smiled and sat back in her chair pushing back the plate of food that sat in front of her.

"TIRAD, WHAT IN THE SEVEN HELLS ARE YOU DOING HERE AND WHO ARE THESE…?"

Tirad's face first showed shock and then he smiled in a sassy way back at his captain. "Got special visitors, thought you would like to see."

"This was supposed to be a secret meeting." Miathis exclaimed as he looked at Tirad with a very cross expression.

"And how did you know where I was anyway?" Miathis asked as he stepped forward and confronted Tirad.

The lad bowed to Dimona. "You seriously think you could have breakfast with someone this beautiful every morning and I wouldn't find out about it?"

Dimona inclined her head at the compliment but remained silent.

"You are incorrigible." Miathis said shaking his head, but he hesitated as he looked over at Etch and Dimi. "Your sergeant will I am sure find ways to keep you on a shorter leash."

Dimona coughed breaking the poisoned mood and then motioned the strangers in. "Well, now that they are here, why not invite them for a bite to eat?"

Miathis nodded and then motioned the two travelers to come in. Tirad attempted to follow them to the table but was stopped by Miathis who grabbed the youth's shoulder. "What in the world do YOU think you are doing? She meant them, as for you – back to your post soldier."

Turning Tirad around roughly Miathis pushed him towards the door, "back to the walls for you."

Tirad turned gracefully as he exited and bowed elaborately. "My lady," he said over to Dimona and then turned quickly before the captain could plant a boot on his backside.

Miathis slammed the door but paused as he heard Tirad chuckle from behind it. "That lad will be the death of me." The captain said as he turned and walked back to the table. "Smart as a whip, and lots of potential but he sure stretches his leash."

Dimona laughed, and stood to greet Etch. "Sit." She said politely. "I believe you have already met the captain, and you are unmistakably of eastern lineage, an x soldier... Roehn I would bet with my last coin." She then paused as she looked over at Dimi. "But as for your friend."

Etch pulled back out the letter from the general and handed it to Miathis. "Not many men within the city." He said questioningly. "Walls are virtually empty and men we have seen are but lads."

Miathis looked down at the paper reading it and after rereading it a second time he nodded and then nodded back to Dimona. Sitting back in his chair he finally responded. "We ran into some Tock; I lost some very good men." While handing back the letter he added "More then that I will not say, if you have more questions the general and his men are only a day away. You can speak to him yourself when he arrives."

"Only if we have to," Dimi added with her soft voice. Miathis looked up, surprised by the timber of her voice. "We do not plan to be here that long, the Mohen are more then a day away and your voice betrays you… someone else is on their way?"

"Mohen," Etch added as he looked into Miathis' eyes. He knew Dimi had guessed right.

"Why did you send a horse and cart east?" Etch asked as he received the parchment and rolling it slid it momentarily back into his belt.

Miathis grumbled and Dimona laughed. "I like these two she said all at once. And I would suggest Miathis you not play cards with them."

"Ruse." Miathis said as he sent a distasteful look back over to Dimona. "We have an unwanted and very large army of Mohen just east of here. We have killed a few of their scouts, but we need to continue to dissuade their army from hurrying here. We sent the cart eastward with hope that we might convince the Mohen general that the city is plagued."

"Given how easily and carefree you both walked in…" Dimona laughed.

"Him I get." Dimi said pointing to Miathis… but who are you?" She looked acquisitively at the woman in front of her. "You reek of deception, you are too sure of yourself…"

"I", Dimona responded politely and with a smile. "I am a friend, nothing more," then turning to Etch she added. "It was actually my cart and man that went east… I am sure he will sell the misdirection better then one of Miathis'.

Etch looked over to Dimona and then back to Miathis. "How many Mohen did you say?"

"Too many," Miathis answered gloomily. "Latest report says between forty to fifty thousand Mohen regulars."

Etch whistled and then inhaled deeply. "Lovely." Etch finally said sarcastically and turned to Dimi. "Glad we aren't staying long."

Dimi stood and looked down at the table set with sausages and ham. "Unhealthy. We had better fare yesterday." Then looking up at Dimona she asked a direct and frank question as if she knew Dimona was more than what she appeared. "Is your man any good, will he fool them?"

Dimona paused and then nodded slowly. "I think so, he is one of my best. His face and arms have been bruised and we have burned him and made his sores puss. It should work."

Dimona then motioned Dimi to a chair, but she refused. Shrugging Dimona looked back down at her own plate and picked up some bread and began to chew on it.

Miathis sat down but didn't eat; instead he continued to stare at Dimi. He motioned Etch to sit down. "Note doesn't say much. But I can guess why you're here."

Etch nodded and sat at the table, and although he was tempted by the stack of sausages he held back knowing that Dimi would disapprove. Instead he tore a piece of bread off of the loaf on the table and took a bite of it. "What have you found out so far? I would be happy for any information."

Miathis looked over at Dimona and then turned and looked at Dimi.

Etch looked up at Miathis and after swallowing said. "Dimi is a close friend and can be trusted." He could see suspicion and curiosity in both Miathis' and Dimona's eyes so added in a light tone. "Dimi is my guide."

Dimona watched carefully Dimi's posture and quick glance back at Etch. "She is also motivated to help, I think." Dimi looked back and their eyes locked, volumes of information few others in the world would have suspected were exchanged in that look.

Dimona then very quickly started to rise, but Dimi was standing again before Dimona had fully risen. Dimona smiled again and holding out her hands with palms open she then pointed to the back of the room. "I think I might have something you might like back there. That is of course if you like Farrow blood oranges?"

"Sweeter, you will never find." Dimona added as she turned her back fully on Dimi and started to the back of room.

"Blood oranges?" Dimi asked hesitantly.

Dimona laughed. "Don't worry, it's just a name because the fruit inside is deep red." Picking one up from the back counter she then turned and threw it with some force at Dimi. The orange was picked from the air by Dimi's small arm as deftly as a frog would catch a fly.

Dimi's hesitated a second while she looked down at it. But after smelling one she looked up and smiled at Dimona. "Thank you." She said cordially.

"You are quite welcome." Dimona said returning to her chair as Dimi sat down and started to peel the first orange. Under the peel, deep red fruit lay dripping with sweetness. Dimi bit in and her eyes lit up.

Dimona smiled and laughed lightly. "Good eh? What you hold there would have been a special treat brought by the Rohen entourage as one of the gifts for the princess that lived here."

Etch looked up and over to Dimona. "What do you know of the Princes' fate?"

Dimona's smile faded and she looked over at Dimi and smiled. Looking back at Miathis who nodded, "Not much, but I will tell you what you know."

***

A few kilometres to the east Bek rode hunched over on his stinking cart. He groaned out loud. He was sore all over. 'Dimona had prepared the ruse a little too well he thought to himself. When she had insisted that he be burned even in parts below his shirt he had thought she had crossed the line.

The old thief groaned, "My whole body is sore." He said as he readjusted his coat. As his coat was repositioned his swift fingers slipped from his pocket the freshly cut Tygor root that Dimona had given to him. Pretending to then cough the root was then brought to his mouth.

Bek looked forward to the soothing feeling the drug would have on his aches and sores. However, he knew that Dimona had given it to him because the root would make his eyes glass over and the black tar like oils in the root would also make his mouth and lips turn black.

As the drug began to work he licked his lips and then began to hum a Mohen song. In less than half an hour Bek confirmed that he was being watched. As he passed the Mohen scout's position he turned in his seat and patted a bundle of dirty clothes that was arranged behind him in the cart to resemble the body of his daughter.

"You feeling ok? Them sores are awful." He said with a sympathetic tone in the Mohen tong. "I feel so bad. Your mum, bless her soul, she did so suffer before she died. Those people in TerranAdd must have been evil to have such a curse placed on their heads!"

Bek pulled his hood off and wiped one of his sores, making sure it wasn't crusting over. It started bleeding again. After burning him Dimona had put soot in it to ensure it would stay open, exude puss and not heal.

He looked up into the sun, hoping that the scouts noticed the extra burns on his neck. He would hate to have gone through all that pain for naught. He almost laughed out loud when he noticed a lone scout's head poke up from amongst some nearby grass. 'Rank amatures he thought to himself.'

The old thief grimaced and pretended to adjust himself as he averted his eyes. If from the distance they were apart, he could now hear the scout crawl forward for a closer look. He coughed roughly and while hacking he pushed in a small piece of blackened root into his mouth. A moment later, for added effect spat up a big ball of gray flem. "Me lungs feel like they's be full of stone." He said to himself as he continued to ride forward along the road.

Out of the corner of his eye, as they approached the scout still supposedly hidden in the tall grass, Bek coughed again loudly and spat, this time the root had ensured his spit was as black as pitch. It went streaming out of his mouth and hit the dirt road. The ruse obviously had some effect for the Mohen scout quickly retreated back into the grass. It took less than an hour before he heard the approach of a small company of soldiers.

The soldiers riding two abreast stopped a good twenty meters ahead of his cart. Holding up his hand a lone well-armoured knight rode at the front

The thief's eyes squinted ever so slightly in surprise as he noted the colors of the knight shield. The shield marked the knight a belonging to General Kikiltoe Mariard own guard. 'I had better carry this off well.' Bek thought to himself as he raised his hand in greeting to the soldiers.

"Hold fast," The knight commanded to him in broken Terran speech as they came closer. Bek reigned in his cart and attempted to look a little surprised and scared as the Mohen knight and scout moved a little closer while his detachment of men stayed behind. He licked his lips and swallowed the remnants of the Tygor root.

Bek was familiar and fluent with Mohen so replied in Mohen native tong. It had been a while, but he tried to throw in a native coastal accent. "Bidde di, lase me und my dochtor aline."

The guards around the knight immediately looked at ease after hearing their native tong spoken without any hint of Terran accent, however, the knight still looked over at Bek with some great suspicion. "Where are you coming from, and where are you going, and what do you have in the cart?" He said in the Mohen tong to Bek.

Bek scratched under his armpit, and then his head making sure that they could see his facial sores. He knew they had seen it when the noble squinted. Continuing with his best south-eastern Mohen tong he replied with a haltingly, concerned reply. "I am Moridar from the village of Mardin by the shore."

"I trade in shell combs. My family and I make combs for the ladies. We came to sell our wares in TerranAdd."

Bek paused and then scratched his forehead again and wiped his hand, now covered in puss on his sleeve. He tried to act conspicuously, inconspicuous. "Trade is bad there now so we are going home." He added with his southern Mohen drawl.

Bek and Dimona had talked at length about who he was to be and how he was to act. He reached down and pulled a large shell combs out from behind him and held it up to the knight to see. "Very good quality and for you; only one Silver Stain."

The knight dismissed Bek's offer with a flick of his hand.

"What is in TerranAdd?" The knight demanded as he moved his horse ever so slightly forward to get a better look at Bek. "And what is wrong with your face?"

Bek put back the shell into the sack behind him – trying to look a little coy he responded to the knight while trying to conceal the marks on his face. "Nothing is wrong with my face. I ah, burned it is all."

The consummate thief continued trying to lie poorly, but not too well. "No trade in Terran Add. Don't know where all the people went."

The soldiers all around the knight stirred and started chattering to themselves. The noble raised his gauntleted hand and bid them to silence. "How many Montterran knights are there?"

"Montterran? I don't know, we didn't see any merchants there, so we left."

The young Mohen knight impatiently turned and addressed a mounted soldier that was sporting a long heavy crossbow. "Mantoth – if this man doesn't speak faster. Air him out with a bolt ok?"

A crossbowman rode forward beside the Mohen noble. As he drew closer Bek turned and looked at the man. Below his visor Bek noted the lads eyes were beaming as if the lad looked forward to using his heavy crossbow.

Bek no longer needing to feign concern for his own safety he quickly blurted out. "Ah, my lord, there is no reason for that. I will tell you all I know. The Montterran soldiers said that their company of men had arrived a week ago, but now all that is left is a few of them and they are all sick with the same disease they said they found when they arrived. "

"Sick? What sickness?" The knight demanded.

Bek shrugged. "I don't know. There were too few to stop me from leaving. The men there cough and then they after a while they die and turn to dust…"

The knight turned back to his man… "Turn to dust? Mantoth put one through the man's arm!"

"WAIT!" Bek yelled out as he waved his arms. "I know, I know you mean business." He blurted with a distressed voice.

"Please sir," Bek pleaded. "My girl, and me we aren't that sick. We didn't stay long there. We came, the gates were open then and we drove in. I noticed a few shops I used to go to and went there. No one is around but a few Montterran soldiers, we talked to them and then we got out of that cursed city as fast as we could."

The scout pointed at Bek. "It is a plague. Look at the sores on his neck and face and he was coughing earlier!"

The knight growled in a suspicious tone, "A sickness that turns people to dust? Never have I heard such a thing!"

The Mohen scout pulled up close to the knight. "It matches what we have seen." He said. "All around the city walls there are corpses. We find them rotting one day, and the next they are gone and in their place is nothing but a stinking, rotting muck."

Still not convinced the knight yelled at Bek. "GET DOWN FROM THAT CART, TAKE OFF YOUR SHIRT."

"NOW, NOW, I AM A CITIZEN," Bek pleaded as he got off of his cart.

"A fellow Mohen," Bek said in a pleading tone as he looked over at the soldiers. "Don't go making me full of holes. I will do what you ask."

Bek stepped down onto the road and then began to take off his shirt. When the shirt was covering his head and face he smiled as he heard the scouts and soldiers gasp.

"I don't think mine are getting worse." He said reassuringly as he dropped his shirt to the ground.

It was cold out and he started to shiver in earnest. "We didn't stay long. I left what I found from that accursed city."

"Please don't shoot me and my little girl." He pleaded. "You will see, in the morning we will be better, I know it for in the city, those with the curse died fast. A few hours are all I am asking to prove it."

"Never heard of this crap before," the knight said but this time with less conviction. Then the knight lifted his visor. Another chill went through Bek as the knight smiled wickedly down at him. "Take off your pants!" He commanded in a slow but confident voice.

Bek purposefully hesitated, raising the knight's temper to a dangerous point. "IF YOU DON'T WE WILL DROP YOU WHERE YOU STAND!"

Hurrying as fast as he could the thief untied the cords holding up his pants, and let them fall. Bek didn't need to look down, instead watched as the soldiers and knight gasped.

'Dimona had done a most thorough job' Bek thought as he stood silently knowing that they were all now looking at the very nasty burn right on his privates. It had hurt like hell, but all of a sudden he was very happy that Dimona had insisted in properly 'preparing' him as she had said.

The scout turned to the knight. "There is proof to his sickness, we should burn him and the cart!"

"NO MY LORD, PLEASE MY LORD." Bek pleaded. "IT is a curse not a sickness! YOU need to believe me! We will prove it is a curse. We will stay in the cart here, right here and not move. It is a curse, not a plague... they were wicked, wicked Terrans in TerranAdd!"

The Knight looked over to the scout and then nodded to Bek. He then turned his horse around to address the bowmen and the scout. "You two will stay here with him, watch him. If they move near you or try to escape – shoot them and burn down the cart and bodies."

Turning his horse the knight motioned to the other soldiers. "Back to camp, we will go no further until we know for sure. Then he turned in his saddle and waved his company to turn round.

Bek pulled pack up his pants and then put on his heavy shirt as his two guards watched him. All evening long he sat and attended his daughter, who remained in the cart above the view of the soldiers; neither drew near enough to suspect anything was amiss. He laid his blanket up by his supposed daughter and fell asleep.

In the middle of the night Bek woke as he heard the scout leave his post. Silent as a mole he slipped down off of the cart and followed the soldier into the corn. It took little effort to sneak up on the lazy soldier who was busy relieving himself. The garrotte slipped easily around the soldier's neck and with a pull and a twist Bek killed the man.

Sneaking back the thief had to stifle a laugh as he approached the second snoring guard. Pulling a small vile from his vest he bent forward to within a hand span of the man's face and ever so gently let drop a few dark drips from it onto the man's lips.

As Beck left the camp he passed the cart, silently he pulled off the back covers where two additional piles of rather disgusting muck sprinkled with black spit sat. Without another smile or glance back at the dying soldier he turned and disappeared into the night.

The night stalkers

Dimona walked through the shadowed back streets of the city weaving returning to the apothecary where she found Dimi still sitting cross-legged on the shop's center table amidst dozens of bottles and pistils.

"Thought I would find you here," Dimona said with a light and friendly, casual tone. Their two like souls had bonded almost immediately. Below both of the lady's quite different exterior lay a deep and dark layer. Indiscernible except to those well seasoned in reading the language of the body warrior's balance and assassin reflexes rippled in each step and motion they made. Mutual respect was the foundation from which quickly grew an almost casually girlfriend closeness one would expect to see in only the young and foolish.

"Cities have some advantages." Dimi replied with her musically high voice. "No forest sounds to hide your steps. You are getting sloppy, I heard you approaching quite some time ago."

Dimona issued a laugh as she walked over to the table Dimi sat at and peered in to one of the pistils that sat beside her. Bending down she waved her hand above it and took a careful sniff. "Interesting," was all she said but a slight twist to the side of her mouth said volumes to Dimi who smiled back knowingly. "You HAVE been busy." Dimona added. "I would have expected a stronger concentration." Pausing a moment as she casually looked down at a red and yellow herb on the table she pulled her dagger and carefully without touching it nicked off the slightest sliver of its leaf. "I wasn't trying to hide from your, and usually in a city there are many sounds to cover one's footfall.

As Dimona looked up inquisitively, Dimi shook her head. "More might make it act faster, but it won't enable the other effects within it to show itself." Thinking a second, Dimona nodded approvingly and with the hand movement of a magician her blade disappeared.

315

Dimona pointed at the brown pasty substance smeared in another very small bowl. "I have never seen the likes of that before. It sure smells foul."

"The smell gets stronger with age, but fortunately so do its effects. Dimi said in a tone displaying just how pleased she was with her rare find." Dimi motioned to the cup sitting half a meter before her. "Adding it to our final toxic soup will make our brew quite deliver some very spectacular effects that come close to matching your requirements."

"Really," Dimona asked excitedly. Then looking at a relatively small bowl of Dimi's finished product frowned. "How much will we need for each, 'candidate'?"

Dimi's eyebrows winked upward and her emerald eyes sparkled mischievously. "Even the smallest amount in their blood will trigger the flesh eating disease and within an hour or two blotchy gray, semi transparent skin will pop like a soapy bubble and like an over ripe melon their liquefied insides will slough out of them."

"I smell curare and hemlock." Dimona added approvingly. "They will be alive, but incapable of moving or even speaking... but if they suffocate will the effects still work?"

Dimi laughed. "Trust me, it will be spectacular, but not," Dimi paused a moment her lips pursed.

Dimona concluded her friend's sentence. "Not pleasant."

"Well," Dimona added with a laugh. Turning she around the table closer to Dimi and softly placed her hand on her small shoulder. "You know if you are ever looking for work."

"I don't usually need money." Dimi added haltingly as she looked up and back. "I rarely go in to cities."

"Well, if ever you want something," Dimona smiled. ANYTHING your little heart desires. Trust me, with talents like yours nothing you might want is out of reach. And you would have to deal with me."

The dryad shrugged and continued mixing the concoction. "I am looking forward to seeing how this works.

Dimona, usually a lone hunter nodded to the window. "Let's hunt together tonight, it will be fun. From what your friend told us you both won't be lingering."

Dimi looked up apprehensively but then smiled at Dimona, "not very sporting."

"But good fun, with dart and dagger from the sounds of it, it will be like grabbing fish from a stream."

"Fish in a barrel," Dimona corrected, but seeing a perplex look added. "It doesn't matter. But tell me, why North? "Looking around Dimona added quickly. "Trust me; I am not staying here to wait for the army to arrive but the payment would have to be very high for me to cross over into Masti lands. They always lived on the edge, being held back by southern forces. Is it worth it? What is the princess to you?"

Dimi laughed, suddenly every tone in her musical voice sounded sharp and sickly. "I care nothing for their princess; I am going to settle a score."

"The best blade is one bereft of emotion."

"A passionate blade twists and cuts that much the deeper." The dryad answered as she set down the pistil and reached for the toxic fluid that was congealing in to an even thicker, pastier substance.

The thief looked away. "After years of suffering the days with morons and incompetents, I finally find two people I actually like and believe could be friends with. People don't typically take me at face value and also want to know who I am. Miathis is stubborn and far too loyal for the good of his own health. We will gain him some time, but it won't be enough. The Mohen will cleanse this city with a wash of fire."

"We will meet again." Dimi stated as a matter of fact but looked down at the bowl now in her hands. "Nothing can stop me from repaying Sarta, and then I will find you and show you areas where no other human has set foot. Places carpeted with jasmine, framed with dark woods more fragrant then any red cedar and covered with orchids and magnolia.

The thief turned away and looked out the window, "sounds very nice."

Dimi looked as she heard the movement but said nothing as Dimona slipped back out into the city, "I will see you at sunset - for the hunt." She heard Dimona whisper back at her. "I want to see just how good those cute ears of yours really work."

***

As evening turned to night Dimona put down her glass of wine and brushing the crumbs off of her jet black vest and pulled on long elbow length black satin gloves. Pushing the fabric in to the small gaps between her fingers she stood, and turning completed the transformation to assassin. With the soft padded footfall quieter then a rabbit she glided to the door and opened it. The evening fog brought on by the cooler night didn't even part but appeared to reach out and embrace her.

"Damn." She whispered as she stopped in her tracks. "That is good." Turning she reached out to her left and waved it parting the fog shrouded darkness. Dimi's pale face beamed, lit only slightly by Detro's cloud covered face. "Dark for a city," Dimi said looking up.

"Assassin's mood we call it." Her voice was hushed, yet she breathed in deeply. I love the stillness of the night.

"Well, then let's go. There are some noisy scouts in need of stilling." Dimi held out her hand and then let slip from her bare hands a small oil bag, "Just a scratch."

The assassin nodded, getting both the instruction and the warning intoned in her friend's voice. Like stalking jaguars each huntress slipped into the tall grass outside of the city. Unlike their pray, the stalk tops neither bent nor swayed. Each moved gracefully, if not almost too quickly to their mark as a competitive edge seeped in to their play.

By sheer luck Dimona's prey had turned and was apparently moving in to the city for a closer look, while Dimi's had by chance had already been moving in a circular pattern with them towards the northern gates. Dimi quickened her pace, jumping from one bare patch trying without much luck to gain ground on her companion's moves. Smiling, she suddenly stopped dead.

Dimona hesitated only a moment feeling that fate had given her the upper hand she stalked forward carefully. The scout she had been stalking had slowed and was only a dozen or more meters ahead of her. Fogged breath soundlessly wisped from her mouth as she reached down and without looking dipped the tip of her dagger into the top slit of the oil sack was now holding. Her had was about to rise, as her legs coiled for the run when she froze and then silently fell to her knees. From the place she knew her friend was came a very audible sneeze. 'What the ?' she thought, bewildered by her friend's amateurish mistake.

But as she heard her mark turn recognizing the sound Dimona growled inwardly, 'The bitch!'

Kneeling in the darkness Dimona held her breath and listened as both Mohen scouts having heard the unintimidating sound turned and headed for it. Knowing that her mark was now on guard Dimona sat and painfully listened as it headed over to where the sound had come from.

The huntress hesitated a moment too long for less than a minute later as she started circling back she heard the dull whisper of Dimi's small reed blow gun.

Decision made, the assassin turned and headed for the more distant mark hoping to reach it knowing that her own was likely now the harder target.

"Over there, can you see something?" She whispered."

Dimi turned and looked in the direction Dimona faced. Out deeper into the corn the dryad sensed more than heard 'something.' She turned and nodded to her friend and then motioned that she would circle round to see what it was.

The thief went down to a crouched stance and started slowly down the end of the line of corn and paused as she came to a small path that separated the one field from the other. Behind her, the city's walls towered high casting tall shadows down into the field before her.

Looking up she smiled at first and then frowned. Halos and Detros both would sleep behind thick billowy clouds this night, making it very dark. Although ideal for a thief with good vision, for those tracking assassins it was a little 'too dark'.

Carefully, Dimona moved across the path and into the second stand of corn. Pausing a moment she dropped down to all fours and listened intently. The corn had been planted in rows circling the city. Passage around those rows was relatively easy, but in order to approach the city the scout would have to pass through the dried out stalks making his passage much noisier.

The thief smiled as she heard the scout move through another line of corn. 'Right to another planted body, keep going my friend.' She thought as she mentally mapped out all of the locations where they had planted decomposing plague victims.

Dimona slowly moved back to the separating path and then slid three rows closer to the castle before working her way back south. When the body was in partial site she dropped down to her belly and waited knowing that the scent created by its decomposition was likely to draw the scout to it.

Silently traversing the rows of corn was nothing for the dryad for they seemed to part effortlessly for her. Smiling she strolled quietly behind the scout as he made his way east towards the castle. The man was tall, and dressed all in black without a cape or jacket to enable him to move quickly unseen. Dimi froze a moment as the scout finally caught scent of the body.

Dimona breathed slow and softly as she heard the scout break through the last line of corn that separated himself from the body. Dimona squinted but could make out little more now than the silhouette of the man. She was immediately impressed with the scout for he appeared not to be too concerned of the plague. He looked over it and prodded the body with his dagger. 'Not good.' Dimona thought to herself as she watched the scout lean forward and sniff the corpse.

Dimona almost jumped out of her skin when Dimi put her hand on her shoulder but she had sufficient training to restrain herself from making any sounds.

As Dimi lay down beside her the small dryad's mouth pressed delicately against the thief's ear. In a whisper that was like the wind itself Dimi cautioned her friend. "Bad news, I think this is a smarter one."

Both ladies lay quietly watching the scout who audibly sniffed the air. Both knew instinctively that if the scout had training as an assassin he might be able to discern the ingredients used to make the body appear as it did.

The scout obviously was not sufficiently intimidated by the body to turn round, or alternatively had been given order to get a closer look at the city and the men guarding it. Slowly, and deliberately the scout rose and started forward again through the lines of corn to the city.

Dimona took a risk and shielding her mouth with her hand turned and whispered back to her friend. As she turned she paused a moment startled by the brightness coming from Dimi's emerald eyes. "I think we should take this one out."

Dimi's eyes bobbed in the darkness and in the blink of an eye she was no longer beside her friend. Dimona rose up and started backtracking to her path hoping to be able to reach it and make her way to the end of the corn before the city walls before the scout could.

Without a moment's pause Dimi moved like a jungle cat through the corn towards the scout. The corn parted soundlessly for her and her light steps made no sound as she stalked the man. She was drawing close again to him when all of a sudden Dimi stopped, having lost the man's scent. She could also no longer hear him or see his movements. For the slightest moments Dimi felt afraid, wondering if somehow he had sensed her movements and was now somewhere close looking back at her, stalking her.

Slowly, deliberately Dimi's confidence and movements forward returned. Smiling she inhaled slightly and then scrunched up her nose in disgust. There to her right was a small sewage creek that ran from under a low grated hole on the western walls out into the pastures. The scout must have dropped down into it and was planning to use it as cover as he made his way to the wall and perhaps via it under the wall and into the city. 'This one is good,' thought Dimi as she smiled enjoying the challenge.

Dimona made it back to the end of the corn and started slowly south. There was virtually no light and she had to work almost blind. Stopping she looked up at the tall walls using the shadows of the towers to orient herself as to where she was. Shaking her head with doubt and slight confusion she took another step.

But the dark, unseen bank of the creek just in front of Dimona gave way and in a tumble she splashed down and into its filth.

Startled, with adrenaline surging through her veins she gasped and tried to listen, but all she could now hear was the pounding of her own heart. Spinning around, assuming she must have been heard by anyone close by she pulled the black dagger from her sheath, its blade glowed blacker still in the night as she instinctively sliced the air in front of her.

Dimona's keen instincts had been accurate. She had almost landed atop the scout who having heard her fall into the creek was already moving forward with his dagger in hand.

The scratch made by Dimona's blade on the scout's forearm felt inconsequential to him as he lunged forward for the kill.

But the scout's hand numbed as it surged forward like a viper to strike his prey. As the tip of the dagger hit Dimona's chest, his hand lost its grip.

As the tip of the scout's blade cut through Dimona's vest and shirt above her belt she braced herself, sure that she was going to die. But instead of pressing forward and parting the skin at her belly the blade stopped and instead of being gutted Dimona felt the scout's now empty hand slam into her.

Although startled the scout's hand had not been clenched tight and did little to impede the skilled thief's own instinctive response. As she fell backward Dimona reached forward as far as she could and sliced her dagger up hard.

The scout, having leaned in for the kill caught the blade under his chin. Dimona's black dagger sliced upward easily into his chin and then into his mouth and pallet.

However, the scout felt no pain. For the poison that had already been delivered to his forearm had been sufficient to paralyse his entire body. His lungs did not even have enough strength now to push forth a gasp of dismay as he fell forward.

Dimi was there a second later stabbing and then pulling off the scout from Dimona. "What did you do to him?" She said in a normal voice knowing that there was little use in trying to conceal themselves now. As Dimona stood up she reached down and pulled out the dagger. Dimi watched as the black dagger slipped from the ridged corpse and took a step back. "You are going to let me take a look at that when we get back." She said simply.

Dimona had barely been able to catch her own breath when both of their attention was turned to motion in the field further south. "Damn the seven hells." She swore softly.

Dimi splashed across the filth but without her wings to keep her high she began to sink. Gasping the sludge sucked on her feet and pulled her deeper down and the slimy excrement crept up to her face. Dimona, longer of limb than her friend was ahead of her in two steps and grabbing Dimi by the shoulder pulled her across the creek and up onto its bank.

The creek's bank crumbled as they both crawled up it. Thinking quickly, Dimona grabbed Dimi's feet and launched her over her head up onto the bank. The thief then proceeded to climb up herself; however, the adrenaline in her veins took that moment to reclaim its loan. Panting and now slightly dizzy the smell of the filth hit her like a sledgehammer. It was too much for her and a moment later she lay against the creek's side wrenching uncontrollably.

Dimi's feet now felt heavy and slippery with slime and muck however, still the dryad moved faster and surer than a spider in sand. Entering the corn stalks again she weaved in and through them using her ears to guide her direction. As she ran, her hand reached down and pulled up the blowgun. Knowing it would be clogged she blew through it as she ran clearing it, and then deftly her slick fingers flew through her belt and it was loaded in the blink of an eye.

The scout had made his mount and was already atop it by the time Dimi reached the path. At a full fifty paces she knew there was no way she could hit cleanly given that he too was likely caked with muck. Cringing with realization as to what she would have to do Dimi brought the gun to her lips raised the barrel high and blew with all of her might.

The scout's horse had just kicked off of its hind legs when the dart hit its flank. Although many time the size of the man, the poison in Dimi's dart worked and after ten lengths the animal stumbled and fell.

Dimi had another dart loaded by the time she reached the scout who was raising from the ground with dagger in hand.

Weaving as she ran Dimi shot without hesitation hitting the only clean spot on the man's neck. The scout's hand moved up as if to swat a stinging fly but as his hand rose to touch his neck, his feet gave way and he crumpled to the ground.

Ten minutes later Dimona found Dimi still sitting there beside the horse crying.

After a very long night's duty, and a very, very long hot bath both ladies stayed up until morning talking. When the sunlight first broke the horizon both walked hand in hand from the private royal baths back to the pub and prepared a feast.

By the time Miathis arrived for his normal breakfast meeting with Dimona all three of his new friends were already engorging themselves. Large stacks of pancakes smothered in syrup covered the entire table before them.

"Am I too late for a little breakfast?" The captain said as he entered the pub and closed the door behind him.

"We worked up an appetite last night," replied Dimona looking up from her plate and then winking at Dimi.

"And I get by your celebration, the hunting was successful?" Miathis said as pulled up a chair to the table and pulled a few pancakes from the platter.

"We had to kill only a few, many appeared convinced." Dimona paused. "It will slow him for a day, but even if your general arrives, you will be outnumbered."

Dimona looked imploringly up at Miathis and she looked as if she might ask him once again to reconsider leaving, however, she remained silent. After a moment of looking at each other Dimona went back to her breakfast.

"Montterran scouts are already here, General Thesera will be here before sunset... after that I will be under his order as to what is next." Miathis said as if in answer to Dimona's unasked question.

Dimona nodded and then motioned over to Dimi who sat beside her. "You should have seen our little friend here move last night."

Dimi's head barely made it over the edge of the table and she was having some difficulty spearing her food with her fork, but she looked up and smiled after Dimona spoke. "We had some fun didn't we!"?

Etch looked up from his meal. "Must have had a fun time, but you girls still do smell funny."

Dimona reflexively brought her arm up to her nose and sniffed, but then as Etch started to laugh realized that he was pulling her leg, having already heard their story.

Dimi's giggles inverted Dimona's frown and she too began to laugh.

"I think the ladies are a little giddy." Etch added to answer Miathis' confused look. "They haven't slept."

"Ah," Miathis answered although he looked still very confused by the verbal jousting.

"Anyway," Etch continued. "We would love to stay, but we too should be off."

Dimi didn't look up but rather continued to eat.

Dimona looked over at her. "I have no idea where you put it all Dimi."

Dimi smiled and winked at Dimona and then readdressed her plate with fervour.

Miathis looked over to Etch who seemed so relaxed and at ease. "When are you leaving?"

Etch put down his fork and looked apprehensively at Miathis, "soon."

Dimi and Dimona looked around again today, but haven't found much. Dimi is convinced that Sarta was through here. What Dimona and her men found up at the keep is definitely her work, although we still only can speculate on how she was able to capture all the people within this massive city."

"The stink of Sarta is greater by the northern gate and roads." Dimi added as she stuffed another piece of pancake into her mouth.

Miathis paused first and then leaned in and spoke quietly. "So, are you headed northeast to the Masti? Are their hands behind this?"

Etch looked over to Dimi who shrugged. He then turned back to look at the young captain, "due north for now. Dimi is fairly sure she is headed north, perhaps to hook up with the Masti, perhaps not. We think she has had help, but Dimi isn't sure it is the Masti."

The captain nodded. "I wish after all this we had known more, but it is good to know what we do I guess."

"Can I ask a favour of you two?" The captain started. Dimi and Etch both paused from their meal and looked up. "We have sent a man north to AnnonTer to beg for assistance, he left two nights ago, but if you see him on the way -" The captain's voice trailed off leading the two to understand fully his request.

Etch nodded in understanding. "If he doesn't make it, I will talk to Duke Rudolph Ygor."

"Thank you." Miathis said. "I am sure King Roehn has already sent runners or birds to Ygor and to Tierie Zarof Count of MinonTer but neither likely know as of yet the Mohen advances to their capital."

Miathis paused a second in thought after noting Etch nod in agreement. "Ygor's sister is Tierei's wife, you might suggest to him to send word to his sister as well."

Etch looked over to Dimi who didn't seem concerned so he nodded again. "It is a long ride from here, and if Sarta's trail takes us elsewhere we will follow her."

Miathis looked deep into Etch's eyes and spoke volumes without a single word. His eyes were filled with duty, and dread and pessimism of the future.

Etch nodded again. "Although Dimi is a great guide it will take several days unless it snows and then it will take longer. If the Mohen are as strong in numbers as we hear, then even should they marshal troupes, they will be a long time in coming."

Miathis nodded and then looked down at his plate and pushed it back from him. "Not too hungry this morning." He said simply and then stood up from the table.

"Well then." Miathis said as he reached forward and extended his hand to Etch, "best of luck."

Etch rose and took both of Miathis' hands in his. "Best of luck to you my friend."

Miathis nodded and then let go of Etch's hand walked around the table and was about to mess Dimi's hair but when she looked up at him he smiled instead. "Thank you for helping us last night."

"Couldn't have done it without her," Dimona added and Dimi turned to smile at her new good friend.

"My pleasure," Dimi replied. But then after thinking she turned to Dimona. "Don't forget to put a rather large pile of muck out where the horse died."

Dimona nodded. "We will bury her in the city." She added making the small dryad smile.

"Will I see you again?" Miathis asked Dimona as he rounded the table to her spot.

Dimona shook her head. "Sorry, no. As I have said before, we are not soldiers." She looked up at the captain and smiled. "Stay alive, I would like for us to do more business together."

Miathis laughed. "How many horses laden with bags are you taking west?"

Dimona smiled back. "Not too many, we only took the good stuff. Besides, most of it already has been sent."

Miathis nodded in understanding. "Well then, I had better get to my men and prepare to receive General Thesera."

"Send him my regards," Etch said and then pushed over a piece of paper to the captain, "My report."

Miathis took the piece of paper and put it into his vest. Nodding one last time to his friends he turned and left the pub.

Dimi, Etch and Dimona all watched him go and then looked from one to the other. Each knew what the other was thinking and all felt as if they were seeing their new friend for the very last time.

"Any chance," Dimi asked turning to Etch.

Etch looked over to Dimona who looked back at the two and simply shook her head. "No."

Out of the pan and into the fire

It was very early morning, and very dark when Etch and Dimi set out. Like the night before the sky was filled with thick clouds obscuring all light from both moons. Bettham opened the North gate sentry door and Etch and Dimi nudged the heavily burdened animals forward out and into the darkness.

Having taken the liberty to visit a few of the shops before departing both travelers were well dressed for the trip north. Etch looked up and then pulled up the collar on his new heavy overcoat. The scent of the coat's heavy felt lined with fur brought to him memories of his home. Some mornings when he rose early to go hunting Alyssa would greet him at the door. He could almost feel the warmth of his daughter's head as it pressed into his shoulder as they hugged silently before he set out. Chad's head might peak down from their loft and he would wave and say good-bye.

It had already been some time since he had seen Chad's smile, smelled Rachel's cooking and heard his daughter say she loved him.

A gust of cold wind hit Etch's face bringing him back from his daydream He spoke without turning around in a quiet voice as if afraid to disturb the darkness. "I might be mistaken Dimi. But I think it is cold enough to snow."

"Yes," Dimi replied as she looked up. "The clouds are full and it is surely cold enough."

Dimi rode behind Etch upon Peppy. The only coat they had found for her had been for a child. It was embroidered with flowers and on its large hood was painted a rose. The front of it was fastened with large wooden pegs.

Etch apologized for its childish appearance however Dimi had taken it gladly saying that she liked flowers. "Besides," Dimi replied. "Should we enter another city it might actually make me easier to explain!"

The two rode forward watching the landscape change about them as the sun continued to rise and warm the frost bit land. The flats of the Terran planes fell quickly behind them as they entered an area with long rolling hills. Large, dark thickets of white pine and maple trees started to spring up on the tops of the hills

Their progress slowed slightly by midday as they climbed a long rolling hill; on top of it stood a small grouping of trees. The tall white pines poked up as if to pierce the clouds above. Once atop the hill Etch glanced around and then dismounted.

Leading Mule back Etch looked curiously over at Dimi who was curled up atop Peppy's back, fast asleep. Etch smiled as he drew near, puzzled how she could remain so balance while sleeping. As he drew near Dimi's eyes opened.

Etch stopped beside Peppy yawned and stretched. "We are making excellent time. If I am not mistaken the village of Tar Fur might be made by tomorrow morning if we continue this pace. I was through this area once, but it was long ago. All I remember now of it was that they made some rather tasty cheese."

Bending over he then looked down at Peppy legs and stroked them. "Peppy has made an excellent recovery. So has Mule. You have really done some magic on them Dimi."

"Not magic," Dimi replied as a matter of fact, "just knowledge of animals and herbs."

Dimi then smiled and stroked Peppy's neck and untangled part of her main. Mule resenting the attention Peppy was getting nickered and pushed Etch with her nose.

Etch laughed as he looked back at his horse. "You are a spoiled one."

"The rest has done them both well." Dimi responded quietly as she sat up and leaned forward to pat Mule's head.

Dimi then stopped patting and instead sat up and looked around the horizon.

"What's the matter?" Etch asked as he looked around himself

"It's weird." Dimi started and then paused. "It's almost as if I feel as if we are being watched."

Etch glanced around and turned a bit more serious to face her, deep in thought. "We are far enough north of TerranAdd; I doubt any Mohen scout would venture this far north. To the north of us the horizon is clear and I have seen no tracks of recent travel."

Etch paused as he looked around and behind them. "Yet, somehow, I feel it too."

Dimi shrugged while scanning the horizon. "But I haven't seen anything unusual."

Etch laughed. "How could you, being asleep and all."

Dimi frowned back at him. "I was resting, not sleeping." She then jumped down and Etch reached to untie one of the large bags tied to the pack mule. He reached in to the bag and grabbed an apple from it and held it up for the mule. The mule grabbed it with its long teeth and Etch held the remains in his palm so it could finish its snack. He then reached up and patted the mule.

Etch pulled out of the bag a two-kilo wheel of white cheese. "Are you looking for something like this to add to your diet of roots and twigs?" Etch questioned jokingly as he held it up and waved it in front of Dimi.

Dimi jumped up and grabbed the dark red cheese from Etch and sat unceremoniously down on a large stone on the hill and started to peal back the wax that covered it. I had forgotten what it tasted like… now I can't get enough of it." She then looked up at Etch. "I don't know if I should thank or curse you for reintroducing it to me."

"Take it easy," Etch said as he watched Dimi take a big bite from the wheel. "We don't have much of it and in case you forgot – too much of it will tie your stomach up in knots." Etch grabbed out of the bag another three apples and after tossing two to Mule he walked over to where Dimi was and sat down.

"This rock is like ice." Etch said after taking a bite from his apple.

"The ground is turning hard. The sun is waning and winter is here." Dimi looked up to the trees behind them. "I still feel it." She said softly.

Etch turned and scanned the horizon behind them; his face tensed as he looked from where they had just rode off into the horizon where other large clusters of trees gathered.

"But I hear and smell nothing." She added softly after a moment and took another bite of cheese.

Etch looked around and then bit down on his apple again. "We shouldn't dally, we are wide open, and anything could be watching us from any one of the large cops of trees that spot the hills." He stood up and finishing his apple grabbed Mule's reigns. "Lets go. Once we hit the tree line in a day or two we will be less easy to follow."

Dimi rose and then looked south. "But it will be harder to see what is following us too." She said.

The consummate woodsman looked south again, pulled by Dimi's own stare.

"Lets see then." Etch said as he handed to Dimi Mule's reigns. "Keep going north over this hill and on to the next. Stop at the next thicket of trees a kilometre down the path and stay out of sight. Wait for me there. I will wait behind these trees and see if something is following us."

Etch pulled his bow and quiver out from under Peppy's saddle bags, strung it with two quick movements and then adjusted his dirk. Crouching down he then turned without looking at Dimi and raced off into the tall pines.

Dimi curiously watched Etch and then shrugged her shoulders and nudged Mule forward back into the denser trees. "Silly man, if anything was that close we would have smelled something wouldn't we have friends?"

Dimi nudged Peppy and Mule forward down the path towards the next group of trees that stood atop the next hill.

"I feel it too." Etch said silently as he worked his way behind the first row of tall pine trees. There was little cover so he crouched down as low as he could. As Dimi and the animals passed him moving on into the thicket the hairs on the back of his neck began to rise.

Spotting a small shrub by another tree Etch crawled to it, hoping it would give him better cover. The branches of the shrub were no longer covered in leaves, but its interwoven branches were thick.

Lying down on the cold needle covered ground Etch pulled a small curved piece of clear glass out from his coat's pocket. Holding it up to his eye he scanned the southern horizon.

"Damn this is good." He said softly to himself as he smiled inwardly wondering if he should have told Dimi of his find.

"Lots of cool stuff can be liberated from empty cities." He said smugly as he surveyed the lands behind them.

After some time sitting and scanning the horizons Etch started to rise but just as he was going to his knees a movement in the distance forced the crystal back to his eye. Down in the valley below them, in the blurry distance the animals walked unhurriedly out from another gathering of trees. The animals exited the thicket in straight line and as each emerged Etch clearly noted that each animal looked to its right and left.

"Animals working as a team to flush game," Etch whispered questioningly as he lay there trying to focus his eyes for a clearer view. "Even wolves don't get that big." He said with a nervous voice after a minute watching them.

The distant images were blurry at this distance and Etch strained his eyes to focus on the animals trying to discern what they were. He looked back and forth among them and then tried to recall how big the trees were that they had just past. All of a sudden the apples in his stomach felt rather heavy. "Too damn big, couldn't be." He whispered feeling uneasy and more than a little concerned.

The animals walked unhurriedly, stepped lightly and yet moved far in a single stride. "By all the hells," Etch swore softly as he stuffed the glass back into his coat. He turned quickly grabbing his bow and started to jog north through the trees to where he hoped Dimi now was sitting with Mule and Peppy.

Etch had taken no more than five steps when a small glint of steel amidst the trees to his left caught his eye. Overcome by curiosity, Etch took a few strides towards it but then stopped dead in his tracks mesmerized by what he saw.

There, just off the path north hidden by a small grouping of trees lay the remains of a soldier and his horse. The man's mail armour had been gnawed through and little remained of him and only the saddle and a few meatless bones remained of his horse.

The soldier's helmet lay with most of what remained of the man's head. Beside it lay a broken shield with the remnants of one arm still within the buckler's leather thongs. Etch walked round the head and took a closer look at the saddle which he noted was clearly marked with a white fist.

Etch glanced nervously backwards and then turned and started to run at full speed.

Down the hill at the start of another thicket Dimi turned Mule round and looked back up the hill that they had just come from. She pushed back her hood and then pulled from her pocket a small piece of cheese that she had broken off of the wheel prior to returning it to the saddlebag.

"Where are you my friend? Why do you dally?" Dimi said absentmindedly as she gazed out.

Dimi's eyesight was impressive, and her expression dimmed as she watched Etch run from the southern thicket at a high pace.

"Something is about." She said as she stood on Mule's saddle to gain a better view through the few branches in front of her.

"Something disturbs Etch, he is running. Should we go get him or stay?" She said as she untied Peppy from Mule. "Just in case, mind you Peppy. We won't leave you, but I might need to ride fast to pick him up."

Etch started panting hard while still only halfway back to the animals. The slope afforded him a good running speed, but the muscles in his legs were already burning from the pounding they were receiving from the hard packed ground. When he made it onto the road his running improved and he regained a bit of his breath and got into the rhythm of the run.

"My god, I am out of shape." He swore between puffs.

Dimi's anxiety increased to a boiling point as Etch drew near; nervously she untied her blowgun and loaded it.

Etch, totally spent bounded the last few strides up to Dimi and the animals. Falling to his knees he looked up at her. "Blood Ferrets," he coughed in between gasps of air.

Dimi's demeanour went from concerned to one almost comical. "Blood Ferrets? Oh come now, you are running like that from Blood Ferrets?" Casually jumping down from Peppy she walked over to where Etch knelt. "What are they going to do to us, jump up and bite our bottom?" She laughed as she looked down at him. "WAIT, I know. They will make lots of cheese and force us to eat it!"

Dimi's laughter trailed off as Etch looked up. The expression in his face said more than his words. "They won't need to jump, each is as big as a horse... and there are three!"

The dryad looked up the hill, and started to walk but Etch caught her wrist. "Let me go!" She said in a chastising voice as she tried to free herself from Etch's hold. "Let me see, I have a way with animals!"

Etch shook his head as he stood. "Not likely, they are pack hunters now. I found a soldier and his mount ripped to shreds up in the woods. They look very hungry."

Dimi looked up at the hill and then back to Etch. "Transformed, Sarta did this in passing! A beast would not have the mind to know what has happened to it, its instincts would be all confused." She looked nervously back and forth between Etch and the hill.

"We should go…" Etch implored.

"NOW," he yelled as he tied his bow onto the saddle and then moved to climb back aboard Mule.

Dimi vaulted back atop Peppy and both turned their mounts north. Etch looked nervously back at the mule. But knowing Dimi would rather fight then leave the animal behind he kicked his horse into motion.

Riding as quickly as Peppy could go they twisted and turned through the thicket emerging to look up yet another hill. With the ferrets still not in sight they started the climb.

"When we get to the top of this one I want to stop and see for myself." Dimi called forward to Etch who nodded in agreement.

"But only quickly." Etch called back to her.

When they reached the top of the hill they hid themselves as best they could behind a few trees and looked down into the valley. The animals continued their methodical pace and had not yet reached the thicket below. Dimi sat mesmerized as she described in detail each animal.

Etch sat upon Mule nervously listening to her until he could bear it no longer. "Ok, I don't need to know how their eyes look. They are Blood Ferrets! What more do we need to know, the animals are insanely vicious at the best of times. I watched one rip off a woman's finger when she went to pet it. And these are as tall at the shoulders as you are high!"

Turning as if he wasn't going to wait any longer for his companion Etch spurred Mule forward. However, he moved only slowly until, from over his shoulder he noted Dimi and Peppy following.

Dimi called from behind Etch. "With time I might be able to tame one."

"Perhaps," Etch called back to her. "But not likely while the other two gnaw on your bones. Time is something we do not have."

Looking back at Peppy Etch shook his head. "They aren't running and they are moving as fast as we are. We are not going to stay out of their sight for long. We need to make it to the village, it's our only hope."

"Why is Sarta doing this?" Dimi called forward.

Shrugging Etch didn't turn around but replied while turning Mule to cut a path around more trees, "because she can. Perhaps she thinks it's fun."

Etch slowed his mount and then threw back a lead to Dimi. "Tie it on to Peppy's lead, Mule will ensure we don't slow."

Dimi reluctantly tied the two leads together and then turned around in her seat so she could watch behind them as they rode down yet another small hill. Her blowgun was still in her hand and occasionally she checked it or the pouch of quills at her side. "They have a lot of fur." She said as she looked back. "Darts are hard to use on animals with lots of fur."

The woodsman looked down at his bow. "They move too fast." His voice was filled with tension as the seriousness of their situation sank in.

"We can't out run them." Etch added. "I think there is a small village to the northeast of us."

A moment later Dimi's voice rang out again in a concerned questioning tone. "How far, I can see them."

Etch kicked Mule's sides as he glanced back nervously. The tether from his saddle back to Peppy's lead was taunt and stretched. "Peppy can't travel as fast as Mule. If they gain any more we might have to leave her behind."

Dimi shook her head. "No, if it comes to that we fight."

Etch shook his head furious at her response. "Are you insane? Better the mule than all of us!"

"If Peppy slows then we will make a stand in the open with a fire." Dimi retorted. "How fast could you make a fire?"

Etch chuckled looking around. "A lot longer than we would have," He said as looked around. Bending forward he patted Mule's neck, "Faster."

Dimi turned around in her saddle. "Throw me back your quiver." She demanded.

Etch pushed Mule's reigns in under his leg and pulled the quiver from off of his back. "Why?" He asked as he turned and tossed it back to Dimi.

"I will put some poison on them." Dimi replied as she took one arrow out and then a pouch from beneath her heavy coat. "Just be careful when you draw the arrow back."

As his dirk bounced against his leg Etch looked enviously back at Peppy's saddlebag where his sword hung.

At the top of the next hill Etch turned Mule to the Northeast and spurred the animal to even greater speeds towards a small creek that lay at the valley's floor.

The water was cold as it splashed up on the animals and friends soaking them. Thirsty Mule pulled hard on the reigns hoping Etch would stop and let her drink. "Sorry girl." Etch replied as he pressed his feet into her ribs and urged her on. "We don't have time."

On the other side they slipped into another thicket of woods but didn't slow or turn to watch if the water had in any way confused their trackers. Instead they continued their long hard ride.

After two hours of hard riding Etch looked back again at Dimi who was still holding his quiver but looking back intently. "And," he asked.

"Nothing," Dimi replied and then turning tossed the quiver back to Etch who caught it and put it back onto his back. "We might have gotten lucky."

"How much farther," Dimi asked, "and how big is the village?"

"I am not sure." Etch answered as he looked to the continually rolling horizon. Glancing to the west Etch watched as the sun began to set. "Days are getting shorter." He complained. Then looking up to the sky he added. "Least it will be a clear night."

For two hours more they rode, occasionally Etch would call back just to be sure that Dimi hadn't seen anything. With the hope that they had indeed eluded the ferrets they risked a stop when they approached another creek.

Both animals drank deeply and Dimi took the time to massage their legs and readjust their bags and saddles. "Mule is ok." Dimi added, as she looked the horse over.

"But this pace is killing Peppy." Etch added looking back at he mule, which was now much, the worse for the forced run.

Dimi spun as Peppy's head came up unexpectedly from the water. The animal's coat shuddered and then the creature whined.

"Damn." Etch swore softly as he ran through the water to Mule and started to climb atop of her.

"Wind is from the west." Dimi added as she jumped back on Peppy's back and threw Etch her reigns so he could tie them once again onto Mule's saddle.

Splashing loudly the four scared travelers left the creek as fast as they could. As they rode Etch untied his bow and checked to ensure it was not wet as a result of their ride through the creek. Rather than replacing it back by the saddle he elected to rest it on his lap as he nervously turned around to look behind them.

Dimi, still facing back did not turn to look at him. "Keep looking forward." She called back to him, "I will tell you if I see anything. You just get us to this village."

The pounding of Peppy and Mule's shod hooves on the hard packed ground echoed over every hill and followed them into every valley. The two friends knew that they now had little chance of eluding the ferrets.

Etch glanced back at Peppy. The mule's bit was fully extended and the animal was gasping, being pulled hard by Mule. "I tell you she isn't going to make it."

"Peppy smelled them, if it wasn't for her we would already be dead." Dimi called back. "They are close but I haven't seen them lately which scares me even more."

"You've seen them?" Etch asked now looking left and right nervously. But the sun had now set, and what light remained in the sky was grey. Shadows flew from every shrub, every hill and every tree.

"Back a ways, we still have a fair lead. How far do you make it?" Dimi asked.

Etch heeled Mule a little more, the mare was tiring as she pulled Peppy as hard as she could forward.

"I hope not far." Etch called back. "With luck we will see it around the next set of trees."

Dimi's voice was nervous as she called forward. "They are running slow, and spreading out, about four hundred meters behind us."

Etch checked his quiver placement and touched the dirk that was bouncing against his leg. He then looked up to the dark sky. "Light is poor already, I hope they have lit torches at the village gates."

As they exited another thicket of dark trees the village formed in front of them. It appeared like a diffused silhouette against the darkening horizon.

There were only flickers of some type of flame from within the village itself; no torches were alight at the gate. At the blurry sight, Etch spurred Mule on urging the animal to expend the last of its energy. Dimi cut loose one of the heavy bags that had been tied to Peppy's saddle. It fell with a thud to the road and broke open spilling its contents on the road.

"My sword was tied to that bag!" Etch swore back at her.

Etch looked back. "And the bag contained no meat; they won't even stop for a sniff."

Dimi stood up on Peppy's rear and with blowgun in hand rode standing and looking back as the beasts drew nearer. "I can see the yellow of their eyes Etch my friend."

"Damn." Etch swore. "The village torches are not lit, so no one mans the gate. We will not make it in!"

Etch stood up as high as he could in his stirrups and yelled forward to the gates of the village in the distance. "HELLO!" He yelled at the top of his voice. "OPEN THE GATES!"

But his voice drew no response. No head popped up from the walls to look.

"Come on Peppy." Dimi yelled down and back to the mule. "Keep going girl!"

Etch kicked Mule hard, but its pace did not change. There was now nothing left in the mule to enable the horse to go any faster.

As they drew within a few hundred meters of the village Etch noted that it was encircled with a dilapidated three-meter fence made out of spiked logs loosely tied together with heavy cord. Not much care had been taken to erect or maintain the wall and Etch wondered if it would hold the creatures at bay if they made it inside.

The scent of the sweating and afraid animals had been inhaled deeply by the massive creatures behind them, and they began to wail and chatter in excitement as they began their all out run to capture their prey before they could enter the walled village.

"TO ARMS!" Etch screamed as they drew within fifty meters of the village.

"HELP US!" He screamed with his lungs almost bursting. He then put Mule's reigns in his left hand with his bow and brought his thumb and finger to his mouth and he blew a long hard whistle. The shrill sound pierced the night, yet the village gates stood closed.

Not having enough energy to stop quickly Mule hit the gate with almost full force. Her heavy shoulders slammed into the loosely knit poles shaking them and bending in the gate by a good meter. Even though an entire length of wall vibrate the gate remained closed.

Peppy, exhausted and being pulled hard by Mule slammed into the back of the horse almost throwing Etch off.

"LET US IN!" Etch demanded in a scream as he sat now upon Mule, his left leg pinned between the horse and the wall. Frustrated he twisted as he felt Dimi's hands on his back and then her feet.

Like a monkey the dryad used Etch as a stepping-stone as she launched herself up. In one graceful, fluid motion she was up and over the wall.

With his free foot Etch pushed Peppy back and freed his trapped right leg. Spinning as he slid off of his horse he ran forward to face the horrors that chased them.

Large dark images raced across the field. Etch stepped out in front of the mule and horse and looked out desperately trying to focus his eyes in the dying light as chattering sounds echoed and reverberated around him.

"Come on, let's get this done." Etch said calmly to him self as the creatures forms started to coalesce out of the darkness in front of him. Only the flickering light of a single obscured torch behind the walls illuminated the ground before him. Etch squinted and filled with moisture as he looked to the left and right trying to judge which creature would reach him first.

Now closer, the ferrets appeared even larger and their sickly yellow and black bodies were covered with filth. Their heads moved eerily up and down as they ran, their long bodies undulated, and in their yellow eyes Etch saw malice and hunger.

Etch pulled back his bow and took aim at the middle creature and let loose, knowing that at best he might be able to draw and loose one more arrow. The arrow flew and momentarily disappeared from his view as he reached around to grab another shaft.

As he notched and let loose another arrow, from the corner of his eye he watched as the first ferret began to fall. The long arrow shaft, stuck firmly in the animal's eye splinterd as it tumbled. Cart wheeling legs and long fur made the other two animals bolt to their sides. Etch knew that his second shot would not hit its mark.

The two massive beasts jumped at the same time and to Etch it looked as if a giant wall of teeth and snapping mouths were approaching him.

With Peppy and Mule directly behind Etch was unable to step back. Feeling boxed in he bent down and at the last moment, with every ounce of energy he could muster, he dove to his left.

Tumbling in the dust Etch twisted and turned. The creature closest to him had slowed in time and its long neck and snapping mouth continued their pursuit of his flesh.

Defensively he brought up his bow and whacked the creature across its massive snout and then without looking he dove again, hoping to get behind the creature.

Peppy screamed loudly as the second massive ferret slammed into the back of her. Instinctively the sturdy mule let forth a massive kick that lifted the ferret, sending it up and over Etch to land behind him.

The mule's blow turned the head of Etch's attacker giving him just the opening he needed.

"AHHHHHH!" Etch screamed as he spun and as the animals head turned back to face him it was met with the tip of his dirk. Bits of teeth, gum and snout flew into the air. Howling the beast jerked back and away from Etch, his arm now totally numb from the impact of blade on bone.

"IN!" Dimi screamed from behind him.

Turning Etch noted that the gate was open. The animals being very eager to depart the company of the creatures surged forward pushing Dimi back through the gate.

Without looking back Etch followed the animals in. With Dimi, then at his side, they threw the gate closed and lowering its long locking bar.

Just as the bar locked in place the entire gate and wall shook as one of the ferrets hit it. Etch and Dimi slumped down to the ground and with their backs against the gate they sat there and panted.

"Took you long enough." Etch said after a moment.

From behind him he could hear the creatures chatter and wine and pace back and forth.

"They sound upset." Etch said after regaining his breath.

"The lock bar was a little heavy for me to lift by myself." Dimi said apologetically.

Etch looked up and back at the gate and then over at the wall. "Not much of a wall, but enough I guess."

Etch was about to ask out loud why no one came to help, but as he turned to look in to the village he didn't. There were in fact no torches lit within the village. The several long poles with torches atop of them were all burnt out. The only light came from three small fires that were consuming the remnants of what likely were shacks. Many of the other small wooden houses had already been burnt to the ground.

"She's been here too." Dimi warned. "I can smell her." Dimi reached round and pulled on Etch's arm. Etch looked to his left, there beside the gate was a corpse, peeled in succubae fashion. The remains of a small woman or older child lay a few feet further into the village, twisted, torn and pulled inside out.

Etch swallowed hard trying to keep his stomach from turning over. Behind him there was silence. Turning to Dimi he spoke softly. "We need to check the rest of the walls, I would rather not have those creature back in here with us."

Dimi nodded and stood up while Etch used his long dirk to help him rise.

"I could really do with a good night sleep." He groaned.

Mule and Peppy were now huddled together to the left of the gate, neither having any ambition to move.

As Etch passed them he patted Peppy. "Well done girl."

In the darkness behind him Etch heard Dimi call. "I told you so!"

"Ears like a bloody bat." Etch whispered.

Dimi ignored Etch's last jest and continued walking down the village's eastern wall. Although in sad shape, her keen eyesight noted no gaps between the tall poles wide enough to let the large ferrets in. However, she knew that if the animals were hungry or upset enough they had the strength, and intelligence to get in through or under the wall.

"It is only a matter or time." She said to herself.

As she made her way around inspecting the fence Dimi occasionally looked back in to the village. Inhaling deeply she tried to catch Sarta's scent, but the air was rank and foul smelling of smoke and old dried blood.

A soft sound emanating from within the village caught her attention. 'Survivors?' She thought to herself. Eager to meet with Etch and search the village for survivors she quickened her pace.

"I heard something." Dimi said excitedly to Etch when they met at the end of the Northern wall.

"Me too," Etch said looking back into the dark village. Then turning to look at the fence he shook his head. "No major holes, but they aren't in the best condition."

As in answer to his statement the two turned to hear the padding of the feet of one ferret that had obviously followed Etch around the wall.

"This one appears lonely and eager to regain my company." Etch said sarcastically.

"I think you pissed that one off." Dimi replied as she looked at Etch. "And I think the other one still lives as well."

Etch looked up at Halos and then down to the dark village. "You had best lead the way, I can barely see my hand in front of my face in here."

Dimi stepped south into the village. "I thought I heard some noises coming from further in to the village."

"After you then," Etch added with some hope in his voice. "Perhaps they can tell us something."

Dimi didn't answer but instead continued to walk into the village.

"Hold on for a second." Etch said stopping Dimi in her tracks. Stepping over and through a burnt out house he reached down and pulled from the flames a burning piece of wood. "That's better." He said as he lifted the flickering flame up high.

As they drew closer to the center of the village Dimi proceeded to lead them to a small group of larger dwellings. Stopping she signalled to Etch to listen. In the distance they could hear the other frustrated ferret chatter and bang against the gate.

"Lovely." Etch said sarcastically, but Dimi motioned back at him with a frustrated expression demanding that he remain silent.

Etch stood a moment longer in silence beside Dimi. And then he too heard the sound.

"Several people are in side." She said as she pointed to one of the larger houses, but her tone denoted to Etch a sense of uncertainty or confusion.

"What is the matter?" Etch asked.

"I would expect whimpering, crying." Dimi started to say but after a moment paused and then shrugged. "I don't know, perhaps I am just a little spooked after being chased by blood ferrets taller than I am."

Etch laughed. "Yes, that can shake up just about anyone."

"Hello." Etch called out to the cabin, "Anyone inside?"

The sounds from within the house grew still and only the small cracking of flames from still burning houses around them disturbed the night. Even the creature outside appeared to be listening intently.

Dimi signalled with her hand, indicating they should investigate and both stepped slowly towards the small house where the sound had come from.

"Is someone there?" Etch called out to the house.

From within the small wooden shack came a heart-wrenching cry. Visualizing his own daughter, hurt and afraid inside Etch set aside his fears and pushing open the door he entered the dark small house. "Are you hurt?" He asked as he raised the torch to look around the room.

"Eiiiiaaaah!" Etch screamed as he tumbled backward out from the room. The torch dropped from his now bloody hand. Pushing and kicking the ground with his heals Etch retreated not so gracefully from the door.

Dimi's blowgun immediately was raised as a scarcely dressed, sickly white form with dirty scraggly midnight black hair crawl out of the house.

Dimi hesitated. "It's a girl." She said simply.

But as the child lifted her head up and looked at Dimi the dryad knew that although what was in front of her might have been at one time a child, it now was nothing less than a horror.

Glowing milk white eyes looked up at Dimi and as its lips parted a long, thin, split tong darted forward to taste the air.

Etch, obviously still in shock screamed at Dimi. "IT'S A SNAKE, KILL IT!"

As if in reply the creature's head turned to Etch. Its lidless white eyes appeared to focus on Etch's bleeding hand and on all fours it bounded forward to him.

Dimi's dart hit the abomination in the back of the neck, but instead of immediately dropping like it should, it continued forward.

Etch, still on his back, kicked the creature in the face sending it backward. Bending forward he picked back up the burning stick.

Dimi stood there in awe as she looked at the dart, clearly imbedded in the creature's neck.

Etch got to his feet quickly and slashed the air in front of him but the creature nimbly jumped backward.

"Try something else then." Etch called to her as he danced back and forth warding off the creature.

Dimi scavenged through her small pouch and a moment later she had another dart loaded in her gun.

The second dart did much better than the first dropping the creature in a heartbeat. Etch, with eyes wide still with fright looked over to his friend. "Unreal!" He finally said.

Dimi nodded as she took a closer look at the body. "It's only asleep." She said as she prodded it. "I had three darts that are more a sedative then a poison."

"Part reptile part snake I would guess." Dimi concluded as she stood back up. "Look at the clawed fingers."

"And part human child." Etch added with a sad tone. "Sarta needs to be stopped."

Dimi spun round as another door behind them opened. "There are more." She said plainly.

"Bloody lovely," Etch swore.

349

"We need to get back to the animals." Dimi pleaded. "They aren't safe."

"Nor are we," Etch added smugly as two more creatures came out from doors beside them. Both of the creatures turned and looked directly at Etch.

"How many do you think there are?" Etch asked nervously as two more glowing white eyes illuminated the doorway of a house.

Dimi looked up as they continued to back away from the creatures. She reached down and loaded her blowgun again. "Too many, I only have two darts left."

"They sure were quiet when we did the once around this village." Etch said in a nervous tone as he waved the fiery brand in front of him slowing the creature's advancement as the two started their way walking back to the front gate.

"They can likely smell the fresh blood." Dimi added looking over to his bleeding hand. Like dogs waiting for a bone the now four white mutated villagers watched intently as drips of blood fell from Etch's wrist onto the dirt.

Etch brandished the burning flame at the closest to him. Both hesitated and backed off.

"Let's run shall we?" Etch said and without comment Dimi took off and Etch followed close on her heals.

The four creatures caught off guard by their sudden departure hissed like cats and then followed in a run behind them.

As they neared the end of the houses another creature jumped out to cut off their path to the gate and their animals. Dimi didn't hesitate a second. With a leap she vaulted over the creature and while cart wheeling she slashed at it. Dimi's dagger parted the white skin and ribs of the creature as if it were nothing more than warm butter. Howling the creature twisted and then ran on all fours past Etch back into the center of the village.

Mule and Peppy stood motionless by the gate. Both animals turned with great fear in their eyes as their masters returned with seven new horrors following them. Peppy howled in warning as the southern gate sagged inwards as a ferret hit it with all its might.

With the Peppy, Mule and the gate at their backs Etch and Dimi ran back and forth scaring away the mutated villagers. "There are too many of them!" Dimi called over to Etch. "And they are fast and weary of us know. Eventually they are just going to wear us down."

"Only for as long as my torch holds out." Etch answered back as he slashed his dirk at another creature. "I still can't believe that you ditched my sword." Etch said as the wiry reptilian mutation jerked back avoiding his short blade.

"Live with it." Dimi said and then laughed.

Seeing the blood speckle down as he waved his torch Etch grinned. "I have an idea." He said.

Looking at his cut hand Etch clenched his teeth. "Hold them off." He commanded to Dimi who without hesitation started to scream and dance back and forth flashing her dagger dangerously.

Placing his dirk between his knees Etch pressed the burning end of his torch into the wound. "AHHHH." He screamed as he dropped the torch. The small blood drenched ember flickered for a second and then went out.

"That's stupid." Dimi said as she looked over at Etch who now was taking the dirk again in his right hand. "They don't need to smell blood anymore, they know where we are."

"Actually," Etch said smugly as he grabbed the animal's reigns and started leading them to the left of the gate waved his dirk back and forth. "I think we should invite our friends in after all."

Dimi looked over at Etch. At first she was puzzled, but then understanding crept to her expression.

After pulling Peppy and Mule to the left of the gate Etch dashed forward and sliced one of the villagers across the belly. It howled, turned and as intestines began to seep out from between its white fingers it ran screaming away from the group, leaving behind it a long trail of blood and guts.

"Messy business." Dimi said as she jumped forward. With her small dagger in her left hand she swiped back and forth three, four times at a creature. The white skin parted and blood began to well up from the wounds. The creature looked down and screeched and then spun and started hurling back towards the inside of the village.

"Bait set." Etch said with a not so calm voice. "You ready?"

Dimi nodded and ran towards the villagers who now were very leery of them backed off while Etch turned and started opening the gate.

At first the villagers hesitated, but as the gate began to swing open realization crept into their reptilian faces and they all turned and started running back into the village.

A lone cry came from beyond the walls. "Here kitty kitty." Etch whispered as together they pulling back the gate so that it would somewhat shield them and their animals.

With the scent of fresh blood the ferrets bounded into the village at a high run following the two massive trails of blood.

Dimi turned and grabbed the reigns of Mule and Peppy as Etch pushed the gate allowing them to get around it.

Etch smiled as the s screeches of the village creatures being chased and caught by the massive; hungry ferrets followed their exit.

"Vicious animals," He as they pulling the gate closed behind them.

"That will keep them all busy for a while." Etch said as he cut off a piece of Mule's lead and using it tied the gate closed from the outside.

Exhausted both sat down next to the gate and listened to the sounds of screeches, hiss and howls as the ferrets feasted.

As the morning sun rose large round snowflakes fell blanketing the land making it sparkle. Behind the gates the sounds of screams had stopped and all that could be heard now was the crunching of bones and rending of flesh.

"I think the ferrets won." Etch said as he looked over at Dimi.

"And I doubt they will be hungry for a while." Dimi replied with a smile back to her friend.

Etch put his arm around Dimi and leaning back against the fence and letting the sun's rays play across his face he sighed. Dimi rested her head against his shoulder and moments later the two exhausted travelers fell into a deep and peaceful sleep.

SanTer and the Cliff Mines

Carton Tunis governor of SanTer heaved a heavy sigh as he looked out over the city's battlements to the long line of carts and wagons that wound its way down from the cliff mines to the city's gates.

A dispirited laugh issued from his throat as he shook his head. "What safety will these people find within these walls?"

The moisture of his breath fogged the frigid air and tiny crystals formed on his well cropped grey moustache and beard. His gaze lifted to the towering mountain behind the castle. There masses of soldiers worked among its pock marked face and sides securing the massive iron gates to lock tight the entrances to the mines.

And above them all hung his greatest leverage, although it would only be used as last resort. High at the top of the mineshafts, held back by kilometres of stacked and bound wood was a wall of rock and soil. With one word, with one call of warning, with one command he could shut down the mines and make the mines inaccessible for years.

"It will not come to that." His wife said as she came up from behind him. Gently she wound her arm under his. Her long warm fur coat pressed tightly to him and he could feel her extended tummy press tightly in to him.

Turning he looked down at her smiling youthful face, her long flowing blond hair wafted up in the cold breeze. He smiled as he looked down, but his joy was not complete as he remembered their first born. 'Darn' he thought as the image of his son flashed through his mind.

"I miss him too." Carel said as her smile faded slightly and she looked to the north and snuggled even closer to him.

"You above all others have always believed that life brings with it eternal hope." Carton laughed, but this time his tone was joyful. "Look here I am at fifty years of age having thought that I would

354

never again see the joy of a child born to us. I had given up all hope, but you never did and here we are."

Carel looked up and smiled but behind her eyes he could see a depth of meaning. "But we must move on from the past, we must look to our future. You cannot focus on the past – Terros is long dead and his son Tar now too is as lost as our own."

"King Roehn has sent word, his men are riding and sailing as we speak to aid the Terran people. The Mohen advances will stop." Carton added but his tone carried little confidence in it.

Carel grabbed his hands in hers and held it to her chest. "Your new son or daughter will need both a mother AND a father. You must put your feelings for Methor aside. Terran lands will not stand even with aid from the west unless we stand together. The other dukes and counts must be all brought together as one and Methor is next in line to the Terran throne – he has the right to these mines AND our loyalty."

"I was THERE." Carton added as his voice rose. "When Methor marched back to TerranAdd and laid the heads of several hundred Masti blood priests at the foot of his father's throne. Oh how arrogant a fool was he, proud with hands drenched with so much blood. I knew then and there, nothing good could come from such an act of atrocity. His mind was set on genocide from the start. What type of future king would act so?"

The governor pulled away a little from his wife, his face was tense once again. "The stain of blood, the stink of it cannot be washed clean. Methor killed Terros and Metrin as sure as he had done the deed himself. It was his ruthless actions in the blood wars that spurred the Masti zealot's hand."

Carel shook her head and smiled. "He was young and impatient, seeking glory at all cost. He too has aged and matured my husband. And you must for once swallow your own pride and bend knee to him for he is the son of your friend, and the brother of the king we have lost. You MUST my husband or not only will this city fall, but with it so too will fall our kingdom and all home for our yet unborn child."

The governor looked back up to the top of the cliffs where the visible line of the wall of wood and stone sat patiently. "I hope, each day I pray that our son stands beside Tar somewhere, perhaps they were pursued by the Mohen and have not the time to contact us." Carton added but again his voice had not been filled with any confidence but rather bordered on self-sarcastic reproach.

Carel looked with her husband up at the line of wood that ran across the tops of the cliffs and mountain. "You tie together the hope of Tar's survival with that of Dar's. Our son is gone as is the king, his wife and daughter and all those within that city."

"There is no need for immediate action. All others know that with one word we can shut down the mines. No one will attack us, our child will be safe." Carton said as his eyes continued to focus on the cliff walls. "We can wait and see."

"The other lords will follow the coin, and you hold the Terran purse. If the Mohen do not take them then civil war will soon commence – either way our country will fall." She said understanding what he was thinking of. "We cannot afford to dally here." Carel said as she pulled from him. Frustration rose in her voice.

"You are so stubborn my husband."

Finally, Carton nodded and stepped forward back to her side. Gently he put his arm around her. "I know. I know."

"We must settle for the lesser of evils." Carel added softly. "He is still your friend's son. And General Kilkitoe will think twice if he knows that the Bloody Duke has the support of the Terran lords and that the Duke has the wealth of the mines backing him… In a fortnight we could secure many mercenaries."

Finally after another long pause the Governor's wife added. "Let pride not slow your hand to an action that is inevitable. Make the offer quick and generously and we might benefit from it."

"All I can see is the boy standing there in court laughing as his men dumped the heads." Carton said but then added. "I will send a rider to Methor in the morning and invite him to inspect our holdings."

"His holding," Carel chided as she nudged him in the ribs.

Carton chuckled and brought her closer to him.

A man coughed as he drew up behind the two. "Excuse me sir." The knight said apologetically as he drew up.

"Sir Nindor." Carton said as he turned to the approaching knight. "What news of our men at arms?"

"All is in place governor." Sir Daros Nindor started as he stepped up to the battlement's wall and pointed down to the massive catapults at the northern gates. "Our new war engines are in place, the cauldrons of pitch are in place and our archers well supplied with shafts. By nightfall we will have taken in all we can and our gates will be closed."

"There will be many not able to enter our city for protection." The governor added looking back at the long line of people and livestock.

"Soon we will have enough men at arms to ensure their safety." Carel added politely then she looked up at her husband urging him to the command she knew had to be made.

"King Roehn's men are many," Sir Nindor added. "But they alone cannot stave the Mohan tide." Then to press the point the knight looked to the east and TenTor. "And to the east there are other dangers."

Carton Tunis looked over at his knight. "In the morning, Sir Tendor Sendin will ride east to TenTor and entreat with King Methor."

"'King' Methor," Sir Nindor asked incredulously as he looked back to the governor for an explanation.

The governor looked back at his knight and nodded.

Sir Nindor cleared his throat and then softly added. "I had never thought I would see the day when the Bloody Duke would be allowed within these walls."

357

"King Methor Bestinor." Carel said in a chastising voice to the knight.

"He is our king." Carton added in a warning tone.

Sir Nindor looked at the governor's wife and then back to the governor. Carton nodded in agreement with his wife.

Flustered and almost unable to maintain his composure the knight took a step back and bowed to the governor and his wife. "As you wish my lord," he said as he turned and stormed away.

Carel, to distract her husband's thoughts pulled his arm and started him to walk beside her along the tops of the battlements. They walked silently until they came to the bridge that would take them to the inner keep and their chambers. Carel smiled knowingly up at her husband and arm in arm they crossed the bridge.

Two young soldiers stood guarding the bridge and both drew to attention as they approached.

"Beautiful day, Eh," Carton asked as the two stopped to chat.

"What are your name soldiers?" His wife asked politely, knowing that her husband hated to look as if he didn't know the name of each and every soldier within the walls. She smiled politely at them as she looked them over trying to judge their age.

Both were dressed in the white of the guard, but neither of their shirts showed wear of more than a year's use. They likely both were well under the age of eighteen and looked a little startled to have the Governor and his wife address them so personally.

"Terrac Mag my lady," replied the taller one to the left. He had a face that had a light dusting of blond hair on it, in need of its first shave. A few strands of dirty blond brown hair hung out from under his pointed helm. Side flaps of leather and mail cascaded from the helm and touched the lad's shoulders.

"Fatin Gors Governor," replied the other on the right. He was much shorter than the other and together they made a mismatched pair to guard one spot. The lad had seen more dinners then summer trainings. He was portly and sported a rounded baby smooth face that was almost hidden by the helmet that was too large for him. Obviously the smithy had to find one large enough to span the lad's enormous head but hadn't adjusted its depth. The only reason it hadn't totally encompassed the lad's head was that his longer crooked nose protruded proudly out and pressed against the nosepiece. The leather and mail splashed around the kid's chest as he spoke."

Both lads remained at attention eyeing the Governor and his wife nervously not knowing what to expect next or what to do. Neither had ever once talked to the governor nor his wife.

"Where you lads hail from?" Carton asked smiling. "Wait, let me try to remember, Terrac right?" Carton pointed to the smaller rounder one on the left. Carton paused to look him over. ""From your eyes you might even have Farrow blood to you as well I think. How did you come to the guard?"

The lad looked rather puzzled but didn't nod. Carton continued seeing he had put the lad ill at ease.

The lad moved a little back and forth on his feet prior to replying. "I was orphaned lord. I was picked up out of the sea. A sailor of the southern docks found me and took me for drowned out on Old Woman's Grief's. I was found in the wrecks. He took me in, him and his wife. He raised me till I could take the pledge."

Carton nodded and then looked over to Fatin and gave him a reassuring wink as well. "Each of us contributes in our own way to aid our city, our country and our king. You obviously have South-Western blood in you for your complexion is as dark as night."

Fatin smiled. "Yes, my family hunts crocks in the marshes."

Fatin paused but then continued on more boldly, "begging your pardon, lord. But is it true; are all the people of TerranAdd gone? Did some Masti curse the city?"

The governor's wife blanched and Terrac immediately realized his friend's mistake. "Sorry to hear of the loss of your son." Terrac said earnestly. "He often came out to train with the knights; he was a gifted swordsman and a man of courage."

"He was a good lad." The governor answered back looking down at his wife. Then turning back to the lads he shrugged. "We don't know for certain what happened in TerranAdd, but as you know I fought with Tar's father in the early wars against the Masti. I know what they can do and this is beyond their capabilities."

A cold wind gusted up and Carel pulled in tighter to her husband. "I grow cold my husband."

Carton looked down at her and smiled and then looking back to the men he nodded. "Carry on men; I must take my wife in."

When Carton entered the inner rooms his wife Carel turned and buried her face into his shoulder and wept. He had been used to her sudden swings in emotion, but he knew that deep down her mind was now on their lost son and not the future.

"There is always hope." Carton said as he pulled his wife deep within his arms and kissed the top of her head. "There is always hope."

Sharks in the waters

Tall waves crashed against the hull of the flagship of the Sieren armada. Duke Sindor Sirthinor stood on its bow looking to the horizon hoping to spot the fabled southern cliffs. Turning he smiled as he counted the fifty tall ships following him. "And how far behind us are the cattle?" He asked with a smile to his general who stood beside him.

Sir Admon Terets, general and chief aid to the Duke of Sirthinor did a double take, but then as he comprehended the question looked to the western horizon. "The Duke of Capris and his horsemen are now more than two days behind.

"Two days eh," Joked the Duke. "That is of course assuming that the old decrepit boats you sequestered for them still float."

The general replied with a sardonic laugh, however, inwardly his conscience was punching him in the mid section making his stomach roll. He did not share his Duke's 'kniving' mind, nor lack of morals and he had a good friend aboard one of those boats back across the turbulent sea.

The general's thought must have been reflected in his dark southern complexion for the Duke's eyes narrowed as if searching for the weakness within his aid. "The road we are on is set Sir Admon. There is no path back to the arms of your old friends or the king."

Sir Admon smiled with his thin lips, trying to muster whatever bravado and confidence he could in his demeanour as his eyes locked with the Duke's. "Never have I doubted that. We are 'all in' for this journey."

The general kept his unblinking gazed lock with the Duke's, hoping that his reply would be fully accepted and that his stoic and unblinking stare back at the Duke would hide the turmoil that he felt deep down. When the Duke's piercing eyes moved back to the north the general started breathing again. It was hard for him to maintain composure. As he looked over the rail to the

361

crashing waves he felt as if another chunk of his conscience had just being torn out of his heart and thrown overboard to crash in the tall waves.

To continue the facade that he cared little of the life or death of those that followed them the general non chalantly raised his hand up and brushed back a long black lock of hair, pulling it back over his head. Being a close cousin to the Duke, the general shared his lord's sharp facial features and long thin black hair that appeared always to look wet.

The Duke apparently sated by the general's response chuckled wickedly; his reply was quiet enough that only the general could hear. "I can almost visualize the Duke of Capris bending knee to help in the bailing of the bilge."

General Terets smiled in reply and then forced another throaty laugh. But his laugh was louder than he had hoped as his conscious again caused him grief. 'Would Bestos Hastinor, the Duke of Capris' general be bending knee beside his Duke?" He thought to himself. 'What would his best friend think of him now? Would he be questioning his friendship and loyalty already, did he suspect yet? They had trained together, and he was closer than a brother,…'

The general pushed his mind to release the errant and disturbing thoughts. "We have set our path," Sir Admon said almost as if to himself. "Duke Hastor, his general and all the horsemen will not be happy the next time we meet them."

The Duke laughed and turned and slapped the general on the back, although the diminutive man needed to almost rise to his toes to do so. "You worry too much my friend. As for me?" The Duke raised his hand to his cheek to wipe off the small tears of glee that had fallen from his eye. "I can see them now, all the proud men of Capris standing knee deep in filth, bailing slop over the sides….hugging their horses as each tall wave hits their small, decrepit vessels."

Then as if the Duke's emotional flow had been turned off with a spigot he turned and looked up again with a cold stare at his general. "'If' we ever meet them again, Personally, I doubt General Bestos Hastinor and his men will survive the winter given the Mohen advances."

The general visible blanched upon hearing his friend's name. 'Can the Duke now read minds?' He thought momentarily to himself.

After a pregnant pause the Duke's piercing eyes moved once gain mercifully off of the general and back to the horizon. "How much longer until we can see the Terran shores I grow tired of this boat?"

General Terrets looked and then pointed to the north and east. "We will move in and through the old woman's reefs where the other ships will wait until they are signalled to continue. There a longboat will take you further up the coast and then to the shore where our man awaits."

"Once at San Ter I will need half a day…" The duke added softly and we will signal you when you can proceed.

Sir Admon Terets tensed, deciding after all to retest the Duke's stance on their current plan. "I wish you would reconsider…" He stuttered. Then after a long pause he spoke his heart. "There are other ways."

The Duke of Sirthinor looked up and his eyes were bright with anger. "Reconsider what? If you are going to have the gall to challenge the plan now, then spit it out man. Don't dance with the words. We have gone through this before."

The General breathed in deep then looked up and around, several of his officers were watching them both intently and sailors buzzed around the deck trying to look busy, however, he realized that many ears were now intently listening to their debate.

The general contemplated how he might reply, knowing that he had to choose his words carefully. However, as he was about to reply he noticed that the Duke's attention was elsewhere. The diminutive man's peaked nose was pointed up and he was obviously captivated by a seagull, which was about to land on the mast above them.

"We are closing to shore." General Terets acknowledged as he watched the Duke study intently the bird high atop the mast.

"Hmmmm," mused the Duke. "All is coming together as planned." The Duke said smiling as he nodded up to the bird. "Get a man up here, fetch me that bird." He commanded as his eyes stayed transfixed.

General Terets stepped over to the holding and pulled it open and yelled down. "Bariston. Come up on the double and bring your bow!"

In a moment a short thin man in leather climbed quickly up out from below decks – he held an unstrung bow in one hand and his quiver in another.

Sir Admon Terrets looked up and pointed at the bird as the archer grabbed the bow and putting it over his leg he bent it back and strung it in one deft move. Then brining the bow up with one fluid motion he notched and let loose a shaft.

The bird was silent as it was struck, but made a dull thud when it hit the deck below the mast. The archer immediately stepped forward to pick it up but the general put up his arm and shook his head. "Thank you." He said motioning the man to return to the holding.

The archer looked over at the Duke, hoping for some statement or note of approval, but the Duke's attention was still set on the dead bird. Shrugging the archer turned and went back down the hatch.

The General walked over picked up the bird. The weight of shot had been perfect and the arrow had stopped leaving the bird fully transfixed by the shaft. As the general pulled the arrow the rest of the way through the bird he noted that the Duke had walked up behind him, obviously anxious to see it himself.

The General absentmindedly tossed the arrow to the mast so it wouldn't be stepped on as he turned and held out the large limp seagull to the Duke. Curiously the Duke smiled and then grabbing the bird roughly he started pulling at its two small legs.

With two small cylinders now in his grasp the Duke dropped the bird upon the deck and then turned and headed back to his quarters.

Reaching down the general grabbed the bird and looked curiously at it. "A seagull courier?" he asked in a hushed and very confused tone. Seeing then that the Duke was not waiting for him he hurriedly flung the dead bird over the railing and turned to follow the Duke. As he walked he wiped the blood on his hands off onto his pants.

The General's eyes dropped as he followed the Duke into the captain's quarters. 'Keep it together man.' He said silently to himself as he followed the Duke in.

As the Duke walked forward in to the large cabin the general quickly grabbed the door and closed it behind them. He stood there a moment as if frozen in place. 'Eyes down…. Keep focus… Don't look up.' He said to himself as he began to turn.

With eyes purposefully blurred he twisted round and walked briskly to the side of the Duke's desk as if intending to stand beside or behind the Duke.

"Have a seat." The Duke offered.

Soft strained sounds came distractingly from behind him, but the General kept his composure as he replied. "I'm Ok." Then after a moment's pause, to ensure the Duke's attention wasn't on him, he quickly added. "What do you have there?"

The Duke looked up beaming at the general. Then in a smug, voice he waved to the two small tubes before him and asked the general his rhetorical question. "Tell me general. What manner of sea gul could deliver a message to a ship at sea?"

The General shook his head, knowing the answer but not wishing to say it. "I would not have thought it possible. The birds are too stupid, and even a courier pigeon can only be trusted to return to its nest."

From his side the Duke of Sindor pulled out a long, thin silver plated dagger. The tip of it was as pointy as a needle; the blade was as long as his hand, but no wider than any one of the Duke's fingers.

With the knife held gingerly in his hand the Duke pried off the top of the first tube. Then tipping it he shook its dark, powered contents onto the table.

Without hesitating Duke Sirthinor pricked his thumb with the knife and pressed out a drop of blood onto the small pile of powder. "Blood to my blood," he said softly as a small billow of smoke curled up from it as the powder began to burn. The flames were small but pronounced and a sickly sweet smell filled the room as the flames dropped and disappeared.

Behind the general there were more noises, but the general refused to turn, and kept staring intently at the spectacle in front of the Duke.

Duke Sindor looked up and smiled at his general. "And soon this act will seem nothing more than a parlour act done by a court jester." He then reached over to the other tube. The second tube held within it a small a rolled parchment. The Duke licked the excess blood off of his thumb and then with dagger in hande he delicately unrolled the parchment and bent forward to silently read the message written on it.

General Teret coughed for although the smell was now dissipating, it still made him want to retch. Then under his breath he said almost inaudibly the prayer he had been taught as a child. "Let our blood stay clean."

The Duke ignored the General's prayer as if he had not heard it. Looking up he smiled at his aid. "All is arranged." The Duke said motioning down to the parchment. "It goes as planned and we are on schedule."

The general nodded but as he did so he swallowed hard fighting off a sudden massive wave of nausea. 'Control man,' he commanded to himself. 'You have seen battle before, you have killed before!'

But the general's mind was slipping and twisting with turmoil as evident within his face.

The Duke's expression hardened as he recognized the turmoil the general faced. "It must be done." He stated without emotion. "And now is not the time to get squeamish. I told you back in Sirthinor that we would have to do certain things you might find distasteful in order that we might succeed."

The general nodded as his eyes connected with the Duke's. "I know… and I know what must come next." He said slowly. "I guess I had always jut hoped there might end up being another way." He was about to turn to look behind him when the Duke reached out and grabbed his wrist.

The Duke's expression was filled with malice as he looked up to his aid. "This is 'my' act, not yours and there is always a price one must pay for power."

The general nodded and breathed in deeply trying to regain his composure. Hesitantly he pulled back his hand from the Duke's hold. With what little willpower he had left, he made his last stand. "What will our allies think if they were to find out the means of our power?"

"STOP IT!" The Duke yelled slamming his fist on the table. After the bang, there was the sound of a whimper from behind the general. The duke's own eyes darted past the general, but the general stood motionless desiring rather to stare into the Duke's hostile eyes vs turning around.

"I TOLD YOU…" The Duke started as he pulled his own eyes away and looked back at the general. Then after a small pause his tone dropped and his body relaxed as he sat back. "It IS necessary."

"Besides," the Duke added, as he looked once again at the twisted, bloody paper in front of him. "There is no other way but the path before us. Only if there is true belief that the bloody duke was involved will we be able to not only obtain, but hold San Ter."

The general looked to plead – "But …"

"ENOUGH ALREADY!" The Duke said stopping the general in his tracks and with a note of finality he looked away from the general and with a flick of his wrist dismissed the man, knowing that any further conversation was futile. "If you do not have the stomach to assist me – be gone. I will do this alone."

The General, torn by command and conscience stood motionless. His breathing was short and broken as his head ever so slightly shook. He was now almost ashamed of himself for being part of this venture. With the last of his resolve he looked up at the Duke; determination and set. "There is no return from your next step. If this act is known, even the Count Palantine will not follow you – every last man in the west will pursue us."

Duke Sirthinor smiled wickedly. "Landor Rutt is a fool, and I need his loyalty only for the moment. Besides, he has already made his bed by not sending his men east as Roehn commanded. I care little now for him." The Duke looked back at the general. "We will not need him or any other soon. The Mohen and Masti will keep the Terran and Montteran forces busy, and by the time they figure out that there is even a greater threat about – it will be too late."

"Besides you must relax my general." The Duke said as he licked his yellow teeth. "In a few weeks the two of us will sit safe within a massive castle drinking imported Ferrow spice wine, eating blood oranges and crisp pork ears while dozens of naked young slave fulfill our every desire. We will care little for the old hags we have left behind or…"

The Duke paused a moment as if his conscience had finally caught up with him. But then when he smiled and there was no sense of hesitation in his vinegary voice…"Or for the product of the lust of our youth."

"Now, my friend." The Duke said as opened the drawer of his desk and removed a pale white wooden dagger. "Do you have the stomach to assist or should I call another to be my aid?"

The general swallowed hard, his eyes transfixed now on the yet unstained Masti dagger... the symbol of almost everything he had ever thought was evil and unclean. The blade and handle were one, made of a rare white wood; it remained for the moment unstained by blood.

The general closed his eyes and turned to look behind him. When he opened his eyes, the very frightened gaze of the Duke's son met his own.

"Lets get on with it then…" The general said with a dispassionate soldierly tone.

The young lad of twelve let out a soul wrenching whimper and then started pull and strain to be free of the hurtful tight leather straps that bound him to the solid dark captain's table. His wrist, already sore, started to bleed as he yanked and pulled on the cruel leather bindings. But as his father rounded the general and approached him smiling, the gagged child stopped his pulling and with eyes wide with horror he started to shake uncontrollably with fear.

"Well then." The Duke said in an almost humourless voice. "Onward and into the belly of the beast we go."

The Bloody Duke

Methor Bestinor of Ten Tor paced nervously around his circular turret study. Shaking his head he mumbled to himself and then suddenly stopped in his tracks and walked over to the room's most westerly window. Flipping the wooden latch he pulled with both hands the heavy weighted frame. It groaned as it opened. Ignoring the papers that flew off of the desk behind him he leaned forward and let the cold winter wind bath his face. The crisp, dry air almost burned as it went up his nostrils and then down into his lungs.

Straining his eyes he looked to the west and to the distant cliffs of San Ter.

"What are you thinking of this night dear governor?" Methor said to himself bitterly. "This country does not have time for us to play childish waiting games. We must be as one, or we will all fall."

Methor, the first son of King Terros and Queen Metrin looked out impatiently at the west. "I can't believe that you would sacrifice everything, everyone just because I was a bit … 'overzealous' when I was young.

Methor stepped back from and pulled the windows closed. He sighed and turned and went back to his desk and sitting down he let his head fall back and he gazed at the ceiling as his memories of the past danced before his open eyes.

The Terran disputes with the Masti had gone on for many a year. Skirmish after skirmish had been fought, and although the Masti intrusions continued to escalate Methor's father had refused to declare all out war.

Methor let his mind drifted back to recall the warm spring day, when the impatience of his youth pulled his arm to act in defiance of his father. News had just reached him that the trade caravan he had sent to Plan Ter had been intercepted. Twenty guards had been lost as well as the entire caravan – to Masti raiders. It was that very day that he had sealed his destiny. For on that day with the arrogance of a future king he stormed from his castle and in less than a week in the mountains north of Plan Ter they had found the Masti raiders.

He had been too over confident for after all he was the son of a king and there was the prey they had pursued, trapped with their back to a wall of tree and rock, quacking in their boots the Masti had turned to face their fate.

He had ordered the charge without a moment's thought. But then, in a blink of an eye, the illusion disappeared and a hundred men and their horses disappeared into a deep and dark crevice where once stood the Masti.

It had just been blind luck that the right flank of his cavalry had made their way up ahead of all of the others, else he too would have perished that morning.

"The horror." Methor whispered to himself as he remembered the screams of surprise and fright and then the horrifying sounds of bone being splintered and flesh being ripped apart by the jagged stones far below.

He had heard of Masti blood priests when he was a child – every boy had. But he had never in his wildest dreams ever had believed that they could by magic create the nightmare that followed.

One moment his men were charging up the hill at an enemy in clear sight and in the next moment his forces were trapped with their backs against a deep crevasse with Masti spearmen dancing among them effortlessly killing at will.

Sir Gadral alone turned the tide by noticing that the soft, now blood soaked earth showed the tracks of their invisible assailants. With his confident commands the tide was turned and as one they moved back down the hill. Finally after still considerable loss, one of his knights got lucky and with a stab, dropped the Masti priest ending his magic. As one the remaining Masti reappeared.

The Terrans had come north seeking vengeance for a simple raid, but they had found much more than that. Everyone within their ranks including him were overpowered with a sense of terror they had never before felt. The thought that Masti priests could ride to their villages and to their homes and kill at will chilled each and every one of them to the bone.

The paranoia that ensued turned quickly to contempt and then hatred. After tearing the remaining Masti apart, limb-by-limb, they were back atop of their mounts and headed north to rid the rest of the world of Masti blood priests.

Methor's head bent down and his hands went up to grip his dark hair.

They went from village to village seeking the priests, but with little success. The hatred and frustration of the army insatiate was brought to a boil as unseen adversaries frequently ambushed them. Soon, what little humanity they had been clinging too was washed away. They began to torture innocents, nailing entire families to walls and tables to convince others to uncover the priests that they were hiding. By the end of the second month, Methos and his men had given up all pretence of civility and chivalry and started to just kill every Masti they came across – man, woman and child.

On the third month after their first encounter with the Masti, Methor's brother Tar had come with force supplied by his father and before the first fall of winter snow, Methor was standing back in Terran Add before his father.

Methor stood up and walked back to the window and opened it again and breathed in deeply hoping the cold air would clean or burn away the memories of the words his father had said that day and the look that his mother gave him. Four weeks later, his father declared an end to the hostilities against the Masti.

His parents had lived less than a year after the ending of the blood wars. A lone Masti zealot serving as their Terran servant killed them in their sleep. Before her beheading she called out that her actions were in payment for the children Methor had killed in his northern raids.

There was a knock on the trap door that led up to the study. Methor closed the window and turning slowly walked over to it and pulled it open. A battle worn officer in his late forties rose up from the trap door.

With a not so convincingly happy voice Methor called out to his friend. "Sir Gadral, good come up and join me, we have much to discuss."

Sir Gadral looked around as he entered the study. The General was wearing heavy scale mail; it creaked a little as he moved uneasily. A heavy metal helmet was held under one arm and his other hand rested on the hilt of the short officers sword hanging from his waist.

Methor motioned his general to the center of the room where a massive oak desk with three large oak chairs sat. It was stacked chest high with parchment maps, although now several were strewn on the floor. The captain bent and picked one up as he advanced and placing it on the desk while Methor sat, he however, remained standing.

"We have been through a great deal together." The Duke started.

The general, stood silently and nodded.

"Done such things," Methor continued looking for a reaction from his captain… hoping to see some empathy to what he was currently feeling. "Thinks that still haunt us – for we are short in allies at this trying time."

The general shook his head. "Had we not ventured north, who knows, they might have risen sooner."

"You are still convinced what happened in Terran Add was as a result of blood magic?" Methor asked.

"Just as you are." The general replied. "We two have seen the potential of their dark arts. Terran Add is the work of those heathens, mark my word." Sir Gadral added quickly. "Unwatched and unchecked by your brother now these years, they grew

373

strong…Our only failing was having stopped our march north. We should have marched all the way North and smashed their broken bodies against the Trukian Mountains."

"But now we are against not just the Masti, and we have too few allies." Methor said sourly as he unrolled a large parchment map on his desk. "And our coffers are too light to hire an army to fight for us."

The captain looking impatient leaned forward, his voice dropped down to a near whisper. "You should take what is rightly yours. We should ride to San Ter and kick the governor out of his cushy bedroom. With the wealth of the mines and safety of the walls of San Ter we could withstand any advances from any foe. You ARE the rightful heir to the throne – you always were – send a message to the other Lord with his demise!"

"NO!" King Methor said slamming his fist onto the table. "Not my own people. I must by action or inaction gain their respect and loyalty – but not through their blood can I lead my people out of this abyss."

Sir Gadral taken back by his grace's sudden outburst remained silent but then he reached into his surcoat and brought out a sealed letter. "A knight of the Temple arrived with this sealed message for you. It is from his holiness."

King Methor looked concernedly at his general and then took the parchment and breaking the seal he began to read the long letter.

Finally after a moment he looked up at his general. "The Tock fell upon MinonTer, he fears it has fallen. Annon Ter too is besieged with Tock."

The general nodded. "I feared as much."

"But what is even more disturbing." Methor added as he looked at his general watching for his reaction. "Is that Wogs and Weer in hordes are descending from the Nasky Mountains."

The general in total disbelief turned and then sat down in a chair with a thud. "What?" He asked incredulously.

Methor smiled. "We have seen so much, and yet you are so surprised that other horrors now walk the land as well?"

Sir Bruto paused as if in thought not knowing quite the words to use. Leaning back in his chair his face looked tired and worried as his right hand went up to the long scar that crossed his left cheek He had been with Methos for quite some time and indeed they had seen great horrors, and also done great evil deeds themselves, yet what his King now talked of was truly unbelievable.

"What of our allies, do you have any other news?" Methor asked his general pulling him back to the conversation at hand. "Have your scouts yet returned from Plan Ter?"

Sir Bruto nodded slowly. "They returned with the Temple knight… they met him just north of Plan Ter – which is a good thing since that city has fallen."

"What?" Methor gasped in disbelief. "How? Who? Tock?"

Sir Gadral shook his head. The Mohen banner of General Mariard flies atop the battlements; the Terran Lord's head and that of his wife and court are spiked on their gates. His troops are this moment pillaging the city."

King Methor sat motionless listening intently.

"The emperor sees our weakness and goes for our throat while we worry about the Masti and Tock?" Sir Gadral said as he pointed at the map in front of Methor. "A hundred thousand and more at his side… "

"Perhaps, but perhaps he is alone in this." King Methor said with a smile. "General Mariard is the emperor's bastard son and raising his own banner over the city gives me pause to wonder. It is still very possible that MiHinDor Perrilos the Fourth is not behind this attack. If not, and if we can stop this man, there might be still hope."

Sir Gadral obviously distraught leaned forward. "Stop him plus the Tock, plus the Masti plus all the other foul things coming from the North. With what?"

Sir Bruto nodded and then motioned with his blade back at PlanTer, trying to remain calm. "Mariard holds Plan Ter now and surely after pillaging they will rest a day or two or more there before riding to TerranAdd. Their knights are much heavier laden then our own and Mariard will not move an army of that size through hostile lands without advance troops first ensuring that they know what they are up against… we could beat them to Terran Add."

Sir Gadral shook his head in total disbelief, "suicide. It would be suicide to ride to face a hundred thousand Mohen or more!"

Methor stood up and slammed his fist against the desk. "If we don't stand and fight then our land will fall for sure. King Roehn has always been our ally. In his last letter he said he was sending us aid… Together perhaps we will have enough forces to fend off our enemies. Have your scouts seen any movement in the west?"

"The only news I have is from our man in Mount Ryhn." The general said dejectedly. " He says the city is abuzz with the news of Terran Add's fall and that all the people say that Tar is paying for the sins of his brother."

Sir Gadral leaned forward to press his point. "And if King Roehn entertains the slightest thought that you had something to do with the disappearance of his daughter, he will not be sending you aid."

Methor Bestinor heaved a great sigh lowered his hands and looked up at his general. "If we had the financial and military support of San Ter – we could hire mercenaries, or perhaps even bribe General Mariard to return home. "

Sir Bruto looked up at his King. "I beg of you one last time. In one day I could send a bird to my man in San Ter and the governor and his wife would never awake tonight's sleep."

King Methor looked down at his desk and then buried his face in his hard, dry, scarred hands. "No. Every man in this land would know it was me that ordered his death. King Roehn would never believe that I had nothing to do with AnnonTer. The Bloody Duke would be blamed again and alone we stand no chance."

Methor stood and walked over to the most northerly window and opened it and looked out. He felt at once impotent and helpless. But then, with the reality of almost certain failure ahead of him he smiled and turned to look at his general. "Send word to the Governor of San Ter once again."

Sir Gadral nodded. "What should we say this time that we have not already said to him in the past? What could you say this time to force him to bend knee to you?"

"That for the sake of our people, the brother of the late king, the son of the greatest kingdom of this land, his friend Duke Methor of Ten Tor rides north to defend the Terran people."

Turning Methor smiled wildly as he looked back to the north. "Within the week, the forces of Ten Tor will ride north to face the Mohen. We beg that he sends us aid, for our fate and the fate of our country are now in his hands."

Sir Gadral stood turned to leave; with shoulders now slightly hunched he nodded as he walked to the trap door. "I will start preparing your forces my grace."

As he heard the general leave the room Methor gritted his teeth and looked out across the cold, snow encrusted lands to the north. Quietly, but confidently this time he whispered to himself. "We will ride north once more and our enemies knees will shake upon hearing of our approach, and their women will lament upon hearing of their deaths."

The cold of the Keeper

The night's perfect silence was broken by the clopping sound of Peppy's and Mule's hooves on the lightly snow covered road. Mule let out a cough and the horse's breath fogged the cold night air. The dark, starless sky above was spotted with the occasional large snowflake that drifted down lazily onto the adventurers. "Winter's definitely been here a while." Etch said softly almost as if he was afraid to break the peaceful silence around him.

He sat up a bit and then tried to drape the front of his heavy cape over Dimi who lay slumped in front of him, with her head resting on the horse's mane. Dimi sighed and sat up and started to look around. Her emerald green eyes sparkled in the darkness as she took in the eerie winter landscape around them. Glancing at the sky she then turned to Etch. "We have been lucky we haven't seen snow already, we are a air bit north but I fear we are in for much more."

Etch nodded as he too looked again to the sky. "Halos and Detros are well-hidden. I love riding in the winter... the snow, it makes the ground look so clean and I love how it bends the bows of the great trees. I almost prefer the ride at night ...." He paused a moment and then added quietly one last word. "Peaceful."

A cold draft of wind rustled the cloak the two shared. Dimi giggled as she leaned back against Etch – "Personally, I look forward to seeing the face of a warm sun." With that she turned her head slightly against him and yawned. "Wake me when you want to stop."

Etch didn't respond, but instead breathed in deeply and let the horse's rhythmic walk drag him back into a lazy half awake, half asleep state.

Hours later the sun had risen but the tall trees still obscured much of its light. Here and there the occasional ray of sun breached the shadows of the trees. The two weary riders trudged along moving along the road that had now transformed into more of a well-traveled trail. Neither stirred until finally after some long while the bright light and warmth of an errant beam of sun lay on Etch's face long enough to coax his eyes to open.

Thick blankets of snow covered the lands as well as the riders. From within the cloak he tapped the robe and the dry cold snow that clung to them slid off. With a flick of his head, he threw back his hood. "My back is killing me." He groaned as he gave Dimi a slight shove. "I think we have gone long enough. I need to get down and stretch."

"Hmmmm." Dimi moaned. "I can smell old trees and water. Not far. Can you ride another hour? We can stop and make camp there and sleep an hour or two in the warmth of the morning sun."

"I don't think so." Etch said as he moved a little in his saddle. "My leg is asleep and I have to pee."

"Great." Dimi groaned as she started to sit up. She then leaned forward inhaled the musky fragrance of Mule's main and gave the animal a hug. "You have been really good. When I get off I will find you a treat."

Without much warning Etch pulled on the reigns and then without much grace slid off. Upon hitting the snow covered ground he staggered and then fell on his butt. Scowling and scolding Etch tried to stand up but the knee-deep snow kept him off balance.

Dimi's laugh rang out around them. With tears of joy in her eyes she howled as she watched Etch struggle to his feet.

Etch looked up with a scowl, but then when his eyes met Dimi's tearing eyes he smiled to himself and then stood and dusted the snow off. "Hillarious." He added jokingly. "See the old man fall down…. very funny." With that he picked up a handful of snow and threw it at Dimi. "Lets see how YOU like the snow."

Dimi moved to the side quickly but the snowball had only been lightly packed and in its flight it had somewhat disintegrated. Although she fended off one of the chunks of snow several others hit her in the face and chest.

Etch rushed forward and tried to grab Dimi's leg with hopes to pull her off the horse. But Dimi was too fast, and with little difficulty she pushed him back effortlessly forcing him to fall back once again into the knee-deep snow.

Dimi laughed. "I would rather remain dry, thank you."

Etch laughed loudly as he stood up and shook off the snow that now fully covered him. Deciding to concede he pulled out his map and looked at it and then looked down the path and pointed at what appeared to be a small offshoot from the road they were on. "That path would take us to a lake… and perhaps back out of the shade of these large trees.

Dimi nodded and then smiled. "Sounds good, wish I would have thought of that.."

After a very short break, Etch was back atop of the horse and they were heading down the winding trail that was bordered by massive trees that reached up and embraced the sky. Dark thickets of brambles, tall roots and small offshoots from the trees interlaced the forest floor making visibility into the woods difficult and setting the two riders to be a bit on edge.

"The Giant White Pines smell so good." Dimi said looking around. But the confidence in her words sounded false to Etch's ears.

Etch strained to glimpse the top of the trees trying to add confidence to the conversation. "Bloody amazing, how tall are they?"

Dimi sat back up and stretched both hands into the air and arched her back. Her head tilted backward until from the tops of her eyes she could see Etch's face. "These are the small ones. The trees around the lake itself will be almost ten meters wide at their trunk. Many stretch up a hundred to two hundred meters. Sniffing she then added with a sour tone. "Your rather ripe and badly in need of a shave." She said to Etch and then looked around."

A loud cracking sound brought their attention to the canopy of trees a few hundred meters ahead of them. A massive branch, unable to bear the weight of the snow upon it, splintered from a tree and started to crash its way through the other branches. The heavy meter thick limb and all the snow it bore added too much weight for other smaller branches beneath it to bear so they too strained and many cracked and joined its sister limb in its descent to the ground. The forest echoed with the sounds of the cracking of wood and breaking tree. A few moments later the ground beneath the two adventurers vibrated as tons of snow and tree hit the earth.

Etch looked around nervously until Dimi hit him in the ribs with her elbow. "Don't worry." Dimi said turning back to look at Etch. "I would feel it long before one around us were to fall, long enough to lead your slow sorry ass out of danger."

"Hey!" Etch said with a sarcastically hurt voice.

As they rounded another set of trees Dimi pointed ahead of them. "We should be close, the ground is dripping faster and I can smell the water.

"What type of twisted person could do that to an entire village?" Etch asked as his minds drifted to the village they had barely escaped from. Then as the thought danced through his mind he added quickly. "Do you smell anything else?"

Dimi smiled shook her head. "Nothing... and I have been consciously searching for unusual sounds or odours...but as for what type of twisted person, well that would be Sarta...."

"She must be beyond mad." Etch added.

Dimi shook her head. "That is what is weird. The magic takes concentration and you can't do that type of magic when you are a raving lunatic..."

"Obviously she has changed." Etch said. "What was she like before when you knew her?

"We never saw her much." Dimi said with a shrug. "As a succubus she was never around during the days and at night she roamed the thick forests around the castle, or along the nearby dark roads searching for her next meal. I only ever saw her lucid once, and that was when I saw her talking to a villager that had strayed out too far from the castle. Sarta walked up to her in her shining glory and started talking quietly to the individual...

Dimi visibly shivered and put her arms around herself and hugged herself at the memory. A moment later she took in a deep breath and then continued the story. "She is lucid for moments only, and those just before a kill."

Dimi paused as she tried to picture Sarta the succubus as a fully functioning mage. "To cast those types of powerful spells would require very long periods of crystal clear thinking. I just don't get it."

With his most sarcastic voice Etch summarized his fears. "Periods of clarity in an insane mind capable of doing massive, horrific acts of magic in the body of a succubus that can suck you dry and turn you inside out. Hmmmm. Somewhat, I don't know let's just say 'unnerving'?."

Dimi giggled at Etch's description. "One thing for sure, she has changed since I knew her and something or someone is giving her new purpose. She used to spend entire days and nights roaming the woods alone living for her next meal and now she is working on schemes and spells that depopulate an entire city? "

"We need to find what motivates her and gives her purpose. It isn't hunger for she didn't eat all those in Terran Add... well not most of them." Etch added in a very confused tone.

"Whatever the reason," Dimi said with malice in her tone. "She needs to be set down."

Etch nodded in agreement, but his confidence was not as high as his travelling companion. "Assuming we 'can' kill her."

As if Mule had understood Etch's last comment and was afraid now to go forward she stopped dead in her tracks. Peppy, with head bent down and somewhat oblivious to their track bumped into them lightly from behind before she too stopped.

Dimi stroked Mule's main "Com on Mule, nothing to fear here."

Mule stood her ground and didn't move.

"The snows too high, I will drop down and lead them the rest of the way." Etch said as he swung himself down off of the horse. Dimi grabbed the reigns as Etch tossed them up to her. But as she caught the rains she raised her head and stopped him in his tracks. "Shhhhhhh". She said and Etch froze. "Another branch," he asked. But in reply Dimi only shook her head slowly.

After a few minutes of standing still Etch started to whisper to ask what she had herd, but Dimi's hand flew up demanding his silence. Only after thirty minutes did her hand drop and she looked down at Etch and spoke in a normal voice.

"Something was watching us. Weird, it wasn't human, and it wasn't an animal... something in-between." Dimi shrugged and then nudged the horse trying to move them again forward.

"Hey, wait a sec." Etch demanded and he watched Dimi start the animal's movement back on the trail. "Not so fast," He called in a semi-hushed voice as he ran up beside the horse and took hold of the mouthpieces. "Like what?"

"It was up originally just ahead on the ground but later was silently up in the trees above . This creature can fly!"

Etch let go of the reigns took a few steps backward and looked to the sky. "Lovely. Bloody lovely," he said as he walked back to Peppi and pulled out his bow from under one of the saddlebags. Reaching into his pocket he drew his string and bent his bow over his leg and deftly strung it.

Dimi looked around somewhat puzzled and then sniffed the air. "Lets keep going. The trees will obscure our view of it, at least by the lake we will have open site." Leaning forward she whispered to Mule and the horse started moving again.

Dimi continued walking slowly the animals down the road. They were no more than twenty meters further down the path when a deer jumped up from behind a tree and in one leap crossed the trail before them. In the blink of an eye, Etch's bow let loose with a 'twang'. The arrow, although well shot only grazed the animals back. Obviously scared beyond belief and in full flight mode it jumped forward with blinding speed dashing into the thicker woods. A large fallen branch lay ahead of the deer creating a final barrio for the animal's escape. The deer pushed down and in one amazing feat jumped up. Etch and Dimi watched in wonder as it rose two meters above the earth easily cresting the branch.

But the graceful animal's feet never touched the ground again. For from above a darkness descended and plucked it from the air. Black as night, it dove in engulfing the deer with folded leathery wings. There was a small thud as the massive black creature caught the deer, then a small snap as the deer was passed from the creature's feet up to its mouth. Then the creature's wings expanded out into all its amazing length and in two leathery beats it and the deer were out of sight, lost in the maze of woods and branches above them.

"What in the seven hell was that?" Etch said as he stood there with mouth open.

Dimi said nothing; she just sat there shaking her head.

Etch paused a moment but then stepped quickly to the leads of Mule and started pulling on its tethers urging it forward. "We need to start moving faster, this snow is too high, we won't outrun it."

Dimi looked back shaking her head. "It's been watching us for some time, if it wanted to have swept you or I away it could have. It wasn't really that interested in us… and I don't sense anything else around."

Unconvinced, Etch urged the group on as fast as he could.

The height of the snow lessoned as they continued their movement to the lower lands however all four were fully exhausted when finally they could see the reflection of water. "Keeper Lake,"

Dimi said somewhat ominously, "I haven't been these ways in a very long time."

"Does the lake have fish in it?" Etch asked eagerly.

"Don't know. Dimi shivered and looked around. "This area always gave me the creeps..." she said as she looked out across the water as they neared the shore. "It is a dark place, there is something here that 'feels' odd and old, unwelcome. I never liked this area, but never knew why."

"Well my weary bones like the look of the sun, we have been riding a long time in shadows and its nice to see its warm face again. And I really would not mind at all if we had some change to our menu. Roots and bread are ok, but some meat now and again would be nice... would have loved to have dropped that deer myself." As they reached the opening that led to the lake Etch reached over and started to untie the saddlebags hoping to get them off the animals so he could then start looking for a line to fish with. "And I am sure you will feel even more welcome when those stones on the bank have a roaring file on it."

Dimi jumped down from Mule and then led the animals to the trees closest to the shore and tied them to one of the many large roots that poked from the forest and rolled along the lake's bank. "Look at these roots." Dimi said pointing at a long heavy strand that interwove in and through the large rocks along the shore and then plunged down into the river disappearing into its dark waters.

"Normal roots don't just go straight into a lake like this." Dimi said straining her eyes to validate that the lake was indeed fully encircled by massive roots.

"Oooo," Etch said with a grin now feeling as if their last encounter with the unknown creature was well behind them. "'Scary weird roots,' Etch restated. "Really Dimi, I thought you had more never, first you are hearing things and now you are afraid of a tree. The ground is probably just too rocky for the roots so they are going straight to the source."

Dimi bent down and picking up a stone licked it but shaking her head she said nothing and instead turned to tend the animals. Finding a brush she started to brush down Peppy. "Mule and Peppy are soaked, they need to be brushed down and blanketed or they won't be of much use to us tomorrow."

The lake surface was as flat and as smooth as black glass. "It is going to be nice to camp here." Etch said looking around. "We don't have to break ice to fill our cooking pans and the tall trees are keeping the wind away… It is definitely going to be a nicer warmer camp then our last one under the shadows of the trees."

Reaching up he scratched the stubble on his chin. "I'll be back in a second, just going to splash some water on my face." He said as he walked to the lake.

Dimi busied herself with the brushing of Mule and Peppy, their coats were covered with chunks of snow that had adhered to the droplets of their sweat. Her brushing stopped mid stroke when she heard Etch yell 'Yahooo.' But then there was a loud splash.

Dimi turned quickly, her emerald eyes flashed back and forth across the shoreline expecting to see Etch's head bob back up and hear him scream just how cold the water was. But there was no sign of Etch. A long moment paused before she dashed forward.

Approaching the small lake Dimi noticed a few of his cloths in a heap by the shore. They had been neatly folded, obviously Etch had decided to clean from head to foot rather then just splash some water on his face… "Damn fool jumped in!" Dimi swore.

With mind reeling Dimi spun, and picked up Peppy's tether and untied it from the stump she had secured it to while brushing her down.

Spinning she yanked on the lead and pulled the animal forward to the bank to where Etch's cloths lay. The mule bayed as its feet banged against the stones and roots as Dimi pulled it forward at a frantic pace.

With deft movement Dimi reach out and with the flick of her wrist her dagger was in her hand and one of the mule's leads had been cut. She tied the two meters of leather onto the other lead and wrapping the lead around her wrist she dragged the mule another step toward the water. Throwing her knife behind her, without hesitation Dimi followed Etch into the dark lake.

Pulled forward and down by the lead Peppi staggered forward to the very edge of the lake. Straining it held its head inches above the water. Its lead, straight and taunt dropped down and disappeared into the black glassy surface of the once again still black water.

The water was beyond freezing cold. It froze Dimi's eyes on contact, her limbs cramped as daggers of cold pierced them. Fangs of familiar, bitter sweet coldness slammed into her stomach making her toes curl. Blind, and in agony Dimi turned and moved pushing her hands and feet outward hoping to make contact with Etch.

Her mind fought the cold. Biting down on her tong and cheeks she used pain to help retain consciousness. "NO" her mind screamed, but her frozen lips remained pursed and didn't move. Kicking out she vainly tried to feel something, anything "I will NOT give up!" She yelled at herself.

But the cold water encircled and embraced her. With cloths saturated and skin turning blue Dimi's thrashing movements slowed. Coldness seeped into every pour leaching away her strength. Cold teeth sunk into her skin and tendrils of its poison dove deep into the depths of her body as if trying to chill her very soul.

To Dimi the cloudy feeling the coldness brought to her mind was all too familiar. "nooo." She pleaded inwardly. "Not again... I cannot." She begged but the persistent cold embrace slothed away her anxiety and will to live and a lethargic, hopeless feeling closed in on her numbing mind as the dark waters pulled her down.

Blood stains

It was very late by the time Governor Carton Tunis started mounting the long stairs to take him back to his chambers. The Governor reached up and rubbed his temples. "My brain hurts."

"It's been a long day." He said to himself as he took another step up the winding stone stairway. He shrugged, rolled his head and inhaled deeply, hoping that the throbbing pain in the back of his neck and head might pass. Realizing that his hands were clenched into tight balls he let them loose and shook them trying to relax.

The mental image of his wife waiting for him by a warm fire in their room pulled him upward. His weary body felt slightly renewed by the mere image. As he topped the stairs and started down the hall towards his room he spotted the two men on guard.

"Is my wife inside?" The governor asked as he drew close to the soldiers who now were at attention. He squinted, his mind was weary, but he had just met these two earlier... desperately he tried to remember their names.

"She went in more than two hours ago Sir." The one young guard replied. The lad smiled back at the governor who was smiling back at him. "Its Fatin Sir."

The governor paused reflecting and remembering the lad's name. "Fatin... right now I remember." He said looking at the shorter heavier lad. Then he looked over and slammed the other soldier on the shoulder. "And Terrac? The two inseparable new men of our garrison."

Both men beamed.

"Weren't you both down in the fields training this afternoon? What did you do wrong to warrant a second duty?"

Fatin grinned ear to ear, "easy duty sir."

Terrac added. "And it wasn't to be for too long."

The governor yawned. "But still a long day you both; as for me I am off to bed to be asleep this very hour." The Governor smiled and slapped the lads again on the shoulders. "I hope you are relieved soon." As he said that he looked down the hall – there walking down its length was his sergeant Sir Nindor. Not wanting to be dragged into another conversation the governor waved to the man but then turned and with Terrac opening the door he entered the room quickly.

Fatin and Terrac both stood to the side of the door as it was closed before them. "Good night Sir." Terrac said as he heard the latch click shut.

The Governor stepped towards the side table and chair where there was a large basin, towels and water. Kicking off his shoes he pulled off his pants and top and tossed them on the chair. Carel had put his nightshirt on his chair – a clear notification to him that she had retired and not wanted him to go searching under the pillow for it.

The stone floor was freezing cold so he hastily pushed his sore feet into the waiting slippers that his wife had put beside the night table. The small act brought a smile to his lips.

Turning somewhat mindlessly he poured some water into the basin and with cupped hands washed his face. With splashes of water he rubbed his face, hoping that he could in some way rub away the thoughts that were creeping back into his mind. 'Methor was now the heir to the throne. Methor, of all people! The world seemed like it was crumbling around him, chaos appeared around every corner.'

As the Governor's mind raced, his nerves increased. Pulling on his nightshirt he decided he would risk his wife's wrath. "Sorry dear, you awake? I need to talk to you, else I doubt I will be getting any sleep… and you know what that means. If I toss and turn, you too likely will get little sleep."

"Carel, you wake?" He called out hoping that his wife wasn't yet in a deep sleep.

Not hearing anything in reply he went back to the wash basin and picking up a towel mopped his face, realizing that in his stressed out moment he had pulled his nightshirt on before he washed his face. Now it would be damp. "Damn. I tell you, "he called over to his wife a little louder. "I am losing my mind with worry wondering what our new King is going to do."

Hearing nothing Tunis frowned, realizing that his wife was indeed likely in a deep sleep. He stared at the basin table spotting a long necked pitcher. With a further frown he picked it up and filled a large pestle with the aromatic red wine. Picking it up he brought it to his lips and drained the wine in one long gulp.

Turning, he looked over at the bed, whose canopies were closed. By the hearth, the bed warmer was gone indicating that Carel already had brought it in with her. He smiled, thinking of his unborn child nestled warmly in his wife's belly. There are better things to think about he said as he felt the relaxing effects of the wine.

Walking back over to the bed Tunis gently pulled back the canopy and sat down on the bed. Kicking off his slippers he pulled his feet up and then drew the canopies closed, instantly he was a bit warmer and the darkness within the enclosure made him feel safe and snug. Rolling slightly he shoved his feet under the blankets not pushing them in too far too fast in fear that they would burn if they touched the bed warmer.

The bed was deliciously warm and soft; he groaned as all the muscles in his body reacted to the familiar feeling and they started to loosen even if ever so slightly. Turning over, he pushed himself over to kiss his sleeping wife on the cheek.

As his lips touched her cheek he stopped. His wife usually was quite warm and often as of late with being pregnant even sweat in bed, but the cheek that touched his lips was cold. "Carel?"

Carton pulled back the covers exposing her shoulders as he went to his knees so that he could better see her face in the gloom of the enclosed bed. Carel remained throughout all of this, alarmingly motionless.

Shaking his head in disbelief he gently reached out and touched her shoulder, and then shook her gently hoping to wake her. His hand stayed in place as the coldness of her skin beneath her silk nightshirt was felt.

"No" was all he could whisper as he pulled her shoulder turning her over onto her back. Her eyes were closed, and although serene as if in sleep her face was as grey as the dust of coals in their hearth and her once red lips were now streaked grey and black.

"NOOOOOO" Carton cried, his pained voice was drenched with despair and sorrow. "NOOOOO!" he sobbed looking at her as he buried his face in her shoulder.

Carton the loving husband then crawled forward desperately reaching out to his love. He tenderly pulled her to him and turned to sit and cradle her head in his lap. Gently he reached down to her abdomen, but there was no movement from within her womb.... Both his wife, and what was to be their new child were dead.

Despair crashed down on Carton and tears sprang from his eyes. He had faced death before. His first wife had died at the birth of their child. But this was too much to handle – his surviving son was now among thousands lost at Terran Add and now his new, young bride and future child both dead as well!

"Why?' He sobbed, "Why have I been cursed so?"

His sob was broken as he heard the door to his chamber open. "FIND THE SURGEON – MY WIFE, my wife. As he reached down and stroked her very cold face he knew that there would be no recovery. Her body was cold and the colour of her face gave him no hope... he had seen death before, he had held his wife just so .. before. In a softer, less urgent voice he called out pathetically. "Call the priest, my wife and unborn child... have died."

There was no response from behind the curtains that blocked Carton's view. Assuming that his news had startled the guard he looked to the canopies. He wanted to pull them wide, but in his heart of hearts he did not have the ability to let go the embrace of his dear Carel.

"My wife has died." He said in a softer, less nervous but still saddened tone. "Please just leave and send word to the priest to come to my chambers." There was no reply from beyond the canopy, only more footsteps that drew closer to the bed.

Sorrow turned rapidly to outrage and anger at the guard. 'Had the imbecile not heard him?' He thought, 'Did they not know the sorrowful state he obviously was in?'

"Fatin? Taramac?" He called out with a commanding tone.

The Governor's mind flashed. Detached words, impressions and fears broke the surface of his consciousness as he looked down at his wife's lips. "Poison?" He said trying to see more clearly. His head snapped round as he reached to his wife's side of the bed, so that by pulling open the curtains the light of the roaring fire would better illuminate his wife's face.

With his left hand still touching his wife's cheek, his right hand parted the curtain. But the light of the fire was silently accompanied by a very long silver dagger. The thin, sharp blade slid into him as easily as it would have warm butter. Carton gasped as he watched as if in slow motion the blade slide effortlessly into his chest.

A moment later the hand that clenched the blade retracted back behind the slightly parted curtains leaving the governor alone with his dead wife.

Incredulously the governor looked down at his stomach. A small circle of blood began to form around the impression in his nightshirt the blade and handle had made.

The pain was not overwhelming, but more like a bad case of indigestion. Shock and confusion masked his discomfort completely. He wanted to say something, to do something, but somehow it all felt so futile and his limbs felt as if they were made of overcooked pasta.

There was nothing left for him. Tunis let fall his right hand and with it, so too fell the parted curtain bringing him back into the gloom of the canopied bed.

Alone with his wife he laid forward and with his last breath he kissed his wife's cold cheek and died.

Cold Awakening

Darkness enveloped and embraced Dimi. Like an old friend its fingers caressed and encircled her rubbing the pain out of her limbs. She knew that the numbness and sense of peace she was feeling was akin to the kiss of an assassin beetle. Just like its kiss this one would drag her to a lethargy to which she would not likely escape. The kiss, the seductive tong would stretch out and tease her into a sense of wellbeing, but behind that red darting tong were teeth that would tear her very soul to shreds. Yet Dimi did nothing as she slowly descended, she had fought this battle once before and just didn't have the strength to do it again.

With all slack expanded, the tether that stretched upward from Dimi's hand drew taunt. Two meters above, a breath above the water Mule's head hovered. Peppy's legs were straight, her neck bent as far forward as possible and there was nothing left to give.

Dimi had survived years frozen in the cave, the feeling she now was embraced with was not foreign. It had bested her will before; her resistance felt futile. Giving up to the feeling of loss of her only friend, not wishing to survive in the state she had before Dimi's hand relaxed and the tether began to slip through her grasp.

But somewhere, way back in Dimi's mind some semblance of what she had once been, some fragment of passion sparked as her leg collided with something solid below. Only one small word danced before the sparkling lights that danced in her brain as it too began to freeze. "no". The word was small, and the voice it was said with was weak, but it was enough. "No." She thought as she willed herself back up from the depths of resignation. Biting her frozen lips, Dimi grimaced and reached down to her leg and with numb fingers grasped what she substance she could and then with the last of her energy Dimi yanked down hard on the lead in her upraised hand.

Peppy squealed as the lead was pulled down sharply bringing the Mule's nose down to the point where it touched the water. As the cold slapped her nostrils she bayed like a banshee. Her hardened hooves slashed and hammered at the stone bank sending shards of rock to splash before her. As she pulled back violently Dimi and then Etch were drawn from the depths.

Dimi immediately began to sputter and spit as she came forth, but she hadn't any strength left to open her eyes, let alone help Etch. There was nothing left within her.

At first Dimi thought the pounding in her ears was nothing more than the blood returning to her eardrums but a moment later she heard a low tenor voice. "Lie still a moment, your friend isn't breathing I must tend to him first."

The warmth of the words was enough for Dimi to let go once again and a moment later consciousness departed her.

"Don't try to open your eyes." The friendly voice said as she was lifted and then set down next to a warm fire. "You won't be able to see for some time, stay your friend breaths but still I don't know if he will survive."

Dimi heard thumping as the large man departed, and then she felt the warmth of the fire on her face. Turning she started to crawl towards the crackling fire desperate for warmth.

"Wooa there little one." The tenor voice rang out a moment later as two large hands picked her up as easily as she might pick up a frog. "You are frozen through. By the time you would feel the warmth of the fire, your fingers would be nothing but burnt bits of charcoal."

Dimi was gently put down. "Say put now. The fire is going well and you are a meter from it – go no closer I can't watch you both."

The giant of a man worked for minutes, but there was no sound that came from that to which he worked on. As hot tears began to run down Dimi's face she heard the tenor voice again, but this time in an almost hushed and somewhat fatalistic tone. "His only chance is if I can get some of this down deep into his gullet… warm him from the inside out. But his mouth, throat… it's all frozen solid. If I push too hard I think I might just break him in half…. Well – I know we can't wait for him to thaw naturally. One more try – it will be do or not."

A moment later a large hand rested gently on Dimi's shoulder. "I have done what I can. He has some of my medicine in him, here drink this, it's all I have left.

Dimi held up her hands and pushed back the cup. From beneath chattering lips she hissed. "Give it to him; make him drink it."

"Hooo!" the loud voice boomed sending Dimi's back into a foetal position with hands beside her ears. "So now you are telling me, my business?"

But then the giant chuckled and the large hand rubbed her hair. "Fine… I think you have enough piss and vinegar in you to survive anyway…" Turning he went back to Etch. "I will push what is left through his lips and down his nose."

As Dimi felt the warmth creep back into her face and hands her shoulders slumped and her body began to unwind. Great fatigue gripped her and pulled her head to the ground. A moment later she was sleeping soundly.

An hour later the massive hands were lifting Dimi up and positioning her a little closer to the fire. "Careful, you are still numb… you don't even know how hot it is but you need to get your circulation fully going now. Your limbs will feel like they have been asleep. It will hurt, but rubbing your hands and stomping your feet is better for them then trying to barbeque them or hoping that they will thaw by themselves."

Dimi's eyelids still heavy were hard to rise, and through the small tear filled slits she could see little but the dancing flames. Squinting she bent forward searching with her throbbing hands for what appeared to be Etch's form. "Is he going to be all right?"

Raging flames danced close, but no matter how hard she tried, Dimi could not see the light.

"Relax and don't look straight at the flames." The voice said.

"Who are you?" Dimi asked. "And you didn't answer my question."

The man laughed, "a new friend." Then after a moment of hesitation he added. "I don't know."

Dimi's head jerked around as heard something else flutter near them. "What was that?" She asked anxiously.

The large man laughed again. "Relax, just another friend. It was Darn that saw your friend jump. It was he that came and told me." The man paused a moment. "Damn stupid move if you ask me. I said that anyone that was that stupid didn't deserve to live and bread, but he seemed to think that you two should be saved."

Dimi sniffed. "That sound wasn't a man moving, and it doesn't smell like a man."

"Smell and sound back in force eh? Sight won't take long then." The giant replied but his voice was cut off as the sound of large wings flapped. Wind blew the faint scent of wet cave to her face as the creature before them took to the air. Dimi tensed at the thought of how large the creature was that had a moment ago sat across the fire from her.

"Relax, he won't hurt you. That was Darn." The man laughed, "Besides, even if you had seen him you likely wouldn't have believed your own eyes anyway."

Dimi squinted to look at the giant man before her. The light seeped in to her mind showing her the blurry image of a towering hulk of a man well over two meters high weighing two to three times what Etch weighed. "My eyes have seen a lot of strange things in my time."

Dimi moved slightly closer to the fire, which not so coincidentally was also slightly farther aware from the towering man. "I hate being cold." She said after a moment. "After this adventure I am going far down south where everything is hot. I think I would like to live in the desert." She said as a matter of fact as her teeth started chattering again. "I HATE the cold."

"No, I don't think you would like the desert. No trees, no flowers, just rock and sand!" The man laughed. His tone was deep but it exuded warmth and familiarity. "But I can't blame you for not liking the cold of this lake... foul place."

"Who are you?" Dimi said as she still tried to solidify the image before her. "Why are you here?" Through her blurred vision she could see the large man sit down next to Etch and holding his arms he rubbed his hands and then legs hoping to coax warmth into them.

"I was on the other side of the lake, two of our acolytes disappeared south of here a few weeks ago."

"You are a priest?" Dimi asked as she blinked, with vision now almost nearing normal she scanned the area. It was already turning dark, but her emerald eyes noted nothing moving near them. "Where is the creature?"

The man looked back at her and nodded. Then looking back into the woods he shook his head. "I have no idea. He told me that there are other rather unusual creatures following both of you... blood weasels the size of horses?"

Dimi nodded her head as she watched the large man bend over and then kneel next to her friend. "Your friend is breathing, but not much else. I gave him all the rest of the tethroot leaf tea. It warms the blood and makes the stomach an oven... "The man's gentle voice tailed off. "Less than one in ten live after going in... and none have I ever seen come back after being in so long as you two."

With a discerning, educated voice he stepped in and took a close look at Dimi. "Surprised you weren't out cold when I got here... or worse. But then you aren't ordinary are you?"

Dimi looked up at the man. "You seem to know a lot about this lake."

Dimi's sight now cleared watched as the giant of a man rose. He was dressed all in a massive flowing brown prior's robes drawn tight around his massive girth with a cord as thick as her arm. The giant of a man looked down at her. "Every fool around these parts knows not to swim in it... "

"We aren't from around here." Dimi said simply.

"Couldn't you 'feel how 'off' this whole place is?" The priest said with arms raised as he turned slowly around. "Surely, one like you can feel it?"

Dimi closed her eyes and breathed in deeply hoping to catch a small sense of what the man spoke of but she could feel nothing. "I don't sense anything."

"Hmmm," the priest said in a disappointed voice.

"What is wrong with this place, and with this lake?" Dimi asked inquisitively.

The man words were spoken slowly and each word was said as if it carried great weight. "The cold of the keeper can freeze and eat a man's soul." For most it is quick and sudden." The priest looked down at Etch. "A few linger but few wake. "Nothing more I can do for him. Just a waiting game now... "

Dimi turned and pushed herself up with her hands groaning as she did so.

"Slow down little lady, your muscles are still cramped from the cold."

Dimi shook off the comment... "We need something stronger than a week warming tea. I have something that might do that."

As the small dryad staggered over to the saddlebags she called over her shoulders. "Who and what are you?"

The man moved next to Etch and started rubbing Etch's legs and then hands. "Mellon, Father Mellon." The priest frowned as he looked down at the man's mottled skin. "I am from the Temple. What are you thinking of?"

"You are a priest?" Dimi said as she grabbed a small pouch from within one of the bags.. "Are you trained in herbs?" Dimi asked said as started back to the fire.

"Some." The priest said with a shrug.

"A few pinches of Brenasal in with the root, the two should produce a little more reactive drink."

The priest looked up and then leaned forward and peered interestingly at Dimi as she removed a small leather pouch from within the leather bag. Untying the pull strings she tapped from the pouch a few flacks of leaf into the small tin mug that sat next to Etch. "Lift his head, lets get this into him."

The large man lifted Etch's hand, his massive palm cradling his skull and his long fat fingers almost encircling his head.

Dimi looked at the gargantuan priests hands and hesitated as she lifted the cup to Etch's lips. Looking up into the eyes of the man she paused. "You are big."

The priest smiled warmly back. "And you are small." Then with his index finger he pushed down on Etch's chin forcing his mouth open and with another finger he pushed against his nose.

Dimi began to pour the warm concoction down Etch's throat. Etch sputtered only once and both of them knew that his lack of gagging was not a good sign.

"Wash your hands, and don't touch your eyes.. you got some on your fingers when he coughed."

The priest set down Etch's head and then put his fingers to his nose and inhaled. "AAAAA Choooooo," the large man's sneeze echoed across the lake. Dimi fell backwards and landed hard on her butt.

"What in the seven hells was that?" Dimi said in a shocked and shaken voice.

The priest with eyes watering wiped his nose on the sleeve of his long flowing poncho. "A sneeze," he said as he rose to his feet.

Dimi watched him with awe for the man was easily three times her size, twice as tall as Etch and likely two hundred kilos or more in weight. His poncho swayed from side to side like the leaves of a large tree as he walked to the lake.

Bending over carefully Father Mellon splashed a little water on his hand and then rubbed them vigorously. Then looking beside him he picked up some loose sand and gravel and rubbed them again. Finally after splashing a little more water and once again rubbing his hands he raised them slowly to his nose and took a small sniff. Satisfied that his hands were clean he rose and returned back to the camp.

"Potent leaf," father Mellon said as he sat down next to Etch and placed a wet finger to his forehead. Then he looked up questioningly at Dimi then back down at Etch. "I once had the misfortune to eat a steak laced with Drekian peppercorns… Nothing like what I just smelled my nose is on fire!"

The corner of Dimi's mouth turned up in a snide smile then she looked down pathetically at her friend. "If this doesn't warm up his blood…. Nothing will."

The priest nodded and then resting his hand again on Etch's head he closed his eyes and after a moment when opening his eyes he sat back down and sighed….

"Where is your friend?"

Laughter rolled out of the friar like beer out of a keg. "Who Darn?" The priest continued to chuckle and wiped his eyes again on his sleeve. "Don't you trust me yet? I told you I am not his keeper, he is free to come and go as he wishes – and if you had ever seen him even given my size you wouldn't be assuming I could control him even if I wanted to. He dropped in on me a few weeks ago while I was walking through a forest. It scared my breakfast right out of me!."

"What is he then?" Dimi asked now more curious then ever.

"When my eyes first set upon him I thought he was the largest damn bat I had ever seen. You know, black as the night, leather like wings supported by an imbedded set of limbs... But, at second look I have to say I am not sure. Obviously its size would make it beyond a freak of nature, but it is more then that. The creature's face is too round, and its eyes... there – "

"Almost human," Dimi said completing the priest's sentence.

The priest looked over inquisitively to Dimi and then scratched his clean-shaven chin. Dimi watched as the man's hand reached up and brushed back the short cut grey hair that encircled his baldhead. "Then the creature did something that really startled me." the priest continued. "It tried as if to talk, but nothing came out from between its long thin teeth. Then it hunched over and started scratching in the dirt.– the creature could write!"

"He was once a man." The priest concluded.

Dimi nodded in agreement. "We have been looking for the wizard that has the power to transform animals and humans. You won't believe some of her other creations – Blood Ferrets the size of horses."

The priest's eyes showed no sign of surprise, "Wizard?"

"Sarta was herself turned to a succubus long ago as penalty for the betrayal to her master and mentor. She is now something very different and also quite mad ..."

"Old stories confirmed now as truths... the only wizard to pass through and return." The priest paused deep in thought, "transformed into a succubus, tormented and crazy wandering the world, preying on innocents. But, how could she do such continued magic, the stories say she remains totally crazy with only fleeting moments of sanity?"

Both sat still in thought for a moment until Father Mellon broke the silence, "through the study of blood magic."

Dimi looked back at the priest showing obvious confusion.

"Don't you see," asked the priest passionately? "What better follower of the blood arts then a Succubus, a creature that by its very nature seeks out and consumes the blood of innocents! What better acolyte could the priests of the blood order find then such a creature?"

"And for Sarta," Dimi continued recalling the years when Sarta patrolled the lands around the castle. "Sarta would seek to gain the ability never to return to her hag state. She had been vain before the transformation, which is why the Wizard picked that specific curse. A curse was put on her that would make her beyond beautiful to others. But when in that state the Succubus looses all control, she loses all will to do anything but to feed on her victims. Only in her resting state has any semblance of control. But in those times she would revert to a withered hag. The priests, through training could bring her balance. Through blood magic she could retain her Succubae state yet enable her the clarity to also perform magic."

Father Mellon added eagerly. "Clarity would come in the early days, but after that would come great power. Blood magic bestowed by Andarduel is strong stuff. A wizard that could tap into it and their own magical abilities, a wizard that could commune with Andarduel herself would be unstoppable."

Dimi looked back at the priest. "She must have started down this path many, many years ago. For she practiced her magic on me before you were born and it is she who we believe is responsible for the disappearance of all those in Terran Add." Dimi added slowly watching for disbelief in the priest's eyes.

The priest's eyes show no sense of surprise. "Yes, yes." He started slowly. "Terran Add. She is combining her powers, possibly able to open lesser doors now at will."

Dimi smiled, but it wasn't a smile that made the priest feel uncomfortable as her evil disposition shone through the veil of the smile. "She must be stopped. We have been following and seeing the path of destruction she has left in her wake. Her sadistic tendencies are growing with her powers. She no longer just feeds, but now goes out of her ways to take pleasure in the perpetual infliction of pain and suffering."

Father Mellon smiled slowly. "It is her teachings. Andarduel's followers are all a sadistic bunch.

"You seem to know a great deal of the blood cult." Dimi put forward in an inquisitive way.

The priest bent his head and looked at the ground, but then nodded his head slowly. "The temple guard was founded centuries ago to watch for and protect against the resurgence of the blood cult. It was the guard that called for early warning when last they rose and it is the guard that now patrols the north seeking out those that have fallen to the accursed followings of Andarduel. When followers are found, they are brought to this very lake for sentencing."

Dimi's eyes lit up…. Dimi looked around the area. "Well now, that explains a great deal." Then smiling wickedly she added with the most sarcastic tone she could muster. "My most pious Father Mellon, you and your kind drowned those you caught!"

Father Mellon nodded somewhat solemnly. "It has been that way for centuries. Their deaths had to be bloodless. The brotherhood could not even risk the noose for fear that it would part their skin and through that trickle of blood they or their kind would be able to curse."

Dimi visibly shuddered. "So gagged and bound you threw them into the lake to drown, and in doing so this lake has been polluted with their powers, and after each death the heart of the lake has grown that much colder. But what has that to do with Sarta?"

Father Mellon pursed and then licked his lips. Before continuing he reached beneath his poncho and pulled out a small pewter flask. He offered it over to Dimi who wrinkled her nose and declined. After taking a long draw from it and returning it back beneath his covering he continued. "We have been hearing rumours of a power that has been drawing out the old blood priests… some power that has taken to the old ways and worships the blood god. But even for a blood priest the rumours of this individual's powers were astonishing."

The priest's eyes turned back to the lake. "A trained and wizened wizard… trained in the blood arts, acolyte, or possibly priestess to Andarduel herself?" His eyes dropped solemnly down to his feet and bending forward he picked up a rock the size of his fist and threw it into the lake. The splash of the stone hitting the water echoed ominously. " And if she can bring forth from behind those locked doors? No, not good… not good at all."

The priest's eyes spoke of fear and unease as they came back to Dimi's but their locked stare broke as Etch coughed.

Dimi, now limber again and free of the lake's cold embrace jumped lightening fast to Etch's side and the large priest again pressed his hand to Etch's forehead, "the lads burning up now."

Etch began to stir, and a moment later his stirring became a thrashing. Dimi could do little but the priest's large hands held Etch tight.

As Etch strained and pulled against his restraint the priest began a slow, methodical chant like prayer. His voice was as low as a drum and almost inaudible yet it rang out and echoed across the waters. Dimi's eyes sparkled reflecting the light of the fire as she felt the priest's spell spread out from his hands and

"Tied to the coldest of cold

"Soul, bound with chains of ice."

"Remember the hearth of home."

"Of family, of wife or kin."

Etch gasped and his eyelids opened slightly exposing the whites of his rolled back eyes.

"From darkness bound…"

"Rise to the light and to the warm embrace of friends."

Etch groaned and his back arched and then he shuddered and breathed in deeply.

"He's past the worst." Father Mellon said with reassurance. "If his body doesn't break from the strain now, or his mind doesn't crumble under the strains of the visions."

"Visions," Dimi asked as she tried to keep Etch's legs from moving.

"Our acolytes come out here as part of their final testing before ordainment. Their last test is to take a sip of the water from the lake."

"The lake imbues them in part? It is how your own order obtains its powers? Somewhat hypocritical isn't it – obtaining power from what you dispose of?"

Father Mellon smiled sarcastically but shook his head as well. "For those that survive the ordeal, the waters from the lake 'enlighten' – it opens their eyes to the natural powers around us all… nothing more."

"Those that survive," Dimi said looking down at Etch.

The priest shrugged. "The priests don't swim in the lake, and take only a mouthful. Nothing is certain for your friend."

There was a swishing sound in the trees and both the priest and Dimi looked back into the darkness of the trees behind them. The day had come and went without their sensing it and shadows danced in the tall woods. But Dimi's keen eyes spotted the large bat hanging far up from a branch twenty meters in through the woods. But as she tried to focus on him, the creature fell from the branch and disappeared into the night.

The night was long as they sat next to Etch trying to keep him warm. As the morning sun's rays cracked through the tree line Etch began to stir. Groaning he raised a trembling hand and touched his now stubble cheek. "I need a shave."

Dimi's laughter rang out like tinkling wind chimes across the lake. In the blink of an eye she as at his side steadying him and trying to coax him not to rise.

Father Mellon stood back and waited until Etch's eyes finally met his own. "Welcome back. It wasn't very wise jumping into 'this lake'.

Etch, somewhat startled by the size of the man sitting near him smiled back wryly. "You should post a sign."

"Who's the giant?" Etch asked glibly looking back to Dimi for an explanation and to obtain from her a sense of her disposition towards the imposing man.

Dimi, still laugh let Etch's head go as she turned so that he could see past her better. "His name is Father Mellon, he is our new friend. He found us after I pulled your sorry excuse for a body from the lake. He has been helping me bring you back."

Etch tried to rise up on one elbow but after trying for a short moment decided it wasn't worth the effort and lay back down. Both eyes were now squinted open and he looked up at the large priest. "I would get up to shake your hand, but not feeling all that great yet."

"No need to rise lad." Father Mellon added with a cheery voice. "Looks like your friend will survive after all. I had better go and get word back to my order. They need to be warned."

Dimi shook her head, "So soon?"

The priest stood and nodded, "Yes, I need to go... It is crucial I get word to the Northern castles and warn them that Tock might be the least of their worries and I need to get word to out as far and wide as I can, we must bring together a force and bring down this creature."

Dimi nodded her head understanding. "I agree. She must be stopped at all costs."

The priest strode forward and bent forward and looked Dimi straight in the eyes. "If her knowledge elevates her to become a high priestess of Andarduel, then all the Masti will rally to her. With those powers, she will be too great for two lone soles to stop."

407

"Yet try to we will none the less." Etch added looking up at the giant.

Dimi looked down and smiled at Etch in solemn agreement. A binding silent pledge had been set that very moment between the two.

"Let not vengeance cloud your thoughts." The priest added, but then seeing the steel determination in their eyes he straightened out and then nodded in understanding. "We must all do what we can I guess." Then, while scratching his chin he added. "We have ways to pass on word that will travel faster than your horse can carry you. I will let others know of you and ask that they give you what aid they can."

Dimi nodded and without any further pause Father Mellon turned and started walking away at a brisk pace. Dimi and Etch watched him walk around the edge of the lake and then without turning to wave goodbye he entered the eastern tree line that surrounded the lake.

Dimi picked up the small cup by the fire and brought it to Etch who took it with shaking hands. "My friend, the mule is smarter then you are. Even she knew not to put so much as her nose into those waters!"

Dimi said chidingly. "Drink this slowly; it's a concoction we brewed that will take the last of the chill from your bones. Lucky for you the father had a herb with him that I needed. Dimi looked down by the side of the fire and noted that the priest had left his small pouch of herbs.

"Nice, 'big' man," Etch added but as he started to drink his expression changed to one of shock and then almost horror. "Oh my goodness.. What in the seven hells is in this?"

"Drink it up!" Dimi demanded as she pulled her blade from her belt to punctuate the command.

Etch with eyebrows still raised tilted back and drained the cup. With tea gone he threw the cup down. "That was disgusting. Then he gasped and coughed and then sneezed. My god girl, if I didn't know better I would think you was poisoning me."

A second later his hands went to his stomach.

"This stuff is like liquid fire!" Etch complained as he grabbed his stomach.

"I need to..." Etch said with a raspy voice. "Pee." He added weekly as he grasped his stomach.

A low growling tone issued from his gut, it gurgled and groaned for the longest of time and at each note Etch's eyebrows furrowed deeper.

"Sooo, Pee." Dimi demanded. "You are already wet with sweat; I will bring you another blanket."

Etch looked up with a grimace. "Ah, ya... NO. I am strong enough to make it to the woods." With that he pushed himself weekly to his knees and then feet.

Dimi jumped to his side and steadied him and then helped him walk to the forest. "I can make it the rest of the way there." Etch said as he put his hand atop her head and turned it so she would face the other way. "Give me some peace. It won't be pretty."

Without any further coaxing Dimi took a few steps back towards the fire. "I will wait here." She said as she heard Etch take a few steps deeper into the forest.

"The cold drew out your strength and shocked your body. You will feel tired soon – don't walk too far and don't get lost." Dimi said as she sat on the stony ground.

Etch felt chilled to the bone but the turmoil in his stomach pushed him on to find a place where he could be alone. He had felt similar feelings in the past after eating spiced meats, but he knew this bout would be worse than any he had experienced before.

Staggering, with week almost fluid legs he half walked half jogged into the woods. The air was fresh with the smell of moss and leaf. Making it to dodge behind a large root he did a quick check to ensure he was out of eyeshot and dropped his drawers. A moment later he exploded.

Etch howled in pain. It was as if a furnace had been burning in his gut for a week, and now hot acidic flames were streaming in great gushes out of his backside.

"What's wrong?" Dimi called over from her place near the fire… "You need help?" She added with a knowing sarcasm in her voice.

"You FOUL WITCH!" Etch growled as loudly as he could through clenched teeth.

"I am," Etch buckled as if hit square in the gut, "on fire!" His back then arched and his head pulled back as once again acidic torrents streamed from him.

In the distance he could hear Dimi laugh. "Better red then dead!" She laughed."

Etch was about to yell again at her, to let her know that it wasn't funny when another rip of pain shot through him like a torch. The air around Etch no longer bore any semblance to the sweet smell of moss and leaf.

After forty minutes of torture Etch already week now felt incapable of standing. With trembling hands he grabbed some moss hoping that its cool moisture might put out the remaining embers below. Then pulling up his pants he took a few steps forward.

A small root caught his right foot and brought him tumbling down to the cold damp earth. Rolling onto his back he looked up to the sky, content to rest there a moment or two. Above him towered a Massive White Pine. 'How many years would it take to grow such a tree?' He wondered looking up at it totally content to stay there for the rest of his life.

Etch closed his eyes and took in a deep, deep breath. Breathing in the sweet smell of life and tree, his stomach felt much better even though his backside still felt as if it was on fire. But even that discomfort couldn't make him feel sad, in fact he felt deliriously delicious. "It is good to be alive'. He said.

It was as if the water had been a straight edge that had scraped him clean. It had scraped so hard that it had scratched off more than just dirt and grime but a part of him that had felt old and soiled. It had seeped into his pored and into his nose and mouth and had burned him like fire. The cold still dwelled deep there in his bones. He could feel it like a knife at the base of his tailbone. Like fishing line it traveled up through his spine to the back of his head where the hook appeared set.

Etch's closed his eyes as suddenly extremely dizzy. He dared not move his head for fear of losing what little sense of balance he was maintaining. With the grim thought of expelling acid from his throat he inhaled slowly trying to regain his equilibrium.

Cold sweat poured from every pore as he grimaced trying to maintain control. As panic set in he set aside his pride and tried to call out to Dimi, but all that issued from his trembling lips was the faintest of words that were lost in the wind.

Cascading shivers slashed through his weak body. Clamping his mouth close to restrict the bile that was rising up from his stomach Etch's hands dug deep into the moss below him as he through every last ounce of will he had into remaining conscious. Bright lights flashed from his brain and danced before his tightly closed eye lids. The harder he strained to keep his eyes closed, the brighter the lights became until as one the spots joined and a large white light shone before him.

'This is 'it' the end.' He thought, and yet with all his might he continued to fight it.

The cold in his tailbone pulsed and cracked like an icicle that fell from a rooftop. It was as if someone had taken an axe and tried to split him from tail to head. The cold axe traveled up the center of his spine and he felt as if the very bone was separating as it worked its way up. The cold slipped into each rib encircling his check and gripping his heart and lungs with coldness.

Tears stream out from beneath his tightly clenched eyes only to slow and freeze upon his frigid cheeks. Flashes of blinding cold light streamed into his brain searing him in brilliance; piercing his skull like a nail would pierce an apple.

Etch gasped in air as the lights twisted and sparkled in brilliance and then dimmed to a dark, but clear image of a withered, shrunken old woman standing in the middle of a large hall, on the dais behind her stood a massively tall wrought iron throne and on each side of the throne two massive buckets of pitch stood sputtered and burn sending dark clouds to the ceiling.

The scarred hands of a Masti acolyte pushed a peasant girl into the throne room. Stumbling, the girl cried out as her knees hit the hard stone floor. Hesitantly, and very fearfully she lifted her face to look up to her captor. The old crone before her was more hideous then the worst descriptions she had heard, yet… as her bones shook with terror she dropped her gaze to the floor.

"Rise!" echoed a gentle motherly voice from the dishevelled heap of rags and withered flesh. "What is your name child?" The voice came to the girls ears as if born upon silk.

Plucking courage from the depth of her soul the young peasant risked a quick look up. Then, as if the world of troubles had dropped from her shoulders she gracefully rose to her feet and smiled "Mara." She whispered back.

The girl had been pretty once, but the last few weeks of bread and water had ravaged her face and soil and dirt smeared her forehead and cheeks. Yet the girl smiled as if she had been freshly bathed and dressed in silks and she took two graceful steps towards the diesis.

Kindness and empathy rolled from the withered lips. "Are you afraid?" The image before her asked slowly.

The peasant girl in disbelief of her own actions shook her head slowly.

"You are not afraid, good." The old lady stated. "Come closer my dear I wish to take a look at you."

The peasant took two confident steps forward and looked up at the beautiful woman before her. "I should be trembling, running with fear? But I cannot take my eyes away from you."

The girl reached out as if to touch the old had, but as her had reached out the image before her flickered for a fraction of a second she saw the old hag again and her had spastically jerked back.

But in the blink of an eye the old woman's hand shot forward, as it grasped the girls wrist. Mara looked down, the hand holding her wrist was once white beyond belief. It was clean and young fresh skin, the fingers long with nails brightly painted in red. Yet the skin on her wrist recoiled at the touch, it was as if damp, cold, old leaves were holding her.

Mara tried vainly to pull back her arm repulsed by the old woman's leathery touch. But the golden image of the woman in front of her held her fast.

"Fear sometimes tastes better then blood." The woman asked. "And surprise can bring great fear."

The girl started again to tremble and tried to violently pull back, using both hands to attempt to pry loose herself. But she was held fast. "Whimpering, she started to tremble."

The hag began to cackle and the girl began to scream the image before her flickered between the beautiful, regal woman and the hag. "Soon I won't even need to transform to feed." Sarta said to the girl as she transfixed her image to the beautiful succubae image.

Mara grew all of a sudden grew calm and stopped resisting. She shuddered and let flow a deep breath out as her entire body all of a sudden relaxed. The most generous and trusting smile upon her lips she smiled up at the woman giving herself freely over to the magic that compelled her.

The bright lady's vibrant form before her was held only back by sheer a silken gown. The low neckline exposed volumes of softness. The beauty of the eyes and face captured Mara's gaze and held them like a vice.

Blond streaming hair flowed gracefully down the lady's shoulders and back. The hair wafted in unseen breezes. Her face was bright, stark white and were contrasted by the endlessly black eyes that smiled at the girl. The lady's lips pouted and them her red, red lips formed the faintest smiles.

"Are you mine?" Sarta said as she pulled the girl closer.

Mara's face was frozen in an endless and mindless smile. The succubus' spell had pulled out whatever will she had from her as easily as water is squeezed out from a soft sponge. Yet, in her eyes still could be seen shock and terror as realization of her pending fate reached her brain. Sarta smiled as she felt the girl treble in her grasp.

Sarta drew the girl in close and on her toes she whispered into Mara's ears. "You will languish in great pain before I will agree to suck the last of your life and blood from your tortured body."

Sarta's hand reached forward and stroked Mara's hair back away from her face a small as tears issued from her almost disbelieving eyes.

A brief gasp issued from the Mara's lips as Sarta's hand stroked again, but as Sarta's hand left Mara's head, with it fell both hair and skin leaving exposing raw red tissue. Mara didn't even flinch as her hair and scalp fell to her shoulder and then the floor.

Then as if the pain had crossed some frozen threshold in Mara's brain her mouth opened and a scream grew up from deep within her throat. The shrill of her voice rose as Sarta's other hand went up to stroke the girl's head again. As each stroke graced the young woman hair and skin fell way exposing more of her skull. Blood spilled down from the girl onto her neck and down the length of her body to start to pool at her bare and dirty feet.

Sarta smiled sickly down as she continued caressing the young lady, peeling her slowly. Her hands slowly and methodically moved from the girl's head, to face to neck to shoulders. Mara stood motionless, screaming as she was slowly flailed alive..

The body, now stripped of skin and exposed to the bone in many places stayed amazingly upright and motionless until Sarta smile at last and bent forward to kiss Mara. The succubus's lips moved forward. Mara, still alive, quivered within the frame of what had once been her body. Her teeth parted as another wail came out from deep within her. The succubus smiled and bent forward, her tong darting out to sample the blood the flowed freely downs the girl's bony face. Finally, as Sarta pulled back what was left of the girl finally collapsed into the pool of blood and tissue at Sarta's feet.

An eerie, dark and sinister, laugh rang out from behind Sarta. Etch looked back to the darkness. Behind Sarta, on the once empty throne now hovered a darkness. The two Masti acolytes previously hidden by the back columns of the chamber dropped suddenly to the floor lying prone before the image.

The dark image coalesced and turned from a charcoal wisp of smoke to a massive black winged creature with horns and tail. The smoky image raised its wings almost in salute to Sarta, tattered and torn and ethereal the air wafted around and through them. "How you please us with your work. Such divine creativity. The creature's fear is so pungent you can cut it with a knife." The creature extended its smoky hand, it elongated like a thin cloud as it reached out to touch the succubus.

Sarta let forth a gasp of ecstasy as the smoke encircled her. The blood upon her face was the first to disappear. It was as if her pours opened up and sucked in the moisture. Then, her hands were clean. Etch gasped as he stared in awe as even her blood red dress drained of colour to turn white once again.

Etch wanted to pull back his mind's eye from the sight, but at once he was seized as if held in a vice. "Who is this one that has come to watch our fun priestess?" The smoke asked without drawing its gaze from Etch.

Sarta turned and stared at him as if he was standing plainly before them.

Anxiety overwhelmed Etch; he tried to turn but couldn't. Etch's heart pounded like a hammer within his chest. He looked down to it, but saw nothing. 'I am not here.' He said to himself willing himself to remember where he really was.

Etch felt a sharp stab of pain in his hand, and this time when he looked down he could see its translucent shape and upon the piece of flesh between his thumb and finger blood began to well up.

The floor beneath Etch appeared to loose its substance and he felt himself plunge back into the darkness. The once clear picture before him swirled and then waned as the pain within his hand pulled him back to reality.

"My god, my god, my god," was all he could say as his breath finally returned and his tortured body began to relax. Opening his eyes he tried to raise his hand, but it was held tightly. Moving his head ever so slightly he turned and looked across to see Dimi sitting there holding his hand, worry and concern showing clearly upon her face.

Etch then began to tremble and shake. All the emotions he had felt while watching the scene flooded back to him in massive waves. Sorrow, loss, outrage, repulsion and fear slammed into his gut. Curling into a ball he turned his face into the leaf-strewn forest floor and began to sob.

MinonTer and the coming of the Weer

"Hold your fire you stupid sots. They are a hundred meters far from your best." Bartholm bellowed at the archers on the wall.

Sir Bartholm Bethos, Son of Duke Baras Bethos of Oathos stood atop the parapet overlooking the northern gates of MinonTer. He was in a bad mood, he and his father had needed to battle hard to get to the gates and they had lost many men repelling the last attack on their new position within the castle itself.

What had set out as a mission of mercy to 'save' the Terrans had now become a battle for survival.

Bartholm Bestinor screamed as another archer on the wall let loose an arrow. It fell a good fifty yards from the enemy, which ran in and out of the bushes just out of reach – taunting and teasing them.

"If you cannot see their eyes amidst their red painted faces they are too far!" He yelled at the archer. He then turned to the other men standing on the walls, all of them were crouched low and only Bartholm's stood tall totally visible from both inside and outside the walls.

Bartholm raised himself and bent over the top of the wall and pointed down. "Look at all those shafts in the dirt below. Damn MinonTers with your pretty colour shafts see what efforts you waste?" He turned and started to yell at the archers that stood upon the wall near him. "The next archer I see let a bolt loose that misses his mark or falls that far short I will have fletching arrows while the rest of you sleep!"

A crossbow bolt zinged just above Bartholm's head; however, he paid it no head and started walking down the walls continuing his inspection of what remained of the troops of MinonTer.

Bartholm, fully clad in the Bethos standard gold and silver chain and scale male armour, appeared as a formidable figure on the battlement of MinonTer. His glinting armour made for a pretty target for the Tocks down below. However, Bartholm was one of those lucky soldiers – no arrows ever appeared to be in the right place at the right time. He walked back and forth on the front wall oblivious to arrows and bolts that flew past his full helmeted head.

The Duke's son was quite the site striding back and forth. He was a massive, burly man and his blond hair hung out the back of his helm and splashed down his back to his backside. What little face could be seen through the slits of his helm was covered with a light brown beard.

Bartholm, first hand and son of Duke Baras Lord Bethos and fifth in line to the Montterran realm swatted an cowering archer on the backside with the flat of his bastard sword sending the man sideways down onto all fours. "Up fool. You can't shoot them if you can't see them!"

The archer grabbed his small bowl leather helmet and put it on his head and peered precariously between the archers slots down to the moat and field below. "I don't have no iron helm and their bolts are sharp." The man retorted low in his breath as Bartholm walked away.

"Unlike 'my lord,'" he whispered. The man jarred to the left and hit his head against the wall as the flat of the Bartholm's bastard sword hit him in the side.

"You won't earn one either by talking." Bartholm replied. "It is actions that gets a man promoted not cowardice!"

The archer looked up and ducked down quickly as a bolt from a crossbow ricocheted off the battlements. Chips of rock sprayed up and clanged off of Bartholm's helmet.

Rather then ducking Bartholm moved up to the wall and looked over still standing tall. "There, there. Down below. Do you see the Tock archer trying to hide amist the bodies? That one is in range. See, he lies down with the wounded by the downed horse." Bartholm looked up and yelled down the line of archers, all of whom appeard to have greater concern to protect their heads then to find out where they were coming from.

"Does anyone see him man?" He said out loud not expecting a reply."

"I can." Came a voice to Bartholm's right. A young lad no older than thirteen walked casually over to Bartholm, he was short compared to Bartholm but looked sturdier than most of the other older archers that walked the walls. Unlike the others on the wall, the lad held a light crossbow, one almost appearing hand made. A quiver of yellow painted bolts were strapped to his side.

"MinonTers with their pretty feathered arrows." Bartholm said sarcastically as he turned to the lad. "I never understand why you all paint your arrows. It takes time and the paint would make the shafts heavier not lighter. Your armour needs much in repair too. It is soft, not boiled and hard."

The lad shrugged and bravely looked over the wall. He pushed back the strange tanned skullcap on his head as he looked down, "which one?"

"The yonder by the black horse or the speckled one?" he asked as he pointed down.

"By the black horse, I doubt you could reach the one closer to the woods. Both sit behind dead horses and pop up only to site. Then they lay back and use their feet to pull back their bows. Never have I seen such a thing, using your feet!" Bartholm pointed down and to the right of the wall. "A good hundred meters – see them?"

The lad pushed forward his skullcap. It was slightly pointed at the front and pushing it forwards it created the slightest of 'V's before the lad's right eye. Bartholm suspected that the lad used it as an aid for arc.

"Our trainers here in MinonTer have disdain for anything other than a straight long bow. Old are their ways. You have to admit though that they are effective, they reach father up then those here can hit shooting downward."

Bartholm snorted. "Well if the trainers here don't like not else than a straight bow, you must be a popular lad?"

The lad shrugged and then sat down and winched his crossbow and set the bolt upon it. Standing he nodded to the knight. "Do me a favour and walk over ten paces down to the left and raise both of your hands above your head."

Bartholm looked down at the lad then shrugged and did as he asked. He paced down the wall ten paces and then turned to face the field and lifted both arms in the air.

In reply from the field below there was a 'twang' as the archer closer to the castle let loose and then another as the farther one fired. Bartholm stood still disregarding both arrows that flew up at him, but instead turned and watched as the lad pulled the trigger on the crossbow and watched as the bolt flew.

The yellow bolt flew like a hornet down at the second archer and just as the Tock looked up to see if his arrow had hit its mark, the hornet stung him – right between the eyes. The bolt entered a good ten centimetres and quivered before the barbarian fell backwards to land behind the dead horse.

Bartholm laughed a big belly laugh that rumbled over the walls. "Well done!" He yelled out loud with hopes that all within the castle would hear him. "Well done lad!" He then walked back over to the young archer. What is your name?"

The crossbowman, a young lad of twelve looked up at the towering knight that approached him. He was a stocky lad, with strong shoulders. The lad had an unassuming look to him, neither proud, nor audacious. He shrugged off the compliment and looked blankly back at the knight that approached him.

Bartholm looked over the peculiar boy. The lad was stockier then most of the other light archers and he assumed the boy could likely yield a good long sword from the size of his upper arms…

yet he noted only the crossbow and a short silver spiked cudgel that was hanging by the lad's side.

"Good shot." Bartholm said as he approached.

Bartholm looked at the lad's leather helm then looked around at the other archers noting that he was unique in its use. "Love the hat." He said jokingly as he tried to knock it from his head in jest. The lad ducked to the side dodging the knight's hand and keeping his hat upon his head.

The boy stood expressionless looking at the knight – un-amused by his comments and actions. In reply he moved the hat back again to its normal position.

"Interesting." Bartholm said out loud when surveying the archer in front of him perplexed somewhat by what he saw. "I asked your name lad; in case you forgotten I am the son of a Duke. The same Duke that has come to keep your Minon Terran derrieres off of barbarian spikes."

The lad looked up, still without much expression at the big knight. "Stansford." the lad said in a low almost inaudible tone.

The other much older archer that hunkered still down behind the wall looked up at Bartholm and nodded to the lad. "He doesn't talk much, our sergeant calls him Mute."

"And what do your friends call you?" Bartholm asked smiling down at the lad.

The other hunkering archer laughed, "'friends'?"

Smether of MinonTeir gave the archer an evil look. You could tell by his look that the lad had a sleeping lion of anger brewing beneath his covers. He then turned to Bartholm defiantly.

Bartholm looked over to the other archer. "Well, he's got one now. I welcome the friendship of any that could shoot like that – especially at your age." He then turned to look at the lad again. "Stansford, it sounds strange on my lips."

"Stans." The lad replied. "You can call me Stans."

The old archer grumbled to himself. "This I have to tell the sergeant. Heard more from Mute today then I have in the three years he trained with us."

Bartholm glowered at the archer then put his hand on Stans and turned them to walk down the walls. "Sergeants dead I think." He said absentmindedly. On eastern wall took an arrow to the head while yelling at his men."

"He wasn't a nice man." Stans started and then in a more sarcastic tone added. "But I think he was well born if that makes a difference."

Bartholm looked down started at the lads bluntness then smiled and laughed a little. "Doesn't much matter to the worms he feed now does it?"

They walked down the walls; fewer bolts rang out as they walked.

"Great shot Stans." Bartholm said as he slapped the lad on the shoulder still trying to size him up.

Stans looked up with a quizzical look, that wasn't quite smiling but wasn't quite straight in face either. "You Montterrans might have saved the day, but we have been here fighting for weeks."

"I heard tell that those of MinonTer were supposed to have the best. But frankly not very convinced after what I saw today." The knight spoke low and looked questioningly back at the lad, "with the exception of your shot just now."

Stans paused and then shrugged. "People here don't count me in because I use this." He lifted up his light crossbow. "But the best archers of the lad did once reside here. Look yonder." Stans motioned with his bow. "We colour our shafts, so at the end of a battle we can count how many each of us have feathered."

"Problem is most of the trainers and archer masters are all dead – having died with our lord. They were ambushed by Weer and Wog."

"Eh?" Bartholm replied. "So what is left here is the dregs?"

Stans nodded pointing at the shafts in the ground outside the walls then at the archers standing on the walls "The shafts you see below bear no colour or are green and those archers you still see upon our walls have either white fletch or are feathered green. White implies little to no training and green marks one as an apprentice archer."

"And yours is yellow." Bartholm noted.

"Highest they would give me, given I use this." Stans said. "I can shoot better than most blues but .." his voice trailed off.

Bartholm looked out and down at the field. Among the bodies, horses and armour lying in the field there were hundreds of arrows sticking up like pincushions. As the lad had indicated most were feathered white or green. Most of the green-feathered arrows were stuck into something… but many were in horses. There were nine or more yellow bolts all of which were stuck into Tocks or Wogs.

Bartholm looked back at the lad who was standing expressionless. He grinned and then slapped the lad again on the shoulder. "Your sergeant only had green shafts I hear.

Stans shrugged. "Rank is bought and sold here like most other places, but feathers must be earned by one and all."

"What feather marks the best? Blue?"

Stans shook his head. "There is one better." He said as he turned to walk away, "black. But none of them are alive anymore"

Bartholm followed the lad. His boots and armour clanging as he walked. They strode past several other archers.

As he passed each archer Bartholm looking down at each man's quiver noting that even if most of their shafts were green each had slight variations in the colour of their feathers.

Stans smiled his half smile. "Most can also catch a arrow in flight."

"Tell you what 'Stans.'" Bartholm started. "Since your sergeant's dead…. Why not I make you sergeant for now?"

Stans shrugged obviously not caring too much..

"Lad," Bartholm started incredulously. "It is sure hard to get a rise out of you."

Stans turned and smiled at the knight then adjusted his hat and shrugged again. Bartholm chuckled and slapped the lad on the shoulder, "done then. Sergeant Stan."

"So tell me Stans." The knight asked as the continued down the wall. "All the others are dead – not one of these great archers of MinonTer returned?"

"Only three men returned from all those that went out with our Lord and his son." Stans replied solemnly. "Only three men of the over thousand archers returned. Two were of our highest ranked archers, but both of those passed after their fever started."

Bartholm nodded. "But one soldier lived? There is someone I should talk with."

"Only Quizler survived." Stans said with a tone Bartholm found disquieting.

"Lucky man that." Bartholm said and looked down to and Stans' blank expression.

"Not too lucky if you ask me." Stans said looking back up at the tall knight.

"The beasts took off his left hand. If it wasn't for his nature he would have been as dead." Stans replied as he turned to continue to walk down the wall.

"You." Bartholm yelled at an older archer on the wall. "You! Wipe down your string. It is wet. If it stays wet it will fray. Oil it some and your bow."

The older archer looked at the knight and the lad and nodded and immediately pulled an oilskin from under his wide leather belt and started to wipe down his bow. However, as they passed him they heard him grumble.

Bartholm stopped dead in his tracks and the man cowered and hushed his complaints.

Bartholm chuckled then and looked at Stans.

"What do you mean, his nature saved him?" Bartholm asked curious about this lad that had gained more respect with these local archers then he had after riding in to their rescue with a thousand men and four hundred knights.

"Quizler is the son of a quicksilver trader. His father traded the Tock and Masti and mountain men for what quicksilver they could find in the mines. Quizler and his dad also worked the liquid metal into the best of blades."

Stans pulled up his spiked cudge and handed it to Bartholm. "It cost me two months salary."

Bartholm took it and twisted it around with his hand like a small blade. "Cute, for killing rats or something small." He said turning it over.

"The spike is smaller then my finger." As he turned it over to hold the cugdge he almost let it drop for the other end of it felt suddenly heavy. Holding the cudgel he tipped one end down and felt the rush of fluid within the shaft slide to the end pointed down.

"Quicksilver is cooked with the coke and imbibes the very metal, but it also is poured to flow freely in the hollow shaft. The spike has the smallest of holes, when I hit something with it a small amount comes out of the point." Stans commented pointing at the spike.

Stans took the cudgel back from Bartholm and tied its string back onto his wide leather belt. "Not all of us need bastard swords to kill with."

"So, what does being in the trade of this liquid metal have to do with saving him?" Bartholm asked hesitantly.

"The metal seeps into the skin. For most, it makes sick or kills over time. Quicksilver traders don't live very long, healthy lives for it gets in their blood." Stan looked up, his expression still somewhat blank but the corner of his mouth raised up slightly in a smile. "The silver kills the Wogs and Weer better than anything."

Bartholm looked at the lad confused and then together they stopped as they came to the stairs that went down to the main courtyard and nodded to Stans.

"Keep well Stans." Bartholm said as he turned. "I would like someday to see you wield that club as well."

Bartholm walked down the fifty steps his sword again sheathed on his back. It was too large to hang at his side. He preferred it over a great sword for with it he was as fast as any with long or even short sword.

"Quicksilver. Interesting." Bartholm said to himself as walked down to the inner city and stopped at the blacksmiths.

Stans looked down into the courtyard at Bartholm strode among the other Montterrans that had come to 'save' them. It wasn't that he wasn't grateful. After the loss of his lord and the majority of their men, they absolutely had needed reinforcements. It was just that theirs had been a proud city and now it was no longer what it had been. Nothing could wash back that which had transpired.

These western men, he feared, were here to stay. Stans noted that deep within the interior the inner keep walls were manned with all Montterrans knights and archers. Bartholms own father Duke Baras Lord Bethos was easily seen standing at the inner keeps lookout and bridge. The Duke's polished armour was hard to miss especially since he was almost as tall as his son and yet had twice the girth. As he looked over the Duke paused mid stride and looked back towards him. Stan shrugged and turned leaving to return back to the wall and his post.

Across the courtyard Duke Baras Lord Bethos looked down at the outer courtyard and city within and then glanced out at the outer wall. He had seen his son descend from the outer wall but had lost him now in the bustle of people running up and down the stairs. He reached up and rubbed his eyes, knowing that they were no longer as keen as they once had been.

The Duke turned to his new squire, Trevor Rutt. During his visit to MountRyhn his 'grace' had saddled him with the Count Palatine's son. Roehn had commanded him to take the lad "To 'strengthen' the binds of our nation". He despised having to train new pages… and Landor Rutt's son was not the type of material he usually selected to page for him.

"Trevor." Duke Bethos growled at the lanky lad that coward before him. "Go out to the outer wall and see what my son is up to. He was to get me a count of archers left."

Trevor, a small skinny youth nodded as he accepted the order and hurried off.

Duke Bethos watched as the lad hurried off, he shook his head. Trevor's parents spoiled the lad having sent him off to serve Duke Bethos with a glimmering youths' set of ring mail. It was as light as a feather with padded shoulders and glimmered as he walked. His mail coif was made of the thinnest but strongest wire Lord Bethos had ever seen and shone like silver as if dangled from his Barbuta helm.

'But what made him look ridiculous,' thought Duke Bethos. 'Was the full faced helm with pointy top. The helm was supposed to make the lad look taller, but in fact it just made him look silly.'

"What garb for a page!" Duke Bethos said shaking his head as he watched the lad bound off.

Lord Bethos smiled wondering what Landor Rutt would say when he heard that the Duke had taken his son along on this quest to take on the Tock. He was probably shitting his britches. Lord Baras Barthos let go gregarious chuckle thinking about the man.

The Duke walked around the wall to the bridge to the inner keep. His guards now were stationed along and through the inner keep. They had fought hard and well to make it to MinonTer and deserved a break.

The Duke sighed recalling the battle. When they arrived the MinonTer line of archers was just folding and the castle was besieged. They had arrived in time to push back the Tock advances but not early enough to stop the massive loss of soldiers that once manned MinnonTer.

Then just when the Duke thought he had the battle in hand – then came down the beasts from the north to reinforce the Tock. He and his men had never seen the like before. Their ranks broke and the best they could do was to run for cover back to MinonTer. He had almost lost his own son in that battle.

Just as the thought of his son washed through his thoughts, he saw his face for real as it rose up from the stairs on his left.

"Ho Bartholm." He bellowed out to his son. "I just sent Trevor out to find you. What took you so long? You were going to get me an assessment of archers?"

Bartholm chuckled and extended and shook his father's outreached hand. "If you sent Trevor out to find me, then you weren't really seriously looking to find out that count all too soon."

Duke Baras laughed out loud and then quickly glanced around ensuring there weren't any soldiers within earshot. He then with his handshake pulled his son a little closer to him. "If I had less sense I would send him out collecting arrows beyond the walls and be rid of him."

"You mean father, if you had more sense." Bartholm said. Both started to laugh.

"So, how many do we have?" Duke Baras asked his son.

"Not as many as we hoped. But worse, they are the least of the skilled. Only one in all the lot was I truly impressed with. The others are not that much better than our own.

Tierie Zarof the great Count of MinonTer must have taken all of his best with him when he marched north to face the Tock. From the sounds of it – none returned…. Only one man that went north of all the thousands is said to have returned.

"Yes, a man called Quizler Far." Duke Baras said nodding. "I heard something about him. I asked them to bring him to me, though I hear he is not in great condition."

"Yes, the man lost a hand in the battle I hear." Bartholm added wanting to go one up on his father in gleamed information.

Duke Baras surprised by his son's knowledge smiled and nodded. "Some day you will make a good Duke." He said fondly to his son and raised his hand and put it on his shoulder.

"Never happen." Bartholm said smiling down at his dad. "I watched you fight this morning. You will live to a hundred. You didn't even break a sweat."

Duke Baras. "Bull-terds. I broke wind and sweat in each swing I made. I was soaked to the bone by the end of it. But what scared me more was watching your reckless charge. Were you mad?"

"I had no idea that the Tock were soon to be supported by those massive beasts. If I was not a little older, I would be saying that nightmares of the past have come again."

"As I believe as well. I have heard stories of old as well, when I was a pup… Some of the creatures appear to alike those descriptions for me not to wonder. Come – enough speculation – the Countess awaits us. She remains of the family that once ruled, she should have more answers. Plus – Quizler Far is to be brought to us there."

The Duke and his son proceeded on over the wall and through to the castle's inner keep. As they walked they looked in amazement at the wealth on open display within the halls, and rooms. Both were simple men, raised with simple tastes. Oathos had within its halls hanging armour and swords, not tapestries made from silk.

Both men stopped for several minutes as they entered the great hall that led to the Noble hall where they expected to meet the countess. In the long hall, bronze busts of past nobles were stationed every five meters, coat of arms were stationed above them made in tapestries woven with silver and gold threads. "Grand place to show past lords." Bartholm said with a little sarcasm.

As the Duke approached the door at the end of the hall it opened and a lady of fifty or more stood before him dressed conservatively in a high collared dress. The dress had a dark red coat about it but under it was an ivory gown stitched with very fine needlework.

The lady smiled at the Duke and his son and motioned with her hand at the busts. "You see before you the shields and busts of the predecessors of MinonTer that have fallen defending the realm. A lord of this castle does not get so commemorated if he dies in his sleep."

Bartholm turned to look down the hall and under his breath added sardonically. "Personally, I hope to die of old age in my sleep after winning and living through a thousand battles."

The Countess smiled at Bartholm as he returned to gaze at her. "Unfortunately, MinonTer has always been guarding the doors of the North."

Duke Baras turned and looked down the long hall. There were at least ten busts on each side of the hall. "A heavy loss you have paid defending these lands." Baras said as he turned back to face the lady and bowed.

"I am sorry to hear of the loss of your husband Countess, and for your sons that rode with him. I heard they too were knighted in the old ways. I am sure they died fighting with valour."

Katrin Zarof the Countess of MinonTer bowed and motioned the Duke to enter the Keeps inner sanctum. As the Duke and Bartholm passed her by she closed the door behind them.

"Please, make yourself at home." She said as they entered a large round room with five doors.

The Duke and his son stood in the middle of the room as the Countess pointed and directed them as to what lay beyond the room. "The door in front leads to the council of the north a room with maps to plan for battles. The door to the left of it is the solarium.

Katrin paused and then cleared her throat. "The door to it's left most side is where our son once stayed and the door to the right of the one in front was my husband and my room."

Without hesitating the Countess bowed her head slightly to the Duke. "I have moved our things out and they are ready for your use. I must apologize for I have neither his, nor my son's sword to hand to you as sign of the passing of rule of this house."

The Duke raised his hand. "No need for formalities my lady. And I must first start by saying that by order of our King Mar Roehn the Third that we have not come hear to take your place, but in aid to you, to your King and to your people."

The Countess looked up very surprised. "Indeed. You surprise me good Duke, and I am not very easily surprised as of late." She turned and led them to the door of the solarium and entered. The two followed slowly looking around at the tapestries and trappings as they did.

"However," the countess continued as she turned to face them again. "My family has fallen, my husband and lord is no more as is my son. Our castle stands besieged and we have the smallest of forces within it. This castle, lands, and all surrounding and all its people I would relinquish my command to you."

Duke Baras looked with great concern at the Countess understanding what she was asking of him. By granting the Duke fealty of the lands, it specifically obligated the Duke to protect all serfs, vassals and others within the surrounding areas…. even if at risk of his own life. Katrin knew that the Duke had the reputation to protect his people above all else.

Duke Baras paused and reflected on the offer. 'If things got 'sticky' here – he could always run back to his own lands. However, if he said yes now – he would be obligated to stay and protect its people as his own.'

"To offer this, you make our situation very dire?" The Duke replied slowly watching every move and expression the lady displayed.

"Indeed I do." The Countess replied slowly. "You yourself have seen our plight. You have seen that the Tock are not alone, that score, new legions of Weer and Wog now roam the north. There is no way what is left of Terran forces can rebuff such evil."

"Weer – childhood myths," Bartholm interjected attempting to lead the Countess on to a further discovery. "We saw some larger than normal war dogs descend behind the Tock… not much more. As for 'Wogs' I know not what you speak of."

The Countess laughed. "I heard that you have seen the start of their forces. Remember, some of my men were there as well, and returned from the same field as you. But what you saw were not your 'fabled' Weer. What you saw was their twisted offspring the Wog. You have yet to see true Weer."

The Countess spoke softly never lifting her head, always looking at Quizler Far. "It is the product of when a Weer mates with a wolf. They might do this when the moon is full and the heat is on them. The wolf bitch will litter within two moons and can have a litter of eight or nine Wog pups. Often times, the bitch dies giving birth for the Wogs are bigger then the largest wolf."

Bartholm 'snarked'. "Weer. My nanny frightened me to be with such stories."

The Countess looked up at Bartholm. Her tone demonstrated that the wisdom she was imparting had been bought for at a high cost. "What you surprised you in battle were a small pack of Wogs. They have not quite the intelligence of a Weer (or as such a man), but are indeed much smarter than any dog or wolf. Did they not charge our forces just at the time you had thought your advantage over the Tock? Was it not their appearance that broke my men's ranks and sent you along with them running back to these walls?"

Bartholm looked over to his father for support. But from his father's returned gaze, he realized that his father was taking this story seriously.

The Countess noted the wordless exchange between father and son turned and walked over to the large stained windows and opened one and looked out. Halos was now up and Detro's evil grin poked up just above the horizon. "Our men ran when they noted their numbers, for they respect the Wogs abilities, and yes do fear them. For the Wog fear silver less than a Weer, as it does them less effect."

The Countess looked up at the sky. "As your nany's stories likely said, and what as of these last months have proven to us. The Weer rose from their dens the first night that Detro's showed us his evil grin…. and appears to come out only when he does."

"However." Katrin Zarof, Countess of MinonTer turned to face the lord and his son. Her understated tan dress suddenly shimmered catching the Duke's eye. In the moonlight silver threads caught the light of Detros and twinkled with its colors. "The Wog cares not what time of day or night it is and we believe cares not as to the phases of the moon. But what is most concerting is their numbers. You see, once a Wog is born, it can then produce a litter of ten or more pubs identical to itself by breeding with another Wog. The pups are born within weeks and mature in weeks as well – not months.."

"What?" Duke Baras said almost out of breath. He glanced back at his son then back at the Countess who was nodding solemnly.

"Their numbers are growing at a staggering rate. A month ago we noticed a few and then only accompanying Weer attacks at the dead of night. But within only a few weeks, we noted them accompanying Tock in significant numbers. Our scouts have seen groups numbering in the hundreds."

Bartholm coughed, "born and mature in a month? Ten pups to a litter?" Bartholm's look was much more serious then it was before.

"And 'True' Weer are being sighted now more and more." The Countess smiled looking at Bartholm. "As you, we thought them only myths until recently. Someone, or something, has started the species once again and they too are proliferating. Further, these are not rouge Weer made from the bite - for those become relatively mindless creatures that single-mindedly and chaotically pursuing their own goal to quench their insatiable hunger when Detros smiles. 'These' Weer all work together and with the Wogs and Tock. Something or someone must be controlling them. But we have no clue."

The three nobles stood silent for minutes on end. Then the Countess walked over to one of the four well-stuffed, regal, high backed chairs that sat within the small solarium. The Duke, looking all at once rather haggard waited until the Countess sat and then too sat down in a chair opposite to her. He looked to the right; the hearth in the room was not lit and was cold. Bartholm remained standing, his mouth open in awe.

"Is there any thought as to who or what holds the strings to these beasts?" Duke Baras said finally after several more minutes.

Countess sighed. "I looked to the east, to my elder brother in AnnonTer... for help. He informed me that TieRei has fallen, the Clansmen have retreated to his hold, beaten and tattered from Weer and Wog attacks. The Clansmen believe some great evil has mastered that castle for other strange creatures now inhabits it and more and different creatures are seen daily. They do not believe that castle as being manned by Tock nor Masti. Further, he mentions that Wog and Weer roam free there in as many as we have here."

"So, no aid from us from the east," Bartholm rhetorically as he apparently woke up. He swallowed hard and looked around. "I need a drink".

The Countess laughed lightly brightening the room dramatically. "I have asked that they bring us some refreshments when Quizler Far is brought to us."

"What do we expect to learn from this man?" The Duke asked sitting even deeper in his large chair. His look brought back to the room a sense of foreboding.

"Quizler Far rode with Lindon who led our second company of men. My husband Tierie was venturing out to crush the remnants of the Tock attack at our castle. He commanded Lindon to head a second smaller company to be as safeguard and ensure their retreat should something unexpected occur."

The Countess looked down at her hands. Only her wedding band remained on her hand, she turned it as she spoke. "I speculate now that the Tock attack and retreat was a ruse to draw us out of our strong hold. They must have feared that with our archers on our walls they would have a hard time to take us here. Quizler spoke only briefly before he went to surgery to repair what was left of his arm. His word then spoke that upon entry to the deeper woods of the Northern pass that a horde of Weer and Wog descended upon my husband's army. Lindon's men rushed forward to break the pincer and allow the retreat – but failed and were consumed in the process. He alone remains alive as witness to what happened."

"We chased a large company of Tock to that northern pass. It is there that they turned and faced my father. He was doing well until..." Bartholm faltered.

"Until the beasts you described as Wogs attacked." Duke Baras continued. "It was then that I was flanked. Our horses were unnaturally spooked. I doubt now that my son's charge had as much to do with our escape then simply that the Wogs were still either engaged or ending the battle with your husband and son."

"Ill timing." Bartholm said gallantly. "If only we had arrived earlier we might have helped your son open a way to retreat home."

"As is," Duke Baras said. "We saw none of your husband or your son's company."

"He returned from the woods alone and in his current state, having lost much blood only hours after your own men arrived within the gates. He was let in while you were manning the battlements." The Countess continued... "As you will see, he was easily identified."

"He alone then can tell us as to their true number, their disposition." The Duke added dryly.

"I have no children left." The Countess said in a heart breaking tone. "My last son went with his father. I pleaded with my husband to command Lindon to stay within the walls, but he would have none of it. But more was his folly to allow my son to take with him the remaining Black and the remnants of our skilled archers - thus leaving us now so utterly defenceless."

Duke Baras mused, not sure on how to answer, on what he could say without consultation with his King and was about to say that when there was a knock at the Solarium's door.

Bartholm looked over to the Countess who nodded, he then walked over to the door and opened it up.

"ENTER." The Countess commanded as her husband's page looked in while balancing a large tray. Another serving lady was behind him holding another tray of soft breads. Behind them stood two of Duke Baras' men supporting a man whose head hung down and whose arm was tied tietly and within a sling.

The page entered quickly and put down the tray of decanters and crystal glasses followed closely by the serving lady with soft breads and sweet meats. Both them bowed quickly and rushed out of the room. The two soldiers looked in questioningly at the Duke who motioned that they should bring in the man.

The two soldiers brought in Quizler far. His dusty silver long hair hung over his face the Duke looked at the pasty grey hand that clutched the bandaged stump and sling restricting its movement as the guards lowered the man into one of the larger remaining chairs.

Quizler Far stayed sitting on the edge of the seat not leaning back to embrace the softness of the cloth. "My Lady," he started. His voice was soft, and choked with emotion. "We failed you. We failed your husband, and I have failed your son. I do not deserve to be in your presence."

"Sit back good Quizler." My son called you friend, and you were within his company for many a year. I have faith that you have done what you could. But there is some urgency to know what you have seen."

The Countess motioned with her hand at Bartholm and Baras. "These two lords are from Oathos, come to aid us. Duke Baras and his son Bartholm are most eager as am I to hear what befell you, what manner of creatures you fought and their number and potential intent."

Bartholm walked over to the tray and poured himself a glass of a amber liquid. The crystal was tall and he filled it to the brim. When his father game him a look of disapproval he reached over and picked up a smaller decanter of black liquid he assumed was Talk and poured some into the same glass. The thick black caffeine rich liquid swirled down and in to the tall amber fluid. Bartholm then picked up the glass and drained it. He neither coughed, sneezed nor winced as the burning liquid splashed down his throat.

Duke Baras coughed and motioned with his eyes to the Countess.

Bartholm looking a tad embarrassed, and also a bit flushed from the consumption of the alcohol raised his glass to the countess. "Can I get you some?"

Duke Baras shook his head in frustration. "Sorry, Countess, my son did not learn well his manners."

"Thank you that would be nice." The Countess said smiling, "but perhaps not so large a glass." She then looked over to Quizlar. "But if you would be so kind Sir Bartholm, please first pour a glass for our wounded friend here."

Quizler raised his good hand up, and raised his head ever slightly. "Talk only please, the surgeon said I was not to have any strong drink on account of my blood. Alcohol thins it, he says and will make me bleed the more."

"Poppy cock." Bartholm said pouring the man a tall glass matching the one he just consumed. "If a man looses a hand in battle he deserves a stout drink or three." He said as he turned and handed the tall glass in to Quizler's good hand.

Duke Baras 'gafawwed' but stopped short of saying anything more.

As Bartholm handed Quizler the man looked up and Bartholm stood motionless, captivated by the man's silvery eyes.

Quizler took the glass and held it until Bartholm broke his gaze, poured and handed the Countess a drink Bartholm motioned to his father who shook his head declining a drink.

Duke Baras looked over at the strange man that now was looking up. He was thin and wiry and his loose white shirt hung loosely from his body. The man's complexion matched his hair and eyes… a pasty, silvery colour. "Can you tell us of what happened to the Count, his son and your army?"

Quizler looked over to the Countess again who nodded. With neck still bent the man looked down at his drink and took a sip. He then grasped it and swirled the liquid within it and watched the talk and bandy swirl but not mix.

Quizler's softly cleared his throat. "The Tocks were lost, disarrayed dispersed and fled before the Tierie Zarof, the might Count of MinonTer. Our archers, running and mounted were bringing the Tock down in scores. They fled and the Count pursued yelling out that never again would they dare to attack our gates. He spurred on his men on foot and mounted to ensure that they could not make it to their stronghold of MarTar Nasky."

Quizler took a little draft and swallowed it. He inhaled deeply and then continued. "I was in Sir Lindon's company, by his side. He was so very afraid that his father would kill all the Tock and none would be left for him that all of our men, mounted and not were almost atop of the rear of the Count's forces.

We stopped them before they could make it to the gates of MarTar… I am sure the Count thought that he had them then and there. Without support, without walls, our archers would make small work of the remaining Tock."

"But then," Quizler slowed. "we followed, we were so close behind the Count's main company Sir Lindon and I could see it plainly even though as you know the sun was just setting."

Quizler's voice was a tear between a whisper and a cough. "Wogs. Wogs. Not the dozens we have sighted roaming the lands, but hundreds, ney thousands of them. From out of the woods around us they sprang."

"Our archers were amazing." Quizler said enthusiastically. "The beasts eyes sprouted arrows like lashes…. But the numbers."

Quizler breathed a deep breath and cleared his throat and sat up a little taller in the chair. "With Icis held high our Lord Count Tierie Zarof sat tall in his saddle. His silver blade cleaving beast after beast."

He paused and then looked over to the Countess and then the Duke. "But. But the light was waning, the sun had set and our light was poor. Halos had not yet risen, yet from the very ground it appeared they sprang. They were massive, ugly Weer to tear down our soldiers.

"How many," The countess asked.

"A score or more, perhaps even as many as a hundred. The wolves had already swept away all of the archers on foot, those on horse were harried having their animals jostle and turn as the Wogs snapped at them, found it hard to let loose their shafts. The Weer cut a bloody path straight for the heart of our Lord's company, straight to Count Tierie Zarof ."

Quizler looked up at the countess and then lowered his head to look within the glass again. "Sir Lindon charged forward our company - but there was little place to go that wasn't packed with Wog or Weer. The Weer feasted on the guard."

'To me' Lord Tierie Zarof cried and all knights still able to him rode. Your son was a blinding light as his silver sword cut a path. Ten Wogs did I see him cut so that he could reach his father."

Quizler halted and slouched slightly. Bartholm picked up the slender bottle of Talk and after receiving a nod from the Countess poured a little more into his glass.

"To this day, I have only heard stories of Weer." Bartholm said as he poured. "Tell me more of them."

Quizler laughed solemnly. "I was raised on those tales, for it was those scary stories that so spurred my father's trade in Quicksilver. Our family knew more of the tales than many. Legend has it that several hundred years ago a great wizard curses a lad that was courting a girl the mage wished for his own. The curse suffered the man to turn to a beast on the long cycles where Detros grins – where he looses his mind and feasts on human flesh. All those that do not die by his bite, too suffer the same affliction. The wizards name was Weerton, thus the cursed was named Weer...."

"They indeed were taller than most men, massively muscled and able to run faster on all fours than a horse. Massive long snouts filled with fangs that extend up and down beyond their gums. The fangs exude poison more vile than any serpent, for if this poison gets into your blood, or even into your eyes or nose... you too will suffer their same curse.. but only when Detros is high in the sky for they are not fully transformed by the curse."

"Wait a moment." The Duke said thinking back. "But you said Detros was not high." Duke Baras said leaning forward slightly.

"Indeed. It was not." Quizler added raising his glass in cheer to the Duke and taking a sip. "Thus, what attacked us were not made from the poisoning of blood... but were True Weers.... Men cursed alike the first."

"It makes sense." Quizler looked up a small smile playing on his lips. "It was heresy to say this within our family, but even we believed that the last of the Weer had long ago been killed. How then could the Wog have re-arisin if they required their sires to exist and how so many now so fast? Plus, those tainted by the Weer become mindless savage beasts, and what we saw was not that. The Weer there worked as a group, flanking and killing in unison working as a pack. The Tock stood and watched so very close yet not once did a single Weer stray from their attack on us."

The Countess paused in thought. "If new 'True Weer' were made, then indeed the worst of what we feared has come to pass. Some great evil mind is behind this and we will have to seek it out before this will end."

Lord Baras Barthos grunted. "Another hand has stirred the pot then."

"And," Bartholm nodded and raised his voice in agreement, "each day their numbers grow at the cost to us and ours. If there is this many 'now' then in six months their horde will be unstoppable by any!"

"Silver is the key to kill them all." Quizler added. "The purer the breed the more effect it has on them. 'Weer' were said to have been able to smell quicksilver for unlike its smelted counterpart, being liquid it has an odor. We sold THOUSANDS of quicksilver vials that superstitious folk would hang around their neck or in their house. Blades with quicksilver are very effective against the Wog; the purer the silver or quicksilver the better."

"But the more diluted the blood, the less the effect. Thus Wogs fear it less." Bartholm added and Quizler nodded in agreement.

Bartholm smiled back. "Bash the head or cut it off and they will die as does every beast."

"True." The Countess responded smirking back at Bartholm. "But arrows do little to it unless tipped with silver for they recover fast from minor ailments, not as fast as a Weer, but fast nonetheless. They can obtain what we would hope would be fatal wounds and yet fight on for hours or even days."

"Go on with how my husband and son died." The Countess asked and drew Quizlers gaze to her.

Quizler swallowed and then continued slowly at first. "With his guards pulled down by Wogs and wolves five Weer pounced all at once at our lord. He raised his mighty sword and screamed "For MinonTer and all Terran men!"

Quizlers voice strengthened. "His giant sword pierced a Weer through its chest and it let out a scram that shook the hills for it was a blade imbibed with the purest silver. But as it fell it pulled the blade that transfixed it, with it to the ground."

"Oh, how the Count did try to twist the mighty blade free as the creature fell but could not and he was pulled down with it to the ground. Then, and only then did the other Weer pounce."

Quizler looked up to the Countess with tears in his eyes. "He disappeared under a mass of fur and fang. Nothing could we see of him, nothing save boot and blood."

The Countess took a deep breath.

Quizler swallowed and then began again with his sorrowful tale. "Your son, my lady – brave was he. For Lindon screamed "For our Lord, my father to me!" and he we charged to where his father had fallen."

"What little remained of the company of men and archers joined with Lindon and we pushed forward to where our Lord had fallen. Man and horse dropped like flies around us! Soon we were fully encircled and we were no more than a dozen Weer and a score or more of Wogs."

"A moment later and it was just Lindon and I that were still mounted. Every other man had fallen to foot and were fighting for their lives as wolves darted between them."

"Yet the courage of the few remained and we hacked and slit so many creatures that their carcasses had to be jumped over by those remaining."

"But hundreds of Wogs still ran about in a circle that continued to tighten around us."

"With Sir Lindon leading I too made it to where the count had fallen. Three Weer sat there over his torn flesh. Each looked up at your son and howled at him in defiance only to defiantly then rip more flesh from your husband's bones."

"Battle fever took your son then. Your son screamed and rode into the Weer that were yet feasting on his father and parted them like water."

"Sir Lindon brought them fear with the cut of his cold sword. They ran like sheep these Weer to hide behind a circle of Wogs."

"Sir Lindon road around the bloody remains of his father screaming curses and slashing at whatever creature dared to come near. His claymore Icicle too had silver within it, but not as pure. Yet it parted several head from Wogs that got to close, and twice he bent low in his saddle and pierced the hearts of a Weer."

"As for me? It was all I could do to help. I sought to keep the wolves off of him for there were so many."

"But there were too many. One of the wolves tore the stomach out from my mount and I fell to the ground and then so too did Lindon."

Quizler paused in speculation. "It was if the Weer were waiting for that to occur." He said almost to himself. "When Lindon started rising from the ground, it was then that they jumped at him."

"With great strength the Weer leapt each ten meters or more and they smashed him back to the ground."

"There was no finesse or honour in their fight. The animals jumped and smashed him to the ground and tore into him."

The Countess began to sob silently with face towards the high back of the chair.

Quizler looked over to the lady and stretched out his hand to her. "My best friend, your son. He showed no fear my lady and

443

asked no mercy my lady. 'For NinonTer' I heard as his last breath was taken."

"And thus I stood alone now. Icis and Iscile lay side by side as the blood of father and son intermingled."

Quizler slowed and the Duke motioned. Bartholm poured the Duke a short glass of amber brandy and handed it to him.

The Countess didn't turn; she remained sobbing silently with head turned away from the men. Only after a few minutes of strained silence did the Countess regain her composure.

Bartholm looked up at the Countess. "Lady, what store of silver do you have within these walls?"

The Countess brushed back a tear from her face with a small kerchief she had pulled from her waist. "My husband loved silver. We have plates and goblets aplenty throughout the castle but it will take time to melt them down and smith them into weapons. . Icis and Iscile were the only blades forged in this city with quicksilver within them, that was for looks and balance alone."

"My shop is within the walls." Quizler stated calmly. There you will find a few barrels of quicksilver. There are more at my home in the Northern hills but with the Weer outside our very walls that would be a perilous quest. Wooden shafts and arrowheads can be dipped in the liquid metal. The arrows and tips are cut and etched and will hold drops of the fluid."

Bartholm nodded and then hastened out of the room closing the door behind him. He could be heard stomping down the hall yelling orders at the two soldiers that had remained outside the door. "Wake my sergeants. We might have work to do yet before we can rest. The stories were true after all. We will be fighting myths I fear before the morning's light!"

The Duke, slowly, carefully looked back to Quizler who sat motionless. "Quizler, how is it besieged by all the Weer and Wog that you returned and non other?"

Quizler paused. "I was done for. Though mostly unhurt, I was too tired to fight any more and after brining down poor Lindon the Weer and Wog turned to the dregs that still lived."

He then laughed and lifted his good hand displaying its colour and brushing back his hair to expose his eyes. "The Countess might have been too polite to say this, but I was adopted by my father, and I too like him have paid for 'this', 'this gift'."

Quizler laughed and then coughed. "I was fortunate. A great beast of a Weer parted the others and walked on two legs to me. It was vast in size and from snout to tail it stood three meters or four perhaps more."

"I had but my sword still, and it was of course imbibed with silver… But the beast jumped so fast, it took and bit it from my arm in one motion." Quizler laughed. "Stupid animal."

Quizler looked down at the stump of his arm. "It howled louder than I did."

"Your blood," The Duke said knowingly.

"Indeed. It is tainted with quicksilver." Quizler said smiling back.

"My bood was down its throat and into its stomach. The beast was doomed and it new it. My own poison was already eating at its mouth and stomach. Its eyes went wild and it ran trying to free itself of the blood seeping down its very throat. And as it ran clearing way all before it in its crazed howling state… I followed."

"But the other Wogs and Weer," the Countess asked.

"My blood, they could smell my blood." Quizler added. "They all parted like clouds before me as I ran with bleeding stump before me."

The Duke gazed at Quizler's bloody stump. "Your blood poisoned the Weer." The Duke stated again in disbelief.

Quizler looked back at the Duke. "And what a poison it was! The beast thrashed and thrashed and then fell to the ground dead."

The Duke gazed back at the man incredulously.

"With bloody stump I ran. I ran and ran and ran until I could run no further."

"Twice Wogs and wolves came at me. Twice I howled back at them and let loose my arm spraying them with my lifeblood! Only a drop or two on their fur sent them running!"

Quizler looked down again at his stump. "My gift, it seems paid me well on that day." He stood and bowed to the Countess and Duke. "If I might, I am very tired and sore and would rest."

The Duke stood and looked over to the Countess who nodded. "Our thanks Quizler Far." She said with great courage. "For all that you have done, for your loyalty to my husband and my son." He voice trailed off a little at the end.

Quizler nodded then looked down. "I only wish I could have done more my lady. My prayers are with them both and with you."

The Duke nodded and then opened the door and let Quizler out, the lady's page was without who he instructed to assist Quizler to return to his quarters.

He then turned and faced the Countess who now stood once again looking out the great windows of the solarium. "I will defend you and yours as my own. Of this, you have my pledge."

With that he turned and walked out. As he strode down the hall she could hear his voice trailing behind him. "Weers and Wogs by the seven hells what has befallen us?

Blood Magic

The image hovering over the dead bodies of the governor and his wife shimmered. A moment later Duke Sirthinor's face and features appeared. With a sickly smile he casually turned and walked over to the nightstand and picked up the goblet of sweet wine that sat upon it. Turning he walked without hesitation, remorse or any feeling what so ever over to the canopied bed and pulled back hard on the curtain exposing the carnage within.

The governor lay, slightly bent over his wife's still form. Their faces were pressed together and Tunis' one hand was outstretched to touch her extended belly. "How touching." The Duke said dispassionately as he took another sip of wine.

Moving the cup to his left hand, he reached forward and put his right upon the hilt of the dagger protruding from the corpse before him. With a hard yank that pulled the body slightly forward the blade came free.

Covered in sticky red blood Duke Sirthinor smiled as he looked at the silver dagger. "For my escape I only need a few drops." He said as he raised the blade and scraped it clean against the top of the goblet. The blood dripped down into the cup mixing with the sweet mulled wine.

Darkness billowed out from Duke Sirthinor's eyes as he raised the goblet to his lips and took a sip. The sickly sweet concoction spilled out from between his lips as he began is gurgled chant. "Gachloch, cochgo, eeii." The Dukes eyes looked down, transfixed upon the image of the dead Governor before him willing his own form to bend to that of the dead man before him.

He could feel the energy coming from the governor's blood as it splashed against his teeth and tong and as it sought out his throat and stomach as he continued the blood spell. "Tee new- na andardial' at the ending note he bit hard the side of his tong mixing his own blood with that of the Governors', then deeply did he swallow as he felt the magic begin to boil.

Small specks of blood spittle issued from his mouth as the burning liquid plunged down his throat to writhe within his belly. With stomach spasms the dark Duke fell to his knees resting his head on the side of the bed. Opening his eyes he tried to regain the image of the governor beside him.

Swallowing once again, he licked his lips and then dried them with the back of his shirt. With eyes now closed he dropped the cup onto the bed and concentrated. In silence he mouthed the rest of the blood rite.

A small glimmering surrounded the Duke and then in his place was the image of the now dead governor. "Aham." The Duke said, and hearing the voice of the Governor he smiled, "perfectly pathetic."

Still kneeling on the bed the Duke, now appearing as the dead governor before him put his hand beneath his shirt and pulled out a rolled parchment. Unrolling it he inspected it once more admiring the forged cigil seal of Methor Bestinor. Above the seal there were only four simple words – 'Traitor to the crown.'

Smiling sickly the Duke picked up unique silver knife and as a means to add an exclamation and homage to his new god plunged it in and through the note and down and in to the belly of Carel. He was sure several of the castle's staff had caught a glimpse of him in his previous form, all eyes and all suspicion for this act would be pointed east!

After admiring his work for a moment he then turned and dropped off of the bed and walked back to the closed door. Opening it he bent forward looked at the two bodies of the guards that had been so easily duped and so effortlessly killed. Bending forward he grabbed the first and pulled him into the room. The second was heavier and by the end of the task he was huffing.

"Killing is such an exhaustive task." He said softly to himself.

A small trail of blood smeared the hall where the guards had fallen but he knew that few people would venture up to the governor's private quarters at this time of the night.

"But soooo much fun," He added as he looked down the long corridor and closed the chamber door behind him. "Panic and suspicions will reign; all I will be welcomed with open arms as the protectorate of the west, the only one to keep them all from falling to the savages that have taken their ruler."

As his footsteps echoed down the hall his mind stepped through his next actions. The Duke smiled as he looked behind him making sure no one could hear him whisper to himself, "Its like taking candy from a baby." Then after laughing a moment added. "But ooh so much more rewarding."

Eyes of TieRei

Dimi looked down looked down at Etch's head now cradled in her lap. Tears were streaming down her face spilling onto her neck and occasionally dropping down to land on Etch's already wet face.

Long shadows brought on by the evening had already consumed the area where they were and Dimi could hardly discern the features of her friend's face. Her hand stroked his wet forehead, he had sweated continuously since she had found him, but what concerned her most was how cold he felt, and that the droplets of sweat that seeped from his pours were cold, almost freezing to the touch.

The night came and went, with little change. She had pulled as much leaf as possible to comfort them, but the place they were in afforded no ability to establish fire. So often she had thought to go back to the camp, yet each time she attempted to rise Etch had clutched her hand, moaned or his breath had shortened enticing her not to leave his side.

Now as the morning's sun began to rise the urgency to move Etch from this pace increased. His cold sweat had not broken, and his shivering was draining the last of his energy. Dimi doubted he would be able to survive until noon unless she could bring him to warmth through fire or sun. The shadows of the forest and the lack of clearing afforded her no ability for either.

Although as she stirred to stand Etch moaned, this time, Dimi continued. Leaves fell off them both in torrents. Pushing the leaves with her foot she made a pillow from the red and yellow leaves that were now in abundance around them. Resting his head she looked around, trying to map out the fastest route out of the forest and back to their camp. She was small and it would be a struggle under normal conditions to pull Etch the distance to camp. However, the massive intertwined roots would increase the difficulty geometrically for her. In many instances she would have to drag Etch up many meters to traverse sections of raised foliage and root.

Dimi looked down as Etch stirred again, his breathing was forced and shallow. She was loath to disturb his sleep but the flicker of sunlight from far beyond the tree line enticed her to action. 'It would be much warmer in the clearing.' She thought as she started to search below the leaves for Etch's arms.

After half an hour Dimi was still huffing and puffing trying to drag Etch up and over the first stump when she heard something stirring in the leaves. She gently let Etch down but as she let go he started to slide back down the root. She reached for him and then stopped as she spotted a movement in between the roots relatively close to their position.

Dimi froze hoping that whatever it was, wouldn't notice her. Inwardly she cursed herself for being so focused on moving Etch that she had not noticed the sounds or movements earlier.

"Hello!" A man's deep tenor voice rang out calling to her from only ten meters away. His voice was loud and deep startling Dimi to spin to face the giant of a man coming from her right almost making her loose her footing on the slick root.

"Don't worry; I am a Priest of the Temple." Came the call as the large framed man disappeared and then appeared between the trees in front of her. He was very tall standing over two meters, heavy set dressed in the white and brown robes of the Temple Guard. He wore a thick gold chain around his neck and his head was bare of a hat. White hair encircled his balding scalp. His face was friendly and sported a big friendly smile.

Dimi stood up, resting her hand on her hip where her quills and dagger hung. "What do you want?" She asked suspiciously.

"Thought you could use my help," the priest said as he continued to wind his way towards her. I was in the area checking on an acolyte on the eastern bank when I was told that you were here and in a bit of a predicament."

Dimi looked around nervously. "Told by whom?"

The priest laughed as he drew near to where she stood, "a friend." The man stood and looked her over, but his face didn't change in expression. His smile was friendly and unassuming. He then pointed to Etch who was slumping and sliding very slowly down the root. "But first, shall we get your friend off the roots and to a fire?"

Dimi looked down and grabbed Etch's shoulder and stopped his slide then looked back up at the priest.

"He looks in rough shape and he will need to be near a fire." The priest continued stepping lightly forward. His long legs helped him crest a few of the taller roots in a single stride.

Dimi looked back briefly at the man and nodded agreement, not knowing what else to do. She knew of the priests, and this man fit the description well. She didn't sense any deception in his words and his face looked friendly although he was massive.

"I could use some help." She said sheepishly as he drew near. "I have been trying to keep him warm, but he keeps getting very deep, unnatural chills and feels very cold to the touch. He is too large for me to carry easily."

The priest nodded and put his arms under Etch's and lifted him up to his large shoulders. Then staggering turned and started carrying him back to the camp. Dimi was shocked and amazed as to the man's strength and just how small Etch looked in comparison to him. "Patrick Mellon, father and Temple Guard." The priest said without turning between huffs as he laboured forward over root and round tree.

"What you two doing in these parts?" the priest asked as he rounded a rather large tree glancing back to Dimi who was dancing now across roots parallel to the priest's route. "Most from around here know that we like people to stay clear of the waters of the Keeper. The Temple has marked them Eyes of TieRei off limits. Most that live around here are aware of that."

"We were following a trail. He went in by no desire of my own." Dimi stated not really wanting to give more information then she had to. "The waters appear very, very cold."

Father Mellon emerged out of the forest followed quickly by Dimi, but in just a few long strides was next to the fire that had already been lit by their camp. He lay Etch gently down only a hands span from the flames and then went and picked up a few leaves and placed it under his head. "Might singe a few hair, but need to get him hot fast." He said looking as Dimi rounded the fire and sat beside her friend.

The priest then went over to a small stack of wood by the fire and threw a few more branches on it. He then turned and went to the pile of bedrolls and supplies stacked by the side of their camp and picked up a small pan that was strapped to the outside of a large bag.

The massive priest then holding the pan as if it were a cup walked over to the lake and filled it with water and returned to the fire. He huffed as he sat down and then immediately his left hand darted under his robes and drew forth a small pouch which he unlaced.

Dimi smiled watching the priest stick a massive thumb and finger in to the small pouch and extract a pinch of old red leaf. Although it was a pinch for the priest, it appeared to be a fairly large quantity. She watched eagerly as he then deposited the pinch of leaf into the pot and return the pouch to under his robes.

"What is that?" Dimi asked as she moved over to Etch and brushed off a burning ember that had landed on his arm. She noted as she brushed off the ember, that it had not burnt his skin. "This is amazing; fire barely touches him in this state."

Father Mellon looked up and at Etch and then nodded nonchalantly as he reached for a small twig from within the flames. He gingerly withdrew it and used the twig to stir the pan filled with water and red leaf. He then placed the pan atop two small smouldering pieces of wood. "Brenasal leaf, little old though – not the best quality." He looked over and shook his

453

head as he watched Etch shiver beside the fire. "Wish I had root. Doesn't do much good to add too much leaf, but the root has something different or more in it."

"This will take a few minutes." He said, his very voice was warming Dimi thought. She touched Etch's head, the skin at first felt hot but then after a moment under her hand it was cold. "From the inside, he has no heat." She said looking down at her friend with great concern.

The priest nodded and then leaned forward stirring the pan. "Hit him hard. Very unusual." He said looking concerned.

"What hit him?" Dimi asked looking up at the priest. Although she was so very small compared to this giant of a man, she felt more at ease every time he talked.

"Well." Father Mellon started sitting back a bit waiting for the pan before him to boil. "Only way to describe it is to give you a bit of information we don't really like to share much." The priest scratched his clean shaven face and looked at her. He then smiled, his teeth slightly yellowed from smoking peeked through his large lips. "But given that I think I know a little about you already, I think I can share some of the story."

The large man leaned back and using his foot pushed another burning branch a little closer to the pan to hurry the process. "We often go through the land to look for men who might one day measure up to joining our brotherhood."

"Men are selected based on what we perceive as latent special abilities." The priest said as he then grabbed the pan's handle and swished around the leaves and water in the pan. "They are trained as acolytes and then after several years they are brought here to bath in the cold waters of the Keeper, or the Eyes of TieRei some call it."

The priest looked up quickly at Dimi ensuring she was following his lead. "Those with the spark receive the gift of sight." Not seeing any sense of disbelief he continued. "Some more than others, and for some – the experience is too much and they die." At the end of the sentence he paused in a sense of almost reflection.

"So, if you are silly enough to jump in the water here you can see visions?" Dimi asked sarcastically.

Father Mellon laughed. His laughter rolled as he spoke resonating in the very trees around them. "No. Most would just feel very, very cold. Others that do have the gift, well frankly most of the untrained people die." He looked over at Etch and then at Dimi. "I will be honest. He hasn't seen the worst of it yet."

Dimi looked up and around. "How did you know we were here? I didn't hear anyone and I have good hearing."

Father Mellon laughed again this time not as hard as the last but still Dimi could feel the tenor resonance in her very body and through the rocks below her. "Not as good in hearing as my friend Socks."

The priest motioned with his hand to the forest. "He heard you before you made it to the lake." He chuckled and pointed at Etch. "Your foolish friend fell right at his feet. At the very tree he makes as his home."

The priest paused a moment and then rubbed his cheek in deep reflection. "Quite the coincidence that …." Then in a much quieter tone he added. "or fate perhaps." The priest then shook his head as if clearing cobwebs, "either way. Socks told me."

"Something in the tree?" asked Dimi.

"Yes, dashed out I guess when you were tending to the lad. You think I can be silent…" Father Mellon said now looking a tad suspiciously at Dimi. He then smiled, having obviously made up his mind on something. "I hadn't thought any of your kind still alive."

Dimi shifted uneasily at the question and change in direction of the conversation. She looked back at the Priest but said nothing.

Father Mellon looked over at Etch and then back at Dimi. "Stymar sent me word about a Mountain man a few weeks back. Said to look out for him.. man name Tarrow?"

Dimi nodded slightly to the priest as he stood, picked up the pan and carried it over to where Etch lay. He looked down trying to figure out how he was going to get the hot liquid into the man. Dimi jumped to her feet and went to Etch's head. "I can hold back his head and open his mouth, but take care with the hot pan." She then glanced at the pan and then quickly back to where she had brushed off the coal from Etch's exposed arm.

"Not too hot?" She asked looking for reassurance from the gentle giant as he bent down beside them both.

"Can't be too hot for him now… even it it does burn him, hotter the better. Bushburn leaf." Father Mellon said. "Wish I had some root, that stuff ground and fresh can ignite the stomach it can."

Dimi looked over and sniffed the steaming tea. "I know a lot of bush and herb. Smelled that plant before, but never used it. What does it do?"

"Well," started the priest. "Some priests back at the temple put small amounts into stew as spice for it can serve better and make it hotter to taste then thrice the quantity of cyan."

The priest then reached down and Dimi held up Etch's neck and pulled open his mouth. Father Mellon poured a small quantity in his mouth. Etch sputtered at first and swallowed little but the process was performed a second time and then a third.

"However," Father Mellon continued remembering where he had left of in the conversation. "It has some wicked after effects." He then laughed, Dimi looked up and noticed that when his belly laughed, so too did the lines around his eyes. "It makes the bowels explode and will make you feel like you are peeing fire the next day."

"But what it does do well." He added after a snort and another attempt of pouring of the tea into Etch. "Is heat the blood up real well. Even weak tea, and small sips can make you sweat."

"If he keeps down these few mouthfuls of this strong brew…." He said bringing the pan back to Etch to attempt another pouring. "He might survive the cold shakes."

Etch sputtered and spat back the last mouthful of tea. Dimi was concerned as to how little was in him as she surveyed that his top and her own cloths were now saturated with the tea. However, almost in answer to the priest Etch moaned lightly – the first real sound he had made in hours. She bent her head to his lips and listened but her hope dimmed as his teeth started to chatter and he started to shiver once again. She looked up hopefully as her hand caressed his forehead.

"Better make up your mind if you want him to live." The priest said looking at Dimi while holding up the tea. "We need to get the dregs down into him. Don't let him spit it up."

Dimi nodded and then bent down and raised Etch's head again and pried open his chattering teeth so the priest could pour the last of the liquid down his throat.

Etch started to sputter and cough but Dimi pressed his mouth closed and held his lips tight. At first a few spurts came out of Etch's nose, but as she rubbed his throat she could feel him swallow. AS the liquid went and hit his stomach his eyes flickered open a second but then snapped shut.

Father Mellon put the pan down and then sat back down and rubbed his hands dry by the fire. Dimi brushed off the little bit of tea on Etch's shirt and off her own pants. The fire was hot and thankfully would dry them out quickly.

There was no other conversation or real movement for hours or more as the day wore on. At lunch, Father Mellon pulled a few apples out of their bags and tossed Dimi one and ate one himself. He then mixed up more of the tea and they spent the next two hours trying to get Etch to drink in between spasms.

As evening approached Father Mellon sat back and dumped the remaining tea onto the fire before him. "That's all we can do." He said as a matter of fact.

"Either he makes it or not. We got what we can in him, any more would not do him good. Now we just sit and watch."

457

Dimi looked up to the darkening sky. The day had passed so quickly. She looked at Etch lying there still cold, even with several blankets piled atop of him.

"What were you doing up around here?" Dimi asked trying not to think about what she would do if Etch were to die now and here. "You said you were on the east shore?"

Father Mellon nodded. "Acolytes know enough to take the tea draft 'before' they go into the water. But even then..." The priest looked somewhat older all of a sudden to Dimi as he spoke as if the years of watching acolytes in their quest had taken the toll on him. " Either I or one of my priests come to check on them if they don't show up within a week after heading out here."

Father Mellon looked down at the ground rather sad, then looked back at Etch.

"The acolyte you were checking on." Dimi asked slowly and then she paused.

"He didn't make it did he?" She asked almost rhetorically.

Father Mellon shook his head and pursed his lips. "I was just finished burying him when Socks dropped by."

"Socks?" Dimi asked. "What manner of creature need I thank for bearing that message to you so quickly?"

Father Mellon laughed as he looked over to the forest and then his hand went up and pointed to the trees. "Look behind you."

Dimi turned slowly to look up at the large root that bent up behind them. At the top of it crouched a large black bat. Dimi turned a little quickly as she noted the size of it. It was the size of a dog. The bats eyes were shut tight and it sat still.

She then looked back quickly at the priest. "Man and beast both it seems grow large in these parts."

The priest laughed and Dimi noted a slight movement behind her and she turned and watched that the priests loud laugh had made the black bat flinch.

Dimi looked back at the priest, her eyes questioningly.

"Guess we two suite each other, but I have never seen the likes of him before. He found me a while back." Father Mellon said as he rose and went to the bag of supplied and pulled out another two apples. He offered one to Dimi but she declined so he sat back down and started eating.

"I was out checking on another acolyte and it was night and this great thing lands right near me. I tell you, I might be big, but seeing his eyes and with his wings all extended in the night… He scared the stuffing out of me."

He finished one off the apple in another bite and then ate the second one with only three bites. He then wiped his mouth on his sleeve.

"When he landed, knew right off that he was something different. AND," the priest said motioning to the large bat still sitting peacefully on the root. "Not just because of his size."

The priest paused a moment then looked at the Bat. "You recall I talked about the sight?"

Dimi nodded and waited for a more descriptive explanation.

Father Mellon paused and then spoke in a rather modest fashion almost bashful. "I don't have as much as some, better then a few. Not why I am what I am, just … for me the gift really comes in what I can see in things…"

"And," Dimi added cautiously. "in you being in the right spot at the right time."

Dimi's statement caught the priest off guard. At first he looked taken back but then he smiled and nodded his head. "You know, never thought of it that way. But now that you say it, I guess so."

"Anyway," Father Mellon continued. "He didn't 'feel' like a bat when I saw him. Right off I thought – interesting seeing a boy that looks like a bat."

"In fact the image came so clear, that I had to rub my eyes and look again." Father Mellon motioned back over to the bat. "Can't talk, but sometimes I can grab fleeting images from him. Just pieces mind you. And not clear, more like 'bat thought'…"

"So once he was a man." Dimi said sounding not too surprised.

The priest smiled back at Dimi. "Guess it would sound stranger to most but not you."

Dimi shrugged in reply.

"Best I can make out of it, wasn't long ago though and that surprised me. For…" Father Mellon stopped mid sentence looking somewhat almost ashamed to continue. He then pushed forward. "For that type of magical capability was said to no longer exist, that all the old masters and their ways are long since past. That the know how was lost."

"We have seen other transmogrophications these last weeks, Etch and I." Dimi said stroking his head. She looked up and smiled at the priest. "His head isn't quite as cold, he is warming up."

Father Mellon shook his head. "Don't get too excited. When they die the cold leaves them just like heat leaves a normal man."

"When I use my sight," He said changing to a easier topic. "I see in him the spark of humanity, transformed. It has been changed by something, different and twisted – almost tainted. Not like you at all. He still has a strong mind…"

"Why do you call him 'Socks'?" Dimi asked looking back over to the bat, but it was no longer there. "Fast and quiet like you said." She looked up to the dark sky. "Guess he needs to do a great deal of hunting to feed such a form."

"I guess." Father Melon said looking around hoping for a glimpse of the bat in flight. "When I asked him that is in my mind… I sort of think about my own name and picture myself. When I do that I received images… images of damaged and torn socks….. I think he is already loosing much of his ability to think like the boy he was. I can tell it isn't quite right by his reaction, but he responds to the call."

Dimi looked back at the stump when she heard a flutter and it was back, with a rabbit clutched in its one wing. The bats black beak went out and started ripping the flesh from the body. "Damn quiet, especially for that size."

Father Mellon nodded and looked to the darkening sky. "Socks will keep an eye out for us. I would sense if he was around and distressed."

The priest motioned over to Etch. "There is nothing you can do now; you must be tired. I know I am." He turned then and lay down next to the fire. "There is nothing you can do now, you should sleep."

Dimi nodded but smiled back and drew a little closer to Etch. "I will keep an eye anyway." She said as she brushed Etch's forehead.

Dimi was still looking down at Etch in the morning when his eyes opened. In the background Father Mellon's snoring rang out cracking the silence of the lake.

"My goodness what is that sound." Etch groaned as he tried to sit up.

Dimi laughed, small tears of joy fell down her cheek as she looked at him from above. "A friend came by in the nick of time to save your frozen ass." She said nodding her head over to the priest.

"Well." Etch started as he raised his head up off her lap and started to sit up. "He snores so damn loud I would wager nothing in this entire forest could sleep last night."

"Nothing save you that is." Dimi retorted with a laugh.

Etch pushed himself up onto his elbows and then sat up. He swayed slightly but his sitting position held fast. Dimi moved round to the side of him and they exchanged a knowing smile.

"Rough night," Etch stated.

"Rough days and nights," Dimi added.

461

Etch shrugged his shoulders and rubbed his neck. He let the blankets that had been piled on him to fall to his side and then he tried to stand. Dimi jumped to her feet to steady him and together he was successful.

"My back, neck… my whole body hurts." Etch groaned.

"You've had the shakes and shivers. Very strenuous on your body I would assume." Dimi added as she held on to his arm, hoping he wouldn't fall.

A very loud grumble issued from Etch's belly. It was loud enough that it overshadowed even the priest's tonsil serenade. Etch's face suddenly turned bright red and he swallowed hard. "o", "Oh." "OH!" he gasped as Dimi watched him go down to his knees and hold his stomach.

"By all the unholy demons…. What is happening to me?" Etch asked. "My stomach, oh my god."

Dimi knelt down beside him, and in an almost chiding voice responded to Etch. "This 'priest' gave you something. It saved you, but he did warn me it would be hard on your stomach." Smiling she added. "I am sure it will pass." Dimi looked over at the priest, but he seemed oblivious to the fact that they were awake.

Etch looked up – "The, who?" With startling speed for a man who Dimi thought almost gone, Etch pulled himself to his feet.

"Where are you going?" She yelled at him as he pulled away from her.

"To the forest. I, I,… Oh my …" Etch ran forward into the twisted roots. "Don't follow me!" He yelled without turning, Dimi stopped in her tracks, understanding finally showing on her face she smiled…. 'It too will pass.' She yelled after him. She turned and walked back to the fire and sat down next to the priest.

Father Mellon was turned on his side, still snoring very loudly. A very large, grey brown thick blanket was pulled up and around him. Dimi laughed. "My family could have all slept under such a large tarp." She then shoved his shoulder, his snoring momentarily halted and then resumed.

"Wake up! It is morning already!" Dimi yelled. She shoved him again. "What is this made of?" She asked as her hand came back from the blanket covered in soft thin hairs.

"Goat hair," Father Mellon groaned as he turned over to face his attacker. He sat up and rubbed his eyes. His face had the slightest of shadows of a beard which he rubbed with his large right hand.

"Alive I see." The priest added as he looked over to where Etch had lay. "In the woods I assume?" He chuckled rhetorically as he got to his feet.

"Didn't think he could move that fast." Dimi answered looking up. She disliked standing next to someone so tall so walked away from him and sat back down next to Etch's blankets.

"If you have any soothing salve, something you might have to help a burn, I would fetch it." The priest said as he walked towards the water. He then knelt down and pulled a straight edge razor from under his robe and unfolded it. To Dimi it looked large enough to use as a dirk. "If you don't a salve, bacon grease works, and is a good by product of a good breakfast." The giant rubbed his belly. "I am hungry."

"For the talc?" Dimi said standing and then walking over to their saddlebags. "Grease solidified."

"Yes, some acolytes say it is actually better than most salves." Father Mellon said as he started to scrape his face with the razor. After each stroke he swished the blade in the water. "I love a cold shave." He added.

Dimi proceeded to the pack and pulled out a large chunk of deer meat that had a thin strip of gristle attached to it. "No pork left, but Etch has some deer meat left, it is lean but might produce some fat." She then went round the camp and picked up the pan Father Mellon had made the tea in. She then went down to the water, washed it out and then began cutting strips of meat which she neatly arranged on the pan. A moment later it was sizzling on the breakfast fire.

Dimi smiled briefly when she heard a load groan coming from the forest. Father Mellon laughed as he turned having finished shaving he walked back to the fire returning his straight edge back under his robe.

"He'll live." He said smirking. "Although I bet given the quantity of what we gave him, right now he might not want to."

Father Mellon laughed. "Side effects will keep him in the woods a good hour or more. I would suggest that we also put out what cheese you might have to lessen the burn of his stomach."

Dimi nodded and walked back to the bags. "Not sure how much cheese is left, but we have some hard bread."

Father Mellon reached under his robe and pulled out a spike of a wheel of dark red cheese the size of his fist. "Blood cheese," he said as he tossed it to Dimi. "I am sad to part with it for I love the stuff. But if you don't have any cheese or milk yourself, he will need it."

Dimi turned and caught the cheese in a nimble move. The priest smiled as she did so with recognition of her agility. "Thanks." She said as she carried it back to the fire.

Dimi had finished cooking and cooling the lard and was almost going to go into the woods for Etch when two hours later Etch returned to the fire.

He was pale and walked with a funny limp. "Oh my. That burned." He said, his face as red and flush as a rose as he walked up to the camp. He looked around, not sure if he really wanted to sit quite yet.

Dimi stood and handed Etch the large chunk of blood red cheese. "This is from Father Mellon." She then reached down and picked up something. She turned and then handed Etch a large leaf covered with a wad of cooled deer lard. "And this." She said holding up the leaf, "is for your other end."

Etch took the cheese, but hesitated when the leaf was held out.

"Best you be doing that or you won't be travelling anytime soon." Father Mellon said glibly.

Etch took a big bite of the cheese and then with his free hand took the leaf and turned. A moment later he was out of sight back in the forest.

"He will be raw a day or two." Father Mellon said as he smiled at Dimi. Better though he walk then ride – if you know what I mean?"

A few minutes Etch returned holding neither the cheese nor leaf. His face was considerably less red and as he walked to the fire he forced a smile. He walked over to the lake and washed his hands. "Don't you go now jumping in again." The priest yelled over at him in jest.

Etch finished washing his hands and then walked back to the fire. "Ah.. Thanks I guess." He said holding his hand out to the priest. "Etch Tallow. I am indebted."

Father Mellon took the hand and shook it although he didn't stand. Sitting, he was almost chest high to Etch and his hand entirely enveloped Etch's when they shook. The priest held on hard to Etch's hand.

"Least I could do." The priest said politely. "Least I could do." The priest pulled Etch's face a little closer and then he smiled and let his hand loose. "Your fun isn't over I am sure."

Dimi handed him a plate of stew she had prepared for lunch and Etch sat down and started to eat. Dimi and Father Mellon followed suite.

Father Mellon stopped eating and returned Etch's curiosity was looking at him attentively. "Western mountains, eh? Stymar said to keep an eye out for you."

Etch became a little more relaxed after hearing the name but still ate quietly.

Dimi broke the silence. "Father Mellon is a priest from the Temple Guard. He was checking on an acolyte on the other bank when he was told we were in trouble. We made a tea of it and forced you to drink it. Brenasal, I think local term is bushburn. The tea heated up your blood… and saved your life."

Etch stopped eating and then looked at Dimi, back to the priest and then back to Dimi. "Miserable side effects though." Etch said smugly. But he looked up and noted both Dimi and the priest were smiling ear to ear.

Etch looked back and did a double take on the priest sitting beside him, "THE Father Mellon?" The priest in response shrugged.

Etch turned to Dimi. "Father Mellon my good friend is none other than the High Drakon… head of the church, and head of the Temple Guard."

Dimi looked back at the priest questioningly. Father Mellon shrugged and continued eating. He then looked up and smiled.

After the meal the three sat down quietly. Etch leaned back as far as he could to be comfortable, but often had to rise and move about. One time when he was standing walking by the priest Father Mellon grabbed his arm and pulled him close to look again into his eyes. He then smiled and sat back. "So, what did you see?"

Etch looked at the father then back at Dimi unsure how to proceed.

"Come now." Father Mellon said. "Everyone that lives through it has a good vision or two. Most are about home or friends, about a child or something. Me, my first time – I saw myself catching the biggest damn fish ever… at this very lake." Father Mellon rubbed his face, and paused a moment deep in thought. "Interesting."

"Can't catch fish here," Etch said suspiciously. "Waters too damn cold for fish."

The priest laughed, "Exactly, that is what was so weird." His laugh was contagious as it rolled in with his tenor voice. His heavyset framework jiggled slightly. "Funny though, I have never fished here, never would think of brining a rod."

Father Mellon's laughter dropped off very slowly. He then wiped a tear from his eye and looked at Etch. "So, tell me what you saw in your vision."

Etch started slow, explaining his experience first as to how it felt and how his vision came… He stopped twice but was prompted to proceed by both Dimi and the priest. Father Mellon said nothing until he was finished. Dimi looked over at him as did Etch not quite sure what to expect.

"Ok. That wasn't the typical vision most get. Also rather disturbing," father Mellon started. He looked at Etch and shook his head. "First, for that clear a vision, that many details…. You should be dead. Secondly…." He paused.

The priest moved uncomfortably in his seat not sure what he was going to say or how he would say it. 'What you have told me creates more questions than it answers – give me a second." With that ending comment Father Mellon turned and sat staring into the campfire.

Finally, after a long pause, the priest looked back over. "Not sure where to start," he began. "I know something of your quest, searching for the princess, and we have suspicions of what transpired with TerranAdd. But, before I go on, let me first ask - What are you pursuing now?"

"Why?" Dimi asked suspiciously.

Father Mellon chuckled and rubbed a small tear of mirth from his right eye. "Such suspicion I rarely face with those that know me. "You see, my little lady. Whatever it is HIS mind jumped to. You see our minds typically lead us to see that which we desire to see or find."

Dimi looked over to Etch; both turned and nodded to the priest but stayed silent.

"Come now." Father Mellon said rather frustrated. "You can trust me. I don't know of this hag, nor this white lady. But I must know."

Father Mellon leaned forward and looked straight at Etch and then glanced at Dimi reinforcing how serious he was. All expression of mirth was gone from his face.

"Sarta Pensor the Mage and Succubus." Etch stated. "We believe she is tied to the events of TerranAdd. We also suspect she is responsible for transforming a number of people – even entire villagers into inhuman beasts."

Father Mellon nodded and smiled at Etch and then Dimi. "I have heard of her before. We suspected she was tied to some goings on but have had little proof."

"Much of this now ties together well." The priest said nodding to himself as he looked down at the ground. "The lady in white dallies with the forbidden blood arts."

The large priest stood up and brushed off his robes. "The Temple Guard was put in place to ensure the Masti would never again rise to their full power. Their worship of Andarduel the God of Deception leads to nothing but blood, death destruction and chaos."

Etch looked up and Dimi nodded back at him. "Tell him Dimi. We need to piece this together."

Dimi and Etch together explained to Father Mellon about all they knew about the Mage gone succubus, about their suspicions of TerranAdd, and about the transformed beasts that had almost killed them. All the while Father Mellon sat back, prodding only lightly to clarify a detail or two.

When Etch disclosed what he had seen in his vision, the Father sat forward intently listening to every word.

At the end of the review Father Mellon sat back shaking his head. "Not good, not good." He mumbled.

"Why?" Dimi asked.

"It's everything. All the pieces are now coming together." Father Mellon said. Looking anxious and now scared he continued. "Do either of you know what a person must go through to be even accepted to study within the Blood Cult?"

Etch laughed. "Years of temple service?" He said flippantly. "Ya, we heard they have to sacrifice one of their kin simply to be granted the ability to study the art."

"That is but how they start on the path to corruption," replied the priest un-amused. "They undergo years of abject humiliation, public debasement, accompanied by physical and mental torture that extends a full decade. Young apprentices to their church are whipped and cut and bled and chained in the public to show the level of their devotion. Only the most insanely devoted and strongest survive the public ordeals to move on to be acolytes."

"Wow." Etch said. "Not a fun club I want to belong to."

"That is what it takes to 'enter' the temple." Father Mellon said emphatically. "And the right to then be baptized in Blood Lake with hope to one day ascend to study their ways and eventually become a Blood Priest."

Dimi smiled. "I guess Sarta's last hundred years or so has in their eyes granted her this privilege... So what?"

"Dimi's right. So what?" Etch said. "Sarta is by nature twisted, sick and sadistic. What could she possibly gain by being baptized in their cult – she plans to learn the ways of the Blood Priests? We have seen her capable of transforming an entire village to beasts... is this Shadow magic that the Blood Priests have so terrible?"

"No. I mean yes." Father Mellon stuttered. "Shadow magic – is based on deception, illusion. Yes, it can be quite formidable. You could make an army believe you are their general and enter their camp. An endowed priest could make an entire army believe it is walking over a bridge yet have them walk over a cliff."

"BUT THAT ISN'T the problem." Father Mellon continued slamming his fist down on his leg. "It is 'what' the cult represent – who they worship. In their final stages, those destined to priests undergo one last ritual. The final passage to Blood Priest is done in secret deep within a dark mountain. We know that a prelude of this even is that the Blood Priest must bring to the goddess a great gift. Many priests have brought to her the polished skulls of their remaining families and friends. If she isn't impressed they don't survive the ritual."

"They 'claim' that in their last ritual each priest is given the gift, they are 'blessed' by Andarduel herself. With her eye on them, they can bring to their aid the power of a god herself! But who knows, if the god is intrigued, and given Sarta's capability – perhaps she could even bring her to our realm."

"We have to stop her, we know that already." Dimi said slowly looking at Etch.

Father Mellon nodded in agreement and looked back at Etch. "Blood Priests are abominations themselves, mentally twisted by their years of torture. But once on this path of worship they regain a twisted clarity in purpose."

Father Mellon produced a small pencil from his waistband and a piece of paper from the small herb bag hanging by his side. Sketching out a map he spoke at he wrote down reference points. "She will be strong; Masti worshipers will likely be at her side along with whatever abomination she might have created. You will need men at arms to even get close to her now."

"We have yet to confirm, but rumours have it she is in the north, held up in a castle she has taken by force. Those towers have a room atop the highest part of the keep that matches the one you described in your vision Etch so I think that confirms what we have heard."

"If Sarta is totally under her control, Andarduel will likely bring forth her own minions into this world. If that happens, all is lost for it will be nigh impossible to beat them for their lives will be tied to their plane and not ours."

"This is rather disturbing." Etch added. "Its hard to go from a world where I didn't even believe magic really existed to one where we discuss gods and demons as matter of fact. The seven hells were only fables, how come so few believe them real?"

Father Mellon Chuckled. "We in the temple work to keep these things hidden. The peasant in the field should not be weighed down with these fears for there is little they can do. And the more we can make these items obscure, hidden and forbidden the fewer the followers of that trail will be. We work with the kings and dukes of the land diligently to squash any signs of blood magic following and to kill rumors, making them in stead myths and fantasies."

Dimi sat watching the exchange but getting rather antsy, wanting to move or do something. "So we track her down and kill her."

"She will be well defended." The priest said as he looked at Dimi and then Etch.

"Start by heading north," The priest said. "up the TieRei and north of AnnonTer there you should find others that will help you. The Clansmen or those within AnnonTer should be swayed to assist if you pass on my note to them."

"The castle Sarta now likely resides in was originally owned by the MiKay. Dwarfish people so it is well built, but also that means there are several secret ways in to it." The priest said. "The Clan took it over when the MiKay so they might know its secrets. The river Tie Rei flows from the Truk Mountains. It passes down and through the twin towers they built and then AnnonTer. This lake is that river's mouth – or ending. We in the Temple calls it the 'Eyes of TieRei, for by baptizing in these waters one can receive second sight."

"So if we follow this river north, we will eventually get to it?"

"Yes." Father Mellon replied.

"But you and those from the temple aren't coming with us?" Etch added rhetorically.

"No. Our members are fewer now and spread out across these lands. I must go east to the libraries of my castle and using what you have told me seek out any information that might help us against Andarduel should you fail to kill Sarta. I will send word by pigeon to Duke Rudolph Ygor AnnonTer if I find out anything that might help you bring her down.

Etch nodded and looked up. Dimi was already standing and packing Peppy and Mule up. "I guess we won't be doddling." Etch said also standing. "My sincere thanks for your aid, I am sure I would not have survived the night without your help." Etch said offering his still cold and clammy hand to Father Mellon.

The priest laughed a big rolling laugh as he got to his feet via Etch's hand. He staggered a bit and then brushed himself off.

Father Mellon shook his head and scratched his balding head. "I regret not being able to help you more then I can right now. But I sense that we cannot delay your attempts for Sarta's powers continue to grow. This might sound harsh, but even distracting her now will slow down her ascension and thus Andarduel's physical appearance in these lands."

Father Mellon turned square to face Etch. "Remember this above all else Etch. Absolute power corrupts absolutely. The more power a creature has, the more corrupted everything they touch is. The hells are chaotic by design with continual shifting of massive powers. Remember that always also that the more power anyone gets, the less they associate with the masses. The more Sarta or any demon has the more omnipotent and apart from the rest of everything they see themselves. It is their arrogance above all else that then makes them vulnerable."

Father Mellon then turned raised his hand and started walking. With his massive strides within only a few minutes he was rounding a set of boulders and re-entering the forest. A second later, and he was gone from view.

Etch turned to look at Dimi. "Are we having fun yet?"

The Bloody King of Ten Tor

The Duchess of Ten Tor Rabina Ferroten Bestinor had seen her husband upset before, but never this upset. She sat, literally shaking in her seat, next to her husband in the main throne room. Her hands were red from the force she was rubbing them with and her normally dark southern face was ashen white. She had been brought up in a family that had domain over much of the southern Terran lands and as such, was accustomed to hearing court. She was accustomed to her father, and then later husband passing judgement on legal matters relating to the district…. But today, this preceding was beyond anything she had ever experienced in all her life.

Several merchants within the city had called on her that previous week - begging that she once again attend court beside her husband who now was ruling as King and not as Duke. They had pleaded with her, all with hopes that her presence would bring common sense back to her husband's rulings. In the last few weeks not only had the Duke now King reinstated martial law but in addition he was dishing out extreme punishments for lesser crimes. The queen had been specifically requested to attend the session today to speak on behalf of an elderly couple that was well respected within the city – and distantly related to a lesser noble's family.

It had taken her days to work up the courage to walk into the throne room this Friday. She had almost lost her nerve when she had met her husband to break fast this morning. He had reminded her that she was to correct anyone that called her Duchess – she was now Queen of Terran lands as he was King. Her response had not been sufficient or fast enough for when she didn't promptly reply his mood soured further. They ate the balance of the meal in silence. If her handmaid hadn't delivered her a small port to wash down breakfast with – she wouldn't have been sitting on the dais now beside her – husband and King.

The first case brought before the Duke and Duchess, now King and Queen was a simple one. Two landowners were arguing about each others right to access a river that ran between their properties. Each wanted to erect a mill that would straddle the lake's supply, however, neither the river nor surrounding farms could support two mills. The resulting dispute had escalated beyond hard feelings and into almost a regional feud.

King Methor ruled quickly. "As the two land owners cannot themselves figure out how to share, we will help them. The mill will be built, and each land owner will pay half the sum that it costs to construct. However, when completed it shall be owned by the crown."

The gallery of merchants and lesser nobles in attendance within the great throne room jeered and jibed the landowners who stood mute before the King. In less than a minute, the two lesser lords were escorted from the room.

The Queen tried to gauge the day by the first case. 'The ruling had only been a tad extreme.' She thought, 'given that the feud between the two lords had already cost the life of a serf who had been killed in a city brawl.'

Rabina's attention was quickly grabbed by activity within the throne room as the great doors opened and two guards led through the next case. She quickly noted that behind the guards were three men she did not recognize – this was not the case for which she had been asked to intercede on. She sat back in the hard cold chair as an older man, dressed in an ancient guard's uniform strode forward.

The Queen smiled recognizing the man as he drew closer to the front of the room and their dais – he was the cities sheriff. A man that had served within the White Guard of the city and as a result of his loyalty and dedication had been named to oversee general policing of the city. The old man had become an iatrical part of the city and now was more that what he had been named. He was their liaison between merchants, serfs and the soldiers of the citadel. She liked the man for he had been more than kind and always ensured she had additional escorts when she was within the merchant district of the city.

The old man walked forward confidently and proud of his status as sheriff. A small bronze badge of office hung pinned on his shoulder signifying his duties. His face was wrinkled and worn but his eyes and very manor of walk showed confidence and of knowledge gained from a long lifetime. As his eyes met the Queen' she smiled and he returned her smile although it appeared somewhat 'forced'.

The Queen visibly relaxed as his name came to mind. "Sendel Sourto" she said softly to herself. The sheriff motioned and two guards led forth three merchantmen to stand before his king. 'This was not yet the case'. She thought to herself as she took in a deep breath.

The clerk read the charges against the men before her husband the King. Three merchants from south of Plan Ter were being charged with theft having sold eighteen barrels of Plan Terran sweet greens to a local merchant who later discovered that the barrels had been excessively padded with hay.

The Queen stifled a chuckle and removed the smirk from her face. 'What crimes to have before a King?'

The sheriff strode forward and bowed to the King. The clerk indicated he was to expand on the charges and present the evidence.

"If it please my lord, putting hay in the bottom of apple barrels is common practice. Farmers do it to absorb moisture and to reduce spoilage." Recited the sheriff calmly.

"However," Sendel continued his voice had risen slightly. "The individuals before us today have been accused of laying excessive quantities of hay and thus short changing the local merchant. The accuser is a merchant of our fair city one Idus Marron." A slight man pushed his way through a few of the individuals at the front and bowed slightly to the King and then Queen.

The King looked over to the plaintiff. "How light do you estimate the load to be Merchant Marron?"

The merchant pushed out his chest. "A good three or four barrels your grace."

"Yes. If it pleases your 'grace'." The sheriff said correcting himself.

The sheriff, looked over to the three accused now apparently somewhat nervous having addressed the king incorrectly. "Not wishing to burden you with such trivial, your grace, I suggested to the three men from Plan Ter that they make good the load so they would not need to return."

The sheriff's confidence grew as the King nodded in approval to his statement and smiled at the older man indicating that he approved in the use of title.

"However, Jonus here," the sheriff motioned to one of the accused. "Refused my suggesting saying the load wasn't light and that he had already spent the money received on salted pork which they were taking north. He also refused to offer pork to offset the light load of apples."

The King's eyebrows were raised and his tone came with a definite tone of sarcasm. "Is that right Farmer Jonus? Is your time that much more valuable then our own?"

The merchant to the right of Jonus, panicked at the King's comments started to blubber. "If it please your grace." The man started.

The sheriff moved forward to stop the man from speaking but the King raised his hand and waved off the sheriff. "Let the man speak."

The man nodded. "Thank you sir, ah great sir."

"Bramby and meeself." The man motioned to the other freeman standing to the left of Jonus. "We were just hired by Jonus. We knew nothing of the barrels save that he needed help carting them to Ten Tor. I told –"

The King raised his hand and the man stopped mid sentence. "I would expect any man to make it his business." The King added slowly looking at the two that stood either side of Jonus. "To know the business and company of men they were in hire with."

The sheriff fidgeted with his right hand as he desperately sought words to say. Methor the King was making it a point of imposing much more extreme punishments these days. Twice in the past two weeks simple street thieves had their left hands removed for their acts… .

"If it please your grace." The sheriff started trying to gain the King's eye and lesson the situation. "We have their carts and salted pork. No overly harm done. We can give the Merchant Marron three fold worth of pork and send Jonus back home."

The King sat back in his stone chair, his fingers tapping on the hard stone arm. The thirty or more people standing in the hall before him were quiet as mice, not one whispered to the other. A sense of dread rose up and through the room in anticipation as the King leaned back and contemplated.

"Theft is theft." Started the King and simply by the tone of his starting words the Queen realised 'why' she was being asked to attend these sessions. 'This should have been a fast ruling.' She thought to herself. 'What the sheriff has just proposed seems entirely fitting.' The Queen tensed up wondering what was now in store for these men.

"All the salted pork is forfeit as is the cart and horses they rode in on." The King stated unemotionally." The sheriff visible cringed and there was an audible intake of air from the individuals behind him. Jonus stood with open mouth listening incredulously and in no doubt a sense of denial.

Jonus the Plan Terrian apple merchant's mouth opened and closed like a fish out of water. "But, me lord." He started. There was a small snicker from the back of the room as someone noted the merchant's mistake at saying anything. "Not all those horses are mine. Two sets were lent to me by the farmers." Jonus added.

"Let us help this good man ensure that when he tells his tale back home that it is supported with evidence – that they know that it was for theft that he lost the carts and horse."

The King motioned to the guards standing beside the sherrif. "Take his left hand and wrap it to return home in place of the pork."

The Queen gasped in surprise. The King turned his head to look at her in surprise of her outburst as in the throne room someone stifled a laugh.

"My apologies my good husband," the Duchess added quickly in her calmest voice. She raised her hand to her mouth and feigned a dry cough. "I appear to have a dry throat."

The King, without taking his eyes motioned to his page. "Aaron, would you be so kind as to bring my good wife the Queen something to drink."

Aaron was there not a moment later with a small pewter cup. The dark metal hid from public view a stout mulled port. It was cold but welcome to her throat as she drained it.

"My thanks my liege," she added for effect as she placed the cup on the large flat stone armrest. She held it tight, hoping that the shaking of her hand would be steadied by its grasp.

The King slowly took his gaze off her as he smiled, "my pleasure dear wife." He then looked out to the sheriff. "Sherriff, what is our next case?"

The sheriff nodded anxiously and waved the two guards to take the stunned Jonus and his friends out of the room. As the guards and defendants exited the back of the room, two more guards entered escorting an elderly couple. The Queen tried to quietly clear her throat in anticipation. 'This one,' she thought to herself and tried to steady her nerves.

As the two new defendants were brought through the crowd of spectators the Queen arched her back and sat up higher. When she caught the first glimpse of their faces she hesitated. Then, slowly she pressed the palms of her hands down and in to her long flowing turquoise dress. Her hands felt the embroidered designs of soft ocean flora and it momentarily put her at ease as she remembered simpler times.

Before the guards and defendants had reached the front of the room Methor turned to the clerk. "What are the charges in the next case." He said impatiently.

"Murder my grace." The clerk added. The Queen sat motionless, not sure if her husband was watching her from the corner of his vision. There were two gasps of recognition from within the crowd as the two defendants made their way forward.

The clerk standing before the dais read the charges. "The two defendants before your grace this day are Siar Bates and his wife Warini. They find themselves charged with the murder of Captain Moirie and his first man one Barno Forr, both of the Ferrow trade ship the Far Sailer."

The clerk then turned to the sheriff who had stayed where he had been. 'After hearing the charges out loud the sheriff looks years older.' Thought the Queen.

The sheriff turned and motioned to the two guards that brought them forward.

"If it pleases my liege," the sheriff started. "These two well respected citizens of Ten Tor stand before this court of justice pleading their innocence. I have known these two myself, for over fifteen. "

"Get on with it," interjected Methor as he sat forward in his stone chair. "Don't try my patience with small talk. Tell me the facts of the case."

"Yes my liege, my apologies." The sheriff said quickly as he bowed.

"My two guards stopped these two at two in the morning the night before last." The sheriff motioned the two guards to come around the defendants to be seen... not at all worried the two elderly defendants would try to escape.

"Mr and Mrs Bates were stopped pushing a wheelbarrow with the bodies of the two men in it. They were heading out the small eastern Tiemo gate. The guards brought it to my attention and although their story is very plausible, I was honour bound to bring it before he court."

Methor looked startled at the sheriff who now looked up with pride straight back to the King. "And rightly you should my good sheriff."

The Queen added feigning ignorance of the facts although she had already been well informed as to their statement. "What explanation did they give you to present before your King?"

The King's neck almost snapped as his head turned to look at his wife a second time. The Queen did not look over at her husband but could feel his gaze upon her. She smiled at the sheriff who was nodding in reply.

"The two sailors, your grace, are well known for being rather obnoxious, loud drinkers and trouble makers." The sheriff added quickly. "AND Siar Bates and his wife are well known to all within the city as they run the Bitter Water Inn and pub down by the Timri Long Docks. It is an inn of good reputation."

The King was now looking at the sheriff, but was sitting back a bit. The sheriff's whose confidence was now restored exploited the pause allotted to him. "When they were brought to me, with the wheelbarrow in the morning I was very surprised as this appeared quite out of character. I am partial to believing their story myself."

"Go on." The Queen replied quickly, not letting time be present for her husband to interject. Inside she felt bile in her stomach rise up to burn her throat.

"Yes your grace." The sheriff said as he bowed briefly. "They says to me that the two sailors had been quite drunk and that the two were in a bit of a fighting mood that night and ended up knifing each other to death."

"Do they have others to back their explanation?" The King asked dryly before the Queen could once again lead the sheriff in the review.

"Ah, well. We have several that can state that they knew the two sailors as troublemakers and those they often fought between themselves and others….. But all the patrons were either passed out or left and haven't come forward to stand as witness."

"So no witnesses to attest to a fact that the two did themselves in?" The King asked.

"No my grace," the sheriff answered.

"Go on. So how do you believe they die?" The Queen prompted.

"Killed each other I believe they did." The sheriff said simply.

Siar Bates' wife blurted out addressing the queen directly. "Fighting drunk they both were. They were both in a foul mood my queen. The first mate got the first stick in, proper up and into the captn'. The captain turned the first mate round and slit his throat nice and clean, but he was dead hitting the table not a moment after his first mate hit the floor."

The Innkeeper's husband looked over surprised at the confidence of his wife. He looked up at the King, but felt cowed and quickly looked down at his shoes.

Rabina Ferroten Bestinor, now Queen, looked at the Inn Keeper with pity in her eyes. 'He already thinks himself doomed.' She thought to herself. 'The people of this city fear us, and have little hope of justice when brought here.' She then looked at the Innkeeper's wife –'Has her addressing me directly doomed them both?' She thought to reply but her husband stepped in taking back control of the proceedings.

"That is a convenient story." The King added with a laugh. "Both up and died at the same time, with no witness dear lady?"

"There were two others still there your grace, but it was late and they were passed out from too much drink." The old lady continued now addressing the King..

Although her face was wrinkled her manner was proud and her face showed that she was a hard working lady. She elbowed her husband who obviously almost more afraid of his wife then the King added to reinforce her story. "Say something you old mule. The king is asking us a question." The man looked up, looked as if he was going to say something but then looked back down at his shoes. His wife groaned. "Damn useless husband." She said quietly to him gritting her teeth.

Her curse brought the man's head up – the queen smiled. 'He fears her more than the king.' She thought to herself.

The old man looked at his wife and then at the King. "As my wife says, your grace, they were arguing and both very drunk your grace. Both stood, and I thought they would be going to bed… then there is a scuffle. I look over and the captain is spitting blood from his mouth. The next moment he has his knife out and has his first mate by the neck and slits his throat – faster than I could blink it was."

The sheriff added quickly on the heals of the man's statement. "The captain had been stabbed in the chest – it hit his lungs."

"Spitting blood?" Methor asked as he leaned forward in his chair. "Spitting blood?"

The sheriff's face turned pale and there were a few whispers behind him. The Queen looked at the sheriff puzzled hoping he could somehow fill her in as to the relevance of the statement.

The sheriff regained his composure and spoke at last. "I do believe the blood was for no other reason than the fact that the captain's lung was pierced by his first mate's knife."

"A bloody mouth says you?" Methor asked cautiously there was a stirring in the crowd behind the dependents. A few of the nobles and guards looked nervously to each other.

"The blade must have pierced his lung." The sheriff added. "Nothing more than that; the captain likely fell to the floor not a moment after his first mate did."

"Are you a surgeon now too?" Methor added with a smile. "You see spitting blood and lightning fast movements – are there no other explanations? I believe you served in our campaign, did you not?"

The sheriff nodded in agreement and remarked confidently. "Yes my liege, more than twenty years I served in the White Guard. And I was in the vanguard you led north. I served under Sir Bruto Gadral who was a lieutenant then. I did march with him to put down the Masti in the north. But that is why I make little of the fact of the blood in the captain's mouth."

The sheriff stood tall as he addressed the king and court. "For I have seen a Masti priest, have seen them with my own eyes chew up their cheeks to issue blood so they could curse and do their fowl magic. I have also been side by side with your own General Bruto as we did catch those suspected of being priests when we entered their capital city."

Then his voice wavered slightly as he continued. "I held down many a man and nailed their tongs to the doors or their houses as punishment and warning against the crime of performing blood magic."

The crown behind the sheriff was deadly silent. Not one individual moved so much as a finger the entire crowd was silent as if they all collectively held their breath. Fear permeated the room.

Recognition finally crept across the Queen's face. 'This trial is now headed towards a discussion of heresy. My husband is now insinuating that perhaps the captain was a blood priest, and that perhaps the two innkeepers were somehow involved with his doings?' "My god." The queen whispered.

The King heard his wife's exclamation and a small smile drew across his lips as he perceived she too was aghast that blood magic might again have been practiced and that such practices might be going on in their very city.

The pregnant paused ended as the sheriff raised his voice in a comment of finality – hoping to coax the King away from this line of discussion. "I have seen knife woods, the man was specifically stabbed in the chest – the man was not a cursed worshiper of Andarduel."

The king looked up from the sheriff's eyes and scanned the crowd. People flinched when his eyes met his and they looked away. He shuddered inwardly. "Continue then." He commanded the sheriff.

The tension in the room visibly broke, as there was a collective inhalation. A few individuals whispered to each other filling in details or suspicions of their own.

"The couple before you, two individuals I do personally trust were simply disposing of the bodies." The sheriff concluded.

"So why dispose of the bodies in such a fashion?" The King asked the two before him. "Why at 2am in the morning cart out the bodies. In the darkest hours why are you slinking out of the city with two dead men in a wheelbarrow? Why not dump them outside the back door and call a grave digger in the morning?"

The sheriff looked over to the two. The old proud woman looked straight up at the King but the older man looked down at his shoes.

"As they should have," The sheriff said, hoping now that the case was moving in a better direction then it had. "My thought is they first thought to protect their reputation as a good and safe place to stay. A murder or two does not well to attract others."

"Plus," the sheriff continued as he turned and looked at the elderly couple. "I suspect that they also sought to save the expense of pine box and grave. If they had dumped the bodies in the eastern forest not a kilometre away they would save the cost of the digger."

The older man standing behind him lowered his head and didn't look the sheriff in the eye. The woman, however, looked the sheriff proudly straight back and didn't flinch.

"They should have called me?" The sheriff said turning back to the king. "That is their only wrong doing my lord."

"We impose laws in this land to protect all – both our own citicens and merchants from abroad. PLUS…" The king continued.

"Had we not caught them in the act, you would not have been able to verify the manner of their death and as such not be able to, as you just did, assure me that there was no relationship with a religion and practices we within this country do not abide with. All man and woman within these lands know the Masti priestly practices and that any time there is ANY suspicions or signs…. They are to report it."

"Yes your grace." The sheriff said meekly agreeing with the King.

"Fortunately," the king continued as he relaxed his tone, "you were able to attest that there was no such relationship." He then looked at the couple. "But only because you caught them in a crime as well. For disposing of bodies in such a manner without notifying the authorities is a crime."

"My king," The Queen interjected kindly trying to steer her husband down a more compassionate path. "These are good people my lord as others will attest to, not common criminals disposing of bodies. They just intended to clean up the mess before others rose to break fast."

The Queen then laughed and smiled. "They are only really guilty of good housekeeping."

The Queen' smile and comments brought forth a few strangled laughs from the others behind the defendants and there was a lessoning of stress within the room but all eyes then turned back to the King.

The king turned to the sheriff. "What sum of money the two now dead did have on their person we will never know for sure. Nor will we know if their deaths were as described. Why would two 'upstanding citizens' risk such scrutiny for a few paltry coin?"

The king, obviously, not wishing to be upstaged by his wife continued exploring another r path. "Perhaps they did in deed kill the two and make it a common practice to waylay passing tradesman that have been seen with large purses. This was a captain after all. Who knows how many other of our visiting captains and tradesmen go missing each week?"

The Queen didn't know how to respond, so surprised by her husband's unbelievable statements. She tried to retain a smile to lesson his stress. "Surely –"she started but before she could continue her husband was standing looking down at the members of the court.

Methor's mind raced around his anxiety clearly visible as his lucidity turned to rambling. He jumped to a second line of judgement and concern. "AND we depend on the Ferrow trade. What are we to do – send the Ferrow boat home without explanation as to what happened to their captain or first mate?"

Methor's voice rose and filled the room as his rambling reached a crescendo. "Or should we tie a cord around their necks and hang them from the mast and send them back home as explanation to the good people of Ferrow?"

The now proud innkeeper's wife turned pale as her husband stood beside her looking down at the ground visibly shaking. There was an audible gasps within the crowd.

"My King. Please. Have reason." The Queen implored compassionately. It was very out of fashion for her to speak so in public. The King turned to her startled by her request.

Methor looked at his wife. She obviously was sincerely distressed. Reality started sinking back into his mind. The tension in his neck and back hurt him and he felt all of a sudden so very, very tired. He sat for a long moment, with the weight of the world on his shoulders… the court stood silent waiting for his decision.

Rabina said softly. "They did error only in judgement my good husband - not to call the authorities, and only due to the harsh times we do now face. I do not see evil in their eyes."

She pleaded now aware that every word was somehow also hurting her dear husband. By speaking out she was challenging his authority, which she hated to do. "I ask that this crime alone they stand for and that the penalty match their error in judgement."

"As you wish," He conceded to his wife finally and then returned to sit upon his hard, cold stone chair.

The king was confused as to how to proceed. He loved his dear wife, and realised she was trying to bring him back down into a non-emotional, rational state. He knew that simply discussing the Masti and blood rituals had brought him to this frenzied state and to a thought of extreme punishment.

The King sighed and then softness returned to his face as he nodded to his wife, reached out and touched her hand in reply. He then turned to the court, "very well."

The sheriff motioned the two defendants to kneel to receive their sentence hoping that their act of contrition might also help lessen the sentence. The old woman went to both knees willingly and quickly.

"All coin that was found upon the Captain and his first mate is to be returned." The King said while pointing at the Inn Keeper and his wife…"

He added emphatically. "Every Bronzen Ferron Saltac you found will be returned by you to be sent to their widows." The king watched as both of their heads bobbed up and down rapidly agreeing to his words.

The King looked over at his wife momentarily and then continued, "Plus fifty golden Teeth in penalty." The King looked over to his wife, whose eyebrows then rose and her head tilted inferring the added penalty as being rather stiff.

"Make it twenty Teeth in penalty." He corrected as he looked back to the sheriff who nodded in reply. He then looked over at the innkeeper's wife who looked up, now visibly shaken.

"For stupidity," the Queen added crossly to the man and woman before them hoping to show to all within the court that she truly stood behind her husband. "You would be best to remember the kindness the King has granted unto you this day."

"Yes your grace, thank you your grace." Siar Bates said quickly and loudly smiling up at the queen and then bowing low to the King. The old man stood up and turned and gave his wife, who knelt still staring at her judge a small push with his foot. The old lady smiled at the queen and then turned to the king. "Thank you your grace." She then rose slowly from her knees and stood next to her husband.

King Methor Bestinor stood up from his throne starteling everyone as they expected the next case to be called. The clerk looked puzzled at his grace and came round the dais.

"Enough for one day," the king said as he rose and turned to round the throne chairs.

Rabina's heart felt heavy as she watched her husband stand. She rose from the hard stone chair and pulled up the hem of her long skirt from the floor and hurried off after her husband hoping to speak with him and help him rationalise why she spoke as she had during the session.

'He is slipping.' She thought to herself. 'Will his past never let him rest? Will he ever forget and forgive himself?' A small tear came to the corner of her eye as she exited the room heading for where she knew she would find him.

Rabina found her husband as she had suspected in his secluded study atop the north-western towers. Cold air greeted her as she entered the study from below. Methor stood before the large western window, it was open and gusts of wind blew back his hair and robes.

Methor looked up as his wife rose out from the trap door that marked the entrance to this tower study. "It is cold up here, you should have brought something warmer." As she approached him the tension in his neck and back lessoned. He turned greeter her approach as she came to the window he encircled his arms around her shoulders to warm her.

"I am fine my husband." She replied as she nestled into his arms.

She looked up at him, but he was now looking again out the window to the west. "What do you look for?" But he didn't respond.

"You do not seem at peace with yourself." She said softly.

Methor laughed but his tone was sad. "I doubt if I ever will find peace." He said as he held his wife in his arms.

"Any news from San Ter and the governor?" She asked carefully looking over at a small rookerie that stood on long legs near the window.

"None as of yet." He replied looking over at his wife wondering how much of his plots and the schemes he had put in place she was aware of. He had in the past confided greatly in her, but in some things – he felt he needed to keep her apart of.

"The one true hope that I have love," he started in earnest looking down at her. "Is that my past and current failings and sins?" He turned and took her hands in his. "That the blood that has and is on my hands… never stains yours."

Rabina looked up at her husband. She raised her neck and head and kissed him on the lips. "We are bound together for better or worse my husband. Is it not time for you to let me in on your past. Even the good sheriff has said more about your past then you and I have ever discussed."

"You have heard the stories." He said simply without emotion. "You know likely as much as anyone of the march north."

He said looking over at his wife. "Let the past lie."

The queen shook her head refusing to let it pass this last time. "Too many times have you said this. It is consuming you – surely you see that.

She replied tearfully full of emotion. "Perhaps if you talk of it your soul will find some rest?"

The king sighed and nodded in concession. "It was hard times." He started. "Desperate times mandated desperate deeds."

"The world was in chaos. I remember." She added coaxing him to continue. "Masti priests ruled their country. They were zealots, and there was no separation of state and religion. All people north of our border were forced to worship the shadow goddess. The priests were merciless to those that wouldn't. They ruled with absolute authority."

The king nodded his head and pulled back slightly from her and looked back out the window westerly to San Ter. "I was not supposed to go, but stand as rear guard to support my elder brother. But I was impatient then and had never fought in a war."

"I led them men of the south through the eastern Trukian mountains. What we found within the first villages…" He halted as flashes of memories were brought from the past.

Rabina hugged him, giving him the strength to continue.

"To even become a priest, I think you must be mad." Methor continued. "But if not from the start, they surely make you mad."

"I knew then and there – at Mrio, that first village we came upon after exiting the mountains… That to succeed the message we would need to deliver would need to be as harsh or harsher." Methor shook his head. "I guess I was a fool."

"No, NO." The Queen said looking up at her husband. "You did what you thought was right at the time. The world knows the outcome… in the end tens of thousands were saved for the war was ended."

The king shook his head and looked out the open window again. "We brought down such horrors upon all of them that their soldiers, and captains risked the wrath of their priestly generals and deserted. Returning home to find and burry the remains of their loved ones."

"But their flight from the lines, enabled our victory." Rabina insisted. "Even your father knew that as did your brother."

"But such evil cannot go unpunished." Methor said as his hand went to his face to brush away moisture upon his cheek. "Tar was able to advance and cut down the remaining Masti forces… but it was my dead that sealed my parent's fate…. When I returned my father said as much to me. What I had done was not in the ways of his Kingdome."

"Even he did not know that a rogue zealot would attempt to revenge his family's death by seeking to kill your parents." Rabina pleaded.

"It's sort of like Andarduel won." The king said half-heartedly. "Andarduel is after all Goddess of chaos and deception. What better deceptive act then assassination, what better act to induce chaos then to kill a king?"

The two stood motionless beside the open window. The cold air whipped through it, the cold and salty southern air hit them but drew them closer together.

"I have and always will love you my wife." Methor finally said looking down at his wife.

Rabina looked up lovingly at her husband the king. "You should love yourself as much. Take heart in love my husband for with it all things heal."

Methor filled his lungs with the air in an attempt to clear his thoughts. His hands clutched his wife to he chest. He then eased his hold on her and reached forward and closed the windows. "Enough cold," he said. "Although I do love the smell of the sea."

"It is the smell of home and hearth." Rabina agreed. "But we need light a fire now." She said as she walked towards the cold small hearth opposite them.

Methor pulled a long cord near the window and a bell rang out from below. "I will have someone start one. You should go below and rest – I have need to talk with our General as to the state of the war in the north."

Rabina nodded and turned and headed to the trap door. As she was about to descend Methor's page Aaron Murdoc's head appeared. She paused as he bowed and passed her and then descended down the stairs.

Aaron was a tall lad for his age with long blond hair. At the age of sixteen the look of youth was all but gone from his face. He sported a scraggly peach beard of a youth,.

As he entered Methor turned to the lad nodding. "Where is my other page? Twice now I have seen you. Are you not a squire now Aaron?

Aaron smiled in recognition and his chest extended showing that he was indeed wearing a large black surcoat, which sported the colours of Sir Casten Ferroten. His knight's coat of arms was a variation off of the Kings. It had the King's two crossed swords on a shield with the TerranAdd shield much smaller above the two shields. But also sported a bow behind the two daggers and the words 'Loyal to the End' embroidered below.

"My brother lies ill today my lord and our mother begs he be forgiven for not being present." Aaron said as he smiled back at the King. He stood proud dressed in his squire's uniform.

Methor smiled at the thought of Casten Ferroten, one of his most trusted knights. Sir Casten had proven his worth and earned his knighthood spurs and first stretch of lands when fighting under a knight in the Duke's own company.

The King continued to look at the lad. How fast he had grown. A 'real' sword hung by his side. Not a wooden practice one, but one of metal.

"Wear those colors well Squire Aaron." The king started. "Sir Casten was but a squire himself when we marched north. It was his act of sword that saved my lieutenant Sir Bruto Gadral and it was for that act of skill and bravery that he received his knighthood."

Aaron nodded and smiled proud of his surcoat, "as I hope to do some day. Follow you north that is and do battle against some great foe to prove my worth."

Darkness momentarily grasped the king's face. Methor looked at the lads face gauging his maturity. Aaron's facial hair was very thin and curly and grew mostly on his chin. "Shave yourself lad. You look younger when you have the fuzz of a peach growing in patches on your face." His tone was colder than it had been.

Aaron startled by the King's sudden coldness, retorted with a rather sheepish reply. "Yes my lord."

Then as Methor smile reappeared Aaron's confidence returned and he returned the smile and added boldly, "Should I retreat and shave this moment or is there another task you would have me do this day?"

Aaron sarcasm lit up the room and Methor smiled from ear to ear. "Don't be so eager to go to war, it is a ghastly job my lad." He said in earnest as he walked towards his desk. "Fetch me some wood and also my general."

Aaron smiled and snapped his heals together as he took the command. He nodded and then as Methor sat at the desk he turned and walked to the trap door.

Methor paused then looked up as Aaron approached the stairs. "So, does Sir Casten speak of battle? Would he march on SanTer this day?"

Aaron stopped mid stride, he had been just about to descend the stairs down. He looked puzzled, not sure if he should voice that which his knight had told him in confidence.

'Is this a test of loyalty to my knight or my king?' He thought to himself as he looked at his king.

"Yes my liege." Aaron finally said. "He does. He says to thomp the governor a good one so that he finally knows a king when he sees one."

Methor laughed and the youth's expression changed from serious to a lighter less serious one.

Aaron, head held high smiled with confidence. "All those wearing the black of Sir Casten's company believe that Governor Tunis is a coward and a traitor. After hearing of your brother's death he

493

should have immediately bent his knee to you – as you are the true heir to the throne. Should Sir Casten have his way, Carton's head would be spiked upon SanTer's walls within the week.

Methor smiled a dry smile. "Indeed, but SanTer is no small thing to walk into and the Governor is no stupid man. " Methor paused, he liked the lad's confidence and also liked that should he make the move that the city believed he was in the right.

"Well, Sir Casten might still get his wish," Methor continued slowly looking back down to his parchments. "But perhaps not today," he ended in a soft voice.

He then motioned that the lad should leave. "Please Aaron, go fetch the General for me."

Aaron nodded and spun on his heels. He had neglected to place his hand on his sword, so as he spun so too did the sword, sheath and chains that held it to his belt. The sword swished round and hit the floor as he started to descend the stairs. "I will find him and return back with him my Lord." He said as he started down the stairs.

Methor looked up and watched the lad leave and noted the lad hadn't shut the trap door when he left. He almost stood himself to do it but decided against it. Instead he turned as he heard the beat of feathers as a bird landed outside the closed window he had momentarily just come from.

King Methor Bestinor stood and marched over to the window and opened it. A large pigion fluttered and then flew past him and to the small birdcage to the right of the window. There it entered the cages open doors and immediately started pecking at some seed strewn within it.

He closed the window and turned to the gage. Reaching in he carefully grabbed the bird and removed the tiny cylinder tied to its leg.

With shaking hands, Methor returned to his desk holding the little cylindrical bottle. He sat down in the big wooden armchair and set the cylinder on the desk that was covered in roles of parchment.

He paused a moment and then opened a small drawer on the right of the desk and pulled out two small silver knives no larger than sewing needles.

He reached for the small bottle and with one knife pried of its top and extracted the thin rolled parchment. Using both small needles he gently spread the parchment. He had to move quite closely to read the very fine print and by the time he finished reading the few sentences his eyes felt strained and sore and were hard to focus. He let go of the thin needles and let the parchment curl back up as he rubbed his eyes.

Methor then looked back at the rolled parchment, although the room was cold he felt hot as his face flushed.

He heard running feet pound up the metal stairs that led to his study. He didn't smile but rather expressionless as his General Crested the stairs to his study. The old soldier looked only momentarily at his King bowed quickly and then turned and closed the trap doors.

As he turned latched the doors he turned and started walking to the desk. His eyes went to those of the king and then down to the desk before him noting the cylinder.

"I have news of my own." The general said. "But first by your expression I likely should hear your own."

General Bruto Gadral's old worn face had a look on it that King Methor had not seen in years - concern. Not since they had been knee deep in carnage surrounded on all sides had he seen Sir Bruto even show the slightest concern let alone fear. But that indeed was what he saw on his general's face now – concern.

As the general sat in a chair in front of the desk the King looked back down at the message before him. He paused only momentarily before reciting what he had just learned to his most trusted friend. "The Governor of San Ter is dead – Sir Nindor killed in the act."

The general paused, keenly trying to observe his king; searching for a telltale sign as to why the message was 'disturbing' rather than 'uplifting'. Finally, after a long pause he nodded. "But there is more…" He looked down and pointed to the message before the king. "More in the note."

King Bestinor nodded. "It appears that everyone in SanTer believe that I was his accomplish… I was seen there in his company, and mysteriously vanished after the act."

"OBSURD," the general bleated out. Then, he recognized the expression in his king's face. "Blood magic at play, we have seen THIS type of work before!"

The king nodded slowly. "How easily the Masti blood priest was able to gain access to my father – disguised as his son. Twice now I have been painted the traitor by blood magic."

"AS BEFORE, YOUR name will be cleared! Fingers and evidence will point north! Many have seen you here! You have not been from this castle in weeks and SanTer is days away even by boat!"

"But don't you SEE!" The king implored. "Just like before, it won't matter. The rumours are out, the suspicions laid. No matter how we proclaim our innocence, there will always be some that remain faithful to the accusation."

"Before, they believed that upset with my father's exile I might have taken to action… at best – they believed that my invasion of the north provoked the Masti priest to kill our king. EVERYONE, knew I was pressing the Governor to bend his knee to me, and that he had rebuffed my requests. How different will the situation appear to the remaining Terran Lords?"

"And there is no way," the general continued shaking his head, "that the captain of SanTer will open their doors to you now."

The king chuckled. "No need to, not for protection. It appears the Montterran Duke of Sirthinor is there to protect them from me and mine."

"The Montterrans sent forces to SanTer too?" The general inquired.

The King looked up surprised and asked, "Too?"

"Montterran sails have been sighted approaching our own port. They will arrive before nightfall."

"So," the king said as he looked to the stone ceiling deep in thought. "King Roehn has sent us aid?" He scratched his face nervously then looked at the window that faced the south. "What houses from Montteran are visiting us this day?"

"Upon their masts hang the coat of arms of Capris – King Roehn's brother-in-law appears to be sailing to our shores."

Methor paused as he stood and then walked round his desk and over to the shuttered southern window. He pulled them open and gazed out and down to their port. "So King Roehn sends us aid. None other than Hastor Karathor, Duke of Capris, the famous horse lord and ruler of the lower plains…"

"SanTer is now as much in Montterran hands as any… after the coincidental assassination of the Governor… Should we make ready for a hostile arrival." The general stood and walked up behind the King. He then turned and surveyed the room nervously. "I will have extra guards posted, and call for members of the Temple … no blood magic will touch any within these walls."

The king nodded. "Call for the Temple priest. I always feel the better when they are around. But as for Karathor, no, I do not fear the Duke of Capris or his lord. Karathor is an honest man, honest and trustworthy above all else – as is Roehn. PLUS, we have no proof of any alliance between Roehn and the Masti. Knowing the man, I doubt that very much… and never forget his daughter."

The general's voice strained as his anxiety increased. "Terran Add falls, and now we have proof of blood magic! SanTer under Montterran rule… Surely we must be concerned that Roehn sees us as vulnerable and seeks to exploit the situation?"

"King Roehn is not an ambitious man, he rules with a soft hand. Above all else he was my father's friend – a loyalty even after his death he would not betray. His own daughter was in TerranAdd at my nieces' birthday party – a party I was not invited to!"

The king shook his head. "King Roehn is not behind this – we do not need to fear him. And you above all others know that what happened to TerranAdd could not by itself be done by blood magic. Deceit and illusions cannot make an entire city of people disappear overnight. There is more to this as we have always said… but what we do not know."

"However, shadow magic can, however, make one man look like another." The general said in retort.

"Indeed… we are in agreement there. What happened at SanTer I believe as you do is as a result of blood magic… The cult is somehow linked to this… or someone has their aid."

"We should have finished what we started years ago." The general added with a great deal of contempt.

"Had we, perhaps…" The King shook his head. "We will never know. The Temple guard supported my claims – together we warned Tar of their resurgence." The king laughed. "He thought me a paranoid, obsessed extremist bent on genocide. He forever blamed me, citing that it was my actions against the Masti that cause our parent's death."

"He never understood…" The general said to console his King. "Your brother never faced the Masti Blood Priests in battle. Your father coddled him, Tar never ventured north to see their temples, how they sacrificed their own wives and children to Andarduel. He never smelled the reek that issued from the river of blood."

The General stood beside the King and looked from behind him out the south-facing window. Snow started to fall making it harder to see the harbour. "So we open our gates to the Duke of Capris?"

King Methor smiled and sighed in the cold fresh air. "Duke Karathor is a very honest man as is his King… I am torn for you are right to have suspicions. There is too much coincidence that the Governor dies and I am implicated at the exact time that Duke Sirthinor arrives at their shore."

They stood for a long moment both looking to the south. Finally the king spoke. "Open the gates to him… but we will tell our priests to be vigalent."

The general nodded. "Yes, but what then?"

The King turned and then looked to the north. "We ride north – to TerranAdd. It is the key to this country, the hub. Whoever has within their control that key has our country's throat in their hands. We suspect that the Masti are involved, we have the Mohen before the gates of PlanTer and there are battles with Tock in the north. We cannot afford to sit idle. That is why King Roehn sends aid. The horsemen of Capris are here to ride with us north – you mark my words for that will be his council."

***

It was very dark and very cold outside when finally the Duke of Capris and his men arrived in the port. Heavy wet snow covered everything on shor and on ship, but the water remained dark and foreboding. Normally, ships arriving late at night might pull into port, however, rarely if ever did they unload until the morning's sun. However, immediately upon arrival the Duke of Capris sent word requesting that his men and horses be allowed to disembark that very night. "We would rather not sleep another night upon these stinking ships!" Duke Hastor Karathor said as he beseached the General, attempting to persuade him to wake his own men so that they might start the docking and unloading of Montterran ships.

The general conceded to the Duke's wishes, and after sending word back to his King as to the Duke's desires he ordered his men to light all the lanterns and firebowls around the harbour. The port glowed earily, the dark waters reflecting the light cast from the shores as Terran workers and soldiers alike assembled.

"I will leave you then Sir Hastor," the Duke of Capris said looking over to his general. "in the capable hands of Sir Bruto Gadral." Turning then to the General of Tentor he added. "If your King is still awake, and as you say bids me meet with him this very night then I will hasten to the castle and his keep."

Sir Gadral nodded and two honour guards and a lad stepped forward. "The Kings squire, his nephew, Aaron Murdoc of TenTor will show you where the King of Terran awaits you. He is eager for your council my Lord."

Trailed behind by two of his own guards the Duke of Capris mounted his horse and following the King's page and honhour guards rode up and through the port and city, which although late at night was fully awake. Behind every shutter and door heads peeped out and watched, occasionally waiving and cheering as the Duke ascended the long road that led to the castle and its keep.

"Many have heard of you in these parts my Lord." Aaron Murdoc said as another few city merchants came out from their stores and waved to the Duke. "The reputation of the Southern Riders is well known – as are your horses."

The Duke waved back in a friendly way, even though he felt ill at ease with all the people staring down at him. "Not much of an honour guard." One of his soldiers said from behind him under a half stifled voice.

Aaron, having heard the man turned in his mount. "The King did not want to alarm you with the presence of many knights. He thought that you would feel more easy should you not arrive to see armour and sword standing ready for your arrival."

The Duke chuckled at the lad's comments. "Right he was." He then turned to his soldier and gave him a stern look. "Especially since we pulled up in the middle of a night and then asked to immediately leave our ships and enter your city."

"Be assured." The lad continued. "You are most welcome, your arrival is well received – no matter the hour."

As they rode up the long rode the Duke of Capris often glanced back at the port which now was filled with his ships. Morning was still hours away, and he knew that most of his men and their mounts would be busy well into the next day unloading.

Aaron, noting the Duke's persistent glances back assured the Duke. "It might take two or more days for your entire fleet to unload… even within a port this size. Space must be made for your horses. We only received notice of your arrival earlier this day, else we would have had more chance to prepare."

The Duke looked forward again just as they entered the massive front gates of the castle. Large spires reached to the sky at at their tops massive gargoils stood with mouths agape. He knew that behind the gargoils large tubs of oil stood ready to be lit. As he passed under them and through the gate he visibly relaxed knowing that had the King not wanted them on his shores, that surely by now he would have done something. Although soldiers were aplenty within the city and castle, not one of them appeared alarmed.

As they passed through the next set of towers and gates that marked the entrance into the inner keep the Duke looked up and spotted two men in long drab robes standing atop the walls looking down – neither looked to be soldiers. "Is it customary to let civilians atop your walls?" He asked the lad.

Aaron, turned and smiled politely. Then looking up he pointed to the two men. "They are of the Temple Guard, priests. They are here to bless your arrival."

The Duke of Capris smiled, inwardly knowing the reason for their presence.

The Terran King awaited the Duke within his large dining chamber. A hearty fire and feast had been laid out on a long table. When they arrived to the room Aaron informally announced them and the Terran King actually stood and strode forward extending his hand in welcome to the Duke of Capris. The Duke scrambled to remove his wet helmet and leather cap as the King approached him with extended arm.

Hastor Karathor, startled by the King's informally placed his helmet upon the floor and bent knee and took the King's hand. "King Roehn sends his regards to the new Terran King and has asked me to bring words of friendship and alliance."

King Bestinor nodded he was dressed in a dark plush surcoat one that was more akin to rest than it was to the entertaining of visiting emissaries. The king's dark and hard face looked unnatural almost as the Terran king smiled and shook the Duke's hand and then turning slightly, iviting the Duke in and to the table.

"Excellent, and well met Lord Karathor." King Bestinor said as he turned and walked to the table. Sitting down – he motioned that the Duke also sit smiling as he did so. "Please sit. You have had a long trip, and you look cold and hungry."

The Duke still very surprised by the King's very friendly demeanour stood up, picked up his helmet and slowly started walking towards the long table that had been stacked with all sorts of breads, fruit, sausages and assorted jams. His guards both stayed at the back of the room not quite knowing what to do.

Before sitting the Duke stood at the side of the table and looked around. Beyond himself, and the King there were no other signs of Terran guards or any other servants. Beyond his men and the King's squire they were alone.

King Bestinor watched the Duke look around, noting that the Montterran Lord was still obviously ill at ease. "You are here as a friend as you say Lord Bestinor, as a welcomed ally. There is nothing to fear within these walls."

The king then motioned to the Duke's guards. "We have much to discuss. Perhaps your men would like some food to break their fast as well?"

Noting the Duke nod he continued quickly. "Aaron take the Duke's guards to the kitchen and have them fed. The hour is very late and I am sure the Duke is also very tired so I will not detain him too long in conversation. Have them return in two hours to escort him to the rooms we have prepared."

"Yes, your grace." Aaron replied smartly as he turned and opened the doors. The guards looked back over to the Duke who, still silent nodded in agreement.

The Duke then seeing the King begin to pile his plate with food sat at the table and placed his helmet upon the floor. Looking up at the food he hesitated but then started placing an assortment of food on his plate.

"I am sure you are eager to get out of your wet cloths, but I hoped to have a moment of your time prior to your rest." The King said after a few minutes to allow the Duke to consume a few first bites.

The Duke still obviously flustered nodded as he swallowed down a bite of sausage. "Thank you your grace. I am honoured by your consideration."

"So what word does your king send – what advise has he instructed you to pass on to me?" King Bestinor said frankly as he placed his glass back on the table. His piercing gaze implying to the Duke that the informalities were drawing to an end – the game of politics had once again been initiated.

"King Mar Roehn the third sends his greetings and has sent me and my men to assist defend the Terran lands. Another company of men led by the Duke of Sirthinor is to land in SanTer."

"Yes, we were already informed of their arrival." The King said plainly. "Go on… what then – what does your King recommend as our next course of action. Does he desire us to march north leaving you here to defend the city?"

"No your grace," the Duke replied emphatically. "He assumed that together we would ride north… We would ride together to PlanTer or TerranAdd."

The king nodded and a smile formed on his lips. "North to TerranAdd was my thought as well – PlanTer is under attack and will fall long before we reach its gates… The Mohen are moving in like vultures on a dead carcass. There are troubles in the north as well – we must hold TerranAdd and the forces you have there will not last."

"Reinforcements are being sent, but will take time to get there." The Duke added. "Should more be needed the Duke Sirthinor will march as well to follow us."

The Terran King, now having baited the hook paused and smiled, his entire attention was focused on the Duke – hoping to observe the subtlest of tell tale signs of knowing. With an even tone he threw out the hook. "From what I hear, the Siren Duke is sitting quite comfortably in SanTer, proclaiming himself as Lord of those lands. Now that my good governor is dead."

Hastor Karathor, Duke of Capris coughed. His hand came late up to his mouth and a few crumbs of breat passed his lips and fell back onto his plate. Startled he sat back and looked at the Terran King. A cold shudder came flew down his back and he shuddered.

King Bestinor smiled, having now received as much information as he needed. "Your surprise appears genuine as I believed from the start." He then reached for and picked up a pice of bread and broke it. With a small knife he spread some jam on it and took a bite. After swallowing he motioned for the Duke to continue eating.

The Duke startled by the information shook his head. "I have lost my appetite your grace." He then looked nervously around. "And if you would be so good, I must make my way back to the port so that I might send word back to my king of the events of the day."

King Bestinor nodded slowly, "And when you send word back to your King, send him my regards, and let him know that we suspect." The king paused and leaned forward again looking for the smallest of reactions from the Duke. 'That shadow magic was involved in the demise of the governor of SanTer."

The Duke of Capris looked over at the Terran King and then down at his plate. "These are ill tidings indeed."

"Much to think about indeed," the King agreed as he took another bite from his bread.

The Clan

Etch bent forward and slid off of Mule's back. He landed stiffly, took a step away from the animal and started to stretch. His back cracked loudly as he flexed.

Dimi winced as she heard his back crack. "Old man, you need to keep move with the horse, not against it when you ride."

Etch moaned as he lifted his hands and touched his toes. "I know, I know. It's just that someone, who shall remain nameless poisoned me and made it rather difficult for me to sit let alone ride!"

Dimi, having forgotten Etch's situation laughed heartily. Her high, echoed over the spectacular countryside. The valley before the small group was covered in green brown grasses. Dark green evergreens dotted the horizon, and a few of which sported snow capped bows. Tall hemlocks pockmarked the hills pointing to a time when in the not too distant past the valley had likely been holding a small lake or bog.

"It smells cold." Etch said as he inhaled deeply and looked around. "Last night snow only barely melted I would guess that we are in for more tonight."

Dimi nodded, but remained seated on the neck of Mule. "No warmth in store for these bones. I would have loved to see our quest turn us south but I feared as much. "

Etch nodded in agreement, "As for me, I hate wet snow or sleet and would far prefer a dry cold snow as long as it doesn't get too deep. Easier to track in snow, but I don't have my snowshoes with me. Looking around he pointed ahead of them. "Two days north, north west to AnnonTer."

"It would only be a day in a half if you can pick up your pace." Dimi replied as she reigned in Peppy turned the mule around to face Etch.

"Wooow Mule." Etch said reigning in his horse next to where Dimi now stood. Dimi reached behind her and grabbed out a few pieces of cooked meet and handed one to Etch and then pulled out a root that she started quietly munching on.

As Etch took the meat he moved uncomfortably in his saddle.

"Tell me the truth?" Dimi asked sardonically as she watched Etch move around in his saddle. "The salve helped right?"

Etch chuckled and nodded and Dimi laughed back, her eyes lighting up as she did reflecting back the sun of the day.

Dimi said. "You gave me quite the scare. I did tell you I wasn't fond of the cold right, what made you think I wanted to go swimming?"

Etch's eyes became somewhat distant for a moment but his focus returned as he smiled back at his small friend. "Scared myself," he agreed. "And the 'vision' I experienced vision really through me through the ringer. It's a little more than just seeing it; it is like almost being there. When I watched Sarta kill…" Etch paused, shuddering at the memory. "I not only could feel Mara's pain. I could feel Sarta's hunger. She relished not only in her feeding, but in the pain she brought to the young woman. She more than enjoyed her feeding, she revelled in it."

Dimi looked back trying to understand as much as she could, trying to be as reassuring as she could to her friend who had obviously witnessed something that had obviously darkened his very soul. "The future is never certain, and 'visions', what you saw might not fully come to be, or not in the same way. But one thing is for certain and that is we will kill her. That will be the end of it."

Etch looked pessimistically back at his friend. "If Sarta was baptized in the blood river, and is now a Priestess of Andarduel… As she feeds and consumes the blood of others, she not only regains her strength, but grows in other ways, her powers grow and she will have the help of the Masti."

Dimi looked back at her friend and smiled. She nudged Peppy closer to Mule and reached out and touched his hand. "We will stop her, she is still mortal."

Both sat still a moment reflecting the rhetorical question that they now debated. 'Was she indeed?'

The sat quietly looking at each other and then the landscape. After a moment Etch sighed and rolled his head letting the strain and stress obtained from his memories ease out of his neck and back. "SO over hill and dale we go." He said without much enthusiasm.

Dimi reached down and patted Peppy. "Have heart Etch." She said with a loftier tone. "Believe in yourself, you question yourself and your capabilities far too often. We can do this, you and I, alone if must be."

Etch spurred his horse forward and followed Dimi and Peppy up the long grass covered hill. As Mule stepped over a stone bouncing Etch slightly he bent backward and groaned. "I am missing a good soft bed. We will stop in Annon Ter for supplies, and a good night's rest."

"We must visit another city?" Dimi lamented.

"Hey, you did well in the last!" Etch retorted now with some levity in his voice.

"I wonder how Dimona is." Dimi reminisced thinking back about her friends in Terran Add. "I wonder if the ruse they pulled still holds the Mohen at bay."

Etch laughed. "She probably is having a great time counting the coins and treasures found in that great city and she likely has even figured out a way to have the Mohen forces pay her a tith so that they can camp in the area before they all scuttle off home with their tails between their legs."

Dimi's laugh danced upon the air. "One thing I do look forward to, warm baths are spectacular and beat out any stream! So to Annon Ter for a bath and a sleep and supplies we go. From there will we head back up the river to the Two Towers?"

"Mmm, a warm bath indeed. The 'vision' of a hot mulled wine and hard oak cheese by my side as I sit in a hot tub." Etch nudged

Mule forward to a brisker walk. "Now that will keep my spirits up in anticipation. I remember back when I used to come down from the mountain…" Etch's voice drained off to a mumble.

"Now you think of home, family and hearth." Dimi said quietly. "Of Rachale, Chad and Lyss."

Etch nodded silently. "When I set out, all I had in my mind was the quest, the chore at hand. I was so passionate about helping. I always get that way, I turn my mind inward and go about my task.

"'But,…" Dimi added for Etch.

"I departed fast," Etch said sadly. "I never measure the cost of my work in advance of starting out."

"And in the end, you question the cost paid." Dimi answered with rhetorical finality.

Etch nodded silently as he thought of his family, and the many times in the past he had left home and his loved ones.

"It is good to remember them." Dimi continued. "Remember, you do this for them too. And not just to return the princess now. We fight for their safety too."

"Yes, I guess we do." Etch agreed. "Sarta is on a bigger path then just the princess. It is much bigger than just her, just us."

"Yes, if she continues to grow strong." Dimi started. "With what she was, she was able to make all within a vast city disappear… her rule and domain will stretch to the very ends of the earth if she is not stopped. Your home, and all you love is in jeopardy as well, perhaps not today, but someday."

Etch arched his back as the mule and horse paced up the long grassy hill towards hills covered in evergreen and tall brown grass. "I hope Chad is chopping wood and Lyss is helping Rachael prepare for winter, for I feel it will be long and cold this year."

The analogy was not lost on Dimi. She knew in his heart that he fought his own demons. That deep down he now questioned if he should be turning about to return to the mountains, to sequester away his family from all humans and demons alike. "Every last creature in this world will feel her touch if she is not stopped." Dimi stated again plainly.

"There is no place to hide." Etch agreed.

Etch gave Mule a small nudge with his heel coaxing the animal not to slow although their climb up the hill became harder. "He stole a quick glance backward from where they had come from, down the long hill and back to the great forest that encircled the lake of Keeper. "Did you see Socks after last night?" Hoping to change the subject and keep his mind apart from his family and home.

Dimi shook her head as she continued riding. "I thought I caught Sock's scent when I woke up, but I don't think he likes going about during the day if he doesn't have to."

Dimi looked back along the path they had just ridden almost as if she expected to see the bat hiding among the shorter trees. "I wonder who or what he was before Sarta found him? I felt," Dimi stumbled for words. "I don't know, something noble... something heartbroken."

Etch looked back along the broken path of long grass bowed and bent down by their passage. "I would be hart broken too if a bitch of a witch turned me into a bat." He then paused, thinking about the ramifications. "Sad." He finally admitted. "Couldn't really go home – could he?"

They reached the top of the rise and started descending the back of the hill. Before them rose another hill, that much higher and steeper then the one they had just crested.

Over hill, through valley the two rode. Their conversation was as light as the cold winter breeze. Silent hawks flew the air, and occasionally a crow would caw, but all of the songbirds and other smaller foul that usually sang within the forest had already flown south for the season. It was a peaceful ride, and they took the time to think deep thoughts and reflect upon their past and on the prospects of their future.

Into the next few days they rode, finally the incessant hills disappeared and the land became flat once again and riding became easier. But the open fields let the wind build up and they had to pull from within their bags additional shirts to wear and they pulled their coats and buttoned them up tight.

They rarely stopped for lunch, halting as they rode only to pick up edible root. No longer were even errant apple trees around, in their place stood tall spruce and pine. Etch sat up in his stirrups and breathed in the cold northern air. Although the air was cold, the scent of pine cleared his sinuses and warmed his lungs.

On the third night after departing the Keeper they at what was left of their food. The meet was still fresh for the cold had preserved it well. They relished the last of it. "Hunger sure is the best spice…" Etch said as he swallowed the last of the meat. He looked over as Dimi chewed down a piece of root she had found.

"Glad you enjoyed our last meal." She agreed. "It is colder here; we won't find much more edible food around." She brushed the dirt off her hands. "Not even these roots. We always had to prepare well for winter when I lived up north. That was one of the reasons I so longed to move to the warmth of the south."

"Tomorrow we will see the city." Etch said. "But until then we will have to feast upon the dreams of a bath, warm wine and cheese eh?" He said jibbing her.

Not having anything left to eat the next morning they broke camp quickly and started off again in their northerly procession. Their daydreams of warm bed, bath and delicacies only found within larger cities drove them on.

By mid day they noted several small single dwelling cabins dotting their path and by evening they came upon the main road that they both knew would lead them to the large city of Annon Ter.

"Can you smell it," Dimi asked wrinkling her nose, "the city?" She asked.

"Ahhh, we must be getting close." Etch said as they wound down the long hard packed road. "Not long now."

Although the acrid smell of burning coal could be noted, it was not until late evening when they finally were able to see the silhoete of the great northern city.

As they approached it, great gusts of wind threw back in their face, the sooty smell of coal fires, the smell of iron being melted and smelted, and the distinct smell of animals being butchered.

"Ahh," Dimi continued sarcastically, "nothing better than the smell of a city." "Well, you might not like it." Etch retorted. "But I can smell a warm bath and bed in those fragrances. Let's push on. It can't be more than ten kilometres." Etch said spurring Mule forward ahead of Peppie.

The four rode on but it was night before they drew up to the edge of the great city. It spread out for miles, and at its heart rose a steep hill and atop the hill stood massive walls and atop them rose to the black starry sky spiked towers. Around its entire breadth fell a great moat, a sole drawbridge pulled up for the night stood as the first sentinel and barrio to the city before them.

"Annon Ter." Etch said as they turned with the road headed for the drawbridge that during the day would span the moat enabling travelers to and from the city. "This city is the gateway to the north it is the last Terran city and fortress between us and the wilds."

It was already dark, but Dimi could make out the city's main walls and the massive white towers behind them that marked the second and greater keep. Dimi looked at the city and towers before her. "Will we find aid there? Will the letter from your king hold any sway here?"

"Hard to say," Etch started not quite sure himself, "unless he died of old age, Duke Rudolf Ygor rules there. He had a reputation of being a real headstrong, fireball… but a loyal man to the last Terran King – Tar and his father King Terros before him. His wife the Duchess Elizabe was Terros' elder sister. Lord Rudolf might be the

Duke, but the real power of AnnonTer is the Duchess. I don't know if they still live, let alone if my note will hold sway with them."

Dimi looked at the city and towers before her as they drew nearer to the moat and drawbridge. "Some of the city looks old and burnt, but the towers are clean and new. They have "

"From the time of the Masti uprising," Etch started, "when the Masti rose up, Duke Rudolf Ygor assembled all of his knights and most of the men from the countryside and marched to rebuff the Masti and to send them again back home. Along the way they picked up forces from the MiKay from the city of Two Towers – where we head to next."

Etch paused turning round to look at Dimi's silhouette. "The Duke and the MiKay did not fare well. The Masti blood priests were getting very good at their magic and hid through magic many of their own soldiers. The Duke and MiKay forces marched north… it appears in the light of day they walked right past an entire legion of Massi."

"That's quite strong magic to hide an entire army." Dimi noted.

"The Massi Blood priests cast shadow spells and hid THOUSANDS of men in plane sight." Etch restated shaking his head. "Can you imagine hiding an entire army through magic? Having thousands of armed me riding past hills spotted with campfires? Deceiving hundreds of scouts?"

Etch shook his head. "It must have been something. One moment the Duke and his men are riding behind a long line of MiKay dwarfs and the next moment their entire combined armies are virtually surrounded. It was a bloody massacre."

"Yet the Duke lived?" Dimi asked surprised.

"Most of his men didn't, and the combined Terran and MiKays forces were decimated."

Etch's voice was sombre fitting the cold dark night around them. "But not all fortune passed them by. The northern clansmen that lived in the hills came to the call of the MiKay war horns. They swept down from the hills and hacked through the Masti lines – breaking through to the encircled troops. With Clansmen blood they opened up a path through the hills to get to the MiKay lord and the Duke."

"Two in ten escaped the Masti trap." Etch continued. "But even then they were not safe for now between them and their home stood almost half the Masti legion – fifteen hundred to two thousand or more Masti soldiers and dozens of ordained blood priests."

"The clansmen were late to the fray, but a full thousand were called from the hills and with their help and ferocity the MiKay dwarfs and Terran soldiers cut a bloody swath back to the Two Towers. However," Etch paused a moment, "it was too late for the Twin Towers had already fallen."

"I can only imagine what the MiKay soldiers found when they returned to their castle." Dimi added knowingly. "Sacrifices to Andarduel, blood rituals performed on wife and child...."

Etch agreed and continued. "It is understandable that the remaining MiKay had no heart to continue the fight... nor to remain after the Towers were cleansed of Masti. What remained of their men departed back up through the hills. West and North seeking to return to their ancestral cities beneath the Trukian mountains.... For their aid at time most needed the MiKay – they left the Clansmen the castle."

"So Duke Rudolph had to fight his way home alone?" Dimi asked shaking her head in disbelief.

"No, Even though before that time the clansmen were only known as raiders and rouges that would waylay merchants going north and south, they surprised the Duke and banded with him in his time of aid. They accompanied and fought side by side with Duke Rudolf and with their help the Duke returned in time to save his fair city."

"But it had been badly torched, the towers of the citadel and keep are white and new, but much of the walls and roofs are scorched and burnt." Dimi said looking past the moat to the great city. The white towers stood now tall in the distance, brilliantly white contrasting many of the larger buildings now visible – scarred badly by flame.

The two weary, hungry travelers stopped their mounts before the massive moat. The drawbridge had been pulled back. No sentries stood near it or appeared in or about the small guardhouse on the opposite side.

"Weird." Etch said looking across the wide moat. "Usually the drawbridge is only raised when battle is imminent, and even then, soldiers are stationed to let other pass to the hale the main gates." He looked to the portcullis a good hundred meters behind the drawbridge a few soldiers could just be seen in the light of torches that flickered on the wall.

"I am not swimming tonight." Dimi said with a laugh looking down into the trench.

"Nor I." Etch agreed quickly looking down as well. "Twenty, no thirty meters wide at the top; ten or more deep, filled with filth and spikes no doubt. NO – definitely not swimming tonight."

"YO, WITHIN," Etch yelled at the top of his lungs. "CAN WE GET ENTRY THIS NIGHT TO YOUR FAIR CITY?"

There was a stirring on the wall as a soldier grabbed a torch and held it up closer to his face as he yelled back. "ARE YOU MAD BEING OUT AT THIS HOUR WITH DETROS HIGH?" There was a distant laugh from another soldier and then his words rang out. "WE OPEN NO GATES AT NIGHT BY ORDER OF THE DUKE. COME BACK IN THE MORNING IF YOU STILL LIVE."

Etch looked puzzled back to Dimi. Both then looked nervously around them.

"I don't sense anything." Dimi said trying to reassure Etch as he continued to look around them.

"Given the comments," Etch said softly to Dimi who sat atop Peppy not two meters from him. "I am loath to yell and argue the point and possibly draw more attention to us."

"Agreed," Dimi said as she turned to Peppy the mule. "Let's spend the night in the thicket of trees we just passed and return in the morning."

Without further argument both turned their mounts and set them to trot back from whence they had come stopping only when they were within a darker part of the thicket of pine and spruce.

They lit no fire that night and sat both awake with sword and blowgun in hand listening to the wind within the trees, jumping at every sound. By the morning, both were exhausted, but relieved when the sun began to shine. They gathered their mounts quickly and returned to the city.

Two soldiers came out from a small door beside the portcullis and slowly walked to the drawbridge. However, they did not immediately tend to the giant wheel that would lower the drawbridge, but instead stood defiantly on the other side of the bank and glowered a the two weary travelers.

"Greetings." yelled Etch as he raised his arm high.

Both guards looked at Etch and then stared at Dimi. She lowered her head slightly and looked off to the forest feigning to have little interest in the pending discussion…. Hoping that at the distance they were would take her for Etch's son or daughter.

"HO THERE." came the hesitant and not that welcoming reply.

"What is your business in our city?" The second soldier demanded of them with his arm resting upon the hilt of his sword.

"Rest and respite," started Etch sounding very positive "to replenish our supplies and to rest a day or two in the warmth of one of your inns prior to continuing our journey."

One of the soldiers turned and looked to head back to the walls. The other held firmly shaking his head in denial. "Only kin from

515

those within the city are allowed passage, and under close review even at that. For over three weeks now our gates have been closed to all others except to farmers and merchants that have done trade with us in the past and who are either kin from those within the walls, or are vouched by them. And even then, great care and watchful eyes are put upon their comings and goings."

The soldier that had turned away looked back and waved the two away. "Be gone with you and waste not our time, unless you can name a man within our walls that would vouch for you."

Etch played his card, realising that entry to the city itself was not assured. "Have times gone so poorly in these parts that you would turn away travelers?" Well then, good soldier I would name your own Duke as having an interest in my presence. For I am an officer of the Montteran forces and have for him information as to the goings on in the south."

The soldier who had just turned round laughed aloud. "Unless you have proof to that end, you will not gain easy passage here." The other soldier agreed and yelled back at Etch. "Only with proof of such claim would we disturb or bring you to face the Duke."

"They are very very leery." Dimi said under her breath over to Etch. "They fear something greatly to stop two innocent travelers from entering such a large city."

Etch put his hand under his travel rob and from the pocket within pulled the letter from his pocket. "I have a letter marked and signed by King Roehn stating my duty and my rank."

The soldier that had headed away took a few steps closer to the drawbridge and the two soldiers conferred. After a moment one of the soldiers turned to the walls and yelled. "Close tight, drawbridge going down."

A few heads popped up from the wall and looked down as the two soldiers then proceeded to the giant wheel. They strained and puffed as they lowered the drawbridge. As its end hit the opposite shore the soldiers immediately put their hands up warning the two not to cross immediately. "Hold one of us will come to see your letter and you had better not be lying."

A few soldiers with crossbows were now apparent on the wall behind the two soldiers nervously watching the two travelers. The second soldier motioned to them. "And if you do anything funny, you will find yourselves stuck like pin cushions."

Etch dismounted and walked over to the soldier and handed him the paper. He roughly took it and then eyed Dimi. "Says nothing here about a son or daughter." The soldier replied as he read the letter and looked up and motioned to Dimi.

"Harmless orphan. Bad war to the south you know? Especially now with the Mohen beating on your capital's door and all." He then turned and motioned to Dimi who had hunched down a little making herself appear even smaller then she was. The hood of her traveling cloak had been pulled far forward hiding all but the front of her face. "I have taken it to name myself the young lady's guardian."

The guard snorted, handed back the letter and then waved to his friend and those upon the gate. "THERE COMING ere coming through." He yelled.

After they passed over the bridge Etch lent the soldiers a hand to raise it; then followed slowly behind the two as they went to the gate which was now being opened.

"These two have asked to see the Duke sergeant." he said as they entered.

"Stay with them until you get to Captain Asnori." Another soldier said as he watched them enter.

Once within the city they were escorted up and through the cities second walls and right up to the keep. There another soldier had their mounts taken to the stalls while another brought them further into the city and the castle itself. At virtually every passageway they were stopped and had to explain why they needed to proceed. Over and over again, Etch reviewed his purpose, and the note from King Roehn was read and then read again and again.

It wasn't until late in the afternoon that they finally made it to the inner keep – at which point they were told that they would next meet with the captain of the guards.

When the last guard finally brought them in to see the captain in his study he rose to greet them and hearing a loud grumble from Etch's stomach he smiled and pointed at a small table by the door which had upon it apples and dark orange cheese. Dimi and Etch put their manners aside and started wolfing down chunks of fruit and inhaled a third of the small wheel of cheese that had been there before even sitting down in the chairs by the captain's desk.

While they ate the captain remained silent, first reading the note Etch brought and then later reviewing a parchment he had before him. When finally the two before him paused apparently with hunger sated he smiled and sat back in his chair.

Captain Asnori was a battle worn older man and appeared to stare incessantly at Dimi. When she finally looked up and their eyes met he smiled. "You have unusual eyes. Would you be so kind as to pull back your hood?"

His voice was gracious, but demanding. Dimi glanced over at Etch who nodded and she pulled back slowly her hood. The guard that had brought them both, still standing by the door they had entered gasped. Asnori looked at the man and smiled knowingly.

"Not type of orphan I have ever seen." He added with a tint of sarcasm in his voice. "And yes, I have been well south in these lands."

The captain then looked back at the guards. "And had my men been alert, you likely would not have made it this far today but would have spent the night in observation before me."

He then leaned forward in his chair and looked at Etch with steel grey piercing eyes.. "Interesting travel partner." he stated slowly.

Dimi shifted in her chair, noticeably uncomfortable as Etch replied. "Dimi is a very trusted friend and advisor. She is no child, but in fact much older then either of us."

After a moment's pause Etch added, "I trust her with my life."

Captain Asnori looked again at Etch's letter from King Roehn and as he handed it back to Etch he said. "In Annon Ter, when a person vouches for another – that is what you do."

"Well here you are." He continued looking back at Etch and then Dimi. Finally he seemed to come to a conclusion that the two could be trusted. "Which by the very fact says you are likely who and what you claim to be…. And also possibly even more – though unlikely less."

He continued now with humour in his voice. "Meaning that you are either brave and strong, or simply two individuals gifted with more luck then sense."

Dimi laughed and the captain turned and looked at her face and sparkling eyes. His gaze lifted and fell to take her in. His expression changed from delight to one of puzzlement. "My men say I have a clansmen dog's nose about me which is why I have this post, for in this duty I see all before they meet with the Duke and his wife."

Still obviously trying to puzzle out what Dimi was he shook his head and then he smiled once again. "A fell creature you are definitely not…. But I would love to spend an hour or two talking with you later to find out more about where you come from dear lady? For never before have I seen such a beauty and I would love to take you to my daughter for she often reads fantasies of dryads and nymphs."

Dimi giggled and Etch's eyebrows rose in almost exasperation at her response.

"But we should not dally." The captain continued. "For the day is drawing closed and no man or woman is brought before the Duke and Duchess after they dine for supper."

He then rose and Etch and Dimi followed suit.

Etch's tone became somewhat serious. "We noted a definite tension here, with drawbridge raised, we came last night but were turned away…"

Before opening the door the captain turned to Etch. "I think it best to let the Duke and Duchess explain after you have told them your story." He then turned and directed them back from whence they had come. He then walked around them and started leading them back out the hall waving off the guard that had brought them.

"Follow me, the Duke and Duchess will receive you in their study." The captain said as he turned round a corner and proceeded to lead them up a long stretch of steps. "If you ask such questions to me now, there is much you will need to know if you plan to travel in these parts."

Etch turned to look at Dimi, his eyebrows rose wondering what events could turn an entire city paranoid.

Before entering the Duke's study the captain turned to the two companions. "If you need any more information or details on the area after talking with my lord and lady come back to my office and I will give you what aid I can." He then turned and knocked on the door – a voice from within said enter and the captain opened the door and led them forward and in to the study.

The study was small compared to what Etch expected. It was laid out like a small library with two walls covered in bookshelves no higher than two meters, above them hung tapestries depicting mountain boar hunting. In the middle of the wall a cozy hearth blazed, radiating heat throughout the room. Four high backed, red velvet chairs sat around the hearth and a blue area rug covered the floor, it was worn, but not tattered. The Duke and Duchess both appeared to have been enjoying each a book looked up as they entered.

The captain performed a short bow and introduced the two. "My Lord and Lady, may I introduce Etch Tallow and 'Dimi'. Etch is a Montterran officer carrying papers from King Roehn. He has asked attendance to present to you information from the south. I brought him forthwith."

The Duchess, a lady in her late seventies looked up from her book. Age and strain reflected from her face. "From Terran Add?" She asked. "Have you news from Terran Add?"

Etch took a step forward and bowed, "Yes, my Lord and Lady of AnnonTer. We have indeed just come from that city."

"You must excuse my wife's brevity. Our son was lost at Terran Add." The Duke said looking back at Etch. "If you have news of Terran Add and the south, please sit." He motioned to the captain who passed Etch's paper to the Duke and then turned and departed. Etch walked forward, Dimi hesitated a moment when the Duke looked her over but then shrugged and went over to the large chair beside the Duchess and sat down.

Etch sat down on the edge of his chair beside the Duke. "Thank you my lord and lady."

The Duke smiled and then looked down and read the letter, squinting at the words. There was a slight tremble in his lips and face as he read.

"We have heard of the fall of Terran Add." The Duchess started looking at Etch and then looking curiously at Dimi.

"We sent a knight and three riders when the rumour first reached our doors." The Duke said looking over at his wife. "We could not afford any more, for already then our men were engaged."

"But none returned." The Duchess said continuing her husband's review. "Then we sent another two men. One returned indicating that he found the bodies of the previous four killed by some large animals. They made it to Terran Add without seeing the beasts, and returned. But they could tell us little beyond that the city was empty and our son, the king or any within the city were not to be found." "Our son was at our King's reception." The Duchess said, turning to look at Dimi beside her. Her voice almost breaking. "He was of age and full of haste to go to the King's court. It was to be a grand event, but we are getting old… and travel is hard for us now."

"We too did barely escape ourselves from some rather…" Etch paused wondering what level of detail to present to the Lord and Lady. He had just been introduced to them and he feared that if he relayed the true events of their encounter with the blood ferrets and transformed villagers he might lose what little credibility afforded to a strange emissary from afar. "Unusual beasts," Etch finally concluded.

Duke Rudolf smiled reassuringly at Dimi and nodded knowingly. "Strange creatures, some harmless and others not are not unknown to us in the north."

Dimi nodded but did not speak. She looked over to Etch, not quite sure what to say, or how to act having not had much opportunity to talk with royalty.

The Duke seeing Dimi's obvious discomfort smiled warmly at her and then at Etch. "Please be at ease good friends. Dire times are upon us; we cannot let the formalities of title stand between ourselves and knowledge."

"We are old, have lived through a great deal and seen much in our lifetimes." The Duchess said. "I witnessed my brother's death by blood magic; he was cursed by a man who spat a curse with blood. I have stood atop our castle walls and watched as our men rebuffed Masti blood priests who through all manner of illusion at us." She motioned to her husband. "Rudolf was old when last we were at war with the north, and he too has seen much."

"What my good wife Elizabe is trying to say." The Duke interjected with a warm smile. "Is that you should not hesitate to speak freely. Fear not that what you say will sound incredulous to our ears."

Etch looked at the Duke then back at the Duchess. Time had not been kind to either, both now looked very tired and drawn out. Etch realised that their son must have been born late in their lives and had meant a great deal to them.

"As you have heard," Etch started. "TerranAdd stood empty and within its walls and surrounding areas there is no sign of man, woman or child. And as you have heard, there is no sign of siege or war."

"That much we know." The Duchess said shortly.

Rudolf looked over to her and motioned with her hand to relax. "Let them continue Elizabe." He then turned to Etch. "Do you have any knowledge, or even suspicions as to how this came about?"

Etch cleared his throat. "We have only speculation." Etch started.

"Tell us what you believe." the Duchess encouraged, "anything, everything."

Etch nodded, "The quest assigned to me by our King Roehn was to find out what has befallen his daughter our princess Elle Roehn. The princess, like your son was at King Tar's celebration."

"In these last few months, I have heard a great number of strange things, and seen things I cannot totally explain. Blood ferrets the size of horses, twisted and deformed residents of villages…. We have been within Terran Add and have consulted with the Montterran knights that now protect it against the Mohen."

Etch paused and looked back and forth to the Duke and Duchess. Encouraged that neither appeared to not believe his words he continued more bravely. "We do not know for certain what exactly befell the city of Terran Add, but we believe that it was as a result of great magic and the magic is being performed by a mage and succubus that we know as Sarta Pensor."

"Sarta," Dimi added, her voice calm and convincing chimed like a songbird in the room, "is old. Very old and once trained under a great master and we now fear she also is a worshiper of Andarduel."

"She is also, we believe quite mad." Etch added in conclusion.

After a long moment of silence the Duchess looked over to Etch. "Could your princess still be alive?" She then turned to Dimi. "Could my son be yet alive or is there no hope?"

"It is possible." Dimi said. "We believe that the magic involved the moving of beings, people and even possibly demons, between planes of existence."

Etch looked back at Rudolf and Elizabe searching for signs of understanding or disbelief. Neither showed surprise, nor looked confused. The Duke looked over and noted Etch's puzzled expression he laughed lightly and then coughed. "You look puzzled that my wife and I are not shocked or surprised by your conclusions."

Etch laughed a little in reply, "Well, Duke Ygor, actually yes. For it took us many hours of deliberation and discussions with many people such as the Grand Drakon to come to such knowledge and understanding ourselves."

"How is Father Mellon." The Duchess inquired with a smile. "When last did you see him, and was he well?"

"He saved Etch's life less than a week ago when he fell in to Keeper Lake." Dimi said in reply.

"He was well." Etch added.

"Perhaps we should tell you what WE have seen these last few weeks." The Duke said excitedly. "For it will explain why we are not surprised by your observations or findings."

Duke Rudolph Ygor, cleared his raspy throat. "Foul creatures of all sorts plagued our lands. Weer creatures, who in the past were just legends now roam the woods around our castles. So many are they and so frequent the attacks that now no man, woman or child now enters this castle unwatched throughout the night for fear that they might turn themselves. Their offspring the Wog attack our outposts and kill the game and cattle… and there are worse to the North."

Etch swallowed hard. "Worse? What of the Two Towers, have any of your men heard of a beautiful or fearful woman or mage within that castle now?"

"Our scouts are few now." Duke Rudolf agreed. "But we do send them north and although none have themselves seen Sarta Pensor, our friends the Clansmen attest that she is indeed resident there and that it is she who is behind the denizens that now issue forth from that unholy place."

"Damn her black soul." The Duchess said harshly. "I knew somehow, that she was behind all of this. My husband hoped beyond hope the two events unrelated."

The Duchess turned to the Duke angrily. "I told you we should have mustered the last of our men and besieged that unholy dwelling and sent that woman back to the hell she was spawned from!"

Rudolf shook his head. "Neither we nor the clansmen have enough men. Perhaps when first the towers were taken, had we known the extent of her reach, had we obtained aid from affar we might have… but not later."

The Duke looked sadly back to Dimi and then his wife. "And surely not now."

"She must be stopped, why not now?" Dimi implored

"She is not alone in that seat of power, is she?" Etch asked knowingly. The Duke looked over at Etch, squinting. Now the Duke wasn't sure how much of the knowledge they had he should give to Etch.

"A demon lord." Etch continued.

"She called him forth, and through him can bring his minions." The Duke said as he sat back in his chair and sighed.

"Andarduel's spawn." The Duchess spat out the words harshly and a slight dribble of spittle flew from her lips. She took a small kerchief from beside her and wiped her mouth.

"You must forgive my wife." Rudolf added. "We do not in fact know from where they come. There are other creatures our friends have sighted atop the castle walls, although they are not many but that is not what holds us back for we know not what they can do. It is simply that the cursed woman is spawning so many weer and wog that even had we the entire strength and support of the armies of the south we would be hard pressed to attack her stronghold. The mountains and forests of the north are plagued by the beasts, thousands; perhaps tens of thousands guard now and roam freely even south of our own castle."

"We were very surprised." The Duchess said, now being back in control of her emotions. "That you did not know. That you travelled up to our lands and were not so accosted yourself."

Etch sat back in his chair, and then he looked at Dimi. The reality of their current situation sank in, there was desperation, and dismay that soiled his very soul. The room was silent save for the crackling of the fire.

"There is always hope." Dimi said plainly after a long silent moment. "And I for one will not be swayed from the task at hand – to kill the succubus mage - to kill Sarta."

The Duchess looked over at Dimi, with certain apprehension. "You speak bravely for one so small."

Etch stifled a chuckle when the Duchess turned to him. "Excuse me Duchess. Its just that Dimi is much more than she seems. And she is quite determined to do harm to Sarta."

"And Etch is much more than he was." Dimi added. "And knowing him as I do, I know he will continue with his quest."

"Even if that quest brings you to a certain doom?" The Duchess asked. "To what ends would you go? Do you still hope to return your Princess to his King? Would you die to achieve this?"

Etch paused and reflected on the question then nodded as he solemnly replied. "As my good friend Dimi has said. There is always hope. And each of us must look in our own hearts some times, to see if within we have the courage to fight the good fight. Even if doing so may cause our own demise."

"Well said." The Duke agreed after another long moment of silence.

"Perhaps we or our friends can help in some way." Duchess Elizabe remarked. "And would only ask in return, that should you find our son…"

It was Etch's turn to clear his throat. He didn't want the Duchess' hopes to rise too high. "We know not know for certain as to what specifically befell them. As to if they yet live, or if they can be returned from where they now are. But we will do what we can."

"Then, good man, we would aid you in whatever manner we can." the Duchess added politely, yet without great conviction or joy.

"Thank you both." Etch responded with a slight bow of his head. "Have you any men to send to assist us in the defence of Terran Add? Montterran reinforcements are said to be coming, but the Mohen are at the city gates and our soldiers are few and will not hold them at bay for long."

The Duke looked deeply disturbed and his voice almost broke. "Two weeks past, I received an urgent message from my sister Katrin Zarof Countess of MinonTer – they were besiged by legions of Weer and Tock. I sent all available men I could to her aid and her defence." Rudolf looked away from Etch and towards the fire.

"Of the men we sent." Elizabe continued with a voice almost inaudible as she looked to her husband. "Only a handful made it to their gates. Katrin's husband and her son, our nephew perished the next day as they sought to rebuff the foe."

The Duke inhaled and then his hand went to brush off tears from his eyes and he turned again back towards Etch. "A bird delivered a message last night. Had it not been for the arrival of your own Duke Bethos from Ortho, my sister would be dead as would all her people."

The Duchess breathed in deep drawing the attention of all. "We sent men, such men at arms that we could not then easily spare. Four hundred mounted knights, and twice as many men afoot.

527

Yet in that force, they could not make it cross the Miror Ter to the castle and lands of Minon Ter."

"And as a result," Rudolf continued bleakly, "our own plight is darker still. We have no men at arms to spare, nor do our Clansmen allies… for they are even more solely done by having lost the majority of their men when the two towers were taken."

Etch visibly slouched in his chair, despair having sucked out what little energy he had left. The room all of a sudden felt so very small to all the four sitting there.

"We will do what we can." Dimi said courageously. "It is better this way for I do not like the idea of traveling in front of hundreds of noisy soldiers only to pound on a mage's door and then waiting to see what she might have in store for us. We need go north in stealth, not in force anyway."

Dimi's courage and brightness brought a spark of hope back to the room. Etch sat forward sighing once again loudly – hoping to shake off the overly warm feeling he was having. He undid the buttons of his coat, and slipped it off and placed it on the floor beside him. He then looked over to Dimi and smiled and nodded back. "Stealth it is then."

"If you plan to go north and to enter the towers then you had best talk to Stephan and his men. The clansmen were given the towers by the MiKay and have held it these last years. If anyone knows how to travel there and get within unseen – it will be the northern clansmen and Stephan.

"Would you be so kind then to direct us to him and perhaps give us such a note that he would assist us in this matter?" Etch asked with determination and courage reappearing in his voice.

"I can do better than that." Responded the Duke as he stood. "For since the tower's fall many of the Clan have made Annon Ter their home. I will introduce you myself to Stephan, for the entire Douglas clan, past defenders of TeiRei sit now in our Northern Towers."

Dimi and Etch stood with the Duke and Etch reached down and picked up his jacket.

"Take care my husband." The Duchess warned. "They just arrived this last night back from another raid and Detros' grin will shine this night and it is time we sit to eat. It is not the time of day to meet with those that travel north."

Dimi and Etch followed suite and stood not quite understanding the Duchess' concern.

"As always, I trust Stephan with my life." The Duke replied but seeing the concern on his wife's face he added. "But I will take extra care."

"Extra care and with two guards I hope." His wife implored.

"Yes my dear." The Duke said as he started towards the door. Etch stepped lively around the Duke and opened the door for them. The good captain of Annon Ter and another castle guard stood outside waiting to return Etch and Dimi they stood surprised as the Duke walked past them. "We are off to meet with Stephan." He said casually to his captain. "My wife bids you accompany us."

"Yes sir." The captain replied in a surprised voice.

Without looking back, the Duke proceeded down the hall and then the stairs. He was taller than the captain, and likely had been a formidable knight in his time. Although still spry for his age, his walk was stiff and a bit forced. However, it was brisk enough that Dimi had to skip every other step to keep up with them.

Etch took a quick step faster and walked parallel to the captain who walked directly behind the Duke. "May I ask, why so much concern as to the time of day? And what did the Duchess fear in visiting the Clansmen now?"

"They returned from a raid last night… and as they do each night after such a raid, they hold a Black Watch?"

"And just what is a Black Watch?" Dimi asked as she skipped up to walk just behind the two.

Captain Asnori looked over at Etch and then back at Dimi. "Sir Stephan Douglas, leader of the Northern Clans and rightful lord of Tie Rie and the twins rides from our gate each week to look upon the towers with hope to know the fate of those still captive within. They have not the force of man to attack it outright, but often they meet packs of Wogs or a Weer or two that they must kill in order to return."

The Duke started to huff as he went down the stairs. "I get the feeling that they know little of Weer and Wog in the south good Captain."

Asnori smiled and winked at Etch and Dimi. "Then you might be in for a sight tonight."

The Duke turned to rest a moment his chest heaved as he breathed in deeply. "I will let Stephan describe his towers, for his descriptions are more vivid having lived there. Plus, the clansmen know more of what is there and what surrounds it then any other. However, you must know this." The Duke paused a moment still out of breath. "He believes that his wife still lives and is held capture within the towers by Sarta. Do not speak of it though, for he will turn dark."

"I tell you this." Rudolf continued. "For because of this I am convinced he will aid you in your quest... However, Stephan must agree with your plan for whatever you do, for your actions could put her at risk."

The Duke reached up and took Etch's arm. "Stephan and his wife courtship was the foundation of Clan legends, he desperately needs to continue believing that she is alive although all others believe by this time that surely she has perished or worse. "

"He fears perhaps she was transformed?" Dimi asked knowingly.

"Yes." The Duke replied slowly. "The evil mage has been busy. The clan has brought back many interesting tales of what they have seen at the twins."

"It is best if Stephan himself describes what he has seen." The Captain interjected. "Let Etch and Dimi hear first hand from him and his men. And as for the 'black watch'…" Captain Asnori let out a cold sardonic chuckle. 'That you will see for yourself, and also understand why we watch our visitors so closely."

Etch turned to Dimi who shrugged and they followed the Duke and his guards as they threaded through the halls and passages and made their way to the large northern towers.

The northern towers and defences of Annon Ter were massive. An outer and inner keep stood only a hundred meters apart spanned only at its top by a massive stone archway. Far below the archway Etch noted nothing but spikes should by some great machine or magic the ten meter thick stone walls be breached below, the visitors would receive little welcome.

The walk went on for quite some time through intricate stone doorways, each with sentries, and each with strong wood and iron doors. To enter from the outer walls through to the keep would be slowed many times. As they passed, each set of guards watched closely Dimi and Etch.

As they approached the first set of doors after the causeway they came upon their first view of clansmen. Two shorter men dressed in brown leathers, with hard boiled leather armour stood guard in front of the doorways passing out to the outer castle walls and towers.

As they crossed over the last stone causeway Etch looked up in awe at the massive white tower that rose to the sky, "amazing, so tall."

The Duke smiled with great pride. "It is our pride. When finally peace was declared, the king sent a thousand stonemasons north to help us rebuild our home. Yet we benefited most from but twenty MiKay stone smiths sent to us from deep within the Truk mountains. It was their plans, and engineering that made this tower possible. "

Dimi craned her neck and peered up… the white stone almost glistened catching the last rays of the day.

531

"When the towers fell I the Clansmen the use of our Northern towers." The Duke continued. "From there they can see up the valley to the first bend and shouldered pass of the Tie Rei. When we enter, we will pass through to the Northern hall where the men who are at risk will gather for the 'black watch'. Stephan is always there during the watch."

The captain turned to Etch and spoke softly as the Duke approached the two clansmen guards and made small talk. "When you enter, stay by our side and stray not far. We will talk and sit with the head clansman Stephan Douglas. It was he that answered the MiKay horns first, and it was HE that convinced the other clans to help our lord return to save our town and his wife. Stephan is a personable man that will speak freely with you but never forget that he rules all the Northern clans. He is seen as a king among his people and others in the room will expect him treated in the same manner as you have Duke Rudolf. Also, it is best you know that his wife was the Duchess' closest friend and that Stephan's love of his wife Wendy was the stuff that legends are based on." With his last words he looked away as a sad memory and interrupted his line of thought.

The Duke laughter brought Etch's and Dimi's attention forward to look as Duke Rudolf slapped a clansman on the back. "Well said my good man. Well said. Now if you would be so kind, I would sorely like to introduce your good leader to two people that have come to us from the south bringing news." He then turned to Dimi and Etch and motioned them forward.

The two clansmen looked Etch over but their eyes, once connecting with Dimi did not come off her. She smiled back at them but neither flinched, "What manner of creature have we here?" One of the clansmen said. He then looked up at the Duke. "You know of course that we just returned and that Sar Douglas sits 'the black watch'?"

"We expected as much." The captain replied to the two. "I will vouch for both of these two." He said nodding to Dimi and Etch. "She is no fell creature and is harmless."

Dimi took a step forward her hand went to her hip to seek out her dagger in a threatening gesture, but then it dropped as she recalled having to leave it behind at a station before meeting the captain. Etch put his hand on her shoulder not so much to hold her back, but rather to ensure she wouldn't do or say anything that might then impact their ability to see the head of the clansmen.

"I wouldn't go and say 'harmless'." Etch said chuckling. "For I have seen her bring down fell beasts herself single handed." He then looked over and patted her back in a companion like way. "But she will not harm any of your clansmen of that I give you my word as well."

The second clansman guard laughed, "Perhaps creatures of the south. Well I fear not she might hurt a clansman, I fear more for the waif's safety within… the black watch is not something we enjoy others to watch, and it is no place for a child."

Etch took a step forward and looked the second clansmen in the eye. "She is many times your own age and is much more than meets the eye. Unless you have a desire to spend the night bent over holding your jewels as you puke into a bucket, I would suggest you choose your words carefully when around Dimi."

The clansman both looked over to Dimi who gave them an evil knowing look back at them. "Eye, pass then. You have been warned." The first guard said a moment later. "We have warned you of the watch, and once within…. NO man or woman exits without Sar Stephan saying so."

The clansman looked over to the Duke who in turn nodded his agreement. "Then enter." Both clansmen then turned and opened the double wooden doors. They groaned and Dimi looked at Etch in a foreboding way.

Captain Asnori moved to the front of the group and led them up a winding stair that would suffer only a single man aside passage. They climbed and climbed and climbed, occasionally the captain stopped and paused allowing the Duke who followed him a moment or two to catch his breath.

Five times they passed other floors and halls that led into the tower, and still they climbed until the end of the stairs was reached ending as it opened up into a small hallway, which again was guarded by two clansmen. Behind them stood a spectacular door its dark cherry wood was interlaced and inlaid with silver runes and writings of the north. Two massive iron bolts were securely keeping it closed, locking all those beyond the door – in.

The Duke, now being severely winded walked to the two guards who barred the group's way. The captain seeing that the Duke was having problems breathing, let alone speaking, spoke aloud for his lord. "We seek the council of Sar Stephan."

"The Black Watch has started." The one guard said defiantly. "You may all go forward, but know that none may exit the room without his approval." He then rested his hand on the hilt of his sword. He looked over to the Duke. Although confident, the clansman obviously seemed apprehensive about what he was about to say next. "If you try to leave before obtaining his approval, even your life good Lord, will be forfeit. It is for the greater good of the city and all within."

Dimi looked over to Etch and pointed to the clansman's hilt… for it too was inlaid with silver. Etch nodded as he started realizing the implications.

"We know," replied the Duke finally having regained his composure, "and approve."

"Then enter." The clansman said. He then turned and knocked hard on the door. Muffle sounds from behind the door could be heard followed by a clear command voice that demanded them to enter. The two clansmen pulled back the two massive bolts and heaved on the heavy door opening it. The captain strode forward, followed by the Duke. Etch paused a moment and then followed in with Dimi close behind.

The top tower room was massive room and the group halted mid stride into the room as all the eyes of twenty or more men and six large black war dogs turned to look at them. The room's silence was quickly consumed as the men turned away from the visitors and started talking among themselves in quiet voices. Occasionally the room echoed with a nervous laugh. The dogs, all sat amidst the group by their feet – save the largest one which sat atop the feet of a man who sat on a large, high back chair.

The Duke motioned that the others should follow him as he wound his way around two standing groups of men to the clansman in the chair by the wall. The bent in sides of the high back chair obscured the man from view as they drew closer.

Dimi's nose wrinkled and her eyes widened as she scanned the room. "Have you seen the walls?" Dimi said pulling close to Etch and tugging on his sleeve.

Etch looked around the sides of the room. The walls were of the same stone as the outside of the tower and should have been all gleaming back in the same shocking white colour. However, all over the walls were mottled spots and splashes. Most of the spots were a dark brown, but several were still red. Etch slipped slightly but regained his foot. He looked down at the puddle he had just stepped in. "Blood" he said casually to Dimi.

"The black watch," Dimi whispered to Etch as they walked behind Duke Rudolf and Captain Asnori across the large room. "Do you know what it is?"

"I am getting the general idea." Etch whispered back to her.

"They wait to see who is infected by bite from Weer." Dimi paused a second as they rounded another group of clansmen and another large black war dog. The dog followed them with its eyes, but the clansmen didn't interrupt their conversation. The men within the room all looked nervous as if they were biding their time for some great event. "When Detros' grin is in the sky all those infected will show signs…"

AS the Duke crossed the last few steps across the room a man sitting in a chair across from Stephan stood. Stephan's head peeped round the chair and then he too rose to his feet, the dog at his feet moving only slightly to let him stand. Stephan stepped forward smiling taking Duke Rudolf's hands within his and shook it firmly. "My good Duke Rudolf what brings up these tall stairs? You had but to send word and I would have run down to see you and your dear wife."

Duke Rudolf took Stephan's hands in his and shook them. They were slender and clean a burn crossed the back of his right hand yet the clansman showed no signs of hesitation to the handshake. "We are sorry to disturb you Stephan." The Duke started and then motioned to his captain. "Asnori informed me you were standing watch." He then motioned back to Etch and Dimi. "And I thought it best to bring these two to meet you as soon as possible for they are anxious to continue north to the towers."

Stephan motioned to the man standing behind him. "Allain, go fetch three more chairs for the Duke and his party." He then turned and motioned the Duke to take the chair that the clansman had just vacated. Etch, Dimi and Asnori the captain stood to each side of the Duke as he sat down. Stephan then returned to his own seat and the massive black dog huddled close and lay down once again atop his feet. Allain a moment later returned with one of the chairs and then went again in search for others.

Stephan's eyebrows rose at the comment, but his smile never lessoned. "North to the towers are you going?" He said nodding his direction to the window by which he sat. "Any idea on the manner of beast resides in the hills north of here?" He looked at Dimi, his smiling eyes looked back at her in particular. "Fiercer things then you can even imagine live north of here."

Dimi without a hesitation smiled back at the clansmen. "Oh I don't know." She started in a sarcastic note. "I can imagine quite the beast these days, having come across blood ferrets the size of horses, and of course… having known Sarta Pensor for these last few hundred years."

With her last words the room again went still as all eyes once again turned to her. Stephan, smile still on, didn't flinch nor pause although his voice dropped down a tone or two in volume.

"We call her the blood witch in these here parts. A few others…" he went on looking to his men within the room who now were resuming their conversation. "Have other choice words for her which I would not say in the presence of a lady."

"How came you by the witch?" He asked. "The more we know of her the better our ability to see her within a grave." His smile but briefly flickered as a sense of deep hate crossed his brows.

As Allain brought forth another chair Etch sat and Captain Asnori motioned to the clansman that he preferred to stand. Stephan looked at Allain and motioned that he preferred to continue the conversation without him. Allain nodded politely to the others and went off to talk to a group of men standing nearby.

"Before we start." Etch asked curiously. "I get from the look of the room the general idea of the watch… but"

Sar Douglas laughed lightly and looked over to the Duke. "Oh that is good my friend. Invite them in, give them a warning I am sure, but let me do the full explaining eh?" He paused and then his eyebrows rose showing more understanding. "Or is it my good friend. That you hope the full force of a visual education is in order?"

He then turned and looked back at Etch and then Dimi a smile flickered across his face and disappeared. "All these brave men and eighty more rode north. And what fun we had when we found thirteen Wogs in a thicket west of the river. It was a good ambush and bloody good fun and not a scratch we had." He looked around. "But then from the woods did come their bitch of a mom and another of her litters. We lost two men right then, Shawn and his brother Timothy. They were good men, both now gone to stand beside their father."

Stephan continued. "We speared her pups right quick, but she was a feisty one this bitch from hell." Stephan motioned around. "Srento was pulled down off his mount by a Wog and then the bitch herself was at him. He would have fallen right then had not my brother Allain jumped down from his mount and fought the bitch with spear and shield."

537

Stephan continued after glancing and nodding at Allain. He then looked over to Dimi again as if he had to convince her of some greater danger of the north. "The Weer bit his shield in two. Hard wood with iron bands, inlaid with silver is as our ways. The Weer's grabbed it in its mouth, bit down and shattered his shield." He smiled back at Dimi proudly. "But as the shards of the shield broke and pierced Allains arm and hand he pierced the bitch's lungs with his silver tipped spear."

There was another banging on the door and then it opened. Two larger clansmen came in carrying a large barrel. "The brandy is here." One yelled out and the men within the room cheered... non-louder than Srento by the eastern wall.

A servant entered behind the men carrying pewter steins draped up and over him, tied together with string. He unloosed the steins from around him, placed them on the ground and darted quickly out of the room. A few within the room laughed as the man left in all haste.

The massive war dog atop Stephan's feet rose and meandered to the group of men on the eastern wall and the few within the room watched it walk. It sat down and they lay its head down on the floor before the group, as if waiting and watching for something.

"Massive dog you have there." Etch said admiring the animal. "Weird, typically in larger groups dogs like that act nervous.... they typically don't do well mingling in with larger groups of humans."

Stephan smiled as he watched the animal move. "Modo's no man's dog. They are like our brothers to each of us, and they are fearless." He then laughed a little. "And good company to warm one's feet on a winter night." He then laughed again a little and then his smile faded a moment. "They really come in handy going north. They can also smell out the Wogs and can keep them from you for the moments that will save your life. They don't get affected like we do if they get bit too."

Dimi turned from her seat and watched the animal slowly walk through and around the room as if it was searching something. It walked slow, its massive body slightly undulating as it strode. Ripples of power waved under its dark black short haired coat. Another dog in the room rose as if in reply to Modo's walk. It too started to meander through the room. And then a third did rise, but its walk was more determined, more direct. Although deathly slow, it walked straight to the group of men surrounding Srento. When the men noticed its approach their conversation momentarily faltered. A clansman who had just refilled his cup hesitated in drinking it, and thinking better handed it Srento who took it with unspoken thanks..

Stephan looked out the window beside him; from behind the glass there was darkness. "Modo is restless. See how Detros is showing his face?" The group by the window looked out the window. The broken face of the second moon peeked over the lower frame of the window as it started to rise to the sky.

"The black watch has begun." Sar Douglas said with a slow and deliberate speech. He then left his chair and walked slowly to the center of the room. His voice rang out clear starting low and then building. "It is dark AND THE FACE OF DETROS DOES SMILE." He said loudly. The clansmen in the room all stood and turned to Stephan. "Wicked is his face." They replied as one in a low tone.

Sar Douglas looked around the room from clansmen to clansman…"So bar the door and let the black watch begin." He then turned and looked at the men in the large room. "And let us show the Duke and his guests how the clansmen of the north fare when facing the devil herself."

There was a loud clang as the doors to the room locked tight…. And a few clansmen purposefully walked apart from others – all the remaining dogs rose to their feet in anticipation to some pending darker moment. Their eyes all appeared to gleam reflecting the torchlight of the room.

Sir Douglas looked over to the clansman Srento whose eyes were nervously darting around the room at the men and dogs. He took a gulp of his brandy and wiped the spilled drops from his lips with the back of his brown leather shirt. He laughed as a man nearby said something, but it was a forced laugh that ended quickly.

Srento's face appeared strained and for a moment there was a flicker of sadness in his eyes when another dog from across the large hall started to meander towards him. A few of his friends took a slow, and attempted polite step back from him – only two of what appeared his closest friends now stood next to them. One was a tall burly man whose blond beard spilled down his face. The beard was tied with a red string in the fashion of the MiKay dwarves. The other man beside him was Stephan's brother Allain… the man that had tried to save him.

The large, bearded clansmen unexpectedly stepped close Srento and gave him a short but strong bear hug and then slapped him hard on his back spilling Srento's drink in the process. The tall bearded man looked down with sorrow, knowing and tears within his eyes. "Ya dad, would be proud had been alive to see you fight." The tall man said in a deep tenor voice." Srento nodded in reply to the gesture as the man then took a step back from his friend.

A moment later the second of the two closest to Srento, Allain, stepped up towards him and and slapped him on his shoulder. Etch and Dimi now noticing just how badly Allain's hands really were. There were massive cuts and bruises on his knuckles and a deep gash across the back of his hand. "You have always fought well…." Allain said pausing, desperately trying to find the right words. "I only wish I was a tad faster with my spear my friend." The young clansmen nodded, but said nothing.

When Allain stepped away from him he laughed again, and then he raised his cup to the others in the room and drained it. "Good brandy." He remarked as the cup lowered. There were a few nods and others still holding mugs raised theirs back in reply.

Srento looked around the room, nodding back to men he knew and had fought beside these last few years. But in between the men stood the dogs, all of which were slowly, deliberately working their way to encircle him. After a moment or two, all his eyes would focus on were the dogs. Their glimmering eyes, and tight drawn mouths captivated him. They were massive beasts, black and foreboding. Quiet as night as their large paws touched lightly on the stone floor. Their mouths were tight shut, but Srento knew that beneath their lips were massive, sharp canines that could rend leather and flesh as easily as his teeth could tear bread.

Someone from his side came forward with another styne of brandy but he shook his head. "No. Thank you." He said to the man without ever loosing the gaze of the largest of the dogs now within but two meters of him.

Sar Douglas stepped forward within arms reach of him and he smiled back courageously.

"They have the scent it appears." Srento said from between clenched teeth while motioning to the dogs that were drawing around him.

Sar Douglas shrugged. "It is far and few between the man that is fully bitten by a Weer and does not turn himself when Detros first draws high within the sky."

He nodded back in reply, still trying to keep a courageous face for his clansmen and for his leader. He then looked up from the dogs and straight into the eyes of Sar Douglas and smiled. "I would follow you to hell and back. You know that right?"

Stephen looked back at the young clansman. Feelings of sorrow and regret fought feelings of pride, knowing and courage in his face. He was about to say something more to the lad, in encouragement and recognition when from his right one of the dogs issued a low guttural growl. He nodded quickly and smiled at the lad. "Good journey." He said and stepped back.

Srento looked around the room, now trying to avoid the gaze of the dogs he sought the friendship of faces he knew. Of courage he sought from other a man standing around him. "When the clansmen once again stand atop the two towers, remember me." He said looking from man to man. Although desperately trying not now to look at the dogs one stepped within a meter of him and growled again. All eyes darted from Srento to the dog, wondering if the lad would run or if he would submit and die bravely. Or if the sickness, the poisoned blood would turn the lad. Several soldiers around now rested their hands on silver handled dirks that hung by their side.

Dimi, now out of her chair standing next to Etch nudged him in the arm. He followed her gaze and noted that two clansmen by the door had picked up short crossbows that had rested against the wall. The winches had already been turned, and upon its shaft rested bolts whose silver tips gleamed.

Srento took a deep breath and then went to one knee and then the other. He set down his cup upon the floor and started to unstring the top two laces of his shirt. There were a few knowing and encouraging nods from within the room as the lad showed his courage.

Stephan still standing within three meters of the lad looked as one of the large black dogs stepped within arms reach of the lad and sniffed him. It mouth opened for the first time as its eyes lit upon the lad. A small drip of saliva fell from its mouth and then it licked his lips. "Don't dally you fool beast." Srento said lifting his eyes and gaze to the ceiling exposing his neck. "FOR THE CLAN." he yelled out. "Now finish it."

Beside Etch and Dimi the Duke's old voice was quiet as from beneath he breath he swore. "Damn Detro's dirty face. I will one day she that witch dead."

Dimi screamed and the dogs dropped as one to their haunches in pain at the sound.

Her voice rang out like the breaking of glass. She shrieked and then men began to drop their cups and put their hands to their ears as the high pitched blast echoed through the massive room. Heads with eyes blazing turned to her at first in disapproval, and then in recognition as they followed her gaze to the wall beside where she sat.

For there, now kneeling upon the floor, hunched over was Stephan's brother and Srento's friend Allain. His face was strained, and teeth clenched. His left hand clutched his stomach as if he had been stabbed as his left arm reached to the floor to steady himself. But at the end of his arm, from beneath his sleave instead of a bloodied and bruised fist there protruded a paw with the black, cat like sharpened claws of a Weer.

Dimi's screech ended as Modo's massive body flew to the air slamming Allain against the wall. Allains' head hit the wall and as it came away drops of blood slid down the white stone. Although dazed, and still in pain his twisted right arm and paw rose and slashed at the massive black dog whose mouth was gapping forward hoping to find Allain's throat. Across the room there was an evil, ominous howl as Srento's lips pulled back horribly wide exposing new massive canines. He head and back arched to the sky and he howled in pain and anger. Every tendon in his neck, every muscle in his face bulged as his arm shot out to either side. The flesh and muscles beneath his shirt and pants twisted and rolled visibly. His chest heaved and extended forward stretching the leathers on his chest until the ties, unable to withstand the pressure pulled apart breaking their knots and bows. A rib stretched chest shot out from beneath his shirt, hair sprouted from it as it grew.

The dog now crouching in front of the clansman Srento leapt forward. With mouth wide open it shot forward looking to tear the soft exposed flesh of his throat. Although the massive animal had been less than a meter away and fully coiled to jump it never made its mark. Instead, the twisted and now fully deformed claw dangling from the massive shoulders of the transforming clansmen slashed powerfully across catching the dog in neck and shoulder smashing it aside and past the clansman.

Two silver tipped bolts shot from the back at the room transfixing Srento in the chest and abdomen. The now half transformed beast howled shaking the very walls and floor. It started to rise as in the background the soldiers by the door frantically started winching their crossbows.

Etch stood up next to Dimi, both felt exposed and naked having had all their weapons stripped from them along their trip to the Duke. They backed away from Allain who now was almost fully transformed into a dauntingly massive beast with elongated snout that ended in sabred canines that protruded from it.

There were yells amidst the crowd of clansmen as they backed away from Allain and Srento. Burly hands pulled forth dirks as others sought unattended swords that had lain nearby by wall or on floor.

As what once was Srento rose two more bolts hit him. One bolt creasing the creature's shoulders deflected and smashed into the wall behind. The other, struck well the creatures throat dropping it to its knees. Then without warning the dogs were upon it tearing, biting and rending flesh from bone.

Dimi pushed Etch aside to gain sight again of Stephan who now strode boldly up to the hunkering form of his brother. A clansman behind him yelled warning as the creature spun and lunged at the clansman captain. But the massive black form of Modo hit the creature mid stride – turning it as both entwined bodies rolled to the side.

Shredded cloths fell from Allain as he rolled entagled with the large black dog. His massively elongated snout snapped in reply to the dog's attack. Modo whelped as the Weer bit down snapping its front leg in two. Blood spilled from the leg as white bone and red tissue spilled out of the broken end of the leg.

A moment later Stephan was above the two animals; a long thin silver blade in his hand. In less time than it would take a person to blink his shoulders were slamming down the the dagger into the exposed hair and bent neck of what once was his brother. No emotion played on his face as he drove the blade down and into the beasts spine.

The creature immediately paralyzed from the neck down crumpled immediately. Sar Douglas left the blade within the creature and pulled back his hand as blood dripped from the wound he had just made.

Stephan looked down at the beast and then reached down and started pulling Modo out from its entanglement with the new, yet now dead, Weer. The dog yelped as it pulled free, but then started licking Stephan's hands as the clansman knelt down and took the large animal's head in his hands.

He stroked the head and looked down at the dog. "Rest, rest my friend, you done well." He said reassuringly to the animal as he petted it. Blood gushed from the animal's leg and momentarily it tried to rise to its feet, but Stephan held his head firmly and hushed it back to rest. In a moment, the dog's heart stopped beating, its life having puddled the floor beneath it.

In all the while, as Stephan sat comforting the dog not a man stirred within the room. As he stood up and gently set the dog's head down on the ground a few other clansmen went over and pulled the other dogs off of the other beast. They came away from the carcas bloodied and the men were careful holding the dog's spiked collar and led them to the guarded door.

Stephan looked over at the questioning guards by the wall and nodded. They promptly opened the door for the clansmen to exit with dogs in tow, obviously intending to clean them off.

Asnori, the captain of Annon Ter looked over at Sar Douglas and then headed towards the doors himself. "I will find someone to help take the bodies away and to help clean this place." He said softly as he passed Stephan.

Duke Rudolf shook his head as he walked up to Stephan. "Such sorry, so heavy is my heart for your loss my good friend." He patted Stephan on the back and both turned to look at Allain, now looking so very different then he had only moments before.

"He was so full of life." Stephan said shaking his head still in disbelief. "I thought his wounds all from the breaking of his shield, or from claw."

"You have said so yourself on many occasions." The Duke added with much emotion within his voice. "Sometimes only the breath of a true Weer is needed over an open wound to infect a man."

"I promised my father I would take care of him." Stephan said looking down still shaking his head. He heaved a sigh and then looked over at another clansman that stood beside him motionless, but with silver dirk out. "My brother is dead; my wife…" He paused, obviously not yet ready to come to grips with thoughts and fears surrounding the disposition of his wife.

Stephan looked down at the bloodied creature before him. "Get this fell beast from my sight." He then turned and walked from the company of men.

North – For friend and country

The knights of Capris busied themselves brushing down their mounts as their sergeants looked on. The cold early winter weather had shut out the sun from view for the last three days. The mass of Montterran horsemen grumbled and moved slowly as the sleet, snow and rain beat down on them chilling them to the bone. The smell of searing sausages wafted through the air making the soldiers of Capris fidget. Although their stomachs roared they knew that not a bite would be taken by any of them until the last of their horses were taken care of. The men and horses of Capris were accustomed to dryer weather having sailed from the dry southern planes. Spirits within their ranks sank that much further as they heard the Terrans in the nearby camp break their evening fast..

It hadn't helped the spirit of the horsemen of Capris to have spent the last three days riding behind the Terran's and their mediocre mounts. They knew that protocol had to be followed and that the Duke Hastor, leader of the horsemen of Capris had acknowledged the sovereignty of Methor Bestinor and as such had agreed that his men would 'follow' the men of Ten Tor.

Needless to say, although the differences were small between the two groups of soldiers there had already been many fights between them. Late in the evening of the previous night after having no success in quieting the fighting that was breaking out along the borders of the two camps Sir Bestos Hastor general of the horsemen of Capris suggested to his counterpart Sir Bruto Gadral of Ten Tor that the Terrans station their horses between the two camps.

Sir Bruto had thought it a sound and unemotional request, up and till the point when Sir Bestos Hastor added in conclusion "His men would far sooner look on the asses of the Tentorian horses, then on the faces of the Terran soldiers."

Atop the largest open hill overlooking both camps Methor Bestinor, Duke of Ten Tor and self now proclaimed king of all Terran lands looked down at both companies of men. He shuddered as a harsh breath from the north assaulted him spraying his face with cold wetness.

Many of the tents from his company were already pulled down, and others were being pulled down as he watched, however, in the valley nearby all the Montteran tents remained up.

"How odd a people." he said to himself looking down. "That they value horse over man."

Methor could 'feel' and 'smell' the tension from the men of Capris as he looked down the hill towards them. He knew that General Bestos Hastor had specifically passed the word that his men should look happy and content, and treat the bad weather lightly to make the men of Capris grumble the more.

"A little competition between armies is a good thing." He said out loud smiling although in his mind he wondered if his general would overstress the relationship.

Barren and stark grey trees sprung up on either shoulder of the large clearing surrounding the Terran soldiers offering little shelter for his troops. A large lance with standard stood up and flapped in the harsh wet wind. The standard measured over a meter and a half, yet its split ends snapped so violently back and forth that the Terran King's new crest on it was almost indiscernible.

The Terran King looked soulfully down at the horsemen of Capris. Rain, sleet and snow had a fast way of sapping the spirit from such a group of otherwise sturdy soldiers and their mounts. He knew the reputation of these men. They had ridden hard before and endured great hardship, but always in warmer, dryer weathers. Facing the wet cold of the eastern lands was unusual for them. Although hardy they were showing the wear.

Squire Aaron Murdoc approached Methor from behind. He had spent most of the night drying out the King's leathers and had dried and oiled the armour but as he approached from behind, he noted that his lord was already drenched. In his hands he had a less stylish but more practical riding robe for his lord. It wasn't embroidered with the King's new crest, but it was heavier and at least dry.

"Your Grace." Squire Aaron Murdoc started as he came close to his king.

Methor turned and nodded to his squire. "Lovely day." He said looking up at the sky. "I wonder when it will finally let up? For three days now it has been this way – what a way to start a march."

"Yes, your grace." Aaron paused as he walked to Methor's side and held up the robe he had brought. "I have another riding robe for you my grace." He said hopefully. "It is thick and dry."

Methor looked at the robe the lad was holding but shook his head speaking with a noble tongue. "None of my nor Duke Karathor's men have second dry robes." He started. "I will keep to what I have."

Aaron didn't want to give up, but knew he had to approach the subject in an indirect and possibly not to honest way in order to convince his king to put on the dryer cloak. "I understand that the horsemen of Capris bring second blankets for their mounts. Plus, I understand that Duke Karathor has several riding robes – one to match each colour of blanket he uses for his mount."

King Methor Bestinor looked at his squire and the dry robe he held. Another draft of rain and snow drenched wind hit him and pierced his armour swifter than any arrow or sword ever would. He stifled a desire to let his teeth chatter and nodded to his squire.

Aaron, happy with the success of his minor mission smiled and reached up and pulled the strings at the King's throat that held fast the robe. Before it could fall to the ground he grabbed it with one hand and threw it over his shoulder. He cringed as the moisture sluiced off the robe, traveled down his own back and into his wide brim leather boots. Hesitating only a moment as a result of the uninvited soaker he then quickly draped the plainer grey riding robe over Methor's shoulders and laced it up.

The squire shook his boot trying to ascertain just how much water had traveled from his lord's wet cape, down his back and into his left boot. The added cold was most unwelcome, but Aaron didn't flinch as his movements produced the effect of having more water drop into his boot.

Methor Bestinor turned to look at the young man squinting as water and snow dropped down from the brow of his helmet. Water ran like a river down his pointed nose guard and onto his heavy, square chin. He licked his lips picking up some of the moisture.

"Quiet bunch." Methor stated out loud to Aaron motioning with his hand out to span the riders from Capris.

"Yes." Aaron agreed. "They sure think highly of their horses."

"I hope some of that will rub off on our own men." The King said with a chuckle.

"I heard that last night a few of their knuckles rubbed off on several of the faces of our men." Aaron added glibly.

Methor grumbled. "Ahhhh... Its this weather, give us a day to dry out and we'll all be friends again... but in the mean time I know we can expect some tension. Hmmm." Methor mused. "See if you can spread a rumor among the troops that the Mohen armies are all said to be tented on dry land eating vast amounts of cooked meats and drinking gallons of ale... perhaps we can get our companies of men more focused on the enemy before us then on each other."

Aaron laughed lightly. "I will try. I have a few friends in the troops that would be more than happy to gossip."

Methor nodded and lifted his arms, granting Aaron access to start stringing together the ties just under his arms. "Sir Casten Ferroten treating you well – are you learning under his guidance?"

Methor looked around the camp below them. "Where is he now?"

"Busy inspecting man and mount for as you know Sir Bruto named Sir Casten's company to ride behind you as vanguard."

Aaron smiled broadly as the Duke looked back at him. "I will ride by him in the van. It will be our swords that first strike the Mohen!"

"Indeed." Methor added looking over at the lad wondering how much of a favour he had done the boy by having Sir Casten take the van. "It will also put first amongst the troops in harms way." He retorted cautiously.

Aaron looked up absentmindedly and then glanced back down to the field in front of them. "Even the horses are quiet." He added. "They too feel that we are getting closer."

"Still a few days ride from the hills." Answered Methos looking northward. "Down the hills well east of Par Tor ... and then from there the planes of Annon Ter."

"Too bad we don't have time to stop in Par Tor for a dry night's sleep." Aaron lamented.

"Count Marrow Bissrod of Par Tor did not respond well to me saying he had already lost many men having sent then north when Plan Ter was besieged." King Methor started with a stern tone in his voice. "It would lengthen our ride by half a day which I do not know if we have. I have sent him word asking for aid, with luck he will send some... if not."

Down below them the knights of were starting to take down their tents. A few Terran squires having completed the grooming were leading the horses to them. The horses moved methodically along their coat's glistening with moisture from the light snow that continued to fall.

Methos pointed to the horses. "Watch their feet. The ground is cold, but soft yet. It will be hard riding."

Aaron stayed quiet and shifted to the Duke's other side and started fastening the long leather ties of Methor's armour ensuring a snug fit so the wet leathers would rub less.

"Have you seen Sir Bruto yet?" Methor asked Squire Aaron Murdoc as the lad started lacing up the second set of leathers on his sides.

551

"Yes, he was down by the horses already when I rose." Aaron started. "He brought with him several knights under our 2nd, Sir Lucient Barronst. Sir Lucient sure likes to yell! The man was yelling at the squires and making them jump. Both were very concerned that the mounts had not had sufficient cover for the night and now were far to wet for good."

"Yes, foul for man AND beast." Methor added once again looking up to the sky with a prayer of his own.

A man in the field was starting to pull down the lance and standard and was moving it to a mount nearby. The wind grabbed the tip and pulled it forward. The soldier had to hold it fast to ensure it wouldn't slip from his hands and strike the ground — something that the soldiers would believe as being an ill omen. Several soldiers nearby turned anxiously to watch the man in his struggle.

Methos cringed thinking that if the flag hit the ground, given how wet it was, it would surely stain it making all around know that it had fallen. "Good man." He yelled out and down to the man as he noted the soldier grabbing the lance hard and keeping it above the ground. Another ran to him and together the carried the standard to where they could secure it to a mount.

Aaron bent to one knee and laced up Methor's greaves. The sides of it were muddy and Aaron used his hands to clean them as best he could. Occasionally, he held his hand to his mouth and blew on them trying to ensure they didn't stiffen with cold. After he finished dressing Methor, he would still need to get back to his small tent and dress himself, and then pull down his tent... Aaron moved as fast as he could, but his hands were slow with cold.

Methor noticing the lad's discomfort attempted to encourage him. "We have now the planes before us.... And possibly even a night within Plan Ter."

Aaron nodded and smiled inwardly. "That would be nice.... A chance to dry out." Silently as he finished lacing one and picked up the other.

Methor nodded but said nothing as he turned his head slightly after heard Sir Bestos Hastor, General of the Army of Capris, approached from around the backside of their tent.

Sir Hastor's helm was off and his long hair was matted and dark with rain. His interlaced leather armour however, appeared strangely light brown as if in some manner it had not been soaked through.

Methor noted that man was alone, which irked him greatly. He should have been escorted in by his guards. He was an ally but Methor still didn't feel entirely at ease with the man.

Aaron, noting the approach of the general looked up enough that Methor could turn to the man.

"Good morning Sir Hastor." Methor said as the general approached. "How fare the Montterran Company, and your wonderful mounts?" Methor turned motioning to the general's horses. "Never have I seen such fine horses!"

Methor noted the general and knight crack a smile for just the quickest moment, before it went back to his normal stern face. As Sir Hastor bowed his head in acknowledgement to the Terran King his hair spilled up and over his shoulders. "Hail and well met, King of Terran." came his cold, soldierly reply.

With a flick of his head Sir Hastor sent the strands of hair that had fallen forward, back again. A long strand of braided hair flicked like a whip and headed to slap against his back. The hair had been braided with red and white string that Methor knew was tied round a strand or two of the knight's horses main.

Methor admired Sir Hastor's armour. His armour was more leather then metal. Long strands of treated and hardened leather were interlaced and occasionally a circle of metal was tied to it. It was several layers thick, yet very flexible and likely much lighter then mail. Long strands of colourful string were laced in consistent patters in and through several of the metal hoops.

"I have seen the colored string these last few days, but am after watching your soldiers more confused then when I first noticed them." Started Methor as he looked at the general's armour. "I thought they might represent the families within your lands, for I noted that some shared the same colors, but after hearing their names my guess was proved in error."

The General of Capris smiled and nodded as he looked down at the coloured cords on his chest. "Each colour tied to the hair represents the lineage of the horse we ride. We can trace the lineage of our horses back fifty or more generations with these colour combinations."

The general reached down and pulled forth one strand of the intertwined colour cord. "Note, the top tied strand at the ends are the longest. Two colors, red and green are intertwined. Then each above it are tied smaller, and different colors run up to the head."

"Many of the horses we ride in our company come from the same lineages, thus many men wear proudly the same colors believing their own horse best." The general let drop his own strands. "The strands also represent the stables the horses are from. If you see any that are wound green and blue at the top – they come from my own stables."

"That's half of them." Aaron blurted out, as he looked up started at the general. The general nodded and winked at the lad in reply but then became more serious. "Your grace might I ask a favour of you?"

Methor looked at the general in surprise. "Depends Sir Bestos Hastor." he replied quickly. "Is it something you have already asked my own general Sir Gadral, and or does this request come from your own Duke?"

General Bestos looked back with obvious discomfort as he came to stand before the King of Terran without his own Duke present. "Duke Karathor knows not that I am here." He started as he shifted his weight uncomfortably from one foot to the other. "And I have spoken to Sir Bruto."

"Go on then. I can see in your eyes that something distresses you. Out with it." Methor said with a light voice hoping to set the man more at ease. "After all, we ride as allies in this.. this." Methor looked up at the drizzling sky. "Wet cold land and march against a common foe. We will soon stand shoulder to shoulder in battle and we must trust each other." General Bestos Hastor looked back and nodded in agreement. "It is of the horses I would speak to you this morning before we ride." added the general. Once again his face was stern and soldierly. "My men see how your mounts are treated, and although most are not well bred it is still an effrontery to them that horses not be sheltered or fully dried before a ride."

Methor looked back at the general not quite sure how to respond. "What is it that you ask of me?"

"This tension between our men is not healthy." Sir Hastor started anxiously trying to spit out his proposal. "All I ask is that Sir Bruto insist that his lieutenants order their men to tend to the horses. If they need guidance some of my men would be more than willing to work with them to show them the many techniques we have learned to ensure the health of a horse."

"I don't see the harm in it." Methor replied slowly.

"Aaron." Methor turned to the squire. "Go find the Sir Bruto Gadral." He then turned back to Sir Hastor. "Consider it done. There is no harm done to increase our efforts in the care of our mounts and keeping the men busy will keep them also warm and give them less time to grumble."

The General of Capris nodded and smiled in reply. "Thank you my grace." He then turned and walked away quickly.

Methor smiled noting the general's haste – 'it's almost as if he doesn't want to be here when my general returns.' thought Methor as he chuckled to himself. But his smirk dimmed as he speculated on how his own general would reply to such a command. He knew Sir Bruto Gadral had little respect for most beasts and thought of them as no more than a tool of the trade.

A moment later as he watched Sir Bestos Hastor wind his way down the hill towards his men he noted his own general Sir Bruto Gadral climbing the hill in front of him with Aaron in tow.

"Lovely day my Grace." Sir Bestos said in his harsh, throaty voice as he drew near.

"IF only it let up for a day." King Methor Bestinor replied looking again to the heavens only to feel icy water sluice off his helmet and down his back. He cringed and then looked at his general who was now but a few meters from him. "What news from our scouts?"

"We must make all haste." Sir Bruto Gadral replied and turned to motion to the North. "Our first riders have just returned. The Mohen Company is well prepared. Their seig engines stand tall for us to see on the planes. They will likely attack within a day or two and we are still two days hard ride from the lower planes. We do not have the time to dally."

"How many strong?" King Methor asked glancing around ensuring few were within earshot.

General Gadral signed, "Ten thousand or more." He said in a low voice. "Well armed, seasoned troops. Their knights ride with full plate. Our men's lances will find it hard to pierce them, and will have to hope that the horsemen of Capris can send their arrows at joints between armour."

The king of Terran's mail jingled as he shook his head. "Has Duke Hastor any news of Duke Sirthinor? Is there any chance the Duke of Sieren will march his men north?"

Sir Gadral laughed. "Duke Sirthinor sits contently atop his treasures in the Cliff mines. Duke Hastor is fit to be tied. It appears as if the riders he sent to speak with the Duke of Sieren have not returned."

King Methor looked incredulously at his General and then shook his head in disbelief. "So. All of work and scheming comes to nothing. All of our waiting and diplomacy only to have San Ter and the mines slip from between our fingers. That the city did not fall to an old foe, but was 'given' to what was to be a new 'friend'." King Methor shook his head in utter disbelief.

"Unbelievable." General Gadral said after a long moment's pause. "Does Sindor not understand how precarious his perch is? That should we fail his head will be piked by Terran, Mohen and now Montterrans alike? Surely he must fear his King?"

"A large gamble for a larger prize." Methor said in a low exhausted tone. "King Roehn's forces have marched either to defend his north from Tock, or are with us or within Terran Add to defend against the Mohen forces moving west. He will not dally by asking the Duke of Capris to war with Sirthinor, even if Hastor would like that best."

"And Sirthinor hopes that we will be too occupied with the Mohen to stop and dispute his act." The general added. "If we win, we will be so weak that we will not be able to thereafter storm the massive gates of San Ter. But is he so stupid to forget what we ride north to face – that the Mohen forces are moving west?"

Methor Bestinor's eyes narrowed and he shook his head as realization came to him. "Sirthinor is one slippery seal it seems and smarter than you give him credit for. If general Kikiltoe Mariard, bastard son of the emperor, is indeed acting along as we suspect – with desires to rule this land. If he succeeds us and our forces are crushed then Sirthinor will sue for peace and bend his knee proclaiming Mariard as ruler of Terran lands."

"With San Ter and the wealth of the Cliff Mines." King Methor continued. "Mariard would be a fool to turn Sirthinor down. If General Mariard controlled the Terran Add, country's crossroads, and the Cliff Mines which is the country's purse he could rule this land."

"He would be the next King." General Gadral concluded.

"If Mariard through this act brings the revenues of our lands to the empire then his father MiHinDor Perrilos the Fourth..." Methor continued after a choked laugh. "MiHinDor would pat the lad on his back, give him a great parade."

"Who knows?" Methor continued. "He might gain such favour from MiHinDor that he is named as his successor. Goodness knows – MiHinDor's eldest son Paxton Perrilos hasn't earned the right to rule the Mohen Empire."

"Duke Sirthinor hopes then that we will fail?" The General answered with a rhetorical question. "If the Mohen General crushes our forces, and if he takes the capital Sirthinor will bend knee to Mariard and hope to be protected later by him."

"We must head then north and east to see if Count Marrow Bissrod as you suggested from the start." King Methor added with a note of pessimism. "I do hope the Count hospitable and that he has men to spare us."

The general nodded approvingly. "More now so than ever we must beg what men of arms we can. We must take whatever means is necessary to secure more forces or we are lost. Our only hope is to sting Mariard so hard that he looses heart and returns home. Then we can deal with Sirthinor… with Hastor's and King Roehn's help."

"Our only hope is to turn them here." King Methor agreed, however, his voice showed strain and concern, "Ten thousand or more Mohen. How many can we hope to get in Par Tor?" He asked his general.

Sir Bruto Gadral shrugged, "With luck, four or five hundred knights. The Count was not very forthcoming with information. He had sent many of his men north when PlanTer was attacked. And we do not have a full count of what General Kikiltoe Mariard has left of his forces after seiging Plan Ter."

"If Terran Add falls before we arrive." Sir Bruto continued. "We will not be able to move Mariard from that seat of power to easily."

"I agree, to stop them here appears the only answer to this riddle." King Methor agreed.

"But for our small army, our only chance is to catch Mariard with his pants down." The king looked down at their men and then at the riders of Capris.

"Surprise, and speed must be our allies." The general continued enthusiastically. "You should send Duke Karathor and his cousin Sir Bestos Hastor apart from us – north and west. Let us ride in all haste to Par Tor and get what crossbowmen we can, then on the eve of the next day as the sun has set let us attack and send the emperor's bastard son back to his mother's teat."

Methor Bestinor's eyes went wide at the remark and he smiled with renewed hope. "It will be a long hard ride across the plain to surprise the Mohen." He added. "And dividing our forces? Should we not break way through General Mariard's men and protect ourselves within the walls of our capital?"

"To what end?" Disagreed the general. "The Montteran riders would be useless within – General Mariard would starve us while he takes Par Tor and perhaps marches to our own city…. It would secure his place in our land. He heads west straight for Terran Add, he knows if he can hold the capital the crossroads of our empire then San Ter and all the other lords will eventually bend knee to him."

"I will talk with Duke Karthor." Methor finally said looking back at the general. "I doubt he has any desire to hide within the walls of a foreign capital… and I get the feeling that General Hastor prefers to ride apart from us anyway."

Sir Bruto laughed, the chains of his armour bounced lightly as his chest heaved. "Damn horsemen." He said with a low voice so not to be overheard. "If we ride two more days with them I might have the kill the man myself."

King Methor laughed back feeling the camaraderie of his long and dear friendship with the general pierce the cold he felt in his bones. "Par Tor it is then – and then north to Terran Add across the planes in the darkness of the following night."

"Prepare our men General." King Methor said dismissing his friend and confidant. He then turned to Aaron. "Let us go and find the good Duke of Capris and tell him of our plan."

The scheme is set
with black and blood

In the morning Etch felt as if his eyes were going to explode. He had spent, if he recalled correctly, much of the early hours of the morning laying face down over a privy hole retching. He had puked so hard, and so many times dryly that he had thought his eyes were going to pop out of his head. His entire body hurt.

Etch looked up, the room was strange. He had no idea what chambers he was in, or how he had gotten there. He was still fully clothed but lay now upon a soft bed. He looked over and a pitcher of water was there and a mug. Groaning, he reached over and with shaking hands poured himself a mug full and started to drink heavily.

Etch sputtered and some of the water splashed down the front of his cloths soaking him. The cold water that soaked through his linen top tingled as it hit his skin sending shivers through him. Etch peered into the mug. The water was cold and fresh, but something had been mixed in to it that tasted bitter. He picked the pitcher back up and looked into it noting a twisted bunch of herbs were sitting at the bottom of the container. As he was about to reach in to the pitcher a knock came at his door.

Etch cleared his throat, it had been ripped raw from his yakking. "Come." Was all he could finally say out loud. It was more of a squeak then anything but the door swung open.

Dimi strode in smiling at Etch. "Drink it all." She said motioning towards the pitcher as she approached the bed. "We are to have a late lunch with the Duke, and Sar Douglas in an hour." Dimi wrinkled her nose at him. "Your saddle bag is by the side of the bed. Take off what you have on now, I will see if they can be washed… my my, look at your eyes!" Dimi giggled and pointed at Etch.

"What is wrong with my eyes?" Etch asked with croaking voice.

"You must have burst all the blood vessels within them with all that throwing up you did last night and this morning." Dimi giggled. "It looks like someone pummelled you good!"

Etch reached up to rub his eyes with the back of his arm as his hands still clenched the mug and pitcher.

Dimi stepped lively up to him and pulled his arm down. "Don't do that, it will only get worse. Dimi reached down and grabbed part of the linen blanket and pulled it up and dipped a bunched up corner into the pitcher in Etch's hand then dabbed the wet cloth on his eyes.

"Just leave them be." Dimi said chiding him in her youth full voice. "Splash water on them if they are sore... Now drink up."

Dimi pushed Etch's mug clenched hand up to his mouth. Etch took a long hard swallow and grimaced at the taste.

"Does all of your medicine have to taste so foul?" He groaned as he fell backwards onto the bed. He kept the mug and pitcher upright nestled beside his waist. "I want to die, just let me die or lie here until I do. What did I do to deserve this?"

Dimi laughed. "After the black watch you and the good Duke convinced Stephan to drink a keg or two of Northern Winter Wine. You deserve every pain you have, you earned it last night."

"I don't remember much beyond you not wanting to offend the Duke so you didn't refuse the first few rounds, but made me drink them." Etch moaned as he lay back on the bed resting his aching head against the soft down filled pillow. "This pillow even hurts."

"They were small shots and I wasn't feeling like drinking. Anyway, no time to sleep." Dimi said as she started to prod him. She picked up one of his boots and marched over to the bed and started trying in vain to put them on him. "Get changed." She finally yelled at him in frustration.

Etch rose, but it took more than an hour to get his boots on. Dimi had to shave him herself, for his hands shook and she worried he might cut his own throat with his trembling appendages.

Finally with Dimi supporting him they strode out together arm in arm down the stairs and across the courtyard to the inner keep where the Duke and Sir Douglas waited for them. Both were drinking beer from tall pewter steins.

Sir Douglas turned to the door as Etch and Dimi walked in and smiled and he attempted to rise from his chair but then thought better of it and remained seated. Instead he rose his mug in welcome.

"Welcome. Our host has set another fine feast before us!" Stephan said motioning to the food in front of them. "But we have yet to eat a bite, thinking more to quell the hammer in our heads."

The thought of drinking alcohol made Etch's stomach do a back flip and Dimi's arm came up to steady his step as they approached the long table.

She helped him round the end and seated him next to Stephan and then poured him a tall glass of the ale. Handing it to him she coaxed him to drink. "Drink up. We don't have time to spend this day laying about."

The Duchess strode in from the other end of the room. She wore a soft brown velvet morning gown. She sat down next to her husband who shied away from her gaze. Flustered she groaned out loud and wagged her finger in his face "You are old enough to know better!" She yelled pointing her finger."

"Not so loud, I beg of you he replied and then promptly raised his stein to his lips and drank deeply.

"Arrrr." She replied shaking her head and then motioning Dimi to come round the table and sit by her. "You seem less the worse for wear." She said as Dimi sat down.

The Duchess gave the Duke a harsh look and then turned back to Dimi. "He drinks far too much, but I tolerate it… for he is old and the nights are cold. But Winter Wine is a potent drink for those unaccustomed to it."

Dimi brought her feet under her and stood on the chair and reached for the plate of red cheese and promptly started filling her plate with it. She glanced at the Duchess who smiled back encouragingly at her. "Please eat, eat."

The Duchess then looked at the men at the table. "For it is unlikely any other here will enjoy this feast."

Dimi sat back down at the table, though it was high coming almost to her neck. She pulled her plate closer and yanked a large piece of cheese from it and began to nibble on it.

"I did not feel like drinking. And the men became drunk very quickly." Dimi added looking over at Etch.

"She didn't feel like drinking, so instead, she made me consume all she wouldn't." Etch groaned laying his head onto the table. "The cold of this table feels good on my face." He said with a dry raspy voice.

The Duke with a surprised look upon his face glanced over at Dimi and then his wife just in time to see her punch him in the arm. "I swear dear…. I didn't know." He said as he pulled back a little from her reach.

The Duchess shook her head and then looked over apologetically to Dimi. "I am so very sorry my dear." She glanced evily back at her husband. "It takes years of practice to hold as much Winter Wine as he can." She then smiled at Dimi. "And it is not much fun to be in the company of drunk men. Had I known you still up after the watch I should have sent for you, you could have enjoyed much better company."

Dimi shrugged not overly concerned as she continued to eat. "No matter," she replied simply. "They hurt themselves more than I ever could have for their vulgarity." Dimi said and then giggled. The Duchess laughed politely in reply but still gave her husband an evil look once again. Duke Rudolf however was now oblivious to her as he drank down another ale.

"So what are your plans now my dear?" The Duchess asked looking over at Dimi. "After what you both witnessed last night, and what our good friend Stephan has told you – what do you now intend to do?"

"We go north this very night." Dimi said looking over at Etch, "Once his head is back on his shoulders."

"Did my husband not talk you out of it then?" The Duchess asked incredulously. She then looked over at her husband and hit him again in the arm. He winced and then reached for another pitcher of ale.

"It was your husband and Stephan that hatched the plan." Dimi said smiling back, "Before completing their fist keg." Then added, "Sounds like a good plan to me… for it involves killing the witch."

"Did my husband not tell you that our own men with many Clansmen left our gates to help his sister in Annon Ter." The duchess started. Her voice rose to accompany her anxiety. "We lost all those men to Weer, Wog and Tock."

Dimi nodded and then shrugged off the comment.

"Did Stephan tell you what number and manner of Weer and Wog lie directly north of here and within the very castles of Tie Rei? Did you not see your fill of what but one of those beasts can do to a man?" The Duchess looked at Dimi her eyes wide in disbelief.

Dimi stopped her nibbling and looked back at the Duchess. "He did, and I too saw with my own eyes. But more is the reason to kill the witch."

The Duchess shook her head and bit her lip. She started to say something but stifled the comment. Frustration built within her eyes and then fear and then finally sorrow as she looked at Dimi. "I wish you the best." The Duchess Elizabe Ygor tried to put on her more courtly expression, but something inside her broke. A small tear appeared at the corner of her eye. "Everyone that goes north dies." Elizabe paused trying to collect herself again. She smiled a sad smile. "I wish you the best." She said and then shaking her head she rose from her chair and started to leave the room.

Before Elizabe reached the door she turned and looked at Dimi. "If there is anything you need… she looked over at her husband. Rudolf will get for you." She then turned sadly and left the room

"She grieves yet for our son Terris. Hope vanishes as each day passes and he does not return. Although we must always hope, this place.. And what we have seen bleeds that hope."

Duke Rudolf paused a moment in grief and reflection. "Perhaps I was too drunk to think straight last night." The Duke added after a long moment of silence. "Perhaps it is best if you do not go." He looked at Dimi, there are things Stephan said last night after you left… there are things worse than Weer at Tie Rei."

Dimi looked from the Duke back over to Stephan who now sat nodding and looking into his beer.

"What does he talk of?" Dimi asked Stephan as he looked up.

"Spiders. Big, hair spiders." Stephan said slowly.

"I hate spiders." Dimi said softly almost to herself.

Etch's head rose from the table. "Whaaa." He said in a bleary tone. "I thought you were at home with any creature that walked or crawled within the woods."

"These aren't natural…" Stephan said. "And they are big, very big and very hairy and yellow and black."

"How big?" Dimi asked. "As big as a fist, as big as a dog.. as big as a man?"

"They are now larger than a man…. or woman. Or rather, larger than the men and women they once were." Stephan added and then drank some more beer.

Dimi sat motionless looking over at Etch who had rested his head on his arm. She didn't know at any moment if he was awake or asleep. "Go on."

"I had led the clansmen out of the twin towers to rid our area of a large group of Tock our scouts had spotted." Stephan began as he straightened himself up in the chair, "We went west, chasing them.. Not realizing it was a ruse to get us from the castle; to get us from our stronghold."

"The Tock turned." Stephan continued his voice getting stronger. "And their numbers were stronger then we had assumed. When they turned to meet us face on out of the woods also came from either side two hundred or more Wogs." He paused a moment remembering the battle. "We won the battle but at a great cost."

"We limped back home, seeking the warm hearth of the castle in which to warm our battle weary bones. To rest and lick our wounds." Stephan's eyes glazed over as he spoke.

"But Tie Rei had fallen in your absence." Dimi concluded.

Stephan nodded sadly. "The witch was atop the portcullis when we drew near. The drawbridge was raised. The top of the walls were Weer, atop the towers Tock archers. And swarming on the walls of the castle itself….." Stephan added now looking up at Dimi in the eyes. "The walls appeared to move as they were alive, covered with great black and yellow spiders. Their bodies bloated, but their heads and eyes…"

"I would assume the survivors of the siege, if you can call them that." Dimi shook her head. "Sarta cast a spell and turned them to spiders? Her powers grow it seems each and every day it seems. Andarduil has now quite the skilled priest. Did you see her?"

Stephan nodded and looked at Dimi. "Grand, and horrifying both she was. All in white, brilliant white… Her voice boomed down as we approached and from the parapet she threw down the bodies of two of our children…. They were…" Stephan inhaled deeply.

"Dead, flailed alive." Dimi ended his sentence for he could not.

Stephan nodded solemnly. "Several of the fathers in our group ran forward… though I commanded them to stand fast. When within reach of the walls, spiders dropped. They were lightning fast dropping from silk upon the men, biting them and then just as quickly returning up the walls carrying my men."

"And atop the wall the witch laughed…. And laughed and laughed. Then she yelled down that we should return later but that right now she had enough to feed herself and her horde."

"In the next few nights we sent scouts to watch the castle… but we lost too many… Those few that did return said they heard screams from high up the eastern tower. She no longer discards the bodies, they are fed to the many Weer and Wog that patrol outside the castle walls."

"What time of night?" Came Etch's voice from down the table.

"Detros is at its peak, when she feeds." replied Stephan looking back at Etch. "My only hope is that my wife she still holds hostage, perhaps as her last meal."

"You hope that your wife Sarta still holds hostage, perhaps savouring her fear and grief as she is made to endure watching others go to their death." Dimi concluded looking at Stephan with sad eyes.

"I don't know how many within the walls were changed to spiders… many. Likely the very old that appear not to satiate her needs." Stephan paused again. "Yes, I still have hope, though each night I fear that the scream from the tower is hers. How many are left we do not know." Stephan said ending his story as he drained the last of his beer.

"Perhaps we shall see ourselves." Dimi said softly understanding now the sorrow in Stephan's eyes. Dimi shivered. "I just hate spiders."

"When they took the men up the wall, one of my lads put an arrow through one. Its yellow slime fell from it down the wall. The Tock above the wall shot at it then, killing it. A second arrow in its tubular body and it virtually exploded spewing the walls with its innards. My guess is the yellow slime isn't something the Tock wanted atop the walls."

There was a long pause at the table. The Stephan reached over and picked up his mug. Noting it was empty he looked for the pitcher. Etch stirred and pulled his mug forward and drained it in one long slurping pull. He then burped loudly and wiped his face with the back of his sleeve. He blinked twice, and Dimi noted that colour was returning to his face. "Feeling better?"

Etch burped again loudly and the Duke laughed in reply. "Much." He said after a moment.

The Duke cleared his throat. "Well, there you have it all." He said as he looked to Etch and Dimi. "A witch holds TieRei, one that flail you alive and make you enjoy it when she does, plus Tock, and lets not forget the Wogs and the Weer and a multitude of spider spawn…"

"Not just a witch." interjected Dimi. "Sarta Pensor was once a student of a great wizard master known as Kaynor the Brutal. Taught by his hands and then later transformed by his hands in to a succubus to punish her. Her pain has made her quite mad."

"And now it seems." added Etch sarcastically. "Now, it seems very likely she has also been baptized by the Masti and worships the god of shadow and deception - Andarduel."

The Duke suddenly rose to his feet. His body shook as his arm reached out and pointed at Dimi. Spittle flew from his lips as he yelled at her. "Say not that name in this house. Say not that name here!"

Dimi and Etch looked back shocked at the old man, now trembling. A moment passed before the Duke sat down but yet his hands continued to tremble. "Stephan and I have seen the blood priests, first hand…. It was for them that I that went north." His trembling hands reached for another pitcher of ale, which he then preceded to spill into his cup. "It was them that killed the thousands of men that called this region their home…. Their worship is vile, and their god will be forever stained in the blood of the innocent."

Stephan didn't reply but instead closed his eyes and nodded. "Shadows and deception to add to her list of powers. Wonderful…

means we won't be able to trust anything we see… Forests become armies; bridges disappear as you lay your first foot on them… Glimmers of massive trolls send armies running in the wrong direction… Its all so bleak, so very bleak."

Stephan looked over at Dimi. "Have you seen her as of late, do you know what blood rites she has performed, how powerful her shadow magic has become?"

Dimi shook her head. "The last I saw of her was long ago when she froze me in a cave."

"I have seen her as of late." Etch said slowly in a not overly convincing tone.

"Eh?" The Duke said looking over at the man who appeared all of a sudden sober.

"I had a vision." Etch started drawing the gaze of the Duke and Stephan both looking surprised at him.

"After falling into the Ice of TieRei…" Etch continued as he raised his hand to his scalp and rubbed it. "Father Mellon helped Dimi save me from the chills." Etch looked over at Dimi as if asking permission to continue his explanation she nodded in reply and looked over at the Duke and Stephan hoping to gauge their response to Etch's story.

"When she feeds," Etch started with a sigh, "each night she calls a young man or woman forward. And upon the dais sits one of An.." Etch cut the word short when the Duke looked back at him with piercing eyes. "One of 'her' disciples I think, weird, it sort of looked like Sarta but wasn't…. I don't know, it appeared to have very feminine feature."

"What did it look like?" Stephan asked eagerly. "I don't suppose it was small, soft and furry like a bunny?"

Etch laughed and the tension within the room eased. "Not even close." he started. "Very strong, ebony skin, horned, with large tattered wings tipped with talons; a tail too I think. Just looking at it made me think it would have almost predatory cat like reflexes...You know, not big and bulky but sleek and fast."

"More joy." Stephan concluded sarcastically. He looked back to the Duke. "Even the blood priests we killed hadn't the power to open a portal big enough to pull as large as that through. Andarduel's hand is obviously at play here and when gods are involved.. It is never fun."

The Duke closed his eyes and nodded. "Not even a high priestess of the old." He then laughed. It was a cold and old laugh. "Mad tortured souls do well in Andarduel's tutelage. A wizard trained succubus.... Sauce for the goose." The Duke said opening his eyes he looked around the table. "YO MONTOIN".

There was a scuffle by the door and a lad appeared. "Yes my lord." He said as he drew near the Duke.

"Fetch me something harder. Whiskey perhaps... and bring lots of it for I have memories I wish to expunge."

The lad hurried out of the room and Dimi looked searchingly back from the Duke to Stephan.

Dimi stood up onto the seat of the chair. "We care not what aid she has found. Through stealth and cunning she will be laid low. Now Sar Douglas – you said last night that ther is entrance below the rivers."

"I just hope it's not as cold as my last swim." Etch said thinking back.

"Colder." Sar Douglas added. "But not with magic."

"Small relief." Etch added soulfully.

Lord Stephan Doug shivered. "Even getting above the towers will be a challenge, many Weer and Wog now roam the woods and along the river.... But even if we get into the castle.... We will need much luck to find and kill the witch for we know she doesn't sleep much at night."

"I will want to talk with her before we kill her to see if there is any chance that our princess yet lives." Etch added. "And we have committed to the Duke to ask of his son as well."

"Are you **mad**?" Stephan asked looking over at the Duke and then Etch and Dimi. "We will be quite fortunate to get in alive, and extremely fortunate not to be sighted by the hundreds of ghastly spiders that roam the walls and corridors… If we get in and find her we plunge a dagger in her heart and be done with it."

"I am for that plan." Dimi agreed enthusiastically.

Etch shook his head. "NO. We must find out what we can… All this feels linked. Terran Add, the Weer, …"

"It is all linked to Sarta." Dimi said plainly. "Kill her and we stop her madness."

"If we 'can' we will question her." Etch turned to Dimi. "We are going to need a potion or something. Something that will make it hard for her to cast a spell… something to give us time to slow her down…"

"We aren't coming out of there alive then are we?" Stephan said looking over at his determined friends. Neither replied, for their eyes said volumes.

"Oh well." Stephan said standing to go to a table by the wall and retrieve another pitcher of ale. He then went round the table and filled Etch's and then the Duke's mug. "Why not then eh? As long as whatever you hit her with causes her great pain I am for it."

Stephan paused as he rounded the table and approached Dimi offering to fill her glass. He looked over questioningly at Etch. "Visions eh? Grand Drakon himself? Didn't happen to see if we make it out of there?"

Etch laughed, as did Dimi in unison. "No." He replied after a moment or two wiping tears from his eyes. "Didn't see anything of the future…Although I appear to be able to see better at night… if I concentrate real hard."

Stephan tilted back the pitcher and drained the dregs. "Well then." He said after stiffening a belch. "Some some thing at least might help us approach the castle tonight.

Dimi looked up and watched the Etch drink his ale as well. The Duke's page returned to the room carrying a small cask plugged with a thin spout. He put it on the edge of the table and the Duke moved to it and began to fill his mug.

Stephan and Etch both started to their feet, but Dimi called them off their advance. "I don't think so boys. You need to stop and take another nap... we go tonight." She said as she looked sternly at them.

Both Etch and Stephan groaned as they watched the Duke raise his glass and toast them. "To the end of bitter memories." he said and then took a long swig of the strong drink.

Stephan looked at Dimi. "I will need to get a few things ready. We will need good rope, and good oiled leathers."

The Duke put down his drink and then rose to his feet. His balance obviously compromised he steadied himself by leaning a hand on the table. "I can help there." He said proudl to Stephan and then winked at Dimi. "Anything within these walls that is mine that can help you is at your disposal. And I know just one thing that will help" His eyes lit up and he pointed at Stephan. "The black shadow blades..."

"That would be generous." replied the clansman. Dimi looked at Etch who shrugged.

The Duke seeing Etch's puzzled face explained. "We caught two blood priest outside these very walls. It was a nasty fight, for we couldn't tell exactly where they were for they can hide themselves, and also cast glimmers in other locations that look like them. So we had the archers launch arrows by the hundreds... until they reappeared... Each had a black blade on them."

"With it can we do magic?" Etch asked hopefully.... "Disappear into the night?"

The Duke hiccupped and then burped, "Ah, no unfortunately not." The Duke continued steadying himself again on the table. "But the blades are all black so they won't glint in firelight and they are sharp as razors, and very strong but as light as light."

Etch looked back puzzled still wondering why the Duke appeared so excited about a couple of what sounded like ordinary tarnished blades.

"They will be good for your swim and venture to the towers in the dark." The Duke said excitedly. He turned and staggered out to of the room. "I will find them and bring them to you." He then turned and looked at Stephan. "Take what rope you want from the storeroom." He then looked over at Dimi. "Our surgeon has some rather exotic plans up stairs… If you need anything, herb or anything for a potion let me know. I will bring you the keys to the surgery."

"Thanks." Dimi said in reply. "Where is that?"

"Right above us." the Duke added as he spun again to head out of the room.

The ale blurred Etch's mind, and he slid into a daydream wondering what his family was doing while he sat here at this Lord's Table so far from home. 'Rachael would probably love to have visited this place, in the summer. The kids likely were busy chopping wood…or No. The snow would already be likely deep on the mountain. Etch might be out hunting game slowed by the snows and Lys would be knitting by the fire while her Mom cooked..

A blurry vision formed in Etch's mind. Rachel cooking pancakes for the kids, he could almost smell them, and there by the hearth was his son Chad teasing mercilessly his sister Lys. Rachel having enough of Chad's activities finally yelling at him to leave his sister alone. How he missed them so.' A small tremor went through his body as he wondered if he would ever see them again.

Etch reached up and touched the side of his head with his left hand, his temple throbbed.

"Now I remember why I stopped drinking." Etch said out loud rubbing his temples.

Dimi and Sir Douglas all started to laugh as they looked over to him. Etch realizing a little late that he had said the last comment out loud. He smiled and shook his head.

Dimi was the last to stop laughing, her musical voice echoing in the large dining room.

"In for a Nail, in for a Teeth." Sir Douglas said looking down at his silver blade. "There is no half way in this venture as you know. Not for us, nor for those left within the castle – which includes my wife." He said building up the courage from within him.

"The twins are well defended." The Duke said as he came back in the door a moment later holding a large cherry wood box. Atop the box was a large silver key. "I will give you what men I have."

"We must in secret go." Dimi said shifting forward in her seat and resting her little elbows on the table. "Gain access to the castle, capture her alone and unaware. There we can torture her until we find out what we need to…"

The Duke nodded and then tossed the key to Dimi who in a blurr jumped up and caught it. She looked at it and then placed it in her belt. As she jumped Etch noted that Dimi had already restrung her blowgun and pouch upon her leg.

Etch visibly shuddered. "The challenge will be getting in with all those spider-spawn running up and down the walls. If we can't dice and slice our way through them without getting poisoned… we are going to need a lot of darts to poison them."

Dimi mused. "But I know some things that will make any creature sleep." She reached up and scratched her blond white hair. "But I need to think of something slightly more creative for Sarta." A slow wicked smile crossed her lips. "Fun, fun, fun." Dimi looked at the two men and then jumped down from the table. "I will be in the surgery. Have a nap if you like, get your other things then meet me there."

Dimi skipped to and out the door appearing in a rather happy mood.

"Interesting lady." Stephan said. He then turned and looked at Etch. "The river current is very strong; will she have the strength to swim it?"

Etch laughed. "She is so light she likely will dance upon the waves and beat us there." He paused then looked over to Stephan. "Seriously? How cold and how deep?"

Stephan laughed; his smile was contagious and brought a smile to Etch's own face. "There is a way as I said before, risky but the only one I believe will enable us entry unseen." Sir Douglas said smiling leaning back in his chair, "Under the icy waters where the support of the arching bridge dives to the bottom of the river."

"As you know TieRei spans the Black River." Stephan explained as he went to the table. He took a few pieces of bread and tore them apart and placed them end to end representing the river. He then put two cups on either side and placed a small sausage in the middle of the bread that represented the river. "Two towers surrounding two small cities, walled and guarded."

Stephan pointed to the big mugs on either side of the river. "Between the two towers runs a great causeway over the river. " He then pointed at the sausage that rested atop the bread. "A single massive pillar supports the two arches of the causeway and runs all the way down into the water. It was why that place had been picked to build the towers, for it was narrow there and yet not too deep in its center, and by erecting the twins safe passage could be made atop of it."

Etch stood looking over the food based model and pointed at the bread. "Hard current eh? How far from shore need we swim to make it so the current carries us to its base?"

Stephan nodded. "Shouldn't be too bad for there is a bend above that pushes the water away from the western shore. We need to enter above the castle and swim with the current to the support.

Then we dive down and up at the back of them where there is an access hole that leads up the support."

"How big is the support and how high up do we need to climb and how will we climb?" Etch asked dryly.

"The pillar is massive. Fifteen meters it spans wide… but it is hollow. A ladder of sorts runs from the causeway and plunges down into the water. In that way the MiKay could check and fix the pillar after the ice flowed down from the mountains. There is hole under the water." Stephan laughed. "The dwarves are a sturdy lot use to the waters deep down in the mountains. They would dive down and fix the stone on inside and out… holding their breaths for tens of minutes."

"Sound like sturdy stock." Etch said impressed.

"Shorter then us by a head." Stephan added. "But burly, stalking lads the lot." He laughed, "Even their women. You can't tell the men from the women, for both have beards and both of their chests are like barrels, rounded with massive muscles."

Stephan leaned in to Etch holding out his hands as if he was grasping an axe. "I watched one MiKay slice so hard with his axe that it passed through 'two' Masti in a single blow… His stroke so fast and his axe so heave that it parted their bones and flesh as fast and as easy as warm butter."

"Too bad we couldn't find one or two to help us on this venture." Etch said looking down at the model. "I can't hold my breath for tens of minutes."

"Its not that deep this time of year. The waters are very low in the winter as the mountain lakes are all frozen already. We need dive only three meters at most."

"In freezing cold water, in the dark after having swum from upstream." Etch added sarcastically. Stephan smiled back and slapped him on the shoulder. "If it was easy, it wouldn't be fun."

"So, swim down the freezing river, dive under and come up the shaft. Then climb up the ladder to the causeway…" Etch said with little joy in his voice. "Hope that we don't get spotted by spiders. Then where?"

Stephan looked at the mugs. "We exit the causeway in a crawl way within the causeway. We should be able to make it across to the eastern towers without notice as long as we are quiet. We exit the crawl way from a trap door that leads down to the 2nd floor staircase. From there, we go down 2 flights to the top of the dungeons... which is at ground level."

"If there are any prisoners left, they will be held in the dungeons with luck we can let them loose." He then pointed to the top of the mug that represented the eastern tower. "From the screams we heard, Sarta is in the judgement room at the top of the tower. There is another flight of stairs for servants to use that go all the way up to a big room where she likely is – it has a massive black dais, heavy metal throne chairs…."

"Lots of brass torch holders shaped like hands?" Etch said looking hopeful.

Stephan looked back a little startled. "Ei. That there is." He paused a moment – 'your vision?"

Etch nodded in reply. "We return the same way?"

Stephan shrugged. "Only if we can do all that unseen and unheard and Sarta keeps quiet. Else, we go out the throne room's front doors and down to the causeway access…. There are no ground level doors at the East tower… the only way out of the castle is through the causeway… "

"Do you know any more of the demon with Sarta?" Stephan asked with more fear then curiosity in his voice.

Etch shrugged. "Just what I told you. He had a single large horn that protruded from the back of his head and curved over and down the front of it but didn't look like he need ever use it. The horn ended with a single point just between his eyes… Big, burly, likely very strong. Skin looks tough and he has some wicked looking claws on him."

The Duke stepped around the table placing the wooden box before the two men. He then took Etch's hand. "You do know the history behind that Lake don't you – the Ice or Eyes of Tie Rei. No sane man from these parts drinks from its waters or would even think of splashing his face with its waters!"

"Little late for the warning." Etch said jokingly. "After having bathed entirely in it. But yes, Father Mellon said as much after he fished me out and I came too."

"Good priest that." The Duke agreed nodding his head. "The Temple guard has been the watchers of the Masti. They were established many, many years ago to keep an eye on them and their blood rituals. Not many of them left after the Masti were put down… I guess as a nation we became complacent."

"That's it, Sarta, this demon, and the throne room. She brings prisoners there to feed which seems to please the Demon."

"I can help by sending a group of men north and west…" The Duke started, "To draw their eye." There are always Wogs in the NorWestern fells. I can send some out to do a quick hit and run. We did that more in the past then now, it won't seem unusual."

"Then," the Duke pointed at he river between the two mugs. "I will have some men in secret wait for your return down the river. We will span it with rope and pull you from it."

"As for a weapon for you two," The Duke added looking at Etch and Stephan. "I have these." He motioned to the dark cherry wood box before them and in a grand way flipped the latch on it and opened the big heavy lid. I

Inside the velvet covered box were two identical black blades. From base of handle to pointed tip the blades were made of one unusual material appearing something between stone and metal."

"Shadow blades," Stephan said in a low tone. "You said you caught up with a few high priests when you came back home…. But I don't recall you mentioning taking these from them."

"Wasn't sure what they really were." The Duke started almost apologetic to Sar Stephan. "When we split to regain Annon Ter my men and I stumbled upon the two – quite literally. One moment we are riding hard with a small group of men North an the next moment two of my men and their mounts have fallen to the ground having collided with two invisible Blood Priests….We were lucky it seems they must have been deep in concentration casing fire or something at the castle, they hadn't heard our approach."

Both Stephan and Etch looked down at the blades. "Magnificent." Stephan said pointing to the blade. "What are the holes for?"

"Rune holes," Etch said looking down at the blades thinking not to quickly touch them. "What properties do they hold?"

The Duke, seeing both men's reluctance to pick up the blade, picked one up. He turned, pretending to battle an invisible form. It was comical to see the older man dance and lunge but both men held back their smiles.

"Not sure what the runes do." The Duke said as he waved the blade back and forth. "But the cuts make the blade even lighter than it looks. No matter what you hit it with, it stays as sharp as ever and never nicks."

The Duke put the blade back in the case and motioned the men to pick each one up. "Don't hold the blade. For even the runes cut into the blade appear sharp. Pick it up always on the handle. The runes are Masti, but we aren't sure what they say."

Etch reached forward and grabbed one. "Amazing, it is as light as a feather!" He said as he turned to admire it. He stood and walked over to a lamp hanging from the wall to inspect the blade more carefully. He moved his left hand ever so softly over the side of the blade; it felt cold and almost moist. "You are right, those runes have an edge turned grove, I would bet you could shave by moving the flat of the blade over your face."

"It would be used to skinning, branding and marking." Stephan added. "Blood priests would likely place the blade flat over a person's arm and move it back and forth slightly."

Etch visualised the picture and cringed. "In the end, the person would have the runes cut into their arm."

The Duke walked back to his seat. "There are black leather sheaths under the velvet... You are also welcome to anything in my personal weapons stores... take what you want. Although I would gladly go with you, I fear I would only slow you down."

Sir Douglas smiled a big smile and chuckled. "Till through the first line of trees my own men will come. But we need to travel few and silently... from there we go alone."

"Tonight as Dimi says then?" Etch said. "Or on the eve of tomorrow?" Etch stood and wobbled slightly having lost his sense of balance.

"There is little here that will change in a night." Sar Douglas said looking at Etch and then the Duke. "Let us rest the day to clear our heads and depart tomorrow night."

"Then I would back to bed and rest now for I fear this ale has had its effect." Etch said standing up. He nodded to the two remaining men and then headed back to his room.

The walls of TerranAdd

The last of the evening's sunlight shot out like fiery icicles over the treetops of the horizon. The clear blue sky was darkening as night approached and in the southern skies the faint outline of Halos could be seen, its pink surface just now showing as the day's light and warmth ebbed away.

Massive smoky flames started to rise to the sky as men lit the meter wide bowls of oil that encircled the tops of the walls of Terran Add. Soldiers in bristling chain mail with pointed helmets gleaming looked down and over the walls at the Mohen forces that spread out over the eastern planes. Many stood side-by-side pointing to the foreboding spectacle before them.

To officers stood atop the highest eastern tower watching as men readied the castle's largest catapult. The scanned the horizon watching the enemy complacently settles down for the evening. Beside and behind them their own men ran about readying the castle for the pending siege.

Sir Beston Thesra Grand General of the Montterran armies put his hand on the shoulder of Captain Miathis derCamp who stood by him looking down at the Mohen forces from the tallest eastern tower. "I bet your old man wouldn't believe his eyes to see you here standing atop the eastern turrets of TerranAdd looking down at likely over ten thousand Mohen."

Miathis smiled as he looked over his shoulder at the general. To him, the man had aged a decade these last few months. Sir Beston's hair had turned from dark to almost white and short, unruly grey hairs poked up through his well-trimmed moustache and cropped beard.

"I wouldn't be here at all," Captain Miathis replied glibly. "Had you and your men arrived even a day later. "Nothing was more welcome than the vision of your army of over two thousand strong exiting the western woods in full gallop."

The General nodded a smiled. "Quite the ruse you put on here Captain. When your message came outlining your plot to delay the Mohen from attacking, I thought for sure we would find this city in ruin with your head spiked at the gates."

Miathis laughed. "We were very lucky. General Kikiltoe Mariard was deffinetly suspicious for we ended up having to kill quite a few of his scouts in the last few nights. It was quite the job making the General believe that his scouts were dying from exposure to some unusual disease. It was the fear of some great pestilence that slowed his sword... just enough it seems."

General Thesra laughed in reply and took off his plate gauntlet and held it under his arm so he could use the bare of his hand to wipe a tear from the corner of his eye. "It still makes me laugh. I haven't laughed that hard in a very long time. I would have given my left nut to see the famous Mohen General's face when his men finally informed him that we were exiting the western fen, and headed straight into the plauged castle."

The Captain laughed again looking out at eastern planes, now totally covered in tents, fires and Mohen soldiers. "We had some help." He added. "Dimona and her men were most helpful in establishing the ruse effectively... and of course in killing the scouts that came too close to look."

"From your description of the talented lady, I would have been very happy to have made her acquaintance." The General said looking over at his captain with a glint in his eyes. "Crafty and beautiful you say?"

"And very deadly." Miathis added with respect. "She and her men were gone from this city before I had even heard that your forces were spotted... They knew you were within distance before we did and then virtually disappeared."

Miathis mused a moment remembering his friend the queen of thieves. "Too bad she left, however, I doubt the aid of a few more knives and bows will make much difference in the next few days."

The general nodded looking out. "General Mariard came well prepared with men able to build great siege engines. The ones being pulled forward now are much bigger than our biggest. They will be able to hit our walls and we will not be able to reach their lines…. Ten thousand or more against two… and some scouts are saying that there is still movement out of PlanTer – we know not if the General even might have more. No, a few more bows won't make a difference."

"Any news from the North or South?" Captain Miathis added almost rhetorically.

"You know as much as I on that. The North is falling as we speak. The Tock were bad enough, but now there appear other things more sinister northward."

"And as for the south," The General added cynically. "I have a bad feeling about Duke Sirthinor… Rumor is spreading north that the Governor of San Ter is dead… As for the new Terran King – Duke Karathor might convince him to march north to our aid, but …"

"Even if they come, even if our forces double in size we will be sorely pressed." The captain answered his own question and a feeling of gloom hit the bottom of his stomach.

"I have faced worse odds." Sir Beston Thesra Grand General of the Montteran forces answered with some finality. "We will stand and make General Mariard pay for every step westward. If we make him pay dearly here the Mohen will think twice before looking even further west to our home and OUR families."

Miathis nodded, thinking fondly of his girlfriend Bess as he last saw her, tending bar in the Porker Barrel; wondering if he would once again feel the warmth of her hug, or the tenderness of her kiss. Miathis shook himself out of the daydream and scanned the Mohen forces. "I wish the thieves were here. Perhaps they could have infiltrated the camps and poisoned the lot, or even just taken out General Mariard. If the Mohen emperor really isn't behind this push, my guess would be that his captains might turn tail should he no longer be holding their whip."

Sir Beston added with a chuckle. "I hope that General Kikiltoe Mariard himself leads the first charge as he has done in the past. I would love to see that 'beggard' with a quill of two feathered in his cap."

"He only leads charges on open ground." Captain Miathis added shaking his head. "He has never put siege to a city such large and as well fortified as this one. I respect him based on what I have learned of his past battles… he will only lead the final charge after he is assured of breaching the walls."

Sir Beston stood with his captain looking down at the Mohen forces. Inwardly, he wasn't confident at all. The worries of the Kingdome were squarely on his shoulders as seen in his tense face. He was dressed in full plate male, new the buffed steel shone and glimmered catching the last of the day's light. Enamelled on the chest was a black shield – and in its center a white unicorn with a red, bloody horn. Specks of red blood had been patterned across the head and neck of the unicorn.

"The Terrans had become complacent." The general said as he looked down the outer walls and at the catapults below them. "These catapults haven't been updated since before King Terros' time. MiHinDor Perrilos the Fourth might haven been a good friend to King Tar's father Terros but even so, Terros should have learned from the Masti uprising that no political situation is forever. Tar and his father before him should have seen the sleeping Lion for what he was – old. That soon another would be at the head of the Mohen forces, one perhaps not so peaceful."

"Their complacency was reinforced by the fact that MiHinDor's eldest son Paxton Perrilos cares nothing for his pipe of dreams and his nine wives… they had no fear that he had ambitions west… they were at peace." The captain added convincingly.

General Thesera slammed his fist on the wall sending dust flying down its length. "Any one of MiHinDor's 32 legitimate children could easily kill his eldest son the man's a pig… what then? A

King's responsibility is to ensure the future health of his nation, and to do so he needs to keep his armies strong."

Captain Miathis remained calm and quiet letting the General vent. The apparent futility of their situation was taking its toll on the general.

"Too many years of peace did they have with their eastern and northern neighbours." The General spat over the wall and watched it fly down until it disappeared from view. "Tar was stupid to think that now was the golden era of peace."

Miathis shrugged invisibly under his own white surcoat and heavy coat of glistening mail. His half helmet face turned to look at the General. His mail face guard was unstrung exposing his smiling face. "They had been at peace for years, solid trade partners, the gates east were open to all traffic without tax. Mohen were seen by Tar Bestinor as friends... a sleeping lion yes, but one also with heavy golden filed pockets."

The General looked up to the standards now flying atop the capital – they ran the colour of Roehn – a black flag trimmed in silver and in the center of those long streaming flags the Bloody Unicorn waved. "The Terrans are all gone now, crawled away hiding.. or dead. We will have to hold the eastern borders in their stead."

"My only hope," the captain added not quite sure how the general would take his comment. "Is that if we pay for this land with our blood and rebuff the Mohen that our King thinks twice before handing it back to Duke Bestinor."

"King Bestinor." General Thesera corrected. "So proclaims our own King."

Miathis reached up, took off his helm and un-slung the mail over his head so that it rested on his neck. He rolled his neck and it cracked in strain. "I expected to fight Tock warriors, or even Masti... somehow deep inside I still never believed we would be fighting fully armed Mohen knights.."

A cold wind hit the top of the walls, and Miathis pulled back up his mail over his head and put his helmet back on. He looked out over the horizon. Large communal cooking fires were sprouting up all along the eastern horizon. They spanned kilometres across. It was unnerving thinking just how many men were before them.

"General Kikiltoe Mariard, bastard son of MiHinDor." The general added. "My guess is that in morning's first light, his troops will marshal and the siege will begin… With ten thousand strong I doubt he will attempt to feign and test our defences. If I were him I would run with all he has in one great attack."

"Go, check on your men at the western gate. You guard the west, the eastern walls will be mine." The general added dismissing Miathis.

The casual, friendly conversation Miathis noted was at an end. The general was dismissing him. Miathis was about to object, to ask why his men after coming to Terran Add first were not afforded the honour to face the Mohen straight on… but after a moment's thought decided to resist his request.

The general looked over at his captain, sensing the man's potential request. He smiled and turned and slapped Miathis on the shoulder. "Do not fret. Trust me. You and your men will have all the fighting you can stomach."

Miathis nodded. Stood tall and then started walking back down the wall. Down the stairs and into the city he went. He wound in and around the empty buildings, continually looking back and around.

The evening was gone and the last glimmers of the dusk had dissipated, the shadows sprung from around him as he moved forward. Halos had risen higher and its ping glow radiated the sky around it illuminating a few wisps of clouds.

Miathis looked up as he approached the western towers. They were alive with soldiers in white surcoat and silver mail. Most carried bow or crossbow but a few held halbards and spear to hold back the ladders and repel climbers.

As he drew near the western walls he frowned as he watched a small group of soldiers wearing surcoats he didn't recognize in the darkness gather round a young noble Montteran lord. General Thesera had indicated that a few had joined hoping to gain glory and riches in the perceived vacant and undefended lands. The captain smiled doubting very much that when they volunteered they had expected they would be facing ten thousand Mohen regulars.

The small group of soldiers looked dishevelled, and a few appeared drunk… "Don't you men have some stations to tend?" Miathis said in his most authoritative voice as he approached them.

The young noble in the center of the group turned to face the captain defiantly. His motion clearly indicated he had spent much of the day drinking. His shiny, clean purple robe looked ridiculous to Miathis as he slowed to see if the man had audacity enough to return a response. However, one of his men stepped forward and pushed his thumb into the captain's shoulder. Miathis looked back incredulously at the man.

"I would have you know, good Sir." The solder said with a slur in his voice. "You address Sir Landin Rutt, the son of non other than Landor Rutt, Count Palatine and lord of the Norwesterns!

The young noble looked squinted at Miathis. His vision obviously blurred as well by many pints of ale. However, his eyes widened slightly recognizing Miathis as an officer under the General. Attempting to keep face, and bolster the bravado of his men the Landin stepped forward himself and attempted a small bow. "Captain Miathis is it? I would have you know, good captain that General Thesera his self has specifically asked that I and my men lead the contingent holding the third turret." The young man motioned to the men around him. "We go there presently." He then paused looking over Miathis' shoulder. "But we were just thinking we might need to take along a barrel or two for I hear it is dry work up on the walls."

Captain Miathis smiled as Sir Landin Rutt's followers laughed as the young noble's jest. But his smile faded and he bent forward to give the young man a stern look. "I think you and your men are sufficiently lubricated."

Miathis derCamp - Commander of the Fist and now captain of the eastern walls looked back to the young noble's entourage and then back at Sir Landin. "And I just came from the General. So I would suggest if he is expecting you on the eastern wall, that you make all haste to get there."

The lord bowed mockingly to Miathis but he almost fell over as he did so. "As you wish good captain." Sir Landin retorted smugly. He then turned and motioned for his men. "Come along then." He then started walking towards the eastern wall.

Miathis shook his head in disbelief and then a smile came to his face. "Forward eastern turret!" he said laughingly. He visualized the pompous young noble and his drunken cohorts standing atop the eastern most point of the castle, watching as the massive siege engines were pulled forward, letting them see the full strength of the Mohen before them. "I bet they will sober up fast." He said as he turned and started walking back to his men.

The Captain slowed as he approached the stairs to the wall – fascinated as he watched scores of men run up and down the staircases bringing up arrows, pitch and poles. It was the largest company he had ever commanded. He wasn't sure if he was happy or disappointed for not standing beside the General on the western walls when dawn came.

"The general is right." Miathis finally said to himself as he started to climb the stairs. He knew deep down that no man would leave this castle alive or un-bloodied. There were over ten thousand Mohen, they might first hit the western walls, but by the end of the first battle they would be fully surrounded and defending every tower, every stone with their blood.

Miathis continued to hustle forward. Under the veil of his mail, he smiled as he approached a group of men atop the stairs. Tunder, stood a good head taller than the others and he was loudly giving them orders. Two of the soldiers nodded and then started racing

589

North up the wall opposite from where Miathis approached. At first he thought the two were Tirad and Bettham, but both soldiers were sporting scale male and white surcoats emblazoned with the King's new bloodied unicorn insignia.

The captain removed his helmet as he approached Tunder, now raised to lieutenant. The large burly man's head was bear of helmet... his new massive shiny axe was leaning against his one leg. Tunder, noticing his approach smiled and raised his hand in greeting.

"So, lieutenant." Miathis said smiling as he approached Tunder extending his hand to shake that of his good friend and 'first'. "How goes it on the western walls? Will we be prepared by sun's next light?"

Tunder was even more impressive looking then ever. He wore new polished gauntlets, small spikes protruded from the knuckles, and his scale greaves shone brightly. His old bloodied surcoat darkened with blood looked out of place compared to his polished armour.

Tunder's smile faded slightly but then returned confidently. "We will." His deep booming voice rang out. "If I can get these laggards to do a good days work." He motioned with the back of his hand to the two men hustling away from him, now almost out of sight running down another set of stairs.

"Was that Tirad and Bettham?" Miathis asked as he watched them run.

"Yes." Tunder replied looking back over his shoulder and then turning back to face his captain. "I am having them search for more oil. These walls have recessed fire pits and massive iron bowls to heat and dump the oil, but we have found little to put within them."

Tunder laughed, his voice echoed down the wall. "If anyone can find anything in this city, it is Tirad."

"I didn't recognize them at first." Miathis asked suspiciously. "They weren't wearing the Fist surcoat, and both wore rather different armour then last I saw them."

"Tirad is a scoundrel." Tunder started somewhat hesitantly. "Found a cache of well made armour in the city." The large man held up his own gauntleted fist. "Gave some away, but traded some so that they could pay General Thesera's smith to do alterations. Tirad and Bettham are now running a regular side business now selling odds and ends they discovered when we first came to the city…. Items too large to be carted away by Dimona's group."

Miathis' expression was one of concern and disappointment. Tunder reached up to put his gauntleted hand to his neck to massage the stress away, however, when his hand was raised he watched the gauntlet sparkle and quickly lowered it and put his hand behind his back somewhat self-consciously. "He has found us a lot and only goes in to the city when he isn't on duty." Tunder added quickly.

"Better him and our own men then the General's or the pup 'lordlings' that came with him." Miathis finally concluded. "But give up the Fist colors? I wouldn't have expected you to stand for it?"

Tunder shook his head in explanation. "Both of their surcoat's were a mess after helping me with the wounded and carrying out the dead. I had none other to replace them. I didn't see much the harm now that we are all serving under the general in this castle together."

Miathis' laughter startled Tunder. The captain reached up and put a hand on the lieutenant's shoulders. "No harm done Tunder. You are right. The Mohen will know no differently when they attack."

Tunder Warmar, 2nd of the Fist and now lieutenant of the Montterran regulars flinched when Miathis reached up, almost as if he expected to be slapped, but then a big beardy smile opened up showing his slightly yellowed teeth. His smile faded as he began to grasp his captain's innuendo. "Is it that bad in the east?

Tunder turned and looked west over the wall and to the forest. A few Mohen scouts were riding in plain sight just outside of bow reach. They galloped around the western walls heading south. "We see little of the Mohen, except for the likes of those."

"The Mohen have taken to the sport of racing the walls." Tunder said looking out at the three Mohen knights riding. "When they reach the southern walls often they are in a rush and pass close enough to lose an arrow after. But mostly all we see is a few now and then."

Miathis pointed over to the fen forests marking the edge of the horizon. "Thesra says that the Mohen General Kikiltoe Mariard has a small company of men stationed in the forest. But General Thesra doesn't believe that General Mariard will split his forces until just before the attack, in that way we won't know how many will come from where. There is also a chance I believe that Mariard might be over confident with his numbers, and decide not to split his forces, but rather attack as one our eastern walls."

"You know I was just about to ask why the general's best company and brightest captain wasn't manning the eastern walls…" Tunder laughed, his eye brows raised in understanding. "But I no longer see it as a slight, but rather as a favour!"

"My thoughts exactly." Miathis replied laughing with his friend. "Especially after I stumbled upon Lord Landor Rutt's son Landin down below. Our good friend General Thesra has placed the pompous fool in point upon the eastern most turret!"

Tunder bent down and put his hands to his stomach laughing hard. The axe handle by his side began to fall and he had to reach down to catch it before it hit the cold hard stone of the wall. "Well deserves the damn drunken pup." Tunder laughed as he sniffled. "Damn fool's been running around ordering my men about, drunk when he arrived and hasn't sobered up yet."

"He will sober up fast when ten thousand Mohen regulars charge." Miathis said turning the conversation back to a gloomier tone.

The conversation waned, as both men turned to look down the walls at their men. Both wondering how many, if any of them would get out of the current situation alive. Finally Miathis broke the silence. "No help expected from the north and no new news from the south… Mariard won't wait too much longer."

Tunder heaved a sigh and then turned to face his captain smiling. "Good!" He said loudly lifting his axe to rest upon his shoulder. The blade flashed, the hollowed runes swished as it past his head. "I have been practicing on wooden posts, but nothing better to work on then real necks."

Both men turned as in the distant east heavy drums could be heard. Then a moment later there was a loud cheer from well beyond their western walls. "It begins." Miathis said.

"It begins." Tunder said in replied turning to the east. "Bout time, I was getting a little board." Tunder lowered the axe from his shoulder and held it in both hands.

Captain Miathis chuckled. "Slow down. At best they will spend the night softening us with stone." He paused a moment following his friends easterly gaze. "Tell the men to relax, send most to bed…."

Miathis turned and started walking back from where he had come, hoping to make his way back to the eastern wall to see what the noise was all about. He paused momentarily and then turned back to Tunder. "But have them up and on the walls before dawn breaks."

Tunder nodded silently, never letting his gaze from the eastern walls. "We'll be ready."

593

North in darkness surrounded

Dimi sat cross-legged on top of a long and high dark granite surgeon's table. Her arms and head were bare of garments and dripped with sweat. Her face was contorted with concentration as she worked the massive stone pistil grinding a multitude of herbs and roots in a large white stone bowl. Yellow 'mustard like' powder wafted up from the bowl as she hammered and ground its contents furiously.

The small nymph like lady had almost jumped out of her skin in excitement when she had first entered the surgery. The grey stone walls were almost invisible behind shelves upon shelves of clay pots, glass containers and boxes and boxes of herb. Bound herbs hung inverted to dry from the ceiling and buckets of fresh dug roots sat under the lower most shelves many still wet with mud.

The surgery hall was long at over thirty meters and it spanned over ten meters or more wide. Down the middle of the hall sets of heavy oak table legs supported five granite surgery slabs. From the ceiling hung five massive lanterns each positioned directly above a slab. A geared pulley system and ropes went from them, up to the ceiling and then diagonally over to the walls. All five of the massive lanterns were lit filling the room with brilliant golden hues.

After a few minutes of hard grinding Dimi pulled out a few quills from the quill pouch that sat beside her and rolled their tips in the mustard paste contained within the white bowl. Smiling Dimi gingerly placed the quills on a small piece of wax paper, rolled the paper and then returned the quills within the paper back in to her quiver.

"How do I clean this up?" Dimi said out loud to herself looking at the pistil and bowl still filled with an obviously dangerous mixture of lethal plants and herbs. She paused a moment and then simply dropped the pistil and mortar along with its contents into a barrel that sat beside the table. As the stone pistil and mortar hit the bottom of the barrel they banged making Dimi flinch a little afraid that the contents might splash up at her.

"And now... for something completely different." Dimi said cheerily. She reached up to her face as if to rub her chin or brush back her hair but she froze mid motion. Looking at her hands she noticed that they were covered in a fine mustard colour dust. Jumping off the table Dimi went to the one of the many shelves and pulled off a container.

"Simpler wine." she said reading the ingredients printed on the bottle. "Wonder why they have this?" Dimi unstopped the bottle and used the clear liquid contents to wash her hands. The granite floor darkened as the wine hit it. She then went over to another large barrel stationed near the surgery slab and pulled out two handfuls of sawdust that she threw onto the wet stain.

Dimi returned to the walls and scanned the shelves and started picking out bottles which she then took in arm over to another surgery slab. In a few minutes the slab was covered with varying sized bottles and herbs much like the one she had just left. Having completed her search for ingredients Dimi jumped up and sat on the second slab. Delicately she picked up each bottle, read its label and then started rearranging the bottles.

Drop by drop, crystal-by-crystal Dimi added minute quantities from various bottles to her concoction. After each drop added to the bottle from another source Dimi would pause and think, then stopper the bottle shake it and think some more before proceeding. So deep was her concentration that Etch's entry into the room was totally unnoticed by her.

"Busy busy I see." Etch stated rhetorically as he looked over Dimi's shoulder at the small bottle she was now peering into.

Dimi gasped and turned quickly almost dropping the bottle in her effort. She flushed and looked furiously at Etch chiding him for startling her. "ARE YOU MAD?" She yelled in her high-pitched voice. "Any idea what would happen if I splashed this on you?"

"Well, actually no." Etch said and then wrinkled his nose. "I would smell bad, that is for sure."

"Idiot." Dimi added then turning back to the bottles she picked up another and added a drop to her concoction. "It needs to be perfect." Dimi added as she went back to looking at bottles.

"I have my first two potions." She added pointing to her small bag. "I have a Brenasal mixture that has saltpetre in it for us to take before we enter the water. I also have mixed a rather nasty poison tipped darts that will dissolve a creature from the inside out if it gets within their blood.."

"Now that sounds like fun." Etch said bending over and opening the flap of Dimi's bad to look inside. "Something special for someone we love?" He added sarcastically as Dimi slapped his hand forcing him away from the bag.

"A special mixture for the mage's minion…. And then after we toy with her, I hope to watch her melt from the inside out." Dimi said with an evil smile.

"What are you mixing now?" Etch asked as Dimi poured out more dark grey fluid from one container into the bottle that appeared to hold almost all of her attention.

"Little trickier potion." Dimi added holding up the concoction to the sky so she could see through it with aid of the light from the lamp above her. "Killing is easy. Immobilizing a Sarta, without knocking her out or killing her will be a little trickier."

Etch nodded with understanding. "Tricky is right. What can you hit her with that will stop her from killing us before we get a chance to ask her questions about Elle."

Dimi's eyes narrowed and her face tightened angrily. "Oh how I would love to know how to freeze her like she did me…. I tell you, I would break off a thing or two from her!" Dimi said wickedly.

"But unfortunately I am not a mage." Dimi added after a pause in a disappointed tone. She then looked back at the mixture that swirled in the bottle. "However, we have to do something to stop her from creating illusions which might enable her to escape."

Etch bent in to get a closer look at the fluid. "Shadow magic." he added ruefully. "Added to all her other skills likely an ability to project illusions and deceptions. What you got?"

Dimi and Etch both turned to look as the door to the surgery opened. Its large door swung wide as Stephan gave them a kick – both his arms were holding large piles of leather that matched the pants and suite he wore. "Hello. Having fun?" He said smiling as he walked forward into the room.

As always, Etch noted the smile on his face. He had seen the man clean-shaven earlier in the day, but now looked like he had a two-day growth on. His eyes were bright as he strode forward.

Etch smiled back at the man as he approached and then hastened around the table to offer Stephan assistance with his load. Stephan handed him one load of leathers and then took the other set and tossed it beside Dimi. "They should fit… they stretch well." He said to her.

Etch took the outfit he had been given to the large slab and laid them out. "What type of skins are these? I thought at first they were just oiled, but the leathers are covered in very small hairs." Etch pressed his thumb down onto the leather and a small pearl of oil came out from around his thumbprint. "What type of oil are they soaked in?"

Dimi looked up and watched Etch hold up a leather pullover. It was long in the waist and would rise up to the neck. The stitching was all along the sides, and the leathers were overlapped.

"Water Lion skins." Dimi added looking up to Stephan who nodded.

"Right." he said looking back over to Etch to explain. "They are small but vicious web footed cat sized animals that swim like fish. Fishermen from the Isles of the Monto hunt them when the waters freeze in the Sea of Tears. They are hard to catch for they usually swim and hunt within the great depths and exit unto the ice flows to give birth to their young. But even on the flows they are tricky to kill. They are small, but even on land they are fast and their teeth are like small knives."

"So, have you guys figured out how we are going to stop Sarta from killing us?" Stephan asked with a smirk on his face.

"As a matter of fact I do." Dimi said proudly. "We get either Etch or you to simply walk up to her and prick her with a pin that has this on it." Dimi held up the completion of her mixture. The grey fluid swirled, shimmers of white and black strands spiralled within the bottle. She shook it a moment and held it up again, but still the black and white strands remained separate from the grey fluid.

"I volunteer Stephan." Etch said with a smile turning to the clansman.

"Gee thanks friend." Stephan said coming up behind Etch and slapping him on the back. "I appreciate the vote of confidence and the recommendation… but I will pass."

"How will we get close enough to prick her with a needle. Why can't you just shoot her with one?" Etch said puzzled.

"Because she will believe you are under her succubae spell." Dimi retorted gleefully. "See while you two slept the day AND night away…. I have been busy thinking and planning and making potions."

"If we are under her spell then we are nothing more then flailed flesh a moment later." Etch said shaking his head and looking to Stephan for assistance in this argument.

"You will be 'pretending' to be in her spell." Dimi added pointing to her bag. "Before you enter the water you will both have consumed a mixture of saltpetre and Brenasal."

"Brenasal!" Etch said out loud shuddering. "Oh no, not again I won't, not willingly anyway."

Stephan looked guardedly at Etch and then Dimi. "What am I getting myself into?" He asked Etch suspiciously.

"A whole lot of discomfort." Etch said looking evilly at Dimi. "Surely there is another way?"

"We are…" Dimi started. "Going back into the river of ice. The source of water that feeds the lake you were in for but a few minutes."

"Yes, but the river has no magic in it." Stephan said. "Only the lake. It is very cold, but I have washed in it before."

"The Brenasal will be week, but will keep your limbs warm." Dimi added coaxingly to Etch. "But mixed with saltpetre it will make you immune to the Succubus' enamouring spell."

"It will stop Sarta from entrancing us?" Stephan asked hesitantly.

"Exactly." Dimi added nodding her head rapidly. "Together the two ingredients will make you both immune to her enamouring enchantment."

"Are you going to take it too?" Etch asked sarcastically.

"I will chew on a small root of Brenasal to keep my limbs from freezing in the cold winter waters. But I won't need one of the same strength nor one mixed with saltpetre." Dimi replied.

"If Sarta sees me, there will be no way I would be able to hit her with a dart covered in this." Dimi said lifting the container again. "If she so much as sees me she would protect herself with illusion, I might end up shooting either of you with the darts. There is no way I can be in the room. Thus little need to take the full mixture."

"Is it so bad?" Stephan asked hesitantly to Etch.

"Let me put it this way." Etch started with a very sarcastic voice. "If while swimming, after drinking that mixture…. And you fart in the river, the river will boil and all the fish will die."

Stephan laughed, he leaned forward bending down holding himself up with one hand on Etch's shoulder. "OUCH! And you trust her in mixing something like this for us?"

Dimi huffed. "I will be taking some Brenasal too!" She pouted a moment and then smiled. "Although a much smaller potency.

You both need more to increase your circulation so the saltpetre will have its full effect."

"I can hardly wait." Etch said continuing with his sarcasm.

"It's the only way I can think of, the only potion that will possibly work to stop the succubus from putting you under her spell. If you walk in there unprotected, you would freely kill for her if she commanded you."

"The salzpeter." Dimi continued. "I put five grams of pure powder in with the fluid. It will… shall we say – put your desires to sleep and make you immune to her commands."

"None of this is permanent?" Stephan asked quickly and earnestly.

Dimi stood up on the table. "No. The potion will last no more than a day."

Standing there she stood but half a head above the men. "We need to get one of you up as if from the dungeons as food. When you get near her, you pretend to be under her spell and approach her and then prick her with a pin I will give you. A moment later and she will be very pliable and do OUR bidding."

"How long for it to take effect?" Stephan asked curiously.

Dimi looked concerned. "It is very hard to say. The potion is pure, but it affects the will…"

"And she is after all crazy." Etch added looking over at Stephan. "Totally twisted, insane and was tortured for years… You sure it will work?"

Dimi remained silent but nodded.

Stephan shook his head in concern. "If she has the skills of a blood priest, we will still need to be steadfast and not believe anything we see until it does." Stephan urged.

"When we were first attacked by the Masti blood priests," Stephan added with a low toned voice. "When the Masti army appeared their blood priests made many of us believe that we were covered in spiders…. So real were they that we could feel their feet upon our faces." Stephan shuddered.

"Not fun." Etch added. "But it is just an illusion, an illusion can't hurt you."

"It can make you hurt yourself." Stephan added. "Men used their own knives to scrape off and stab the spiders cutting themselves."

"Once this potions effects start." Dimi added anxiously. "We can command her to stop her illusions and she will. She can't harm you as a succubus as long as you aren't in her spell. Her curse is that she can only feed on willing victims."

Stephan looked over and picked up a large bottle from the table. "Truklite? I hope there isn't any of this in what we drink."

Dimi laughed, her musically high giggle. "No, I thought we might be able to use it to battle whatever we find within the castle, but there is no safe way to transport it on us when we swim. Even if we put it in the thickest jar, just the smallest amount of moisture would set it off."

"Boiling waters and dead fish again." Stephan joked. He looked up and around the room. "What do they use it for here?"

"Small amounts are poured onto stumps after amputations are performed." Dimi said taking the bottle from Stephan and putting back on the table. "When it touches anything moist like blood or an open wound it burns hot and fast, cauterizing the wounds closed."

Stephan looked over at Etch. His eyes looked glazed as if in deep concentration. "What are you thinking about?" He prodded.

Etch shook his head. "No, I am just not looking forward going back into the water. I haven't felt warm since I fell in to that lake."

"I am almost done here." Dimi said as she took out some more quills and dipped them into the bottle. "Start changing." She suggested to Etch.

As Etch dressed Dimi completed packing up her quills and then leaving her cloths on put the slick leathers overtop of them.

"They won't keep them dry." Stephan said as he watched her dress. "But they should keep you warmer."

"The quills are well wrapped." Dimi added noting his concern. "And I have more of each potion within small bottles. I will reapply the potions to the darts after we get out of the water."

Etch pulled off his leather vest, and his linen shirt, and started pulling on the oiled leathers. Stephan laughed as Etch half way through became somewhat stuck. His hands were waving in the air straight up. Stephan walked over to him and grabbed the bottom of the leather long shirt and pulled. Etch's head popped up and through the long neck. He was red and panting from the effort. "Thanks." He said as Stephan turned.

"Come over, I have something for you to drink." Dimi said as she held up a bottle for them. Etch winced but walked over. "One mouthful," Dimi said coaxingly.

Etch obliged and shuddered and then handed the bottle to Stephan. He then picked up the leather pants and sat on the floor. "These are a little to tight for me to put over my own."

Stephan looked hesitantly at the bottle in his hand.

Dimi laughed lightly. "It will save your life."

Etch chucked as he laboured trying to put on the pants. From below the tabletop his head popped up and he smiled at Stephan. "Trust her, but get ready to piss fire." Etch said jokingly as he began to rise.

Stephan looked up from the bottle and back at Dimi. His smile returned, from ear to ear. With a slow and deliberate action, without taking his eyes off of Dimi he raised the bottle and poured a large mouthful into the back of his throat.

Dimi noted a slight widening of eyes, but his smile did not falter as he then closed his mouth and swallowed.

"I like these leathers." Etch said admiringly as he stood and turned his upper torso around to inspect his backside. "Snug but they feel warm."

"Don't forget this." Stephan said handing over to Etch one of the black sheaths with long dangling leather straps attached to it. "Cords are made so that you can strap the sheath on your back."

"Very light overall." Stephan added as he watched Etch pull the blade out.

"All Done…" Dimi said as she started walking to the door. "Are you boys finished playing with your new toys?"

Etch laughed as he slid the blade back into its sheath and strapped it on his back. Both men started walking to the door.

Stephan slapped Etch on the back as they approached Dimi and the door. "Did we forget anything?"

Etch looked at Dimi who shrugged indifferently. "We have a plan, but executing it …. We just need to focus on each step of it… and the first part is even getting to the Twins unnoticed."

"Leave that part to me… just follow my lead." Stephan said confidently. "Wait."

Etch stopped in his tracks and Dimi paused looking up at the clansman. "What now?" she asked him – what did we forget?

"Silver," Stephan said turning and looking back at the surgery. "We are going to need lots of silver blades, or arrows… ….. Silver and good luck. We can stop off at the armoury for a few items… "

"And as for Luck," Etch added starting again out and through the door. "We shall make our own."

Raining Stones

"Double or nothing!" Tirad Mismar said as he turned to watch as Mohen started to reload the catapult in the distance. "Double or nothing, PLUS an added forty silver nails that the catapult fourth from the left makes it not only to the wall, but crests it."

Bettham paused and looked at his best friend who was now intently watching the activities of the Mohen.

"That would be eighty six Terran Silver Nails," Bettham said in a low, incredulous voice." He paused and then with sincerity added. 'Or, or sixteen Golden Teeth. Are you sure my good friend?"

Bettham stared at his friend, with great concern. "That is the same as forty eight Montterran Golden Talons, you know that right? You could buy yourself a piece of land in the western vales with that!"

Bettham Bethos was son to the Duke of Oathos, as such he had lived well all his life and money had never been a great concern to him. But even for the son of a Duke what they were betting now was a great deal of money. He also knew that for his best friend Tirad, it was a fortune.

Tirad smiled back at his friend. "Call it Bettham; I know you are good for it. Or chicken out and say pass - just do it soon." Tirad pointed over the eastern wall, they were standing at the highest central tower overlooking all of their own eastern towers as well as the entire eastern field – currently covered with Mohen soldiers and siege engines.

Bettham looked at the siege engine, not sure how to proceed. He desperately searched the landscape looking for a way out of the bet. Stretched out into the horizon were eight thousand Mohen soldiers and hundreds of mounted knights. Dozens of massive siege engines rose up menacingly from the ranks. The campfires of the soldiers made the entire horizon glow red. "Shouldn't we secure the oil Tunner sent us for?"

"I told you on the way here." Tirad said in a frustrated tone. "It is already on its way. I knew he would be needing some, I already arranged to have two gatemen pull the cart to him… it was loaded up yesterday."

Bettham shook his head. "You are a merchant at heart aren't you?" You know after all this…" Bettham said motioning out to the Mohen before them. "If you ever would consider living up in the Casten Mountain area… We could go into business together. With my connections and your skills we could have a lock on the NorWestern trades!"

"What and miss the excitement of all this?" Tirad said jokingly. "Live a life of safety and luxury as opposed to wondering if your stomach will have a blade in it before sunrise?"

Tirad sighed silently he scanned the horizon and then the Montterrans running along the walls.

Bettham looked down the walls to the other lower towers. He noticed a few of the Montteran soldiers readying their own catapult. "Check out the men down at the most eastern towers."

Bettham said pointing down and forward to the towers that stood out slightly from the rest of the castle. He chuckled as he watched the soldiers bumbling and running frantically around the devise. "Idiots, running around like a bunch of chickens with their heads cut off."

"They won't stand a chance." Tirad said shaking his head. He leaned forward over the side wall to get a closer look.

Bettham walked over beside his friend and looked down. "They don't look like they know what they are doing… and there is no officer there to assist."

Bettham, thinking he had found his diversion jabbed Tirad in the shoulder. "Come on. It will be fun, let's go down and help. I would love to send a few lobbies back!"

Tirad turned and looked back at the Mohen siege engines then back to the walls. "That spot is almost exactly where those engines are now pointing at." He said rather concerned. "Besides - watch!" Tirad said with great anticipation. "They load up the stone now and are preparing a bucket of pitch for it… you have about twenty seconds before they set it alight and let it loose. Better make up your mind now if you are a betting man on a northern fowl."

Bettham looked at his friend trying to figure out if he should make the bet or not. They both had sneaked out into the city during off duty hour and had both found quite a sum of Terran coin as well as a few rare gems. It was Tirad however that had made the most of it – trading larger goods he wouldn't be able to take with him like fine armour and swords, to others within the barracks. In his trading and dealings with the Montteran regulars he had made a small fortune – how much Bettham wasn't sure.

Bettham knew Tirad very well and he laughed at his friend jokingly. "Gold never stays long in your pocket does it Tirad?" Bettham said looking back at his friend. "When we go into business together, I will I guess need to be our banker. Are you sure, that is a great deal of money?"

Tirad shrugged off the comment still intently looking at the Mohen catapult. "Keep watching brother. Your odds are good, take the bet. The last several have fallen well short."

Bettham looked over at the Mohen siege engine, "Your money, which soon will be mine." Bettham answered nervously.

Tirad turned and the two men shook hands. "But seriously Tirad," Bettham added. "Keep some of it for your future, you needn't blow it all away. Plus now that the lordlings are romping through the city, there isn't as much there to snag."

"PLUS – remember them." Bettham said pointing his thumb out at the Mohen. "They won't be sitting out there long… we won't have many more night excursions to find more loot."

Bettham looked over to his friend, and then turned and sighed looking at the catapult being aimed now at the city's wall. He paused a moment more deliberating…

"Here we go." Bettham said as he continued to eye Tirad nervously. Tirad turned and nodded to Bettham confirming the bet once again.

Bettham was afraid to win. The sum was large and it wouldn't be a trivial loss to him. His findings had been small and amassed to only around thirty silver nails. If he lost this bet his only recourse would be to hand over to Tirad the ruby he had found in one of their earlier trips through the city. Together they had found two such stones secreted away within a nobleman's house. They each had kept one. Bettham had right away thought to keep give it to his mother when he returned home. If he lost the bet, he would likely have to part with the beautiful stone.

Tirad glanced back at Bettham and winked as if reading his mind. "Don't worry, I know you are good for it."

Bettham tried to shrug off the comments. "That is a big sum is all."

Tirad's arm shot out and he touched Bettham's armoured shoulder making him look up. "There watch, it lifts." Tirad said anxiously.

Bettham turned once again to watch the catapults. When they had first arrived, the line of catapults were just starting to be tested. They had bet at first only on which of the catapults would throw the farthest, although each never coming close to the walls.. they all were getting closer. Tirad had his 'favourite' catapult and had been betting on it – loosing to Bettham in the process as Bettham stayed more objective and bet based on what he observed in previous throws. He had the benefit of having been a Duke's son and had as such experience in formal training in the art of catapults. It was another unmentioned factor that made his winning less appealing – he felt almost as if he was cheating his friend.

The Mohen had continued busying themselves making changes to the ropes and counter weights and each time of the last few throws, their massive projectiles came closer... Each time Tirad had bet that the next time his favourite catapult would exceed the others. Bettham knew that although the catapult that Tirad had picked as his champion was the largest, it would never likely out throw another by its side. The second one in the line although smaller was better built and had a much heavier counterweight… and those that manned it knew what they were doing.

In the darkness before them they watched. "See!" Said Tirad. "This shot my men are loading this time is not of stone, but of pitch. They used the others only to guage the shot. This one will be lighter and surely fly over the walls!"

"The weight is needed to offset the counter." Bettham started. "If the stone is too light the arm will travel too fast and when released will fly in a lower arch."

Tirad's face grew stern with determination watching the Mohen men prepare to pull the lever and let loose it's load.

The massive twenty meter long arm lurched forward and up, the massive counter balance pulled down lurching it forward and upward. Pitch sprayed out from the metal basket that held the burning ball.

Just as Bettham had feared and hoped the catapult's arm moved too quickly, the stone within the basket was too light. The Mohen manning this engine should have pulled the bars that would stop the arm forward but instead had left it as was set for the heavier load. As expected the arm raced forward faster than it should have and when it hit the retraining bar the pitch flew forward in a low arch landing less than a hundred meters forward – well short of the walls.

"Damn, damn, double DAMN." Tirad yelled out of the walls. "DAMN MOHEN FOOLS." Other Montterrans along the walls had also been watching a few yelled cheers and jeers back at the Mohen.

"Common. Let's go down to the eastern towers and see if we can help the men send a reply back." Bettham said hoping to steer Tirad away from dwelling on his loss. "Lets go down to the other tower."

Triad put on his best game face and smiled at Bettham and hit him on the back as they both turned to the stairs that would lead them to the eastern tower lower walls.

"Besides," Bettham laughed as he looked out over at the long line of siege engines and ammased Mohen forces. "We might not live to spend it anyway." He reached down and picked up the chains and handle of his morning star. It jingled as he pulled the chains togeterh so that the spiked balls wouldn't bang on the floor as they walked down the stairs.

Tirad didn't laugh in reply but continued down the stairs. "We will get out of this my friend." He then turned and winked at Bettham. "Nothing is going to stop me from winning back that money... not even eight thousand Mohen regulars."

Bettham laughed somehow feeling that no matter what assailed them, if any man would walk from the castle it would be Tirad.

It took them almost an hour to walk down the walls and climb up to the most eastern lower parapet. By the time they arrived the Montteran regulars were still running around the catapult not sure what to do with it. There were no sergeants or officers within sight.

"Hey guys – what you doing?" Tirad said mockingly. "This thing hasn't even been cocked yet."

"Need some help?" Bettham added more sincerely.

The six men working the catapult looked over suspiciously at the two new men. One of them walked forward he looked very nervous. "None of us have ever worked one." He explained as he walked towards the two lads. "They looked simple enough from afar, but there are many more ropes and pullies when you get up close."

Another of the eight men stood forward and moved in front of the first soldier. He appeared much cockier and bolder then the others. "Who are you anyway?" Looking at Bettham and Tirad "Go back to your moms Lads and let the men work the machines."

The first soldier put his hand on the man's shoulder and pulled him back a little. He turned to look at the first man and spoke to him – as intended as a personal conversation although clearly audible to the other six men behind them as well as to Bettham and Tirrad. "That is Duke Bartholm Bethos' son you address. Mind your lounge."

"Just a pup lad from what I see." The man responded sourly. "No rank on his shoulder…. What do want me to do bend a knee?"

The first soldier shook his head then turned and held out his hand to Bettham. "Josh Kline." He said nodding his head. He then turned back to the other soldiers. "Lads son of Duke Bethos – if anyone knows a catapults front from its tail, it would be the son of the Northern Duke…. They have the tallest towers and largest machines and it is said that Tocks don't venture closer than a kilometre for fear of getting stoned."

Tirad looked over at his friend. "Bastard…. You didn't tell me you were some kind of expert." He then turned to the soldier to explain. "I lost a fortune betting on the Mohen throws just now, which I had known that earlier friend." He then walked round to the siege engine leaving Bettham to stand and shake hands with the soldier.

"I did warn you!" Bettham said as Tirad walked away. "That I had some experience with them."

Bettham stood forward and shook the soldier's hand. "Hi Josh, pleased to meet you."

Josh smiled and put his second hand to shake Bettham's in warm and friendly way – drawing him closer to the catapult. "We were supposed to have a lord and another eight men here, but they haven't shown up yet. None of us have ever manned such a contraption."

Bettham and the soldier walked up to the large machine. "Looks like thousand kilo counter weight on those beasts." He motioned over to the far wall where ten massive stones were piled. He gazed up at the tall arm that stretched high above them.

"We tried to crank the wheel." Another soldier said motioning to the two wheels on either side of the siege engine. Large heavy wooden poles were set into holes there to enable leverage to rotate the wheel. "But the gears don't hold. We pull and the gears let go."

Bettham nodded and stepped through and into the massive wooden structure. On the inside he found two ropes as wide round as his arm. He took their looped ends and placed them over the sprockets of the gears. The men peered in at him as he threw wound the heavy cords around. "The ropes need to tie to the gear that is what causes the tension."

Bettham climbed out from under the large wooden arms and posts and then motioned for the men by the wheel. "Try turning it now; it will take many turns clockwise before you feel any tension."

A man on either side of the wheel started turning their end. Three men on each side of the massive machine started pulling down the levers turning the giant cog and wheel. After a few turns the strain showed on the men and others joined to help turn the wheel and in less than a minute six of the eight men were work the two weeks. The massive wooden machine groaned and the gears clicked loudly as the long wooden arm started to descend to the ground.

When finally the arm was touching the back of the tower floor the men let go of the wheel and headed to the pile of massive stones. Two very large wooden rounded poles rested by the stones, and a man went to each end. After placing the poles under the first rock they lifted it and then in a staggering walk placed it into the basket of the catapult.

Josh, eyeing the limited number of existing boulders by the back of the tower looked over to Bettham. "Shouldn't we keep them for when we are attacked?"

Bettham shook his head. "You need to know where it will fly and how to operate the machine. We won't miss one stone." He then waved Josh closer to him. "Let me show you the safety rope and how to let it loose."

Both men walked over to the machine when they turned to see a group of men led by an apparently drunk nobleman climb up the last few stairs to their tower.

"HOLD THERE." Landin Rutt commanded as he crested the stairs. "What do you think you are doing? This is MY tower." He bellowed as he and his men moved forward. "I was assigned to run this catapult."

A broad smile crested Landin's face as he spotted Bettham. "If it isn't Bettham Rindorith." He walked defiantly up to Bettham and Josh and then pushed Bettham's shoulder. Bettham stood up tall and turned to Landin but didn't say turn or say anything.

"What is he saying?" Tirad said marching up beside Landin.

Josh turned and looked at Landin, recognizing immediately by his attire that he was some lordling. His eyes widened slightly as he noted the family crest sown on the lads red and black field robe. "You are Landin Rutt." He said without thinking.

"Obviously," came the reply from one of Landin's men behind him. "And you had best address him as Sir if you know what is good for you."

"The 'lord' must then surely know this is Duke Betho's son Bettham?" Tirad added in a incredulous voice.

"ALL I see before me is the grandson of a commoner." Landin replied looking smugly still at the face of Bettham. From the family Rindorith… common tailors the lot." He said with a defiant tone.

Tirad looked at Bettham, watching his face darken with colour. Betthams' fists clenched, balled, but hanging at his side. He totally expected to see Bettham reach forward and deck the Count's son… yet Bettham stood his ground.

"You pompos.." Tirad said figuring if Bettham wouldn't say something and knock this ass down he would.

But Bettham reached up an unclenched hand motioning Tirad to stand his ground. "We were just leaving." He then stepped to the side and walked around Landin. The men behind him made his progress to the stairs none too easy and all jeered as he and Tirad made the top of the stairs and started walking down.

"What in the seven hells is wrong with you?" Tirad demanded before Bettham hit the second stair. Bettham didn't turn around but rather lifted his hand again pleading for silence.

Tirad had to quicken his pace down the stairs to keep up with his friend. "None of his men would have dared to hit you if you had decked Landin... and had they I and Josh and the others would have fought by your side."

They went down thirty or more stairs that twisted around the back of the tower. Tirad, then, was having had enough racing after Bettham put his hand firmly on his friends shoulder and turned him around. "What in the hell is going on Bettham? Never had I thought you lacking the courage to stand up for yourself."

"It's not that simple." Bettham said shacking. His face was still flush red and his teeth were clenched in anger. "I can't'"

"Why? You afraid." Tirad prodded.

"NO!" Bettham said defiantly. "I decked Landin three years when he stopped me in the city of Narway...." Bettham paused. "You don't understand."

"So if you know you can beat him?" Tirad said now very confused. "No I don't understand so explain it to me my friend. Explain to me how the son of a Montteran Count can bully a Duke's son around."

"Count Palantine." Bettham retorted. "Son of the Count Palatine..." He then shook his head furiously. "But that isn't it."

Tirad looked at his friend. "He called you something... Rindorith."

Bettham nodded. "My mom came from the Casten Mountain area... Lindor Rutt's lands. She was born to my Nanna and Opa Rindorith."

"So?" Tirad said looking more puzzled then ever.

"My mom was born a commoner. My dad when visiting Narway met her. She worked the front store that my grandparents ran – they were simple tailors."

"So." Tirad shrugged. "So what - I still don't get it." Tirad said frustrated.

"He thinks he is superior because both his parents can trace their lineage back to other noble houses…. On my mom's side.." Bettham's voice trailed off.

"Who gives a hoot?" Bettham yelled looking back up the way they had come. He turned as if he was going to return back to the top of the tower. "We should knock him on his ass, teach him a lesson."

Bettham reached up and grabbed Tirad's shoulder and stopped him turning him around forcibly. "WE CAN'T" He implored.

"Why not?" begged Tirad.

"When last we met I decked him. And I did it in front of a few of his pompous friends." Bettham began. "After I left the city we received a letter from my Nanna… her store had been broken in to by thugs, they destroyed the place and hurt my grandfather."

Tirad looked back at his friend, his mouth open in shock.

"My grandparents still live under his father's rule." Bettham pleaded. "WE have tried to convince them to move back to the North with us… but they refuse. They have lived their whole life there; they are old and fear our lands too cold…. "

"So as long as they live," Tirad began. "He holds that over you? You think he was behind your grandparent's place being broken in to?"

"I can feel it. I know it, but I have no proof." Bettham said. "My father doesn't get along with Count Lindor and he is not one to go to Roehn on a family matter – especially one he cannot prove."

Tirad looked back up the wall and then back to his friend. "Me personally, I would stick him. Just say the word and he disappears this night." Tirad winked at Bettham – won't cost you a penny more than what I owe you."

"I would give that gladly." Bettham began. "But too risky. If Lindan is found with a blade in his ribs, especially NOW after that scene… and a small war might break out back home. We can't afford that now."

"Besides." Bettham said looking up the tower wall to where Lindan likely stood. "Perhaps the Mohen will solve my problem."

Bettham and Tirad reached the lower courtyard and looked back as they heard a loud CLANG as the eastern catapult was released.

"oh my." Tirad started as they heard a man's terrified scream echoing down from far above. In the darkness both stood aghast as the catapult let loose – and sitting atop the arm they heard clearly Josh scream as he was thrown upward.

Bettham took a step forward to return and then let unfurl the chains of his Morningstar. "This time he has gone too far, I will put an end to that ass."

Tirad jumped forward and put a hand on Bettham's shoulder this time restraining him. "Now is the time." He said in a quieting voice.

Bettham turned and looked puzzled back at Tirad. "Josh didn't deserve "his words were cut short as Tirad shook his head.

"No – but now is not the time." Tirad said once again.

As in reply from the east came the reply from the Mohen catapults. Massive burning stones roes up, visible high over the eastern walls. A few descended well short, but one massive burning stone crested the wall and smashed into the ground before them. Fire and pitch spraying the area.

Both men jumped back in surprise although it was well short of their mark the size and concussion from the massive burning stone was staggering.

"We should get back." Tirad said coaxing his friend to turn westward. "Tunder will be looking for us."

Bettham took a last look at the eastern tower. Tirad pulled with his hand coaxing him to walk with him back to the western walls. "Another time…" Tirad added. "Assuming he lives the night."

Bettham turned and started following his friend back to their post on the western wall. "Assuming any of us do." He said softly to himself.

Darkness Falls

The sun was setting, and darkness was falling light a blanket on the horizon. Shadows played across the Terran hills, clouds filled out the sky blocking the light from moons and stars above.

The hills before General Bruto Gadral and the Terran Southern army rolled up and down in the horizon. It was the last bit of cover they would have before descending down to the Terran Planes. From there on, only darkness would protect them from view. From there on, each sound they made and the continuous sound of their riding would eventually let the Mohen's know of their advance.

Sir Bruto looked up at the dark, cloud filled sky praying for snow. "All week long, it has rained and snowed and now the sky is bereft of rain or sleet that might muffle the sounds of our advance." He cursed to himself. As if in reply a singular snowflake fell before him as he rode. He bent down slightly so it would hit the mail on his face. Inwardly he smiled. "It will snow. It will snow." He said to himself as if trying to convince himself.

The general sat up in his saddle and looked quickly behind him hoping to share his observation with his king, but Methor Bestinor was nowhere to be seen. He wondered when the King would return from his ride back to the newly acquired Par Torian Company – hoping it would be soon.

Their visit with Count Marrow Bissrod of Par Tor had been brief. The King had suspected that the gates of Par Tor might be shut to him so they had in secret had discussions with the Count's captain, who among other things had once served under Gadral's command. The Count had indeed ordered the gates shut when he had found out that Methor's army was approaching, however, his captain Sir Trious Printon failed to execute the order and in stead had stood fast with a strong contingent of soldiers loyal to him and ensured the gates were open when King Methor and General Gadral approached.

Confronted by King Methor Bestinor, General Gadral and their entire army the Count quickly bent his knee to Methor and offered up the remaining four hundred mounted crossbowman he had. The discussion was brief, there was little the Count could do or say.

Less than three hours later the crossbowmen of Par Tor rode from their gates led by Sir Trious Printon following the general and their King. Sir Bruto couldn't have been happier. The bowmen's armour was heavy and they carried great heavy crossbows – exactly the type of augmentation they would need to put a serious dent into the Mohen regulars who sported heavy plate male.

Sir Bruto was also excited having Sir Treious Printon under his command having had the pleasure of his aid when last the Duke had ventured north against the Masti. Sir Bruto hoped that soon Sir Printon would leave his company of men and ride forward so that they could talk, however, knew in his heart that the good captain would not likely leave his men – knowing that their moral was important. They had woken up this day, only to find that they were to leave home and heart and venture north to face a force many times their size.

Sir Bruto rode smoothly forward, his large brown stallion, Midra, kept an even pace as they moved up the next hill. Midra moved almost effortlessly up the hill, for sport he manoeuvred him up and through a few spaced out trees. From the top of the hill he hoped to sight one or more of the twenty-four scouts he had sent out in advance of the army. They were the best men he had. Their mission – to remove whatever ears or eyes the Mohen might have stationed south of their forces. As he rode up the hill, he wondered if they had seen anything, or if he might see signs of their passage.

The general heard the beat of fast hoofs from behind him and looked back. A man wearing the whites and grays of his scout was spiriting his horse up from behind him. Sir Bruto slowed Midra and turned to face the rider. However, the man's head was bear of hood and his face showed panic. With one arm he held up a finger and pointed to the top of the hill. Sir Bruto spurred Midra and wheeled him to face again the top of the hill. He could see nothing, but knew instinctively that atop the hill must sit or stand a Mohen sentry. He leaned forward in his saddle and pressed his knees in to his mount "Haste" he said forward to the waiting ears of his stallion. His horse responded immediately by pumping its large muscular legs tearing the soil beneath it the beast and rider surged up the hill.

From behind him he heard his scout yell. "Atop. Atop" His voice sounded hoarse as the man was likely winded having had to run back to his mount. Sir Bruto wondered what had gone awry and why he had been able to ride ahead of his own scout. 'If the Mohen beast was awaken, the Mohens would be sure to exact their payment for this folly in blood.'

As the general approached the top of the hill still he saw nothing out of the ordinary. The snow and ice were unmarked showing no prior rider or man had gone where he was riding. It wasn't until he topped the hill that he noticed anything... There fifty meters or more down the hill was the broken body of one of his other scouts. The man lay beside his standing horse. An arrow neatly standing out from either side of his neck – the man had been expertly slain by a marksman. No note of fear, nor call of warning would have been issuable by the man. The tracks before the horse showed that the scout had been riding fast from the west, and had been shot while horse and rider were in full flight..

"But from where?" Sir Bruto said out loud as he continued his charge over the top of the hill and then down the hill towards the man. Behind him he heard his other scout riding hard, trying in vain to catch up.

He wasn't sure if it was the slightest of movements, or a sound that drew his eye to a small clump of shrubs twenty meters to the right of him, but instinctively he turned Midra to charge directly the position from where he noted the motion.

The Mohen sentry, had used the clump of shrub to shoot his man from, but was already running at full speed east towards his mount which Sir Bruto realized was lying tied and hobbled below an evergreen thirty or more meters to the east. He immediately pressed his knees guiding Midra to cut off the scout from his mount. As Sir Gadral and his mount turned, an arrow hissed past. Looking up he searched the landscape but noticed no other movement so stayed his course and moved to pull his sword out from the sheath.

The scout dove and twisted as Midra drew close hoping to roll out from the raised perch of the general. Midra, reading the general thoughts turned mid stride and the General leaned low out of his stirrups and swung his long blade down and at the dodging Mohen scout.

Sir Gadral's blade caught the scout in the mid of the man's back. Propelled by Midra's charge and the generals strong shoulder the blade sliced through the scout's white robe like a hot knife through butter. The blade sank deep until it jarringly met the man's spine and then skull.

The long sword yanked and pulled violently out of the general's hands pulling him almost out of his saddle as Midra passed by with continued momentum past the Mohen soldier.

Sir Gadral reached up pulled himself back onto his saddle and then reeled Midra to slow and turn. He sat up in his seat desperately searching for where the arrow had come from. He looked behind and up the hill and noticed the body of his second scout lying in the snow and ice now blotched with the man's blood.

Blood pounded in the general's ear as the adrenalin pumping in his veins started to force his body to demand payment in extra oxygen. He breathed in heavily through his mouth, moisture fogged in front of him partially obscuring his vision. He kneed Midra forward and around, hoping to make a more difficult target to hit.

Seeing nothing the general spurred his horse forward, down further into the valley. Hoping that the second scout, was alone and now headed back to his hidden horse hoping to make it back to report his findings. Sir Gadral knew the general direction and healed Midra into a full gallop.

Evergreen trees passed by the general occasionally slapping him as Midra exploited every last step of free space between the trees. Soft snow and ice flew up from behind him as they raced down the hill. The General stifled a howl of delight as he finally spotted horse tracks running up the hill and into the thicker set of trees at its rise.

Midra pumped and they rose up the hill in a continued, unwavering flow. UP, UP, UP they went, in and out of trees – never slowing, never faltering.

At the top Midra jumped over a fallen tree and Sir Gadral bent forward and into the saddle as his horse sought footing on the steep slope. Ahead not fifty meters before him now he spotted the white robe of another Mohen scout. The Mohen soldier, obviously well seasoned didn't slow, nor turn in his saddle, but raced at top speeds to spirit away from the Terrans.

The general grunted as Midra jumped another smaller clump of shrubs. Inwardly he smiled as he realised that he was quickly gaining on the scout and his smaller mount. His mind flashed with thoughts as his hand throbbed, sending a reminder to his brain that he no longer had a sword. Instinctively, he reached down and pulled his Dirk from his side. His hand ached; his grip on the blade was light at best.

Just as the general had expected as the Mohen made it half way up the next hill, he was almost directly behind him. Midra instinctively leaned in and gave Sir Gadral the added boost of speed he needed. The stallion's neck shot out and its plated face bent forward as its teeth snapped at the hindquarters of the Mohen's mount. In the next moment Midra's shoulders were beside the Mohen's mare's hindquarters and Bruto Gadral turned his mounts head ever so slightly.

Midra's shoulder touched the lighter horses flank tripping it sending the Mohen horse and scout tumbling. The Mohen scout flew from his horse as it crashed head first into the ground. He rolled and tumbled, first forward and then backward down the hill.

Sir Gadral pulled back the reigns lightly and Midra turned round a small tree then started bearing down to where the Mohen had fallen. The scout, still alive started to rise. Gaining momentum descending the hill, the general bore down on the man. Midra's chest hit the rising man and crumpled him under the stallions crashing hoofs.

Four strides further down the General turned knowing already what he would see in the darkness - the Mohen scout's broken body lying in the snow.

The general's chest heaved as he inhaled great gulps of air. Dark amongst the thicker trees and starless sky his eyes flashed. Searching, he hoped to catch the remaining light of the day. Deathly silence enveloped him; neither a bird, nor rabbit stirred. Even the Terran forces could not be heard being shielded by the undulating hills behind him.

He turned his mount and nudged the great brown stallion to climb to the crest of the hill.

Atop the hill the General stopped and looked down. There at the end of a long sweeping hill lay the Terran Flats. Although still many kilometers away, he could make out the Mohen fires which stretched out ominously far to the east. The capital city was dimly visible.

From down below another Terran scout rode up the hill to him. The man moved methodically and without panic reassuring the general. As he drew near he turned to look down with him to the sweeping planes. "He wouldn't have made it past me." The scout said softly. "But thanks for saving me the bother."

"There were two." The general remarked casually looking over at the scout who was nodding.

"We thought there were." The scout agreed. "Quite good, fast and quiet. We could see their signs, knew they were about but needed to flush them out. We got behind them and a few circled in to push them forward."

"Did we get them all – are you sure?" Sir Gadral asked looking over at the man and then pointing to the north. "If they wake that beast early there will be hell to pay."

"There are none other." The scout replied as he turned slightly hearing the sound of the hoofs of the Terran regulars in the not too distant south. He looked to the sky and smiled.

"I will leave you here then to await the army while I go below." The scout said as he moved slowly down the hill. He turned looking back. "I went out a ways, the dark hills will hide us and the wind will be in our face to hide our sounds."

"And snow as well." the general said looking up to the sky. "Dark night, flat ground, and snow…"

"Couldn't ask for any better." the scout agreed. "Except perhaps that our numbers were reversed."

The general chuckled softly in reply and looked backward. "I had best go retrieve my sword." He said turning his own mount. "I might have need of it this night."

River's edge

Stephan reached down to the dark forest earth, picked up a handful of dark soil and began rubbing it on his face and the back of his hands. His voice was low, not quite hushed but low enough that Dimi and Etch had to stop moving in order to hear him. "We need to obscure as best we can our scent."

Stephan bent down and picked up a fistful of dark loam. "The oiled leathers are warm and we are sweating. Wogs and Weer will smell our scent within a kilometre."

Etch and Dimi following the clansman's actions reluctantly reached down pulling up fists of dark, marshy smelling dirt and began to coat themselves with it.

"Smells heavy after Malt, sure the Wog's aren't drinkers?" Etch said with a smile.

"It has a heavy oil within it, it should last for a little while even when we get wet." Stephan chuckled as he looked over to Etch. "Most of my men would sniff you out, but the Wogs won't." As he turned his voice turned to a tone stressing how serious he was. "The last few kilometres we will be crawling in the river itself, water hide our scent a bit, but these dogs can track anything so we need to be very careful."

"How far away is the river?" Etch asked softly.

Stephan looked around him before responding. "I would guess, at the speed we are going no less than two hours away from the Tie Rei river's edge, and less than four hours from there to the two towers."

"From here on we should expect the unexpected." He continued with a grin. "When we make it to the bank of the river, get wet and remove what scent you can. The less we smell the safer we will be. It will be dark out when we get to the towers, and we know for certain Weer patrol the base of the castle."

Sar Douglas looked over at Dimi's side noticing her slim silver dagger. "We can't confront them. If they see us or smell us going in we will be swarmed." He paused a moment his face grew solemn. "You might be fast, but remember what it took to bring down my brother."

Dimi and Etch nodded in understanding and after a short pause Stephan turned and continued walking northeast.

The forest was unusually quiet. The late fall rains had softened twigs and roots and the snow muffled the sounds of their movement. There were virtually no sounds of birds or other animals.

When they reached the river's bank Dimi pointed at Etch and then pinched her nose indicating he should be the first into the water. Etch exited from the tree line and crawled to the stony bank while Dimi and Stephan scanned the area looking to see if they were being watched.

Crawling over large stones, trying to be as inconspicuous as possible Etch moved slowly to the river's edge and then turned and started to lower his legs into the water.

The water flowed up Etch's pant legs and down into his soft soled leather shoes. The current was light and tugged only gently. He looked up and scanned the opposite bank over two hundred meters away. Turning he looked back checking to see if Stephan and Dimi had seen anything.

Dimi yelped suddenly catching Stephan's attention. Looking over Stephan froze, startled as he watched Dimi unexpectedly bound without concern of being seen over rock and tree towards the river's edge. Confused he looked around expecting to see a Wog or Weer, but saw none. Then he realised Dimi's concern, Etch was no longer to be seen anywhere.

"Damn. He fell in!" Dimi said in a half whisper, half normal voice as she bound forward.

Stephan, overcoming his concern about being seen bounded after Dimi franticly scanning the river's edge searching for Etch. His eye caught the colour brown mixed in between a few larger boulders ten meters downstream and his feet instinctively propelled him forward.

Dimi jumped and danced upon the tops of the rocks as she too caught sight of Etch, now face down within the river, lodged between two boulders. From one stone to the other she leaped until she was by the shore looking over at her friend, submerged and lifeless.

Stephan reached Dimi's side a moment later. The rocks where Etch lay were green with moss and looked treacherously slick and he was too far out to reach. Without concern as to how deep the water was before him Stephan jumped forward and into the river.

"We are lucky the stones stopped him." Stephan said as he splashed forward in waist deep water. "Currents slow, but still fast enough to have whisked him away." He said as he reached forward and down to grab hold of the scuff of Etch's leather jacket.

Stephan gave the jacket a strong pull dislodging Etch from the front of the rock. The current grabbing hold of Etch pulled Stephan forward almost dragging the two further downstream. Determination and a streak of concern crossed Stephan's face, then it blurred showing nothing more than great determination as he heaved hard and pulled back.

Dimi laying as far forward as she could upon the last rock by the river reached forward from the bank and grabbed onto Stephan's shoulder pulling him to her. "K", Stephan said as he huffed. "Almost there." With a great pull he floated Etch around so that Dimi could get a grip on him.

""Push." Dimi said as she pulled up. Stephan went under the water and under Etch's torso and then pushed up with all his might lifting Etch out of the water while Dimi guided it to lay upon the rock by her.

As Stephan came out of the water he looked around. "I don't see anyone, but we need to get back into the forest, we made a lot of noise." He reached down and grabbed Etch's unconscious body under the arms and started dragging him to the forest. Dimi, grabbing one foot pushed while Stephan pulled until together the three were once again within the shelter of the evergreens.

"What in the seven hells happened?" Stephan asked as he and Dimi turned over Etch.

"Don't know." Dimi replied as she bent down and turned Etch over slightly on his side and started prying apart his mouth. "One second he was there, the next he wasn't." She looked at him confused. "I don't see an arrow. Could it be magic?"

Stephan looked up and around in concern then back down at Etch and shook his head. "They would have been on us I think by now if there was any foe about."

Dimi glanced around. "We are unseen. For now." she said as she bent down to listen for signs of life. Etch sputtered and coughed all of a sudden and Dimi looked up smiling at Stephan who smiled broadly back.

"Well he is alive." Stephan said.

"Good, now I can kill him for scaring the hell out of me." Dimi said half jokingly.

A second later Etch's eyes opened. He lay on his back gasping for air and trying to clear his thoughts. "What happened?" Etch sputtered and then he started to shiver.

Dimi immediately went to her pouch and pulled the flash from it. She held it to Etch's lips and Stephan tilted his head back. A stream of the liquid spilled down his throat. As he swallowed Etch's eyes widened. He coughed twice and then sneezed. "Oh my, I am going to pay for that." He said in a choking voice.

"You ok?" Stephan inquired as he looked down and then around at their surroundings.

"We said wash off, not jump in." Dimi added. "What is it with you? Every time you are near water I wait to hear a splash."

"That was weird." Etch said shaking his head uncertainly. "I was fine; water didn't even feel remotely cold. Then it was like a cold metal hammer hitting me in the head." he added coldly.

Dimi looked back frustratingly to Stephan who looked startled and then responded with an unconvincing shrug.

"What happened?" He asked looking around. "How long was I out?"

"Seconds," Stephan said reassuringly. "A minute at most."

Dimi drew close to Etch and put her hand on his forehead and felt his cold wet cloths. "The water is cold, I think it triggered something. Perhaps you should follow by land?"

"Wasn't cold at all...." Etch said shaking his head. "And i remember feeling a sense of dread, the Weer are out but they are distracted by something in the castle.... something is keeping them at arms lengths from the castle, something they fear." Etch looked up at Stephan.

Stephan sighed and although smiling shook his head back and forth. "That i guess is good news and bad news. There will be more out then in i guess, but it does make you pause as to what type of ill wind blows to keep a large pack of blood thirsty Weer away, Eh?"

Etch moved to his knees and then stood up and tried to brush himself off. "I am ok, lets keep going, whatever i felt won't keep them disoriented for too long." He reassured his friends but he staggered as he took a step forward. Dimi and Stephan grabbed his arm to steady him.

Dimi took a sip of the dark liquid and then handed the bottle over to Stephan who, after Dimi nodded took a swallow. He winced when it went down. "Strong stuff." he said. "And it burns all the way down." Looking over at Etch she raised the bottle but Etch simply shook his head. Dimi shrugged and return the bottle to the bag at her hip.

"If Sarta is the cause of the feeling, once we do away with her.... the Weer from all around these parts will be running back. Trust me, there are many more in the hills that we see, cowering, only the very brave or highly disoriented are not in the caves."

"... lets keep going." Stephan said as he turned and started back to the river.

"Disturbed, disoriented or not, just remember." Stephan said in a quiet voice as they approached the river again. "No speaking if at all possible, not even whispers, Wogs have better hearing then dogs. And Weer hearing is almost on the border of magical. And their sense of smell is amazing. We need to walk up the shoreline a bit and then enter the river and crawl along the edge of the river the rest of the way. With luck they won't be able to smell us, and the motion of the water should make us very hard to see in the darkness. Just watch me, follow me and keep the noise down and yourself clean of sweat, keep slipping into the water to ensure our scent is week."

Stephan shivered, he then turned to Dimi. "Will the potion last?"

Etch chuckled as he heard the question come from behind him. Turning he nodded back to Stephan. "Trust me." Etch said sarcastically. "It will, but you ass will pay for it in the morning."

The sky was darkening as the sun set. Shadows filled the forest on either side of the bank. The cold river water now felt refreshing against their heated bodies as it sluiced around them.

The three walked in a crouch from bolder to bolder quickly looking around for signs of sentries. As the river narrowed the water's speed increased. The sound of rapids soon was all they could hear. The evening sky darkened making visibility limited.

Like a trio of mink the three friends walked and crawled along the river's edge and within the river itself – passing areas of rocks, fallen trees and larger pools of water. Hunkered low they crept forward silently. Beside them the continued movement of the river raced as the banks drew closer together.

As they passed each bend in the river, their progress slowed. Crawling increased and only when necessary did they stand up and race from one bolder to another. They dripped as they entered and exited the cold racing river.

Stephan stopped the team as they came up and behind a massive tree that had fallen from the forest to lay overtop the left bank. The evergreen was bare of needles having been stripped by the elements over the years, but the many intertwined branches of the top of the tree still afforded the three good cover.

"Catch your breath." Stephan urged the other two. "Around the next bend we will see the towers."

Etch looked up and around his pupils consumed his iris. "Dark." he whispered. "I can hardly see a thing." He turned and looked at Dimi's whose emerald eyes reflected a little of what remained of the light of the day. "How are you doing?"

Dimi's eyes moved up and down before the two. "I can still see very well." She looked up to the cloudy sky. "But not for long. It is going to get very dark tonight. Halos should already be visible but its light is fully hidden. When Detros rises it might get a little better."

"Trust me." Stephan added in a sarcastic whisper. "Detros never helps man. When he rises, then the Weer are at their strongest."

Their breathing calmed as they rested. After a moment Stephan touched Dimi's shoulder. "You need to take the lead. Just follow the bank, another curve and with luck the towers will be high enough up out of the forest that we will see them still. Pass under the great causeway along the shore and past the castle to a point where we can talk again."

He turned to Etch and touched his shoulder. "From here on even breath softly." A sense of urgency was in his voice. "The river runs faster as it narrows, with luck they won't hear us." Stephan said. "Keep low too to the water their sight is good but the motion of the water should obscure us. But don't splash."

"Ok, let's go." Dimi said as she moved deeper into the river so she could pass under the fallen tree. She came up quietly on the other side and then waited a moment until Etch and Stephan rose up out of the water.

Dimi proceeded forward very slowly with Etch following occasionally touching the back of her legs to ensure he knew where she was. His blood felt like it was on fire and he occasionally bent forward to let the cold river flow over his face and head.

As Dimi led them round the next bend in the darkness she stopped and turned to them. Before them down another two hundred meters the tops of the two towers punched out of the forest on either side of the river. Between them, high above the river spanned the bridge and from its middle dropped a single supporting pillar framed by two stone arches.

To Etch and Stephan the towers loomed as giants ghostly silhoets against he night's poorly lit sky. Like giant arms they reached to the sky and between the arms hung a massive stone causeway. The river could be heard racing from ahead as the shores drew further together. But below the horizon the shadow of the castle itself obscured everything else.

Dimi proceeded slowly drawing the other two forward. Like turtles they pushed themselves through the shallows on the side of the river, trying to avoid the stronger currents, yet also trying to stay as far from the shore as possible.

When the three were within less than fifty meters Dimi stopped. Her small hand darted back to Etch and then Stephan as he drew closer to her. She tapped them both on the head indicating that they should wait while she returned. She then turned to explored ahead.

Dimi's eyes were wide open, but even her excellent vision now could distinguish little below the great causeway. The towers and archway cast a black shadow that obscured everything. She crawled forward inhaling slowly and moving her head back and forth hoping to sense or see whatever might lurk ahead.

Sensing, more than seeing or smelling anything Dimi stopped and held her breath. A few torches far above on the towers cast small golden rays down but they flickered and the light they cast, diffused made her wonder if she had stopped out of fear. But then, out of the corner of her left eye she noticed movement. Something lurked, something walked along the shore and was proceeding under the great causeway.

It walked slowly forward, quietly on all fours into the deeper darkness as if it was to lay in wait for some unsuspected pray. When it was a little further off, Dimi breathed once again. She took in deep, long drafts of breath. Quietly she deliberately, yet quietly hyperventilated until her mind grew almost dizzy with oxygen. Then she held her breath and stalked forward. Her hand every other moment reaching down to check the position of her blowgun attached to her leg, and her knife in its sheath by her side.

As she entered the pitch blackness Dimi felt again the sense of presence. It was large, and forboding. She sniffed softly catching its scent for the first time. Dry and musty was its scent. It smelled of matted oily hair, and of crusty dried blood and saliva. 'It smells of things foul and corrupted.' She said to herself.

Slowly Dimi moved forward, hand over hand she moved quietly up the riverbank stopping often and listening, and smelling. Over the rapids she heard a stone clatter as something else moved on the opposite bank. 'One on either side.' she thought to herself.

The beast before her also hearing the sound on the opposite shore moved and then inhaled deeply.

Dimi closed her useless eyes and concentrated, trying to hear the beast breath, trying to locate it.

'Dry and musty.' she thought to herself. 'They don't like water so won't get too close for fear of getting sprayed.' Dimi smiled to herself.

Dimi paced her inhalations to match and mimic the rhythmic sound of the rapids around her. There was no movement from ahead granting her some confidence. She moved forward ever so slowly listening to the sounds bouncing off of the causeway around her.

Dimi stopped just shy of where she thought the beast now stood. After her last move and breath the beast had held its own breath giving her the feeling that it now sensed her presence, but likely was not aware as to where exactly she was.

'There is no way the others will pass by here unnoticed.' Dimi thought to herself. 'If it can sense me, the other two would be doomed.

Dimi paused a moment contemplating how she should proceed. To her right the river dropped off and was too strong to swim against. But the tower was too close to the river bank... and to close to the creature.'

Realising her only course of action Dimi rolled slightly to her left so that she could gain access to her quiver which had been tied securely to her leg and sealed. The lid was watertight, but she needed to ensure that the dart extracted wasn't washed of its poison before it was used. Gingerly she delicately raised her leg enough out of the water that she could safely open the top of the quiver. Every muscle in her body was tense as she tried to manoeuvre silently.

Painfully, and painstakingly she removed a dart from the quiver and then replaced the lid on the quiver. Before lowering her leg her other hand brought up the blowgun tilting it to drain it of water. With split concentration Dimi listened trying to ascertain if the beast that stood almost beside her was noticing her actions.

Dimi paused a moment with concern. 'I must keep it pointed down until firing.' She thought to herself... 'Else the poison will wash down and in to my mouth!'

There was no easy way forward for Dimi. The water was fast and deep and her blowgun had limited distance and her vision was blank. Holding her breath she moved forward... then froze. The scent of the beast was powerful, almost overpowering – it must have either drawn closer.

'It was close. Very, very close.' Dimi froze again mid crawl wondering how far away it was. The air currents under the bridge wafted back and forth and she closed her eyes and let the air played and dance in her nostrils. Stars of light danced behind her tightly clenched eyes.

Finally, after an excruciatingly long second or two the beast moved giving Dimi all the information she needed. In one fluid motion Dimi raised the blowgun and blew.

The creature jumped, but missed its mark landing several feet behind Dimi. Dimi reached down to her belt for her knife as she heard its snarl turned to a cough. Her hand came away from her belt as next she heard the beast fall forward, a small splash indicating that perhaps its arm or paw had hit the river's edge.

The small assassin paused and listened intently – searching to hear if the beast still breathed. She inhaled, searching for a sign of scent that indicated her poison was working.

Dimi froze hearing from the opposite bank some obvious movement. But after a moment there was silence. Then to her nose came the scent that her potion was working – she smiled and turned round and started back to her friends.

Passing the beast Dimi paused a second ensuring that the massive beast was down and breathed no more. Dimi, contented, turned and quietly slipped back into the water taking a moment to rinse her blowgun. She then slipped it back into her leg sheath and started crawling back to her friends.

Five minutes later the trio were passing under the bridge. All three had to hold their breaths as they passed the corpse.

As they passed under the opposite side of the bridge all three looked up to the causeway. What little moonlight made it through the clouds illuminating the back of the causeway and towers. Large spidery forms that ran up and down the back face of the tower walls silently.

When they passed another fifty meters upriver Stephan risked a whisper as slowed Dimi with a whisper. "We are far enough up I think."

Dimi and Etch drew near to Stephan to hear his muted speech. 'That was a Weer you slew.' He said to Dimi. "But it smelled much worse than any I have seen."

Dimi's head drew close to the other two. "The poison makes them rot very, very fast from the inside out. In less than an hour all that will be there is a puddle of goo and its bones."

So close together were the three faces that Dimi and Etch could feel Stephan nod. "Good." He added. "Less to stumble upon and it could buy us some time."

He started looking back at the pillar. "Let the current work for you…" He looked at Dimi. "Sure you can make it?"

Dimi returned his comment with a harsh whisper. "Don't worry about me. Just don't get too closer to the other side, there is another Weer there."

Stephan nodded while he uncoiled the rope that had been wrapped around his shoulder. He tied one end of the rope to his waste and handed the other end to Dimi. He then smiled back at both and pushed himself from the shallows into the strong current. His strokes were strong but silent as he started swimming with the current downstream to the opposite shore. A moment later Etch followed him followed closely by Dimi.

The current pulled them all fast downstream towards the pillar. Stephan after a few strong well timed strokes stopped swimming and let the current pull him to the eastern side of the pillar while Dimi and Etch held on to the cord coasted along the eastern shore.

As Stephan passed the pillar his rope pulled taunt and Dimi and Etch held on fast. Less than a few seconds later all three found themselves at the end of the rope bobbing five meters behind the pillar.

Etch reached out and grabbed Stephan and together they started pulling up the ropes, bringing the three to the back of the pillar. Dimi grabbed the slack rope and tied the ends together.

"Found it." Etch whispered to Stephan and then Dimi as his foot reached down and found the opening below the water.

Dimi, unfettered by rope went first. Holding on to Etch's leg she followed it down to his soft leather boots until she found the lip of the hole, then pulling herself further down she entered it. Inside the pillar the water was still and she rose slowly so to ensure no sound would be made.

There was an eyrie echo of water and from inside the tower the rapids could be heard. It was dark, very, very dark within the tower, but at the top of it. Way, way up Dimi could make out what she thought was a crack in a floorboard and above it was a torch.

A moment later Etch and then Stephan rose up out of the water beside Dimi. Treading water the three silently attempted to look around and to listen if their entry had been detected. Hearing nothing Stephan swam forward.

A long iron ladder descended to the depths and rose to the top of the tower. Stephan grabbed it and started to slowly climb giving his leathers a moment or two to drain of the majority of the water as he ascended out of the pool. Surprisingly, he still felt warm and his body warmed up considerably as he exited the water. He felt limber and did not feel still as he had expected.

Behind Stephan out too came Etch and Dimi as they all three started to ascend the ladder. Drops of moisture fell from them back down to the water and the sound of which echoed through the tall pillar.

The ladder ended at a landing and Stephan helped the other two onto it and over to the base of the wall. Above, clearly visible by the very small cracks in the floor above was a trap door. He drew the others close his face visible from the small beams of light that seeped through the floor. He put his hand to his ear and all three listened.

Finally Dimi held up two fingers in front of her face. She then put a flat palm up and with her other hand she ran her fingers imitating the shape of a spider. A small shiver went down Etch's back but then the warmth from her potion returned. Both nodded as Dimi went to her quiver and pulled up her blowgun.

Holding two darts in her hand she placed a third in the gun and then she motioned for Etch to bend over and afford her a perch so she could more easily reach the trap.

Silently the three waited until Dimi nodded. Stephan pushed up slowly but firmly on the trap and Dimi's blowgun poked up and through the crack he made. 'PFFFT' a dart was loosed, and then down went the trap door.

There was silence from above, and then there was a scraping sound as spindly legs scraped against the walls or ceilings above. Dimi nodded quickly and Stephan pushed up. However, instead of opening a crack the trap door flew violently up. There above the three was the massive hairy body of a orange and black spider. Its mandibles snapped down and in through the hole in the floor as Dimi fell backward getting out of its reach. Stephan reached down and pulled out his blade, but before he could reach up and plunge it into the beast another burst of breath was heard and a dart passed within centimetres of his ear and then stuck into the bulbous body of the spider.

Stephan looked down at Dimi lying on her back, with blowgun still in her mouth. He then looked up in time to see the spider sag and fall through the opening onto Etch who was just trying to rise.

Stephan kicked the spider's body and sent it hurling over the edge of the lading. A second later there was a loud splash as it hit the water below. Without waiting Dimi was up and jumping over Etch and then pulling herself out of the hole.

"Clear." Came her voice a second later as Dimi's head flashed in and then back out of the pillar's entrance.

Etch climbed out first, followed by Stephan. All three stood a moment crouched down looking down the causeway. It was over five meters high, entirely made of stone. Small arrow slits were placed on either side. To either side the causeway ran. Stephan hesitated only a moment then dragged the other spider over to the hole and threw it in. They heard another splash just as Etch closed the trap. Etch smiled over at Stephan and then Dimi. "You know." He whispered. "I don't relish the idea of getting back into that water and dive down between two massive sleeping spiders."

"They are dead." Dimi assured him. "Besides." She said confidently. "The water might be a little oily, but there won't be much of their bodies left in a few mintues."

Stephan cringed as he thought of what melted spiders would fell like. But shaking himself of the vision and feeling he turned and headed east towards the end of the hall.

The causeway's end was closed off with a massive wooden door. Stephan put his ear to it as did Dimi. Convinced nothing was beyond Stephan opened it slowly. Dimi's eyes widened and she bounded forward unexpectedly past Stephan. Etch and Stephan pushed through the door as they watched Dimi lunge towards a dwarfish red demon that was moving at lightning speed.

Pincer

"STILL NO SENTRIES, HOW CAN THIS BE?" Methor yelled out so that Sir Gadral could hear him above the sound of the army that rode behind the two.

Even though heavily armoured in scale male, Methor noted the general's shrug and shaking of head. "TOO BUSY WATCHING THE SPECTACLE I GUESS!" The General yelled back to his king.

Methor smiled as he glanced behind him to look at the army stretched out on either side behind the general and himself. There air was alive with the sound of thundering hooves.

He was still very perplexed. They were now not all that far from the Mohen lines, Terran Add was clearly in sight and yet they had not ridden into any other sentries since the last set of hills, nor had they seen any sign of forces in the distance being assembled to face them.

The king looked into the distance at the Mohen forces stretched out well into the eastern horizon and the massive city of Terran Add which stretched out to the west. 'Perhaps.' Methor thought to himself. 'They were indeed too over confident and all the Mohen forces were watching the spectacle of lights being delivered by their catapults.'

As they rode forward to Terran Add and the Mohen the King watched as another massive fiery mortar was launched from a Mohen catapult at the city. It lifted up and flew in a long high arch. A long tail of flames followed it in the sky. The ball arched and then fell – hitting beyond the walls of the city. A moment later even from the distance they were at there was the sound of a discernable thud.

Before the King had even heard the sound of the impact he was watching himself another start to rise from the Mohen field. The show had started half an hour before, and was continuing. And in the distance now clearly audible was the resounding cheers and jeers that the thousands of Mohen soldiers were issuing as each fiery ball flew.

"THE MOHEN CATAPULTS ARE PUTTING ON A SHOW! PERHAPS ALL THEIR EYES ARE LOOKING AT THE SPECTACLE, BUT ARE THEY DEAF AS WELL?" The King yelled over at his general.

"PERHAPS AFTER ALL THESE YEARS WE HAVE GOTTEN LUCKY?" The general replied. "EACH SECOND CLOSER WE GAIN ADVANTAGE." He yelled looking forward.

Massive Mohen siege engines were still far enough away from TerranAdd that nothing from within the capital could touch them. The Mohen had started their siege by sending wave after wave of burning pitch into the city. Within the city itself a few fires had already started making the city glow and atop the walls Montteran soldiers scurried back and forth in panic.

One after another-fiery balls of pitch and stone were launched, and wave after wave of cheers followed their impacts into the city as the thousands of Mohen soldiers egged on those manning the siege engines.

From the distance King Methor could not see clearly those upon the walls yet, but he grew concerned about the damage already done to the city and wondered what type of defences might be left..

"I WOULDN'T WANT TO BE INSIDE RIGHT NOW!" Methor yelled over at the general – it must be like hell."

The catapults were being loaded fast enough that as the last one fell upon the city, the first one was ready to fire again. "NO TIME TO EXTINGUISH THE FLAMES." He added.

The general pointed with his sword to the east. "Look how deep they span?" He called out. "They have received reinforcements… DAMN THE MOHEN SOULS - theY are more than WE HAD FEARED – thousands stretch behind!"

"Not so lucky after all." Methor said to himself looking at the forces spread out to the east. "Closer to fifteen then to ten." Cold sweat dripped down the hollow of Methor's back as he glanced back at his own men.

Methor turned back to look at the ever approaching city and Mohen soldiers. Before them the night was dark, their cover had been fantastic. He still absolutely believed that until this very moment that they had not been seen nor heard. However, fear penetrated his confidence. "So many." he said to himself.. 'Should they now turn and retreat to live another day?'the Terran king asked himself. 'Do I abandon my kingdom?'

He then looked over at his general who was looking at him. The same question he just asked himself was now clearly in the eyes of Sir Bruto. But then those eyes narrowed and the general's lips from beneath his helmet let forth the spark of white as his teeth reflected his grin… "How many times had the two of us ridden into battle not expecting to survive – five times?" He yelled over as a reply.

"WHO WANTS TO LIVE FOREVER?" The general replied.

"THEN LET US MAKE SUCH A DIN. THAT MEN WILL SING BALLADS A THOUSAND YEARS FROM NOW." Methor added loudly.

"PROCLAIMING That this night Methor, King of Terran AND HIS MIGHT MEN did ride to glory." The general yelled in reply. Sir Gadral then stood up in his stirrups and waved round his sword and pointed forward. Not caring now if they were heard by the Mohen forces or not – for their approach was too close. The twenty five hundred knights and bowman behind the general cheered as they set their spurs to their mounts.

The sound of hoofs on hard cold soil became a thunder as the Terran army charged.

"FOR KING AND COUNTRY." The General yelled and from behind him came a roaring reply. "**FOR KING AND COUNTRY!**"

All Terran eyes were looking to the horizon – to the castle, to the catapults and their fiery projectiles and to the Mohen forces still un-massed, unassembled. Most of the soldiers were still standing or sitting around watching and cheering on the catapults.

King Methor's smile turned to one of shock as Alixier's lungs expanded, and his back legs pushed off. King Methor clutched with his knees, and reached down with his left hand to his large front stirrup as his steed leapt unexpectedly. As he took to air the only thought that went into the King's mind was started recognition that they had finally reached the first Mohen sentry post.'

Sure enough as Methor and his steed took to the air, below him standing gawking looking still towards the city was a line of entrenched Mohen sentries.

Shiny Mohen faces and helmets all turned to look up and back as the first line of Terran riders attempted to jump their position. A few screamed, but in most cases the Mohen soldiers stood there mute with surprise. Their mouths hung open in complete shock.

The first line of Terran's and their mounts had seen the general and their King's horse take flight, and they had enough time to react. However, those directly behind them did not. Four of the next ten horses with knights atop fell down and into the trench smashing in to the Mohen soldiers, and the wall behind them.

Methor turned to look back and watch, and listen. He cringed noticing the black surcoat of Sir Caston crested the trench, but there, behind the knight was his former page Aaron Murdoc.

From Aaron's perspective it was all a blur. One moment, he was riding along atop his armoured mount behind his knight and the next moment he was plunging forward into darkness. There was glimmer of light reflected off of a Mohen helmet before the sounds of his horse's legs cracking came to his ears. Forward he pitched uncontrollably. His lance previously vertical now dipped uncontrollably forward with him. It impacted first driving the butt end of the lance back and into his leg. The long, hard shaft of wood flexed and pressed and then poked through his armour as his weight and the weight of his horse continued forward.

Aaron inhaled deeply in shock, and then there was the peace of silence as his helmeted head hit and his neck snapped like a dry twig.

The King didn't have time enough to breath out a warning or a prayer, but watched in dismay as the young lad went crashing down with his mount into the mass of Mohen guards.

Methor turned to face forward once again as he heard the Mohen soldiers within the lines finally start to yell as they turned to see their assailants. A thin grip of blood lust played across his face. "Too late you poor bastards – for we are hear!" He yelled out as he pulled his own sword out.

Sir Gadral, the Terran general was a horse length ahead of his king waving his long sword in the air "FOR THE HONOUR OF TERRAN!" He yelled as they approached.

A yell swelled up from the two thousand men behind him. It started like the growl of a dog but ended like the roar of a lion. In one loud voice they called, "**FOR OUR KING!**"

Methor nudged Alixier faster gaining a length and drawing parallel to his general once again. He too lifted his sword and pointed with it at the line of siege engines at the head of the Mohen forces. As was their plan – they would sting this day the Mohen. Not as a flea, but as a wasp stings and tarantula. They would this day draw such Mohen blood that the bastards would turn tail and run back to the mothers snivelling in pain and agony.

Methor risked a last glance behind him noting that the company was as they had planned splitting in two – the forward line of knights that would include himself and the general would charge in front of the siege engines with a goal to set them alit, while the majority of their forces would ride to its rear protecting them and giving them time. They would both strike and continue through to the North and escape – to attack another day once again.

A confused conglomeration of yells and shouts were coming from the Mohen forces. Dozens, then hundreds of men, some armed with nothing but an axe and wearing no armour at all ran to place themselves between the catapults and their attackers. Others could be seen standing up beside fires, trying to quickly lace on breastplate, or tie on boot or mail.

Commands were being yelled out to them by their officers, some not dressed others just exiting tents that had been erected for them. Pandemonium and chaos ruled the moment as the Mohen soldiers at the forefront of their lines watched their death approach on horse.

Methor smiled as the General yelled. "WE HAVE THEM!" He veered his horse slightly to the right and leaned forward and down to slash down at a knight that was running as a madman with waving sword at the Terran riders.

The Mohen soldier's sword rose up too slowly and Methor's blade hit his breastplate sending out such a clang that it shattered the night like a church bells first toll on a Sunday morning.

Without even knowing if the Mohen was dead, or how he had by luck retained his sword, Methor continued forward. He passed the first catapult, and then the second. Others at the end of the line would take these; he would stop much further down the line. Then a third passed, and as he passed a lance was thrown wildly at him. He bent in his saddle easily avoiding it.

A moment later Sir Gadral was again beside him catching a Mohen archer with his blade, and slicing open the man's neck and head as he passed.

A few arrows and bolts began to flash through the night at Methor. Most were not close, yet their buzz was often ended with a thud as it hit man or beast behind him. But then he heard the reply as the skilled ParTorian crossbowmen behind him. "Chang, chang, chang rang out their reply as bolt after bolt sped ahead of the charging group nailing the Mohen soldiers that were assembling to bar their way forward.

Methor counted out as he passed more catapults and then eyed his own target. Teams of men were established, each under a captain or senior knight whose task it was to set light to a specific siege engine… 'And this one – there ahead – was HIS!' He thought as he returned his sword to its sheath and held out his hand as if in a command.

The Par Torian crossbows cut a path through the soldiers ahead dropping many and scattering the rest. Most of the Mohens were racing back east to their lines and to the safety of numbers leaving many of the siege engines relatively unprotected. Only the catapult crews and stanch, brave Mohen soldiers now guarded them.

As Methor approached his target Sir Gardal drew up close to him, their horses breathing heavy they raced forward. The general reached back and pulled out from a bag on his saddle a large round glass bottle, its neck was short and stopped with a plug of wax.

"Careful!" The general yelled. "Its pure Trucklite!"

Methor reached over and grabbed it roughly from his general. Then as he drew near to the catapult he threw the container up and at it. The glass hit the catapult square and shattered sending white powder down around it and onto the remaining three men that stood their ground to protect it. Smoke immediately began to rise from everything the powder touched. The Mohen soldiers coughed gagged and one fell down covering his eyes with his fists – yelling as he did so.

Then from behind the King a skin pierced and streaming water flew and as the drops of water touched the powder in the air and on the ground or Mohen soldier, there immediately appeared a white flame. As the bag descended Methor and Sir Gadral turned to watch as they passed to see the spectacle. AS the bag of water hit – the nights sky turned as if the mid day sun had risen and perhaps even fallen to the earth before them. It was spectacular – There was a concussion that sent the water bearer and his horse flying, the Mohen soldiers disintegrated and then the catapult itself blew apart in great shots of gasping white flame.

Juan Crazy

The flash made Methor gasp in pain as he winced and closed his eyes. Turning he looked forward, but could see nothing but swirling white as his eyes burned with pain.

"TOO MUCH!" Methor yelled. "My eyes!" He yelled to his general.

"HOLD ON." came the general's voice from his side.

It was like the sun had exploded. Methor gasped as fear took hold of him and he continued his frantic charge forward into darkness. Stars swam in his tearing eyes. "I AM BLIND!" he yelled.

"I AM HERE YOUR GRACE!" The general yelled over reaching down and grabbing Alixier main in order to guide it. "I will lead your horse." He called over to comfort his King. "We are almost half way through and before us I can see Duke Hastor Karathor's men!"

"HOW DO THEY FARE?" Methor yelled out anxiously.

"NOT WELL." The General yelled back above the roar of battle. Smashing shields, crashing swords and explosions echoed in the night and to the east there came a continued building of sounds as the Mohen mounted man and beast and began in groups charging.

"The horsemen charged after we did." The general added as he veared their mounts to the west closer to the walls of Terran Add hoping to find an easier passage north. "The Mohen assembled faster in the north and they have not reached as far to the center as we have."

Fear rose as a dark beast in the King's heart. Questions of strategy raced through his mind, and they were followed with fear. Fear of their charge, fear of their enemy, fear for their allies, and mostly – fear that he now was blind for ever.

Methor's fear grew to panic 'How could he command if he was blind?' As he raced forward he threw off his left gauntlet and held his reigns with his right hand. Franticly he reached up and pulled off his helmet and started rubbing his eyes – desperate for sight.

It was just then that the assembled four thousand Mohen archers let loose. Sight could not have assisted nor saved the Terran King, or his General from the volley of four thousand of arrows. Darkness in shape of feather and shaft fell upon the thin lines of Terran and Montteran riders... the black sky fell as one upon them, devouring their lives and pinning them and their mounts to the hard, cold ground.

The fall of Terran Add

General Beston Thesra stood passively as a fiery load of pitch flew over his head and into Terran Add. He listened, waiting for the thud of its impact. Perchance like many of those before it the sound of the impact would be accompanied by the sounds of splintering wood, or crumbling stone. It didn't matter much now; he wouldn't even turn to look behind him even if the sounds were followed by a scream of dismay, shock or pain.

The General knew that alone his forces could not possibly withstand the pending Mohen attack. The rest of General Kikiltoe Mariard's men must have come during the night from PlanTer. A full second line of archers stretched across the far eastern horizon. Before him were well over fifteen thousand Mohen knights, archers and infantrymen. He had likely now within the castle itself no more than a thousand – and those numbers were dwindling with the incessant and very effective rain of stone and pitch. When General Kikiltoe issued the command to storm the castle – they would breach the walls in a heartbeat. There was no use in thinking of retreat or surrender – they had advanced here first, there would the Mohen General would give no quarter.

General Thesra shook his head in realization of the fate before his troops. "If I were him I would cut every soldier down as a warning that I was here to stay, to send such a scream out of Terran Add that Roehn and all other lords, all the Masti and Tock knew that I intended to keep this land."

The general stood impassionate, staring out to the south – waiting. 'Would they come, and if so how many?' he thought. 'If General Bestos Hastor and his troops were not too far a few of his men might live out the night, and if by some miracle the King of Terran and Duke or Sirthinor were with him – they might actually have a small chance.'

The general looked down the eastern walls to the south – squinting in an attempt to improve his vision. The light from the fires from the city behind him and the light from the thousands of massive Mohen campfires before him made the southern planes look very dark.

Sighing Thesra looked up to the dark, cloudy, moonless sky and the light snow that was falling from it. "If they come, there might be hope yet for a surprise.' Shrugging off a feeling of doom and gloom he focused on the night, on the cold, on the oncoming battle steeling himself, tearing emotion and compassion from his consciousness so that he would do what was right, for his men, his king and his country.

'Would they be enough?' He pondered. 'Would King Methor rally his men as King Roehn had hoped? Would the Montterran soldiers ride from the southern shores and make it in time?'

Then on the edge of the darkness he saw them. At first it was nothing more than a line of movement on the horizon. Frantically he scanned the southern edge of the Mohen forces wondering if any had seen what he had.

The Montteran General leaned over the tall tower wall straining forward to watch the Mohen. Behind the siege engines, sat thousands of unsuspecting Mohen soldiers cheering as they watched catapult after catapult fire at the city. Their army stretched out into the horizon and within the center of their massed troops sat a very large tent topped with the banner of the Mohen General.

"Are you with your men, drinking and watching us burn?" Sir Thesra said to himself jokingly. "Or do you sleep, preparing for tomorrows charge?"

He looked around, searching for one of his officers in which to share his elation with but found none upon the tower where he stood. He glanced down the wall and watched his officers running up and down the walls dodging boulders and burning pitch, and ordering men frantically try to put out the fires that now were raging upon the walls and within the city itself.

"Too busy to take note of the shadows to the south." he said to himself excitedly turning to watch the southern shadows coalesce and turn into a discernable line of riding horsemen. The line faltered a moment but then appeared to continue forward – moving as if to ride to each side of the Mohen catapults. "Brilliant." He said still trying to gauge the size of the forces coming to their rescue.

Another roar of cheers came from the Mohen before him as a massive ball of burning stone and pitch flew from a catapult and arched high in the air. The General watched it passively as it flew over him. He cringed as he watched it crash into the barracks below – there wails and screams issued forth as men ran from its doors, bruised and burning.

Thesra turned back to watch the charge as the sound of hooves filled the air. Groups of Mohen soldiers were now noticing the approaching riders, panic was apparent upon their southern lines as men started running for their swords and armour and officers started issuing orders. Like a wave he watched as the Mohen forces started standing and running from their comfortable spots among the many campfires.

Then, clearly distinguishable even from his vantage point he heard the sound of metal on metal as the Terran troops connected with the first of the Mohen soldiers.

"WOOOOWA!" Came a yell from down the wall from one of his men upon the next tower. He looked down the wall line to the tower and smiled as the young man turned and waved up to him. "WE ARE SAVED!" Young Landor Rutt yelled up to him.

General Thesra smiled and then pointed to behind the young lord to the catapult which the knight had fully winched and set ready with stone. "SEND IT NOW OR NOT AT ALL" He yelled down to the young officer. "DO NOT HIT OUR ALLIES!"

"The stupid fool!" the general cursed to himself as he watched the young lord look around confused. Then much louder he yelled at the top of his lungs. "GET BACK TO THE CATAPULT RUTT! YOUR STONE IS SET, IT MUST BE RELEASED!"

Young Landor Rutt turned to his catapult, which had been set alight and was ready to fire. He spun, and signalled his man to release the lever. The catapult lurched and lunged, throwing its burden forward and up. The stones flew up, however the the aim was too high and Thesra watched in dismay as the stones landed harmlessly half way between their walls and the Mohen forces. "IDIOT!" He yelled shaking his head in disbelief.

The flag of King Bestinor flapped as it followed him and General Gadral who led the charge a good three horse lengths before their men. Behind them - their line of riders split as it charged; half of the Terran riders followed behind their King and General, but the other half veered slightly to the right to separate the bulk of the Mohen forces apart from their siege engines.

The Terran forces surged forward. Surprise was on their side and within moments bottles of Trucklite and water were hitting the first few catapults. The evening night turned as if the sun had once again risen. Massive splashes of white flashed as the powder ignited.

The general looked to the north as from the corner of his eye he spotted more riders.

"HO HA!" he yelled when he sighted the Sigel of Capris. "LOOK!" He yelled in elation to no one in particular. "THE SOUTHERN RIDERS ARE HERE TOO!"

But in almost a blink of an eye, the general's elation turned to one of concern and then fear. The Northern Mohen had already started moving in response to the charge, they were not as asleep and disoriented as he had hoped. In seconds Mohen soldiers were assembling in cohesive lines with lances and halberd they marched forward to protect their rear. The riders of Capris slammed and crashed into the first line of Halberds, long spears and glaives, many men fell to the pike and spear and then were quickly cut down by infantrymen that swarmed them. With their momentum halted the Riders of Capris swung wildly batting away the axe heads of the Halberds and dodging the points of the long spears as they were thrust forward. Yells came up from among them to retreat for their restricted movement was making it that much easier for their foes to spear them. Those at the front of the lines began to fall like autumn leaves and as each line dropped the Mohen spearmen pressed passed the fallen Montterran mounts and attacked the next line of riders. Confusion and then fear cursed through the Capris riders. Then like a flood from deep within the west long lines of Mohen regulars swarmed northward and then westerly around the back of the knights of Capris cutting them off from retreat.

"DAMN!" The general Thesra swore as he watched the Mohen forces swarm as if ants forward and around the horsemen of Capris. There were yells of mercy from below intermixed with the screams of knights that were falling pierced by long spear. Long shafts holding deadly axe heads waved in the air and then descended down upon the riders rending armour and flesh. In less than five minutes there was only a small circle of men left – totally surrounded. The cold white earth was awash with the red blood of his friends and comrades.

To the south and east the Mohen chaotic state coalesced into the well-oiled army they had been known to be. Within the horizon lines of men appeared, shoulder to shoulder they stood as regiments of soldiers assembled. Brigades of archers stood and could be seen stringing their bows and readying their arrows. And behind them were thousands that sat upon the ground cranking up their massive heavy crossbows. Arrows the height of a man were stuffed in the earth beside them, ready for flight.

General Thesera paled as he looked down and to the east of what remained of the Terran Company. The Terran King's charge was had also been halted mid way through the Mohen lines. Long lines of Mohen soldiers with Glaives were racing through what little remained of the Terran forces towards the King, his general and their advanced group. Hundreds of Mohen soldiers with long pikes backed by archers surrounded what remained of the catapults.

"BACK TO OUR GATES!" General Thesera yelled down to the Terran King. "TO US – THE WAY NORTH IS CLOSED!"

Someone down below must have given an order for far down below the Terran battle horn sounded retreat and the Terran King and what was left of his men turned and started racing for the gates of the city.

General Thesera turned and yelled as loud as he could down at the gate – "KEEP WATCH AND OPEN THE GATES FOR THE TERRAN KING!" He then turned and yelled down to a small company of men by the gates – "ALL DEPENDS THAT YOU CLOSE IT FAST!" A knight far below raised his hand up in recognition and ordered his twenty men to the gate and they began the process of unbarring it.

Fewer than two dozen Terran knights remained to make it to the halfway mark between Mohen surging forces and the castle. The rest were dragged down or speared by pike.

For a brief moment General Thesra watched in horror as across the planes the last of the Terran soldiers fell, each being pulled down or shot by arrow. No quarter was given to them and as each fell a cheer was heard by the surrounding Mohen soldiers now fully in the blood fever.

At first he thought the Terran King might make it as commands from below slowed and then stopped the Mohen soldiers from pursuing their foe. The Mohen soldiers pulled back into their now well formed lines. The general ground his teeth, knowing what that meant.

A second later he saw the bows behind the infantry lines lifted to point at the sky, and then the air was filled with the noise and sight of thousands of thousands of arrows. UP UP they raced in a graceful arch, and then down and down they fell. Many of the thicker bolts shot from way far back in the Mohen company hit the castle wall itself. However, thousands rained down upon the King of Terran and what remained of his men.

General Thesera shook his head and then turned to look back down at his men at the gates. "BAR IT CLOSED!" HE yelled down. "AND BAR IT TIGHT."

The officer below waved acknowledgement as he turned and ordered his men to replace the long bars and chains.

General Thesera turned to look back down at the slain Terran bodies each man and horse struck by dozens of shafts. For a moment there was a stillness, a massive silence fell over the battlefield but as the general looked up he saw General Kilkitoe ride out from the depth of his army to stand in front of the foremost infrantry and catapults. He raised his sword high in the air, and as one – the Mohen forces cheered.

"And so the ending song starts." General Beston Thesra said to himself as he watched the sky fill once again with arrows – but this time – their aim was higher, farrer… their aim was at the very walls of the castle itself and on and into the city.

Bettham and Tirad had made it half way back to the eastern walls when the first volley of arrows engulfed the eastern walls. They turned with shock at the sound of clashing point of arrow on stone and metal and man. Both sets of eyes looked up high to the top most turret to where General Thesera stood. He had dodged the first set of arrows, but the second was already descending and many could be seen in a tall arch headed towards the parapet on which he stood. The lads cringed as they watched him stand defiantly, waiting for the arrows to fall. Just as they were about to hit, he raised his gauntleted fits up in to the air and raised his middle finger pointing down at the Mohen forces and their general in one last great act of defiance. And then the arrows hit as one slamming the man down and back onto the stone floor of the wall.

Tirad and Bettham watched incredulously, unable to comprehend at first. Then they turned to each other. "Why did he not turn and run?" Bettham said almost rhetorically for he knew the futility of trying to outrun that many arrows.

"Not good." Tirad said in reply. He turned and pulled hard at his friends shoulders. "Bettham - This is NOT good."

Bettham remained silent a moment more looking up in disbelief, but then he heard the Mohen forces in the east. There was a rumbling thunder as thousands of men beyond the wall started moving forward as one.

Both lads looked at each other a moment, realization grabbing them deeply. They then both turned to look to the east and started to run.

"WE NEED TO HURRY." Tirad yelled as he ran. "I am not leaving my stuff here for the Mohen."

"WHAT?" Bettham replied shocked. "What are you talking about?"

"My stash." Tirad urged as he pulled his friend up towards a city street. "I found even more the other night. But I didn't want to bring it to the barracks. I'll be damned if I am going to leave it to the Mohen!"

"Where are we going?" Bettham replied in a confused voice as he pulled away from the grip of Tirad. "We must return to our posts!" Bettham replied as he turned to point to the western walls and towers.

"Are YOU MAD." Tirad yelled as he turned to look at his friend. "ITS ALL OVER BUT THE DIYING. LOOK AROUND YOU!" Tirad gestured with his hands behind them. The eastern walls were empty – the only thing standing were arrows that had stuck into the cracks between the stones or protruded upward from fallen comrades. Massive flights of stone and burning pitch were soaring in the sky and thudded into the city crushing buildings and setting others on fire.

Back on the western wall there was chaos as officers tried to regroup their men – not totally sure what to do "We are doomed." He said finally to his friend turning. "But we have friends there."

"Just a few strides more to my cache, and then we will find Miathis and Tunder."

Tirad pulled on the arm of Bettham who still refused to move forward. "They are all dead, but don't know it yet, and we don't hurry will be too as will our friends – I know a way out that won't be watched as much!"

Bettham looked around, noting the chaos, confusion and dismay. The heart and courage had been sucked dry from the Montteran forces within the city. Most of the city was now burning, and the men had given up trying to put out the fires. Arrows continued to stream up and over the walls snagging what few soldiers remained atop them. The din of Mohen forces now likely scaling the eastern walls was unmistakable.

Bettham looked back at the eastern wall. "We should go back and find Miathis and Tunder."

"In a moment." Tirad replied grabbing Bettham's arm again. This time, he successfully got Bettham moving behind him. With friend in arm he pulled forward, deeper into the burning city. "Not far, I promise." Tirad added.

Smoke billowed and wafted down and into the streets. Soot fell down upon the lads like snow making both chock and cough. Almost blindly they went forward, two, three then four streets in. Finally, Tirad turned to a door and looked up at the sign. "Here!" He called as he opened the door with a key he held.

Tirad ran in and over to the house's singular bed. "Not many would look inside a common house, nor attempt to pick its lock when other better dwellings are about." He said as he fell upon his knees and reached under a bed that hugged the far wall beside a small fireplace. A second later he stood up with a small brown leather bag.

"What you got there?" Bettham asked. "Is it worth our lives?"

Tirad looked down and then reached within the bag. Out came his hand and upon it was a golden sheath, encrusted with diamonds and rubies. "What do you think?" He asked as a smile crossed his lips. He tossed the blade over to Bettham and then tucked the remaining smaller bundle under his armoured coat. "When we get out we can split the rest. But that should pay off what I owe you."

656

There was a loud bang as a nearby burning building fell in upon itself. "IF we get out." Bettham said. "I think you are forgetting that there are ten thousand or more Mohen soldiers about to storm the city."

Tirad nodded and headed for the door. "Better not doddle then." he added.

As they ran towards the western gates Bettham, almost out of breath looked over to his friend who looked confident even though the sound of the Mohen assault continued to rise. "They will breach the walls with ladders, and then the gates will be lifted. Others will encircle to the western gates they likely have a few hundred now in the forest just west of the castle waiting for soldiers to run from these gates along the road, hoping to make it back to Montterran lands."

Tirad looked over and winked at his friend. "We won't be running like sheep to the slaughter, but riding out of a small north-western door by the sewage grates." Tirad replied glibly. "There haven't been many within the city so the creek is shallow. It will be a filthy, smelly ride, but it will give us more cover then riding upon the road. With luck we can make it to the north-western tree line before anyone sights us."

"We need to get to Miathis and Tunder." Bettham pleaded as he slowed looking to the west. "We owe it to them."

Tirad looked at his friend, as he bit his lip he looked up the streets and then back to the eastern gate. Mohen were streaming over the walls in hundreds, several were already down inside the walls working to open the gates. "OK, but if we die, don't hold me to blame." He then winked and started running to the western gate where he had last sighted Tunder who towered above the other soldiers. He was pulling and swearing at his soldiers attempting to turn them from their chaotic state.

In a few breathless strides they were before the towering man. His massive axe was on his shoulder and his voice boomed out to men around him. "FORM LINES. FORM LINES. WHEN WE OPEN THE GATE WE RUN TO THE TREES AS ONE FORCE!

Tirad looked back at the gate, the massive metal gate had already been pulled up and the bars from the western gate had been pulled down.

Miathis stepped up on the second step of the wall and looked down at what remained of the Montterran forces – there were less than a hundred men standing around him several others were running from the eastern part of the city back towards them.

Miathis stood tall and yelled out to the remaining forces. "WHEN THE DOORS SWING WIDE – THERE WILL BE MOHEN SCOUTS AND ARCHERS LIKELY, BEYOND THAT NOTHING IS CERTAIN. RUN FOR THE SAFETY OF THE FOREST AND WE WILL REGROUP WEST OF THE TIREN TO STAND AND FIGHT ANOTHER DAY."

All the men turned as in the distance they watched the eastern doors slam open and thousands of Mohen surged through. Miathis nodded to the men on the gate wheel which turned making the gates groan as they started to open. Impatient and frightened Montterran soldiers closest to the doors put their shoulder to them pushing them open faster. What remained of the Montterran regulars surged past them out and onto the road.

Miathis jumped down from his step and ran over to Tunder as the last of his men ran through the gates. "LET'S GO." He said turning to lead Tunder, Tirad and Bettham.

"NO I HAVE A BETTER WAY!" Tirad yelled stopping Miathis in his track. Tunder turned and looked back at the advancing Mohen, now less than five hundred meters away.

"TRUST ME!" Tirad yelled. All eyes turned to Miathis who nodded. Tirad turned and started to run down the western wall. Tunder looking back turned and hesitated. He then took three long strides to the gate and swung his mighty axe.

Tunder's heavy axe sang as wind flew through its hollowed runes. It flew in a sideway arch through the air slamming into the arm thick rope that reached up and back to hold up the iron inner gate. The sliced the rope neatly in two and clanged as it bounced off of the stone wall behind it.

As the massive Iron Gate slammed down Tunder was already turning to follow his friends who were waiting a few strides ahead watching him. Miathis nodded in approval and then turned to follow Tirad who took off in a full run.

Bettham turned right of Tirad spotting a Mohen scout putting arrow up to his bow, aiming at Tirad who led the small group down the street. Bettham raced forward to the archer, his left hand held his flail, but in his right now shone the sparkling dagger that Tirad had just given him. Without hesitation he slammed the blade up and under the man's arm into his ribs and lungs. Without slowing he spun and twisted the blade out and then hastening to catch up to the others.

Tirad wound down the base of the western wall jumping over debris and rounding carts. The three friends followed quickly behind. Houses in the east burned brightly and smoke wafted through the city choking them as they ran. Behind them they heard the calls and hoof beats of Mohen knights racing through the city. Every now and then there were calls and then screams as the last of the Montterran soldiers were found and killed.

"HERE!" Tirad called out in a half yell as he rounded another cart and pointed to a door. "Tunder, I will need you to help open it."

Tunder came round Miathis to stand beside Tirad and the door. Tirad looked down at the small iron lock and Tunder smacked it easily shattering it with the butt of his axe. He then grabbed the small iron handle and started pulling on it.

Bettham wrinkled his nose as he turned to the right following the stench with his eyes. Five meters to the right of the door a long wide iron pipe followed the western wall as it rose up and over to the tower. He followed it and noticed that it was mounted under the stone bridge that crossed over to an inner keep. "Well at least it is royal filth we will bath in." Bettham said with a smirk.

Tunder heaved hard on the door and it opened with a load groan. But all four turned as they heard horses approaching through the burning city behind them.

"Hurry." Miathis pressed as the door opened showing a long dark passage under the western wall.

Tirad smiled and winked at the captain. In his right hand he held his sword and in his left a long needle thin silver dirk. Miathis shook his head and almost laughed as he looked at it. After he turned and looked at Bettham holding the gold gilded dagger, wet with blood he shook his head. "You two sure have been busy."

Tirad shrugged then bent down to get under the low doorway as he entered his hushed voice could be heard. "This leads out beside the sewage creak. It drops quickly and the bank is steep ridged with stones and leads north and west to the forest where there is a larger pond now used as a cesspool. Keep low."

Tunder stood aside to let Miathis go through next but his captain hesitated and looked to the north. "The stables are not that far from here." He said to his friend. "Koal?"

Tunder shook his head and grabbed his captain's arms and pushed him to the gate. "You know better than that, and I won't be having our brave captain die on account of trying to liberate his horse."

"Besides," Bettham piped up from behind them. "Horse is so damn tall we will surely be seen."

Miathis groaned and then drew his sword, bent his head and followed Tirad into the darkness under the wall. Bettham smiled at Tunder who looked to the heavens for strength as he passed.

When all were within the darkness Tunder pull closed the door. The floor was damp with seepage that had obviously passed through the mortar and bricks. Metham wafted through the passage making Bettham cough.

Tirad slowed as he neared the end of the tunnel. He reached knelt down and in the darkness started working on the latch that held shut the door. Quietly the other paused until they heard the sound of the lock and latch slowly being opened. They all knew that beyond the metal door any number of Mohen might now be sitting in wait for them.

Tirad leaned forward and carefully opened the door a crack and peered beyond. Seeing nothing he pushed it open a fraction more. Those behind him moved restlessly as they could see nothing but his silhouette. Finally, after being comfortable nothing was beyond he turned and nodding opened the door wide then stepped forward and disappeared into the darkness beyond. The others, following his lead anxiously bent low and followed.

Tunder spun as he hit the bottom of the less than two-meter deep filth filled creek, stifling a curse he heard Tirad ahead of him whisper. "Second step is a doosy, sorry, couldn't see it. I can't see over the edge – take a look."

The giant rose up off of his knees and poked his head over the top and scanned the horizon. The other three pressed next to him as they watched the remnants of their company run westerly down the road in all haste to the tree line. Behind them, quickly catching them Mohen knights rode.

A few of the stragglers, likely men wounded or simply winded from the long run were cut down unceremoniously by the Mohen knights who didn't slow after slashing down or riding over their friends.

"Bastards." Tunder swore softly. "The city is taken; they should at least give quarter."

"Kikiltoe is a bastard for more reasons than being just the illegitimate son of MiHinDor Perrilos the Fourth." Miathis said sorrowfully as he watched men that had served under him and fought beside him be cut down as little more than stocks of wheat.

Tirad grabbed Bettham's shirt and pulled him. "We have to keep moving. The knights will be walking the lines looking for strays. We cannot hide here long."

Bettham followed Tirad and Tunder pulled Miathis forward. "Keep moving. We did all we could for them." In the distance screams of men being ridden down could be heard and behind them, they could hear the cheering of the Mohen soldiers as they raced in and through the burning city.

The four crawled forward down the sewage creek, away from their friends, and away from the slaughter and pain. TerranAdd had fallen once again, but this time there were a few remaining to tell the tale.

Dungeons and Spiders

"Bastard!" Dimi hissed through clenched teeth as she jumped past Etch and Stephan. Her blade was out as she dove forward into the large round tower room.

Keek twisted and ran with blinding speed for the iron staircase. He screeched as he ran, "MISTRISS!" But close behind and faster still was the determined Dimi. With a twist and a turn she had the demon by his ears and threw him into the wall. Keek hit it, and although dazed quickly rose and like a rat started back towards the door Dimi had just come in.

However, close behind the dryad Etch and Stephan followed, entering the room both paused. Both had their black dirks out and stood ready. Keek screeched and nervously dove under a nearby desk. As Etch stood within the open doorway, Stephan ran to the opposite door and pressed his ear to it. "Dimi make quick of it, we haven't the time, nor do we want the entire castle coming to investigate."

Dimi smiled back at Stephan and then dove under the table herself, but Keek seeing her progress jumped up onto the desk's top. "Bitch!" Keek screamed in frustration.

"Stephan look up!" Etch yelled. Stephan turned to look at his friend and then up to where Etch was looking. At that very moment a massive, hairy dropped from the chandelier above Stephan. Just as the tips of its long legs touched Stephan, he rolled and ignoring the snapping, dripping mandibles drove his dark blade into the spider's face. Then just as quickly his hand was pulled back leaving the blade behind. "I hate spiders." Stephan swore as he looked at his goo covered hand. The creature's body continued to quiver and twitch, green venom dropped from its fangs.

Keek screamed in frustration as it danced and dogged Dimi who appeared to be having fun circling the desk, her own dagger drawn she poked at the creature. "Mistress will tear you all apart!" Keek screamed.

Dimi dove forward sliding atop the desk, Keek twisted and turned, but Dimi grabbed the creature's tail. The tail was slick and thin and slid like glass through her small fingers. But as the tail came to an end, Dimi finally held it tight. Then, firmly in hand she yanked the tail hard backward sending Keek falling to the floor.

Keek let out a high-pitched yelp; in response Stephan with ear still pressed to the opposite door exclaimed with teeth clenched. "Stop playing with it. Etch help her we don't have the time. As Etched stepped forward Keek, seeing his opportunity twisted in Dimi's grasp and lashed out with his clawed feet. Dimi released the demon's tail in order to get out of reach of the razor claws that reached out to her face.

But as the creature turned to get to its feet, Dimi dove onto its back and brought her blade up to its neck.

"I Knew your wife!" Keek screamed over to Stephan. Dimi reached down and pulled Keek's small forward back exposing his neck further to the blade held in her opposite hand.

"STOP!" Stephan called to Dimi just as the dagger was about to be dragged across his throat.

Dimi's blade stopped her hand and looked over at Stephan. "Nothing this devil could say would have a gram of truth to it." she replied sarcastically.

Stephan ran over beside Dimi and put his hand on top of the hand holding the dagger as if to stay her strike. "We need more information. We had no other real plan, hear him out. Looking down to Keek he pointed his black blade at the creature's eye." His face was hard and his words were without compassion. "You will tell us what we need to know."

Keek looked up incredulously at Stephan and then smiled wickedly. Its high pitched, scratchy voice spoke out with great sarcasm. "My mistress will rip your soul from your body and tear it to shreds...." He looked at Dimi and then back at Etch.

"Your mistress is not here my little fiend," Stephan began, "only a painful death is here should you not tell us what we will find behind those doors."

Etch looked at the creature and then back to Stephan. "What of his wife, Wendy." Etch asked as he stepped closer to the two. Stephan showed no emotion as he stood with blade pointed. But there was a small quiver in his hand. "The lady of this place," Etch continued, the mistress of this castle before it fell to you and yours."

Keek laughed sickly looking up at Stephan and then Dimi. "I don't fear death I will pass quickly through the other realms into the arms of my mistress Andarduel."

Turning to Stephan the creature smiled wickedly. "Everyone that you loved are dead, they were the first to go. You find her bones in the weer shit pile in the eastern towers."

Now fully straddling the little creature she pressed her hard small fingers into the creature's throat she then twisted and pulled slowly. Dark, viscous fluid leaked out of the creature and it shook in disbelief. Its eyes widened as Dimi removed her other hand from the creature's mouth.

"No more sickness." Dimi spat out.

"Great," Etch said, "He won't be able to tell us much without his vocal cords cut."

Dimi shrugged, as she looked down at the creature who was baring his bloody teeth at her and hissed. "He wasn't going to talk his master's leash was far too tight around his throat."

Etch looked down at Dimi. "Don't dawdle." Turning to Stephan he motioned to the iron staircase.

Dimi whispered into the creature's ear. "I will make it seem like a lifetime."

Etch glanced back as he stepped down onto the first step. There was a faint smile on Dimi's face, and the little creature beneath her twitched and shivered with fear.

As they slowly wound down the stairway Stephan whispered to Etch. "Why?" "Why does she care, why would a god even be interested in a Succubus of this world?"

"Sarta first went and trained with the Masti." Etch concluded. "Without conscious or reservations she would have been revered and ascended fast in the Masti ranks.

Stephan stopped and turned in his tracks. Obviously still shaken by the little creature's remarks about his wife, struggling internally to find an answer to questions that mike make sense about the loss of his wife. "And what better or more ideal a priest to Andarduel the goddess that rules Chaos then a succubus, a creature that lives and breathes death, blood and destruction."

Andarduel can bestow many favours. We must be careful we will not subdue by direct force."

"There were no bodies in Terran, no blood from tortured?" Etch said in a puzzled tone.

"Andarduel is a god, she pulls them in some manner to her."

"We can't fight a god. But we can silence her priestess." Etch said as he put his hands on Stephan's shoulder. "And we can seek a little revenge in the process."

The doorway to hell

Sarta knelt before the TieRei Judgement Dias looking down at the large bronze cauldron before her. Every inch of her skin tingled in anticipation of the feast, every exposed pore in her impeccably perfect ghostly white succubae form glistened reflecting the flames that beat against the golden container. She felt in control, more in control then she had ever felt in her life. No longer was she the servant of her hunger, now her hunger would serve her. And with this final great sacrifice, she would transcend.

"Soon, very soon." she said as she threw a handful of blood soaked herbs into the cauldron. "All seven hells will hear the roar of suffering and the screams of tormented souls as they depart this plane!" The cauldron cackled and hissed as if in reply.

The soon to be high blood priestess to the god Andarduel swayed slightly in her translucent gown. Her eyes looked down into the cauldron. There behind the smoke, within the bubbling blood and gore images swirled. Red hills rolled and tumbled as far as the eye could see, and upon those hills black winged creatures swayed as if moved by some invisible wind. "These would be her legions, waiting, waiting for her command."

A cold breeze wafted through the throne room rippling the sheer fabric of her dress, the silk danced against her hardened nipples. Shuddering under the sensation her mind wandered as she as she let the sensation envelop and take her. Back and forth around the cauldron four men swayed in a ghoulish dance. Silently they looked down at her as they pushed their hands into their abdomens disembowel themselves. As their intestines completed their spill, they slumped and fell.

Sarta's thoughts were broken by the sounds of approaching footsteps and the images in her mind vanished, but those within the cauldron stayed.

Licking her blood red lips she pulled her mind back to a state of calm, to the center of concentration the priests had taught her to find. Her hand reached down and cupped a handful of the boiling mixture before her disturbing the image briefly, her skin hissed as it entered the scalding boiling mass. Not flinching or hesitating for even a fraction of a second her hand continued its descent into the red mass. Slowly, methodically it dipped and then the cupped hand rose up, torturous red, blistered skin peeling from the bone still tightly cupping a small amount of the red ooze rose up. Tilting her head back to face the ceiling she raised her hand above her head and then let the muddy red concoction drip down through her fingers over her face and in to her mouth.

Blood mixed spittle sprayed from her mouth as she began to chant the old rituals that would start her transformation and open the gates. "Dresan ti, within me, through me – open wide." Eyes opening up she looked up to her hand, now once again as pale and silky smooth as it had once been.

Sarta closed her eyes again and began her chant. Blue forked flames appeared beneath the cauldron licking it. "Andarduel, with the powers bestowed by the blood of innocents, and in your name we beseech you."

"For powers granted, for powers yet to come." The dark red fluid within the cauldron began to boil all the more. Great bubbles rose and burst from the pot covering Sarta with blood and hissing entrails. Screaming in agony she fell to the floor a bloody mass of writhing flesh.

Through clenched teeth, the succubus gasped and groaned. "Goddess, lend me your strength. Let me be your vessel, and in your name will we burn, kill, and rend the flesh of all mankind. Let me be thy vessel here upon this plane. Through me let Chaos reign supreme."

The succubus' head bent back and a great scream arose from her as her spine ripped through her skin. From the broken, bloody mass of her back massive leathery, talon tipped wings unfolded and reached for the ceiling. Sarta grunted with a twisted almost sensual sound of suffering, her entire body quivered and she sank to her knees. The skin on her head began to stretch and split as two horns sprung up. Great chunks of flesh slid off her growing form and fell to the floor taking with it the last fragments of her blood trenched gown. Beneath the blood onyx black skin glistened. Dark as the darkest night Sarta rose back to her feet, the transformation to demon form complete.

The fires beneath the cauldron glowed red-hot and the fluid within it sizzled. Bending forward, she gazed in to it seeing her reflection she reached up and turning her head watched her reflection intently. "If you could only see me now old wizard, what would you say? I have shed my skin, and with it your curse. Finally, I am free."

With head turned sideways weighed down by newly sprung horns Sarta growled as she rose and lifted up her voice in praise. "In return of the gift you have given me great Andarduel, I will suck the morrow from this world's bones and feed upon its children."

In a throw of ecstasy as the blood power began to posses her she lifted, her sharply clawed black hands in to the air above her. "Let the faithful prepare to cross." In her mind hundreds of thousands of dark, leather winged creatures looked back at her from across the great expanse, slowly they began their walk towards her mind's eye.

Blood splattered up and around the cauldron creating a circle of blood around it. As the blood splashed out and hit the cold white marble floor it turned black, and started to issue a dark and acrid smoke. In seconds the dais in front of Sarta was hazed. Dark thick cords of smoke jumped from the cauldron to encircle the dais, twisting and knitting together to form a large, gray sphere. Then the smoke from within the twisted black cords turned translucent showing the image that had once only been in her mind.

A calm and distinctly female voice issued from behind the curtained image. "I sense." The voice paused, and a pang of hunger pulled at Sarta's black, rotted heart. "I sense great anticipation and urgency in your voice? Dear priestess, there will be time enough to enjoy your new form, but now – for this last step – complete submission and subjugation."

Sarta smiled and whispered with great reverence. "I exist to serve you Andarduel."

"Seek not just to satiate your new desires." Returned the voice in a chastising way but then in a kinder more sympathetic voice the goddess continued. "Slow down my dark child, your eagerness, your thirst will betray you. There will be time a plenty to rend the flesh of men. Savour the dark boiling powers I have granted you but let them not intoxicate your thoughts. If you fail to open the door, I will not be please."

Sarta dug her elongated cruelly sharp nails into her now hardened hand, but the pain did little to clear her mind. Two sets of distinct footfalls continued to come down the hall. "A guard and her final sacrifice, one of the last of those captured with the castle. Soon, very soon she would dine on hundreds, entire cities screaming in panic would serve as her sauce! Her delightful thoughts broke as she listened intently hoping to hear the man's racing heartbeat. The door behind her being to open and she had to stifle the desire to take a deep breath.

"Slow priestess," Came the voice from the coils of smoke that billowed from the floor all the way up to the ceiling. "To ensure a wide portal this next sacrifice must be well timed." Sarta looked at the smoke nodding to the insubstantial form that wafted in smoky tendrils.

Her white cheeks flushed slightly in anticipation her new, stronger form shuddered. Intoxicated by raw power Sarta gasped, a slight chuckle issued from the cloud as if it was amused by the momentary loss of control. "I see you enjoy this new form, do not disappoint me."

Sarta smiled as she felt the mental presence of her god knowing that with her eyes, Andarduel would see and through her she would feel all.

'Control, she could not let her new insatiable hunger for blood and death drive her to a rash act of rapid consumption. Sarta thought to herself. 'With the succubae skills she would drive this last slave to the brink; balance it between horror and love – then, only when commanded that the time was right! Let Andarduel see how strong she could be and NOT feed until bidden!'

Sarta shuddered as she realized that she was already losing control, that her new stronger all consuming desires for the taste of flesh and blood were pushing aside all other thought that her bloodlust was beginning to consume and betray her.

The transformed succubus pushed her mind back and away from the hunger as she heard the guard enter with his captive behind her. There was a sound of a scuffle and then a thud as the guard pushed the captive hard toward her and the hard marble floor.

They had entered with heads bent, trudged forward as captor and captive. Upon entering the sickly thick smoke had burned their eyes and throats but the scene, the gore and broken bodies of men and women had burned their very soul and captivated their attention.

The succubus, which they had spent so much time hunting was not there. In its place almost lost against the darkness was something else, much bigger. Stephan looked down at Etch who lay sprawled on the floor before it.

The pit of Stephan's stomach gave a lurch as his mind and body was grabbed and held fast by the fabulously beautiful, yet evil and twisted image of the winged creature before him. "IT IS YOU!" He exclaimed. Somehow he knew it felt it sensed it. That which he had come to smite, to throw his ruin against had changed, but he knew her none the less.

The dais was ablaze like a sun behind her, the succubus's pale flesh twisted, burnt and remade. A whip like tail twitched between her legs, with talon hands stretched out as their eyes met, she bent forward and poised like a lion ready to pounce.

Her eyes were like mirrors, at once dancing with the flames, and then blank and staring back at him as if a window to another world. In that moment, Stephan's will was sucked from him; he stood there transfixed to the spot.

Etch lay sprawled on the floor, and gathered his courage. A small gasp issued from behind him, his friend now held fast by the succubus' spell had to be broken fast or all was lost. Keeping his eyes to the ground in avoidance of the gaze, and as if in an act of great supplication he grovelled slowly forward.

Sarta's voice rose to fill the chamber. "You are not my guard, but I recognize that scent." Pausing a moment Sarta inhaled a great breath. "The smell of your fear gives you away clansman; did you come in hopes for revenge?"

Sarta breathed in deeply, letting the smell of the man before her fill her nostrils. "Your wife held a similar scent." Sarta's laugh shook the hall. "A smell I savoured." Sarta continued, her tail twitched like a tiger ready for a great meal. "So totally enthralled was your wife that in the end, even when the last of her life was spilling from her skinless corpse did her hand rise to touch my breast.

The succubus's voice felt like slimy hungry maggots, they echoed and twisted and bit into Stephan's brain. Yet he was held fast within her trance.

Seeing something flicker from the corner of his eyes Etch smiled and then slowly reached to the small of his back. Rolling and twisting Etch brought his hand up and let loose with all his might his dagger. Handle over blade it flew but its tip failed to penetrate the onyx hard flesh of the beast's breast. As the blade clattered to the floor, Sarta lowered her eyes and sought him out. With wings unfurled, the beast flew forward and kicked Etch in the gut sending him a dozen feet slamming him to the wall.

A small dark form darted across the room and Sarta smiled. "Keek, prepare a second wraith. Two will be making the journey to Chaos."

However, as the small form crossed into the light Sarta's smile turned to a frown.

Dimi paused only a moment and then diving she rolled and bringing up her blowgun, she let loose a dart at the demon's head.

Sarta's talon wings rose ever so slightly and brushed aside the dart.

"I killed your pet." Dimi spat in a taunting response to Sarta as she jumped and rolled drawing her to the left and away from her friends.

Sarta howled in frustration, but then turned and with cheeks bulging, she belched forth a blast of sickly green acid. Cracks appeared in the floor where Dimi had once stood as the acid landed it burning through the grout and stone as if they were made of nothing more than frozen lard.

Standing tall Sarta's great black horned wings fully unfurled, cruel talon tips curved down to frame her now furious face. "See what we have made with your precious wings?"

As Dimi danced in the shadows, her voice rang out with contempt and hatred. "After I killed Keek, I ripped off its head and shit down its neck. Now, think of what is in store for you and your new wings, you pathetic whore."

Stephan pulled himself from Sarta's weakened thrall. Raising the knotted meter long cudgel and with unbridled, undiluted, unwavering hate he lunged forward and swung it with all his might at the demon's head.

The stocky, knotty club hit Sarta in the side of her face issuing a dark and deep thunderous knock that echoed in the great room. Slightly dazed, the creature shuddered but only a short moment later, she turned, and stared straight at the Clansman.

Stephan stood aghast; the vibrations from the club still resonating in his arms and back his hands felt as if they were aflame. Incredulously he looked down its shaft and then at the beast, with heart sinking into despair he too late realized his error – once again held by her gaze.

Sarta smiled and stepped forward. Claws slashed forward with blinding speed and ferocity splitting Stephan's ribs like dried kindling her hand plunged deep into his chest. Stephan's broken and torn heart spilled and shot blood in spurts across the floor as Sarta ripped it from his shredded chest. Shrouded by the darkness by the far wall, Etch groaned.

The succubus smiled and bending forward kissed him on the cheek, her horns and hair framing their faces making the kiss seem sickeningly private "In the end, it was I, not your wife who held your heart after all." Then without looking she flung the heart, it hit with a splash as it entered the cauldron. She slowly licked clean her talons as she watched Stephan slump to the floor.

Sarta smiled as gloriously new, dark powers poured into her. With a casual turn, her wings rose deflecting another of Dimi's darts. In the darkness, the dryad cursed as she circled, dogged and danced around the room.

Raising a black hand a swirling ball of fire appeared in her palm. It grew, and as it grew Sarta's smile expanded. "There will be nothing left of you but a little pile of ash."

Etch lay bent and bruised. His side was aflame and each breath he took brought excruciating pain to his chest. Without opening his eyes, he felt blood drip from his nose.

"Die already!" Sarta yelled to Dimi as she threw another ball of flame at the dancing Dryad, but in response, Dimi laughed gleefully as she dodged it.

Etch pulled himself up to lean against the wall. Each breath was purchased painfully as he felt life fade from his limbs. 'Is this it?' he thought to himself in perfect stillness as he filled his heart with the passion required for one last great effort. Thoughts of Rachael, Chad and Lyss burned his heart overshadowing the pain of his body.

Etch paused as he breathed in steeling himself. 'Is this what my passion has led me to?' he thought to himself. The reality of the years of sacrifice and the lost, lonely years thundered into him shaking his soul. "I always ask the same questions and always too late." He whispered. From deep down, he pulled every gram of strength he had left, and with it came the numbing cold of the Keeper and a sense of unrivalled unadulterated hate for the creature that now threatened everything that he loved.

Looking up with renewed clarity determination seeped back into his mind, and his body surged with power he did not know he had left. A smile of realization crested his dirty bloody limps as the old hunter's eyes drifted to the dais and the cauldron. 'It was the tie to her god made her strong!' Dark ropes of smoke still danced and whirled from it to linger around an ever expanding and clarifying portal. Perhaps with that tie broken there was still a chance.

Etch gathered the last of his strength and with icy determination sprang forward. Every shard of energy and passion left within him was drawn upon.

Sarta screamed in realization as she turned to watched Etch lunge to the daises. Twisting fast she let loose a massive fireball hitting him in mid flight. The room shook, both ceiling and floor cracked and the concussion and smoke blasted Sarta back and to her knees and where the dais was, now hung a cloud of smoke so dark that it obscured everything.

Dimi screamed as the smoke cleared, around the dais a singular wraith spun and then suddenly it disappeared and with it, Etch's burnt and broken body.

As Sarta started to rise, Dimi launched herself at the demon's back, her small form lunged forward with such speed and ferocity that Sarta bent forward. Sarta twisted and flapped her great wings, her hard leathery tail cracked like a whip hitting Dimi who screamed as it slit open her back. Dimi screamed again, but this time not with pain, but with hatred and determination. Pulling herself up the beast's back she reached forward and pressed her dagger to the corner of the Sarta's mirrored eyes which now were glowing back.

"Move again and I will drive it home." she threatened. "Now, bring him back."

"BRING HIM BACK!" she screamed into Sarta's long wickedly tipped ears.

Sarta smiled and then laughed. "On this realm I am now immortal."

Sarta smiled and glanced behind the dryad. "And in a moment, the very gates of hell will open and swallow you whole. You will be with him at the feet of my beloved god soon enough."

Dimi, puzzled looked at Sarta, behind her she could hear a multitude of beating wings. "Wrong answer bitch." the Dryad screamed as she drove the tip of the small blade up and into Sarta's eye.

Sarta screamed and the room shook again as her large wings batted feverously.

Pushing off, Dimi back flipped landing lightly in a crouch. "The poison might not kill you, but it WILL make your bones reject the very flesh upon them for all of eternity!"

Sarta screamed as she twisted and pulled herself away. Clawing she pulled the blade from her eye and let it fall to the floor. Howling she reached up to her face, the onyx black skin around her eye was already crackling and splitting.

"Your friend is in the realm of Chaos, in the arms of her demons and as a second passes here, hours of torment he will feel there." The demon growled, and spat. "But it will be nothing compared to the suffering I will put you through."

Sarta staggered in pain as once again her flesh began to peel away, but unlike before now under it was simply sinew and bone. Blind she turned and reached for Dimi who stepped backward quietly out of reach.

"I will send you straight into the arms of my unforgiving goddess." She bellowed in frustration as she sank to her knees.

A thin tear welled in her eye as Dimi looked to the floor where Stephan's broken body lay and then up and back to the dais where her friend had been.

Sarta's now almost skeletal form turned and started towards the dais. Her claws and bones scraped ineffectively the floor making her progress painfully slowly. "Mistress," she begged as she halted before it. As in response, above the cauldron, the portal grew, and within its twisting black bubble, the legions of Chaos approached. Thousands of hungry eyes set within unforgiving faces, upon black winged shoulders they came.

Dimi inhaled sharply then wiping the tear from her eye, she turned and ran.

Epilogue

Chad looked up at the ominous dust filled sky as he caught his breath. Detro's evil face was barely visible through the clouds that choked the sky. It was now two years since their father departed and Chad and Lys were headed up the mountain to the small sheltered cave. Each of the siblings knew that this journey was meant to escape the growing heat and reminisce about their missing father. However as thoughts drifted they both struggled not to wonder when or even if their beloved father would return. Rachael never wanted to go up. During this time of the year, she just wanted to be alone or distracted helping others. She was going to a neighbours, the lady was expecting and Rachael figured she would pick some berries and drop them off. Food, especially berries were harder to find these days but Rachael knew where she could still find them.

It was evening by the time Chad and Lys arrived at the cold stone cave. It was small, damp, and very smoky. The walls were encrusted with soot from the campfire. But the smells reminded them both of Etch, and that was all it took to make them feel at home. The evening was cold enough to force them light another fire as they sat the entire night talking. It had been a while since they had time enough to devote to doing nothing. Game and crops were continually harder to find, they had to work so very hard to find even scraps to eat.

The temperature in the morning was a good 20 degrees less then what it would have been down at the cottage. Walking out into the warm morning sun and leting the fresh cool mountain air wash over their pale faces brought a calmness to their hearts. Chad was glad Lys was happy, he hadn't seen her smile for such a long time. She was literally beaming as she let the cold air permeate her. No red dust brushed her face here, nor did dust continue to stain her blond hair.

Lys spotted it first, pointing to the distance she called out his attention to an unusually black cloud. They sat in awe as it drew nearer and nearer, "Those are not clouds.' she said in a voice that quivered with unadulterated fear. Chad felt a sudden panic so raw that he felt his balls pull themselves up and into his belly. His body reacted to the danger that he could sense was very real, and very close. A few seconds later, he could see them too and he knew his fear was justified.

Frozen there he strained his eyes to see. "Back inside. Quick!", Lys said in a hushed urgent voice as she reached round and grabbed Chad's shirt. She started pulling him frantically back to the stone doorway of their cave. Chad, still enthralled, could not be sufficiently restrained by Lys, who was now getting frantic. "Now, now, please now." Lys urged pulling Chad in deeper to the cave.

But, he couldn't keep his eyes from them. He poked his head out slightly and watched a hoard of great black winged beasts fly past within a hundred meters their cave. The beating of the wings created a thundering banging sound. And the beasts screeched and shrieked at each other as they flow. A few in flight would spin and dash within their group and thump another beast or attempt to rake their long dangling talons across another's wings. Several flipped and inverted to avoid the errand attacks, but ever as a single unit they continued their progress as with great determination. There were hundreds, thousands. It took minutes for them to fly past. First they went east, but then they banked and started flying straight down the mountain... down to the village below.

They were far up on the mountain face, but even though they were kilometres away from the village, minutes later the screams reached them. The horrific cries of men, women and children were lifted up and out of the valley to drift and bounce off the mountains. Each scream, distinct to itself, echoed against the mountains colliding with other screams to create an almost drone of sorrow.

The sound of these horrors chilled them to the depths of their souls and for days on end, they dared not even open the heavy stone door of the cave. Lys's constant worry about their Mom made them depart down the mountain a day or two before Chad felt they should have. But Lys would have none of it and said she was going even if it meant she went alone.

The trip down the mountain was quiet, neither sibling uttered a single syllable a word the entire trip. Only when they crossed the threshold of their home did Lys speak. "She isn't here." She said simply. "We need to.. she went to see...on the outskirts of the village." She took a breath and tried to steady herself. "I'm certain they were able to get out in time" Lys turned back to the door "We have to find them."

Chad jumped to the doorway and put his arm across. "We, should stay safe. She would be livid if you or I got ourselves killed."

Lys could only pause in thought and gaze at her feet.

"I will go. I can pass through the woods to the east side of the village. I will find her." Chad said in his most convincing voice. But deep down inside his stomach was doing back flips wondering what he would find down in the village. He could not muster the hope which he could clearly see in Lys' eyes. "You will be safe here. No fires. Stay inside."

"Be careful." Lys walked over to the fireplace, with her back to him almost as if she was steeling herself to the thought that by the end of the next day she might be on her own "What are they?"

Chad shook his head. "I don't know. But one thing is for sure, they aren't delivering good news."

"I don't want you to go." Lys said, "I don't want anything to happen to you."

"But we have to know, whatever the outcome we must know." Chad said firmly. He turned and started gathering his things, "No time to waste".

Lys pulled together a small back of bandages, and ointments and handed it to Chad as he picked up his bow.

"Down, and back fast." Lys said, "Find her and straight back." she let out a short empty laugh, "But do not let her convince you to go try to find another family or anything."

Chad grimaced in reply but it didn't lower his gaurd at all.

"It's quite down there now, think they left?" Lys asked as she went to the boarded window and peaked out through the cracks.

"Find out soon enough."

"Perhaps you shouldn't'"

"We would never know, she could be lost…hurt…and we need to find out what happened. We should find out if they are all gone from the area, or if some are still around. Plus, we are low on supplies, we need to stock up with the thought that at any time we might need to hunker down."

"It would be good to have a few stashes in the caves and hills around us." Lys said. "If we had some well wrapped, goods we could create caches that would keep us alive should they see this place or…"

"Yes, but for now finding Mom is all that matters." Chad took a good long look at his sister, then gave her the biggest and longest hug of either of their lives and dashed silently through the door.

Chad knelt, taking deep long quiet breaths, he knelt and he listened to the forest. The thickets half way down to the village were typically brimming of life. Chipmunk squeaks, woodpecker hammering, finches chirping, there were always noises. But not today, had there been a few feet of snow on the forest floor and some hanging in the trees he could have understood it but it was a clear summer day. The silence unnerved him.

Reaching up he grabbed a low hanging pine branch. The needles fell off the limb and dropped to the already covered forest floor.

Hot arid winds had sucked the life out of the ground and trees – the forest was dying.

Wiping his brow, Chad came up off his knees and back into his half crouch. With deft skills of a seasoned woodsman he started forward through the forest, easily passing over branches and twigs that for others would have cracked and broken sending sounds out to the world around them.

Every half hour or so, he would pause and sit, and just listen. It was something his dad had try to drill in to him. "Patience Chad for patience gets the catch. Running rapidly anywhere spreads your sounds and smells so fast it warns everything and everyone. Your very sweat born in the wind will give you away. Slow, controlled, keep calm and dry, dirty but not stinky. Take on and be part of the forest and it will protect you in turn."

Chad reached down and grabbed a hand full of moss that grew in a broken tree trunk. Reaching under his damp shirt he wiped his arm pits with it. He had always laughed at his dad when he had seen him do it, and now he was following suit.

Within a kilometre of the village, he plucked up enough courage to climb a tree. Many of the branches creaked; bereft of moisture the branches themselves were starting to crack. The village was quiet, and still and appeared to be empty. There was no smoke coming out of the baker's chimney, several of the houses' doors were open, but there were no parents out yelling at their kids. It was hard to see from where he was but overall he could see nothing unusual except for the absence of people.

At five hundred meters he crawled to the end of the forest that surrounded the village. The trees were smaller and wider spaced, so he went especially slow. Still nothing, he almost just stood up there but then he noticed movement. His breath, froze in his nostrils, every tendon, every muscle in his entire body popped tensing up and riveting him to the ground.

The rooftops, were black, not reddish brown, he had just thought the cedar had been turned darker with the dust. It wasn't until one of the creatures had moved that he had noticed. Lying there, Chad began to slowly breathe again. Then upon regaining composure he slowly pushed himself backward. This was going to be a challenge. The home he had to go to was on the west side of town. But, his hopes were not being raised, only his eyes as they darted back and forth to the rooftops.

Chad backed out a respectful 300 meters more giving the town a wide berth. Then slowly, carefully he crept with the greatest of ease through the forest. His fears grew as he rounded the back of the village. There was chattering and snapping noises that were piercing the thicket to which he stood.

Crawling forward he approached slowly. With his face inches above the forest floor he slipped forward like a reptile. Something caught his eye, shoes, or rather a shoe. By itself, in the forest by the village it shouldn't have caught his eye. But he knew that shoe, or at least he thought he knew. Taking a small detour he crawled forward, ensuring he wouldn't disturb the markings around it.

The shoe wasn't alone; there were other objects around where he now knelt. A club, a pan, even a knife. All dropped in one area, the blade had a trace of blood on it, yet the shoe captured his entire attention.

Closing in on it, he looked at the ground. Several people had run here, run and twisted turning as they ran. They had run. And then. Nothing. There was no trace of them, no trace of broken twigs, scraped ground or footmarks. The shoe was the last in the line of things on the ground. It was just there, abandoned as if mid stride, its owner had taken one step and then...gone. Chad had never paid much attention to shoes, but these, he thought these looked familiar. He pushed the idea out of his mind, there was no way he could know or be sure, his mind was playing tricks.

Edging back to the village, he moved now with some hidden meaning, hidden drive. Compassion which to Chad felt more than unusual drove him onward and somehow it empowered him, filled him with purpose. These had been his parent's friends, his friends. There were some whisperings ahead that drew him in like a bee to honey. Chad tried to check himself, but the sounds were too humane, too desperate, too pathetic not to be pursued.

The west part of town was the blacksmiths, a big building with lots of wooden spoke wheels waiting to be banded or fixed, old shovels, stacks of wood and coal for the furnaces, in other words plenty of places to hide. Chad moved quickly up and around and then froze again, but this time not out of fear. There, not twenty steps ahead of where he now crawled was a child no older than nine. Huddled there with her were three others all of them filthy, with outfits torn, some bleeding from minor cuts and all scared out of their minds.

The eyes that caught his were filled with fear, but something more. There was an ageless knowing there, a knowing that only comes when someone has seen their own death in the eyes of another. The eyes, those captivating blue eyes implored him, begged, and pleaded. But as snaps and scratching permeated the air around him the eyes moved up and around then slowly back to him. With tears the head shook, issuing him a small, honestly untrue plead for him to go, to leave now, to live.

A diminutive creature crawled from the doorway next to Chad almost startling him to the point of gasping. But the creature's attention was fixated on the children in the center of the street. The oldest child's eyes narrowed in disdain as it looked back at its killer and then she smiled, it was the child's last act of defiance. Doom was crawling towards her and there was nothing left, no strength except her strength of will. The two younger kids with her started to cry. She turned and pulled them to her and under her arms. Her hands reached up and lay gently across their forehead covering their eyes. "Hush. Hush. Its ok".

The smell of fear must have been an intoxicating scent for creatures from all about the rooftops started to chatter. Several rose, their talons letting out scratching sounds as they cracked the cedar beneath their feet.

The small devil darted forward on all fours, its wings laid slick back and its tail, long and leathery with a lighter covered thick hair flicked excited snapping so hard it cracked like a whip. It was within a arms reach when something much larger, and much darker, fell upon it with a thud so hard even the ground pressed against Chad's stomach vibrated. The massive black beast ground its one large toe talon deeper into the smaller one's head and the twitching of the tail stopped.

Turning, the creature's massively extended belly blotted out Chad's view of the children in the street. His eyes darted up and around. Screeching erupted as the large beast pulled back his foot fast, ripping the head of the other creature off. It appeared to Chad that having obviously fed on the entire town, they were now more interested in the current spectacle then in the food. The massive beast's wings went wide and arching his back he bellowed. Turning he flaunted his massively muscular arms in a wide sweep to the audience above him. They screeched with approval. But the beasts turn was slow and deliberate. The creatures were bloated to excess.

Bravado, such bravado, and hopeless abandon filled Chad. The eyes had captured his mind and his soul in one moment he had gone from a boy, to feeling almost a father of all mankind. The desperation, the determination filled him and without knowing it, he was on his knees and then feet. He would run, grab them and run. The fat shits would not be able to catch him, he was fast, he was strong, he could do it.

This wasn't a battle, it was a snatch and run. He let his bow down, and, taking one deep breath he sprang forward with all abandon. As Chad hit the open space a noise rang out louder and colder than any noise he had ever heard. It was if the sky itself was being rend into a billion pieces. Wind from the hundreds of wings above him belted him with buffets of foul stench.

One stride, two strides, three; and in four he was half way there, and two steps to the side of the great beast who, as luck had it was turning to the left while he circled on the right. He could make it, he thought, this 'will work'.

The ground started to shake, as beast by beast dropped with heavy thuds to the ground. Each of their bodies heavy and swollen they still moved with alarming speed and with each open mouth, needle teethed screech they appeared to move faster and seem so much less bloated.

Committed he ran, his legs pumped like iron rods, his feet ground the dirt up as he pushed fast. As he drew near the tree, it encircled the others. He would reach them, but then, he would need to turn and come back from whence he had come, turn to possibly face that first large beast. But there was no fear in his eyes, on in any part within his being, only raw courage and compassion.

With one step away he felt pain, great pain in both his shoulders. His feet gave way as he was pulled off balance. The pain was excruciating that his mind clouded as shock hit him like a sledge hammer in the middle of the forehead. His feet gave way from beneath him, but rather then falling he started to rise.

Looking down his toes brushed the three children as he passed over them. Two wings above him pushed down the air so hard in great fast beats that the children became somewhat obscured by dust, but still there, within the cloud were the eyes, their eyes shared with him something hidden. In one instance they shared a lifetime, and then a departure.

He jerked up; each beat from the wings above pulled him up sent shooting pain through his shoulders. Looking down Chad looked to see a talon, pushing so hard against his shoulder that they were starting to sink deeper in. Shock dissipated, realizing he wasn't yet dead, he pulled his knife from his belt and reaching up he started to slash franticly at the long legs that held him. With all his remaining strength he started to twist and turn and hammer.

The creature holding him was less than half the size of the beast in the courtyard, it was struggling to stay aloft with his weight.

"BITCH I'll rip you a new one before I let you eat me!" He screamed with all his might as he started to stab blindly upward.

A moment later he was happy to feel the pain disappear from one shoulder. He was half way free, but, as he stared down, he was also fifty or more feet in the air. They were flying up and up towards the mountains. The thought of freedom, the fear of being ripped apart, and the fear of bone crushing landing below, all mixed together as one.

A growl came from above as the creature's eyes first met his own. "Stupid child", it spat down at him. "How bad do you want to die? First running in there like a fool, and now wanting to drop to the rocks below. Etch said you were foolish, he didn't say I was to rescue an insane child!"

Chad was speechless; looking up the creature's face had turned from his own. He could see it was taking every ounce of strength she had to keep them flying.

"They smell your blood; we need to keep going, until they loose interest."

"The children", Chad said hesitantly

"Small fortune for you, and they felt nothing. The excitement you brought boiled their blood to such frenzy that those children were eviscerated and fully consumed in seconds."

The wings beat half a heartbeat slower and they began to descend. At ten feet he heard a grunt from above and was let go. He broke a few small evergreens before landing hard. Heaving, he inhaled great gasps of air as his lungs ached. Rubbing his shoulders he looked up. There sitting on a branch overhead was the creature.

"After centuries, your dad remembers you as a smart kid. If I ever get to recite these moments to him, he might think the less of you."

"You know my dad? When, how?"

"Yes" the creature spat as it dropped silently with wings extended to the ground next to him. "Long story and I don't wish to repeat it. So let's first find your sister, and then Dimi. By now she should have re-grown her wings. Then with my story told, together the four of us must figure out how to convince a demigod to open the gates of hell so we can bring your father home. Unless of course, you have something better to do?" The creature bent down, and extended a talon offering to help Chad up.

"My name is Elle."